In Stornas
King Hector Berras
Gysa, *the dreamer*
Lord Gudrum Killi, *now of Ottby*
Edrik, *his man*

Gods & Goddesses
Thenor, *Father of the Alekkan Gods*
Sigurd Vilander, *his son*
Valera, *Goddess of Love & Fertility*
Eskvir, *God of War & Vengeance*
Eradis, *his healer*
Alari, *Goddess of Magic & Dreamers*
Vasa, *Goddess of Death*
Hartu, *Goddess of the Sea*
Hykka, *God of Weather*
Solla, *Goddess of the Sun*
Omani, *Goddess of the Moon*
Ulfinnur, *God of Winter*
Eutresia, *First Goddess of the Sun*
Tikas, *Messenger of the Gods*

Tulia Saari, *Warrior of Gallabrok*

THE LORDS OF ALEKKA

EYE OF THE WOLF

MARK OF THE HUNTER

BLOOD OF THE RAVEN

HEART OF THE KING

FURY OF THE QUEEN

This novel is entirely a work of fiction. The names,
characters, and places described in it are the work
of the author's imagination.

AMAZON ISBN: 9798830547567

For more information about A.E. Rayne
and her upcoming books visit:

www.aerayne.com

www.facebook.com/aerayne

FURY OF THE QUEEN

THE LORDS OF ALEKKA : BOOK FIVE

A.E. RAYNE

CHARACTERS

In Slussfall

Alys de Sant
Magnus de Sant, *Alys' son*
Lotta de Sant, *Alys' daughter*
Lord Reinar Vilander
Lady Elin Vilander, *Reinar's wife*
Stellan Vilander, *Reinar's father*
Gerda Vilander, *his wife*
Bjarni Sansgard, *Reinar's best friend*
Agnette Sansgard, *Reinar's cousin*
Ludo Moller, *Sigurd's best friend*
Berger Eivin, *warrior*
Helgi Eivin, *his cousin*
Solveigh Brava, *Tarl's wife*
Jonas Bergstrom, *Alys' grandfather*
Vik Lofgren, *Jonas' best friend*
Eddeth Nagel, *dreamer & healer*
Raf, *dreamer*
Stina Arnborg, *Alys' best friend*
Ollo Narp, *warrior*
Ilene Gislar, *warrior*
Estrella Bluefinn, *former Queen of Alekka*
Ilyia & Maia Bluefinn, *her daughters*
Lady Katrine Hallen, *former Lady of Tromsund*
Ragnahild One Eye, *spirit dreamer*
Torfinn Bellig, *Sigurd's friend*
Beggi Bellig, *old scout*
Martyn, *Stellan's steward*
Puddle, *the puppy*

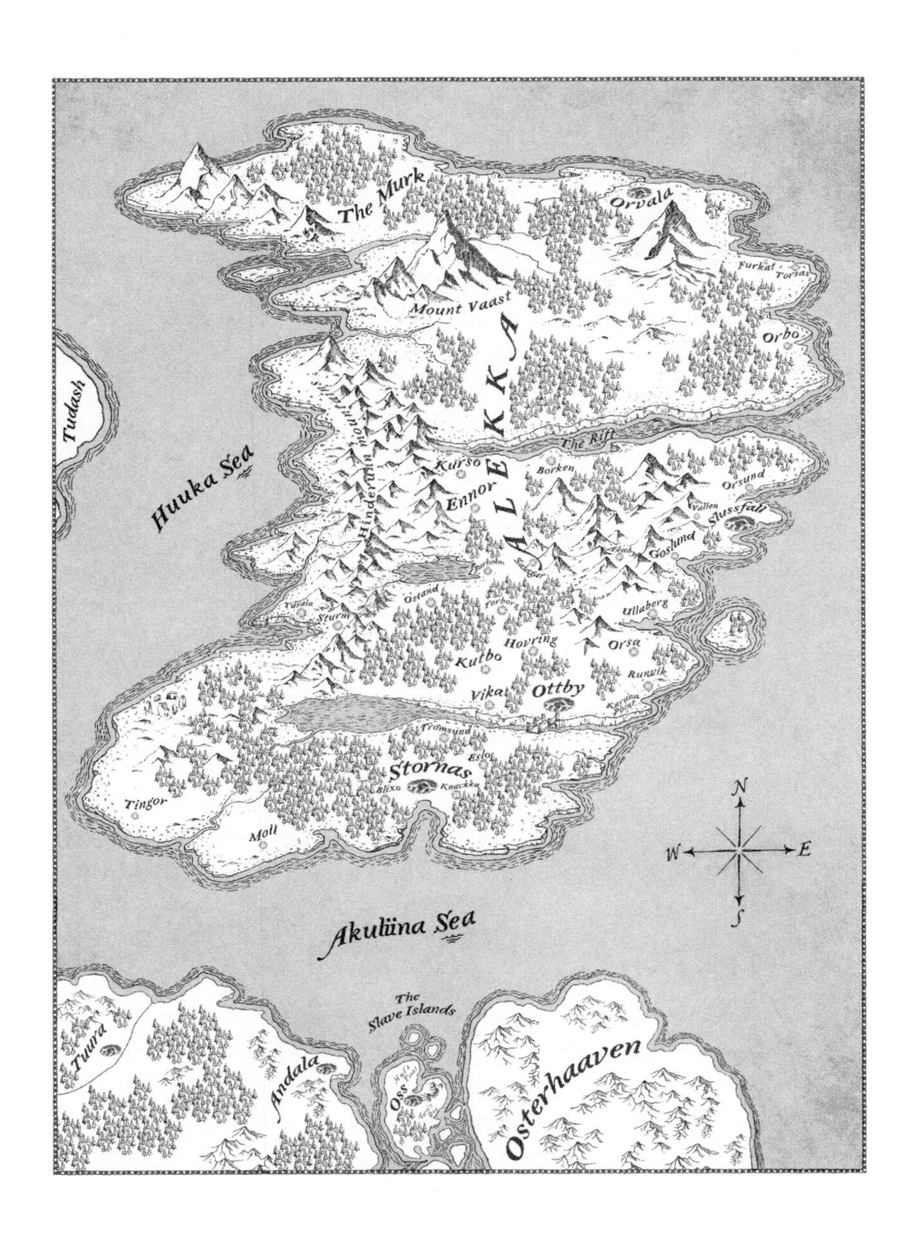

The Murk
Orvala
Mount Vaast
Furkat
Torsas
Orbo
ALEKKA
The Rift
Tudash
Huuka Sea
Kurso
Borken
Ennor
Orsund
Vallen
Slussfall
Goslund
Östand
Torborg
Sturm
Ullaberg
Hovring
Orsa
Kutbo
Runvik
Vika
Ottby
Karuna Point
Tromsund
Eslo
Stornas
Blixo
Knackka
Tingor
Moll
N
W
E
S
Akuliina Sea
The Slave Islands
Tuura
Andala
Oss
Osterhaaven

PROLOGUE

Rain washed over him until he could feel his tunic clinging to his back. His boots filled with water, beard dripping, eyes blurred.

Blinking through the rain, he stared at his king, barely noticing any of it.

His king?

Gudrum snarled, spitting on the slushy ground. 'And you'll do nothing? *Nothing*?' His anger seethed like flames through the rain, fighting its chilling onslaught. 'She killed my son, and you'll do *nothing*?' He wanted to release his clenched fists, to pummel the man standing before him, dark eyebrows jutting out over a stern face. Ranuf Furyck was a beloved king, admired throughout Osterland, yet Gudrum saw only cold eyes, devoid of sympathy. 'But he was my only son! My *boy*!' He unfurled his fingers now, body vibrating with rage.

Stepping closer.

'You'll do well to think that through, Gudrum Killi.' The king's deep voice crashed through the rain like a hammer. 'For though your son is dead, you are still mine to command. Still here to obey me.'

Gudrum's breath was ragged, and squeezing his hands into white-knuckled fists, he rubbed them into wet eyes, rubbing and rubbing until he could no longer tell if it was rain or tears flowing down his cheeks.

'I am sorry for your loss.'

The king's voice was softer now, though Gudrum didn't look up, not wanting sympathy.

Sympathy?

He wanted justice!

'My loss is nothing to you, my lord. I see that clearly.' And now Gudrum dragged up his head, eyes full of pain and hate, and anger most of all. 'My son was worth nothing to you, for he wasn't a Furyck, was he? *Was*?' An odd sound escaped his twisted lips – something between a cry and a roar. 'He was nothing in your eyes!'

Ranuf felt oddly uncertain about what to say. The boy's death had put him in a terrible position, and he felt his own anger at that, though that wasn't for Gudrum to know. 'Your boy is dead, and you must honour him now. That is where your focus must be, not on this.' He opened his hands, furrowing his deeply-lined brow. 'On this anger. It won't bring him back.'

'Honour him?' Gudrum scoffed. 'Here? With her gloating? Watching? *Here*? In Andala?'

Ranuf stiffened. 'My daughter –'

'Killed my son!'

'It was retribution.' Ranuf's tone hardened again. 'It was retribution and nothing more, so I will hear no more about it. Your boy took something of Jael's, and she had the right to make him pay. She is the king's daughter. *My* daughter. He should have known the terrible mistake he was making, the risk he was taking. He knew what Jael was capable of. He'd been beaten by her enough times to know what she could do!'

Gudrum sucked back every word screaming inside his head. He shook with cold, trembled with anger, desperately needing to get out of the rain. He wanted ale. He wanted to get away from Ranuf Furyck and his revolting family. Away from Andala and every reminder of his son.

And her.

The girl who had murdered him.

Jael Furyck.

He would go, but he would return. Of that, Gudrum was certain.

Retribution?

Ducking his head, he drew his sodden cloak around his shoulders, turning away into the downpour.

The king didn't know how right he was, for Ranuf Furyck's daughter had taken something from him, and he would never rest until he made her pay.

PART ONE

Standing Still

CHAPTER ONE

'Your dog! Ate my sausage! My sausage! I...! My *sausage*!'

Alys turned around in surprise, seeing the shouting man, his face screwed up in annoyance, ruddy cheeks pumping in and out. He was filthy, bedraggled, his wild auburn hair almost standing on end, his bushy beard touching the top of a torn tunic. She stayed where she was, one eye on him, one on Puddle, who had run back to her, gulping down the hot sausage with a guilty look. He dropped his head, quickly disappearing beneath the wet hem of her black cloak.

'I'm so sorry,' Alys said. 'He can't have had enough breakfast.' She shrugged, attempting a smile. It was still early, and Puddle had only just eaten a plate of scraps, though no meal was ever enough to fill the energetic ball of fluff, and he'd taken off looking for more as soon as the cottage door had opened.

'Sorry?' The man's scowl deepened as he stomped towards her, hands on hips. She was a pretty woman, he saw as he got closer; a pretty woman with a bad-mannered dog. 'Do you let your dog eat everyone's food? Have you no control over it at all?'

He looked cold, Alys thought, noticing a blue tinge to his hairy lips. The snow in the square was fresh, not all of it cleared, and he shook and shivered as he stopped before her, tapping a boot.

'Sorry doesn't buy me another sausage!'

Alys was surprised by his venom, or perhaps madness? Maybe he was a beggar, and Puddle had taken away his only meal in days? He certainly looked hungry. He wasn't wearing a cloak, and his clothes didn't appear to have been washed or repaired in some time.

The square was heaving with people, a few of whom were now turning her way, wanting to know what all the noise was about. Alys felt her cheeks warming, glared at by the big shouting man, peered at by Slussfallers going about their business. She hurried a hand beneath her cloak, finding her purse, though a quick ferret around revealed no coins; nothing bar a ring, an arm ring, and one of Eddeth's roots. 'I have nothing, I'm afraid. Nothing on me.' Alys lifted her hands, holding them open. Her face burned as she offered a crooked smile, but now the man's scowl turned into a snarl.

'I was attacked,' he grumbled. 'In the forest! By a band of men. Warriors! They were armed. Attacked me, took everything I had! Took my coins, my weapons, my c-c-cloak,' he stammered. 'But not my boots.' And now he straightened up with a hint of pride, a glint of a smile in his hazel eyes. 'You see I always keep a coin in my boots. Just the one. And when I arrived here, I knew that coin would buy me something hot to fill my empty belly.' He looked down as Puddle popped his furry brown head out from under Alys' cloak. 'And your dog ate it. *Ate* it!'

Alys didn't know how to extract herself from the conversation. The man looked ready to throttle her. She hadn't worn her sword since they'd arrived in Slussfall, though her right hand hovered where her hilt should have been. 'I...' Turning her head, she searched for a familiar face. It was a bitterly cold morning, gloomy and grey, and those who weren't staring were trudging through the snow, heads bent against the wind, trying to find the energy for another day. 'I'll find you a coin, I promise. I just don't have any with me. Who are you? I... I will come and find you. Don't worry, you'll have your sausage.'

The man's mouth opened wide. He looked ready to sneeze or scream, and then he was flying through the air, landing face down in the snow with a grunt of surprise, Berger Eivin on his back.

Alys looked on in horror.

Berger rolled the man over, and with a whooping shout, he

kissed his forehead. 'Helgi!'

Solveigh, who had been walking with Berger, turned to Alys with raised eyebrows, a puzzled look on her face.

Helgi spluttered, scooping snow out of his mouth, and though he felt slightly dazed from both hunger and the bang on his head, he almost smiled. 'You're here,' he panted. 'I wasn't sure you'd be here.'

Berger stuck out a hand, pulling him to his feet. They were the same height, Helgi just slightly taller. Or maybe it was all that wild hair, Alys thought, seeing immediate similarities between the two men.

'This is my cousin Helgi,' Berger grinned, turning Helgi around to face the women. His eyes held Solveigh's for a moment, and his smile widened. 'He's from Napper. Down South.' He turned to Helgi, patting him on the back. 'Did you walk all the way here?' And now he laughed, pulling his cousin close, giving him a squeeze. 'You look like shit!'

Helgi sneezed. 'I could do with something to eat, Cousin. Somewhere to sit. A f-f-fire.'

'And a few jugs of ale!' Berger decided, and though it was early and a day's work lay ahead of him, every other thought left his head as he pointed his cousin in the direction of the tavern. He turned back to Solveigh with a hint of regret in his eyes. 'You can come. With us.'

But Solveigh quickly shook her head, hating the smell of the tavern. The sweaty, damp, hot stink of it all turned her stomach. 'I'll stay with Alys. I'm sure there's something I can do.' And rubbing her rounded belly, she smiled.

Berger frowned. 'But not too much.' Then looking at Alys, he directed his next words to her. 'I'm sure Alys won't let you do too much.'

'I won't,' Alys promised, slipping her arm through Solveigh's as Puddle took off after a gull. She thought about calling him back, but he was quickly turning down an alley, so shaking her head, she led Solveigh away.

Berger watched them leave, forgetting all about his cousin

until Helgi sneezed again.

'About that fire,' he mumbled.

Berger laughed. 'I can't believe you came!' He steered his shivering cousin around the market stalls. 'I thought you'd never leave Napper. You swore you'd never leave!'

Helgi could smell the sour tang of ale in the air, and his attention narrowed on a newly built hut in the distance. His eyes flickered to the great stone hall beside it but quickly returned to what he could see was clearly the tavern. Snow started falling, and he quickened his pace, thick flakes settling in his coppery beard. 'Napper? Ha, Napper was never the problem, Cousin. No, it was that bastard brother of yours. You knew that.'

Growing up, Berger had idolised his older brother, Rutger, which had often put him at odds with his favourite cousin. Though, in the end, Rutger had proved to be what Helgi had always warned: a reckless, violent idiot. So now Berger chose not to think about him at all. 'Well, he's dead.'

'I heard. Good news travels far.' Helgi trembled in his torn tunic, seeing a woman carrying two jugs, eyes low as she traversed the freshly cleared paths leading from the tavern to the tables and braziers clustered outside. A few groups of red-cheeked men had already made themselves at home, ensuring they got the best seats. 'It's why I made my way here. Thought you might need me.'

Berger was surprised but pleased, and he pushed Helgi ahead of him, through the narrow doorway, into the tavern.

Helgi blinked. The gloom outside had been dull, but inside it was like stepping into a cave. The stink was intense but mostly pleasant: fish and ale, damp and smoke. He sighed, then remembering his lost sausage, he turned to his cousin. 'Who was that woman? With the dog?'

'Alys?' Berger laughed, manoeuvring Helgi towards the serving counter, already slick with ale. 'Ha! Don't go looking at Alys now. That would only end in heartbreak, Cousin.'

'What?' Helgi spluttered, shaking his head. 'No, she owes me a coin. I want to know where to claim it. Nothing more. That woman? No!'

Berger laughed, ordering a jug of ale, and then, looking at his dishevelled cousin, he added two pots of fish stew and a plate of flatbreads to the order. 'Let's sit down, over there, and you can tell me what happened. How did you end up here, Helgi? In Slussfall?'

***

It had been four months since their victory at Tromsund, yet Stellan Vilander felt older by decades. He stood on the balcony with Reinar, watching the square. His eyes followed Katrine Hallen, former Lady of Tromsund, as she walked alone, eyes down, inviting no company. The day was typically cold and grey, but her hair flamed like a bright fire. She wore it the same every day, he realised: plaited in one long braid that swept around the nape of her neck, over her shoulder, falling to her waist. She never tied it with ribbons. She wore no embellishments, bar the brooch securing that red cloak, which flapped behind her, flaming like her hair.

'What are we going to do?' Reinar muttered beside him. He'd seen Alys disappear with Solveigh. She'd been talking to a man he didn't recognise, but someone Berger obviously knew. He had questions about that and more, but most of all, he wanted to find a way out of the darkness. A way to Stornas, where his destiny awaited him.

According to the dreamers.

'We came to Slussfall to get everyone to safety, but now what? What can we do to change things from here? Hector Berras grows more powerful while I sit inside this fort and stew. While the sea remains frozen, and we all slowly starve to death. We have few allies and more enemies than we ever imagined. And Sigurd's gone.' Reinar shivered, remembering the deprivations of the journey from Tromsund, through swathes of dense forests, over the seemingly endless Hinderunn Mountains. It had taken weeks.

Weeks of walking and riding in treacherous conditions, fighting the cold and the snow, struggling with sickness, the injured, accidents...

He thought of the day he'd faced Gudrum at sea, on their way to Ottby. And if he'd just killed that arsehole, none of this would have happened. For Reinar was certain that without Gudrum, Hector Berras' grip on Alekka would have been tenuous. But with Gudrum whispering in his ear, a newly-crowned Hector had pushed onto the front foot immediately, sending his men out of Stornas, conquering those settlements around the capital, killing anyone who still claimed loyalty to Ake Bluefinn and those considering giving their oath to his chosen heir.

Hearing word of this, Reinar had urged his people on, realising that they needed to get to Slussfall in haste, for Slussfall meant walls and gates and the promise of warmth and food. Shelter too. They couldn't return to Ottby and hope to keep it secure when its gates were off and its weapons' stores were low; when its catapults were wrecked, and its walls were damaged. Ottby wasn't secure, but Reinar had known that with Lief Gundersen in charge of Slussfall, the impenetrable Northern fortress was their best hope of finding a safe haven. A safe haven, a chance to regroup, and an opportunity to plan what to do next.

But months had passed, and he was still undecided.

Stellan patted his son's shoulder, turning away from the square as the snow swept in. He quickened his pace, heading back inside the cavernous chamber Reinar had turned into their war room. It still felt odd to be without Sigurd, and he often expected to find his lanky son smiling at him from a doorway or following behind Ludo. 'Come and have some ale,' Stellan grinned, heading straight for the fire. He saw his steward, Martyn, who, having read his mind, was already filling two cups.

'My lords,' Martyn smiled, handing one to Reinar, and the other to Stellan. The order used to be the other way around, Martyn thought wryly, though now Stellan's eldest son was the chosen one, the man who would be king.

Bobbing his head, he stepped away from the enormous map

table, leaving the two men to talk.

'Any lord who wishes to be king can't hide,' Reinar said. 'And no lord can claim victory by cowering behind walls, hoping they'll hold against his enemy. Hoping his enemy will just freeze to death beyond them.'

'Though with the sea frozen, we can't bring the Islanders into our fight. And without the Islanders, we don't have enough men,' Stellan insisted, seeking to cool his son's impatience. Reinar was becoming more irritable by the day, though he knew his son's fractious mood wasn't all about his enemies. He eyed him, trying to encourage a smile. 'It's not cowering if you have intentions to fight. But to do so now would risk too many lives. To try and force Hector's hand before we're ready? But we've half the men he has, and even that's a hopeful guess.' Stellan sipped his ale, which was surprisingly warm. 'Though I defer to you, of course.' And now his smile grew. 'My lord.'

Reinar snorted. 'Is that so? Defer to me?' He sipped his own ale, not thirsty, not hungry, not hot or cold. He saw Alys' face when he looked in the flames, wondering again who that man had been. He'd stepped close to her, threateningly, and for a moment, Reinar had feared what he might do. Closing his eyes, he took a deep breath, turning back to his father, knowing that if any woman could handle an aggressive stranger, it was Alys Bergstrom. 'Being trapped in this fort will turn us all mad soon. There's no sign of spring, no sign of The Thaw. It's overdue by a month.'

Stellan sighed, running a hand through his bristly beard, which had grown considerably longer since they'd left Ottby. It was turning white, he saw, remembering that he needed to ask Martyn to find him a new comb. He'd broken a few teeth in his old favourite, and with a beard this long, he needed something to keep it in check. 'It is, though if Ulfinnur's still missing, spring won't be coming any time soon.'

Reinar frowned. 'Do you think it's Alari's doing?'

'That's what Raf said, didn't she? That's what she saw. Alari took Ulfinnur, and without him to bring The Thaw, we're winter's prisoner. Keeping the sea frozen means there's no chance of us seeking help. I imagine that's what Alari wants. That's how she'll keep her king on the throne.'

Reinar left his ale on the map table, heading to the hearth, where the fire Martyn had spent a good deal of time over was bright and blooming. A reluctant Raf had often been brought to him by Eddeth since their arrival in Slussfall, though she'd mostly spoken in mumbles, and even now, she wouldn't meet his eye. Reinar didn't know what to make of her. Eddeth had rescued her from Stornas, and now she lived in Eddeth's cottage, helping both her and Alys with dreaming. Though it was hard to trust someone who had once been so close to his enemy, and Reinar feared that, even now, she wasn't entirely on his side.

He turned back to his father. 'Hopefully, Thenor's doing something about Ulfinnur. Or Sigurd. They must be, mustn't they? We can't survive an endless winter.' The thought of what that would mean clenched Reinar's insides until his stomach started cramping. He was responsible for so many lives now – those from Tromsund and Ottby, Slussfall and beyond. Not to mention the families who had headed North to escape Hector's brutal attack dog, Gudrum, busy scouring the South, looking for traitors. And allies. Reinar was sure he would've found both. 'We need to talk to the dreamers.'

Stellan agreed. 'I'll go and find them. You stay here. It'll give you a chance to think. You need that, I imagine, what with so many things on your mind.' He smiled sympathetically at his weary-looking son. 'Or perhaps just sit by the fire and fall asleep?' The giant table in the centre of the chamber had been painted with a detailed map of Alekka, and though Stellan could see his son's blue eyes widen at the thought of sleep, they immediately shifted towards the table.

'I'll wait for them,' Reinar said with a tense smile. 'Hopefully, one of them had a useful dream.'

***

Raf was still sound asleep when Eddeth left the cottage for the second time that morning. She smiled as she closed the wobbling door, trying not to knock her head on the wind chimes. It was a cold morning, another grey day of heavy snow clouds fencing them in. Little wind, though, Eddeth thought as she sneezed, slipping on an icy pebble, whacking into the chimes that immediately started playing a crashing melody in her ears. She became tangled in the strings, batting her hands in annoyance, determined to cut the annoying things down. She thought of Aldo Varnass, as she often did, still surprised that he was no longer there, hovering at her elbow, waiting to help.

'Need some help?' came a voice.

Eddeth twisted around to see a grinning Ludo Moller with his knife out.

'Oh yes. Yes indeed!' Eddeth exclaimed. 'For Reinar needs me. I sense it! And if I...' She gave up speaking, becoming even more entangled in the chime strings. 'Oh dear!'

Ludo laughed. 'Will you miss the chimes?'

'I will not!' Eddeth insisted. 'Stupid things. If I'd wanted all that noise, I'd keep birds in cages, squawking at me all day long. No! They're not mine. No, they're not! Poor Raf. Not sure how she's still sleeping in there.'

Ludo glanced at the cottage door, thinking of Sigurd. He still felt lost without his friend, though wherever he was, Ludo just hoped he was happy. And safe. He cut through the strings, freeing Eddeth, who touched his arm with gratitude in her eyes and impatience in her voice.

'I must go!' she blurted out, eyes bulging in the gloom. 'To the hall! Reinar will want you there. Oh yes, he will! What Raf saw last night will have us all on our toes!'

Raf heard them leave, Eddeth's voice rising in excitement, though she had no desire to go after her. She felt tired after another mostly sleepless night, fighting the urge to fall back to sleep. The cottage was almost warm, Eddeth having been up early setting a fire that crackled noisily. Opening one eye, Raf spied the breakfast spread waiting on the table. She saw boiled eggs and slices of meat left over from supper. There was a shrivelled apple, a tiny pile of nuts, and a cup of what was likely goat's milk. Eddeth had bought a little goat when they'd arrived in Slussfall, calling her Agnes, and letting her sleep in the cottage with them. Raf could smell her earthy odour, though the goat had been let out earlier, taken to the paddocks outside the walls to run around while Eddeth ferreted through the snow, searching for any herb or plant still thriving. Though after such a long winter, it was rare to find anything of use.

Raf closed her eye, seeing Sigurd's face hovering above hers. It made her sad and wistful, for there was no Sigurd in Slussfall. He hadn't come to visit his family once. Or her. She saw a glimpse of Gudrum's face where Sigurd's had been, and opening both eyes now, she panted, feeling pains in her chest. Reaching down, she dragged the fur up to her chin and then over her face, wanting to disappear.

***

Helgi had downed four cups of ale and two pots of fish stew while listening to Berger tell the story of his journey from Ottby to Stornas to Tromsund to Slussfall. He'd embellished it here and there, Helgi was certain, knowing he would have done the same, but still, it was a story worthy of his silence, so he'd mostly sat still, asking few questions. Though when Berger had finished, there were some notable omissions that Helgi felt inclined to pursue further. 'And the woman? The pregnant woman? Who's she?'

Berger dropped his eyes, fixing them on his empty cup, tempted to order another jug of ale, though he didn't want Reinar catching him stumbling out of the tavern half-drunk. That would hardly encourage his future king to see him as one of his most valued warriors, a leader of men.

Eventually, he looked up at Helgi with a crooked smile. 'Her name is Solveigh. Pregnant by Tarl Brava of Orvala. Soon to be my wife.'

Helgi narrowed his gaze. 'Tarl Brava? She's his woman?'

'She was. And Gudrum's.'

'Gudrum? The new Lord of Ottby?'

Berger nodded. 'Though she loved neither. Tarl Brava burned her family alive, forced her to marry him. Gudrum then took her and raped her and forced her to marry him too.'

'And you?'

Berger smiled. 'When she's my wife, I'll treat her like a queen. And when Reinar Vilander makes me a lord, she'll be my lady.'

Helgi looked bemused. 'You want to marry? Have a family? *You*?' He laughed out loud, head back. 'In all your stories, Cousin, *that* is the most surprising!' He laughed some more, slapping the table, his good humour returning thanks to the warmth and the food, and especially the ale. 'You think you can commit to one woman?' Helgi shook his head. 'Two or three I'd expect but one?'

'One woman can change everything,' Berger insisted, auburn eyebrows knitting together in annoyance. 'If anyone knows that, it's you.'

Helgi froze as though struck by lightning, all amusement gone. And swallowing, he looked past a table of loud men jostling over the company of the serving women towards the fire pit. It crackled and spat as snow drifted down the smoke hole, teasing its flames.

He didn't speak.

Sensing trouble, Berger leaned forward, patting his cousin's arm. 'What happened, Helgi? What really brought you here? I doubt it was just missing me.'

Helgi shook his head, and heart thumping, he attempted a smile. 'You don't think your pleasant company's enough to tempt me up here, Cousin?' He had a big mouth with full lips, and his smile was wide, revealing straight teeth.

Berger peered at him. 'Away from the farm? Away from Sahra?'

Helgi turned around as the tavern door creaked open, hiding his reaction from his cousin long enough to compose himself, and when he turned back, he was grinning. 'I decided not to die a farmer. You warned me, of course, though I thought I could tame the land, or perhaps, I thought it could tame me. Though neither happened, so here I am.'

'And Sahra? You were finally wed?'

The door swung open again, and this time, Bjarni stood there, motioning with his head for Berger to get going. Though it was Helgi who was on his feet first, and though unsteady, he turned away from his cousin without a word, heading for the door.

CHAPTER TWO

'It's that woman! The dreamer! Raf saw everything. Oh yes, she did!' Eddeth began loudly. 'She's not as she was. Not anymore! She's a new woman entirely!'

Stellan had gathered Bjarni, Berger, Ollo, and Vik into the war room. Ludo had brought Eddeth and found Alys and Jonas. No one had seen Lief Gundersen, though Alys mentioned something about Falla feeling unwell, which might explain where he'd disappeared to. Eddeth had assured them that Raf was busy dreaming, so there was no point waiting on her. And so she hadn't, blurting out everything she'd seen in a disorderly mess that made it impossible for anyone to follow.

Which wasn't new, Alys thought with a smile, tapping Eddeth's arm, having some idea of what she was talking about. 'Do you mean Hector Berras' dreamer? The burned woman? Something has happened to her?'

Eddeth's eyes rounded as she turned to Alys, nodding, then shaking her head. 'Raf said she's not burned anymore. No! She's healed! And not half-dead either. She's entirely whole, with hair and lips and two eyes. Attractive even!'

Alys stepped back in surprise. 'Why? How?'

'Magic,' Eddeth whispered, as though they were alone, just her and Alys standing by the map table. As though there weren't eight pairs of eyes staring at them, impatiently wanting to know what was going on. 'Goddess magic!'

Reinar frowned. 'What does it matter, Eddeth? Whether the dreamer is burned or covered in feathers... what does it matter to us? To Hector or Gudrum?'

His question had Eddeth flummoxed, for though Raf's dream had been fascinating, she wasn't sure what it meant for their hopes, which had been sinking since they'd arrived in Slussfall. She swallowed, searching for answers, suddenly acutely aware of those eight pairs of eyes.

'It's a reward,' came a quiet voice as the door creaked open and Raf stepped inside, mostly hidden beneath her long fur cloak, which swept across the flagstones as she headed for the table. Immediately intimidated by the gathered crowd, she fixed her attention on Eddeth, not speaking again until she was standing by her side. 'It's Gysa's reward for helping Hector. Alari has rewarded her. I remember Gysa saying something about it once. About what Vasa and Alari had promised if she helped Hector become the king. She's done their bidding, and now she's claimed her reward.'

'So will she go away?' Vik wanted to know, gnawing a toothpick. 'If this woman's got what she wanted, will she leave?' It was a half-hearted question, for they could all guess the answer. Those with evil intentions rarely walked away without claiming everything on offer. And the lure of further power and riches was still in sight for Hector Berras, for though he'd claimed Stornas, he hadn't yet conquered all of Alekka. And while Reinar commanded Slussfall, he had no chance of completing his victory. No chance of proclaiming himself the true king of the land.

'Gysa?' Raf blinked. 'No, she won't go away. She wants more. More than anyone ever realised.'

***

'Ake's wife called it the parlour,' Hector said with a smile, scanning the generously appointed small room with its luxurious fittings, his eyes finally settling on Gysa, who sat quietly opposite him. Her transformation was astonishing. No longer did she hide herself away, masked by a hood so opaque that he could only guess at her true disfigurement. He had caught glimpses of her ruined face over the years, but rarely. He'd seen her hands, dark and slender and scarred. He'd heard her voice, deep and rasping as though she was a dying crone. Her body had been wrapped in a thick cloak, her hair - whatever was left - was hidden away. She'd worn tall boots, long skirts, and woollen stockings to cover her legs.

But now?

She was mesmerising. Exquisite.

Hector was enchanted by her smooth skin, her full lips, her soft voice.

It soothed him in a way her old voice hadn't.

Gudrum leaned across the table, blocking his view, hoping to focus the king on something other than his dreamer. 'We should talk, my lord, about Slussfall. If we don't leave soon, Reinar Vilander will establish a real foothold there. It's already been months. Months since he escaped Tromsund.'

Hector swung around, eyeing his new Lord of Ottby. 'He didn't escape,' he snapped. '*Escape*?' Now he snorted, sensing Gysa watching him. 'He's exactly where we want him to be. He's cornered, like an animal. Alekka's locked in by ice, and with Alari on our side, that won't change for some time. Reinar Vilander has no allies, dwindling stores, diminishing hopes. What? You think this wasn't all part of my plan?'

Gudrum knew it definitely wasn't part of his plan, though he dropped his eyes, helping himself to a slice of bread. Taking up his knife, he cut off a thick wedge of cheese, adding it to the warm bread, and folding it in half, he funnelled it into his mouth, letting Hector's anger cool as he knew it would. All he had to do was wait. Eventually, Hector would realise that he'd crossed the line, and after a mumbled apology of sorts, he would retreat back behind it. For Hector needed him. If he wanted to remain on his throne, he needed Gudrum prowling Alekka, rounding up his enemies, preparing for their assault on the Vilanders. Hector was far too enamoured with the warmth and comfort of his castle, with its giant stone hearths, high beds, and fluffy pillows. He was far too busy sitting and eating and drinking, getting fatter by the day, to do the work himself.

Looking up as the silence dragged on, Gudrum reached for his goblet, draining it, swallowing the doughy bread with a gulp. He turned his attention to his nails. They were dirty, and he picked at them as Gysa sat on one side, silent, Hector on the other, squirming.

Eventually, Hector spoke. 'When winter eases, we will assault Slussfall, of course. But to do so before The Thaw makes no sense. We have ships in our sheds. So many ships! Why waste the opportunity to transport our army with speed and comfort? And in warmer weather, with the sea flowing? Why does everything need to be hard?'

Gudrum bit his tongue. He was impatient, hungry for war, thirsty for blood. He wanted a great final battle to seal the defeat of Reinar Vilander and his family. He didn't want to sit around feeling comfortable at all. 'When winter eases?' He stood, smoothing down his new black tunic, annoyed with Hector and his castle comforts and his wet-lipped simpering over the dreamer. 'When winter eases, the Vilanders will bring their allies to Alekka. They won't hesitate to strengthen their forces. If we wait, who knows what we'll be facing. Certainly the Islanders. And who else? The Brekkans? The Hestians? What are you thinking, Hector?'

Hector lifted an eyebrow, surprised to be addressed so... casually.

And catching hold of his temper, Gudrum smiled, sitting back down, suddenly conscious of the silent dreamer watching from the sidelines. Her eyes were oddly blank, her lips pressed together, and he saw nothing to indicate her opinion on the matter.

'I am thinking of our men,' Hector said coldly. 'I'm sure you're aware of the dangers of sending an army to Slussfall. While winter still clings to Alekka with icy fingers, it makes no sense to throw away the lives of able warriors, archers, and livestock. We would have to camp in the snow while the wind wailed around us, shivering and hungry. And when the food ran out? Where would we take it from? What? Do you imagine those farmsteads and villages around Slussfall will have storehouses filled to the brim, waiting for us? That we'll shop for it like we're at market? No, they'll already be starving, eating their livestock, watching their weakest turn to bone. You're not from here, I know, but surely a few winters in The Murk showed you what cruelty Alekka is capable of!' Hector's irritation had him vibrating, but seeing his calm dreamer sitting opposite him with a hint of disapproval in her eyes, he tried to cool his temper. It was generally not quick to rise, though it had been simmering for some time, sensing that Gudrum Killi was becoming too ambitious.

He sat back, dabbing his beard with a fine linen napkin, and taking the time to steady his breathing and still his raging thoughts, he tried again. 'We will use our time to prepare for the assault on Slussfall, for when we are there, we'll only have one chance. One chance to deliver a defeat so resounding that there'll be no talk of Reinar Vilander again.' Hector speared a hotcake with his knife, and dropping it onto his plate, he reached for the honeypot. 'When you return to Ottby, you will continue to cleanse the South, wiping away all old loyalties, installing my new lords. And, in the meantime, the fletchers and the armourers will continue their work here, and I will ensure that our walls remain secure. I'm having that postern gate replaced, as Ake should have done. And what else? There's more to being a king than running around cutting off your enemies' heads.' Hector spat out his last words, wanting Gudrum on the back foot, though Gudrum only smiled in that irritating way of his.

Gripping his eating knife in annoyance, Hector wondered when things had gone so wrong between them?

When had he started doubting his most loyal ally?

Sighing, he sliced through the hotcake, stuffing a large, fluffy piece into his mouth. Though it was cold now, not nearly as moreish as before.

Gysa turned to Gudrum, finally breaking her silence. 'Alekka is a kingdom in desperate need of a ruler, my lord. If word gets out that the king is merely set on killing everyone who offends him, that will cause both tension and unrest. He must create a sense of stability, as though he has arrived to steady a rocking ship.'

Gudrum turned to the softly-spoken woman with interest, still intrigued by her face. It didn't look as he'd imagined it would, for though she was barely forty, her voice had tricked him into imagining that a grandmother had lingered behind her hood. Now, though, he saw a desirable woman with almond-shaped brown eyes and enticingly plump lips as she spoke in that new lush voice of hers.

Hector noticed Gudrum's interest in the dreamer, which incensed him further. His new Lord of Ottby had barely taken his eyes off Gysa since his arrival in Stornas. 'Let us finish our meal,' he snapped. 'Then we will head to the map table. I wish to discuss the next steps and what I require of you.'

Gudrum forced his eyes away from Gysa, smiling at Hector. 'Of course, lord king. Whatever you desire.'

***

Reinar left the hall with Bjarni, bumping into Lief Gundersen, who fell in beside them, eager to hear the latest news.

Bjarni explained what Raf had seen, leaving Reinar to fret and frown beside him. It was hard not to feel frustrated. There was still no clear path forward, and despite the revelation about Hector Berras' dreamer, there'd been no further information from their own dreamers, nothing to help him decide what to do. His brother was still gone, the sea was still frozen, and Hector was still warming the throne meant for him.

Lief had little to say, and eventually, all three men were consumed by silence.

After heading through the square, they'd left the fort behind, making their way through the tent village, where many of their people were now living, suffering in the cold with the Tromsunders and other homeless villagers. They had taken the icy path to the harbour, though the journey had revealed no new insight, just as Eddeth, Alys, and Raf had revealed no new insight.

Reinar turned to his best friend. 'Bjarni? What is it?'

Bjarni peered at him in surprise. 'What's what?'

'You're not speaking,' Reinar said. 'Something must be wrong.'

Bjarni shrugged. 'I'm just thinking about food.'

Now Reinar laughed, surprising Lief, who hadn't heard him laugh in weeks. 'I should've known. When aren't you thinking about food?'

But Bjarni shook his head without even a hint of a smile. 'I'm not thinking about food for me. We need spring, Reinar. I'm no dreamer, but last night I dreamed of a winter that lasted a year. And how would we survive that?' He swallowed, eyeing Lief, who looked his way with eyes so black that Bjarni couldn't tell what he was thinking. 'Slussfall's stores are dwindling at a faster pace than we can endure, and the days are growing shorter than ever. The trees are still lifeless, the ground still frozen.'

Lief nodded solemnly, feeling as concerned as Bjarni. 'Hakon focused on growing his weapons' stores above all things. I worked hard to do what I could, but the land around the fort isn't amenable to farming. There's little that's arable. The weather doesn't help. It rains.'

They'd all discovered that, and both Reinar and Bjarni sighed.

'We can't take the ship out, so we have to do more ice fishing,' Reinar said. 'More hunting.'

'It won't be enough to sustain a fort overflowing with people,' Bjarni insisted. 'And more coming. More are coming every day. You've seen that. Soon there won't even be enough room for tents.'

Reinar had seen it, and it worried him. 'We're rationing food.'

'But for how long?' Bjarni's stomach growled to reinforce his point. 'We can't just get by on smaller and smaller rations. Not if winter continues. You need to talk to Sigurd.'

That surprised Reinar. 'Sigurd?'

'He's out there somewhere, being a god. He must know something. Must know what's happened to Ulfinnur and whether he's coming back. For if he isn't? If it's Alari's grand plan to kill us all? If that's the case, why bother about Hector and Gudrum?'

Lief was a man who venerated the gods, yet the idea that Sigurd Vilander was Thenor's son was something he was still struggling to accept. Though being stubborn wouldn't help them survive, and with a wife, a stepson, and another child on the way, he had to do everything he could to help. 'Can you find your brother? Call for him to come somehow?'

Reinar didn't know. He'd lain in bed many nights, wanting his brother to come into his dreams. He'd walked the forest, talking as though Sigurd was there with him, hoping he would appear from behind a tree. He'd thought about him constantly and even considered going to Eddeth to ask if there was a way to contact Sigurd, but every time he'd stopped himself. He didn't know why, except that Sigurd hadn't come to him. Reinar was sure his brother could see what was happening in Alekka, so if Sigurd hadn't come before, why would he come now?

Reinar thought of his parents, his wife, and his people, and he sighed. 'I'll try,' he said, barely opening his lips. And turning away from both men, he trudged back to the fort.

***

Alys felt sick. Her breakfast porridge sat in her stomach like a stone, the meeting in the war room having unsettled her. She wasn't listening as Magnus and Lotta walked beside her, both talking at once.

They were heading to the stables with a few rubbery carrots for the ponies. Daisy and Clover were sharing a stall, neighbours with Ulrick Dyre's giant horse, Skuld, who Lotta had brought a carrot for too. Closing her eyes, she saw Ulrick's grizzled face, his long beard flapping in the breeze, Bergit walking beside him, muttering in his ear. She frowned, then cried out as she fell over.

'Why were you walking with your eyes closed?' Magnus grumbled as he stuck out a hand to pull her up. 'Again?'

The shock passed immediately, and Lotta started crying, unwrapping her cloak. She saw the holes in her stockings, which Stina had only just repaired, and her crying became louder.

Magnus looked up at his mother, who seemed slightly removed from them both as she ran her eyes over Lotta's bleeding knees and then a hand over her daughter's hair.

Taking Lotta's mittened hand, Alys quickly sought to distract her. 'We can get a sausage,' she smiled. 'On the way back to the cottage.'

'Sausage?' Magnus' eyes glistened, for he was always hungry.

And though Lotta's appetite was patchy, she'd developed a particular taste for the Slussfall market, where a nice lady called Pia cooked sausages over a brazier every morning. Once, she'd sold them wrapped in warm flatbreads, but now there was little bread as the grain was being rationed. Still, the thought of one of Pia's sausages promptly stopped her tears.

Alys was relieved, encouraging her limping daughter towards the market. She remembered coming here to find Magnus all those months ago, wondering then if she would ever feel safe again.

She still didn't.

In fact, with Hector Berras on the throne, Gudrum roaming Alekka, and a dreamer helping them both, she felt more unsafe than ever. But, trying to smile for her children, she pulled two small silver coins from her newly replenished purse. 'Go and order two sausages, Magnus. Lotta and I'll catch up.' But Lotta's limp magically disappeared, and handing her mother the carrots she'd been squeezing in a mittened hand, she ran after her brother, Puddle bounding along behind them.

Alys' smile grew, the fog in her head clearing slightly. She didn't feel safe, but being with her children made her happy. She pulled up suddenly as Reinar, Bjarni, and Lief crossed her path, nearly knocking into her.

Reinar grabbed her arm. 'Alys!'

She turned to him with an open mouth, quickly aware that

his hand was wrapped around her arm, the white smoke of his icy breath drifting from his lips, his blue eyes so full of concern. Then, just as quickly, she saw Bjarni and Lief watching, and tugging her arm out of Reinar's grip, she stepped back. 'Serves me right for not looking where I was going.'

Reinar just stared.

It was impossibly hard to be locked inside Slussfall with Alys. Elin was so angry about her presence, so vicious whenever Alys was around, that Reinar had worked hard to avoid the dreamer. He'd mainly sought Eddeth's advice, not allowing himself to be alone with Alys. Not once. He didn't want Elin finding out. He didn't want her feeling betrayed, for despite any feelings he had for Alys, Reinar didn't want to hurt Elin any more than he already had.

But then Alys was before him, and it was as though the brightest sun had emerged to change a gloomy winter's day into summer.

He couldn't take his eyes off her.

Bjarni coughed as Lief slunk away, wanting to find Falla.

'I should go,' Reinar decided, not moving. 'There's a lot to do.'

'I imagine there is,' Alys murmured, turning her attention towards her boots, pushing them further down into the snow. 'Though it's hard to feel enthused about any of it. Every day feels much like the one before.'

'Soon they won't,' Reinar said quietly, revealing his fears. 'Soon it will get so much harder.' Alys looked up, and he searched her eyes for clues, quickly finding what he feared the most.

That he was right.

'We'll keep looking for answers, for ways to stop Hector and Gudrum, but with his dreamer watching...' Alys' words were lost beneath a shout in the distance, and they soon heard punches being thrown.

Reinar glanced at Bjarni, wanting him to go and sort it out. Bjarni frowned back, motioning with his eyes that Reinar should really come with him. But Reinar stayed where he was, forgetting his pledge, and turning his eyes away from Bjarni, he brought them back to Alys.

Muttering under his breath, Bjarni turned into the crowd.

Alys squirmed. 'I should... we should...' She clasped her hands together in front of her black cloak, glancing around. 'The children...'

Reinar nodded. 'You should go and find them.' Though as she turned, he turned with her. 'I need some insight, Alys. Some sense of the future and how to reach it. We're feeling our way in the dark. Well, I am, which isn't helpful when I'm supposed to have the torch to light our way. Though I feel no different than anyone else here. No more capable, no more knowledgeable.' He saw Magnus and Lotta in the distance, throwing snowballs for Puddle to chase, the smell of cooking sausages and smoke turning his stomach.

'Hector's dreamer is powerful,' Alys said, knowing that was hardly the reassurance Reinar was looking for. 'She's woven spells all around Stornas. Around Hector too. It's hard for us to see. We've all been trying. The fact that Raf saw her is hopeful. Perhaps she'll see more? Perhaps, finally, Gysa wants us to?'

Reinar hoped that was true.

'There'll be a way, a way to fight, to weaken the enemy. It's just a matter of finding –' She stopped abruptly, seeing that odd man again. Berger's cousin. She'd forgotten his name, but seeing her, he turned, heading her way.

'What?' Reinar peered at Alys, not understanding why she'd stopped, but then he saw the man himself, coming towards them with Berger, and he stiffened.

Alys opened her cloak, taking a coin from her purse. 'Here,' she said, holding it out, wanting to get it over with. 'What I owe you.'

Helgi ran a hand over his beard, so much more unkempt than his perfectly groomed cousin's. He looked slightly confused but mostly embarrassed as he stared into Alys' eyes, truly noticing them for the first time, and quickly feeling even worse. 'I... well, I've had a bite to eat since earlier.' He shook his head, his hairy cheeks flushed pink, thanks to four cups of ale and the shock of the cold morning. 'You keep it. I'm sure that dog will get into more trouble, so you might need it soon.'

Reinar didn't know what they were talking about, but Alys nodded, still holding out the coin, a look of uncertainty in her eyes. 'If you're sure?'

'I am,' Helgi insisted. 'Yes, definitely. Besides, my cousin tells me you're a dreamer, so perhaps there's another way you can repay me?'

He was watching her so intensely that Alys slunk backwards, not sure what to say.

But Reinar said it for her. 'Alys is no fortune teller, as Berger well knows. She's my dreamer. Not for hire. Not for any reason.'

Helgi rolled back his broad shoulders, lifting his chin as he considered the man before him. A blonde-haired, fur-cloaked beast, he saw, though just a man. He narrowed his gaze, eyeing Reinar sharply.

'My cousin,' Berger put in, amused by the tension. Helgi and Reinar looked like two stags ready to clash. 'Helgi Eivin. I left him behind in Napper when we came to Ottby. Now he's found me again. And this,' he said with a nudge of his glowering cousin, 'is our lord and future king, Reinar Vilander.'

Helgi's expression didn't alter as he rubbed his dripping nose.

'Another Eivin?' Reinar mused coldly, his attention briefly on Helgi before returning to Berger. 'Not like your brother, I hope?'

Berger laughed, seeing the flare of jealousy in Reinar's eyes. 'Ha! Rutger? Nobody hated my brother more than Helgi. It's why he didn't come with us to Ottby. They fell out years ago. Helgi wanted nothing to do with him in the end.'

'Well, I hope that's true,' Reinar muttered as Alys looked to step away, seeing Magnus and Lotta already disappearing with their sausages. 'For I need help, not more problems.'

'So I've heard,' Helgi said, and though he was speaking to Reinar, his eyes remained on Alys.

Which Reinar noticed, and his voice deepened. 'And no distractions. We have to defeat Hector and Gudrum before they claim every part of Alekka.'

Helgi finally drew his eyes away from the dreamer, resting

them on a clearly simmering Reinar's face. 'I've some information about that, if you want it. I saw a few things on my way up here. Heard more.'

Reinar looked surprised, at first, then reluctantly grateful. 'I do. Any information is welcome.' And nodding at Alys, he ushered Helgi and Berger towards the hall.

CHAPTER THREE

Gysa found Gudrum leaving the hall.

It had rained steadily throughout the morning, and finally fed up with squeaking boots and dripping clothes, Gudrum had returned to his chamber to change. He had many clothes now. Not the roughly stitched together rags he'd worn in The Murk, but proper clothes, expertly finished and embroidered by tailors. He had a steward and servants, many of whom had travelled with him from Ottby. He had his own guest chamber in Stornas' castle, with a copper tub, a giant bed, and a hearth big enough to sleep in.

He had everything he wanted, but no Raf.

And after seeing her every day for years and curling up with her nearly every night, he felt an emptiness that grew whenever he was alone, but especially when he was in Stornas, reminded of the last glimpses he'd seen of her. Memories of the catacombs, of the battle at the postern gate, still flashed before his eyes. He regretted that he'd thought so little of her in those moments, casting her aside as though she was a thing of no value, not a precious dreamer with the power to help him both rise and survive.

There were brothels in Stornas – more than one – and Gudrum had made full use of their services. His servants were more than accommodating, too, though none of the women who graced his bed could help him with anything more than a few moments of pleasure. There was no one to talk to. Ilmar was gone, Ahlen, too, and though others filled the void, he missed the familiarity of a friendly face, of a comforting body and real friendship.

He turned to Gysa with a forced smile, though he wasn't unhappy to see her.

'You are dry,' she noted, having seen him dripping as he'd entered the castle earlier.

'I am.' Gudrum strode across the flagstones, his dry boots thudding loudly in the echoing corridor. He paid little attention to the grandeur of his surroundings now. At first, everything had been jaw-dropping, his eyes constantly filled with wonder and surprise. The size of the city and the luxury of the castle had left him grinning for days, though when he returned to Stornas now, it was with a sinking feeling, conscious of the ever-tightening leash Hector was keeping him on.

'But though you are dry, you are not happy,' Gysa murmured, touching Gudrum's arm as she strode quickly to keep pace with him. Hector, she knew, had gone to visit the ship sheds, firmly focused on his plans for spring. 'Not happy being made a lord? The king's most powerful man? And after all that effort? How disappointing for you to just be unhappy.' She shook her head in mock concern.

Gudrum turned to her, stopping beneath the flaming torch protruding from a copper sconce. 'You are Hector's eyes and ears, Gysa. I no longer have my own, so just say what's on your mind, for I have to get back to my men. My time here is nearly done, and I must return to Ottby. I've no time for games.' The dreamer's hair shone like ebony before him, pulled back tightly from a full face, though the way the light fell above her shadowed her eyes. He couldn't see what she was thinking.

'And nor do I, but your little Raf is busy playing games in Slussfall, I assure you. It's no wonder you're so keen to go there and get her back.'

Gudrum snarled, not enjoying having his thoughts mined. 'She made her choice, and it wasn't me.'

Gysa purred, stepping closer. 'You may think she ran away, but when I saw her in my dreams, she was screaming. They took her from Stornas. She didn't go willingly.'

Gudrum was surprised, though he didn't know why Gysa felt compelled to tell him anything about Raf. Her eyes were dark, but her voice was lightness itself. He frowned. 'What use is telling me that? Either way, I can't do anything about it. Stuck here? Waiting for a spring that never comes? What use is thinking about a dreamer I no longer have?'

Gysa smiled. 'But what makes you think you no longer have her?' And laughing playfully, she turned around, heading back down the corridor, certain that Gudrum's eyes were following her every step.

***

After a morning spent in constant distraction and ending up with little achieved, Reinar had taken Ludo to the training ring where they'd attempted to beat each other to a pulp, though neither man had had their heart in it. Eventually, as the afternoon darkened and the cold intensified, they returned their wooden swords to the training shed and headed to the tavern.

It had been repaired as soon as Lief had taken command of the fort, knowing how fond the Slussfallers were of the tiny shack. Repaired, and in some places rebuilt, though it still wasn't big enough to fulfill the ever-growing demand for ale and hot food. So now, another was being built on the opposite side of the fort. There was talk of opening a brothel, too, though Reinar wasn't sure how he felt about that. Nor was Lief. But neither man could deny the need to find some relief. The weather and the walls and the threat of enemies above and below made it hard to even breathe.

Ludo blew on his hands as he walked, then lifted one in the air to Torfinn in the distance. 'It's strange to be here sometimes,' he sighed. 'I keep thinking we're in Ottby, though everything's different.'

'And Sigurd's not here,' Reinar added, which was the strangest thing of all. 'That should've been him in there, training with you. Not me.'

Ludo agreed, dropping his head as his boots sunk into the snow. It had come down in heavy waves as the sky darkened, and now the path to the tavern was hidden beneath a thick layer of white powder. 'Though I'm not sure I want to train with a god,' he grinned, looking up.

Reinar laughed. 'True, and who knows what he's capable of now? We certainly don't.' He paused, frowning as the raised voices of those deep in their ale cups reached them through the swirling snow. 'I thought he'd have come to see Stellan and Gerda. I didn't imagine Tromsund was the last time we'd see him. The way things are going here? What Hector and Gudrum are doing to Alekka? It makes no sense that he hasn't come.'

'Maybe it's not his fault? Maybe Thenor's forcing him to stay?'

'Or Alari's captured him?' Reinar suggested. 'Just like she's captured Ulfinnur.' He peered up at the dark sky, and mouth open, he let the snow melt on his tongue, wanting to feel like a carefree boy again for just one moment. 'Whatever the case, I wish he was here. I wish I knew he was alright.'

'Well, he's a god, so likely he is. Alright, that is.' It was strange to say, and Ludo shook his head.

Reinar patted him on the back, seeing a familiar silhouette in the distance. 'You go on. I'll catch up.' And leaving Ludo behind, Reinar pulled his hood over his head, weaving through the square until he was standing before a shivering Raf. 'You and I need to talk.' Raf looked ready to run, big blue eyes darting about beneath a flapping hood, but Reinar grabbed her arm, holding her in place. '*Now.*'

***

Valera returned to Gallabrok in the same way she had left –

breathless and frowning, shoulders hunched up to her ears – and Thenor felt his own tension mounting. He quickly called a meeting, requesting the presence of two of his most loyal gods: Tikas, The Messenger, and Omani, Goddess of the Moon. He needed all the help he could get to find Ulfinnur. Valera had done nothing but search for the God of Winter since they'd discovered him missing. Thenor had tried himself. He'd had every god loyal to him out looking, searching through the waves of time, delving into that space between the realms. They had scoured every known lair of Alari's, even known haunt of Vasa's, though there'd been no sign of them. It was becoming a problem so grave that they were all on edge.

Sigurd sat to his father's right, studying the drawn faces in silence, uncertain whether to speak. He'd been mulling over an idea for some time. Gallabrok was warded against Alari and Vasa, so Sigurd knew he could speak freely, though he was hesitant to do so. He was a god now, but a god of nothing. He felt self-conscious speaking up at all.

Though Thenor could sense that he needed to.

And soon Omani, Valera, and Tikas turned his way too.

They sat at the round table Thenor had installed in a new chamber. He didn't want to meet in the public hall. He wanted these meetings to have extra layers of protection, so he'd worked with Valera to create a windowless chamber adjoining his own, warded with intricate symbols and spells. Though he still felt wary. Seeing Valera sitting opposite him, eyes moist with tears, Thenor tried to focus. 'Speak,' he said to his son. 'Tell us what is on your mind. I feel a weight upon your shoulders, as though these thoughts have been with you for some time. You won't feel any better if you keep them to yourself.'

Sigurd was reluctant to admit that was true, but eventually, he nodded. 'Alari took Ulfinnur because of me. I feel it.'

Valera blinked. 'You do?'

Sigurd squirmed, uncomfortable with the unwavering attention of so many gods. He had grown used to Thenor's ways, and Valera was kind to him, but Omani and Tikas were new, and there was little in their eyes but mistrust and doubt. 'She wants to stop Reinar seeking help. If he's frozen in, no ships can sail. No messages can be sent.'

'Well, not by sea,' Tikas pointed out. 'Though there are other ways to communicate.'

'But we will not interfere,' Thenor insisted sharply. 'We will not go to the Slave Islands, to Osterland, to the Fire Lands. We cannot seek help on behalf of one man, for we are the guardians of this land, not its servants.'

Sigurd bit his tongue, having heard that many times before, forced to remain in Gallabrok as his brother struggled and his family suffered. He'd seen their frustration and heard their fears of what would come when he'd looked into Thenor's waterfall. And yet he'd turned away time and time again, knowing what Thenor would say.

The gods could not interfere.

But Ulfinnur? If they could rescue him from Alari's clutches, he would bring The Thaw, which wasn't interfering at all. It was time for spring, well past time for Vuli to emerge from her slumber. And when she did, the sea would melt, and Slussfall's solitary ship would sail for the Slave Islands and hope.

'I want to reveal myself to Alari,' Sigurd announced.

No one spoke, though Thenor gripped the table with rigid fingers.

'She wants to beat you, to defeat you, and if she captures me...'

'She will kill you!' Thenor growled. 'And what sort of plan is that?'

But Sigurd wasn't deterred. 'She'll certainly try, but not if you stop her in time. There must be a way to track me once she captures me? She'll take me to where Ulfinnur is, won't she? To where she's keeping him?'

Thenor sighed, though he had considered the plan himself, many times.

As had Valera, who looked up with hope in her eyes. She turned to Omani, white-haired and grey-eyed, still and stoic beside her. 'You could follow Sigurd. If you place a symbol on him, Alari won't be able to see it, but you will. You could show us where he is.'

Omani was hesitant. 'I have been looking for that evil witch for many moons, though she has made herself invisible to me. To *me*?' The ivory earrings hanging from her ears tapped together as she shook her head. 'I see all, as does Solla, though we cannot detect her. I could try placing a symbol on Sigurd, but I fear she is already many steps ahead of us.' And swallowing, she turned to Thenor, placing a smooth hand on his weathered one. 'Alari appears to have outthought us all.'

Thenor leaned forward, realising that, of all of them, Sigurd had the clearest, most direct way to proceed. It had only ever been fear stopping him from choosing that path himself. Sigurd was here in Gallabrok because he needed to stay safe. And now, if they followed his plan, he wouldn't be safe at all. He sighed. 'Though you will try, Omani,' he said solemnly, pushing a finger into the crease between his eyebrows. 'Sigurd is right. Alari wants to capture him. And if not her, then Vasa will come as soon as he reveals himself. Either way, we'll be one step closer to finding Ulfinnur. One step closer to ending this interminable winter.'

Sigurd felt relieved that he didn't need to press his case further but suddenly very aware that he'd just volunteered to enter the dragon's mouth.

***

Reinar almost pulled Raf off her feet as he tugged her through the dark square. Slussfall irritated him. Everything felt close. The houses and worksheds ran down either side of the square, almost leaning over it. The great stone hall commanded one end, the main gates, the other. He felt a constant need to escape the walls and the eyes that followed him everywhere he went. Though he knew that if winter continued, there would be no escape at all. 'I need you to find Sigurd,' he said when they were finally alone. He had taken the little dreamer around the back of the hall, down by the harbour gates, into the dark passage where he'd killed Hakon Vettel. The memory of that was still strong, as was the stench of fish in the air, drifting in from the harbour. While the weather remained mostly clear, fishermen were trekking back and forth across the ice, making holes, looking for perch and pike, maybe even some cod. He tried to focus, turning Raf to him, though she pulled against his hold, wanting to escape. 'You need to find him for me.'

Raf thought that through. 'How?' she asked with a sullen pout. 'How do I do that? You don't think I've been trying? Trying to find him since...' Raf bit her lip, knowing that she'd barely tried. She feared that Sigurd didn't want to be found by her. Her few attempts had resulted in nothing, and she'd quickly decided that Sigurd was happy where he was, happy with who he was with too. She'd seen glimpses of him standing with his flaming sword, a dark-haired woman beside him. And that woman was likely with Sigurd in Gallabrok. One of Thenor's chosen.

After that, Raf hadn't tried finding Sigurd again.

'Here,' Reinar said, slipping off an arm ring. 'This was Sigurd's. He gave it to me when I saved his life. It meant a lot to him, this arm ring. Stellan gave it to him when he became a man. It was our grandfather's. A family heirloom.'

Raf's hands were curled into fists by her sides, but Reinar grabbed one, forcing her fingers around the silver arm ring. The passage before the gates was barely lit by torches, and Raf saw nothing but the glint of metal, though she felt it, cold in her hand, and she saw a flash of Sigurd's smiling face.

'Do you think we can live like this forever? Stuck behind these walls with a powerful dreamer watching us? A king and a lord bent on revenge? Another lord above us wanting to take the South and the God of Winter missing?' Reinar was almost spitting in Raf's face, not understanding the difficult girl.

Surely she cared for Sigurd? Surely she wanted to see him again?

Reading Reinar's angry thoughts, Raf dropped her head,

tightening her grip on the arm ring. Sigurd's arm ring. She felt his presence, hearing his laughter. 'He has his woman back,' she whispered, chin on her chest. 'He's a god now. I'm not sure Sigurd wants to see me anymore.'

Reinar worried about that, too, but he wrapped his hand around Raf's. 'Though you must try. We saved you from that man in Stornas. He would've raped you. That's what Eddeth said. What Vik and Ollo saw. And Gudrum wasn't protecting you. He yelled at you and tossed you about. You can't still be loyal to him, can you? Can't be trying to help a man like that? Gudrum just used you to further his own ambitions, but I need your help, Raf. Not for me, but for everyone here. They'll all starve if winter goes on much longer.'

Raf stumbled back as though struck, yanking her hand out of Reinar's.

This wasn't about Gudrum at all!

'I don't care about him,' she snarled. 'Gudrum? He'd kill me if he caught me. I don't want to help *him*!' Though her voice quavered, her heart fluttering in confusion.

Reinar didn't hear it. He heard the whistle of the wind through the passageway. He heard the hum of the tavern in the distance, the odd creak from the frozen sea, his heart thudding in his chest. He tried to push those feelings away most of the time, but in the darkness, they often found him. He felt panic that Ake had made a mistake or that Thenor had. That he wouldn't be enough. That he couldn't save his people and rescue Alekka before it was too late. 'Then prove it,' Reinar demanded, lowering his head, trying to see Raf's eyes. 'If you're loyal to us and not Gudrum, find Sigurd. I promise you this, Raf, he thought about you all the time. He talked about you, wondered about you, got angry about you. He didn't understand you, but he wanted to be with you. We could all see that. Ask Ludo. Ask Eddeth. We all saw it.'

Raf was surprised, though she quickly dismissed Reinar's words. 'I'll try,' she said shortly, and sweeping her cloak around, she disappeared into the darkness.

Reinar stared after her for some time, wondering what he was doing. Was he so desperate for an answer, for some great revelation from the dreamers because he had none of his own?

Yes, he knew.

The answer was yes.

***

Solveigh braided her long hair by the fire.

Braiding soothed her mind. There was something hypnotic about that repetitive motion. It reminded her of her childhood and her kind mother, whose fingers had worked with skill and speed, braiding her hair every night. Most women wore their braids during the day, but Solveigh's mother had believed that hair was made to fly freely, like the mane of a wild horse. She would braid it at night instead to stop it tangling while her daughter slept. And now, feeling her own child moving within her, Solveigh had started that childhood ritual again, wanting to feel close to her mother, to feel some connection to her past. 'Oooh!' she exclaimed as her baby flipped inside her. 'I think I'll give birth to a fish!'

Stina laughed as she turned down the beds, shooing Winter off her pillow. The white cat jumped down, joining a sleepy Puddle by the fire, where he was whimpering in his sleep. Lotta sat beside him, drinking a cup of warm milk, occasionally stroking the puppy to soothe him. 'Puddle must be having a good dream,' Stina said absentmindedly.

'I think he's having a nightmare,' Lotta decided. 'He doesn't sound happy.'

Alys had peeled off her wet stockings, slipping on a pair of dry socks, and she padded over to the fire, listening. 'I think you're right, Lotta. Though is it Puddle having the dream or Ragnahild? We just don't know.'

Lotta shrugged, handing the empty cup to her mother with an enormous yawn. 'We haven't seen Ragnahild in weeks. Maybe she's not even here now? Maybe Puddle's just Puddle?'

Alys smiled, stroking Lotta's hair, fearing her daughter was right. 'Well, there's not much she could do either way. It's up to us to find a way out of here, isn't it? Not Ragnahild.' And catching Lotta's yawn, she ran her eyes around their cottage. It was twice as large as the one they'd shared in Tromsund, with two windows and six single beds hugging the wattle-and-daub walls. The walls were mostly covered with old tapestries that Stina had to repair often, trying to block out the determined drafts. A cooking fire was stationed at one end, where Stina could usually be found, flanked by the children and Puddle, and in the centre of the long room, a generous fire pit kept them warm. The cottage was tidy and pleasant, lit with lamps that reeked of fish oil. Stina had tried masking the smell by hanging bundles of dried lavender from the rafters. Though Alys smiled, still smelling that fishy odour as strongly as ever.

She stared at her bed with longing, enjoying the peace of the approaching night with Stina, Solveigh, the children and the animals for company. It was as though nothing else existed when they shut their door on the cold and the snow and the fear most of all. As though, for a few hours, they could pretend they were safe and free.

'What did you think of Berger's cousin?' Solveigh wondered with a smile as she tied up her braid and picked up her comb, encouraging Lotta to come towards her.

Magnus was already in bed, lying on his side, half asleep with exhaustion after a day spent training with Jonas and Vik. He had just turned eleven and was growing obsessed with becoming a warrior like them; like the older boys he watched training, too, many of whom were now his friends. Having seen his mother fighting in Orvala, he wanted to do everything he could to help her. He didn't imagine they'd come to the end of their journey. Sometimes, it felt as though, despite everything they'd been through, they were barely at the beginning.

Winter jumped onto Lotta's lap as Solveigh placed a hand on her head, gently pulling the comb through her hair. She thought of Ulrick again, feeling sleepy. 'What do you think Tarl Brava is doing? And Mirella? Are they watching us?'

Solveigh shuddered, trying not to let her mind wander back to Orvala and the life she'd been forced to share with Tarl.

Alys shivered as she crawled into bed, feeling the cold sheet meeting her bare legs. She no longer slept in her cloak, though she looked at it for a moment, considering popping it on. Though, knowing she would warm up eventually, she slid under the fur, teeth chattering. 'I would guess so, though I don't imagine Mirella can do much about us until spring. Unless she can fly!'

'If spring ever comes,' Stina sighed, finishing her own cup of milk. She returned it to the kitchen table, twisting her neck from side to side, trying to relieve the ache in her shoulders. She rolled them, using her hands to loosen the knots, though her fingers were stiff with cold, and she gave up quickly, deciding that sleep might be the only way to find any relief.

'It will come,' Alys promised, wanting to instill them all with confidence. Stina, who had been through so much. Solveigh, who was terrified about giving birth, fearing what would happen to her baby. And the children, who rarely spoke their fears out loud, though she could read their thoughts, and they were both frightened of what Hector Berras would do if he came to Slussfall. 'Spring will come, and hope will follow. Once the sea flows, everything will be different, I promise.'

CHAPTER FOUR

Raf hadn't spoken through supper. She hadn't spoken as they'd cleaned their dishes and banked the fire, bringing Rigfuss and Agnes inside and locking the door. They'd prepared their beds, adding extra furs, for their cottage was drafty in a way that made no sense. Eddeth kept muttering about evil spirits playing tricks on them, for as soon as they'd plugged up every hole and tucked themselves into their beds, the wind would find a new way in, whistling loudly.

'How do you think you saw Gysa?' Eddeth wondered suddenly. 'And why? Did she let you in? Does she want us to know that she's changed? That she's more powerful now? Do you *think* she's more powerful now?'

Raf closed her eyes, not wanting to answer questions about Gysa. She didn't want to hear Eddeth's voice at all. She tried to listen to the fire, which spat, and the cat, who snored, and the door, that creaked and rattled as the wind blew.

But Eddeth?

Raf sighed, having spent enough time with the dreamer to know she couldn't ignore her forever. Eddeth rarely gave up when she'd fixed her mind on something. And Raf knew that if she didn't stop her talking, she'd never be able to sleep. 'I think Gysa wants me to see her. She took some of my hair when Gudrum and Hector parted in The Murk. She wanted to be able to reach out to me, she said. To find me.'

'Did she give you anything of hers?' Eddeth asked, yawning as she stretched out her legs until her gnarled toes cracked. 'A way to reach her?'

'No, but I took something anyway. Strands of her hair. I have them in my purse.'

Eddeth sat bolt upright. 'I didn't know that. You never said that!'

Raf kept her eyes closed, smiling. 'Why would I say anything about some old bits of hair? Why does it matter? I don't want to reach out to her, do I?'

'No, of course you don't, but you have her hair, and she has yours. Oh my, but that is both a wonderful opportunity and a terrible problem.'

Now Raf rolled over, opening her eyes. 'What do you mean?'

'Because with her hair, we could hurt her, but with yours, she could hurt you!'

Raf swallowed, staring across the fire pit into Eddeth's blinking eyes.

'She hasn't, though, has she?' Eddeth mused, picking her wart. 'She hasn't hurt you at all. She's even let you in. She let you see her! And what does that mean?'

Raf didn't know.

But Eddeth did, and she lay back down, keeping her thoughts to herself.

Raf didn't answer. She needed to find Sigurd for Reinar but also for herself.

It had been too long of wondering and questioning and doubting.

It was time to go and find some answers.

***

Sigurd reached for the trousers he'd tossed onto the floor. 'I should go.'

Tulia frowned, remembering their chamber in Ottby's hall. When they'd lived there, Sigurd had been the son of a lord, and she had been his woman. They would fight and eat and talk and spend every night in each other's arms.

Here, he was the son of the most powerful god of all, and she was...

They spent most nights like this, in her cottage, in her bed. Sigurd would eat with his father, then leave Thenor's hall behind, seeking her out, entwining his fingers with hers, kissing her neck, wanting her body. He spoke little, and though she had many questions, she never asked them. She'd missed every part of him, and when they were naked, tangled up in each other, noses touching, eyes full of desire, she felt as though he'd missed her too. Though the moment it was over, Sigurd became restless, eager to leave.

It was starting to get on Tulia's nerves.

'Why do you come here, Sigurd? To my bed? There are pretty girls in Thenor's hall. Servants, who wouldn't say no to a god. Who couldn't. So why come here for me?'

Surprised by the question, Sigurd jerked around. 'What? What are you talking about?'

'I don't remember how we were in Ottby anymore, but it wasn't this.' Tulia sat up, breasts exposed in the firelight, eyes sharp. 'You weren't like this.'

'Well, we were both different then,' Sigurd insisted, body tense, his focus sharpening. 'A lot's happened since we were in Ottby.'

He didn't elaborate, though Tulia didn't need him to. What he hadn't said since he'd returned to her bed had spoken louder than any words. 'It has,' she agreed, her voice stripped of all emotion. 'With a lot more to come.'

Sigurd watched her, guilt swirling his guts. She was fierce and strong and beautiful. She was his friend, and he loved her. He had always loved her, but every night he left her to go back to his own bed because he wanted to dream about Raf. He couldn't bring himself to do it lying beside Tulia. He was betraying her either way, he knew, but those hours he lay in his bed, searching for Raf, were for him alone. 'I'm leaving tomorrow,' he announced, realising that he should have said something earlier. Tulia's face quickly told him that.

'What? Leaving? For where?'

'I don't know,' Sigurd realised. 'Leaving Gallabrok. I... need a break. Some... time alone.' He was reaching for explanations, not having thought any of it through. Thenor had told him he would sleep on where Sigurd should go to draw out Alari. He needed to find a logical spot. He couldn't just leave his son dangling like an apple from a tree, hoping to tempt her. Thenor had insisted that it needed to make sense, though they couldn't risk putting anyone else in harm's way.

Tulia waited, but Sigurd said nothing further, so she lay back on the pillow, closing her eyes. 'Well, I hope you find what you're looking for. And when you return, we'll talk.'

Sigurd nodded, watching her, hoping he would.

Return.

And taking a deep breath, he stood, tugging up his trousers, doubting he'd find any sleep.

Wondering if Alari would come for him tomorrow.

***

Gudrum stared at the rafters, one arm extended across the pillow beside him.

The empty pillow.

The chamber he stayed in when visiting Stornas was enormous, grander than anything he'd seen in all his time in Brekka or Iskavall. He smiled, thinking of Ranuf Furyck's brother, Lothar. Lothar would have laughed to see him now. He would have clapped him on the back, amazed by his luck. His luck, which had seen him escape death on countless occasions. And yet knowing that was true, Gudrum felt anything but lucky as he lay there.

The bed was comfortable and his tired, aching body sunk into it in a pleasing way. The stone walls kept out much of the cold. The blazing fire in the hearth helped, and the generous array of different coloured furs stacked on top of him did too. Though Gudrum didn't feel at ease. He'd once shared jugs of ale and goblets of wine with Hector as they'd plotted revenge and dreamed of success, refining their plans, trying to outthink their enemies. But now Hector had what he wanted - almost all of it - and Gudrum...

He felt hungry for so much more.

He hadn't cared about Ake Bluefinn. He hadn't cared about the Vilanders in the beginning, though running his hands over his face, feeling the new scars Reinar had given him, he desperately wanted to end that idiot's life.

But vengeance?

Gudrum hadn't even sniffed it yet.

He closed his eyes, seeing Andala's training ring and that smug bitch swinging her sword at his son, taking his life.

And opening his eyes, Gudrum felt his heart beating as though it would burst from his chest.

Jael Furyck.

He saw those green eyes glaring back at him, and clenching his hand into a fist, he thumped it into the pillow.

***

Gysa stared into the mirror, transfixed.

There were other things to do, tasks of great importance, though she couldn't help but take the time to sit at her table and admire her appearance.

She laughed out loud, still stunned to be herself again.

Though was she really?

'You have exceeded my expectations,' Alari had beamed, that

blue eye sparkling like a jewel. 'And now I shall exceed yours, Gysa, for the King of Alekka must have a dreamer of unrivalled power by his side. I cannot be with him, helping him rise even further, defeating every enemy, so you must. I will not only return your face and your body to what they once were, I shall enhance your abilities beyond anything you now possess. That will make you my most powerful dreamer. Hector will have Gudrum standing before his enemies, striking them down with his blade, and I... I will have you.'

Gysa smiled, picking up her comb. Her hair was wiry, and released from a tight bun, it sprung out to resemble a bush. It was hard to manage, almost impossible to tame, though she couldn't have been happier to see it again. She saw wrinkles around her eyes and embraced them, frown lines between thick eyebrows, and she frowned more, watching them deepen.

It was a joy to have a face that moved, skin that reflected her moods.

Eyes to see everything.

And now she turned both eyes to the low table placed before the hearth, where her servants had stoked the fire, layering it with wood until the flames were tickling the top of its embellished stone rim. She welcomed the fire's light and heat, enjoying its angry noise. Standing now, deciding to forgo combing her hair, she moved towards the table with a smile, and bending down, she lifted the silver goblet to her full lips, drinking with pleasure. Stornas had a supply of wine from the Fire Lands far better than anything she'd drunk before.

Closing her eyes, she inhaled, picking out each note, every hint of flavour. And savouring the full-bodied liquid, she placed the goblet back on the table, kneeling on a silk cushion, sweeping that wild hair away from her eyes. She took a slow, deep breath as Alari's whispers and Hector's grumbles faded away. And reaching out, she pulled a stone bowl towards her, picking up her pestle, pushing it down into the pungent herbs and seeds.

And blood.

***

'Who is your enemy?'

Raf swung around, horrified to hear that familiar grating voice.

'*Me*?' Alari grinned at Raf, who stared at her in horror. 'What? Did you think you could escape me so easily? That there was a happy ending awaiting you and Sigurd? Is that what you thought, little Raf?' She laughed loudly, stepping forward to clasp Raf's trembling hands. 'Oh, but I haven't finished with you yet, my dear. Not at all!'

Raf's eyes snapped open, though she saw nothing but darkness. She heard Eddeth's snoring and the goat's snuffling, and that gave her some comfort. Her dream had gone, though it echoed for a time, Alari's laughter still vibrating through her body. She curled her hand around Sigurd's arm ring, feeling confused.

And afraid.

How could Alari still be inside her head?

Every time she'd tried to escape her, to find the freedom to dream and help Reinar and Eddeth, there she was again, face to face with the goddess.

Who wouldn't set her free.

She was afraid to tell anyone. She couldn't even tell Eddeth, for she didn't know what Alari wanted from her. And she didn't want to put Eddeth in danger.

Eddeth snorted, calling out as she rolled over, though after a moment's pause while Raf held her breath, her snoring resumed its steady rhythm.

Raf felt her shoulders drop, though she lay perfectly still, afraid to think anything.

Afraid to fall back to sleep.

***

Sigurd stopped before Thenor's waterfall, Hyvari, wondering if he could bring her to life himself. And though he'd often thought of attempting it, he'd never actually tried.

'What are you hoping to see?' wondered his father as he joined him.

Sigurd jumped, startled, stumbling away from the great stone bowl, filled to the brim with rippling water.

'I thought you would be used to me turning up by now,' Thenor chuckled, enjoying the silence of the evening and the opportunity of finding his son alone.

Before tomorrow.

'No, you're like air. I don't hear you at all.'

'Well, that's something,' Thenor supposed. 'I was beginning to think I was losing my touch.'

'You were?'

'Of course. Alari and Eskvir are threatening to overthrow me, and Mirella Vettel... she saw my end. I have been contemplating my immortality, wondering if my descent would be slow and torturous, a gradual decaying of mind and body? Or would I simply die, ended by a more powerful enemy gloating over my corpse? Would I even have a corpse?'

'You don't know?'

Thenor smiled. 'I have killed my enemies, as have you, but in all the thousands of years I have lived, I have only ever killed one god. A goddess. Eutresia. She bled like a human, I remember, her body turning white like snow. And then she was gone. Bones, skin, hair. All of it gone. I could have sent her to the Gallagrim, imprisoning her soul, though I knew that would not be the end of things, so I took her life myself. I destroyed every part of her.'

'But you are not like her, are you? You're a more powerful god.'

'I am. I am one of Daala's children. She has many. Some are dead, others are full of hate, weighed down by years of resentment and pain.'

Sigurd looked confused.

'We are like any family, I suppose,' Thenor laughed. 'We have our problems, but, ultimately, we try to stay together. We try to stay strong. It is our place to be above those who struggle, not to engage in the struggle ourselves.'

'Yet your brother and your daughters want to kill you,' Sigurd reminded him.

But Thenor didn't need any reminding of that. 'They do, and perhaps they will, and if that happens, Sigurd, you will remember my words.' He turned his sharp eyes away from the puzzlement in his son's towards the waterfall. 'You want to help Reinar, I know. I see you watching Hyvari, hoping she'll reveal what is happening in Slussfall or what Hector and Gudrum are planning in Stornas, but that is not our purpose. The war we are fighting is not that of men. Your brother must earn the crown on his own. He must claim it with his sword, with his skill.'

Sigurd sighed, having heard those words more times than he could count.

'Hector took the crown from Ake, a man who showed what it meant to be a true king. A man who fought up a mountain that seemed to grow in size every year. And though I knew he wanted to quit, he never did. He never gave up or gave in, even in the face of death, and now Reinar must prove the same. He has help, more than enough help, so he doesn't need yours. We cannot defeat Hector for him, nor Gudrum. We must focus on our own problems, of which, my son, there are many. You must leave Reinar to defeat Hector Berras on his own.'

***

Hector opened his chamber door, surprised to see Gysa smiling at him.

Surprised but not disappointed. She looked exquisite in a dark-red gown, cinched at the waist, hair loose around her shoulders, dark skin burnished by the firelight. 'Has something happened?'

he wondered, suddenly anxious as she made her way into the chamber. And then he became even more nervous, rubbing a hand over his head, wanting wine. 'Have you had a dream?'

Gysa laughed. 'I've been far too busy to even sleep,' she said, turning to face him, her back to the fire. 'You and Gudrum have been making plans for months, my lord, as have I. We may be frozen in by winter, though a dreamer has many tools at her disposal, ways to make things happen, to... speed things along.'

Hector was intrigued. He bent to pour wine into a goblet, offering it to Gysa, who shook her head. His steward had topped up the jug, he saw, pleased that the man had thought to bring an extra goblet. 'You will at least take a seat?'

Again Gysa shook her head. 'What I have to tell you is of great importance, my lord. I don't wish to delay.'

Hector's mouth was dry, though, and he gulped down the wine, quickly refilling the goblet. It was flavoursome and refreshing, and feeling his nerves settle and his confidence return, he joined Gysa by the fire, where she had turned to warm her hands before the flames. 'Do you not fear it?' he asked softly, stepping close enough to smell the heady scent of spice-infused oil she had dabbed around her neck. And feeling slightly intoxicated, he inhaled deeply. 'The fire? After what it did to you?' It was a question he'd often wanted to ask, for his dreamer appeared so transfixed whenever she was near a fire that he found himself becoming curious.

'I am part of the flames, and they are part of me,' Gysa breathed, turning to Hector, seeing a sheen of sweat glistening on his bald head. 'For what happened to me cannot be erased by Alari's magic. The fire killed me but also renewed me. Fire brings death but rebirth too. I stand at the altar of both, a mistress and a servant, always humbled by its power.'

Hector smiled, though her words meant little to him. It was her voice that kept him enthralled. It wove threads of mystery around him until he felt wrapped in her spell. He'd barely known a woman's touch since the death of his wife. He had loved Cotilde with every part of his body, with his entire soul, and the thought of being with another woman had almost repulsed him.

Until now.

Reaching out, already feeling the effects of the wine, he gently touched Gysa's cheek. 'You are quite exquisite. All these years, I longed to see beneath your hood. To know the real you.'

Gysa didn't shy away from his touch. 'You were wise to wait, my lord, for that woman wasn't me.'

'I can see that. You even sound different,' Hector murmured. 'Though you helped me then and now.'

'I did, my lord, for I felt your pain. What had been taken from you spoke to me. I knew how it felt to lose a family, to be alone, to feel empty.'

Hector leaned forward, kissing that smooth, round cheek.

His lips barely brushed her skin, and Gysa smiled at the king's shyness. She saw desire in his eyes but fear too.

She stepped closer.

And suddenly hot all over, Hector stumbled back, immediately losing his confidence. He guzzled another goblet of wine. 'You had something to tell me,' he remembered, wiping his moustache. 'Something important?'

Gysa nodded, eyes sharpening. 'We have a way into Slussfall. Gudrum's dreamer, Raf. I let her into my dreams last night, and she was... open.'

Hector's eyes widened. 'She isn't loyal to the Vilanders?'

Gysa shook her head, watching Hector's cheeks flush a deep pink. He stepped back, once again rubbing a hand over his sweaty scalp, the intense heat of the fire becoming too much. She reached out, touching his arm. 'Loyalty is fragile, my lord. You can never truly trust anyone's intentions. Not even mine.'

Hector was puzzled. 'Not yours?'

'Are you well, my lord?' Gysa wondered, touching his other arm now. And holding her hands there, she expelled a long, slow breath over his face.

Hector almost fell backwards, blinking rapidly, but Gysa held him firmly in place, her hands pressed against his arms. She wasn't grabbing him, but somehow, she held him with a strength he couldn't fight back against.

'You seem unsteady, my lord. Here, let me help you.' And now Gysa wrapped her fingers tightly around his arms, crushing him with force.

Hector screamed. 'What are you... doing?' he spluttered, staring into her eyes, looking for answers, the flames rising behind him, crackling now.

'Do you remember how much you wanted to take Ake Bluefinn's head? How many dreams you had, imagining the different ways it could go? And yet, in the end, that boy, Skoll, took the pleasure from you. He took everything you'd dreamed of, snatched it away, leaving you without that moment. *This* moment.' Gysa's eyes danced like the flames, deep and full of meaning.

But Hector remained confused. Fearful too. She was stronger than any man, her hands almost breaking his bones. He started panting, chest tight, unable to catch his breath. His vision blurred, the dreamer's dark eyes jumping out at him. He tried to pull away, to escape her penetrating stare and her crushing hands, but he couldn't move.

She had him in her grip.

His tongue swelled, his lips burning. He stared at her but couldn't speak.

'No, you can't, though I don't need you to, Hector, for what would you say?' Gysa laughed darkly. 'You don't remember me, so what could you possibly say?'

Hector frowned, frantic thoughts warping his mind. He didn't understand what was happening. His racing heart hurt his chest, his arms throbbing now.

'You were there, I remember,' Gysa said. 'I remember your voice, ordering your men to clear my village. And your men were so loyal to you, weren't they, Hector? They obeyed every word you uttered, eager to earn your praise and rewards, for you have always been such a generous, giving man. And when they started hurting the women and children? Innocent farmers? Craftsmen? Not men wielding weapons, but those trying to protect all they loved and held dear. Did you stop your soldiers? Tell them to just take the lord? To take his warriors, the ones with weapons? Or did you watch and say nothing? Did you, in fact, join in?'

Hector scoured his memory, trying to understand what she was talking about, but Gysa's voice grew as loud as thunder, and he cowered before her, struggling to think at all.

'You encouraged them to fire my village, *Hector*,' Gysa snarled. 'The resistance of my people, those loyal to the Vettels, became too much for an impatient lord trying to impress his new king, so you ordered them to fire my village. To kill us all!' Now her voice rose until Hector was crying in pain, begging for mercy. 'I watched my children killed, my husband's head taken from his shoulders. And me? I didn't want to live, that I promise you. But I wasn't killed, not quickly. First, I was defiled by your loyal men, my dress torn from my grief-stricken body. My body, that was pawed at and assaulted, scratched and cut and *invaded*!' Gysa took a breath, squeezing Hector's arms until his thick neck reddened, his eyes bulging.

He started foaming at the mouth.

Gysa laughed. 'That would be the wine. You do so love your wine, don't you, Hector? Though perhaps you are not as fond of the little *flavouring* I added?' Her pleasure grew, her body vibrating, watching his fear intensify. It was exploding now, almost powerful enough to kill him. 'I waited so long for this moment, as you waited for yours. But unlike you, my vengeance belongs solely to me. You are the king, your enemy is dead, and though you long to sit on the throne and bask in your victory, I am delighted to inform you that your life ends here.' Gysa's smile was replaced by a look so menacing that she saw Hector tremble. 'I let you have it all, my lord, my little lord, because the higher you climbed, the greater I knew your fall would be. And now, I'm afraid, it is time to fall all the way to your death!' She released Hector's arms, pushing him with anger and force, with hate in her eyes and strength in her hands, feeling the power of the potion she had drunk herself.

Hector felt the release of pressure, the pain in his arms intensifying. The dreamer's words swam around him, crackling his eardrums, the noise of the flames behind him growing louder. And then he was falling, unable to hold himself up, arms cartwheeling, mouth open, eyes catching one last glimpse of Gysa's triumphant face as he fell backwards into the fire. His terrified screams rose up the stone chimney like a bird's cry, arms flailing in the heated flames, unable to save himself.

Throwing back her head, Gysa laughed, listening to Hector's dying panic. She could hear his heart thumping in terror, his skin sizzling. She could smell the stink of him cooking in the fire.

'Now the past is complete. Over. And I am ready to begin again.'

CHAPTER FIVE

Despite the dreamers' nightly efforts, no one could see what would happen. The future remained masked by snow clouds so thick and heavy that neither Alys, Eddeth, nor Raf could penetrate them.

Though they tried.

'What did you dream of then?' Eddeth wondered, splashing a bucket of water down onto the hard mud floor. Her nose was red and dripping, and realising it, she wiped it on her sleeve, grinning at a squinting Raf, who lay in bed, peering at her as though seeing a ghost. 'Something bad, I think. Nothing good is lurking in those eyes.' Now Eddeth left the bucket and headed back outside to retrieve Agnes, who bleated noisily as she trotted inside. 'Onto your bed now, there you go,' Eddeth cooed, pushing the little white goat towards a freshly laid bed of straw. 'Won't be long till Raf will be up, giving you a nice milking.'

Raf closed her eyes and rolled over, facing the wall with a moody scowl. She didn't want to do anything, and she certainly didn't want to get out of bed. It was too cold to move at all. Though the darkness quickly frightened her and her eyes sprang open.

Agnes bleated some more, and eventually, listening to Eddeth grunting and scraping about inside their small cottage, full of good humour as always, she rolled back, surprised to see her dragging a stool towards the bed. 'What?'

'It's me who asked first,' Eddeth grinned, sitting down. 'What did you dream of then? Something must have brought those dark clouds.' She leaned forward, pressing a red finger into the crinkle between Raf's dark eyebrows. 'Was it Sigurd Vilander, perhaps?'

Raf's scowl deepened as she edged away from Eddeth's frozen finger. 'It was supposed to be,' she grumbled. 'Reinar asked me to dream about him, and I had this.' She lifted up the arm ring, still in her hand. 'Though I didn't see him.'

Eddeth looked disappointed, though seeing Raf's frustration, she was quickly smiling again. 'But you will, won't you? It's likely Thenor's doing. He'll want to keep Sigurd safe. I expect he needs to, what with Alari prowling around, searching for him. He can't have everyone turning up in Sigurd's dreams. I imagine that's why. That's why you couldn't find him.' And now Eddeth's eyes widened, her thoughts running away with her, forgetting all about Agnes and the water she'd fetched, eager to make a tea. 'Thenor will be keeping Sigurd away from Alari. And Valera! Oh yes, they'll all be working hard to keep Sigurd safe. That's something, isn't it? Something to hold onto?'

Raf eyed her miserably, remembering Alari. She saw Gudrum's face, too, hearing his laughter as he gloated over her. If only she hadn't run away, he taunted in her ears. If only she hadn't left him. She could have been the dreamer of a king.

Raf sighed, listening to Eddeth muttering something about needing eggs for breakfast, and then she blinked.

A king?

***

Having spent years in Raf's company, Gudrum was used to dreamers. He'd often been woken by her shouts and panicked splutters. Sometimes, she had whispered in his ear, sliding a hand beneath his tunic. He'd welcomed most of what she'd discovered in her dreams, so he'd rarely begrudged the loss of sleep, but still, it was a surprise to be woken by Hector's dreamer.

Gysa touched his shoulder with a warm hand, and he jerked away as though struck by a shield. Pulling the furs over his naked chest, he panted, squinting and blinking, trying to understand what was happening or where he even was. Then he saw the woman smiling at him, fully dressed, the light seeping in through closed shutters. It was still a shock to see her face. She was mostly a stranger, yet here she was, sitting on his bed, touching him as though they were old friends. 'I...'

Gysa stood, gliding towards the windows, where she opened the shutters, inviting more light into the dim chamber. 'You didn't come down for breakfast. I was worried.'

Gudrum was puzzled. 'You couldn't see I was asleep?'

'I could, of course, though I didn't understand it, for a king must lead by example, not lie in bed all day snoring.'

Gudrum's puzzlement grew. 'King? What? Where's Hector?' He sat up now, glancing around the chamber, feeling the chill of the air despite the fire burning in the hearth. Seeing his robe lying on the floor, he reached for it, wrapping it around his shoulders as he slid out of bed. 'Why are you here, Gysa?' Though he couldn't deny that she was an attractive sight to see first thing in the morning, dressed in a flattering yellow gown, her dark hair pulled back from a smiling face. Her eyes sparkled, her cheeks showing hints of colour.

She looked radiant.

Then she pulled the crown out from behind her back.

Hector's crown.

Gudrum started, unsettled now. 'How long have I been asleep?' he joked, tying the robe around his waist with fumbling fingers.

'Too long,' Gysa breathed, eyeing him intently. 'But now is the time to be wide awake and ready for what comes next, my king.'

Gudrum's mouth dropped open, his eyes unblinking as she stepped forward, reaching the crown towards his head. And without thinking, he bent to her, aware that he hadn't bathed, that he stunk of wine, that he wore a robe.

That he was shivering.

'My lord king,' Gysa smiled, stepping back. 'Your people await you.'

***

Eddeth knew better than to let Raf hide away in the cottage, so after a quick breakfast, she took Agnes and Raf for a walk, leaving the goat tied up outside the hall while they went inside to find Reinar.

Who looked happy to see them as he pulled on his gloves and hat, preparing for his daily inspection of the sea ice. Though after listening to the dreamers, it quickly became apparent that he had nothing to smile about. 'But if Sigurd can't help us, if we can't reach him, what are we going to do?' he wondered as Eddeth trotted along beside him, Raf hanging further back, letting Eddeth answer all the questions.

Eddeth clutched Reinar's arm as they walked down the icy steps towards the goat. 'The answers to your questions won't come from the gods, Reinar. Not even from your brother! They must come from you.' She smiled sympathetically up at him, feeling his fear, hearing his worries and doubts. 'Your brother will be watching, I'm sure, but there is a reason we can't reach him. You are on separate paths now, so you must let Sigurd go.' And sighing loudly, she untied Agnes' rope, giving the little goat an affectionate pat.

Reinar saw Berger and Bjarni on their way towards him with that man, Helgi. He glowered, remembering the way he'd looked at Alys. And feeling good about nothing at all, he threw up his hands. 'Then I will! I will! I'll let him go! I'll let all of it go!' And stomping away from Eddeth and Raf, he pushed past the three men, heading for the stables.

Bjarni approached a stunned Eddeth with concern in his eyes. 'What's wrong with Reinar?' A baby was crying loudly, and he glanced around, wondering if it was his daughter, though he saw no sign of Agnette. Though he did catch a glimpse of the sausage lady readying her brazier. She was much friendlier than Slussfall's mean but accomplished cook, and her sausages were always perfectly charred.

'Reinar?' Eddeth nibbled her bottom lip. 'He's the man destined to be king, but that's no easy task. Just ask Ake Bluefinn! It's not easy to claim a throne, harder to hold one, devastating to lose one. No, most men think power is a prize, but the truth is, it's more of a curse. A terrible, glorious weight that not everyone is born to bear.' She looked after Reinar, wondering if Ragnahild had been wrong. Reinar was struggling to find himself, to locate the strength needed to propel himself forward. He was angry and short-tempered and frustrated, most of all, but it had to be him, Eddeth knew. The answers were his to find.

It had to be him who found them.

Bjarni followed her gaze. 'But Reinar is, Eddeth. That's what Ragnahild saw. Reinar is destined to be a great king. Our king. The High King of Alekka.'

Eddeth smiled with some sympathy, knowing how Bjarni felt about that old prophecy. 'Indeed she did, but destiny isn't reached through dreams. It's reached through actions. Dreamers only see what could be, not what *will* be. What happens now is up to Reinar and to him alone.'

***

The stables smelled of horses and hay and manure, though Lotta was happy to be hidden away where no one could find her – at least for a while. Puddle was rolling in some dried manure, Daisy and Clover were nibbling the apples Lotta had stolen from the cottage, and she was brushing Ulrick's horse, thinking of Orvala, when the door slammed open and someone stomped inside.

She couldn't see over the stall door, so she didn't know who it was. But then she heard a man muttering and cursing, and thinking he was alone, he started talking louder.

It was Reinar Vilander, and Lotta didn't know what to do. She wasn't afraid of him, but she didn't want him to find her. He would tell her mother, who would drag her off to do some terrible chore. She clamped her lips together, not wanting even her breath to escape, hoping Ulrick's horse would stay quiet too.

'Where are you?' Reinar cried. 'Why have you left me? Why won't you help me?'

Lotta heard him opening a stall door, greeting his horse in a softer voice.

She didn't know what was going on.

She heard the jingle of bridle and bit, the snorting and jostling of Reinar's horse, Riga, excited for his ride.

And then Puddle escaped under the stall door, barking happily.

Reinar spun around in surprise. 'What are you doing in here?' he grumbled, bending down to lift up the wriggling puppy, who had doubled in size since they'd sailed away from Orvala. Though he still wasn't very big, Reinar saw, getting licked as though he was covered in honey. And now his grumbles were interspersed with protests and laughter as he held Puddle at arms' length. 'Where's your mistress then?' He stepped out of Riga's stall, dropping Puddle into the straw, watching as he scampered away, slipping under a stall door, barking some more.

Reinar heard an annoyed, 'ssshhh!', and smiling widely now, he went to investigate.

Lotta looked up as Reinar leaned on the stall door. 'Puddle's a very annoying puppy. A big-mouthed, silly puppy.'

Reinar laughed at her sullen face and pouting lips. 'Why? Because you're hiding again? You don't think your mother could find you? I imagine there's no point hiding from a dreamer, is there? They'll always find you.' His smile faltered then, thinking of Hector Berras' dreamer, wondering if she was powerful enough to see what they were doing? Eddeth, Alys, and Raf had worked to cover Slussfall's walls in symbols, though none had appeared confident that they would keep the woman out.

'Is that why *you're* hiding? Are you trying to escape dreamers?'

Reinar blinked. 'You think I'm hiding? No, I'm just getting Riga. Going for a ride.'

Lotta shook her head. 'Not now. Other times. You're always hiding, aren't you? Here, in the fort. To stay away from the king and Gudrum. Away from Tarl Brava and Mirella too.' Reinar didn't know what to say, but silence was never a problem for Lotta to fill, and she went on. 'I hide sometimes, but it never lasts long. Magnus or Mama always find me. Even that mean Katrine. They always find me, in the end, making me do things I don't want to do.'

'And what don't you want to do today?'

'*Everything*!' Lotta sighed dramatically, as though she was too exhausted to go on. 'Everything they ask me to do. I don't want to do it. I just want to do things my way. I don't want to be told what to do. I want to *choose*! And when I'm grown, I will. I'll choose to stay in bed all day!'

Reinar laughed. 'Which would get no breakfast on your table and no wood for your fire. You'll be cold and hungry in your bed. Lonely, too, for everyone else will be outside working. No one stays in bed all day. Not even lords or ladies.'

'Or kings?'

Reinar peered at her. 'No, kings can never stay in bed, not if they want to keep their people safe and happy. There's always something to be done.'

'But what about the bad ones?' Lotta wondered. 'The kings who only care about themselves? They don't want to keep their people safe, do they? Or make them happy? I think they'd probably stay in bed all day and do nothing.' And realising what she'd revealed to herself, Lotta went quiet.

Puddle became frisky, digging a hole, flicking straw all over her. And then he scuttled under the door again, racing out of the stables, leaving them both behind.

They stared at each other.

'There's a lot to do,' Reinar said, studying the little girl. 'Though a ride would clear our heads before we begin, don't you think? I'm sure your mother wouldn't mind if you went riding with me.'

Lotta blinked.

'We could take Magnus, too, if you like?'

'Oh no, no, Magnus doesn't like riding. I don't know why he even has a pony. Poor Daisy, he barely visits her at all.'

Reinar knew that wasn't true, but he nodded, heading back to Riga. 'Get your pony saddled, Lotta de Sant, and we'll go for a ride. But be quick about it now. Riga doesn't like waiting on anyone.'

***

The surprise still hadn't left Gudrum's face when he stepped into the square. Slightly dazed, he walked in front of a horse, which reared up with ironshod hooves, nearly catching him in the face. And blinking to clear his thoughts and his vision, Gudrum lifted his head, aiming for the ramparts. He walked with his eyes up now, head swivelling, noticing the looks of surprise as Stornas men and women passed him, staring with open mouths at the crown perched upon his head.

It was garish, designed by Hector, who had melted down Ake's simple golden band, making a bolder, brighter statement by adding blood-red garnets and perfectly-white pearls. It didn't fit Gudrum, who still had a thick head of hair, sitting too high upon his head, making him feel slightly ridiculous, as though he was merely pretending to be the king. Hector had been entirely bald, and the crown had fitted him snugly. He'd worn it daily, proudly showing it off. Though Gudrum wasn't Hector, and he suddenly tore it from his head, changing direction, aiming for the metalsmith's workshop. He would get the crown remade, and then...

It didn't feel real. That Hector was dead? And not just dead, but murdered by the dreamer. She had admitted it freely, wanting to quickly earn his trust, to offer herself to him.

A murderess?

A powerful, murderess dreamer who could see into his mind and kill him whenever she felt the urge. That was unsettling in a way that was most unfamiliar to Gudrum Killi. He had faced every challenge head-on, sword and shield in hand. Not everything had gone his way. He'd battled uphill for much of his life, but he'd never felt afraid, never felt like a victim.

But now?

Gysa hadn't threatened him. On the contrary, she had smiled and flattered, holding his hand, speaking with enthusiasm and confidence about how she could help him. He could become the greatest king Alekka had ever known, she'd suggested with bright eyes and soft words. Perhaps even the high king?

His head swam with memories and possibilities until he didn't know what to believe.

'My lord?'

Gudrum turned, squinting at the man approaching him. One of his, he knew, recognising the thick scar across his chin. 'Oddrun?' He coughed, clearing his throat. 'What is it?'

'Word from Adalen, lord. Scouts say we defeated them all. Tore through them like wildfire. They surrendered immediately, half-starved, begging for mercy.'

Gudrum saw the filth on the man now. He smelled the long days on the road, and he straightened up, remembering who he was. What he was. 'And you left Horst in charge?'

'Yes, lord, and brought back prisoners, as you said. There's at least fifty of them.' Oddrun's weary eyes moved away from Gudrum's, drawn to the golden crown clasped in his lord's hand.

Gudrum followed his gaze, and finding it lingering on the crown, he lifted it up. 'There have been a few... changes while you've been gone.' And now he smiled, feeling his confidence return. He was the King of Alekka, for there were no other contenders - not in Stornas, at least - and there was nothing the King of Alekka couldn't do. 'Get some food and dry clothes, then meet me in the hall. Find Edrik, Valda, Lari too. It's time to gather my best around me and plan my next move.' He turned around, seeing the open harbour gates, the docks and piers beyond. And the sea, frozen and pointless.

But hopefully, not for long.

***

Reinar had sent word to Alys, though not enough words to make sense of why he had taken her daughter for a ride. She was still puzzling over what it might mean when she banged into Helgi Eivin, who was walking so quickly that he knocked her over.

'Oh!' Alys cried, falling backwards, head thumping onto the freshly cleared path.

Magnus rushed forward, glaring at the man who had bent down to help the dreamer up.

'So sorry!' Helgi apologised, immediately flustered. 'I... I'm a fast walker, you see, always have been. I hate standing still. Don't see the point in it. Death will come soon enough, so we may as well keep moving till then.' He grabbed Alys' hand, pulling her to her feet. 'Though with the ice, I should've... slowed down?' He shrugged, feeling embarrassed.

Horrific images flashed before Alys' eyes in a frenzy of colour and noise, and she immediately felt nauseous. Yanking her hand out of Helgi's, she stepped back.

'What? Did you see something?'

Alys shook her head as Magnus took her hand. 'I... I think I hit my head.' She felt the back of her head, which was wet, but bringing her hand around to her face, she saw no blood. 'I...' Turning her eyes away from Helgi and then her body, she hurried to escape him entirely.

'I think you saw something about me!' he called, pursuing her. His legs were long, and he quickly caught both her and Magnus.

Alys didn't answer as she moved with speed, squeezing Magnus' hand as he kept pace with her, still glaring up at the man.

Then Berger emerged from an alley with Solveigh, and Alys

was forced to stop.

'Are you alright?' Solveigh wondered, seeing the panic in Alys' eyes, noticing her slightly dishevelled state.

'He knocked her over,' Magnus said, feeling cross about that.

Berger looked surprised, peering at Helgi. 'On purpose?'

'Of course not on purpose!' Helgi snorted. 'Why would I do that?'

Berger laughed. 'Well, Puddle did steal your sausage.' He winked at Solveigh, who wasn't smiling.

'Forget the damn sausage!' Helgi snapped. 'I... don't care about the sausage. I was just walking!'

Berger clapped his hands together with a hoot. 'You were just walking. *You*? But your idea of walking is most people's idea of running. You're like some mad dog, Helgi, the way you move. Always trying to get somewhere in a hurry.'

'What's happened?' Stina asked, coming to a stop behind Alys. 'Have you been rolling in the snow? You're wet through. Come on, don't stand out here freezing to death. Come back to the cottage and change your cloak.' She took Alys' hand, which prompted Helgi to lurch forward again, touching her arm.

'I need to know what you saw,' he demanded, acting as though Stina wasn't there. As though Magnus, Berger, and Solveigh weren't there either. As though they were alone, just him and the pretty dreamer.

Alys felt it, too, and she backed away, letting his hand fall. 'I saw nothing, as I said.' And not wanting Helgi to say anything further, she grabbed Stina's arm and hurried away, Magnus following closely behind them.

'Who was that?' Stina wondered when they were out of earshot. She kept glancing over her shoulder at the odd man whose eyes continued to follow Alys. Seeing that no answer was coming, Stina went on. 'And where's Lotta this morning? I haven't seen her since she left with Puddle.'

Alys still didn't answer, her mind crowded with disturbing images, seeing Helgi Eivin in the middle of it all.

'There's something wrong with him,' Magnus muttered as

they turned into an alley. 'He could have killed you!'

'What?' Alys woke up, looking down at her angry son. 'No, he just wasn't looking where he was going. I'm fine. I am.'

Magnus thought back to his first time in Slussfall, when his friend Leonid had knocked a man over. That man had hit his head and died, and Magnus had been thrown into the prison hole with Leonid, and eventually, Jonas too. He still remembered the smell and the rats and the overpowering fear of impending death. 'But he might have hurt you,' he said, quieter now. 'The ice is hard.'

Alys pulled him out of the path of a woman and her daughter. She smiled at them, receiving smiles in return. 'But he didn't, and I'm fine. It was just an accident, Magnus.'

Stina tried again. 'But who is he?'

'Berger's cousin, Helgi. He's a... little odd.'

'And what did you see about him?' Magnus wanted to know. 'He said you saw something.'

Alys clamped her lips together, jaw clenching. She didn't answer until she felt both Stina and Magnus staring at her. 'Nothing,' she lied. 'Nothing at all.'

CHAPTER SIX

Sigurd adjusted his swordbelt, seeing *Fire Song's* hilt sitting proudly in her scabbard. He thought of the first time he'd used her at Tromsund, feeling embarrassed that he'd been able to do so little. Now she was truly his, and they knew each other well. Thenor had shown him much, but Sappa, Gallabrok's armourer, had shown him more. And between them both, Sigurd had become adept with his sword and more weapons besides. Though, despite any new skills he'd acquired or weapons he'd mastered, he doubted he could do much against a goddess as powerful as Alari.

'Don't be so certain of that,' Valera said, reading his thoughts. She stood beside her brother, shuffling her feet, struggling to know what to do with her hands. 'There are many ways to hurt Alari. She may be an expert in symbols and spells, but you can wound her in ways she won't see coming. I have woven protective symbols all around you. She won't have all the answers, I promise.' Valera felt sad, thinking of how she had tried to protect Ulfinnur. Whatever she'd done obviously hadn't worked, though she didn't want to tell Sigurd that.

He needed to leave with confidence.

Thenor clapped his hands around Sigurd's arms. 'I remain unconvinced that this is our best approach,' he said gravely, then looking down at *Fire Song,* he sighed. 'I think it best if you leave her here. I would hate Alari to get her hands on her. I'll have Sappa bring you another.'

Sigurd nodded, agreeing, though as he removed the sword from its scabbard, he became more aware of his vulnerability, feeling nothing like a god. He felt the strength in his father's hands, as though they were made of stone, and that strength calmed him. He saw Tulia enter the hall, and he smiled, pleased that she'd come to say goodbye. She didn't look happy, though he didn't blame her for that. He'd danced around their relationship like a boy since he'd arrived at Gallabrok. One moment, he was taking her in his arms, the next, pushing her away.

He wondered why she'd come to say goodbye at all.

She waited near the open doors while Thenor finished speaking to him. 'I will send you to Slussfall. Near Slussfall. I can't risk anyone in the fort. I want you merely heading towards it. Alari will see you if she's watching. I imagine she'll expect you to come for Reinar eventually. She'll be waiting for that.'

Sigurd took a deep breath, excited by the prospect of seeing his brother, though his father was right – he couldn't risk leading Alari into Slussfall. He thought of Alys, remembering the wall she'd made in Tromsund, and Eddeth, hoping they were both helping Reinar and Stellan.

And Raf.

He wondered if she was helping Reinar too.

Then, looking at Tulia, who was watching the thoughts sweep across his face, he blinked, clearing his face entirely.

'I hope Alari will be there. I want to lead you to Ulfinnur. It's all that matters now. We need to stop winter before it kills everyone.'

Thenor nodded, though he didn't agree. What mattered most was that his son returned, for he sensed that soon he was going to need him more than he'd ever anticipated. 'We will. As soon as Alari touches you, Omani will be able to follow you. She'll show us where you are. It may take some time, though, so do what you can to hold on.'

'Will Alari realise it?' Sigurd wanted to know. 'That she's being followed? That I am?'

Thenor hoped not.

'No,' Valera assured them both. 'She might wonder, of course, seeing Sigurd appear from out of nowhere, but she won't find the symbols.'

Sigurd felt slightly better, though he adjusted his cloak, fiddling with his brooch, nerves making him restless. 'What will she do to me?'

'She wants me,' Thenor reminded him. 'You are just a way to get to me, so she will not kill you because I wouldn't come to her then. She will keep you alive, use you as bait. It's all she wants. To beat Eskvir to my death, to take my throne, to command the gods. To be the victor.'

Now Valera looked as worried as Sigurd.

Thenor turned as Omani swept into the hall, her long face absent any joy, Tikas beside her, smiling and impatient. 'But she won't. Omani will follow you, and we will find Alari and Ulfinnur before I ever have to put myself in danger.'

'Do not forget about Vasa,' Omani warned. 'I will watch Alari, but you, Valera, must look out for Vasa.'

'And I will do what I can,' Tikas promised with a confident grin, eager to do his part. He was cheerful and boyish, filled with energy that never appeared to ebb, and, like the rest of them, fuelled by a desperate hatred of Alari, who had hurt and killed more than one of his friends over the years. 'My allies are listening. They will hear if Vasa or her creatures are on the move.'

Sigurd nodded, ready to leave, though he wanted to speak to Tulia first. And sensing it, Thenor stepped away, leaving him to go while he poured mead for his guests.

'Will you come back?' Tulia wanted to know when Sigurd reached her. 'From wherever you're going?' She inclined her head to where Thenor watched them. 'Seems like you're doing something important.'

Sigurd shrugged. 'Thenor doesn't want me to leave,' he lied. Although when he thought about it, he realised that was true. 'But I need to see Reinar.'

'Though what about Alari? Doesn't she want to hurt you?'

Sigurd felt terrible for lying. He felt terrible for his disloyal thoughts, for everything he'd done since Tulia had died. Though he didn't want to put her in danger. It was better if no one else knew.

'Thenor and Valera will keep me safe, and Reinar needs me.'

'What? You and your magical sword?' Tulia's arms were crossed over her chest. Her scowl hadn't budged.

Sigurd liked that scowl, though, and he smiled, kissing the tip of her nose. 'You leave my magical sword alone. She's more powerful than you know.'

'I hope so,' Tulia said. 'For who will I talk to if you don't come back?' She wanted to say more, to ask why he left her bed every night, returning to his own. She wanted to know who Raf was. He'd called out that name in his sleep once. She wanted to know why he'd kissed her nose and not her lips.

Though Sigurd turned his head, looking over his shoulder at Thenor. 'Oh, I'm sure you'd find someone,' he grinned. And now he turned back, seeing that she'd moved further away. 'When I return, we'll talk, about everything. I promise.'

Tulia nodded, though she didn't like the sound of that. 'See that you do, Sigurd Vilander. I'll be waiting.'

Sigurd smiled. 'I will. I won't be long.'

***

'You were gone so long!' Magnus exclaimed when Reinar returned Lotta to the cottage.

Lotta held her head at an angle, as though whatever nonsense Magnus was spouting was far too trivial for her important ears. Her chin was in the air, her nostrils flared.

She looked bored.

'Mama got pushed over,' Magnus announced.

'What?' Reinar looked from Magnus back to Alys.

Who rolled her eyes. 'It was an accident. I just fell. I'm not sure why Magnus keeps mentioning it.' And now she turned around to glower at her big-mouthed son.

'You didn't fall. Helgi Eivin pushed you!'

And hearing it, as Magnus had intended, Reinar was incensed. 'Helgi Eivin? Why?'

But Alys laughed, almost relaxing for the first time since she'd touched Helgi. 'He walks fast.'

'What?' Reinar looked confused.

But Alys didn't have time for his confusion. With Stina rushing off to find fish for supper, she was alone in the cottage with the children. And with the number of gossips in Slussfall, it wouldn't be long before someone was whispering in Elin Vilander's ear about her husband lingering at her door. 'You need to leave,' Alys said, shooing him away. 'You have things to do.'

'Do I?' Reinar looked annoyed and then bemused, not minding the feel of Alys' hand on his as she pushed him into the alley. And then, seeing Lotta's face peering at him from behind her mother's skirts, he nodded, winking at the little girl. 'Of course, I do, but...' He held his ground, meeting Alys' eyes. 'If Berger's cousin gives you any more problems, come to me. I'll deal with him.' His eyes drifted to Magnus, who looked pleased to hear it. 'I won't have him pushing anyone over.' He lowered his voice to a whisper. 'Especially you.' And with the slightest of smiles, Reinar turned into the dark alley, disappearing with a flap of his cloak.

Alys watched him go, barely aware of anything until Lotta poked her waist. She jumped. 'Ow! What are you doing that for?'

'I'm hungry,' Lotta complained. 'It's hard work, all that riding.'

'Is it?' Alys snorted, coming back into the cottage and shutting the door. 'And why were you off riding with our future king then? Did you bribe him to help you escape your chores?'

Lotta's face reddened. 'I didn't. No, I didn't! He needed me, Mama. I helped him to see things better. He *needed* my advice!'

Alys blinked at her daughter in surprise, seeing the truth in her words, and bending down, she kissed Lotta's head. 'Well, that's more useful than carrying some firewood, isn't it?'

***

Gudrum felt slightly displaced when he returned to the castle. The weather was wild, and he wanted a hot fire, eager for some ale. Both were immediately supplied, and he pushed a fur-covered bench close to the hearth, wondering if he was dreaming.

Spinning around, he took in the hall with its curved rafters and circular candelabra, the beeswax candles flaming like tiny lights overhead. And he thought of the day he'd left Ranuf Furyck behind in Andala, seeking a new life. Needing a new life. For if he was ever going to claim vengeance for the murder of his son, then he had to be something more than the king's lackey, forever standing in a shield wall, waiting for the gods to strike him down.

He'd had little to show for his life. He'd been entirely alone. Mostly broke.

He'd been humiliated, his son taken from him, offered nothing but a few meaningless coins. Though he'd used those coins to find men, knowing that that was the first stepping stone. For if a man wanted to rise, he needed steps to walk up. And each one of the steps he'd taken since leaving Andala had led him here.

Gysa swept into the hall with a beaming smile. 'Hiding from the rain, are we? My lord,' she added, stopping before him, her eyes immediately fixed on the fire.

'What are we going to do about Hector?' Gudrum wondered. He motioned Gysa closer, pulling her down onto the bench. 'What have you done with his... body?'

She laughed. 'You haven't been paying attention if you think anyone here will miss him, my lord. He sat in this castle, stuffing his face like a greedy dog. He barked orders because it made him feel important, but he sent you off to do all the work. There was little respect for him here and certainly no tolerance. Not after a king like Ake Bluefinn. The people of Stornas were quickly growing weary, seeking something more.'

'But he *was* the king,' Gudrum said sharply. 'So we must honour him. I don't intend to drop him into the midden heap with the rest of the scraps.'

Gysa tried not to smile at the thought of it. 'I had him removed to the kitchen garden. He's out in a shed. Well, what's left of him. There wasn't much, to be fair, which was surprising given the size of him.'

Gudrum seized her arm. 'And who's to say I'm not next?' he snarled, not enamoured with her smug gloating. 'Perhaps that's your plan? To be the queen? To take the throne yourself?'

Gysa had never thought of such a thing, and she looked at the new king in surprise. 'But why would I want that?' Now she was purring, her eyes catlike, her hand resting on Gudrum's knee. 'I do not seek to rule. All that hard work? All on my own? Oh no, my lord, I certainly don't wish to spend my life carrying such a weighty burden.'

Gudrum was surprised and more than a little unsettled, by both the woman's hand and her words. 'We can't work together if I can't trust you. Look at Raf. At what she did to me!' He almost rose off the bench, feeling the sting of that wound, still sharp, though the warmth of Gysa's touch was distracting.

Gysa laughed. 'She's barely a woman, that one, and I am on my second chance. Do you really think I would risk losing it all? Now? But Alari is always watching. Soon she will come, seeing what I did, and I don't want her for an enemy, or you. Hector was responsible for the murder of my family. My husband, my sons, they died by his orders as much as by the hands of his warriors.' Gysa's eyes glittered with tears now, her voice faltering. 'I have had my revenge, finally, after all these years, and now I will gladly help you. I've done Alari and Alekka a great favour by removing Hector. You saw that yourself. As soon as he reached Stornas, which *you* had claimed for him, he just wanted to eat and drink and bask in the glow of his victory. He wanted a throne and a crown, a gilded reputation. But the man was weak and vain, not equipped for what lies ahead. You, though, will be the king to deliver Alari and her allies everything they've dreamed of. You will defeat Reinar Vilander in a way Hector never could have.'

Gudrum sat back in surprise, mouth open, though it wasn't

long before he was smiling, placing his hand over Gysa's, staring into her eyes.

***

'What did she say to you?' Bjarni wanted to know as he leaned on the ramparts beside Reinar, staring at the forest in the distance. 'Lotta? You don't look like the same man I saw this morning.' He blew on his hands, dreaming of a hot bath. It was bath day in two days, and he couldn't wait to fill up the tub, hoping Agnette would join him this time, though she still wouldn't let the baby out of her sight. She didn't need to, he supposed, thinking their daughter could just stay in her basket beside the tub.

Reinar smiled, remembering his entertaining ride. 'Lotta's wiser than she realises and very confident in what she says.'

Bjarni laughed. 'She reminds me of Agnette in that way, not Alys. Alys is shy.'

Reinar thought so, too, though he didn't say. They'd come up to the ramparts to get a better view, hoping to escape the noise of the square, though the archers were busy running drills, and he was distracted by their calls, thinking about Ottby. 'Lotta told me to stop hiding, to stop standing still. To stop waiting for someone else to help me.'

Bjarni looked shocked. 'She's what? Seven?'

'Eight.'

'And she said that to you? The future king?'

'In a roundabout way, she did. Yes.'

'She takes after Jonas then. He never shies away from saying what he thinks.'

'No, and nor did Lotta, and she's right. I can't wait for someone else to solve my problems. To melt the ice, or find Ulfinnur, or bring my allies to help. I can't wait on the dreamers or the Islanders either. It's time to leave the fort, Bjarni. I need to defeat Hector on my own.'

'Well, not entirely on your own,' Bjarni suggested with a grin. 'You might need an archer or two, a shield wall, some horses?'

Reinar started towards the guard tower, having had quite enough of the wind twisting his cloak in knots, drilling into his ears. Thinking of what Lotta had said made him eager to get to the map table. He needed to find a way to neutralise Hector's obvious advantages. From everything his dreamers had seen and his scouts had reported, Hector had stayed in Stornas, sending Gudrum out to do his bidding. So, if he could try and defeat Gudrum, he would have a better chance of beating Hector. And beating Hector was now about so many things: avenging Ake, putting his chosen heir on the throne, steadying Alekka and resetting the balance of power again. But more than anything, Reinar thought, taking one last glimpse at the great village of tents sprawling ever wider before Slussfall's forest, it was about returning the grieving and displaced Alekkans back to their homes and families.

***

When Stina returned with her hard-fought-for fish, Alys left the cottage to visit Eddeth. Eddeth rarely came to see her, so Alys knew that the only way to hear about anything Raf or Eddeth had seen was to seek them out. They kept to themselves, mostly in their cottage, which had belonged to the evil dreamer, Mother Arnesson. She wondered why either of them wanted to stay in such a small, dark pit, but Eddeth seemed to like it, and Raf never spoke much. In the few months they'd been in Slussfall, Alys hadn't been able to penetrate the shell she protected herself with. She saw pain in Raf's eyes, unhappiness and fear, embarrassment, too, though she was yet to find a way through.

Alys shook her head, realising how impossible she found it to stop worrying. She thought of Solveigh, fearing she was making a mistake with Berger, who had made his intentions so loud and clear. She wanted to prod Stina to say something to Ludo, who was the complete opposite, not revealing his feelings about her at all. She thought of Falla, who was terrified about the impending birth of her daughter, too afraid to tell Lief that he wasn't having a son. And Eddeth, who had become much quieter since Aldo's death, and like Raf, less willing to share what she thought.

Her head was full of questions, though Alys had few answers as she walked down the alley, knowing that she had more important things to think about, like Hector Berras and Gudrum, like Ulfinnur and the threat of an endless winter. She shivered, hoping it wouldn't get any colder, for if Alari was controlling the God of Winter, there was a lot more she could do to terrorise them all.

She held out her arms like wings, trying to steady herself as she walked down the path to Eddeth's cottage. It was sheltered from the wind but also from the sun, and the ice was deadly. Eddeth was always tumbling down the path, collecting bruises that she proudly showed off. Alys smiled, then lost her balance, falling onto her arse. 'Aarrghh!' she cried, feeling foolish, and picking up her cloak, she attempted to stand.

'Well, this time you can't blame me,' said a voice.

Alys looked up in horror. 'You again,' she sighed, reluctantly taking the hand Helgi Eivin was holding out to her. 'Are you following me?'

He laughed as he pulled her to her feet for the second time that day. His hair was brushed, his beard combed, though his hazel eyes looked as wild as ever. The alley was dark, but slivers of light shone through rents in the overhanging porch roofs, and Alys clearly saw Helgi's eyes. There was fear and curiosity in them and desperation most of all.

'No, just familiarising myself with the fort. Berger's off with your friend again. The pregnant woman. I didn't think they'd want my company.' He took his hand away, motioning for Alys to move ahead of him.

'Perhaps you could go to the tavern?' Alys felt flustered as she started walking, hoping to leave Helgi behind, but he tapped her arm, quickly stepping ahead of her. And turning around, he forced her to stop.

'I'm not a forward man,' he admitted. 'Though I know you saw something when you touched me earlier. We had a dreamer two villages over when I was a boy. My mother took me to see her once. I remember the way she looked at me, blankly. She saw nothing. But when she gripped my mother's hand, her eyes changed, as though she was seeing something that wasn't there before us.'

Alys didn't move, though she desperately tried to avoid Helgi's searching eyes. People walked past them - an old couple with their old dog - and Alys' eyes flickered towards them. She wondered where Puddle was.

Helgi took her hand, and she blinked up at him in surprise, quickly tugging it away.

'You don't know me. I'm strange, odd. I don't know. Aggressive? I've knocked you down, accosted you, and I'm sorry for all of it. You know my cousin, though, and he's a good man. I just... I need to know what you saw. It's important to me.'

He'd rambled at such speed that Alys had struggled to keep up, but eventually, hearing the sadness in his voice and feeling the depth of his despair, she nodded. 'I.. yes, alright, I'll tell you what I saw, but not here, please. Not now. I need to see Eddeth.' Alys paused, trying to think. 'Go to the tavern. I'll find you there shortly.'

Helgi looked pleased. 'I'll wait for you.' Looking up, he saw that the day was nearly done. 'Though don't be long.'

Alys nodded, moving past him with care, hands out, remembering the horrors of what she'd seen, wondering what she was doing trying to help a man like Helgi Eivin.

***

'And this is how you repay me? After all I did for you? Another chance at life? A new face and body? And you cast my king into the fire as though he's some carcass! Some sacrifice! To who? Not me! What were you thinking, you stupid bitch? You self-serving, vain and ridiculous woman!'

After disposing of Hector, Gysa had been anticipating Alari's arrival, though she hadn't been looking forward to it. The goddess had spat and snarled and threatened to strike her as soon as she'd arrived in her chamber, too furious to stay still for long. Too wild with rage to listen to anything Gysa tried to offer in her defense.

Alari laughed maniacally, her eye bright with anger. 'You thought you could hide your true intentions from me?' That wasn't true. Gysa hadn't just thought to hide her plans for Hector, she *had* hidden them, successfully, and that was what bothered Alari most of all. That she had been bested by a dreamer? Another one? 'Why did you seek to do such a thing? *How*?'

Gysa didn't intend to reveal that, so she sought to distract Alari, trying her best to look remorseful. 'I knew you wouldn't let me anywhere near Hector if you knew the truth of what he'd done to me.'

Alari paced back and forth, so angry that she thought about pushing the dreamer into the fire herself. But Gysa stood before her like a serene goddess, a powerful, clever woman. It would make no sense to dispose of such talent.

Though her ambition...

'But what did Hector really do?' Alari sneered. 'Order his men about as his king had asked him to? Why blame a lord for doing what every lord has done since the beginning of time? For following his king's orders? For defeating his enemies? Why blame Hector for that?'

Gysa's anger sparked, and she curled her fingers, squeezing her hands together, though her smile remained firmly in place. 'Because it was *his* idea, not Ake's. It wasn't what Ake wanted, not what he ordered at all. Ake Bluefinn instructed Hector to take the lords loyal to Jorek prisoner or kill them if they refused to surrender, though not their people. But Hector became as battle drunk as his men, and he made his own choice. If he hadn't, my husband would be alive today, my children too. The men who followed his orders were mere pawns. What else were they going to do? No, it was only Hector I cared about killing.'

'But a king? You killed a king! *My* king!'

'Though he wouldn't have made a good king. He was too weak, too uncertain, too full of his own self-importance. Gudrum will make a better ruler. He's a warrior, a man with ambition and skill, not some old lump with vengeance on his mind.'

'I'm not sure that's true,' Alari sneered. 'From what I've seen, Gudrum Killi's full to the brim with dreams of vengeance, just as Hector was. Just as everyone is! Including *you*!' Alari didn't dispute that Gudrum would make a useful king, one she was happy to own, but the idea that Gysa had thought to take matters into her own hands? As though she had any say in the future of Alekka?

It infuriated her.

She blinked, turning her head.

'But Gudrum –'

Alari held up a hand, staring at the chamber door.

Through the door.

And then she was gone.

CHAPTER SEVEN

The urgent call from up on the wall had Reinar pushing through the darkening market with impatience. There was a sudden flurry of activity on the ramparts, though he didn't know what was happening. He couldn't make out the calls – the noise in the square was too loud, and it was growing darker by the moment. He'd been with Vik and Ollo, talking to the smithy, and they followed him, as curious to find out what was going on as their lord.

Reinar took to the stairs, quickly out on the ramparts, staggering to a stop, mouth falling open as he recognised the figure walking towards the fort.

Sigurd.

His brother's head was raised, searching the ramparts. 'Sigurd!' he called, arm extended, and turning, he yelled to one of his men. 'Ingur, get my father! And the gates! Open the gates!'

'No!' Sigurd threw up a hand. 'No!'

And with his brother's voice ringing in his ears, Reinar called back his men, not understanding what was happening but well aware that Sigurd would know more than him.

Sigurd stopped, hoping Alari would come quickly, though he felt rising fear. Would she kill him outright or just torture him? It was a risk, but one he needed to take to save everyone in Slussfall, and not just Slussfall, he knew, but Alekka too. For the Alekkans needed a good king again – a fair, just, honest king – and he needed those people to be alive when Reinar claimed the throne. 'I don't know if it's safe!' he cried. 'I want to speak to you, Brother, but is it safe?' Sigurd didn't know how long it would take for Alari to register his presence. He could see the ground darkening rapidly around him now, noticing the first hints of moonglow.

Up on the ramparts, Reinar was surprised by the sudden arrival of night. Looking up, he saw the moon watching them before turning back to Sigurd. 'Let me come out! We can speak outside the fort!'

Sigurd couldn't risk that. He shook his head. 'You must get your dreamers to make the fort safe first. I'll come again tomorrow. I'll be here at this time tomorrow. And then –'

A flapping cloak announced Alari's arrival. She didn't wait, didn't hesitate, and whipping out her hands, she moved quickly, white light flaring from pointing fingertips, trapping Sigurd.

He couldn't move. His arms fell to his sides – pinned there. A weight as heavy as iron slags pushed down on his shoulders, as though driving him into the earth.

And then they were gone.

'*Sigurd*!' Reinar bellowed from the ramparts. He pushed past a gaping Ollo, running to the guard tower. He almost fell down the stairs as he ran, stumbling, knocking into surprised men and women as he made it to the gates, screaming at the guards to let him out.

Though when the locking beam was removed and the gates were scraped open, Reinar could see that there was nothing he could do.

Sigurd was gone. So was Alari.

And Slussfall was plunged into darkness.

***

Thenor dropped his head, feeling Valera's hand on his arm.

'It is as we hoped. She came immediately,' his daughter said calmly.

'Yes, as we hoped, and yet what will it mean now? For Sigurd? For Ulfinnur?' Doubts swirled in Thenor's mind, and he wondered if he'd made the wrong choice.

'Sigurd has Omani's mark. She can find him, and when she does, she will follow him. We only have to wait until she reveals Alari's hiding place.' Valera was nervous, despite her confident words. She feared that Ulfinnur was already dead. It had been so long without him now. Why would Alari keep him? Unless, like Sigurd, she wanted to lure Thenor away from Gallabrok?

'We must prepare,' Thenor decided, not wanting to delay. 'For the moment Omani reveals Alari's location, we have to be ready. Though perhaps Alari is already one step ahead of us?'

'She hasn't been so far. You've managed to outthink her every time,' Valera reminded him.

Thenor nodded, though he was barely listening to anything more than his own fears, which thumped like a heartbeat.

He needed to get to Sappa.

It was time for his spear.

***

Slussfall's hall was abuzz with what had happened outside the gates.

'But why did Sigurd come?' Falla wanted to know, tugging Lief's arm. She was exhausted, her belly heavy and pendulous, but she had waddled out of her chamber, wanting to know what was going on. Though her husband was his usual tight-lipped self, and she got no information out of him. So, spying Alys and Eddeth entering the hall with that little dreamer, Raf, she shuffled towards them.

'What has happened?' Eddeth wanted to know when she reached them.

'I was about to ask you that,' Falla sighed wearily. 'Didn't you see?'

'No, but we heard the kerfuffle loud enough. Someone said Sigurd was here.'

'And Alari,' Agnette said as she joined them. 'That's what Bjarni said. Alari came and snatched Sigurd away.'

Raf felt ready to faint or run. She heard the fire spitting and popping, the raised voices suddenly muffled, and Alari's victorious laugh echoing in her ears.

Eddeth nudged her. 'What about you then? What did you see? Can you see something now?'

Raf stared into those familiar bulging eyes, unable to speak.

And realising that she'd put a stunned Raf on the spot, Eddeth turned to Alys. 'What about you? One of us needs to be of some use, don't we?'

But Alys hadn't seen anything either.

Having caught a glimpse of Eddeth, Reinar strode through the rapidly filling hall, wanting to speak to his dreamers. All eyes were on him, though before he answered any questions, he needed some answers. So with a quick look back at his father, who had gathered his council together, he headed into the war room.

When they were inside, Reinar closed the door and turned around with a frown, his attention on the dreamers who stood together, backs against the table. 'Sigurd said he wanted you to make it safe before he came again. He said I needed to get you to make the fort safe. That he would be back tomorrow.'

Eddeth glanced at Alys, feeling confused by that.

'But Alari was there in a heartbeat,' Vik put in, still shaking his head. 'He stood no chance.'

'*Was* it Alari?' Ludo wondered. 'In the forest, we thought it was Alari, but it turned out to be Thenor.'

'It was her,' Reinar said, motioning Eddeth forward. 'Her white braid. I saw her white braid.'

Eddeth blinked, her mouth absent any words.

And sensing it, Alys spoke. 'Perhaps Sigurd didn't come to you before because he knew it was dangerous? So there must have been something important he needed to say.'

'And he couldn't come into my dreams? Or one of yours?' Reinar asked, his frantic eyes finding Raf.

She squirmed silently, ducking her head.

'It would only be Thenor holding him back, knowing he was in danger,' Eddeth promised, patting Reinar's hand. 'And he was. Oh dear, but what will happen now?' They all looked at Eddeth, hoping she knew, but she shook her head, not having any answers. 'That goddess has plans,' she warned, 'so we can only hope she keeps Sigurd alive. That her real target is Thenor.'

Stellan joined his son, feeling equally frantic. 'But is it? What do you think, Alys? You've spoken to Thenor.'

Alys blinked, trying to speak with a confidence she no longer felt. 'Alari wants to defeat Thenor, so I don't think it helps her to hurt Sigurd. He's valuable. If she came so quickly, it's because she was watching, waiting for him. She'd know that this was where he wanted to be. She would've been watching.'

Eddeth nodded vigorously, trying to edge towards the welcoming fire, though a wall of burly men blocked her way. 'We must leave Thenor to save Sigurd,' she decided as that theory settled in. 'Yes, it is something only Thenor can help with. What could we do? Against the Goddess of Magic? Oh no, but we mustn't risk our lives to save Sigurd's. Thenor wouldn't want us to. He would want us to keep Reinar safe, to keep his people safe. To keep our eyes fixed on Stornas. On the throne.'

Reinar didn't care about the throne, he cared about his brother, who was always getting into trouble. And despite Sigurd being a god now, he felt real fear, wondering if this time, he had finally run out of luck.

'Eddeth's right,' Stellan said with some reluctance, placing a hand on Reinar's shoulder. 'Thenor is the Father of the Gods. If anyone is powerful enough to find Sigurd, it's him. We can't risk Slussfall now. There are too many people in here. We can't expose them to whatever magic that goddess is stirring up.'

Reinar clenched his hands into fists, staring at Alys. Then, drawing himself away from her worried gaze, he turned to the map table. 'We must focus on Hector then, on Gudrum, on making some inroads. We can't wait for spring, for Vuli may not come for months. We have men, weapons, enough stores if we ration carefully. We'll hunt and fish before we go, but whatever the case, it's time to leave these walls behind.'

Berger looked pleased, especially now that he'd have his cousin for company. Ludo was distracted, still wondering what was happening to Sigurd. Bjarni felt a tingle of excitement, followed by a tremor of fear at the thought of leaving Agnette and Liara behind.

'I'll stay,' Lief offered immediately. He was as eager for battle as the rest of them, but he'd promised Falla that he wouldn't leave when she was so close to giving birth. And Slussfall was his responsibility.

It was he who should remain.

Reinar felt relieved. 'Good, we'll need you here, keeping everything secure.' He stared at his father. 'I want you with me this time.'

Stellan nodded. 'I've no problem with that, and I do want to get my hands on Hector. I think we all do,' he added, eyeing Jonas, Vik, and even Ollo, who he'd softened to since they'd left Tromsund. Ollo Narp had proven himself a useful pair of hands, and his experience would be welcome.

'We do,' Jonas agreed. 'While that traitorous turd sits on the throne, Ake will never be at peace.'

'No, and nor we will,' Stellan said, thinking of his sons and his wife, his niece and her daughter. 'We can't hide.'

'We can't hide,' Reinar echoed. 'And we won't. We must leave soon, though. Five days. That should give us enough time to prepare. Eddeth, Alys, you need to find Hector and Gudrum for us. You too, Raf. We need to know what they're planning and where they are. The rest of us will focus on gathering supplies and sorting out weapons.'

'And ale,' Ollo put in. 'We'll need a good supply of ale.'

Reinar agreed. Keeping their men happy while they trekked back down Alekka looking for their enemy was going to be very important indeed.

He turned towards the flames, seeing glimpses of his brother's face. He still heard his voice in his ears, trying to remember if Sigurd had given even a hint of why he'd come or of what was wrong. But realising that he couldn't give one more moment to trying to help his brother, Reinar turned back to the map table, attempting to focus on his next steps.

***

It was as though Alari was sniffing a corpse.

She had chained Sigurd to a chair in one of her dungeon chambers, imprisoning him inside a great stone circle, its symbols glowing, warning her prisoner that he was very much at her mercy.

She smiled as she stepped back, though there was annoyance in her eye, her lips pressed together, jaw clenched. 'Why reveal yourself now?' she wanted to know. 'What great insight did you have to share with your brother? Something about Thenor? Something that might be wrong with Thenor? *Our* father?'

Her black cloak shimmered as she swept back and forth before him.

Sigurd didn't speak. He felt afraid. Alari hadn't dropped her knife since she'd strapped him into the chair. The blade glinted, newly sharpened, and Sigurd saw the odd symbols etched along its haft.

Alari couldn't find any symbols protecting Sigurd, which surprised her. 'Did you escape?' she wondered, though before Sigurd could speak, she dismissed that idea. 'No one can escape Gallabrok. And yet there you were, trying to see your brother.'

Sigurd shuffled his boots, feeling tense. He feared she would cut him or use magic to draw the truth out of him. Though he didn't plan to reveal anything to this witch.

His sister.

Then, remembering how much everyone was relying on him,

Sigurd swallowed, clearing his throat. 'I wanted to warn Reinar. Thenor tried to stop me, but, in the end, he let me go. Unlike you, he doesn't keep prisoners.'

'Warn him?' Alari leaned forward, lips parting. 'About what?'

Sigurd didn't flinch. He barely blinked as he braved that searching eye. 'About Ulfinnur. That we couldn't find him. Thenor has been looking, though there's no sign of him. I wanted to warn Reinar that spring wasn't coming. That we didn't know how to stop winter. That he needed to prepare, to ration food.'

Alari lifted an eyebrow, seeing no lies in Sigurd's eyes. She couldn't read his thoughts, which didn't surprise her, knowing Valera would have gotten to work on him as soon as he'd arrived in Thenor's hall. Though the lack of symbols on his armour and body was still a mystery. 'You have been in Gallabrok,' she said, straightening up with a smile. 'You'll know everything about it, I expect. My father would have spoken in great detail about his fortress, about his plans for me, and you. So if you wish to live, Sigurd, you will tell me everything you've seen, everything you've heard. I want to know it all.' She brought her knife up to Sigurd's eyebrow, surprised when he didn't even blink. He held her gaze, unflinching. 'Perhaps you're as stubborn as our father, or perhaps you are smart like me? For I can help you, Sigurd. If you tell me everything I need to know, I can send you back to Reinar and your family. I can give you everything you want.'

Sigurd hadn't been expecting that, and the surprise registered on his face before he could stop it.

Alari laughed, nicking his eyebrow, watching him bleed. 'Are you all god?' she wondered. 'Or mostly a man, just pretending to be one of us? Well, soon we'll both find out!'

***

Alys left the hall with Eddeth and Raf, eyes down, hoping to avoid

Elin Vilander. Reinar's wife had become increasingly likely to accost her if she crossed her path, and Alys hated coming to the hall, knowing there was a good chance of bumping into her.

'We have much dreaming to do. Oh yes, we do!' Eddeth announced into the darkness. She pulled on her gloves, yanking down her hat over her bouncy hair. 'Perhaps you should come and stay with us for a few nights?' she suggested, looking from Alys to Raf. 'With those children and animals, not to mention Solveigh and Stina, how will you ever focus your mind? How will you focus your dreams?'

Alys was certain she was going to refuse Eddeth's offer, not enamoured with the thought of sleeping in her dank cottage, though she found herself nodding. 'It makes sense. We have to do everything we can to help them before they leave.'

'And will one of us go, do you think? I imagine Reinar will need a dreamer.' Eddeth felt excited by the prospect, doubting Alys would leave the fort. With Reinar's wife raging with jealousy and Alys feeling so protective of her children, it was much more likely that she would be invited along. Eddeth squeezed Raf's arm, planning to bring the girl with her. Then, remembering Aldo, she fell silent, not wanting to place Raf in danger.

'I'll get my things,' Alys decided, shivering in the darkness. She knew Stina would be more than happy to look after the children for a few nights, and the children would barely notice she was gone. Not while Stina was cooking for them, and Puddle was racing around the cottage, inviting them to play.

'I've got hare and turnip stew for supper!' Eddeth remembered gleefully, then she frowned. 'Though perhaps you should eat first, Alys?'

Alys almost laughed, knowing how Eddeth hated to share. And nodding, she headed away from the hall, a sense of doom immediately descending upon her. She remembered standing in Slussfall's square when Thenor had come to her. She remembered Hakon trying to rape her, Ivan dying to save her, and her mother, Mirella, who had threatened to kill her children. They were safe behind Slussfall's walls, she had told herself since they'd arrived on Lief Gundersen's doorstep.

But now?

And stopping suddenly, Alys turned, hearing the raucous noise of the tavern crowd spilling out into the square.

And she remembered Helgi.

***

'Is Ulfinnur safe?' Sigurd cried through the pain of his wounds, wondering where Thenor was. Surely his father should have been here by now? Alari had sliced her knife across his face, his chest and arms, digging its lethal tip into his thighs, and now she was threatening his fingers.

'Ulfinnur? What do you know of him?' Alari was becoming bored. She was the Goddess of Magic, and cutting her prisoner seemed unimaginative. Beneath her. So, throwing her knife onto the table, she wheeled around to face her prisoner, her tattooed necklace of symbols glowing white around her neck. 'What do you care for him?'

'I care that Alekkans are freezing and starving because you have him here.'

'You think so?' Alari laughed. 'Is that because you are a god, Sigurd? The god of what?' she wondered suddenly, peering at him. 'What has my father made you the god of? Not magic. That much is obvious!'

'The God of War,' Sigurd spat, wanting to keep her distracted. He was in agony, his eyes watering, powerless to keep himself safe. He had learned much during his time in Gallabrok, but Alari had symbols carved into the iron fetters clamped around his wrists and ankles, around the circle too. There was nothing he could do to stop her. He remembered being Gudrum's prisoner, feeling his anger boiling now, annoyed at always being on the back foot.

He glanced at the door.

'Hungry?' Alari wondered, trying to read his thoughts. 'Or looking to escape? I can bring you food, of course. A bounteous spread awaits, as does freedom, *if* you give me the information I need.' She leaned closer now, pressing her hands to the sides of Sigurd's head. He tried to pull away from her, to twist and turn out of reach, but soon he was unable to move his head at all, and taking a deep breath, Alari closed her eye, stepping into the darkness of Sigurd Vilander's mind.

CHAPTER EIGHT

Helgi was easy to spot in the dark. He was taller than most of the men gathered outside the tavern, and his shock of auburn hair made him look even more so. Alys walked up to him with obvious reluctance, knowing she couldn't go back on her promise. She would tell him what she'd seen, though it was dark now, and she hesitated to walk anywhere with him. Not alone.

Sensing that, an impatient Helgi drew her away from the crowded tavern towards the square. 'We can just walk here, by the braziers. There are people around.'

Alys nodded, following him as he strode out quickly.

Though realising she wasn't walking with any speed, Helgi dropped back to keep pace with her. 'I was nine when my father died,' he began. 'Leaving my mother alone with my three younger sisters and me. She took me to a dreamer to see what I was made of. Perhaps she was hoping I'd be the answer to all her problems?' He laughed sadly. 'Instead, the dreamer saw that my mother would soon die, leaving us all alone. Me, at eleven, with three small girls to care for. So do not fear, Alys, I'm well aware of the disappointment a dreamer can deliver.'

Alys felt some sympathy for Helgi then, and it relaxed her. He seemed less strange in the dark, more quiet and still. 'I'm sorry. That must have been hard.'

'It became hard very quickly, yes. We were taken to live with my aunt, Berger's mother, and she hated children, so yes, it wasn't the best turn of events. My mother was a dear woman, a kind woman. I was never the same again. Never that boy. From that day on, I was a man.'

Alys thought of her own son and how much he'd changed since that day on the beach. At Slussfall, he'd made older friends, barely spending any time with her and Lotta, though she didn't want Magnus to lose his childhood yet.

He was still so young.

'You don't have to worry,' Helgi went on as the dreamer remained silent beside him. 'I can handle any bad news. Hard to tell, I know, but there's a surprising amount of strength up here.' And grinning nervously, he tapped his head.

Alys didn't know how to begin. What she'd seen was so disturbing. She didn't know if it was a horrifying glimpse of the future or a memory of Helgi's past. 'I can't tell when it was,' she said. 'It was just flashes, and they came so quickly. I heard loud noises, saw violent images. It was over before it began. I'm not sure it will help you or what you even want to know.'

Helgi swallowed, stopping.

'I... it was in a house, inside a house, with floorboards. I... saw a foot.' Alys felt sick remembering. 'A foot and then a hand. They'd been cut off, lying on the floor in pools of blood.'

Helgi sighed now, his shoulders dropping.

'Screaming. I heard a lot of screaming. Crying too. Men were there, you were there. A woman. And just... violence. There were bodies. I...' Alys shuddered, not knowing what else to say. 'It was a bloody mess.'

'Yes, it was. Though I remember little of it. It comes to me whenever I close my eyes, but like you, I see only flashes.'

Alys gulped. 'So it happened then? You were there?'

Helgi saw a bench pushed against the wall of the metalsmith's workshop, and ushering Alys forward, he motioned for her to take a seat. He shivered, memories threatening to tie his tongue as he sat down beside her. 'I loved a woman called Sahra.'

That was all he said for some time, and when Alys eventually turned his way, she saw tears in his eyes.

'She knew I had a farm, left to me by my mother. While I was with Berger's family, there was little I could do about it. It became wild, overgrown, but it had been a profitable place when I was small. Sahra was a girl from Napper, a beautiful, ambitious girl. She'd been left with nothing when her parents died, forced to work as a servant for no more than scraps. I loved her and promised that one day we'd make a go of the farm, but to do that I needed to make my fortune. So I headed off with my cousins. We'd spend years away, at sea, raiding, and then return to Napper, and I'd make my promises to Sahra. Eventually, I fell out with Berger's brother, Rutger, but I had enough silver stashed away to start my dream. Well, Sahra's dream, I suppose. So I bought livestock and equipment. I spent months repairing the farmhouse, the sheds and storehouses. I ploughed and dug. I hired farm hands and servants. It took nearly a year.'

Helgi paused as a small child ran up to them, sobbing.

Alys looked around, ready to get up, but a young woman appeared, breathless with fear and then relief as she picked up the child, hurrying him away. Alys turned back to Helgi. 'You were saying?'

Helgi didn't want to go on, though he knew he would find some relief in the telling of a tale he'd kept to himself since it had happened. 'When the farm was ready, I went to Sahra, told her that we could marry.' He felt numb. 'It was all arranged. We would have a feast at the farm, invite the neighbours, my sisters and their husbands...' Looking down, he took a deep breath. 'The night before, though, Sahra came to the farm, wanting to stay with me. It wasn't the first time, and I thought nothing of it until I woke with a knife at my throat and a stranger leaning over me.'

Alys blinked, lips parting, and realising that Helgi had stopped speaking, she was forced to ask. 'And what happened?'

'It's the last thing I remember, that face. And Sahra's. They laughed, talked about their plan for the farm. How it had been their plan for two years. Other men were there. The man's brothers. I still don't know who he was. There was so much laughter. And Sahra?' He cut off the sobs that stuck in his throat. 'Hers was the loudest of all.'

'They tried to kill you?'

Helgi nodded. 'They had the weapons to, though something Sahra never knew about me, something I never told her, was that I'm a bear man. The spirit of the bear lives in me. It comes like lightning, and when it does, I'm someone else. Something else. I can do things I couldn't do otherwise.' He dropped his head, taking a breath. 'I woke in the forest, covered in blood, the remains of the farmhouse smoking in the distance. I didn't know if Sahra lived or if I'd killed her.' Now the sobs came freely, and dropping his head to his hands, Helgi let it all go.

Alys edged towards him, patting his back. 'I saw no sign of her,' she promised. 'No sign that you'd killed her. It wasn't in my vision, I promise.'

He looked up at her, swallowing, rubbing tears from his eyes. 'I don't know if that should make me feel relieved. She tried to murder me. I gave up everything for her, made my life just for her, and then she laughed at me as her lover threatened to take off my head. Just laughed!'

'We don't always fall in love with the best people,' Alys said with some sympathy. 'I know that myself. What we think is love can sometimes lead us astray. Though everything's a lesson. An opportunity to learn something about ourselves.'

Helgi scoffed. 'What? That I'm a gullible fool?'

Alys shook her head, seeing other images of Helgi now, with his sisters and his mother. She saw a happy boy playing with his cousins. She saw him with his shirt off, working on his farm. 'No, I don't think so. That woman, Sahra, had the problem, not you. You need to keep going and carve out your own destiny, pursue your own path. Perhaps it's not waiting for you on a farm?'

Helgi turned to Alys, taking her hand, immediately sensing her desire to pull it away. Though he felt gratitude and warmth towards this woman for her sympathy, so he held on for a moment. 'It's not something I want Berger knowing. You're close with Solveigh, but I... Berger hated Sahra. He warned me about her from the very first day, but I thought I'd prove him wrong. I don't want him knowing.'

Alys slipped her hand out of his. 'I won't tell a soul,' she promised, taking a breath of cold air, hearing the joyous laughter of those gathered outside the tavern. Looking their way, she smiled.

'Can I buy you some ale? Something to eat?' Helgi offered. 'To say thank you. To apologise for how I was before.'

Alys shook her head. 'I don't think that would help me find any dreams tonight. I'm sorry, but more than anything, I need a dream.' Though thinking of Helgi and the horrors of what had happened in that farmhouse, she doubted she'd find one.

***

Reinar remained in the war room long after everyone had left for supper.

Eventually, Elin came to find him. 'You should eat, Reinar. No matter how distracted you are, you must eat.' She smiled as she swept into the room, looking radiant. She'd been spending a lot of time with Falla Gundersen, who had put her servants to work on Elin's appearance. For if Reinar fulfilled his destiny, Elin was aware that soon she would be a queen. And having seen the way the glamorous Lady of Slussfall carried herself, Elin was determined to leave her plain Ottby gowns far behind.

Reinar tried to smile. 'I'll eat later. I just wanted a moment to myself. There are too many voices fighting to be heard, all trying to get my attention. Ideas and arguments and strategies. I just... needed a moment.'

Elin took his arm, turning him to her, and smiling again, she kissed him. 'You haven't mentioned my new dress,' she said, stepping back. 'What do you think? The tailor delivered it today.' And she spun around in a circle, giggling.

Reinar was confused, wondering if his wife even knew about Sigurd. She appeared thoroughly oblivious to his tension. 'Your dress?'

Elin nodded, running her eyes around the chamber, deciding that it needed more lamps. It was a wonder anyone could see in here. 'I thought you might have noticed, though you are always so busy. I'm beginning to think you don't see me at all!'

'I... my brother,' Reinar began, temper sparking. 'Have you heard about Sigurd?'

Elin looked past her husband to the door, distracted by the noise of the hall. 'Of course. It's all anyone's talking about out there. That, and your plans to leave. Though neither are new, are they? Sigurd's always getting himself in trouble, and you're always riding off, looking to save someone.'

Elin spoke as though none of it was important, and Reinar grabbed her hand, peering into her eyes. 'Are you well?' Elin's behaviour was becoming truly concerning. It was as though she wasn't aware of what was happening around her. As though she was never in the same moment with him.

Elin glared at him. 'Sigurd will be fine. He's a god, isn't it, so can't you stop worrying about him for once?' Smoothing down her dress, she stepped out of Reinar's reach, muttering to herself. 'I must get back to the hall. Everyone will be wondering where I am. They're already missing their lord!' Reinar frowned at her, though rushing forward, Elin kissed his pouting lips once more. 'Don't be long. You should be out there, my love, sitting at the centre of the high table. It's your place, and you must take it.'

Reinar watched as she glided out of the chamber, not once looking back. He stared after her, feeling both puzzled and even more concerned, though it was too much to sift through now. Now, when he had to prepare his army to leave the fort. He couldn't remain on the back foot any longer.

It was time to go and prove that he was truly worthy of becoming Alekka's king.

***

Panic wasn't in Valera's nature, but there was still no word from Omani or Tikas, and she couldn't see any sign of Sigurd in Hyvari.

Nor could Thenor, though he sought to remain calm as he stood before her, dressed for battle, armed with his famous spear, *Folnir*. He felt out of place and far too old, his heart thumping with urgency, caring only for Sigurd. His son was everything now. He couldn't let anything happen to him. Though while there was no word from Omani or Tikas, there was nowhere to go and nothing to do but wait and hope.

Valera placed a hand on her father's arm, patting it gently. 'We will find him,' she insisted, feeling sick with worry. 'We can do more than Alari, I promise you, Father. We will find him.'

***

Alari finally came across Sigurd's symbols when she started exploring his mind. It was locked, warded against her, and though that came as no surprise, she felt a burst of irritation as she stepped away from her prisoner, watching his head loll forward. She had rendered him unconscious, and for a moment, she thought about simply killing him. Holding out her hands, she curled her fingers, twisting them as though turning a lid. But stopping, letting her arms fall by her sides, she knew that one moment of pleasure would lead to many more of regret, for Sigurd was a chest of gold, and Thenor was a poor, old God of Nothing.

He would come if she showed him the way.

'You wait right there,' she smiled at Sigurd, laughing as she turned around, sweeping her cloak behind her. 'I won't be long!'

***

'But how long will you be?' Lotta wanted to know, feeling unhappy about her mother going to stay with Eddeth and Raf. 'How *long*, Mama?'

Alys looked down at her daughter, who had wrapped her arms around her waist as though keeping her prisoner. 'What? Are you saying you'll miss me? I didn't think you even knew I was here, what with Stina cooking for you and Solveigh combing your hair and picking out your clothes. What use do you have for me?'

'Well...' Lotta didn't have an answer.

Alys laughed at the perplexed look on her daughter's face, and bending down, she kissed the top of her head, inhaling smoke. 'You keep thinking, and I'll see you in the morning,' she promised. 'And until then, be good. Remember, Solveigh's busy growing that baby, so she needs a lot of rest. And Stina's old, and the old get very grumpy if they don't get enough sleep.'

Lotta looked up at Stina with serious eyes.

And though Alys was trying to lighten the mood, she could see that Stina didn't look happy as she walked her to the door.

'Stay with Eddeth as long as you need,' Stina said. 'We'll be fine.'

Magnus wasn't there. He was eating supper with one of his friends, though likely he would appear soon, asking if he could spend the night. Alys thought about Helgi again, remembering how quickly his childhood had been taken from him. And then she was focusing on Stina, who truly looked upset. 'I was only joking,' she said quietly. 'You're not old.'

But Stina laughed, a bitter sort of laugh. 'I'm nothing but old. Have you seen my hair?' She had untied her long brown hair, threaded with a few silver strands. 'I look like a grandmother.' Stepping outside with Alys, she turned to close the door.

'Be good!' Alys called over her shoulder, catching a glimpse of Lotta waving to her, though her daughter was quickly giggling as Puddle chased Winter around the cottage.

'You're not old,' Alys repeated as Stina stood on the front porch, arms wrapped around her chest. 'I shouldn't have said it.'

Stina shrugged. 'You're only telling the truth. No wonder

Ludo doesn't want anything to do with me.'

'What? That's not true. I don't imagine Ludo would care that you're older than him.'

'But he'd want children, wouldn't he? A wife and children, and I'm..?' Stina sighed, shivering. The wind tore down the alley, and she didn't want to linger outside, though she had wanted to reveal her fears to Alys for some time.

'You're thirty-eight,' Alys smiled. 'And women give birth at all ages, if that's what's worrying you. You're not too old for anything.' Now she drew Stina into her arms, giving her a reassuring squeeze. 'And what's to stop you asking Ludo? What does it matter if he says no? It's your life, Stina. And if you've set your mind on Ludo Moller, then go and tell him.' With that, Alys kissed Stina's cheek, releasing her with a smile. And taking a deep breath, she headed down the alley, her mind overflowing with everyone's worries.

Too busy to think of her own.

***

Reinar had reluctantly made his way to the high table, in no mood for eating, though it wouldn't be long before the comfort of a chair and a table was a thing of the past. Walls too. He looked around the cavernous hall, feeling no affection for Slussfall. It was a gloomy place, and with Lief Gundersen as its lord, gloomier still. He smiled then, seeing Falla whispering in Lief's ear. Lief didn't appear to be listening, though he occasionally nodded at whatever his wife was saying.

Falla looked unwell, Reinar thought, hoping she would deliver her child safely. And remembering the traumatic birth of his own sons, he turned to Elin with a smile. 'You do look beautiful,' he said, eyes sweeping the elaborately embroidered dress. It was made of silk, finer than anything she'd worn before. 'Gold suits you.'

Elin agreed, and she beamed, thrilled to have finally claimed his attention. The evenings were always her favourite time of day, when she invited Reinar's most prominent warriors and their wives to eat with them. She took great care over the menu and the appearance of the hall, as well as of herself. Though Reinar barely noticed. To him, meal times had become a chore, something to suffer through, for he always wanted to be riding, or in his war room, or by himself, thinking.

Elin froze. 'Will you take a dreamer with you?' she wondered sharply. 'South? I expect you'll need one to guide you.'

'We will,' Reinar said, though he didn't meet Elin's eyes. And picking up his knife, he aimed it at a slice of mutton.

'Who will it be? Eddeth? It makes sense, doesn't it? She's helped you before.'

Reinar kept his eyes on that mutton. 'I imagine it does, though it might be too much for Eddeth alone,' he warned.

'But surely you can't trust that Raf? She hasn't proven herself loyal to anyone other than Gudrum. And you won't take Alys. She won't leave her children. So it must be Eddeth. There's no other way.'

It sounded decided, Reinar thought, knowing he hadn't decided anything. And then his mother tapped him on the shoulder, and he turned away from a vibrating Elin, relieved to end the conversation. His thoughts veered from his brother's disappearance to his plans for leaving.

He didn't want to think about dreamers at all.

***

'Here we are, all together!' Eddeth declared cheerfully, poking the fire that blazed with intensity in the centre of the dark cottage. 'Three dreamers and many problems before us. A bucket full, I'd say. We should divide them up, yes indeed. Like eggs! Decide who'll take what.'

Alys left her things on the floor, joining Eddeth and Raf on a stool by the fire. The cottage smelled surprisingly pleasant. The remnants of the hare stew lingered, mingling with hints of rosemary and thyme. She saw a tiny wreath of dill nailed onto the back of the door and dried lavender scattered amongst the reeds covering the hard mud floor. 'Well, I don't think there's anything we can do about Sigurd,' Alys decided immediately, surprising Raf, who blinked beside her. 'Unless you want to try and dream about him?'

Raf quickly shook her head. Alari could come and go as she liked in her dreams, so she felt hesitant about every word she uttered, awake or asleep. She didn't want to cause problems for any of them, and especially not Sigurd. 'We have to focus on helping Reinar.'

And though Alys saw that Raf's body was almost protesting her words, she nodded. 'Then we need to find Hector and Gudrum, and Gudrum's dreamer. I think that's the best place to start, don't you?'

Eddeth ran a finger inside the cauldron, scooping up the last dregs of stew. 'I'll look for Hector. That old buffoon won't be hard to find if he's left Stornas' walls behind. I only hope he's decided to act like a king and finally emerge from hiding.'

'You should try and find Gudrum,' Alys suggested, looking at Raf, who didn't appear keen on that idea. 'If you think it's possible? And I'll go searching for Gysa. Who knows where we'll end up, but it's a start.'

'She'll lock us out,' Raf warned. 'Gysa. She can open or close the door whenever she wants. We'll only see what she wants us to.'

Alys knew that was likely true, but it was the obvious place to start. 'Well, she can try, but we have friends, don't we?' She thought of Winter and Puddle, wondering if she should have brought them along. 'We might get some help. If not, we'll try again and just keep looking till we find the answers. It's all that matters now. Reinar's leaving Slussfall without enough men. We have to do everything we can to improve his chances.'

Raf nodded, wanting to help, though as much as she knew it

made sense to look for Gudrum, she couldn't stop her mind from wandering back to Sigurd, fearing what Alari was doing to him.

CHAPTER NINE

When Sigurd finally emerged from whatever spell Alari had placed upon him, he felt groggy, confused, and then immediately in pain. Though with his hands bound behind his back and his legs chained to the chair, there was nothing he could do. The pain washed over him, and he simply had to endure it. He couldn't flinch or move, rub his aching wrists or hold his pounding head. He moaned and murmured, waiting for it to pass, trying to distract himself with thoughts of Ottby, though his memories of Ottby were forever tainted by the knowledge of what Hector Berras had done there.

He thought instead of Raf, wishing she'd been standing on the ramparts with Reinar. She wouldn't have looked happy, he thought, imagining her glowering down at him. Much like Tulia.

And then Alari returned, and though she quickly unchained him from the chair, pulling him to his feet, his arms and legs were still bound, and he remained her prisoner.

'We will leave,' she said in a clipped voice. 'You will leave with me.'

'To where?' Sigurd groaned, unsteady on his feet. The witch had dug her knife into his thighs, carving deep, invasive symbols, and his legs wobbled, barely able to hold him up. He began to wonder if he was any sort of god, for how could he be a powerful god if he was unable to hold Alari off? To fight back? He knew Alari's magic was too powerful for most gods to resist - Thenor had said as much - which was why he'd been so reluctant to let him leave Gallabrok. Though Sigurd had known that this was the only way to free Alekka from the devastating winter. 'What about Ulfinnur?' he demanded with a croak. 'Where are you keeping him?'

But Alari only laughed as she doused the glowing symbols of her circle, and with a firm grip on Sigurd's arm, she pulled him out of the chamber towards the stairs.

***

'Are you prepared to kill?' Thenor stood by his noisy waterfall, waiting for word. He eyed Valera sharply, knowing that he was.

Valera nodded. She was dressed in a plain black cloak, her golden braids tucked inside it, covered by a hood. She wore a belt of golden links, and from that hung two long knives. 'I am. I am prepared, Father.'

Thenor saw two of his warriors talking quietly by the circular fire pit, and he drew Valera close, lowering his voice. 'That is good, my daughter. My sweet, sweet daughter.' He lifted her chin, staring into her gentle lavender-coloured eyes. 'But know that it is I who must kill Alari. The burden of murder should never rest on such loving shoulders. I will kill her when I get my chance. I only ask, for if something were to happen to me, or to Sigurd...'

Valera swallowed. 'I know what to do, Father. I have been at your side all my life, listening, learning. I have never sought to be your heir, but I will not hesitate to lead if the worst were to happen.'

Thenor kissed her cheek. 'You are the best of me, Valera. I regret that I have not been a better father. A better father to all the gods. If only I had...'

Valera took his hand, kissing it. 'But we are here for a reason. As gods, we know that better than the humans. The threads weave together in the most perfect way. Pain, failure, and regret are as much a part of the tapestry as happiness and love. We cannot retreat, and we should not dwell on our mistakes. We must be open to what is coming, for only then will we see the true path forward.' She kissed his hand again. 'I will be by your side, whatever happens, I promise.'

The waiting was hard to bear, and the fear of not being able to see Sigurd was growing. Thenor felt it acutely. It was an unfamiliar feeling. Uncomfortable in a way he wasn't used to. It gnawed at him.

Fear.

He had waited so long to claim his son, and they'd had so little time together. There was a lifetime more to say, so much he still wanted to teach Sigurd.

Thenor turned away from his daughter, inhaling deeply, resettling his cloak as he walked back to where he'd left his spear, *Folnir*, lying on the high table. And picking it up, he gripped that golden shaft with a trembling hand. Rage burned. Rage at Alari and at Eskvir, and at Eutresia, who had set the devastating fire in the first place.

No, he realised, shaking his head. He had done that.

But those flames had burned for too long now. It was time to put them out.

A crash had them all turning towards the entrance to the gardens as Tikas came running, arm in the air.

'I know where they are! Omani showed me! Come, we must hurry!'

***

Sigurd regretted that he'd never been honest with Tulia or even himself. He regretted that he hadn't told Raf how he felt or that he'd never known his real mother's love.

Thoughts zigzagged through his mind, faces jumping out at

him. He felt sick, spitting out bile as he lurched along beside Alari, who had taken him out of a building. He swung his head around, wanting to remember every detail. Through his blurred eyes and his muddled mind, he tried to see where he was.

There was a narrow stone tower lit by a quarter moon.

The moon.

He blinked up at it, hoping Omani could see him.

Alari tugged him back around. 'We will wait,' she said, leading Sigurd into another circle. Sigurd tried to push his boots into the snow, hoping to slow her down, fearing what that circle meant. 'What? You're not afraid, are you? A mighty god cowering in fear of a little circle?' She laughed. 'No wonder Thenor hid you away. He must have known what a trembling coward you are!'

Sigurd *was* trembling, his body weakened by Alari's knife, his legs almost going in different directions. He was a god, so why did he feel like a man?

'Magic.'

He heard Thenor's voice in his ears, knowing that to be true.

His hands were bound, and he shuffled along, chains jangling loudly in the darkness. He heard water lapping gently, the call of owls.

He was on an island.

His swordbelt was gone, his cloak, too, and he shivered, his tunic flapping around his legs, cold air creeping underneath it, chilling his skin. 'You think I'm a c-c-coward?' he asked, working hard to stay upright. 'But you're the one hiding, Alari. Hiding away so our father won't find you.'

Alari threw Sigurd into the circle like a sack of grain, enjoying his yelp of surprise as he hit the ground. He was a tall man and strong, but the magical fetters had sapped his strength, leaving him as weak as an old man. She laughed. 'Is that what you think I've been doing? But you are so wrong, Sigurd. I want our father to come and find me. More than anything!'

***

Reinar's father found him on the ramparts, staring at the moon.

'Looking for advice?' Stellan wondered with a cough. A crumb was still tickling his throat from supper, so, opening the waterskin he'd brought along, he tipped the icy liquid into his mouth, swallowing repeatedly.

'Always,' Reinar grinned.

'It's a risk, leaving the fort.'

Reinar waited, knowing his father had never been shy about sharing his opinions.

'But why die here, pointless and powerless? I know what Ake would say, what he'd tell us to do, but it was only ever you who could decide your fate, Reinar. Without help? With a frozen sea and no hope of rescue? Well, we're just going to have to make our own luck.' Stellan wiped a hand across his dripping beard, sighing. 'I fought every day of that Ten Years War beside my best friend, and for most of it, we were on the losing side. Many battles we had less men, fewer resources, facing an enemy intent on wiping us off the map. But in the end we won. And that's what you have to hold onto now. Start here.' Stellan tapped his son's forehead. 'Be strong here first. Win your battles in your mind before you ever take to the field. An enemy will exploit every hint of weakness, so never show any. Lead like you're a god. Like Thenor himself.'

Reinar nodded, thoughts of Thenor leading to worries about Sigurd. Though he pushed them away, knowing that Sigurd was a god.

His brother could take care of himself.

***

Alari tipped back her head, seeing the glare of Omani's moon, and closing her eye, she drew her hood over her white hair, chanting angrily.

Sigurd had struggled back to his feet, watching as she strode around the circle, muttering and growling like some creature from Vasa's Cave. The wind whipped him, and he wobbled on the uneven surface. Soon the clouds came rushing overhead, and the moon was hidden from view, the only light now coming from the fire Alari had brought to life in the middle of the circle.

'Better!' she declared, returning to Sigurd. 'Don't you think?'

The circle was drawn crudely in the snow, Sigurd saw, ignoring her. He staggered as the wind picked up further.

'Shall I bring you a chair? A blanket?' Alari laughed. 'Though surely we won't need to stay long? It's why you revealed yourself, isn't it? To find me? Ha! But do you think I'm a fool? We may not know each other, *Brother*, but I can assure you I will never be a fool!' She walked away from Sigurd, searching the darkness, her neck tingling in anticipation.

***

Thenor, Valera, and Tikas landed on a beach of snow-covered sand. It was cold and soft, and they sunk into it as they moved towards a rocky outcrop. Without Omani's moon to guide them, progress was slow, but no one wanted to use their powers to reveal their presence.

They communicated without words, each god able to read the other's thoughts. Even Tikas. For though he was the Messenger of the Gods, he was half-god himself, and he nodded, leaving Thenor and Valera to walk the path to Alari's tower alone.

***

Sigurd fainted.

Alari watched him in surprise and amusement, laughing out loud. But the sound of her ravens cawing high up in the tower drew her attention away from her pathetic brother to the path. Her servants cleared it every morning, and though there was a fresh covering of snow, there wasn't enough to hide it. She could see where it led through the woods, towards the beach. She had walked that path with each sun's rise, thinking of Eutresia, imagining this moment.

Her father had outthought her countless times over the years. She had been embarrassed and humiliated, losing out at every turn, while he returned to his hall, gloating over his victories. But not this time, she knew.

He would not defeat her this time.

Lifting her hands to the sky, she swept the clouds around like a whirlpool until lightning sparked. Then, drawing it down from the sky, she sent it shooting from her hands, down the path, lighting up the forest.

'You are looking for me?' Thenor said, standing far behind her.

The surprise and speed of her turn unbalanced Alari, who stumbled.

'Or perhaps me?' Valera asked, causing Alari to turn again.

She hissed and snarled, jerking her head around in snapping movements.

'Though I doubt you were looking for me,' came the third voice.

Now Alari laughed, seeing the pathetic sight of Tikas, the boy who wished to be all god. 'And you intend to do what, child? But you are no more use than a pair of socks! Why are *you* here?'

Thenor was immediately aware of Alari's circle. The flickering flames revealed the line he couldn't cross. He saw Sigurd, bloodied and pale-faced, lying in the snow, though he could hear his son's heart still beating, and drawing his attention away from Sigurd, he sought to focus.

'I am here to defeat you!' Tikas cried in anger, wanting to claim Alari's attention. Thenor had asked for his help, and he was determined not to let him down. He carried a shield on his back, and now he drew it into his left hand, sensing what was coming.

Alari beat him to it, shooting a lightning bolt at his chest. Tikas was fast, though - above all things, he was fast - and he jerked away before it struck him. Alari tried again, and this time, he caught the lightning on his shield, sending it back to her. Alari didn't move, knowing her circle would protect her, but the lightning bolt struck her left arm. She roared in confusion, arm burning, not understanding. And then Sigurd was on his feet, unable to move with any speed, his ankles still locked in the fetters. Though he had enough strength to stumble out of the circle, through the hole he'd made when he'd fallen over.

His mind and body had struggled to coordinate, but once he'd pretended to faint, landing near the circle's edge, a few quick movements while Alari's back was turned had helped him break it.

Now, he was free, and Alari was vulnerable.

Though realising what had happened, Alari was quick to respond. She swung around in a flash of cloak and snapping white braid, the gust of wind she generated knocking both a surprised Valera and a weakened Sigurd over. Thenor held his ground, pushing one leg back, and Tikas was too fast to be caught.

Alari's ravens swept from her tower like a storm cloud, sleek feathers and sharp beaks, as silent as the night as they aimed for Thenor. But Thenor had sensed them coming, and he swung around fast, *Folnir* cutting through them in one murderous motion. He didn't stay to finish them off, knowing Tikas was there, smashing those still flying with his shield. 'Valera, take Sigurd!' Thenor cried, rushing into the circle to confront his one-eyed daughter, who appeared so vulnerable now.

But this was Alari. He would take nothing for granted.

Valera reached Sigurd quickly, seeing that his legs were bound as well as his wrists, though she saw no obvious way to unlock Alari's magical fetters.

Alari was too busy fighting off her father to celebrate that small victory. Thenor had brought his spear, and she knew what that meant. *Folnir* was a god-killer. Thenor had killed Eutresia with that double-bladed spear, so she had to be careful now. Everything was so finely balanced. She couldn't make one wrong move, one reckless decision.

Stepping back, she extended her arms, raising her hands to her father as he swung that shining weapon. Its twin blades gleamed, sharpened until deadly, cast in gold. She quickly made a shield of light, but Thenor's blade cleaved it in two. Alari stepped back again, sensing that her ravens were dead. She saw Valera working to free Sigurd.

But Tikas...

Where was he?

The pain in the back of her head as Tikas struck with his shield was blinding. For a moment, she couldn't hear. Then slipping a hand beneath her cloak, she pulled out her belt, whipping it behind her. The belt appeared to lengthen as it flew through the air, and Tikas couldn't outrun it. The leather felt as though it was made of sharpened steel, and it struck his cheek like a blade, taking out his right eye, nearly shearing off his jaw.

'Aarrghh!' Tikas fell into the snow, the shield tumbling from his hand. Alari snapped her belt at it, and soon it was flying towards her. She didn't hesitate, hurling it at Thenor, who came for her again.

'Father!' Valera cried as he twisted to the side, only just avoiding the spinning shield.

'Leave me!' Sigurd insisted. 'Help him!'

So Valera whipped off her cloak, flinging it at Alari. Striking out with her hands, she wove them in circles, the cloak wrapping around Alari's head, obscuring her vision.

Thenor lunged forward, *Folnir* poised to strike, and then he was falling, the earth undulating as though struck by a boulder. Though it wasn't a boulder, it was Ulura, Vasa's wolf, who had landed nearby, five times bigger than any normal wolf, and no illusion at all. She lunged into the circle, past Alari as she tore off

Valera's cloak. Ulura's mouth was open, teeth bared, aiming for Thenor, who rolled at the last moment. *Folnir* fell from his grasp, and the giant wolf was at him again, snapping at his boots as he scrambled away, trying to get back on his feet.

Tikas, one-eyed and unbalanced, searched for his shield.

Valera wanted to help her father, though she had just discovered how to undo Alari's spell, and she hurried to Sigurd, grasping the fetters around his wrists, chanting quickly, eyes closed. The iron locks sprang open, and Valera bent down, repeating the chant, freeing Sigurd's legs. But though Sigurd could now stand freely, he had no weapon.

'You do!' Thenor urged in his ears. 'Hurry!'

The flames flickered brightly, revealing *Folnir* lying in the snow.

Valera ran to protect her father. Arms extended, she brought her blue wall to life, working to hold Ulura back, though Alari quickly shattered it with her belt.

'Aarrghh!' Valera stumbled down onto one knee, wishing they'd brought more gods with them. They needed help.

She drew herself upright again, calling her cloak back to her, wondering what else she could do.

Ulura grabbed a mouthful of Thenor's sleeve, tearing the fabric. Thenor was surprised, knowing how strong and ancient the magic woven into that cloak was. He heard Sigurd coming and threw himself to the right, falling to the ground behind Valera, who was whipping her cloak at Alari.

Sigurd drove his father's spear up towards Ulura, who looked as big as Ottby's hall, struggling to do much more than tickle her belly. But he didn't stop moving, sensing that Thenor was already back on his feet. Valera was battling Alari. He didn't know what had happened to Tikas. It was too dark to see much, and Sigurd couldn't afford to take his eyes off the wolf. He slipped in the snow, avoiding its snapping jaw, smelling its foul breath as it pounced, knocking him over. Lashing out with the spear, Sigurd cracked Ulura's foreleg, breaking bone. The spear was powerful, magical, and as the wolf howled, Sigurd rolled quickly, striking her other leg with even more force, rolling further, hoping that without the strength in its legs, the beast would fall.

He saw Thenor rising, heard his father's voice in his ears, and quickly up on his feet, Sigurd threw the spear into the air, launching it high over the wolf's head. Thenor caught it, wrapping cold fingers around its golden shaft, and as the beast dropped forward, he jumped onto its back, stabbing *Folnir* into its neck. He drew the bloody spear out, hacking down again and again, until Ulura roared, jerking beneath him, her growling turning to gurgling, eventually going limp.

'*No*!' Alari screeched, aiming bolts of lightning at Valera's chest.

Valera threw up her cloak, but Alari's spell cut through the fabric. 'Aarrghh!' she screamed, flung backwards, head slamming onto the ground.

'No! *Valera*!' Sigurd cried, running to help her.

Alari knew she'd lost the wolf, but she could finish Valera, and then Thenor would lose the will to fight. She drew her hands together, taking a deep breath, preparing to deliver the fatal blow, and then something struck the back of her head, and she was thrown forward into the snow.

A now one-eyed Tikas, face coursing with blood, called back his shield, preparing to throw it again. The clouds masking the moon finally shifted, and Omani shone beams of bright moonlight down onto the island, revealing that Alari was outnumbered, her ravens were cut to pieces, and the wolf's spilled guts had turned her circle red.

Then Thenor was before her, *Folnir* in two hands, a one-eyed Tikas taking up his position behind her. A dishevelled Valera joined them with a free Sigurd.

Alari took a deep breath, hands slipping beneath the folds of her cloak, and spinning around, she disappeared.

CHAPTER TEN

Raf thought of Alari as she crept down the dark corridor. She'd become increasingly fearful of her dreams, and falling asleep was becoming more of a challenge each night. She would often lie in the darkness, listening to Eddeth and the goat snoring. Cold and frightened, she wouldn't speak or move. Often her mind wandered to Gudrum, remembering when she'd spent every night lying in his arms. She hadn't felt entirely safe, for she knew that Gudrum wasn't a good man, but he'd looked after her and kept her by his side.

Until he'd just thrown her away.

She kept walking, realising that she was in Stornas' castle. It was enormous, like a great mountain of stone. Looking up, she saw the rafters crossed above her head in a dark lattice pattern. She saw the flickering candles, their warm golden light dancing across the ceiling, filtering down to the floor. And swallowing now, fearing what she would find, Raf dropped her head and moved forward, seeing a vast empty room. Looking down, she was surprised to find that her bare feet were buried in snow. And then she blinked, turning, realising that the castle had gone now. There were no candles or lamps, no tapestries or flagstones. She was standing in a big field, thick with mud and snow, littered with bodies. Most appeared dead. She saw rivers of blood. She heard whimpering, pleading sounds of frightened men. And spinning around, trying to discover where she was, Raf saw a chair.

And a man perched upon it, staring at her.

***

They ran towards the tower, not knowing where Alari had gone. And there they faced more trouble. Alari didn't just have terrified servants doing her bidding, she had some of Vasa's death collectors, whose job it was to be her last line of defense.

'Tikas! Go with Valera! Find Ulfinnur. Sigurd will help me.'

Sigurd nodded, pleased when Thenor handed him *Fire Song*. 'I thought you might have need of her. They're death collectors,' he added. 'Can you see?'

Sigurd could. Unlike in the forest, though, their dark hoods were down, and he saw gaunt, skeletal faces; patches of greyish skin hanging off bone. There was no hair on their heads, none on their faces. And for eyes, Sigurd saw only dark holes. He gripped his sword, steadying himself. Thenor and Sappa had taught him more about how to fight than he'd ever learned in Ottby.

Valera glanced over her shoulder, seeing the line of death collectors advancing on Thenor and Sigurd. Every instinct told her to turn back and help them, but she could hear her father's voice in her ears, urging her to find Ulfinnur. So, grabbing Tikas' arm, she pointed him to the right of the tower. 'I sense there's another way in, around there, though these walls are thick with Alari's protections. I have to find a way to break them before she comes back!' Glancing over her shoulder, Valera took one last look at Thenor and Sigurd, now fighting off the dark-cloaked death collectors, before disappearing around the corner.

***

Raf recognised the man on the chair, and she didn't move forward. He wasn't looking at her. He was drinking from a silver goblet, a golden crown encircling his head. He appeared tired but happy. Victorious, she realised, seeing his bloody face.

Standing now, he raised his goblet and with it a smile that stretched from one side of his heavily scarred face to the other. 'To you!' he called with bright eyes. 'For I couldn't have achieved all of this without you, my love!'

Raf blinked. He wasn't talking to her, was he?

Hearing a faint cough, she turned around, seeing Gysa, the newly restored dreamer, standing behind her.

'No,' Gysa laughed. 'Why would he be talking to a filthy little rag like you? For what did you ever do to help Gudrum? And after he saved you? All you did was abandon him and turn your back on him. Though...' And now she stepped forward, her voice teasing and light. 'Though now he has a proper dreamer. A dreamer who will help him achieve all of this.' Sweeping her arm around the bloody field, she licked her lips. 'I gave him a crown, and soon I will deliver the ultimate victory. You see that, don't you, nothing girl? You chose the wrong side, and soon you'll discover what a terrible mistake that was.'

Raf gasped in horror, recognising a familiar face amongst the dead.

Gysa leaned forward, touching her forehead. 'Back to sleep you go, pointless thing. But don't worry, I'll see you soon!'

***

Thenor hadn't needed Sigurd's help in dealing with the death collectors, though he'd wanted his son to play his part, and after killing all twelve together, they'd hurried after Valera.

'How can we break through Alari's protections?' Sigurd wanted to know, seeing the symbols carved into the tower walls revealed in Omani's moonlight.

'That is where your sister comes in. She's been studying Alari's magic for years, knowing we would have to defeat her eventually. She has far greater symbol knowledge than me. Do not worry, Valera will get us inside.'

They moved with haste, running through an archway into a courtyard, where they were greeted by another circle, a well, and more cawing ravens. Thenor gripped his spear, now dripping with the dark blood of the death collectors, listening to the noisy panic as the birds scattered high up into the eaves of Alari's stone tower.

'Is she still here?' Sigurd wondered.

'I don't know, but stay alert.'

Sigurd nodded, and together they ran into the darkness, following the gravel path to where Tikas stood guard behind Valera.

'She's trying to neutralise the symbols,' Tikas explained, holding a hand over his empty eye socket. It bled, the pain growing more intense by the moment. He felt embarrassed. Useless.

'Here.' Thenor took away Tikas' bloody hand, holding his own over the eye socket. 'I cannot return your eye, but I can seal the wound and take away the pain. Stay still now.' He added pressure to his hand until he felt warmth beneath it.

Tikas gasped, one arm out to steady himself, feeling Thenor's hand vibrating, trying not to imagine the disfigurement he would have to endure for the rest of his life.

'You are the messenger,' Thenor gently reminded him. 'Your ears are of most use to you. Remember that.' He took his hand away, pleased to see that he'd staunched the flow of blood.

'Father!' Valera called breathlessly, glancing over her shoulder. 'We can go!'

'Hurry!' Thenor implored. 'Alari will return. We must find Ulfinnur quickly.'

He took the lead from Valera, who fell in behind him, Tikas and Sigurd bringing up the rear.

The interior of Alari's tower was almost as dark as its exterior, and they struggled to see where to go for a moment, no one having been there before.

'Find stairs!' Thenor ordered. Then, '*wait*! Everyone wait here! Valera, keep your eyes open.' And then he was gone, a cold rush of wind in his place.

Sigurd blinked in the darkness, narrowing his eyes, seeing shadows moving at the end of the corridor. 'What about Vasa?' he breathed. 'Is she here too?'

It was a good question, Valera thought, knowing that Ulura was Vasa's wolf.

She saw the shadows herself.

'No!' came a cry from the end of the corridor, followed by a sudden burst of white light.

Alari had returned.

Sigurd moved ahead of Valera, holding Tikas' silver shield, protecting all three of them as Alari pounded it with white flames, sparks flying. She lunged forward, the ground rippling beneath their feet.

'Move!' Valera barked, and Tikas and Sigurd spun away as she lifted her arms, drawing bricks down from the ceiling, hurling them at Alari. One by one, they pummelled her sister in a shower of rough stone, forcing her back.

Forcing her to think.

Alari smiled, seeing a familiar figure appear at the end of the corridor, and eager to box in her enemies, she started chanting, stepping forward.

Sigurd felt Vasa's presence before he turned around, and drawing his sword, he threw the shield back to Tikas, who caught it, moving ahead of Valera again, while Sigurd spun around to face Vasa, flames streaming from *Fire Song's* shimmering blade.

Though after the murder of her beloved Ulura, Vasa was fire itself. 'You will all die!' she howled, her two ravens launching from her shoulders, aiming for Sigurd. They flew through his fire as though it was water, beaks open, snapping for his neck. Sigurd swung wildly, claws raking his face, and stumbling backwards, he bumped into his father.

Thenor had returned amidst the chaos with an unconscious

Ulfinnur slumped over his shoulder.

Valera turned to him, fearing that Tikas' shield wouldn't hold for long, listening to Sigurd screaming as he fought off Vasa's determined ravens. 'We have to go!' she cried.

Her father nodded, sweeping his cloak around them all, and then they were gone, and Alari was left in the darkened corridor, facing a screaming Vasa.

Alari's arms fell to her sides, breath heaving in her chest, and dropping her head, she slumped to the ground.

***

Raf awoke from her dream with an urgency that had her jumping out of bed, immediately falling over Alys, who was sleeping on the floor. Alys screamed in fright, and then Eddeth was sitting up clasping a knife, jabbing it into the darkness.

'Stop!' she bellowed. 'You stop right there!'

'Eddeth, it's me,' Raf panted, pulling herself up on Eddeth's bed. She turned back to Alys. 'Sorry, I forgot... I had a... dream.'

Eddeth slipped the knife back under her pillow, and hurrying to grab Raf's hand, she pulled her onto the bed. 'Sit down now, sit down, and tell us what you saw.' She was breathless, her heart racing, for it was so rare for Raf to be forthcoming that Eddeth feared she'd seen something important.

'There's a new king,' Raf said, blinking in terror. 'It's Gudrum. His dreamer... I saw him. He was victorious. He defeated Reinar. I saw it. Reinar was dead!'

***

Reinar woke early, as he did most mornings. Lately, he'd tended to try and slip out of bed before Elin woke. He felt bad for avoiding her, but he was finding it hard to be close to her. Something had broken between them, and whether it was guilt or discomfort or a lack of desire, he now felt happier away from his wife.

Standing at the door, throwing his cloak around his shoulders, he glanced back at a serene-looking Elin, who lay on her stomach, one hand under her pillow, eyes closed. Guilt flooded his veins, and he thought about returning to the bed and being the husband he'd promised to be at their wedding feast all those years ago. Then, remembering that they were departing Slussfall in a few days, he felt impatient to find his dreamers, hoping they'd discovered something useful. So, quietly opening and closing the door, he disappeared into the corridor, deciding to head straight to Eddeth's cottage.

Elin opened her eyes, seeing only darkness in the chamber, then squinting, she began making out familiar shapes. She felt cold, drawing her hand out from under the pillow, tucking it beneath the fur. She saw the door, hearing the soft thud of footsteps, and rolling over, she saw the empty pillow her husband had left behind.

***

Eddeth's tea didn't help.

Alys sipped it, tasting lemon balm and elderflower. It would have been pleasant, she knew, if she hadn't felt so ill. That nauseous feeling had been building for days, she realised now. Perhaps this was it? Perhaps she'd always feared what Raf had actually seen?

That Reinar was about to die.

'Hector!' Eddeth announced from the stool where she was milking Agnes. 'What has Gudrum done with Hector? How has he become the king?'

Raf shrugged. 'I don't know, but there was no sign of Hector, just Gudrum and Gysa. I imagine he's dead.' She thought for a moment, the feelings settling in her chest. 'He is dead. I feel it.'

Eddeth released one of Agnes' teats to scratch her chin, immediately regretting that as warm milk spurted over her trousers. She quickly reapplied her hand to staunch the shower, receiving a scolding bleat from Agnes. 'I think we underestimated that dreamer,' she muttered. 'For I sense that Gudrum didn't kill Hector on his own.'

Raf nodded. 'It felt that way, as though they were together. He called her my love.' She made a face, feeling disgusted.

Alys sat on Raf's bed, cradling a cup of tea, trying to think. 'And who else did you see? Anyone you recognised?'

Raf shook her head, sipping her own tea. 'Just bodies everywhere. But I saw Reinar's. He was looking up at me. Dead.'

The knock on the door had Eddeth screaming so loudly that Agnes kicked out with her hooves. Eddeth lost control of both teats now, milk spraying everywhere, the little goat crashing around the cottage like a bucking horse.

Raf hurried to help Eddeth grab Agnes while Alys opened the door.

To Reinar.

He stood in the doorway with a look of confusion, seeing the rioting goat and a milky-faced Eddeth, and Raf, who quickly dropped her big eyes, turning away. 'Everything alright?' he wondered with a crooked smile. 'I thought you might still be asleep, but I see not.' He looked at Alys as Eddeth calmed Agnes down, though Alys wouldn't meet his eyes. He glanced at Eddeth, who quickly started muttering about needing more firewood. 'What happened?' he asked, pulling a stool towards the fire. The walk from the hall had been brief, but the early morning air was icy, and he was frozen solid. 'Something in your dreams?'

Only Agnes spoke, bleating as Eddeth resumed her milking, keeping her eyes low.

'So it's something bad then? About me? About us leaving?'

Alys joined Reinar by the fire, and taking a deep breath, she turned to him. 'Raf had a dream. She saw Gudrum as the king, with Hector's dreamer by his side.'

'Gudrum had a crown and a throne, and he sat in a field of bodies,' Raf added quietly.

Reinar frowned, sitting back as the fire popped. 'And what of Hector?'

Raf shrugged. 'He wasn't there.'

'Do you think Gudrum's the king now?'

Raf nodded.

Silence.

'That's not all,' Alys said, knowing it wasn't a secret they could or should keep. Reinar needed to know everything before he left Slussfall – if he still chose to leave. 'Raf saw you on the field. She saw your... body.'

Reinar felt as though Alys was talking on the other side of the fort. Her voice suddenly sounded so distant, so faint. He had always feared the words of dreamers as much as he'd been enticed by them. The day a dreamer revealed how he would die had loomed on the horizon, but to hear it now, when so much was at stake? He kept his head up, his expression neutral, though his body started vibrating. 'And Gudrum was the victor? He defeated us?'

Raf nodded. 'He defeated you.'

Finishing her milking, Eddeth gave Agnes a pail of barley and oats, and picking up her bucket, she headed to the kitchen corner, searching for a cup. Filling it with warm milk, she handed it to a distracted-looking Reinar before dragging her stool to the fire. 'Well, that's one way of looking at things,' she said into the silence. 'Another way is to be grateful for the message. It's a chance to think carefully, to see what your real problem is. And it's not Hector Berras. Not anymore!'

Reinar couldn't even nod. He remained frozen in place, watching the flames.

'Gudrum is strong,' Alys added. 'I sensed that in Orvala and in Furkat. He has the face of a man who knows how to survive. I think he's lucky. He must be to have escaped death so many times, and luck is like a talisman. He carries it with him, believing he'll escape danger every time.' Alys' words tumbled from her lips as she saw Gudrum's eyes glowing in the flames. It was as though she was staring into his mind, seeing the man so clearly. 'He believes in himself, in his ambitions. He won't stop until he achieves everything he desires.'

'Which is what?' Reinar asked. 'What does Gudrum truly want?'

'Revenge,' Alys breathed, feeling Gudrum's rage burning inside her now. 'More than anything, he wants revenge.'

***

Breakfast as a king felt different.

Gudrum couldn't put his finger on why, but as he sat where Hector had been sniping at him only days before, in his high chair, dressed in his finest tunic, he felt a pleasant warmth radiating in his chest. He sat a little taller, feeling more important than he'd ever felt in his life, realising that every opinion he uttered was now the most important opinion in the kingdom. His subjects, of which there were thousands, were all obliged to bow down before him, the king. The king with his unrivalled, unquestionable wisdom.

He smiled at Gysa, who sat beside him, dabbing her lips with a napkin, having pushed her plate away. He eyed her sausages, which she hadn't touched, thinking about helping himself, though, being a king, he knew he could simply demand more.

'What is it that you want, my lord?' Gysa wondered, hoping to focus him. 'For I am here to make your dreams come true.'

Gudrum felt the warmth in his chest spreading until his arms tingled and his thighs throbbed. His body stirred until he was struggling to sit still, remembering how long it had been since he'd had a woman in his bed for longer than a few hours. Since Raf. Though she hadn't really wanted him, he knew. She'd just been biding her time, waiting for someone better to come along.

Someone younger and more handsome.

Someone called Sigurd.

Snarling, he bit into a runny egg, bright orange yolk dribbling into his beard, and picking up a napkin, he rubbed it away. 'What do I want?' he mused, and turning to the dreamer, he dropped his napkin, taking her hand. 'I want you. And when I've had you, I want my enemies' heads. Tarl Brava's most of all, I think, and Sigurd Vilander's.' Then he thought again, seeing the hulking shape of the man who stood in his way to claiming all of Alekka. 'But first, his brother's. Yes, that's what I want, Gysa. I want Reinar Vilander's head. And now that Hector's gone, there's nothing holding me back.'

CHAPTER ELEVEN

Ulfinnur was weak, his body bruised and scarred. He hung his head, unable to lift it as Thenor's healer, Emina, placed a hand under his chin, tilting it so Valera could pour a bitter tonic into his mouth. His auburn hair was lank and long, plastered to his face, which was ashen.

He looked terrible.

'Alari took his powers,' Thenor said, his hands hovering above Ulfinnur's body. Ulfinnur had closed his eyes, resting his head against the wooden headboard of the bed they'd carried him into after returning to Gallabrok. 'He needs time to heal before I can restore them. But I will. Do not fear, Daughter,' he smiled, touching Valera's arm. 'I will.' He turned away from the bed, heading to the chamber door, where Sigurd hovered, watching. 'You look ready for bed yourself.'

Sigurd turned into the corridor, his father following behind him. 'I don't feel bad. Better than I look, I suppose. She weakened me, but since we returned, I feel strong again.'

'Magic is more of a weapon than many realise. When you enter someone's mind, you can control them entirely. You can make them fearful, make them hurt others and themselves. You can cause any number of problems.' Thenor peered at Sigurd, wanting to ensure that he was alright, which he appeared to be, bar the odd scratch. 'She tried to get in, I see, though what Valera and I did protected your mind. As for the rest of you?' He sighed, concern giving way to frustration. 'Of course if I had killed her before now, we would not have to try at all.'

'But you saved Ulfinnur,' Sigurd said. 'That's the most important thing. You saved him, and now he can release winter, and Vuli can come with spring.'

Thenor smiled, knowing that Sigurd's mind always returned to his family, no matter how many times he thought he'd become comfortable in Gallabrok. 'Of course, and he will, but give him a day. He needs to rest, and we must go and see Tikas. Another wounded hero. If he hadn't hit Alari with his shield...' Thenor shook his head, feeling strange. He wondered who would finally emerge as the victor, starting to fear that it wouldn't be him. And then, annoyed at himself for entertaining self-defeating doubts, he lifted his head, striding onwards.

Sigurd had to walk fast to catch up. His ankles, which, only hours earlier, had been trapped in Alari's magical fetters, were once again moving with ease, free of pain. He swung his arms, remembering what she'd done to him in her dungeon chamber. He'd feared that she would lose patience and kill him. He'd feared he wouldn't be strong enough to withstand her interrogation. But he had, and now he had a choice to make.

A choice about what he really wanted to do.

***

'Reinar!' Alys called, slipping as she hurried down the alley to catch him.

He turned with a frown, though he wasn't unhappy to see her. They avoided each other where they could, though it didn't stop him thinking about her or looking for her every time he stepped outside the hall. Alys was like sunshine, and seeing her filled him with a warmth not usually present. Though after what Raf had revealed, Reinar hadn't stopped shivering. 'Do you believe her?

Raf? Is she telling the truth?'

Alys nodded, eyes wide and blinking with worry. 'She is. Raf doesn't speak up often. She doesn't reveal much that isn't asked of her, but she jumped out of bed when she woke from that dream. She told us immediately.'

Reinar saw the end of the alley approaching, the dawn sky dull in the distance. He heard the sounds of the square coming to life, a woman screeching at her children in a nearby cottage. And he stopped, touching Alys' arm. 'But what do you think? Raf may have seen my death, but can I change it? Is it possible? Can I change it?'

Alys didn't respond; she didn't know. 'I... I'll try and ask Ragnahild. She saw you as the king, so she must know if something has happened to change that.'

Reinar dropped his head, fearing that the threads of his destiny were unravelling now. There'd been an oddly certain path to follow since he was a boy, Stellan's son. He'd been raised to be the next Lord of Ottby, planning to marry Elin since he first laid eyes on her. Gerda had always whispered Ragnahild's vision in his ear, and though he'd never sought such a role, it had been in the back of his mind his entire life.

But now?

He lifted his head, searching Alys' worried eyes. 'I'm not letting Gudrum defeat me. Gudrum as king? Can you imagine what he would do to Alekka? I won't let that happen, Alys. I can't.' He thought of Sigurd then, fearing for his brother, waves of terror and frustration threatening to distract him entirely. 'Ake chose me, and whatever happens, I can't let him down.'

'It won't come easy,' Alys warned. 'Though you mustn't give up. And stay safe. You won't take the throne if you don't stay safe.'

'You're saying I shouldn't leave the fort now? I shouldn't try to attack Gudrum?'

The screeching woman came running out of the cottage after a howling child, who took off in the opposite direction, and seeing her lord staring at her sternly, the red-faced woman bobbed her head, disappearing back inside.

Alys felt distracted, but as Reinar's words echoed back to her, she tried to focus. 'No, that's not what I'm saying, but let us see more before you go. Please. Delay your departure until we know more. What Raf saw...' Alys leaned closer, wanting a twitching Reinar to hear her words. Then realising what she was doing and sensing the woman peering through her shutters at them, she stepped away. 'I have to go back. I'll talk to Eddeth and Raf again before I see the children, and I'll try to find Ragnahild too. Please, Reinar, just wait a little longer, until we see more. We will see more.'

Reinar didn't want to delay his departure, but he also didn't want to throw away his life, putting his people at risk. He sighed. 'I'll wait, but please hurry, Alys. I need to turn things around quickly, one way or the other.'

***

Solveigh was quiet as she walked behind Ludo and Helgi, her arm through Berger's as he munched an apple beside her.

Seeing her studying him, he offered her the apple. 'Hungry?'

She shook her head, struggling to smile.

He frowned, carrying on. 'Is it the baby? Is something wrong?'

Again Solveigh shook her head, causing Berger to squeeze her arm. 'It's that... you're leaving,' she sighed.

'I am.' And though Berger couldn't wait to leave the suffocating fort behind, he felt unhappy about leaving Solveigh. 'It won't be easy, but it's what we must do,' he said, throwing the last of the apple to a mangy-looking dog. 'If Reinar stays behind these walls any longer, Hector and Gudrum will swallow us whole.'

Solveigh gripped her belly, feeling anxious. 'And what about Tarl? He'll come soon, won't he?'

Despite his own worries about that, Berger laughed. 'I'd like to see him try. Perhaps he's a good skier, but it'd be some journey!'

Solveigh dropped her head, eyes on her belly, shoulders

slumping. 'You want me to trust you, Berger. You offer yourself to me as a protector, yet you dismiss my fears as though I shouldn't even have them. But I have two violent husbands, and I'm carrying Tarl's child. My entire family was burned alive. I was raped.' Tears stung her eyes, hands shaking. 'I... I'm scared for a reason.'

Berger stopped, holding her arm, letting Ludo and Helgi disappear around the corner. Any humour was gone from his eyes now as he searched hers. 'I do want to keep you safe, Solveigh. I don't want you to worry. I want to keep the worries for me, not you. You should only concern yourself with the child. With looking after the child.'

'Tarl's child. Who he will come for. He will.'

Berger knew that to be true, and this time he didn't try to laugh it away. 'He can't come now, though, can he? The sea's frozen. He can't come. And as yet there's no child to claim.' Now he smiled, kissing Solveigh's quivering lips. 'But when there is, and when the sea's flowing, I'll protect you. So will Reinar. We need to make him the king, get him into Stornas, shore up that city, and then you'll be safe. We'll all be safe in there together, behind those walls. You, me, and the baby.'

'You're very confident,' Solveigh frowned, peering at Berger's handsome face. 'For I haven't even agreed to marry you.'

'No, but you will,' Berger decided, sweeping an arm behind her back. 'When you're free of your bastard husbands, you will.'

Solveigh shook her head, though she found herself smiling. His confidence was oddly attractive, and though Berger was no dreamer, she wanted to believe everything he'd told her.

***

Raf wasn't speaking, which was nothing new, Eddeth thought with a crooked grin as they tidied the cottage, preparing to start the new day. 'I'll take a look through that book, see what else I can learn,' she decided loudly. 'What about you? Perhaps you need to go straight back to sleep and find out more?'

Raf shuddered. 'No, no. I don't think so.'

Eddeth bounded towards her, tugging her down to the bed. 'I can't read your thoughts, Raf, and you can't read mine. I suppose that means we're doing something right, wouldn't you say?' She chuckled, slapping Raf's knee, though seeing that the little dreamer was so anxious, she tried to look sympathetic. 'But you have a lot on your mind. Too much, I'd say. You could halve it right now just by sharing. By telling me what's in there.' And she pointed to Raf's head.

Raf's black hair had grown long, now hanging well past her shoulders, though it was still a neglected tangle. Eddeth offered to brush it every night, but mostly Raf rebuffed her efforts. She didn't care. She wasn't one of those women – the pretty ones with finely coiled braids and colourful, elegant dresses. Eddeth had found her a new dress when they'd arrived at the fort – one of Falla Gundersen's cast-offs – though now it was stained and torn like her old one had been.

She didn't feel like one of those women at all.

'There's nothing to tell,' she whispered. 'I told you about my dream. That's all I saw. There's nothing else.'

Eddeth tried not to look disappointed. Raf was a hard nut, but she was determined to crack her open. One day. And smiling now, she wrapped an arm around the girl's shoulders, feeling her flinch, trying to squirm away. 'You have a home, with me. And Agnes. Rigfuss too. It's not the most pleasant smelling place, I know, but a few more sprigs of lavender will sort that out. You have a home now, Raf, so there's no need to be afraid. I won't let anything happen to you.' Eddeth's voice faltered as she thought of Aldo, and picking her wart, eyes on her lap, she started muttering to herself. 'I'll look in that book, I will. There'll be answers in there. Don't you worry now, I'll find the answers!'

***

Alys headed back to her cottage, hoping to convince Ragnahild to make an appearance, wondering what the spirit dreamer would make of Raf's dream. For it was Ragnahild who had first seen Reinar on the throne as the King of Alekka. But had everything changed? It was most unsettling, and Alys was distracted, hand reaching for the door handle, when she heard someone calling her name.

Helgi.

She felt more sympathetic towards him after their talk, and he seemed calmer as he approached, as though sharing his secret had reduced his tension.

He didn't speak until he was standing before her.

And then, he didn't speak at all.

Alys could read his thoughts, though, and she smiled. 'You're welcome.'

Now he laughed, teeth showing. 'Being married to a dreamer would be an unusual experience, I imagine. I'm not sure I'd sleep easy with a dreamer seeing into my soul!' He grinned, noticing her frown. 'Though I'm not suggesting...' And now he was flustered, tapping Alys' arm. 'No, after what happened, I... no, you've nothing to fear from me. You haven't!'

Alys stayed where she was, seeing Ilene walking with Elin Vilander in the distance, both women turning her way.

Helgi followed her gaze. And looking back at her with some sympathy, he smiled. 'According to Berger, if we can kill Gudrum and put Reinar Vilander on the throne, everyone can finally escape this place and go back to their lives.'

'Though you've only just arrived.'

The door opened behind Alys, and Lotta popped her head outside. 'What are *you* doing here?' she grumbled at Helgi, then fearing he'd come for Puddle, she hastily turned back inside and closed the door.

They heard the lock turning with a loud click and Lotta calling

Puddle's name.

Alys blinked at Helgi. 'You didn't make the best impression when we first met.'

He could see that, and he shook his head. 'I wasn't myself, though please assure your daughter that I don't want to hurt her dog.'

'Puddle?' Alys laughed. 'He's too fast to be caught, even by someone as fast as you.' And though she felt an urgency and fear for Reinar, she stayed where she was, talking to Helgi Eivin for some time, enjoying the conversation.

***

Gudrum quickly realised that, as king, he had a lot of questions to answer. It was all well and good wanting to dress in fine clothes and sit in the highest chair in the land. He could enjoy the increased level of respect, the terrified looks and grovelling subservience of his people. Stornas' wealth was his. He could take what he wanted. No one would deny him.

Power, women, gold...

It was everything he'd sought when he left Osterland.

Now he had it all.

And yet he spent his day with a frown carved between twitching eyebrows, for everywhere he turned, someone came rushing up to him with a question or a problem. And though his opinions carried more weight than anyone else's, it was his answers that were sought most of all.

Gudrum had walked the city for some time, enjoying the surprise and confusion that greeted him, basking in the glow of his sudden ascent. He'd organised a pyre for Hector. They would burn him that night, and he, as king, would be there, presiding over the ceremony. That gave him pause, realising how quickly a king could become tossed out scraps, honoured briefly, forgotten quickly. He'd felt sorry for Hector as he watched his scorched remains being wrapped in a funeral shroud far too big for what was left of him. He was a crumbled ruin of what he'd once been – a man, a friend, and a king.

Though had Hector really wanted to be the king? Or had he just thought he could mend his broken heart by killing Ake?

Edrik walked beside Gudrum. In the months since he'd claimed Stornas for Hector, Edrik had filled the void left by Ilmar and Ahlen. He was a young man, barely thirty, and though that kept Gudrum on edge, he enjoyed the benefits of having a quick-minded advisor beside him. Edrik's skin had a sickly pallor, though he brimmed with energy and ideas, darting around the city in the service of his master.

'Gather every scout, the leaders of the army and the fleet. Gather them all into the hall. I will hear about our situation. Bring the head fletcher and armourer too. Hector may have wanted to wait out winter, but the kingdom will never truly belong to me if I sit here growing fat while the snow falls!' He took the castle steps two at a time, feeling a renewal of energy as he left the cloying crowds behind. He would go inside his castle, sit in his chair by his fire and make his plans.

He was no Hector Berras.

A little snow wasn't going to stop him.

***

Elin feared what might happen when Reinar left Slussfall, though the thought that something might change was also uplifting. She'd been trapped in the fort in the bleak, bitter winter for over three months, forced to see that dreamer every single day. Shuddering, she tried to focus on Reinar, who was pulling off his socks beside her. Turning for the poker, Elin prodded the logs, moving them around in the great hearth, hoping to release more flames to warm her husband.

'You'll be safe here,' Reinar promised, wiggling his frozen toes, extending his feet towards the fire. 'I'll leave the biggest garrison I can. And dreamers.'

Elin scowled. 'I don't see why we need those.' Though she quickly thought that through, not wanting Alys to leave with Reinar. 'It makes sense, I suppose. Your enemies do like to play games.'

Reinar knew that to be true, but hearing the tension in his wife's voice, he didn't pursue the subject further.

'It will be dangerous,' she said, leaving her chair to sit on his knee. 'What if...'

Reinar smiled. 'You know what Ragnahild saw. I was born to be a king.' The words were empty, and he said them seeing Raf's face, knowing what she'd seen. He shivered as Elin leaned on his chest, nudging her head beneath his chin, wrapping her arm around him.

'You must come back to me,' she whispered. 'And we can have a child. It will be a new beginning for both of us.'

Reinar forced himself to lift his arm to her, to hold her there as she nestled into him. He felt numb, the sound of the fire loud in his ears.

Like a pyre, he thought, closing his eyes.

***

Gysa's bags were packed when Gudrum knocked on the door. She had dressed in her finest gown: a blue silk with draping sleeves and a plunging bodice. Hector's desire for his dreamer had blossomed when she'd revealed her new face, and being a famously generous man, he'd showered her with gifts. Gysa smiled, remembering her last glimpse of Hector, and running her hands over the silk bodice, she jiggled her breasts to ensure they were sitting straight.

Opening the door, she laughed, pleased to see that Gudrum, too, had made an effort with his appearance. He had tamed his wild hair and beard, dressing in a black tunic and matching trousers, both free of mud.

Even his boots looked clean.

Inhaling deeply, he stepped into the chamber. 'What's that smell?' he wondered with a deep voice, his hand brushing against hers. 'Spice?'

'Something like that,' Gysa purred, turning after him as he strode immediately to the fire, eyes darting to the bed.

'You are packed,' he noted. 'Because you know what I'm about to say?'

She smiled at him. 'I do. Of course.'

'And you think it wise? Leaving the city? Attacking Reinar Vilander while winter remains such a threat?'

'Reinar Vilander *is* a threat, and a king should lead from the front. A show of force is necessary after Hector's misguided efforts. If you wish to claim the entire kingdom, as a king should certainly wish to do, then you must be bold. The Vilanders are hiding because they fear you. They fear winter too. And now you need to show them how right they are on both counts.'

Stirred by her bold words and her breathy voice, Gudrum turned to the dreamer in the blue dress. And sweeping an arm around her lower back, he pulled her forward until their noses touched. 'Do you fear me, Gysa?'

Her lips parted as she stared into his eyes. 'No, my lord. Not at all.'

***

Puddle crawled back to Alys, almost on his belly, certain he was going to be told off. Though relieved just to have found him, Alys tucked him under one arm and hurried back to the cottage. It was empty and quiet, so locking the door, she placed a sausage-smelling Puddle near the fire and turned to her bed to take off her cloak.

'She's not wrong! No, she's not wrong!' growled a newly-arrived Ragnahild, glowering at Alys as she paced before the fire. 'And what does it mean? What can it all mean?'

Alys spun back around, mouth open, mind whirring. 'You mean Raf? Raf's dream?'

But Ragnahild had turned away, muttering to herself.

'Do you see the same?' Alys wanted to know, hurrying towards her.

The old spirit dreamer's shoulders heaved. 'Alari is evil but so clever. Some sit back and bask in their power, doing little. Alari, though, she plays games but with a purpose, for she has a singular goal. And we both know what that is!' Now Ragnahild turned around, and beneath all her bluster, she looked worried. 'Alari is always seeking knowledge, much like Mirella. They are two peas in an evil pod! And who knows what they've discovered now? Who knows why it's all changed?'

Alys swallowed. 'But what can Reinar do? Surely there must be something? Before you said he would be the king, and now?'

Ragnahild's sigh was long and deep. 'We dreamers are a link between the gods and the humans. The gods want to help, though unlike Eutresia, they do not seek to become involved themselves. But with the knowledge they give us in dreams, we can help. We can see the paths into the future, both dark and light. It gives us all a chance to act, to grow, to change course. Though dreams are not cast in iron nor carved in stone. The three Goddesses of Fate have been reliable for centuries, though there have recently been questions asked about their loyalty to Thenor.'

Alys felt sick. 'So everything could have changed? What Raf saw could come true?'

Ragnahild stared at her with puzzled eyes. It was as though she couldn't hear her. And then, hand out, mouth open, she disappeared.

***

Ulfinnur looked up at Thenor with a furrowed brow. 'I let you down.'

Standing over his bed, Thenor inhaled a long breath. 'You are not the first god to fall foul of Alari, my friend,' he promised, placing a hand on Ulfinnur's head, and closing his eyes.

Ulfinnur pressed his lips together, stopping the next words from coming out.

'We only have now and what will come,' Thenor murmured. 'What has been is informative, but no more than that. We know more about Alari, and that helps all of us. Thanks to you, we know where she lives. I imagine she'll want to do something about that if she ever returns to her tower.'

Ulfinnur shuddered. 'I can still smell the place.'

Thenor opened his eyes. 'Though you have recovered quickly,' he said. 'Thanks to Emina and Valera. You are certainly strong enough for your powers again.' He pushed aside Ulfinnur's tunic, still seeing the marks Alari had carved into his flesh, cutting through his symbols. Her magic was powerful, and Thenor knew that Ulfinnur would likely bear them forever. Though it never hurt to have a reminder of the past; a warning to always remain alert to danger. 'Vuli needs you to release your grip on winter so she can usher in spring. She is one of my more patient goddesses, as you well know, but even she has been clamouring for your return.'

Ulfinnur pushed himself upright, nodding. 'Yes, it's all I thought about while I was there. Well, not all,' he admitted. 'But I feared the passage of time and what it would mean for the seasons. For the humans, at least.'

Now Thenor was smiling. 'Then let us not delay. If you feel you are ready?'

Ulfinnur took a deep breath, straightening his shoulders. 'I am.'

'Good.' And placing a hand on either side of his friend's head, Thenor started chanting.

PART TWO

Spring

CHAPTER TWELVE

The buds on the trees in the kitchen garden had Eddeth hopping from one foot to the other in a dance of noisy delight.

Falla stared at her from the doorway, the cook grumbling beside her. Eventually, the old woman turned inside, for though the first hints of spring had appeared that morning, it was cold enough to strip the skin from her bones, and she was eager to return to her hot kitchen.

Falla agreed, wrapping her thick woollen cloak over her enormous bump. She had started spending more time in her chamber as the birth approached, though her baby seemed reluctant to leave her warm belly, and Eddeth had suggested that walking would help. That and a special tea she was gathering the ingredients for. Though now Eddeth appeared so distracted by the welcome news that spring was finally on its way that Falla was losing hope for the tea.

'We're saved!' Eddeth declared. 'I feel it! We're saved from the bleakest winter in memory. Oh, it's felt like years! So long of only feeling cold. So long of the darkness!'

'Have you got everything you need?' Falla snapped, finally losing patience. 'For the tea? It's too cold to stand out here. There may be a few buds on the trees, but it's still cold enough to kill us all!'

Eddeth agreed, and grinning, she bustled past Falla into the kitchen, grateful for its busy warmth.

Falla turned to follow her, feeling slightly off-balance. She was tired and irritable and desperate for her child to come.

'Well, that's where you're wrong!' Eddeth declared, nudging the dark-haired Lady of Slussfall. 'You don't want this child to come at all.'

'What?' Falla glanced over her shoulder, seeing the old cook, Margren, staring her way. 'What are you talking about?' she huffed, waddling past Eddeth, out of the kitchen, into the narrow passageway that led to the hall. 'I'm days overdue. You said it yourself. I've been ready for some time.'

It was mostly dark in the passageway as Eddeth snatched Falla's arm, stopping her in her tracks. They were alone. She heard nothing but the raised voice of the short-tempered Margren barking at her kitchen staff to get back to work. 'You're fearful of what your husband will think. The child's a girl! Mother Arnesson saw it, and I've seen the same. She's a lovely little girl, but you're holding tight, keeping her locked up in there because you don't want that husband of yours knowing the truth. You're delaying her appearance. *You* are, Falla!' Her voice had risen considerably, and sneezing, Eddeth tried to calm herself down.

Falla blinked, readying a retort, though her shoulders slumped, fearing that Eddeth was right. 'I'll tell him. I will. I...' She didn't want to tell Lief at all. He'd done nothing but talk about the son they would have since she'd revealed her pregnancy. Borg wasn't his, and though he was protective of his stepson, Lief needed an heir of his own. Falla believed that to be true, and she was no longer a young woman with years of childbirth ahead of her. She feared she wouldn't be able to give him what he desired most of all.

Eddeth patted Falla's hand, feeling her fears. 'It won't help to worry. A healthy child is what you should wish for now. Boy or girl doesn't matter. It won't to your husband. It won't!' Now she was moving past Falla, wanting to leave the hall. 'I know where I might find some mugwort!' she decided. 'You go and find the lord and tell him everything. That should move things along. And I'll make that tea. Rest, and I'll find you in your chamber.' And shuddering with purpose, Eddeth hurried away from the exhausted Lady of

Slussfall, wondering where she would find Alys.

***

Alys and Lotta stopped on their walk to watch the men training. It was mostly men, Alys saw, though there were a few women in the ring, one of them being Ilene Gislar.

'Why aren't you in there, Mama?' Lotta wanted to know with a tilt of her head. 'You should be training too.'

Alys grinned. 'That's not the sort of training I need. I need Ragnahild's training. I need to learn with Eddeth and Raf. I don't need to fight with my fists.' Though seeing Ilene swinging a staff at Ollo, Alys felt a flicker of desire to be standing face to face with the beady-eyed woman, knocking her down. She blinked, resting a hand on Lotta's shoulder. 'Look, it's Ilyia and Maia.'

Lotta sighed, pushing closer to her mother until she was under her arm, as though Alys was keeping her prisoner.

'Lotta!' Ilyia Bluefinn called, stopping some distance away in the slushy snow. 'Come and play. We're going to dress up!'

Lotta didn't say anything as the two dark-haired sisters stared at her with expectant looks, and eventually, realising that she wasn't going to, Alys smiled. 'Lotta's not feeling well today, girls, so I'll keep her by me. She'll come and play tomorrow, though.' She sensed Lotta frowning at this, and when the girls had run away, slightly disappointed, Alys bent down to find out what was wrong. She heard Ilene shouting in victory as Ollo spluttered and grumbled, knocked to the ground, but ignoring them, she ran a hand over Lotta's hair, trying to get her attention. 'Why don't you want to play with them? They're very nice girls, the same age as you, and they're lonely here, missing their father and their home.'

Lotta thought about her own dead father, though she didn't miss him at all. 'I don't want to play with anyone.' She dropped her head even lower, knowing that wasn't true. 'I want to play with

Magnus, but he's...'

'Your brother's growing up,' Alys sighed, feeling the pain of that herself. 'He's barely in the cottage these days. I never know where he is, and now he doesn't even say. He's always disappearing with that boy, Emil. They have a lot of fun, I think.'

Lotta's shoulders slumped, remembering when Magnus had had a lot of fun with her and Puddle. Now he barely noticed either of them. She heard the puppy barking at another dog and turned away. 'I have to go, Mama. Puddle needs me!' And sliding out of Alys' grip, Lotta ploughed through the slush as if nothing was wrong.

Alys shook her head. Then, hearing her name, she turned around to see Ilene looking her way.

'I never see you in here, Alys,' Ilene smirked. 'Perhaps you're too important now? Too worried about ruining your dress?' She ran her eyes over Alys' new blue dress, sneering. 'Too busy scheming and plotting to be the queen one day?'

Alys felt the heat of anger warming her cold limbs, though she didn't speak.

Ollo joined in. 'Wouldn't hurt you to have a turn, Alys,' he decided, wiping mud out of his eyes. 'I've taught Ilene a few things. She could teach you.'

Ilene snorted behind him. 'You? Taught me?'

She was a loud woman with a sharp voice, which quickly turned a few heads her way.

Ilene laughed, enjoying the attention. 'But Alys wouldn't think of getting dirty with the likes of us! She's a lady now, can't you see?'

Ludo came over, wanting to shut her up. 'I'll fight you, Ilene,' he offered, holding out his staff.

But Ilene didn't even look his way.

Ollo slipped out of the training ring, eyes on the tavern. He lowered his voice as he passed Alys. 'I'd walk away if I were you. Ilene's a real warrior now. She'd hurt you. And besides, you don't want to ruin that pretty dress.'

'Though perhaps it's not the dress she's worried about losing!'

Ilene went on, raising her voice. 'Perhaps she doesn't want to get smacked in the mouth? For how could she kiss Reinar Vilander then?'

There were hoots of laughter and gasps of mock horror, all eyes snapping to Alys.

Who turned around. 'I'll fight you, Ilene,' she decided, every other thought leaving her head. 'If it will make you feel better to defeat me, go ahead, try to.' Slipping into the training ring, she unpinned her cloak, and leaving it over the railings, she held out her hand for Ludo's staff, which he remained firmly holding onto.

'Alys...' he warned, looking her over. 'Think this through.'

But Alys didn't want to think. It had been months of feeling hurt and lonely and scared and sad and brokenhearted. She thought of Arnon and her mother, Hakon and Reinar. She thought of Alari and Elin, and she knew that more than anything, at that moment, she wanted to defeat Ilene Gislar, the smuggest, most irritating woman she'd ever met.

Ludo released his staff with a shrug. 'Watch the surface,' he muttered, following after Ollo. 'Find your balance first.'

Alys barely heard him, her mind absent any thoughts as she approached Ilene, out of practice and dressed like she was going to a feast. She caught a glimpse of Berger and Helgi approaching the training ring and quickly dropped her eyes.

Ilene swung her staff hard, cracking Alys' arm with such force that she fell onto her arse with a thump.

There was an audience, Alys realised, hearing a combined intake of breath and a few chuckles. Her eyes watered, the pain pounding as she dug the staff into the snow and pulled herself back to her feet. 'I wasn't aware we'd started.'

Ilene laughed, wanting to put on a show. 'What do you imagine happens in battle, Alys? Should I have waited for an invitation?'

Alys caught a glimpse of Jonas approaching, but quickly turning away from his surprised face, she saw Ilene coming at her again. She ducked, feeling the whoosh of the staff skimming over her head.

'What's happening?' Jonas asked Berger. 'What's Alys doing?'

Both Berger and Helgi shrugged, intrigued enough to stop on their journey to the fletcher's.

Ollo, too, had decided to remain watching. 'Ilene offered to train your granddaughter since you don't seem to have been helping her lately.'

'What? Train? Doesn't look like training to me.' Jonas didn't take his eyes off Alys, who was weaving about in a long dress. He shook his head, seeing that Ilene looked far more comfortable in trousers tucked into boots, her yellow hair pulled back from her face in a single long braid that whipped around as she moved.

Alys quickened her pace, working for balance in the slush. And eventually, finding some stability, she jabbed Ilene in the waist with the tip of her staff. She moved fast now, poking an unbalanced Ilene again. But Ilene had been training all morning, and she was confident on her feet, skipping away from Alys as though she was on hard ground. And now she swung for Alys' head.

Alys cursed herself for giving in to her emotions. Ilene meant nothing to her.

What was she doing?

She lifted her staff, blocking Ilene's blow, dropping low as a grinning Ilene went for her again. Their wooden staffs clacked together, parrying each other's shots. It became almost rhythmic as Alys realised that she could anticipate where Ilene would aim next, as though she was in Ilene's head.

And the knowledge of that had her smiling.

Then the wind swept in, tangling her dress around her legs, and losing her balance, she fell to the ground. Ilene laughed, driving down with her staff, but Alys rolled away, wet through, trying to untangle her dress. Finally back on her feet, she swung for Ilene's throat, though Ilene jerked away, almost losing her own footing.

Ilene saw Berger watching with his handsome cousin, Helgi. Helgi Eivin looked a little untamed, but he had that same tall swagger as Berger, and she hoped to catch his eye. 'There's quite a crowd!' she taunted. 'Though no Reinar. What a shame, but likely he's with his wife. You do know he has a wife, don't you, Alys?' Aiming high, she once again swung for Alys' head. Alys was just that bit taller, though, and Ilene had to push up onto her toes. That unbalanced her, and she stumbled forward, tripping past Alys, who spun quickly. Bending low, she struck Ilene across the back of the legs, knocking her onto her knees.

'Up, up!' Ollo cried. 'Get up!' He nudged Jonas with a grin. 'Ilene won't be beaten. I've been training her.'

Jonas laughed. 'Poor woman. She's got no chance. I trained Alys.'

'When was she a child, maybe. Though she's no warrior, Jonas. You must see that.'

Jonas watched his granddaughter tiptoeing around Ilene, and he saw the little girl he'd been so desperate to keep safe. 'Come on, Alys!' he called. 'Move faster!'

Helgi Eivin was wide-eyed as he watched beside them.

Berger looked to be enjoying himself too. Ilene was fury itself, but Alys wasn't backing down. He turned as Reinar approached. 'Just in time.'

'What's everyone standing around for?' Reinar wanted to know. 'Thought we were meeting at the fletcher's?' He heard a familiar shout and saw Alys down in the slush, Ilene dropping onto her, swinging a fist.

Jonas grimaced, hands on his face.

'What's going on?' Reinar demanded, then just as quickly, he was gripping the railing. 'Alys! Move!'

Ilene swung for Alys' cheek, but anticipating it, Alys jerked her head, and pushing up her pelvis in three quick movements, she knocked her away. Scrambling to her feet, hair hanging over her face, dress wet and torn, Alys scooped up her staff, aiming it at Ilene's face. 'Enough?'

But Ilene rolled, and quickly up on her feet, she grabbed the staff, laughing. 'I'm sure you've had enough, Alys de Sant, but I can't claim victory until I defeat you, *bitch*.' And she tugged the staff, trying to pull it out of Alys' hands.

Jonas almost had to hold Reinar back. He looked ready to

launch himself over the railings, though they both knew what a terrible idea that would be. 'Don't worry,' he murmured. 'Alys knows what to do.' He felt nervous but confident, barely blinking as he watched the two women fighting over the one staff.

'Do you really think you're stronger than me?' Alys taunted, hoping to provoke a reaction. And Ilene quickly obliged, yanking the staff with gritted teeth. Alys immediately let go, watching Ilene's eyes widen as she flew backwards, head thumping the hard earth beneath the thin layer of melting snow. Alys was quick to move, grabbing the staff, and with one foot on her chest, she jabbed it at Ilene's pulsing throat, pushing until she saw pain in her eyes. 'You're not stronger than me, Ilene. You've just got a bigger mouth.' And with a growl, she threw the staff away and strode towards the railings, one ear open to any attack coming from behind.

Though Ilene had hit her head so hard that she was having trouble even seeing. She lay there, trying to focus on the grey clouds drifting silently above her head, until Ollo bent over her with a grin.

'Time for the tavern?'

Reinar stepped away from the railings as Alys slipped through them, quickly wrapped in her black cloak by a beaming Jonas.

'Not bad,' Jonas decided with a wink. 'Though you're a little rusty. I hate saying that Ollo's right, but you could do with some training.'

Alys' legs wobbled, suddenly aware that she hurt all over. She ignored her grinning grandfather, already feeling foolish for giving in to her temper. It had been years since she'd felt free enough to express it, but, like her grandfather, she'd always possessed a spark of fire. It was just so surprising to feel it rear its head again.

'What has happened?' came a booming cry as Eddeth pushed through the crowd, her attention on a bedraggled Alys. 'Are you hurt?'

Alys dropped her eyes, shaking her head. 'No, just stupid.'

'Not stupid,' Ludo decided as he joined them. 'Ilene would make anyone snap.' He looked back at the sour-faced woman being comforted by a fussing Ollo, though she was mostly pushing him away.

Berger came towards her with his cousin, and Alys squirmed even more. 'So now you're even!' he laughed, knowing that as one of Solveigh's closest friends, it made more sense to congratulate Alys than console Ilene. And besides, Ollo had happily taken over that role now.

'Even?' Alys remembered Ilene thumping her in Ottby, but she shook her head. 'Now I'm just cold,' she said. 'I need a fire.'

'Or a walk?' Eddeth suggested. 'I'm heading into the forest to look for some herbs for Falla. You can come with me. Two pairs of eyes are better than one.'

Reinar frowned. 'It's best not to keep wandering into the forest, Eddeth.' Though seeing Eddeth's determination and not feeling like a fight, he sighed. 'I'll send someone with you.'

'We'll be fine,' Alys insisted, not wanting any company. 'I'll go and get my sword.' And having seen how well she'd handled herself in the training ring, no one could argue with that.

Helgi stared at her, remembering what had happened to him on his way to Slussfall. 'I wouldn't mind a walk in the forest,' he decided. 'I'll come along.'

Eddeth turned to peer up at the man, mouth open. 'Who are you?' she wondered, though she quickly saw his resemblance to Berger. 'I'm not sure we want the company, do we, Alys?'

Alys felt caught, though she didn't want to be rude. 'We have a lot to discuss, Eddeth and I. It's best if we're alone, but thank you,' she said. 'Perhaps another time?' She took Eddeth's arm, smiled at her grandfather, ignored Reinar, and headed away from the training ring, sensing countless pairs of eyes following her.

Reinar turned to glare at Helgi, eyeing the man with a look that said many things, none of which he felt entitled to say. 'Alys can take care of herself,' he muttered eventually, patting Berger on the back. 'Let's head to fletcher's.' And striding away with speed, he forced himself not to look over his shoulder as Alys and Eddeth disappeared into the crowd.

***

'The gods are truly with us!' Gudrum declared, eyes on the dripping boughs of fir trees lining the road. The sun was barely breaking through the tree canopy, but there was a sudden sense that spring had arrived, and Gudrum's smile grew as he rode at the head of his army, Gysa by his side. 'Ha! If only Hector had been bolder. If only he'd been brave enough to leave Stornas' walls behind! Perhaps the gods were only waiting on him?'

Having left Stornas, the army was now on its way to Ottby, where it would replenish its supplies further before heading north to Slussfall, sweeping aside any enemies foolish enough to remain in its path. This would be Gudrum's statement of intent, a ringing warning to all that the true King of Alekka now reigned, and anyone who thought otherwise would soon find themselves under his lash. He saw images of burning villages and piles of bodies, treasure rooms brimming with gold and silver. He saw cowering Alekkans, grovelling Alekkans, and ultimately, subservient Alekkans bending to his will. He wanted them to see his face, to see his men, and feel his power. Though spring would melt the sea and snow, freeing up his ships, he wanted every lord and villager alike to see the face of their new king.

Gysa wasn't smiling as she listened to Gudrum's rambling thoughts. 'You are impatient for victory,' she began, 'though so is your enemy. You can't get lost in numbers now. Alekkans are brave and loyal. They know what it means to fight, and so does Reinar Vilander.'

Hearing the reproach in Gysa's voice, Gudrum turned to her with a surprised frown. 'Reinar Vilander? He'll be shitting his breeches when word of my approach reaches him, looking to escape. Though not with ships. Ha! He won't get far with just the one ship!' Gysa appeared unmoved as Gudrum turned his head, seeing Edrik spurring his white horse up the line. 'Why so grim? My army grows by the day, Reinar's stores are diminishing by the moment, and our hopes of a resounding victory are rising. How can you grumble about that, for you will be the dreamer of a famous king. Perhaps one day even a high king?'

Gysa saw rays of sunlight glittering across their melting path, and she took a deep breath, having been thinking for some days about how to broach the subject she needed to discuss most of all. 'Though Reinar Vilander is not the greatest threat to your ambitions.'

Gudrum swung around, eyeing the dreamer with sharp eyes. 'What do you mean?' He flapped a hand at Edrik, keeping him back. 'What threat?' Nudging his horse until he was almost touching Gysa's, those sharp eyes demanded an answer.

Gysa lowered her voice. 'Now the sea is melting, Jael Furyck will soon discover that you're the King of Alekka. She will seek to kill you.'

Gudrum's worried face lightened, and he laughed. 'But that would be my dream come true! I hope she does. Imagine that?' He patted his horse, moving him away, laughing even louder. 'What? You think a few Islanders could defeat me? That they would come here, seeking to destroy my plans for Alekka? Why? Because their angry queen doesn't like me?'

Gysa knew that ego was a mountain to be climbed every day, especially with men like Hector and Gudrum. Their egos were fragile, easily bruised, in need of constant assurance and pandering. She pressed her lips together, trying not to look as bored as she felt having to soothe the king as though he was a boy. 'Yes, of course. Though Jael Furyck is a powerful woman with strong allies. She will not let you remain on Alekka's throne.'

Gudrum inhaled a sharp burst of cold air, drawing it deep into his lungs. 'Powerful? From what I've heard, she's been hiding on that island. Not the same as she was. Not the hero they sing about.'

Gysa smiled patiently. 'Do not underestimate either of your enemies, my lord,' she urged. 'When Hector reached the throne, he believed himself invincible, though the truth is that a throne makes a man more vulnerable than he ever was before. For now you are as much of a target as Ake Bluefinn was or Jorek Vettel before him. You are not Alekkan, and that will work against you.

Reinar Vilander and his family are respected, working hard to generate loyalty amongst those lords still to be reached by your men. And Jael Furyck...' Gysa straightened up, pleased to see curious concern where once there had been only cocky arrogance. 'You must decide what to do about that woman before she takes away all your options. And believe me, it won't be long until she sees exactly what's happening here.'

CHAPTER THIRTEEN

'This is nice, just the two of us!' Eddeth exclaimed as they walked between two rows of thick-trunked ash trees.

Lotta looked up at Eddeth with a scowl.

'Well, three of us,' Eddeth amended. 'Three dreamers off for an adventure!'

'Is there anything to eat?' Lotta asked, peering up at her mother, who hadn't spoken much since they'd left the fort behind. 'Why do you have your sword?'

Alys squeezed Lotta's mittened hand. 'I often wear my sword.'

'No, you don't.'

Alys sighed as Eddeth scampered off ahead of them, sniffing the air, clutching her staff, which reminded her of the training ring, and she felt odd. And sore. 'Reinar said the woods mightn't be safe, so I'm wearing it in case I need it. Nothing to worry about, though. We'll be fine.'

There was a real sense that spring was coming. Snow usually meant a slightly deadened feel, a more silent world, but Alys heard a buzz of activity amongst the trees, feeling heartened by that. The weather was as bleak as ever, but she felt hope stirring within herself as much as in the forest.

'Here! Here!' Eddeth called gleefully from somewhere up ahead. 'Alys! Here!'

'You could have stayed behind with Stina,' Alys smiled at her miserable-looking daughter. They'd left Puddle in the cottage after he'd gotten into trouble, frightening a little girl cuddling a kitten. Alys shook her head, remembering the sad look in Puddle's eyes as they'd closed the door. Though he was quickly following Stina to the fire where she was frying onions and bacon.

'But you might need me,' Lotta decided, thinking about Magnus, who most certainly didn't need or even want to be with her anymore. She grabbed her mother's hand. 'What's wrong?'

Alys had frozen, staring into the trees, feeling everything become oddly dark; wondering if it was just her. 'Something,' she whispered, realising that Eddeth had gone quiet, the birds flitting above their heads had stopped chirping, and the creatures rustling amongst the forest floor had stilled.

And then Lotta saw it herself as two men emerged from behind a tree in the distance. 'Mama!'

Alys drew her sword. 'Behind me. Stay there.' She thought about sending Lotta back to the fort, but she didn't want her daughter out of reach. And who knew how many more men were lurking about unseen?

Another two stepped out from the trees on the opposite side of what was often a road, now just a mess of melting snow.

'You look lost!' one man called. His straggly hair hung over a ragged cloak, and he was shivering as he approached, a starved look in his eyes.

'Eddeth!' Alys shouted. 'Eddeth! Get back to the fort. Hurry!'

That had the men looking around, wondering who she was talking to.

'Mama!' Lotta shrieked.

More men appeared behind them. Two more.

Alys' limbs felt heavy, trembling with fear. Six men.

Six?

Then there were eight, another two coming from the left with a squealing Eddeth thrashing about between them. She clutched her staff to her chest, eyes on Alys, who held out her sword in one hand, using her other hand to shield Lotta.

'What do you want?' Alys called. 'We're not alone out here! People are coming and going from the fort. Someone will come soon!'

'Then I guess we'd better hurry!' laughed the smallest man, though he had the biggest head, thatched with thick orange hair. He was the one who'd found Eddeth, and giving her a sharp shove, he thrust her towards Alys and Lotta, the rest of his men quickly forming a circle around their three captives.

'We're not alone!' Eddeth echoed. She glanced Alys' way, wanting to read her thoughts, hoping she had some ideas, desperately trying to find some herself. 'My friend will hurt you!' she warned. 'She's a warrior!'

The men laughed. They were ragged and dirty; some shook with cold, their thin cloaks not warm enough to withstand an Alekkan winter spent entirely outdoors.

Alys saw glimpses of Helgi, knowing immediately which cloak had belonged to him. She saw that man attacking him, punching him until he fell backwards, scrambling away.

'She's prettier than any warrior I've ever met!' said Orange Hair. 'You, I'll happily gut, after I've cut out your bleeding tongue, you ugly old bitch. Her, I'll have some fun with first.'

Lotta was too afraid to cry. She gripped her mother's hand, hoping she could do something, though fearing it was impossible. She thought about running to get help, but those men were big, and they'd be fast. If she ran, they would kill her.

The circle of men tightened around them.

Alys kept turning, occasionally jabbing with her sword, wanting to keep them back, stunned by the turn the day was taking. 'If you hurt us, you'll have the future King of Alekka hunting you for the rest of your lives. You think he won't find you? But I'm a dreamer!' she shouted. 'I can contact him when I'm dead. I can go into his dreams and tell him all about you. I can show him your faces!'

That had a few of the men second-guessing themselves, Alys could see. So could Eddeth, who joined in, hoping to further play with their minds.

'You don't want to hurt us,' she said in a soft, quiet voice, so unlike her own. 'For we can give you something.'

Orange Hair cocked his head to one side. 'You think we want your cloak? Your furry hat?' He laughed, though he was intrigued, wondering what the women had to offer.

'I've got this!' Eddeth declared, holding out her staff. 'I'm a dreamer, too, just like my friend. It's magical, this staff is. I could give it to you. You could sell it. A dreamer's staff! Sure to fetch you a pouch of good silver coins. Perhaps some gold?' She edged slowly towards the orange-haired man, holding out the staff. 'See the symbols,' she said, her voice like a soothing balm, warm and comforting on such a cold morning. 'Can you see the symbols?' Orange Hair stared, noticing a few symbols glowing on Eddeth's knobbly staff, and he blinked in surprise, quickly transfixed. Then Eddeth was moving around the circle, showing the staff to each man. 'Valuable, it is. Powerful too. Can you see the symbols? They're like the sun, they are, making you feel warm inside. So warm. And you've been cold, haven't you? Oh, but it's been a long, cold winter. Wouldn't you like to be warm? So toasty warm...'

Alys held her breath, watching as Eddeth swept around her and Lotta, holding her staff out as though she was going to drive it down into the snow. The symbols glowed above her hand, reflecting a bright golden light in each man's eyes as she passed. She moved with surprising smoothness and grace, and soon even Alys felt entranced by her melodic words.

Finally, Eddeth shoved her. 'What do you think about that then? Eh?' And proudly opening her arms, she pointed her staff at the men, each one of them staring into the circle as though seeing the most beautiful sight.

'What did you do?' Lotta whispered, afraid to wake the men, who all appeared to be in a trance. She felt a bit dizzy herself, wobbling against her mother.

'Do?' Eddeth chuckled. 'Just a little magic I learned from that book of yours, Alys.' And now she patted the dreamer's arm. 'They're fixed here for now, but we shouldn't wait around. You should kill them!'

That woke Alys up. 'What?' She shook her head, looking down at her sword, then back up at Eddeth. 'No, I can't just kill them. I...

no!'

'Ssshhh,' Lotta hissed.

'Well...' Eddeth peered at Alys' sword before shifting her eyes to her staff. 'I'll stay here while you get help. I'm not sure the trance will hold without me and my staff, and I don't want them chasing after us!'

Alys nodded, thinking that was the best plan. 'I'll run as fast as I can, Eddeth.' And sheathing her sword, she grabbed Lotta's hand, slipping through the circle of spellbound men, running through the trees.

***

Sigurd and Tulia walked into the forest, looking for somewhere to be alone. Sigurd felt an odd sense of purpose, ready to finally confront something he'd long avoided.

The boulders they found in the clearing were like nothing he'd seen before. They were smooth and round spheres, inscribed with rings of symbols. Large too. Sigurd ran a hand over one, delaying the words he'd waited so long to speak. 'I'm sorry,' he finally began as Tulia took a seat on the boulder opposite him.

'Sorry?' She was confused. 'Why? Why have you brought me here, Sigurd? Are you leaving again? Is that it?'

He smiled, half wishing he was. He missed Ludo and Agnette, Alys and Reinar. He missed his father and Bjarni. He missed being human. 'No, I just wanted to explain why I've been acting... differently. It's because...' Words failed to come. He cleared his throat. 'Because...'

'Of a woman?' Tulia prompted, then seeing the look in his eyes, she laughed bitterly. 'You don't think I knew? All this time? You don't think I knew?'

'I... it was a surprise, seeing you again. I didn't know what to say.'

'Well, something would have been useful,' Tulia sighed. 'Don't you think, Sigurd? Or did you imagine I'd enjoy being your second choice?' She stood up to leave. 'Don't make the mistake of thinking the dead have no feelings,' she hissed. 'That *I* have no feelings. Being dead for me feels mostly the same. I need and I want. I feel and I hurt. It's no different from when we were together in Ottby.'

'I didn't know the truth,' Sigurd tried. 'Not at first. I felt things for her... Raf. But she chose someone else. I thought I could just ignore it, shut it out. I wanted to, and when I found you again, I tried to. But it won't go away. I leave your bed every night because those feelings won't go away, and I don't want to lie there with you, dreaming about her.'

Sigurd Vilander had the most annoying way of making her feel sorry for him, Tulia realised, fighting the temptation to simply leave and return to the training ring. She wanted to rage at him, but he looked embarrassed, sorry, and hurt. And then she sighed, realising that she was dead and Sigurd was very much alive, and the dead couldn't keep the living imprisoned with them, no matter the circumstances. Any hurt feelings or sense of betrayal she might feel was irrelevant. *She* was irrelevant to the future Sigurd wanted to forge.

Sigurd braved Tulia's eyes, taking her hand. 'I should have told you about her. I'm sorry I didn't.'

'And what is she then?' Tulia grumbled, resisting the urge to tug her hand away. 'Another warrior?'

Sigurd shook his head, seeing Raf staring back at him with those big blue eyes. In his mind, she looked as angry as Tulia did, though he tried not to smile. 'She's a dreamer. From The Murk.'

'And she doesn't want you? Son of the Lord of Ottby? Brother of the future king?' Tulia snorted. 'A handsome man like you?' She felt jealous, mad at herself for still caring.

'Seems that she doesn't or didn't. I don't know. She's in Slussfall with Reinar now. With Alys and Eddeth. I don't know if she wants to be there or if she even wants to see me again.'

Tulia wanted to change the subject, though Sigurd was her only friend in Gallabrok, and despite a strong desire to knock him out, she didn't want to lose him. 'Why not go to her then? Find out the truth? Why slink about in the shadows like that snake, Torvig? You're not that sort of man, are you? Cowardly? Too afraid to speak the truth? To demand answers?'

Sigurd bristled at the comparison, though he couldn't deny that he'd avoided the truth. 'After what happened with Alari, I can't risk it. And now that we've stolen her prisoner, she'll be watching Slussfall even more closely.'

Tulia snorted. 'Are you a god or a mouse? If you want to find out what this woman feels, then go and ask her. You'll find a way, I'm sure. I'd rather be in the light any day, than scraping about in the dark, feeling like a fool.' Sigurd stepped closer, but Tulia swung away from him. 'I'm happy you told me, but I'm not happy about *what* you told me, Sigurd. You'll need to give me some time.' And with that, she slid between the trees, leaving Sigurd alone, staring after her.

Seeing Raf's face.

***

Raf had run out of the cottage in a fluster, charging down the alley, nearly falling over a crawling toddler whose mother quickly scooped him out of her path. And finding Vik Lofgren, she told him what she'd seen.

Vik hadn't spoken as he'd spun away from her, calling for volunteers. He found fifteen, not wanting to take any risks. And seeing Jonas and Ollo, he shouted for them to join him too. Ollo was a reluctant team member, though he knew that he couldn't rebuild his reputation by sitting in the tavern with Ilene. She had hinted she was open to marriage with the right man. A rich warrior, she'd suggested, eyeing Berger. A handsome, rich, famous warrior. That had put Ollo's back right up, and he'd done everything in his power since then to try and better anything Berger Eivin could do.

Though he doubted Ilene would thank him for trying to rescue Alys.

Not long after they'd ridden into the forest, a breathless Alys came running towards them with Lotta, who was red-faced and crying with tiredness. Alys pulled up immediately, waving Jonas and the men on, throat burning. She dropped forward, hands on her knees, unable to speak. It had already been a strange day, and she was certain the sun hadn't even reached its peak. Straightening up, she attempted to slow her breathing, pulling Lotta close.

Lotta couldn't speak either, so they clung to each other, breath smoke snaking around them, eventually deciding that they had enough energy to keep walking back to the fort.

'Who were those men?' Lotta wondered, head swivelling, searching the trees. 'Why did they try to hurt us?'

Alys didn't know. 'Outlaws?' she guessed, just as interested in what might be lurking in the trees as her daughter. 'Desperate men. Cold and hungry men.'

'They looked like animals,' Lotta thought. 'Like starving animals.'

Alys agreed. 'Winter's been tough for everyone, but many don't have a warm cottage to return to at night. Some people don't even have a fur.'

Lotta felt bad about that, though not about those men. 'What will Vik and Grandfather do?' she asked next. 'Will they kill them?'

'I'm not sure, but those men chose their path. We can't walk it with them, can we? We're too busy trying to walk our own!' Alys was still breathless, her chest aching from so much running. 'And our path is to save Alekka from whichever king is trying to hurt us.'

Lotta looked up at her mother. 'It's Gudrum, isn't it? I dreamed about him.'

Alys was saddened to hear it, not wanting her daughter terrorised by that grinning man. 'You saw him in Stornas? On the throne?' She fell into a hole and stumbled, nearly pulling Lotta over.

Lotta laughed, tugging her mother upright. 'Not in Stornas.

He was coming here. Coming to Slussfall.'

Alys' mouth fell open as Lotta scurried away from her, having seen a red squirrel.

***

'Decisions, decisions, decisions,' Gudrum muttered, feeling the weight of the kingdom resting on his shoulders. Having listened to Gysa's fears about Jael Furyck, he'd brought his army to a halt by a stream. It was a welcome change to see water running freely, and many crowded its banks, bending over with waterskins and buckets while others encouraged their horses to drink. Gudrum had a steward organising servants to do that for him, so his attention remained on Gysa and on Edrik, who he'd invited to join them.

'It will be hard to fight a war on two fronts, my lord,' Edrik warned, tugging his whispy brown beard, eyebrows sharpening. He looked from Gudrum to the dreamer, not convinced that she was serving the king by distracting him now.

Gysa stared pointedly at the man before turning to Gudrum with a smile. 'Hard, perhaps, but necessary, my lord, for no king should turn his back on an enemy as dangerous as Jael Furyck. We've all heard what she's capable of, though none of us has the first-hand knowledge you do.'

Gudrum lifted a hand to his cheek, feeling his scars. 'Well, she's persistent, though I don't intend to let her get in the way of my plans. No, Gysa's right, soon that bitch will find out what's happening in Alekka, and knowing her as I do, she won't hesitate to act.'

Edrik blinked.

'Where will I find a ship?' Gudrum asked, his decision made. 'Ottby?'

'Stornas is likely closer, my lord.'

'Then Stornas it is,' Gudrum grinned. 'Find me a messenger, Edrik. A man I can trust.'

Gysa touched his arm. 'I will need some time with him before he leaves. If this plan is to work, I will need to be involved.'

***

Reinar shook his head in surprise when he heard about the rest of Alys' eventful morning, though he resisted the urge to remind her of his warning at the training ring. Eddeth bubbled away loudly beside him, still in shock that she'd managed to enchant eight threatening outlaws before they hurt anyone. Reinar was in shock himself. 'Where did you learn how to do that, Eddeth?' he asked as they headed to the map table. 'With your staff?' After Alys had revealed Lotta's vision, Reinar had called a meeting of his dreamers, and though he wanted to discuss the future, what had happened in the forest consumed their initial conversation.

'That book!' Eddeth grinned. 'The book Alys found in Ottby is so helpful. I read it every day, I do, wondering when it will come in use. Though I can't say I was expecting that. Eight men? They were desperate, they were. Who knew what they might have done!' She shuddered then, the hum of her success finally giving way to the fear of how things may have gone if she hadn't had her staff with her. 'And thanks to Raf, we didn't have to find out.'

Raf didn't smile, doubting she'd done much at all. She was in awe of Eddeth, though, thinking about getting her own staff. She didn't want a sword like Alys had or a cloak. But a staff sounded like a weapon she could wield.

'They're all in the prison hole now, so I'll have to deal with them shortly. But that's not why I've brought you here, Eddeth, Raf. It's because of Lotta. She's seen Gudrum on his way to Slussfall.'

Eddeth's mouth dropped open.

'She couldn't say where he was,' Alys added, moving towards

the fire. She was still wet through from her fight with Ilene, and holding her red hands to the flames, she welcomed their heat. 'Though she said Gudrum was the king, which ties in with what Raf saw.'

Eddeth glanced at Raf, both of them moving forward to join Alys by the fire. Any optimism that had risen was quickly doused by the silence of the three dreamers.

Reinar watched them for a moment before turning back to the map table. 'I can draw him away,' he suggested, his finger moving, an idea sparking. 'If I take my army out of Slussfall quickly, his dreamer will see it, his scouts will hear about it. Would Gudrum rather besiege a fort or fight me?' Reinar didn't wait for an answer, though he could read Alys' eyes as he glanced back at her. 'He'll come after me. I know he will.'

Alys nodded. 'It sounds like something Gudrum would choose, though he may want to play games.' She looked at Raf, who knew Gudrum better than any of them. 'What do you think?'

Raf nibbled a fingernail. 'He wants victory,' she began, 'above all things. He was always impatient with Hector. He called him an old slug. They were allies, maybe friends, but mostly, Gudrum wanted Hector to hurry up. Hector spent years planning how he would defeat the king. He took his time, he didn't rush, and no matter how many times Gudrum insisted he had enough men, Hector always wanted more. He wanted to be guaranteed his victory. He didn't want to risk anything.'

Reinar turned back to the map. 'So without Hector, Gudrum will be quick to act. There'd be nothing holding him back, especially with the sea flowing again.'

Raf remembered her time in Gudrum's tent, lying on his bed of furs. She remembered feeling protected by him once. Then she saw him throwing her to the ground in Stornas' catacombs; the way he'd killed that old dreamer. She felt disgusted by him and disappointed in herself for ever following him. Though she didn't say. She didn't know if Alari was listening. 'Hector was obsessed with how he would kill the king. He let it distract him.'

'And Gudrum?' Reinar wanted to know.

'Gudrum has scores to settle too.' She shrugged. 'I'm not sure anymore. I can't tell you what he'll do.'

Reinar knew he couldn't rely on the dreamers to make his decisions for him. He remembered that Raf had seen him dead, Gudrum perched on a throne, victorious. But whatever was true, or however he might feel personally, Reinar had to make the best decision for all those he'd sworn to protect.

It was time to leave Slussfall.

CHAPTER FOURTEEN

'I'm back!'

Jael Furyck turned around with a scowl, studying the sodden figure who'd stopped before her. 'Were you gone?'

'Course I was gone!' Thorgils grinned, ignoring her foul look. 'Didn't you miss me?' He bustled past his sharp-eyed queen, who stood in the doorway of Oss' wooden hall, searching for her dogs. It was a damp day, and his long red curls hung limply around an enormous, cheerful face.

Jael turned after him, closing the doors, deciding that wherever Ido and Vella were, they didn't want to be found, and no amount of calling was going to change that. 'Where were you then?'

'I thought Eadmund would've told you. I went to Hud's Point. Took some supplies, went to see how things were looking.' Thorgils threw the long, wet sack he'd carried from his horse onto the floor. 'Brought back a dead body.'

Jael lifted a dark eyebrow. 'So that's the smell. Thought it was you.'

Thorgils was about to laugh, though he was superstitious enough not to joke around the dead, certain the gods wouldn't look kindly on a man who did that.

'Who is it?' Jael wanted to know, picking out a hazelnut from the bowl on the high table.

'Dagbert. Ulla said he died in his sleep. She woke up, and there he was, stiff as a spear beside her. Blue too. Though who isn't in this weather!' Again Thorgils had to remind himself that, although Dagbert Holmen had been a miserable old arse, his death deserved all the respect he could muster. 'Ulla can barely lift her arms these days, and with the ground frozen solid, I offered to bring him back here, give his shitty son the pleasure of burning him.' He glanced around, hoping the quick-tempered Garvi Holmen wasn't lurking inside the hall.

The hall had been relatively quiet throughout the morning, though with the arrival of Thorgils Svanter, Jael knew her welcome peace had come to an end.

'Where's Eadmund?' Now Thorgils scanned the hall for ale. His ride had been long and wet, and though his stomach felt like an empty bucket, more than anything, he wanted ale.

'No idea,' Jael said shortly. She aimed for the green curtain concealing the bedchambers, deciding to find her cloak and go for a ride herself. She'd woken in a terrible mood, which only a ride on Tig would cure, that or beating Thorgils to a pulp in the Pit. Stopping, she turned back to where he was guzzling from an ale jug by the fire, her eyes moving past him to the long sack on the floor. 'You're not going to leave him there, are you? Someone will trip over him. Likely Biddy.'

Thorgils laughed. 'Course I'm not, but give me a chance to catch my breath. It wasn't an easy ride with Dagbert slung over Vili's back.'

Jael left Thorgils to his ale, slipping through the curtain into the dark corridor. She heard the servants cleaning a bedchamber, the faint hum of noise from the square, the patter of light rain on the roof, and Thorgils calling after her. But entering her bedchamber, she shut the door and slid down with her back against it until she reached the floor.

She'd barely spoken since dawn had broken. Not to her husband or her children or to Biddy, who had looked after her since she was a baby.

She couldn't.

She was still half in her dream, still lost there with Aleksander.

It had been over three years without a real dream, so had that finally been the return of them? Had it been one of *those* dreams? A dreamer's dream?

She didn't know, and sighing deeply, she pulled her knees to her chest, resting her head on them. And closing her eyes, she immediately saw his face.

Aleksander.

***

After taking his leave of the dreamers, Reinar found Bjarni, and saddling their horses, they headed into the forest.

'I wish I'd seen Eddeth working her magic,' Bjarni laughed, eyes on the path ahead. 'Those men had no idea who they were dealing with!'

Reinar laughed with him, though his attention was mainly on the trees, seeking out any further threats lurking in the forest. Riga thundered down the path with urgency, having grown bored with being stabled, though with so many people seeking Slussfall's protection now, Reinar felt the need to keep his precious horse safe. 'No, they didn't,' he agreed, feeling proud of Eddeth. She had already grown in confidence since the morning she'd first revealed her gifts to him; since she'd had them revealed to herself. He felt confident bringing her along, though he had to work hard to ignore the voice that told him to bring Alys instead.

He was thoughtful for some time, giving Riga his head, and then, eventually, wanting to speak, he slowed him down, eyeing Bjarni.

'You're not going to ask me to stay behind, are you?' Bjarni panicked, suddenly wondering if that was why Reinar had wanted to go for a ride.

But Reinar shook his head with a grin. 'Course not. I wanted to talk to you, that's all. You're my closest advisor, Bjarni. I wanted to know what you thought, whether I'm making a mistake. I've made so many lately, so I wanted your advice.' Reinar had thought about asking his father, though Stellan was fond of pointing out his son's failings, as fathers often did, and Reinar knew that Bjarni would offer a less abrasive approach. 'If we leave Slussfall and head to Salagat, it's sure to draw Gudrum out. We'd be making our intentions perfectly clear. Well, I would, at least. A man like that? I doubt he'd pass up the opportunity to come and fight me.'

Bjarni looked pleased to have been asked for his opinion, sitting back in the saddle now, his frown easing. 'Well,' he began, patting his grey stallion, who looked happy to slow down, unlike Riga, who shook his head in annoyance, his sleek black mane sweeping over Reinar's gloved hands. 'I think it makes sense if what the dreamers have seen is right. But to trust a small child with a big decision like that?'

'Lotta may be a child, but she's a dreamer too. I trust all the dreamers. They're trying to keep us safe. Even Raf.' He hadn't told Bjarni what Raf had dreamed about him and Gudrum. He wouldn't tell anyone about that.

'So you'll bring them all along?'

'No, just Eddeth, though likely she'll want to bring Raf.'

Bjarni was still surprised that Eddeth had become someone to rely upon. He'd grown up seeing her as an oddity, mostly scattered and confused, useful as a healer, but even then, she could be unreliable. Now Reinar was putting the future of Alekka in those twitching hands. He shook his head, so full of worries and tasks to do that it pounded.

'You needn't worry about Eddeth,' Reinar said, reading that familiar frown. 'Granted, she's noisy, but if I can't have Alys, there's no one I'd rather have snorting and sneezing behind me.'

Bjarni rolled his tongue around his mouth, not speaking the words he felt so tempted to say. It had been an odd few months: the defeat at Ottby, the death of Ake, the destruction of Tromsund, and then a long, cold march to Slussfall, where no one wanted to be. And through it all, Reinar had become more removed, and Elin had become odder. At first, it had just been Agnette making sniping comments about Reinar's wife, but Bjarni had come to see the change in Elin himself. There had been flashes of it before, of course – most notably after the death of her sons – and she had run away, which in itself was odd.

But now?

She seemed to live more and more in a different world, always muttering to herself, unaware of what was going on, her emotions never quite fitting the moment.

He tried to avoid her, which was mostly impossible with the amount of time he spent with Reinar.

'What?' Reinar could almost hear the noise in Bjarni's head. He ducked under a low bough, turning to his friend. 'Something.'

But Bjarni only smiled. 'Just thinking of the last time we had a race. The horses could do with a run. Maybe us too?'

'I think so,' Reinar agreed, and not waiting, he tapped Riga's flanks with his wet boots, turning around to grin at his friend as he took off down the road.

***

Stellan Vilander was ready for action.

Returned to life by Salma, the spirit dreamer, he longed to be free, yet he heard his wife grumbling beside him, and he saw the square of people milling around him in fear of impending death. Slussfall's walls were high enough to block out everything but the clouds, which were once again dense and grey. He saw the faint glow of the sun at times, but mostly it was a blanket of neverending gloom.

'You're not listening,' Gerda sighed, tugging his sleeve. 'Why are you never listening to me these days, Stellan?'

'I expect it's old age,' he said lightly, bending down to pick up a rag doll. He winked at the apple-cheeked girl, who spun around to take it from his big hand before hurrying after her mother.

Gerda couldn't argue with that. She felt it herself: that aching creep of age. She was stiff and sore in the mornings, everything hurting so much more in the cold. She felt more of an old crone than ever, and with the flame-haired Katrine Hallen ever-present in the fort, she was suddenly more aware of her behaviour. She tried to smile. 'Though we're not that old. Not ready for our pyres yet.'

'I hope not,' Stellan chuckled. 'I've only just come out of that stupor. There's more I want to do before I'm back in it, dribbling and wetting myself or sizzling to a crisp in my funeral shroud.'

Gerda cringed, remembering exactly how that year had gone. She gripped Stellan's arm as they crossed the slushy square towards the hall. 'I fear for Reinar,' she said. 'It's all I think about, day and night. Once, I thought it was a gift, the idea that he was fated to be the king. A great honour. Now, after what happened to Ake and what's happening to Alekka, I fear it's only a curse.'

Stellan wasn't sure. He nodded at Ludo, who was walking with Berger and his cousin, pulling Gerda out of the path of a shepherd trying to manoeuvre his noisy flock through the crowded square. 'It depends on how you look at it. Being a king is hard, and I'm sure Ake would have agreed with you there, but nothing worthwhile ever comes easy. And knowing our son has a chance to make Alekka safe and whole again? Well, it's both frightening and worth fighting for all at the same time.' Stopping, he turned Gerda to him, feeling oddly affectionate towards his morose wife. 'I'll be with Reinar, right by his side this time. I won't let anything happen to him. I'll be with him the whole way.'

Gerda snorted. 'You can't promise any such thing, and you know it, Stellan Vilander.' Though she didn't pull away, enjoying the feel of his hands holding her, giving her some comfort. 'It's only Reinar who can save himself. It's only Reinar who can be strong enough to survive.' Her eyes shone with tears, though they didn't fall, and straightening her shoulders, Gerda almost smiled. 'You need to do everything you can to prepare him for the journey. To prepare him for his enemies.'

Stellan patted her arm. 'I will, of course, but try not to worry, Gerda. It gives no one confidence to see the Lady of Ottby full of fear. We both feel it, of course, and I'm sure Reinar does, but we're the leaders here. We must hold our heads high.'

'Lady of Ottby?' Gerda sneered. 'And you think I will be again?'

'Oh yes. I choose to keep the faith, my dear. When our son becomes the king, we'll go home. Don't give up now. We will return to Ottby.'

***

Gudrum stopped his men as dusk was falling. The air had chilled so quickly that, despite the warmth of his fur cloak, eventually, he'd thought of nothing but a fire and something hot to eat.

Now he sat in his tent before a roaring brazier, having eaten a tasty venison stew, while Gysa stood beside him, admiring his new sword.

'A unique blade,' she murmured, transfixed by the shimmering patterns as she turned it towards the flames. 'A blade fit for the King of Alekka, my lord.'

Gudrum stood, heavy with the pleasure of his meal. He turned to his beautiful dreamer, running a finger over her cheek, and trailing it towards her bottom lip, he held it there for a moment. 'Mmmm,' he mused, nibbling her lip. 'I think you can call me Gudrum.'

Gysa smiled. She was becoming more than simply attracted to him. His scars, though terrifying and gruesome to many, didn't bother a woman whose flesh had been melted by fire. She lifted a hand to his face, holding it gently. 'Gudrum,' she breathed. 'I think I should take your sword.'

He stepped back with a raised eyebrow. 'What? Why?'

'There's a lot a dreamer can do to help. More than you can imagine.'

'What sort of help?' Gudrum wondered, remembering Raf.

'I'm not looking for you to win my battles, Gysa. I'm not weak like Hector was. I can win this war on my own.'

'Yet you are only the king because of my magic, so please do not dismiss my help, my lord. Gudrum,' she corrected herself, purring now, eyes narrowed to slits. 'There is much I can do, but I won't do more than you ask. I just want to help.'

Gudrum was transfixed, though not enchanted – his head was perfectly clear. 'And what do you want in return for all this help?'

'Freedom, a life to call my own. I don't wish to belong to anyone, be beholden to anyone. I want to be free.'

Gudrum wasn't sure he believed her, though he smiled nonetheless. Those eyes were mesmerising, and it didn't hurt to let her think she had some sway over him, some influence in his thinking. 'Then take my sword, though I shall need it back soon.'

'Yes,' Gysa said, running a finger over the gleaming golden hilt before returning her eyes to Gudrum's. 'You most certainly will.'

***

The ride didn't help, which was odd, Jael thought as she returned to Oss' dark fort. Leading her beloved horse, Tig, to the stables, she dried his coat while he munched a few old carrots. Her dream still clung to her; she couldn't shake it. Perhaps it was because she didn't want to? She'd tried to outrun it and ignore it, but she hadn't let herself think about it, and maybe that was the problem?

Maybe she just needed to decide what it all meant?

Eadmund found her, shutting the stable door with relief on his face. 'What?' he asked, quickly seeing his wife's disappointment. 'You don't want to be found?'

'Not today.'

'Not by anyone?' Eadmund stayed by the door, feeling concerned. He knew Jael was often distant, and he usually just had to give her time.

Though that look on her face...

'Not yet,' Jael decided. 'I've things on my mind. My things,' she added quickly, not wanting him to ask.

'Well, the children were –'

'Tell them I'm not feeling well, that I'll be there soon. I just need some time. And soon you've got your big day. I have to clear my head before then.'

Eadmund nodded, looking forward to it. The annual Thaw Day was all the Osslanders had talked about for weeks – a day of games and competitions and feasting for all. A day they thought would never come after the longest, bleakest winter in memory. 'Think then, and do what you need to. The children will be fine.' He smiled at her, hazel eyes twinkling. 'I'll be fine, too, in case you were wondering?'

'I wasn't.'

The stables were dark, but Eadmund caught the hint of a smile as he slipped outside.

Jael watched him go, fingering one of her dark braids, now knotted by the wind. And she sighed.

***

Agnes was noisy, Rigfuss was irritable, and Eddeth was having a hard time packing, unable to think at all.

Eventually, she sighed loudly, following that with an explosive sneeze that had her eyes watering. Though neither got Raf's attention. The little dreamer continued to sit perfectly still on her stool, staring at the fire as though she wasn't even in the cottage.

'You should come,' Eddeth decided. 'With Reinar. With me. I want you to come!'

Raf looked around in surprise. 'Why? You don't trust me to stay behind?'

Eddeth was confused by that reaction, so leaving her bags on the bed, she sat on a stool next to Raf, patting her knee. 'I think we could work together. Help each other and Reinar. After what you saw, I fear he needs more than just my help.'

She looked nervous, Raf thought, wondering if that's why Eddeth wanted her there. 'What about the fort?'

'Alys can look after the fort,' Eddeth insisted. 'Don't you think? After what she did in Tromsund, and with those spirit dreamers lurking about, I think we both know that Alys can handle the fort. But what's coming for Reinar and the army? Well, I... I think it's best if you come along, Raf. I want you to.'

Raf hadn't been expecting that. It was strange to hear everyone's thoughts but never each other's. She felt unsettled by the surprise. 'Does Reinar want me to come?'

'Who knows, but I do, and I'm his dreamer, so it's up to me who I bring along. He wouldn't say no. Of course he wouldn't!'

Raf wasn't so sure. Reinar Vilander doubted her true intentions towards him and towards his brother, she knew. But she wouldn't change anyone's mind by hiding away, shirking responsibility. She was a dreamer, and there was a lot she had to offer. A lot she could do to help.

She nodded before she could change her mind.

Agnes bleated loudly, and Eddeth sneezed again. 'Good, good! But you'll have to get packing and find a horse. No, of course you won't. You can ride Wilf!' She thought that through, picking her wart. 'Perhaps Rofni? Although Rofni is wary of strangers. But then Wilf...' And Eddeth began rambling about the horses, quickly jumping to worries about who would milk Agnes and keep an eye on Rigfuss.

Raf's attention drifted. She kept seeing Gudrum's face. He was staring at her, smirking, the dreamer by his side, and she felt powerless, as though she was being propelled towards them both.

She shivered, knowing for certain that, soon, she would see Gudrum again.

***

All the talk in Slussfall's hall that night was about what Gudrum would do and what they would do in return.

Reinar heard his name every now and then. He noticed the looks, the quickly averted eyes. He saw doubt in some, perhaps grudging respect in others. Eventually, he turned his attention to his plate, seeing only smears of gravy left. It had been a fine meal, putting a smile on Bjarni's face, which had gotten a lot rounder since they'd arrived in Slussfall. Margren was a snarling old woman, though she did what she could to please her biggest admirer, Reinar knew. He smiled at Elin, who hadn't said much throughout the meal, not even to Agnette, who sat on her right, chatting away. And even now, as the plates were being cleared and the goblets topped up, she kept her hands in her lap, her lips pressed tightly together. 'Are you feeling unwell?' Reinar asked, leaning towards her. He tried to smile, fearing it was his fault. That she'd caught a look he'd given Alys or heard some gossip about them talking in the alley.

Sometimes, there was too much to think about, Reinar decided, grabbing his goblet. They would leave in two days. He had written his message to the Skallesons, asking for their aid, and soon their only ship would set sail for Oss, though Reinar couldn't wait for a reply. He had to draw Gudrum away from Slussfall, so he needed to leave the fort in haste. Gudrum's dreamer and scouts needed to see that he was leaving for a fight.

Reinar felt a twinge of fear, remembering Raf's dream, but seeing his father raising his goblet and inclining his head for his son to stand and speak, he shut it away. And smiling now, Reinar gripped his goblet tightly and stood. He didn't see Lief, which was a surprise, though he saw other faces he recognised, including a sullen Ilene's. His smile grew as he cleared his throat, waiting as the hall hushed before him. It was a crowded space, the number of tables having doubled since Hakon Vettel's time, but then there were so many more people in Slussfall now. Lords and ladies burned out of their forts by Gudrum and Hector had led their people north seeking safety, just as Reinar had. Lords and ladies who now looked his way, waiting for him to speak.

Reinar barely knew what he was going to say, though the silence gave him little choice but to begin. 'We will depart in two days!' He saw a few smiles then, for the prospect of escaping the confines of Slussfall's walls was welcome, despite the threat of death and defeat. 'And once Gudrum hears about it, he'll come. Come to try and take what was never his in the first place. First, there was Hector, who killed our beloved king!' He saw a flash of pain in his father's eyes. 'And now it seems that his loyal ally wasn't so loyal after all, so it's that mauled dog Gudrum we must defeat. Gudrum and the Ennorians and any Tudashi still willing to fight for a kingdom that isn't theirs. Or perhaps they're still in Ottby, looking for where Bjarni hid the Vettel gold?' That received a few laughs and a raised eyebrow from a red-cheeked Berger, who glared at Bjarni, hoping he'd hidden it well. 'Spring is coming, The Thaw is here, and tomorrow we'll send to Oss for help. Our allies will come! And if Gudrum thinks he's lucky to have the Tudashi on his side, wait till he sees what the Islanders can do!' He'd hoped to inspire confidence then, but the Slave Islanders had more often been enemies than allies over the years, and there was little interest in that comment.

Taking a breath, Reinar smiled down at a silent Elin, whose expression hadn't altered; she wasn't even looking his way. 'And once we defeat Gudrum, we'll return to our homes. Some of us will start again. And me? I'll take my family and go to Stornas to await the gods' blessing. For Alekka belongs to no one man, to no one king. And by taking the fight to Gudrum, we'll all have a say in who sits on our throne!' Reinar lifted his goblet up to the glowing wheels of candles, an explosion of sharp pains in his chest. He felt excitement and fear, and impatience most of all. Victory or defeat loomed on the horizon, but either way, he just wanted to begin. 'To Alekka!' he cried. '*Our* Alekka!' And looking at Stellan, he saw his father's nod of approval.

CHAPTER FIFTEEN

'The Vilanders are finally leaving their walls behind,' Gysa announced at breakfast. After a night spent in Gudrum's bed, enjoying the comforts of Ottby's stone fort, she had returned to her own chamber to dress and fix her hair, eager to keep the king's attention on her.

Sometimes, Gysa saw flashes of Estrella Bluefinn, a beautiful, elegant queen, and she entertained the thought of a surprising twist to her tale. Thrown into a fire, her family murdered, dragged out of Vasa's Cave and gifted another chance. Could she rise to become the most powerful woman in the land?

Though entering the hall, she had struggled to command Gudrum's attention.

He was talking to Edrik, who sat beside him at the high table, loudly regaling his king with the story of a pretty pair of Ottby servants, who, according to Edrik, had been more adventurous than any of Stornas' whores.

'You'll have to point them out to me!' Gudrum laughed, reaching for his cup, banging it into Edrik's.

And just like that, Gysa's dreams of the future slipped out of reach. She shook her head, chiding herself for thinking like a poor maid dreaming of a husband to save her from some miserable existence. No, Gysa realised, from now on, her future would be crafted with her own hands. She wouldn't rely on any man. Not again.

Gudrum turned to her. 'You were saying?' He'd let himself become distracted by Edrik, though he sensed his dreamer was growing impatient.

'Reinar Vilander is leaving Slussfall. He's sent word to Oss. He will seek to draw you into a battle, I imagine. That's what lords do, isn't it? Fight until the last one standing claims the prize?'

Gudrum winked at Edrik, pleased by the speed of developments. 'Leaving Slussfall? And where will he go?'

'To find you, I expect. His dreamers will have delivered the news of your own departure, so I imagine he had no choice but to act. If he wishes to be the hero of this saga, he must defeat you.'

Gudrum turned his back on Edrik, staring into Gysa's eyes. 'And can you stop him reaching Oss? Reinar's messenger? Can you do anything to help me, Gysa?'

She smiled, pleased to have finally claimed his attention. 'Yes. I can certainly try.'

***

It was early, Jael thought with a yawn, though with the days being painfully short, those on Oss had to start early if they wanted to get anything done.

It was cold too.

'Cold, Mama!' Bo Skalleson shivered, tugging her mother's fur cloak. 'Want to go inside!'

Jael ignored her two-year-old daughter, jumping to her feet, seeing the first competitors finally coming up over the rise. They'd been standing around waiting for what felt like hours since those taking part in Oss' famous sled race had rushed away from the fort in a flurry of barking dogs and bragging men, while wives, mothers, and daughters waited in the cold, looking for a familiar face.

'That's Eadmund!' Biddy cried beside her, smiling down at the little girl. 'That's Papa!'

'Up!' Bo demanded. 'Want to *see*!' Her mother had already scooped up her older brother, Sigmund, and Bo was jumping with impatience as Biddy put down her cup of mulled wine and picked up the dark-haired little girl with the cross face.

Just like her mother, Biddy thought with a grin as she lifted her high.

'Eadmund!' Jael yelled. 'What's he doing?' She turned to Biddy in despair. 'Slowing down? Come on!'

The crowd was cheering, watching the race tighten as the competitors drew closer to the finish line. The snow was deep, though a track had been carved out the day before and then cleared as dawn was breaking. And now Eadmund and Thorgils rode their sleds, leading a long row of competitors up that track behind ragged lines of panting dogs, tongues lolling from open mouths. Thorgils' tongue was lolling, too, as he tried to edge his best friend. His hair bounced wildly as he shouted a stream of insults at Eadmund, hoping to distract him, though Eadmund was too busy concentrating on his dogs to listen.

'Hike! Hike! Hike!' he called, and rocking forward, he urged his sled on. The dogs were tiring, though, the last stretch of the race up a long incline taking a toll.

'What? You think you can beat me? Oss' champion dog sledder?' Thorgils laughed, though one look at his friend slightly unbalanced his sled, causing his dogs to lose their rhythm. Only momentarily, but then Fyn was there, shooting past both men.

'Fyn!' Jael roared in surprise. 'Fyn! Yes! Go!' She turned back to her daughter, who didn't look happy.

'Papa! Go fast!' Bo demanded, screeching in Biddy's ear.

Eadmund tried to. Thorgils fell back, cursing and moaning as his dogs became a tangled mess, leaving Fyn and Eadmund to battle for the line.

'Fyn!' Jael shouted. 'Go!'

And hearing his wife cheering against him spurred Eadmund Skalleson, King of Oss, onwards. He leaned out even further, whistling at the dogs. All four responded to his call, charging faster up that snowy climb, dragging him over the line, just ahead of Fyn Gallas, who shot his king a look of annoyance at placing second for the third year in a row.

Bo looked triumphantly at her mother, whose green eyes were bright with fun as she dropped her son to the ground. A golden-haired Sigmund was quickly lost in the crowd, running for his father, Bo not far behind him.

'That was close,' Biddy sighed, cheeks flushed. 'Now perhaps we can all go inside and get warm!'

Jael laughed. 'The day's only just started, Biddy. You know how it goes.'

'Well,' she grumbled, 'maybe for you. I was up with your daughter well before dawn. Never known a child to wake so early. Can't think what to do to convince her that the sun has a purpose, as does the moon. No point waking up when everyone else is still asleep. What's she going to do?'

'Play with you?' Jael grinned. 'You being so much fun.'

'Hmmpph,' Biddy snorted. 'You're in a good mood. Surprising after how you've been lately. Something's on your mind, though. Something you're not telling anyone.'

'That's what you think,' Jael shot back, and turning away, she left the viewing platform to join in the congratulatory huddle, though there were so many Osslanders crowding the competitors and their dogs that she couldn't even see her husband.

Biddy followed her. 'Think? No, after thirty-one long years, it's what I know, Jael Furyck. You're stewing about something. And keeping it to yourself won't help.' Biddy Halvor pulled her cloak around her chest as Oss' infamous wind threatened to rip it off her entirely. She shivered, unable to remember what the sun felt like or even looked like.

'Who says sharing makes everything better? Not me.'

'No,' Biddy sighed, 'never you, I know. But maybe, just once, you might realise that you're not alone, Jael. We're all here with you.' Biddy inclined her head around Oss' busy square, noting the happy faces, mostly hidden beneath swirls of white breath smoke. 'We're all here with you, Jael. We can help. We can.' It was a plea

Biddy had uttered many times throughout Jael's life, though she knew it wouldn't make a jot of difference, and as she thought it, Jael gave her one of those scowling smiles and pushed through the crowd to congratulate her red-nosed husband.

***

Elin kissed her husband as though she would never see him again.

His leaving this time felt different. There was so much more at stake.

The new king commanded twice as many men as Reinar. He had powerful allies, and Reinar didn't even have the assurance that the Islanders wanted to join his fight. He was leaving with a prayer to the gods, some hope...

And not enough men.

'Is it the best decision?' Elin wondered, wishing the servant would leave. The man had been fussing over the fire for some time, on his knees, silent, but very much present. She wanted to be alone with Reinar, and eventually, she flapped her hand. 'Henk! That's enough. Please, go and... do something else!' Her voice rose until it rang in the chamber.

Reinar stared at his wife as the abashed servant bobbed his head, slipping outside. 'I have to attract Gudrum's attention,' he said when the door had closed. 'If he comes here, it will be hard to hold him out. After what happened in Ottby and with his dreamer?' He smiled, pulling Elin close, not wanting to upset her further.

She pulled away from him. 'What dreamer did you decide to take then? Not that bitch, I hope.'

Reinar bit his tongue, seeing the flash of hatred in Elin's eyes. 'Whatever you feel about Alys, she's...' he began quickly, then slowing down, he tried to choose his words more carefully. 'She's helped me from the beginning. You shouldn't speak about her that way.' He felt himself vibrating with anger, some at Elin, most at himself. It wasn't fair on Alys or his wife.

He'd made a mess of everything.

Elin looked ready to hit him, but lunging forward, she threw herself into his arms instead. 'I don't care about her. I don't want you to care about her. I just want you to come back to me, Reinar. To *me*!'

He held her tightly, feeling slightly removed. 'I will, Elin. You just need to focus on looking after everyone here. And yourself. I will come back, I promise.'

Elin's tears ran down her cheeks. She feared a life without her husband, she feared his death, but most of all, she feared losing him to the dreamer. 'I love you,' she sobbed, pulling back to stare up at that handsome face. A face she had loved for most of her life. He was still hers, she told herself. Whatever he felt for Alys, it would disappear. She just had to remind him of everything they'd once had together.

'I love you too,' he replied, kissing her gently. 'I do, Elin. We've been through a few hard years, and though it may not get easier for some time, eventually, things will improve. They will. And then we'll start over again, in Stornas.'

She peered at him through blurry eyes. 'Do you really want that?'

'I... yes. I do.'

She smiled, crying some more, hearing the lie.

'I have to go,' Reinar said, one eye on the door. 'There's a lot to prepare. I'll see you again, though, before I leave. Down in the square.'

Elin nodded as he extracted himself from her arms. 'And will you say goodbye to her?' she asked bitterly. 'Is that what you need to do so urgently, *Husband*?'

Reinar froze, though he didn't answer, and making his way to the door, he dropped his head. 'I... I'll see you soon.'

***

Estrella Bluefinn fussed over Vik, convinced that he wasn't going to be warm enough. Quickly bored with their conversation, her daughters had disappeared into the square, hoping to find Lotta and her puppy to play with. Estrella barely noticed, all her attention focused on Vik.

'I'll be fine,' he mumbled, though he wasn't unhappy with her fussing. Estrella had ducked back into her cottage and come out with the fur she was now trying to tuck into his bedroll.

'It won't hurt to take one more,' she insisted. 'Think of how jealous Jonas will be.'

Vik's face fell. 'He's not coming.'

'What?' Estrella looked surprised and then worried. 'But who will look after you? Who will keep you out of trouble?' She took the bedroll to his horse, frowning, trying to decide where it would fit. Though between weapons and food and food for his horse, there was little room. She turned back, shoving the bedroll at Vik, and throwing up her hands. 'How are you still so reckless? After all these years? I thought you might have stopped wanting to die!'

Vik laughed. 'I'd have Jonas with me in a heartbeat, though he won't leave Alys and the children again. But don't worry, I'll have Ollo.'

Estrella snorted. 'Well, now I'm reassured. You go, off you go then, into the safe hands of Ollo Narp!'

Vik kissed her flushed cheek, his eyes moving to her pregnant belly, hidden beneath layers of fabric and fur. Estrella hated the cold more than anyone he knew, and despite how much effort she put into being warm, she rarely was. 'Very kind of you to care.'

'Care? It's the children I worry about. They expect you to come back, Vik. And you? Well, you want to be a hero, no doubt. Not content to die in your bed like the rest of us.'

Vik's smile rarely faded when he was around Estrella. Since they'd come to Slussfall, they'd spent an increasingly large amount of time together, and though Vik told himself that he was simply trying to care for a pregnant widow and her grieving children, he knew he would miss her dearly. 'I have to go.'

'Of course you do! But first, tuck that bedroll somewhere. I mean it, Vik. You can't just throw it away when my back's turned!'

'What? Why would I do that?'

'You've done it before! Don't you remember? You and your obsession with travelling light. What? You don't think I remember?' Taking his hands, heart pounding, she tried to smile. 'Just come back. I don't want to lose you too. Who would chop my firewood then?'

He grinned. 'Hopefully, I've chopped enough to see you through till I get back.'

'In this place? Hmmm, a few days at most,' Estrella decided, suppressing a grin, and then, fearing that he would be left behind, she bundled Vik out of the way and started stuffing the bedroll behind his saddle herself.

***

Eddeth found Alys in a fluster and feeling mostly in a fluster herself, she dragged her away from the children, the puppy, the cat, and Stina, who appeared in a bad mood, snapping at them all in a most unlike Stina sort of way.

Alys was almost relieved, surprised to see Raf standing there with a stack of bulging bags. 'Are you going? With Eddeth?'

Raf nodded, still unsure about that. 'Unless you need me here?'

'No, it's better if you go along,' Alys said, struggling to breathe. Her chest was tight, her arms trembling by her sides. She kept seeing flashes of a dead Reinar, and it worried her. 'Better that Reinar has all the help he can get. I'll be fine here.' But though she tried to project confidence, she felt only worry.

'You'll have Ragnahild,' Eddeth reminded her. 'And Salma.'

Alys smiled. 'Of course. I'll be fine.'

'And don't you worry about Reinar. We'll look after him, won't we, Raf?' Eddeth shivered, nudging the little dreamer. 'And there's this. We made you this.' Turning around, she bent down to one of the bags, pulling open a flap to reveal a small leather pouch. 'Everything you need is in here, Alys. To find us. To find a way to us!'

Alys took the pouch, nodding. 'I'll give you something of mine,' she said, trying to think.

But Eddeth shook her head. 'No need! I took some of your hair when you were sleeping.'

'You did?'

'Oh yes, you never know when a little hair might come in handy!' Eddeth insisted, smiling broadly, big teeth showing. 'Now, you must look after Agnes. And Rigfuss. Well, Rigfuss can mostly look after himself, I know, but Agnes. Oh...' Tears filled Eddeth's eyes. 'She's like a baby, she is. I can't just abandon her.'

'It's alright,' Alys murmured. 'I'll go and get her. She can sleep in the cottage with us. We can have fresh milk without ever having to go outside.'

'Exactly!' Eddeth said, sneezing all over her. She wiped her nose with her hand, sniffing loudly. 'I'll try and see everything, I promise. I'll try and keep Reinar...'

Alys took Eddeth in her arms, holding on tightly, seeing how awkward Raf looked behind her. 'I know you will,' she breathed, trying not to cry. 'I want to say goodbye to him, though it's probably a terrible idea.' Standing back, she shrugged sadly. 'It is a terrible idea.'

'It's not,' Eddeth whispered. 'No, it's not, because you never know, it might be the last time.' Then realising what she'd said, she brightened her worried face. 'Though likely not!'

Alys felt as though she'd spun around in a circle of emotions, ending up where she'd begun.

And that was nowhere good.

Eddeth glanced around with as much subtlety as a lightning strike, pushing up onto her tiptoes, mouth gaping open. She saw Elin with Karolina Vettel, and grabbing Alys, she spoke quickly. 'I'll go and keep Elin busy. You find Reinar. Quick as you can now. I can't give you long!'

Alys didn't think it sounded like a good idea, but she felt real fear. Not just worry, but a deep-seated fear that what Raf had seen would come to pass.

She had to say something before it was too late.

So, slipping through the crowd, eyes down, watching her step, she made her way to Reinar. He looked surprised to see her suddenly appear beside him, a little nervous, too, so she spoke quickly and quietly.

He appeared hesitant but nodded, and Alys left, weaving through the crowd again, feeling guilty and upset, the pain in her heart stabbing her as she walked. It hurt, which made her feel even more afraid.

He wouldn't come back.

Everything screamed at her that he wouldn't come back.

She took the alley to Eddeth's cottage, slowing suddenly as the slight descent threatened to unbalance her once more, though the path had been thoroughly cleared, the ice scraped away. She reached Eddeth's door, opening it to a bleating greeting from Agnes. And then Reinar was there, slipping inside, quickly shutting the door behind him.

'I shouldn't be here,' he said, though he took Alys in his arms before she could speak. And looking down at her, he said it again. 'I shouldn't be here with you.'

'I know,' she breathed. 'I just... I had to say goodbye.'

He felt her trembling, and now he kissed her slowly and softly, drawing her closer, feeling her arms slip around his waist. He heard nothing but the pounding rhythm of his heart, and looking into her tear-filled eyes, he felt a jolt of fear. 'You don't think I'll come back.'

Alys knew she should step out of Reinar's embrace, but the feel of his hands on her lower back, the great warmth of his fur cloak covering his broad chest, touching hers, was a comfort she hadn't known in some time. If ever. It was as though, in his arms, she finally belonged.

'I will come back,' Reinar promised. 'With one leg, one eye, one arm. Half dead, bleeding... I won't let anything stop me.'

'Sounds painful,' Alys smiled. 'Hopefully, Eddeth and Raf can help you with that.'

Reinar heard noises outside the cottage now, and he glanced over his shoulder, feeling guilty for hiding away. For being alone with Alys.

For kissing her again.

Though it was what he wanted to do most of all. To be with her, look at her, listen to her.

Touch her.

'I'm so sorry,' she said, hearing his racing thoughts. 'I shouldn't have made you come.'

Reinar laughed, his attention solely on her again, and holding a hand to her cheek, he stroked it. 'Make me? It's all I've wanted to do. Since I met you, Alys, being with you is all I've wanted to do. And when I return, I'll talk to Elin. It can't go on like this. It's not fair on her or you.'

Alys stumbled away from him, mouth dropping open in horror. 'No... I...'

Reinar stepped towards her, holding her hand. 'Alys?'

She blinked at him, face wrenched in pain, heart heavy with guilt. 'You can't, can't do that... your wife?'

'But I love you,' Reinar admitted, realising that he could no longer live a lie, and faced with the fragility of life, he knew he didn't want to. 'I love you, Alys Bergstrom.'

Alys' lips parted, tears spilling from her eyes. 'I...'

Reinar heard Bjarni shouting his name, and he kissed Alys before she could say another word. 'Know that whatever happens, I love you, and when I return, everything will be different. This will all be different, I promise.' And with one final kiss, Reinar turned away, pushing open the door, leaving Alys alone with Agnes, who bleated at her with mournful eyes.

CHAPTER SIXTEEN

'Where has Reinar gone?' Gerda wanted to know, nervous tension making her even more uptight than usual. She prodded Agnette, who held Liara in her arms, looking as petrified as Gerda felt.

'No idea,' Agnette snapped, wanting to focus on finding Bjarni, who kept disappearing. After months of planning and debating and delaying the inevitable, why did it have to be such a frantic rush out the gates?

Gerda peered at her. 'You're worried? About Bjarni?'

They stood near the lead horses, where Stellan was talking to Jonas and Ollo. There was tension in the air, a few nervous smiles too. The men appeared happy to be leaving. Most of the women looked upset. There was pride on some faces, fear on others, and a general buzz of excitement that they were finally taking the fight to their enemy.

'Course I'm worried. He's liable to do something silly, get himself hurt again.'

Gerda didn't think she was wrong, and then all thoughts of Reinar and Bjarni left her mind as Katrine Hallen arrived. She stiffened immediately, which didn't go unnoticed by Agnette, who looked past her sour-faced aunt to the Lady of Tromsund.

'The fort will be so much emptier soon,' Katrine noted. 'I will ask Lief about bringing some of the families inside. There must be cottages free, or perhaps some could share? The fewer stuck outside the walls, the safer we'll all be.'

Agnette nodded, though Gerda didn't even look Katrine's way.

Stellan approached with a tense smile. 'Have you seen Reinar?' Agnette had trimmed his hair and beard, and he looked slightly self-conscious, though she could still see that familiar twinkle in his eye. 'It would be nice if our future king was here, organising our departure.' He was grumbling but not cross, certain that Reinar was busy solving some last-minute problems. Still, he wanted to get moving. Smiling at Katrine, he glanced over the tops of furry hats and streaming breath smoke, finally seeing his son appear. He thought of Sigurd then, feeling the ache of his absence. It didn't feel right to be going anywhere without Sigurd by his side.

'Where's Reinar?' Vik wondered, joining them. He bobbed his head to Katrine and Gerda before turning back to Estrella, ushering her forward. 'You'll have plenty of company while we're gone,' he smiled. Her pregnant belly was becoming more pronounced by the day, and Vik had asked Jonas to keep a close eye on her while he was gone.

Agnette kissed her daughter's head. 'Soon Liara will have plenty of friends to play with.'

Estrella nodded, though her attention was on Vik, who was now looking around for Jonas.

'There you are!' Gerda sighed as Reinar came towards her with Elin on his arm. 'I thought you'd changed your mind.'

Reinar slipped his arm out of Elin's firm grip, embracing his mother. 'You'll help Elin, please. With Falla close to giving birth, she'll need your help around the fort. And you, Agnette,' he added, seeing his much more useful cousin.

'Of course,' Agnette said, though her smile was forced. She spent most of her time avoiding Elin these days, not inclined to suffer her sniping about Alys. 'Go, Reinar, and stop fussing.' She kissed her cousin's cheek. 'We'll be here when you return. Don't worry.'

Lief pushed through the crowd. 'Falla's gone into labour,' he said abruptly, his face almost ghostly. 'I... I wish you a safe journey, but I can't stay. I...' He was too flustered to go on.

Agnette was pleased to hear it. 'I'll come and see if she needs any help.'

'Don't tell Eddeth,' Reinar warned, feeling warm with guilt as his eyes met Elin's, the memory of Alys' lips still lingering. 'She'll try and delay us, wanting to help.'

Lief nodded, disappearing into the crowd again, Agnette following after him, wanting one more goodbye with her husband.

'Well, come on then,' Stellan grinned, stretching his back. 'Let's get these horses moving before we're standing in a field of shit!' The stench of fresh manure was ripe, turning already queasy stomachs.

Gerda kissed his cheek. 'Take care of yourself.'

Stellan smiled, kissing her in return. 'And you, my dear.' He heard a yelp in the distance as Eddeth fell over, and grinning now, he patted Vik on the back, nodded at Reinar and turned away.

Reinar sought to follow his father, but Elin slipped an arm around his waist, and looking down at her, he saw the same fear in her eyes that he'd just seen in Alys'. Guilt washed over him, and he felt his shoulders tighten, his body almost protesting her touch. He fought the urge to tell her right then and there that he wanted a divorce. That he loved Alys. That he wanted to be with Alys. But swallowing, he pulled Elin closer, knowing that if this was the last time he was to see his wife, he owed her more than that.

'Come back to me,' Elin breathed against his lips. 'I need you to come back to me.'

Reinar nodded, and though he knew his heart had made up its mind, once again he found himself saying what she wanted to hear. Looking over Elin's shoulder as she clung to him, his attention was suddenly on Helgi Eivin, who appeared to be saying goodbye to Alys.

Alys was struggling to know what to say to Helgi. Having delved deep into his past and being the only one he'd shared his most devastating secret with, he spoke to her as though they were friends. Or perhaps more? She felt uncomfortable, not wanting to lead him on, though at the same time, she didn't want to be rude.

She blinked, realising that he was waiting on an answer to a question she hadn't heard. 'I'm sorry, what did you say?'

Helgi's bearded face broke into a grin. 'Just that I look forward to seeing you when I return.' He leaned closer, peering at her, gauging her reaction.

Alys leaned back. 'What is it?'

'Just wanting to see whether you think I'll return.'

Alys laughed. 'I see nothing about you at all.' Though that hadn't come out right, and she could see that he looked offended. 'I mean, I see nothing bad.'

Which cheered Helgi somewhat. 'I'm glad to hear it. I feel as though this battle might be a new beginning. A rebirth. A chance to touch death and recommit to life.' His eyes rounded as though he was seeing beyond Alys.

Who stared at him. 'Though try not to touch death too closely. I'm sure Reinar will need you. Berger too.'

Berger had finally finished his long goodbye with Solveigh, and as he approached, he slapped his cousin on the back. 'Bet you wish Reinar was bringing Alys instead of Eddeth!' he laughed. 'Though Eddeth's a single woman, and I'm sure she wouldn't say no to a handsome fellow like you!'

Quickly irritated by his cousin's terrible timing, Helgi mumbled at Alys and headed for his horse, Berger trailing after him.

Stina and the children arrived.

'I'm going to see Falla,' Stina said. 'See if I can help with anything.'

'Good idea,' Alys decided, her eyes finding Reinar as he mounted his horse, remembering his hands, his lips, and his promise to come back to her most of all. She didn't move until Lotta grabbed one hand and Stina the other, and soon they were leading her towards the hall.

***

Jael stood on the cliff, her dogs barking behind her, chasing each other in circles, tongues and tails flapping. Her attention, though, was on the tall stone spires guarding Oss' harbour. They posed a challenge for every helmsman, no matter their experience, and many ships miscalculated their entry, foundering or even sinking. It was no easy feat to traverse those spires, especially when the wind was howling and the sea was foaming as it was today.

She saw the ship slow its approach, and shaking her head, she felt tension like blades in her neck. Reaching up a hand, she tried to rub it away, though perhaps only heat would do that? She thought of hot water with some longing. There was a hot pool, of course, conveniently located next to the hall, but she wanted to be alone with her thoughts, which would be impossible once the children found her.

Or Eadmund.

Now she smiled.

One of them always did.

Bending down, she called to Ido and Vella, who quickly turned to her, bounding through the snow, eyes bright, ready for more fun. They attacked her with paws and tongues, leaping on her as Jael dropped into the snow, rolling onto her back, letting them jump all over her.

She closed her eyes, feeling that cold snow soak through her cloak, and then she was back in her dream, standing in the field, bodies all around her. Jael didn't move, aware that she had one foot in Oss, one somewhere else.

But where?

Was it the Vale? The future?

Her breathing slowed, and in her dream, she saw herself looking around, trying to find an answer to what she kept seeing.

'Need some help?'

Jael groaned, the dream sliding out of reach as Thorgils loomed over her, blocking the sun. 'Why are you always where I least want you to be?' she grumbled crossly, batting away his hand, quickly standing on her own. 'Doesn't your wife need you? Or one of your children? Or even your king?' Now she was striding away from him at speed, heading back up the rise to the fort.

Thorgils trotted after her, and with such long legs, he was soon by her side. 'My wife's happy enough, as are my children, and who could blame them, blessed with my presence as they are! But you, my queen? Something is badly amiss with you.'

Jael turned to him with sharp eyes, long dark hair whipping around her face. 'And what if it is? Why do you need to try and fix it? Why not just leave me alone? I don't need your help, Thorgils Svanter. I don't need anyone's help!' And shivering, she stomped away from him, immediately regretting lying down in the snow. She saw a lanky Fyn coming towards her with Bo in his arms.

'Ship, Mama!' Bo screeched happily. She was like a little bird, always calling out the latest news as though it was her responsibility to alert the fort.

Jael smiled. 'And what will it bring then? What treasure will it have for us?' She glanced at the spires again, seeing that the ship had finally escaped its dangerous puzzle, though she couldn't make out anything about it. 'Perhaps something to eat?'

Bo nodded with big eyes, hoping so.

'I want a bundle of furs,' Fyn decided.

'So you and Fria Sanvik can cuddle up under them?' Jael joked, unable to stop prodding that sensitive topic, for though he had recently turned twenty-three, Fyn remained as shy as a teenage boy. He blushed as Thorgils approached.

'Who's coming?' Thorgils wanted to know.

Fyn shrugged. 'We'll have to wait and see, won't we?' And now he tickled Bo until she wriggled in his arms, screaming and giggling and trying to get down.

Jael watched for a moment before turning back to the ship. She lifted her eyes, seeing that the burst of sunshine that had briefly washed over the harbour had gone, replaced by a dark cloud.

***

The squealing baby girl made Lief smile.

An exhausted Falla was shocked, cradling her daughter with weary arms. Eddeth had promised that her second birth would be quicker, easier, though it had lasted for over a day, and now she felt ready to sleep until summer. 'You're sure you don't mind?'

Her husband snorted loudly. 'What? *Mind*? That I have this little creature? All mine?' He looked down at his dark-haired daughter, feeling his heart throbbing with joy. Falla's son, Borg, was becoming more difficult as he grew older – a disobedient, quick-tempered boy. Sometimes, it was easy to imagine that he belonged to someone else. To wish for it. Though this baby? His daughter?

He smiled again.

'I want to name her Madalen,' Falla said shyly as her servant came back into the chamber with a bucket of hot water and a cloth. 'What do you think?'

'Anything. I don't mind. It sounds...' Lief stared at the baby, wishing he could see her eyes, wanting to know if she truly looked like a Madalen.

Falla peeked into the layers of wool and fur, uncovering the squashed up little face. 'She looks like me,' she decided.

'I'm glad to hear it.'

Now Falla was smiling, her body vibrating with exhaustion. 'I need to change, to tidy myself up.' And pleased when Lief stood to go, she took his hand. 'But come back for supper. We can eat in here, together.'

Lief nodded. 'There's a lot to do, and now everyone's gone, it's once again up to me to do it.'

'Well, I'm glad of that. Fewer mouths to feed for a while too.'

Madalen Gundersen opened her tiny mouth, letting out an impatient cry.

'That's the only mouth you should be worried about feeding,' Lief reminded her. 'For now, just rest and focus on our daughter. Leave the fort to me.' He shifted his cloak around, adjusting his silver brooches, and bending over to kiss both Falla's and Madalen's heads, he slipped outside.

***

Alys shuffled her boots in the snow, staring up at the hall. Despite the emergence of spring, it had snowed heavily in the night, and she shivered in the bright glow of morning sunshine, thinking about Eddeth and Reinar and everyone who had to sleep in the snow.

'Looking for something to do?' came a familiar voice behind her.

Alys turned around with a smile, seeing Agnette loaded down with baskets, Liara gurgling against her chest. Most mothers strapped their babies to their backs so they could work with ease, but after what had happened to Liara, Alys knew that Agnette wanted to keep her daughter where she could see her at all times, though it did make things more challenging for her. 'Here, let me help. Aren't there servants in the hall for that?'

'No, these are gifts,' Agnette smiled. 'Some of Liara's clothes. Some things I found useful. I doubt Falla will want any of it, of course.' And now she was laughing as they walked up the steps together. 'But I thought I may as well offer.'

'I think Falla's changed,' Alys decided, listening to a happy Liara sucking her fist. 'She's gotten what she wanted. She's a lady, with a husband who loves her and two children. She has what she wants.'

'Well, lucky her,' Agnette sighed. 'Not everyone can say the same. Most just get by with whatever's thrown their way. Look at poor Estrella or Solveigh. Not everyone can be as lucky as Falla Gundersen.'

Alys nodded at one of the guards, who pulled open an enormous wooden door, ushering them into the hall. A cold draft rushed under the door as he shut it, and Alys shivered, hearing Hakon Vettel's drunken laughter echoing around her.

Sensing her stopping, Agnette turned back. 'Alys?'

'I...' Alys saw Elin coming towards them with Lief. 'I'll leave these baskets here. Perhaps one of the servants can help you?' And turning away, she rushed back outside, unable to breathe. She stopped on the stairs, the cold air quickly waking her up, though the voices intensified, swilling around her like sour ale. Hakon's laughter grew loud and mocking, so loud that Alys pressed her hands against her ears, stumbling down the steps, seeking a reprieve.

Stina came towards her with Lotta, who was crying. And seeing her daughter, Alys pulled her hands away from her ears, the noises receding now. 'What's happened? Lotta?'

'We can't find Puddle anywhere,' Stina said, worry creasing her forehead.

But Alys only smiled. 'Likely he'll be tracking a cat or on the hunt for more sausages. It can't have been long since you last saw him.'

'No, but something's wrong. He's in danger. I know it!' Lotta panicked.

'You do?'

'In my dreams last night, I... I saw him! He was dead!'

Alys frowned. 'Let's look for him together then. We'll find Magnus, and he can help too.'

Lotta was barely listening, more tears flooding her eyes. 'I can't lose him, Mama. He's too important!'

Alys agreed, feeling a jolt of fear then that Lotta might be right.

CHAPTER SEVENTEEN

After leaving the comforts of Ottby behind, Gudrum had stopped Gysa riding beside him, not wanting to give his men the impression that he was overly reliant on the dreamer. He had relegated her to a sleigh with her servants, leaving him free to ride with Edrik and talk over his plans. They were a long, slow-moving column of men on horses and those on foot, archers and scouts, drummers and bannermen, followed by clusters of servants and livestock. It was a stinking, noisy, rabbly mess, and he tried to shut it all out as he listened to Edrik, who was young enough to still be full of ideas. Gudrum didn't think he was anymore.

He laughed, surprising Edrik.

'My lord?'

Edrik's clear blue eyes never stopped moving, his ears sharp enough to pick up barely whispered gossip, and Gudrum felt flutters of doubt for inviting the man into his confidence and giving him some power. For now that he was the king, there was nowhere to go but down. Though not wanting Edrik to see anything other than confidence in his eyes, he grinned broadly. 'Just thinking of the fun that still lies ahead. And that's before we reach Reinar Vilander!'

Edrik peered at his king. Gudrum was an intimidating man, who'd survived more brushes with death than most, which made him lucky, and a lucky man was always worth following, especially if he was a king. So Edrik was conscious of trying to impress Gudrum, seeking to solidify his position by his side. 'They will try to outthink us, lord.'

'I imagine so,' Gudrum said, jiggling in the saddle, trying to reposition the sheepskin, which had become bunched up underneath his frozen legs. 'With half as many men, they'll have to. Though our dreamer makes that harder. Harder to surprise us.'

'But they'll have a dreamer, too, won't they, my lord? Perhaps even Raf?'

Gudrum tightened his grip on the reins, thinking that through, wondering whose bed Raf was warming now. Perhaps she was the woman of a god? He shook his head, not willing to believe that Sigurd Vilander was anything more than a useless fool. But Raf?

What trouble was she going to cause him?

Or, he thought, smiling again, seeing those big, blue, traitorous eyes, what trouble could Gysa cause her?

***

It was boring. There was no other word for it.

Raf hated the slow, plodding pace as she rocked from side to side on Rofni, who was more even-tempered than Wilf, though every now and then, he would shudder with a burst of energy and try to take off like a bird. Raf knew she had to keep alert to that, but mostly, she felt like falling asleep. Eddeth had been murmuring beside her for some time, practising chants. She was trying to memorise the book of spells and symbols that Alys had found in Ottby. Eddeth had become obsessed with it, especially after what she'd managed to achieve in the forest.

'Don't you worry you'll do something?' Ludo wondered, bringing his horse up beside them, having checked in with Ollo and Vik, who rode at the back of their column with Berger and his cousin. 'All that chanting? What if you put a spell on someone without realising it?'

Eddeth immediately clamped her lips together, sitting up straight. 'Don't you have something to do?'

Ludo looked surprised. '*Do*?'

Eddeth quickly regretted being snappy, and she smiled. 'You must miss talking to Sigurd on these rides. Though you've got Reinar, I suppose. And Bjarni? Berger?'

Ludo shrugged. 'It's not the same, though. Reinar talks to Bjarni. Berger's with his cousin.'

'Well, there's always Ilene,' Eddeth joked.

But Ludo only frowned. 'Do you think Sigurd will ever come back to us? We don't even know if he's still alive.'

That was true, and with so many things on her mind, Eddeth felt bad for not trying to see what had happened to Sigurd. She glanced at Raf, who was looking on with curious eyes. 'Have you seen him? Seen if he's safe?'

'I can't see Sigurd,' Raf muttered. 'No one can. Especially now Alari's taken him.' She felt fear then, knowing how eager Alari had been to get her hands on Thenor's son. And now she had. She wished more than anything that she could hear Sigurd's voice or see his face.

Just a glimpse.

She needed to know that he was safe.

***

Sigurd felt his frustration mounting as another day in Gallabrok dawned.

In the beginning, everything had been new, and there'd been so much to learn. After Tromsund, he'd taken his mind off his family by joining in the collective worry over Ulfinnur's disappearance. But now, any curiosity he'd felt about Gallabrok or the gods had lessened to the point where every day and place felt just like every other. There were gods to talk to, gods and their helpers, their allies and friends. Thenor's chosen warriors were always open to training with him and sharing cups of ale in the hall, but Sigurd felt hesitant about getting to know them. He wasn't one of them; it felt odd. He knew Tulia, but since his revelation about Raf, she had, quite rightly, shunned him.

Thenor was always busy with Valera, and though he was left with instructions and willing instructors to guide him, Sigurd felt mostly rudderless and barely present. He still saw Reinar up on Slussfall's wall. Bjarni had been there, he remembered, and Ollo. He'd known he was only there to lure Alari out of hiding, though in that dusky moment, he'd wanted to run through those gates more than anything. Slussfall was no Ottby, and he had no affection for it, but the people?

When he closed his eyes, he saw Ludo and Stina, and Alys and his father. He saw Berger and Jonas and Vik. He saw Agnette with her tiny baby and Eddeth and Elin.

And he saw Raf.

He saw Raf most of all. Lost in a cloak too big for her, all moody scowl and messy hair, big eyes that revealed so much pain. And fear. She was hiding the truth from herself, he thought, wondering what that meant.

Since he'd been in Gallabrok, Sigurd had learned much about his mind and how to use it to draw information to him; how to master his senses, to become more aware, more alert, more responsive. And using everything he'd learned, he had dug into his memories of Raf, seeing so much more than he'd noticed before. She was confused and scared. Lost. Though despite his best efforts, Sigurd could never discover what she truly thought of him.

Thenor approached with a frown. 'Reinar has left Slussfall.'

Sigurd turned around so quickly that he stumbled. 'Why? He doesn't have any allies yet. What's he doing?'

'He needs to attack Gudrum because Gudrum is heading to Slussfall.'

It unsettled Sigurd that Gudrum was now the king, for Gudrum was a slipperier foe than Hector would have been. Luckier too. 'But Gudrum has twice as many men. That would be a mistake.'

'That would be Reinar's decision,' Thenor warned sternly. Sigurd stood by Hyvari, as he often did, hoping for some great revelation. Thenor turned with him, and in the blink of an eye, the water was gone, and they stood before a dry stone wall.

Sigurd jerked in surprise.

'What Reinar and Gudrum do is between them. Between them and their armies. Between them and their dreamers. You will not interfere. You will not place your finger on the scale, Sigurd.'

Sigurd swallowed, anger rising. 'But –'

'We have our own war to wage, and though we may have rescued Ulfinnur, Alari still needs to be caught and dealt with, and Mirella Vettel has disappeared.'

Sigurd didn't care.

'You may not care, but she is helping Eskvir, who is most certainly not going to wait much longer before launching his own attack on us. We cannot help Reinar. We cannot fight his battles. I will support him as king, as I supported Ake, but his fate is in his own hands, and that crown is one he must earn for himself.'

Thenor's words had no impact on Sigurd, who felt just as intent on doing whatever he could to help his brother. 'The sea has melted.'

'It has.'

'So he'll have sent word to the Islanders. To the Skallesons.'

Thenor turned away. 'Come,' he called. 'Sappa has something to show you.'

But Sigurd remained where he was, staring at where the waterfall had been only moments earlier, wondering what he could do to help his brother.

***

The man was dripping on the floorboards of Oss' small hall.

He smelled of salt, Eadmund thought, as he listened, hands

behind his back.

'Everything is in here, my lord,' the dark-haired man explained when he was done, handing over a small scroll, tightly rolled, remarkably dry. 'I kept it in my pouch,' he added with the bob of a wet head.

Eadmund took the scroll as the doors opened, and his daughter ran inside with Ido and Vella, who beat her to reach him, though soon all three were pawing his legs. 'Hello, there,' he grinned, bending down to kiss Bo's head. He shooed the dogs away, seeing his wife coming after them with Thorgils.

'Who's here?' Jael wondered, striding around the fire pits, up to the fur-covered dais, where her husband stood, staring at her with a stern face. 'Alekkans?'

Eadmund nodded. 'They need our help, apparently.' He'd quickly scanned the scroll, which repeated what the man had already said.

'For what?' Jael frowned at the dripping man. 'You need a towel.' She turned around to find Biddy nodding at her before disappearing behind the green curtain.

'To save themselves from a... surprising enemy,' Eadmund said, feeling slightly awkward. 'Apparently, Hector Berras turned on the king, gathered himself an army, and now he's threatening the whole of Alekka.'

'Hector Berras?' Thorgils scratched his bearded chin, recognising the name, though his memories were hazy. Then one familiar face popped out, and he cocked his head. 'Oh. Hector Berras with the –'

Eadmund glared at him, wishing Thorgils didn't have such a good memory and such a big mouth, though Jael appeared too busy reading to pay much attention.

'Ake Bluefinn,' Jael said when she'd finished. 'He wants our help? To do what? Defeat this Hector Berras for him? Why does one lord threaten him so much?'

The messenger looked slightly surprised by the question. 'My lady.' He turned to the queen, lifting his eyes. 'I am only here to pass on the message, and I hesitate to speak on my king's behalf, but Hector Berras has many powerful allies. He has the Tudashi and the Ennorians too. The king is rightly concerned. He has been fighting his enemies for many years now, and his forces are greatly depleted. He needs urgent assistance from his allies.'

Jael crumpled the scroll in her hand. 'Assistance.' She said the word slowly, rolling it around her mouth. '*Our* assistance.'

'You have ships, my lady. You will be able to help now that the sea is flowing.'

Jael glanced at Eadmund, who appeared mostly eager to help, and at Thorgils, who looked ready to go and pack. 'Of course,' she said. 'We would be delighted to.'

***

There was still no sign of Puddle as the sun dipped behind Slussfall's western wall. Alys felt real fear then, wondering what could have happened to him. She had searched for Puddle herself, going so far as to hide away in Eddeth's cottage, trying to reach Ragnahild, but to no avail. Magnus and his friends hadn't stopped looking, and even Agnette had helped. Stina had searched the fort with Solveigh and Lotta until Solveigh's feet started throbbing, and she had to go and lie down.

But there was no Puddle.

Alys wondered if he had escaped the fort.

She kept staring at the gates, thinking of the men who'd accosted her in the forest, wondering if there were more lurking in the trees. Men like that would have little need for a fluffy puppy. Perhaps they'd eat him?

She looked down at Lotta, who was staring up at her with swollen eyes.

'He's gone!' Lotta cried hopelessly. 'He's never coming back!'

'We don't know that,' Stina insisted, eager to get back to the cottage to start supper. 'Come on, we need to go and warm up.

You're turning to ice.' She tried to grab Lotta's mittened hand, but Lotta slid away from her.

'He's dead! Someone took him, and now he's *dead*!' she shouted hysterically, drawing the attention of the traders packing up their market stalls. There weren't many now, winter having stripped most of any goods they were willing to sell, though some still had the odd item to trade.

Alys had become increasingly worried throughout the day, both surprised and disturbed that she hadn't seen anything herself, though maybe Lotta had. 'Have you had a vision?'

Lotta shook her head as Magnus returned, having said goodbye to his friends. 'But I feel it.'

'Feel what?' Magnus wanted to know, his eyes reflecting the worry they all felt.

'Lotta thinks someone took Puddle.'

'What?' Magnus looked horrified, at first disbelieving, then seeing Lotta's tear-stained face, he became even more worried. 'Why would anyone do that?' He glanced around, feeling as though they were being watched. '*Who* would do that?'

'Someone who wants to hurt us,' Lotta whispered. 'A mean person.'

Alys glanced up at the hall.

'Maybe the same person who tried to hurt Agnette's baby?' Lotta suggested with wide eyes.

That had Alys feeling even more unsettled.

Stina had had enough. 'Well, standing around here isn't helping. Let's get back to the cottage. I'll think about some food, and we can talk it through then. We'll probably find Puddle sitting inside with Solveigh, waiting for us!'

'I'll come soon,' Alys promised. 'I'll just see how Falla and the baby are.' And turning away before anyone could offer to go with her, she headed to the hall, Lotta's words ringing in her ears.

***

Biddy had taken the children to eat supper in the kitchen, knowing that Jael and Eadmund had a lot to discuss. News of the messenger had spread through the fort like sea-fire, and everyone was buzzing. Most were keen to pull out their weapons, ready for some excitement, a chance to enhance their reputations and come home a few coins and trinkets heavier.

Though not Jael, who had made her decision quickly. 'I'll stay here.'

Thorgils bit his tongue, which immediately started bleeding, and everyone was forced to search for napkins as he tried to staunch the flood, moaning loudly.

Eadmund had to raise his voice. 'Why do you want to stay? *You?*'

'Why not me? One of us has to look after the island. All the islands. And the children and the fort. So why not me?'

'You?' Thorgils echoed, pulling a bloody napkin out of his mouth. 'Doesn't sound like a Jael Furyck sort of thing to do.'

Jael could see Fyn and Bram looking just as surprised on Thorgils' right, and she dropped her eyes to her empty ale cup. 'I'm a mother now, a queen. I've got responsibilities. I can't just grab a sword and go wherever there's a problem. Eadmund can help Ake. He's perfectly capable.'

'Kind of you to say,' Eadmund grinned, aiming a kiss at his wife's cheek, though it was mostly hidden beneath her hair and with her not budging, he ended up kissing her braids. 'Though it will be strange without you.'

'Strange?' Thorgils snorted. 'It makes no sense! What about Arlo? He should stay behind. He's done it before.' Thorgils inclined his head to the end of the hall, where the popular archer was telling a story, surrounded by enthralled men clasping cups.

'Though he doesn't need to,' Jael insisted. 'I'll be here.'

Thorgils didn't understand it.

Nor did Eadmund, but he decided to leave it, planning to talk to Jael when they were alone.

'I'll stay with you, Jael,' Fyn said.

She didn't argue, which, she could see, disappointed him. 'It's best you do. Learning how to be a warrior is about more than just battles. You have to learn how to keep your people safe in their homes too. Who knows, maybe one day you'll have your own fort to command.'

'What? This weed here?' Thorgils laughed. 'Can't imagine he'll ever stop clinging to your cloak long enough to find his own woman, let alone a fort.'

If she'd been sitting any closer, Jael would have whacked Thorgils across the back of the head.

Thankfully, Eadmund did it for her. 'Maybe I'll leave you behind too,' he grinned.

'Not likely!' Thorgils exclaimed with a loud belch, rising from the bench. 'I'm off to pack my sea chest. I'm guessing we'll leave in the morning?'

'What?' Eadmund looked up at him in surprise, inhaling a whiff of stale fart. He wrinkled his nose. 'The ships need preparing. We have to haul out our weapons and armour. I have to decide who to take and organise supplies. I need time to think, you big idiot.' But Thorgils was already heading away from the table, patting a few backs, aiming for the doors.

'Change your wife's mind!' he called when he reached them, wondering how he was going to tell his own wife. 'I'm sure you know how to do that!'

But Eadmund turned to Jael and sighed.

CHAPTER EIGHTEEN

Alys could hear the meal underway in the hall. She heard Estrella Bluefinn's voice and then Lief's. She thought she could make out Elin and Gerda, too, though she didn't want to be seen by any of them. So, hurrying down the corridor, she turned towards the glowing light in the distance, quickly coming to the two steps leading down to the enormous kitchen.

'What are you doing here?' Margren, the cook, grumbled at her, not liking the dreamers, who were so fond of fleecing what little was left of her winter garden. 'And at this time of day?'

'I was looking for my dog,' Alys almost whispered. 'He's small and fluffy, mostly brown. His name's Puddle.'

Margren hated dogs with a passion, very familiar with the little dog who was always sneaking about looking for food. 'Why would your dog be here? In my kitchen? You think I'd let a dog in here?'

Alys quickly realised that she wasn't going to get anywhere but into an argument with the snarling woman. 'I thought I could check your garden.'

Mostly-toothless Margren thought about simply throwing her out, though rumours of how fond the future king was of this dreamer had reached her ears, so she took a moment to think things through. 'He's not there. I've been out there just now. Nothing's there but shadows.'

'But have you heard a dog? Here?'

Margren lurched forward, finger wagging. 'What are you saying? You think I cook dogs?'

'No, of course I don't, but I think... someone's taken him.'

'Well, it's not me!' Margren snapped, turning around to her red-faced assistants, sweat-soaked dresses clinging to them in the intense heat of the kitchen. 'What would I do with a mangy little dog?'

Alys didn't know, but something had led her here. 'If you see anything, please send someone to find me,' she pleaded. 'You may not like dogs, but my children do. They're very upset.'

'Well, I like children even less than dogs, so that's cut me deep, that has,' Margren cackled. 'I'll need to find a handkerchief, if you'll excuse me.' And cackling some more, she waddled away.

***

Eddeth kept swaying towards Raf as they sat on a log before the fire. 'We need to have good dreams tonight,' she murmured sleepily. 'Reinar needs us to.'

The pressure to always be dreaming made Raf want to run away. She saw the dark trees surrounding their camp like a towering wall. But that wall had many holes in it, and if she could just slip away...

She blinked, turning back to the fire, where they had just been joined by Ollo and Ilene. Raf's shoulders slumped, unable to think of worse company.

And lifting her head, Eddeth agreed.

'Got any ale?' Ollo wanted to know, eager to keep his good mood afloat. Reinar had been tight with the ale since they'd left Slussfall, and though he'd promised Ilene that he'd be able to find some more, they'd gone from fire to fire without any luck. No one was inclined to share, and Ilene's attention was waning, Ollo could see, as she glanced over her shoulder, eyeing Berger's cousin.

Eddeth sneezed. 'Don't come sniffing around for our ale, Ollo Narp. Company and conversation we'll provide, but no ale!'

Ilene sneered. 'We could find better company in a latrine full of turds.'

Eddeth's mouth dropped open, and she turned to Ollo with eyes full of disgust. 'I fail to see what you're doing with this foul-tongued creature. Trying to redeem yourself in the eyes of the gods?' She snorted. 'Good luck with her by your side.' And now she glared at Ilene, who stood in a hurry and spat on the flames, leaving Ollo behind.

'Well, thank you very much!' Ollo snapped. 'How did that help?'

'*You*? I think it helped more than you know,' Eddeth insisted, wide awake now. 'Nothing but trouble leads down that path. With her? Oh no, only heartbreak and embarrassment. She's got no heart, that one.'

'What? And you think I do?'

Eddeth remembered how Ollo had carried Aldo's body up the hill in Stornas at great risk to his own life. 'Yes, though maybe you've misplaced it. Keep looking, though, and you'll find it again. And when you do, take my advice and keep it well away from that woman. She's only looking your way because Berger's got his eyes on Solveigh. She feels nothing for you, nothing for anyone. Not even for herself!'

Eddeth's words dampened Ollo's joyous mood like a torrent of icy rain, and he staggered to his feet, eyeing her sharply. 'And you think *you* should be telling people about who to be with? Ha! But I've heard all about you, Eddeth. All about the husbands you chose and what they did behind your back! So do you really think I should take advice from you?' He turned with a snap of his cloak, disappearing after Ilene.

Eddeth blinked, tears pricking her eyes, heart thudding dully in her chest.

Raf shuffled closer, nudging her arm. 'He's blind with lust for Ilene and dumb with it. He doesn't know what he's talking about.'

Eddeth didn't answer, waiting for those old memories to

recede again. They lingered, though, taunting her, Ollo's words mocking her loudly.

Raf became more incensed, raising her voice. 'He should look at himself! The things he's done!'

'Ssshhh,' Eddeth warned. 'We don't need to make enemies, and Ollo Narp's not one. He's not. It's that Ilene. He's trying to make himself good enough for her, and the man is nothing if not prideful.' She picked her wart, once again aware of the fire and the sounds of the camp.

'Maybe he should buy himself a mirror with all the coins jingling in his pouch,' Raf snarled. 'He's got nothing to be proud about.'

Eddeth turned to her with a smile, glad to have the girl beside her; grateful to have another dreamer to share the burden with. 'We've work to do tonight, oh yes, so let's leave everyone behind now. Shut them all out. We have to find a way to help Reinar, so we can't be worrying about petty squabbles and Ollo Narp.'

Reinar watched the dreamers from a distance, leaning back against a tree while his father chatted to Ludo, Vik, Berger and Helgi. Bjarni was sound asleep in the tent he was sharing with Reinar, having eaten too much, drunk too much, and generally been too tired to keep his eyes open for long.

'It's all those sleepless nights with the baby,' Stellan chuckled. 'You'll be like that soon.' He nudged Vik.

'What?' Berger was looking at him, too, and Vik's frown deepened. 'You mean Estrella? You think I'd...' He shook his head. 'It's Berger who's got a thing for pregnant women, not me.'

Berger laughed, thoughts of Solveigh making him smile. 'Well, not all pregnant women. Just one in particular.'

Helgi didn't smile often. He was a thoughtful man, and though Reinar didn't particularly want his company, Helgi tended to go wherever Berger went, which was generally wherever Reinar went. So it made sense to try and get to know him. 'What about you?' he asked. 'Do you have a woman back in Napper?'

Helgi's lips parted, though he didn't utter a word.

And seeing his cousin's discomfort, Berger tried to help him out. 'He's... between women,' he grinned, slapping Helgi's leg. 'Wouldn't you say?'

Helgi nodded. 'Something like that.'

Which didn't ease Reinar's frown at all.

'No point thinking about women,' Vik decided, wanting to change the subject entirely. He couldn't deny that he'd never stopped loving Estrella, but Ake had been one of his closest friends. He didn't want anyone thinking he was disrespecting his old king or trying to take advantage of a grieving widow, and Vik knew better than anyone how much Estrella was still grieving. 'We need to think about tactics.'

Stellan chomped into a cracker. He'd found it in his pouch, though being a few days old now, it was a little chewy. 'We do indeed. We need to draw Gudrum to Salagat. Hopefully, his dreamer will see where we're going and point him in the right direction.'

'And if he doesn't care? If he goes on to Slussfall?' Berger wondered. 'Maybe he wants to play games? That would certainly do it.'

'It would,' Reinar agreed, knowing every man had someone they cared about in Slussfall, apart from Helgi, who still looked on with a curious frown. 'But it won't help him defeat me.' They were bold words, though Reinar worried he'd miscalculated.

Fearing that Gudrum wasn't interested in finding him at all.

***

Gudrum flopped back onto his pillow, entirely spent. He glanced at Gysa, whose body glistened with sweat. She was panting and smiling, looking deliciously dishevelled beside him. 'You are an adventure,' he sighed, running a finger over her lips, trailing it down her collarbone, touching her breasts. 'A glorious, mysterious adventure.'

'Well, it's one way to pass the time.'

'Better than any other,' Gudrum decided, feeling lighter and younger than he had in years. 'Almost any other,' he amended, thinking of a few things he might rather do.

Gysa turned onto her side, reading his thoughts. 'You must remain focused, though. We stand on the precipice.'

'Precipice? We?'

'Well, you do, of course, though I am by your side.' She kissed him, seeking to soothe his irritation. 'But don't worry, I won't steal away your victory or claim it for myself. I merely want to help you, Gudrum. Alari enhanced my powers because she knew I would be useful to her new king. And now that new king is you, so I can't sit back and wait for you to find your way in the darkness. No, I must be your torch. Alari needs me to be.'

'Well, who could say no to a goddess?' Gudrum grinned as Gysa edged closer, fingering the hairs on his chest. They were grey now, he knew, though his scarred body was firm and muscular, like a man twenty years younger. 'You will be my torch then, and I will be your...'

'King.'

There was no hesitation in Gysa's voice, which filled Gudrum with both confidence and desire, and smiling broadly, he pulled the dreamer on top of him, kissing those perfect lips.

***

Jael had rolled over, which made it much harder to kiss her, Eadmund thought with a laugh.

'What?'

'Just thinking about how much I look forward to coming to bed every night.'

Jael rolled back over. 'Why are you saying that?'

Eadmund stopped smiling, hearing no humour in her voice.

'Nothing. It was nothing, just trying to... I'm not sure.' He gave up, sensing that his wife wanted to be alone. Alone in a bed with her husband, who didn't want to be alone at all. He wanted to touch her and hold her and tell her that he loved her.

He loved her, but it wasn't easy.

'Have your dreams returned?' he asked suddenly, wondering if she could read his thoughts. Sometimes, it was easy to forget that his wife was a dreamer as well as a warrior.

Jael didn't answer.

'Jael?'

'No. Why are you asking?'

Eadmund sighed. 'I think sleep's the only way out of this mess,' he muttered, turning over, pulling the furs with him.

Jael let him take the furs as she rolled onto her back, staring at the rafters. Ido and Vella kept moving around at their feet, deciding whose company they wanted most. She hoped it was Eadmund's, for they both had a way of blocking her in, stopping her from moving even a single limb.

Quickly cold, she edged towards her husband, annoyed at herself for always shutting him out. 'Who's Hector Berras?'

Now it was Eadmund's turn to squirm. He didn't roll over, though he felt Jael moving his way, tugging at the furs.

'You looked strange when that man mentioned his name, so did Thorgils, so who's he to you?'

Eadmund flopped over with a sigh. 'It was before you.'

'What was?'

'When Ake came to make an alliance with my father, Hector Berras came along with his daughter.'

'Oh, and you what? Fell in love with her? Why don't I know about this?'

'I didn't fall in love with her, no. I just... she was nice. Though it didn't work out.'

'Oh?'

But Eadmund wouldn't reveal any more. 'Lucky for you it didn't, or you wouldn't be the happy woman you are today, joyous in your marriage.'

Jael smiled. 'I hide it, but it's there.'

'I'm not sure that's true anymore.'

'Don't be silly, I've just...' Jael didn't know. 'Sometimes, I want to disappear, I suppose. To be somewhere else.'

'Like Andala?'

She nodded. 'I miss my family. I miss the sun, the grass. Summer.'

'But now the sea's flowing you can go back. We both can. When I return from Alekka, let's go to Andala.'

Jael remembered Aleksander, and she became quiet again. 'Maybe.'

'You're sure you don't want to come to Alekka?'

'Positively sure.'

'It's just strange. You're our best warrior.'

Jael laughed loudly, surprising a sleepy Vella, who popped up her head, looking around. 'I thought you were our best warrior now?'

'Ha, not likely. Though how will we ever find out if you won't fight me?'

'Never again, that's what I promised.'

'You did, but you won't fight anyone, Jael. No one but Fyn. And you don't go to the Pit, you just keep to yourself. I don't understand, I suppose. I don't understand why you...' Eadmund sighed, knowing there was no answer to his question. There never was.

'Busy day tomorrow,' Jael said abruptly, turning back over, taking the furs with her. 'Best we get some sleep. No doubt that daughter of ours will be coming in soon, pretending she's one of the dogs, curling up by our feet.'

Eadmund tried to smile, but he felt sad. He tried to tell himself that his wife was still there, that she still loved him, still wanted to be here on Oss with him, but after all this time and feeling her slipping further away, he wondered if he believed it anymore.

***

'Dreamers, dreamers everywhere,' Gysa mused, brown eyes twinkling.

Though not with fun or happiness, Raf thought, watching her closely.

Those almond-shaped eyes shone with menace.

She felt afraid.

'Though *I* am the most powerful dreamer of all!' And now Gysa spun on one foot, staring into Raf's eyes, her full lips set in a slightly crooked smile. 'Isn't that right, little one?'

Raf didn't answer. She had gone to sleep looking for Gudrum. She didn't want to play games with this woman.

'But you won't touch Gudrum,' Gysa warned. 'Not again. He's mine now. In *every* way.'

Raf started, surprised by that, though she felt no jealousy anymore. 'We are coming for him. Coming to stop him,' she warned, holding her ground as Gysa stepped closer, peering at her, inspecting her, looking for...

Raf didn't know what.

'Is that what you think you're doing?' Gysa laughed. 'Well, if you say so. I'll be sure to let him know.'

'We're going to Salagat,' Raf went on, sensing that, for all her games, Gysa was more than a little interested in what she had to say. 'Reinar will wait for Gudrum there.'

'Oh? But I thought Reinar Vilander was destined to be a great king?' Gysa's voice rose, brimming with mockery as she circled Raf, enjoying the game. 'A great king throwing his life away?'

'You –'

'*Me*?' Gysa lunged forward. 'But you have seen everything, little girl. You have seen Reinar Vilander's grim and gruesome future, yet he is still coming! What sort of dreamer does that make you? One who helps her new lord throw himself onto his own pyre?' She laughed, thinking of Hector. 'Gudrum's luck certainly turned the day you disappeared!'

Raf twisted away, wanting to escape Gysa's grinning face as much as she wanted to reach out and slap it. 'Reinar will take his destiny into his own hands. He knows what I've seen, and it doesn't scare him. No man who wishes to be king can run from destiny. It walks with us always.'

Gysa laughed some more. 'I would stay and chat, Raf dear, but Gudrum will wake me soon. You know how he can be. So needy, so... demanding.' She lifted a hand in the air as though swatting away a pestering fly. 'I'll be sure to tell him of your lord's plans. Perhaps he will care?' And now she was tittering, turning into the darkness, her black hair and dark cloak merging into the night.

Raf looked up at the moon, listening to the pounding of her terrified heart. Gysa was more powerful than anyone had ever realised. She could feel her confidence like a shield around her. It almost glowed. Though she knew Gudrum, and he wasn't the sort of man to blindly follow a dreamer.

No, despite Gysa's supposed indifference, Raf knew that Gudrum would come for Reinar.

Of that, she was certain.

***

Stina couldn't sleep. The cottage was cold, and she was worried about the missing puppy as much as the children. Eventually, deciding there was no point lying in bed, frozen solid, she got up to bring the fire back to life. She had a jar of herbs from Eddeth that often helped her sleep, and deciding to try those, she headed for the kitchen.

When she turned back to the fire, Alys was sitting there, black cloak draped around her shoulders, eyes half-closed.

Stina bit her tongue in surprise, just keeping hold of the jar of herbs. 'What are you doing?' she hissed.

Alys grinned at her. 'Same as you, I suppose. Can't sleep.' It was strange in the cottage without a snuffling Puddle. Though there was Agnes, who rustled around occasionally in her little box of straw. Winter was restless, too, getting up to wrap himself around Alys' legs.

Stina tried to catch her breath as she left the jar on a stool and filled the cauldron with water. 'Tea might help.'

Alys nodded. 'Sometimes, as tired as I am, sleep isn't very inviting. I'm afraid of what I'll find in my dreams.'

Stina found two cups, scooping a generous helping of the dried herbs into each one. 'I imagine you are. I don't know how you do it.' She sat down, shivering, thinking about going back to her bed for a fur.

Alys sighed. 'Most nights the dreams aren't useful, just terrifying.'

That didn't comfort Stina, who looked worried. 'I hope Reinar's going to be alright. It seems like a risk, don't you think? Taking your men to face an army twice the size of your own? Betting you can outthink Gudrum somehow?'

'Reinar knows Alekka better than Gudrum, and Vik and Stellan know it better than Reinar. They've got ideas, good ideas about how to defeat him, but I worry about Gudrum's dreamer. If she sees everything they're planning, it will be impossible to use the element of surprise.'

'But can't Eddeth lock her out? Her and Raf?'

'I hope so.' Alys dropped her head, rubbing her hands together, feeling tears coming. She looked up, meeting Stina's eyes, desperate to share her secret. 'Raf saw Reinar in a dream. He was... dead.'

Stina looked horrified. 'Dead? And he still left? But why?' Her fears rose, worrying for Ludo. 'But if...'

'Ragnahild saw Reinar as the high king, and so far, he hasn't even sat on the throne, so he's holding onto the hope that Raf was wrong, or perhaps that...' Alys stumbled, tears blurring her eyes. 'He felt he had no choice. If he doesn't lead him away from Slussfall, Gudrum will come and crush us here. It will take days to reach Salagat. Reinar will find more allies on the way, and hopefully, the

Islanders will come. Once they get his message, I'm sure they'll come.'

Stina didn't feel confident, though she nodded, leaning over to check the water. When she sat back, she saw tears shining on Alys' cheeks, and reaching for her hand, she held it gently. 'Reinar has so many experienced men around him and two dreamers. They'll help keep him safe.'

Alys saw Stina's eyes in the firelight. 'You're worried about Ludo?'

'Of course. He's a good friend.'

'Just a friend?' Alys wiped away her tears, wanting to think about something other than a missing Puddle and Reinar's imminent death.

'He's never said anything different.'

'Then you should,' Alys said, smiling encouragingly. 'If you feel things?'

Stina's dreams were still corrupted by memories of what Torvig Aleksen had done to her in Ottby. She wasn't sure if she was ready for something more than friendship with Ludo, but she thought about him constantly. She saw his face when she closed her eyes, his sweet and kind face. 'I'll speak to him,' she mumbled with little confidence. 'When he comes back, I'll speak to him. I promise, Alys, I will.'

Alys nodded, sensing that Stina didn't mean it. 'It's always better to open your heart. To share it.'

Stina felt her nerves tingling, wondering if she'd get the chance. 'Tea,' she whispered, reaching for the cauldron as the children stirred in their beds. 'Hopefully, Eddeth's herbs have the answer to getting us both back to sleep.'

CHAPTER NINETEEN

Eddeth was up early, talking loudly, wanting to encourage Raf out from under her fur. They'd slept in a tent, which had kept the worst of the wind and drizzle at bay, and Eddeth felt refreshed and eager to get moving. She'd already saddled Wilf and Rofni, made a yarrow tea for both her and the little dreamer, collected a handful of acorns, and a few hazelnuts, before giving a quick offering to Raald, God of Travellers, to protect them on their journey. She thought of the vatyr and the death collectors and shivered, fearful of the forests they would encounter as soon as they set off again. Dense forests and then steep mountains. It was going to be the most challenging part of the journey, though at least they could move with something resembling speed, not having to keep pace with hundreds of tired villagers moving their livestock and families.

Reinar came to join her, pleased there was someone else awake to talk to.

'I saw nothing!' Eddeth announced, quickly cutting off what she predicted would be his first enquiry of the day. 'Nothing but dogs and cats!'

'Dogs and cats?'

'Oh yes, it was a strange old dream. I was wandering through a field, newly cultivated, animals running past me, gulls flying in to peck through the earth. Dogs and cats. A goat. Ravens!'

Reinar held his hands over Eddeth's bright fire, thinking of Gudrum. 'Ravens? They're birds of the dead. That doesn't sound good.'

But Eddeth chuckled. 'Birds of the dead they may be, but I've never had a problem with them. They helped us in Furkat, didn't they? No, it's not a bad omen. It was just a field, a perfect field, and I was free, and the animals were running. We were all running.'

'Running from what?'

Eddeth became flummoxed, not understanding why Reinar was trying to upend her perfectly enjoyable, non-threatening dream. 'From nothing, of course. What? Do you never just run?'

Reinar grinned. 'No. Not since I was a boy, I suppose. Not unless someone was chasing me.'

Eddeth peered at him, shuddering suddenly. Then Raf was behind her, wrapped in a fur.

'Why are they taking down the tent?' Raf croaked, inclining her head to where the servants were pulling down the tent she'd only just stumbled out of. 'It's still dark.'

'Well, it's one way to get stragglers like you out of bed, my girl,' Eddeth laughed as the bleary-eyed dreamer came to sit beside her. 'Come on now, a nice cup of tea will get your blood flowing.' The snow was melting, but the air was icy, and they all leaned towards the flames. 'What did you see then?' she asked. 'Something by the look of those eyes. Busy night, was it?'

Raf was always reluctant to speak about her dreams, though she immediately remembered Gysa's smug face, and feeling incensed, she told Eddeth and Reinar everything she'd seen. By the time she'd finished, Bjarni had joined them, belly growling loudly as the servants stirred porridge in great iron cauldrons, cooking flatbreads and eggs on skillets held over the flames.

'Hopefully, Gysa will tell Gudrum that we're going to Salagat,' Reinar decided. 'But will he care?'

'I'd say so,' Eddeth breathed. 'He's a man, isn't he? A man with a big appetite for battle. I've seen that face. Oh yes, I have!'

Bjarni's frown was deep and exhausted. He'd tossed and turned all night, missing the familiar comforts of his wife's warm body. He'd even missed the sounds of his baby daughter, which had surprised him, having thought he'd at least enjoy more sleep while he was away. 'Gudrum may want a fight, though we're at a disadvantage, and he knows it. He doesn't have to engage on our terms, does he?' He directed his question at Reinar, who turned his head, raising a hand to his father, who was approaching with Vik.

'No, he doesn't, but the temptation will be great. He can't rule as a true king while I'm alive. He has to try and finish me. I imagine he'll come, find us wherever we are, so we have to get to Salagat fast. And first. Then we'll get to make all the decisions.'

Eddeth blinked at Raf, knowing what she'd seen about a big field, though sensing Reinar watching her, she smiled brightly.

'You have to keep looking for him,' Bjarni said to Eddeth. 'We need some warning if he's going elsewhere. Like Slussfall. We can't let him slip past us.'

Reinar agreed, hoping Alys was hard at work, trying to find Gudrum too.

***

Winter was waiting at the door when Alys woke.

She took some time to open her eyes. Her sleep had been disturbed. She'd seen her mother, Mirella. Tarl Brava had been there. She'd seen Arnon too. It had been a horrible swirl of bad memories of her time in Orvala, and she felt so worn down by it that the thought of getting out of bed and leaving the warm furs behind was too miserable to contemplate. Though Winter was scratching at the door, and she heard no indication that anyone else was awake. So, getting out of bed, trying to wrap the fur around every exposed part of flesh, Alys tiptoed across the cottage, almost falling into the fire. There were flames, so Stina had obviously woken earlier. Still, Alys could see her breath smoke streaming before her as she reached the door.

Opening it, she stood back, smiling down at the cat between yawns.

Winter stayed where he was, though, turning his head to look up at her. And bending down until her face was almost touching his, Alys blinked, surprised by her dimness. 'You know where Puddle is,' she whispered. 'You know, don't you?' Salma hadn't revealed herself since they'd been in Slussfall, though Alys knew the white cat carried the dead dreamer's spirit.

He stared up at her for a moment before rubbing himself against Alys' fur-covered legs. But not for long as Alys rushed back to her bed, dropping the fur to the floor, hurrying on her clothes.

***

Eadmund Skalleson sent word to the lords of the seven islands he commanded, telling them to ready their ships, for they would be sailing with haste to aid the King of Alekka. All in all, he expected to command a fleet of some twenty-eight ships and close to one thousand men.

'Where will we land?' Thorgils wondered, peering over his shoulder as Eadmund studied the map.

'Here, apparently,' Eadmund muttered, pointing to the eastern coast of Alekka. 'Ake's ship's still down in the harbour. His man, Harran, says he'll lead us there. But first, we'll meet at Bara. Once all the lords arrive, we'll depart.'

Thorgils grunted. 'Should be in Alekka by next winter then! You think you can rely on those old farts to get themselves together in a hurry? Especially Gulvi Lundberg. He won't have finished fussing over his ropes before summer.'

Eadmund grinned. 'That's why I chose to meet at Bara. Once I'm there, I'll hurry him along.'

Thorgils glanced around the hall, his attention drifting past the servants wiping down tables to the green curtain. 'And you're sure Jael won't change her mind? Seems odd, don't you think?'

Eadmund followed his gaze, agreeing, though he didn't say.

'She's a mother now. She doesn't want to leave the children with no parents.'

Thorgils' eyes snapped back to his best friend's. 'Confident of how things will go, are you?'

'I'm just trying to guess what her thinking is.'

'You mean she hasn't said? Not even to you?'

Despite three years of marriage, Eadmund Skalleson was still constantly surprised by his wife. She was rarely predictable, and though he hadn't said it, he felt more concerned than anyone that she didn't want to come to Alekka. Since the great battle at the Vale of the Gods, Jael hadn't spoken much about fighting, training, or war. In fact, when he thought of it now, she'd become so much quieter about everything since then. So much more removed. He didn't blame her, still feeling the painful echoes of that day himself. Though for Jael it appeared different. She seemed haunted by it, unable to move past it.

To let go.

It had changed her, and he feared that the Jael he'd known, the woman he had married, just wasn't there anymore.

She ran out of the curtain after Ido, who had a flatbread in his mouth and a twinkle in his eyes as he circled one of the fire pits before dashing under the tables, past Eadmund and Thorgils and out the open doors.

Jael came to a puffing stop. 'Why are those doors open? It's freezing!'

'Well, to help our friend Ido make a hasty escape, of course,' Thorgils grinned, receiving a raised eyebrow in return. 'Needing some more breakfast, were we?'

'No, that was Bo's, though she'd already had far too many. She's got an appetite like her father.' Jael turned to smile at Eadmund, who looked surprised to receive it, though he happily smiled back.

Thorgils frowned at her. 'Changed your mind yet? You know you won't be able to live with yourself if you stay behind.'

'Ha, you think so?' Jael snorted, looking supremely comfortable with her decision, which, she could see, didn't sit well with either man, and that made her smile some more. 'I'm going for a ride with Fyn. We'll be gone all morning. We can talk when I return, go over your plans. Hopefully, you'll have some by then!' And now she turned as her other dog, Vella, came racing out from beneath the curtain, wondering where her brother had gone. The little dog slipped through the open doors, closely followed by Jael, who didn't let her smile drop until she was well into the square, heading for the stables.

***

Winter moved with urgency, bounding past the stables, slipping under market tables, aiming for the gates.

Lotta and Magnus ran ahead of Alys, breathless and red-faced, almost knocking into their great-grandfather, who'd been up on the ramparts as dawn was breaking, searching for any sign of the lost puppy.

'Is this some form of training?' he chuckled, looking from Magnus to Alys, who pulled up with a smile. 'Running around the fort?'

'Winter knows where Puddle is!' Lotta exclaimed, spinning around, realising that there was no sign of the white cat now.

'There!' Magnus called, and the two children hurried to the gates.

Jonas peered at Alys, who nodded, just as breathless and hopeful as the children.

'Come with us,' she urged. 'Looks like we're leaving the fort.'

Elin Vilander stood on the balcony, watching them, surprised when Agnette joined her, Liara strapped to her chest. Reaching out, Elin stroked the baby's fine blonde hair. 'She's growing fast. Soon she won't fit in there.'

Agnette wrapped a protective arm around Liara's sling, smiling. 'Then I'll find another way to keep her close. Almost losing her once was enough to never let her out of my sight again. I'm not sure I'll even let her get married!'

Elin laughed, though her eyes hardened as she turned back around, hearing the gates being scraped open. 'Did you want something?'

'I want your help. We need to bring as many families into the fort as possible. The fewer people outside, freezing in tents, the better. There are children out there. Pregnant women too. Katrine is desperate to get the Tromsunders some accommodation inside, so I'm helping her.'

'I imagine Gerda's thrilled about that,' Elin smirked. 'The way Stellan is around her?' She shook her head.

'What?' Agnette had noticed Stellan's attentiveness to Katrine Hallen herself, though she didn't blame her uncle for enjoying company that wasn't Gerda's. 'He's only trying to help. She's had a terrible time, losing her husband and then her home.'

'Mmmm.' Elin's lips almost disappeared as she pressed them together. 'Well, it looks as though she's got her sights set firmly on another husband already. There are always women like that, of course. Women who prey on weak men.' And slipping past Agnette, she headed inside.

'Weak?' Agnette muttered, striding after her. 'What do you mean weak? Stellan's not weak.'

Elin swung around. 'Weak, kind, it's all the same. Men who can't see past a pretty pair of eyes. They might know how to outthink an enemy, but a scheming woman looking for a new husband? Against that kind of threat, they're helpless! Stellan, Reinar... before long it will be Bjarni. And what will you do about that, Agnette? Stand back and smile? Let some woman steal your husband out from under your nose? Be nice and agreeable and friendly to her?' Elin's temper ignited, remembering all the times she'd seen Agnette and Alys together, laughing and smiling as though they were best friends. 'I wish you luck if that happens, but know this, if you don't want to lose your husband, the only thing you can do is fight.'

'Fight?' Agnette swallowed, worried by the glazed madness

in Elin's eyes. 'How? What do you mean?' But Elin turned away, sweeping through the chamber with speed, not waiting for Agnette to catch her.

***

Reinar rejected all company but Eddeth's for the first stretch of the morning. She was pleased about that, though slightly nervous, for she had nothing to say that he didn't already know. She looked back at Raf, who was riding with Berger and Helgi, thinking that Reinar should have spoken to her.

Though it was the little dreamer Reinar wanted to talk about most of all. 'I don't trust Raf,' he began in a low voice. 'I want to. I know how Sigurd felt about her, I know why you rescued her, but I can't bring myself to trust her.'

Eddeth nodded gravely, waiting impatiently while Reinar spoke. And then, inhaling a deep breath, she began. 'Poor Raf's desperate to belong. Yes, I feel it. I *see* it! She's nervous because she thinks we don't want her. It's how she's felt her whole life. Unwanted! It will take time, more than a few months, for her to trust us. But she wants to, I'm sure. Oh yes, I'm sure she does!' She glanced over her shoulder, beaming toothily at Raf, who peered back at her in confusion.

'They're talking about you,' Berger laughed, eyeing Raf. 'No one's got a bigger mouth than Eddeth. They could hear her back in Slussfall.'

'Or in the forest,' Helgi grumbled, not enamoured with the dreamer's booming voice. He felt far too big for his horse, his long legs dangling as though he could almost touch the ground. Though she was a fine mare, even-tempered and steady, and he gave her rich chestnut coat a rub. 'How's a woman like that a dreamer? I thought they were quiet and secretive? Mysterious? Like you,' he said, nodding at Raf, who he'd been observing all morning. She was an attractive creature beneath all the filth, though that scowl...

Raf ignored Helgi, too busy reading Reinar's thoughts. Though she didn't need to. It was obvious what he thought of her. From the first moment they'd met, she'd seen the mistrust in Reinar's eyes. When he saw her, he saw Gudrum, and that feeling had never gone away. She supposed she couldn't blame him. She hadn't been forthcoming, for the most part, and that had only made everything worse.

Now she frowned, watched by both Helgi and Berger. The cousins were quiet for a time but full of questions for her. She sensed that. Questions waited everywhere she turned, but Raf didn't want to answer any of them. She needed to see what lay ahead or what lurked behind them. She had to be the eyes and ears of the entire army. For Slussfall too. She couldn't let Eddeth down, and despite Reinar's doubts, she couldn't let him down either. He was Sigurd's brother, and that meant something to her. In her heart, she still kept a place for Sigurd Vilander, so it didn't matter what anyone thought of her.

She would do what she could to keep them all safe from Gudrum.

***

'Gudrum will engage with Reinar,' Sigurd said, walking beside his father as they crossed Gallabrok's busy training ring. He felt warm all over, having worked hard practising his sword skills with the armourer, Sappa, who had arms like slags of iron. And though he was some sort of god now, Sigurd felt bruised from head to toe. 'Won't he?'

Thenor shrugged, not wanting to encourage further conversation about Reinar's plans. 'I cannot read Gudrum's mind, though he likes to play games, so who knows how many steps ahead of your brother he already is.' And belatedly realising that

that wouldn't have helped things, he frowned, hurrying on.

Sigurd sucked in another breath, too tense to say much more. He wanted something to eat, though it hadn't been long since breakfast. But having thought it, his steward was immediately by his side, offering his master a bowl of fresh yellow pears. Sigurd grinned, taking one and waving the man away. He couldn't get used to feeling so powerful that his mere thoughts commanded actions from those around him. It was unsettling. Though, he realised, taking a bite of the perfectly sweet pear, quite satisfying at times.

'Good?' Thenor wondered with a smile.

Sigurd nodded, juice dripping into his beard. He wiped it away, glancing at the wooden cottages to his left, recognising Tulia's, though he didn't stop.

Thenor noticed, but he didn't say. 'I have to leave,' he said instead. 'I want you to look after things for me.'

'What?' That was a surprise, and Sigurd lifted his head with confusion in his eyes. 'Me? But what about Valera?'

Thenor laughed, opening the gate leading up the path to the hall. 'You don't think you need the practice? No, Valera will never rule Gallabrok. She has made that perfectly clear over the years, and now she has more work to do than ever.'

Sigurd looked further confused, following his father through the gate, still eating the juicy pear.

'I have made her the Goddess of Dreamers and bestowed upon her many new gifts. It makes sense. Alekka's dreamers have long needed guidance from above. Alari has worked so very diligently to corrupt them, and I need Valera to right that wrong. She will be coming and going, barely at Gallabrok, I imagine, so it is you who needs to command here, for me. It is not hard, as you have seen.'

Sigurd's frown intensified as he climbed the steps behind his father, trying not to stand on Thenor's boots. He felt nervous and uncertain. It was a great responsibility, and he feared he wasn't ready.

'You are,' Thenor assured him. 'I wouldn't leave otherwise.' He pulled open the hall door, standing back to usher Sigurd ahead of him.

'But where are you going?'

'To find more pieces of the puzzle. Gudrum may pose a threat to your brother, but *our* enemies pose a threat to all of Alekka. To every god and goddess too. If Alari or Eskvir get their way, we'll be gone before the year's out, so I must find out more. I have some clues, so I will not be away long, just long enough to see a few old friends. Old friends who may know more than me.'

Sigurd felt a tremor of worry then. 'About what?'

But Thenor didn't say as they entered the hall, which was bright and warm and resplendent with food, wine, and ale. He strode ahead of his son, spying Ulfinnur standing by the fire pit. 'How are you?' he grinned. 'Impatient to leave?'

Ulfinnur appeared hesitant. 'I am not, no. I had hoped to stay awhile longer, if you'd have me? I'm not certain I trust myself after what happened. Not yet.'

Thenor nodded gravely. 'It wasn't your fault, but you are right. I am thinking about gathering our allies together and bringing them here. Until I have Alari, no one is safe.' He turned to Sigurd, scratching his beard.

'It's a good idea,' Ulfinnur said. 'We cannot afford Alari to cause more chaos. Her power is far greater than anyone anticipated.'

'It is,' Thenor agreed. 'But ours is growing too. I will have Tikas round everyone up. We will talk about what to do with Alari when I return.'

'You are leaving?' Ulfinnur turned away from the flames in surprise, following Thenor, who was aiming for the banquet table.

'For a short while. I need more information. More than Hyvari can provide.' He glanced affectionately at his waterfall, her clear water flowing once more.

Sigurd looked Hyvari's way, too, trying not to let any thoughts enter his mind as his father turned back to him. 'Tikas will bring everyone here, and Sigurd will take my chair until I return, and you, Ulfinnur, will rest. It is what you must do to conserve your energy for the coming winter. It will not do to be fretting about Alari, pacing my corridors night and day.'

Ulfinnur nodded. 'Of course, though they are especially nice corridors.'

Thenor laughed, and the two gods headed to the nearest table, where jugs of wine and mead awaited them.

Sigurd remained where he was, staring at Hyvari, his attention abruptly shifting away from his father to his brother, consumed by the sudden fear that Reinar was in danger.

CHAPTER TWENTY

Stellan and Vik joined Reinar, wanting one last opportunity to talk before they began the climb up Mount Norvist. They would have to concentrate more as the path up the mountain became challenging, narrow in places. But before then, Stellan wanted to know what was on his son's mind. Reinar had been quiet since they'd left Slussfall behind, revealing little. He seemed to be stewing over something, and Stellan wanted to know what. 'Have the dreamers had much to say?' he wondered, beginning gently. 'I'm not sure I could find my way through the maze of Eddeth's mutterings and that Raf seems the opposite, barely making a noise. I suppose you wish you'd brought Alys? She's the most plain-spoken of the three.'

'Or Lotta,' Vik grinned. 'She's not afraid to say what she thinks.'

Reinar laughed, then remembering how he'd said goodbye to Alys and his fears about never seeing her again, he went quiet. Riga pushed ahead, sensing the challenge that awaited him and eager for it. Reinar had to tug him back, not wanting to tire him out too quickly.

'Though I don't imagine Eddeth or Raf would keep anything from you, would they?' Stellan prodded. He kept his voice light, a smile on his face, certain Reinar knew more than he was letting on.

'I couldn't say, but I hope not,' Reinar said, his eyes on the mountain rising before them. 'It's not easy trying to pull visions out of the darkness every night. I imagine they'd like some sleep.'

Which didn't answer his question, Stellan thought, sitting back in the saddle, eyeing Vik.

Vik decided to try himself. 'Eddeth must have seen something, though? I imagine she has. Or Raf? Something more than darkness in all these weeks?'

Reinar took a deep breath, looking ahead to where the path was narrowing. He saw pale sunlight streaming through the trees crowning the cliff on his right, now mostly free of snow. 'They've seen things, of course, but nothing that helps us. We just need to keep going and hope for more information. The scouts are out there too. Someone will see something of Gudrum, I'm sure. We just need to be patient.' And not wanting to hear another word about the dreamers, he clicked his tongue, urging Riga ahead of the two men, wanting to be alone with his thoughts.

Stellan blinked after him in surprise before turning to Vik. 'Likely you'll have more luck with Eddeth. Why not pop back and see what she knows? Seems like my son's being tight-lipped about something, though he fails to realise how much a father knows about his son. The boy may become a king one day soon, but he'll never be able to fool me.' And grinning at Vik, he spurred his horse after Reinar.

***

'How long will it take our island friends to organise themselves?' Gudrum wanted to know, for though he was on his way to find Reinar Vilander, he'd woken up with dreams of Jael Furyck still lingering.

Gysa had no answer for him.

She had joined him by the stream, which flowed freely before them, sparkling in the sunshine. It truly felt like spring, and that lifted everyone's spirits. 'I think you've more than one enemy to worry about,' she warned, shaking out her cloak as one of her servants approached with a basket. 'And if you take your eyes off either, you may end up being defeated by both.'

Gudrum wasn't sure that was possible, and he laughed. Gysa looked radiant, and the sun was generous with its warmth. He felt optimistic as he basked in it, encouraging his horse to drink. He saw servants dashing back and forth from the stream to the horses, hurrying to fill waterskins before the call to get back on the road came. It was nice to stop and stretch his legs, to give the horses a break and those men who'd been marching since dawn a chance to sit down. Gudrum may have spoken with confidence, though he felt a sense of urgency stirring, fearing that on the cusp of victory, he was, as Gysa had so bluntly pointed out, in danger of making a mistake. Orvala loomed in his thoughts. He hadn't been thorough enough after claiming the city. He hadn't checked that Tarl Brava was dead. He'd listened to unreliable men and a manipulative dreamer and nearly ended up dead himself. As it was, he'd been humiliated, run out of a city he'd only just claimed, his new wife stolen from him, his forces halved. Though realising that he was tumbling down a steep hill of regret, Gudrum spun around, taking in his army of thousands, and he smiled.

The new Lord of Ennor stood nearby, a confused expression on his face. Like his predecessors, Bor Bearsu was blunt, aggressive, and humourless, though Gudrum wasn't intimidated as Hector had been, and he squared his shoulders, eyeing the man sharply.

'A fine morning, lord king!' Bor bellowed, though he looked as miserable as ever.

'A perfect morning, my lord. We will make great progress today. Edrik says we should reach Somma by nightfall and camp by the river. That should see us all with a nice fish supper. Hopefully, some trout. I haven't had trout in weeks!'

'And do you have further information about where we are heading, my lord?' Bor wanted to know. He was a particularly ugly man, his thick skin rippled with scars, much like Gudrum's. He was as big and imposing as Svein had been, though slightly more pragmatic.

Gudrum turned to Gysa, who smiled back at him. 'We're going

to Salagat, where we'll catch ourselves a few Vilanders. The heads of more lords too. We all want to enhance our reputations, don't we, Bor? And Alekka won't truly be mine until we've cleansed this land of everyone still loyal to Ake. Of everyone who follows Reinar Vilander too. So I'll need the help of my loyal Ennorians.'

Bor looked hopeful, knowing that he needed to solidify his claim to Ennor. Svein's son, Skoll, had died without a living heir, and though there were many Bearsus in contention for the lordship, Bor had quickly staked his own claim, bringing his army back down from Ennor, ready for war.

For this would undoubtedly be the battle to claim all of Alekka.

***

Winter led them deep into the forest, past the caves Jonas and Magnus had hidden in when they'd escaped Slussfall's prison hole.

All the way to the quarry.

Magnus and Lotta were both hungry by the time they arrived at the great stone pit, though neither complained. Still, Alys offered them water, and Jonas dug a handful of nuts out of his pouch while they decided what to do.

Winter had stopped on the edge of the cliff leading down to the quarry.

It had started raining.

'I can't see anything,' Alys fretted, holding Lotta's hand. 'Can you?'

Lotta shook her head, feeling scared.

'Well, nothing else for it then,' Jonas decided with a cheery grin as he started unpinning his cloak, tucking long strands of wet hair behind his ears. 'Time to start climbing!'

Magnus was ready to join his great-grandfather, but Alys held him back. The sides of the quarry were terrifyingly steep, and with the rain sweeping in, Jonas needed to keep his attention on his own hands and feet, not on having to prevent Magnus from falling.

And thinking of falling, Alys stepped back from the edge.

Lotta didn't want to watch. She disappeared with Winter, sheltering under the nearest tree. And cuddling the cat, she dropped her head onto his, trying to see if Puddle was alive.

***

Falla and Agnette sat in front of the main hearth in the hall with Karolina Vettel, whose turn to give birth, Falla was certain, was going to be next.

Karolina wasn't looking forward to it, having heard Falla's screaming cries of agony ringing through the hall for an entire day. She smiled, though, watching her son and Falla's playing with a new litter of kittens mewling in a basket by the fire. The kittens were more interested in suckling their mother, though Borg was trying to tempt them out of the basket with swirling ribbons.

Karolina was listening to Falla and Agnette describing their aches and pains when she saw Elin Vilander sweep into the hall from the kitchen corridor and then stop as though struck. Her eyes lingered for a brief moment on the two women holding their babies, and then on Karolina, the great swell of her belly promising another to come.

Then, hand over her mouth, Elin turned and ran from the hall.

***

Lotta stumbled in a stuttering fluster back to her mother, who held onto Magnus, occasionally looking down into the quarry, trying to see Jonas. 'I, I, it's, it's a... bag!' she cried, catching hold of her mother's hand. 'He's in a bag! A sack!'

Alys frowned, calling down to her grandfather. 'Puddle's in a sack! Look for a sack!'

Hearing a grunt in response, Alys moved back to Lotta, pulling her close. 'What did you see? How did he get in a sack?'

Tears in her eyes, Lotta started to shiver. 'A boy tricked him. I saw him feeding Puddle sausages. Small pieces. He kept dropping them on the ground, moving away and then...' She sobbed loudly as Alys and Magnus looked on. 'Puddle ran into the forest, and then the boy grabbed him and put him in the sack!'

Magnus was furious. Fearful too.

'And then what, Lotta? What else?' Alys wiped Lotta's eyes, stroking her wet hair, trying to calm her down.

'He... he threw the sack down there!' Now Lotta pointed at the quarry, her sobs wracking her shivering body.

Magnus started crying, too, and Alys pulled him to her.

'But why?' Magnus wanted to know, tearful eyes full of despair. 'Why would he do it? And who? Who was it, Lotta?'

Lotta didn't know. She didn't recognise the boy, though she did see a sudden glimpse of him wrapping a filthy hand around three silver coins.

***

Having seen Elin run out of the hall, Agnette hurried to see if she was alright. Though it was quickly apparent that she was more than alright. She was delirious with happiness as she wiped her mouth, her body still heaving from vomiting up her breakfast.

'I am with child!' Elin declared with a beaming smile, taking Agnette's hand. 'I hadn't wanted to even think it was possible, though I felt things. Familiar things. I didn't want to say anything before Reinar left as I've thought those things before. But now I know. I truly am carrying his child!'

Agnette tried to show happiness at Elin's news, though she could barely raise a smile. Since their arrival in Slussfall, Agnette had become increasingly aware of how unhappy Reinar was. He would smile when he saw her, much like Stellan would, but there was a profound sadness lurking in his eyes now, something she saw when he thought no one was looking. Unless Alys was around, and then his face was pure joy or furious frustration.

She had thought of talking to him about divorce, for despite knowing it wasn't her place, she feared Reinar would end up like Stellan, stuck with a bitter, angry wife he didn't love.

But now?

'It's wonderful news,' Agnette said hesitantly. 'I... a cousin for Liara.' Taking Elin's hand, she kissed her flushed cheek. 'You must take care of yourself now. Reinar won't want anything happening to you while he's gone.'

Elin barely heard her, already imagining Reinar's face when she told him. He would be so thrilled. A child? And this one would live, Elin was certain, shutting out every other voice ringing in her ears.

This one would live.

***

Creeping his way along the quarry wall, Jonas soon saw a sack on a ledge. The rain stabbed him like cold little blades, and his hands were shaking as he reached the rocky outcrop. Knowing how much the children cared for the puppy, and Alys, too, his heart started thumping, fearing he was too late.

Bending down, blinking through the rain, he saw no movement in that sodden sack. It was old, ripped with holes. Air to breathe, he thought, trying to cling to some hope, though there was no sign of life as Jonas reached for the sack.

And then he saw a little black nose poking out a hole.

***

'Leaves in the wind,' Gysa mused, fingering her fine woollen cloak. 'There are so many leaves in the wind. But which will blow our way?' She had given up the warmth of the covered sleigh, returning to ride beside Gudrum, shooing away Edrik, who looked annoyed to have been replaced by the dreamer.

'Well, are you going to tell me?' Gudrum wondered with a smile, and though he hadn't wanted to make a show of their relationship, he was pleased to see her. 'Or will you make me wait until we're in my tent, lying under the furs?'

'Is that what you imagine will happen, my lord?'

'I do, for as king, I can command it.'

Gysa laughed, feeling as happy as he looked. Gudrum was a powerful man, adept in warfare, leading with vision and strength, and she was a skilled dreamer without peer, thanks to a generous Alari. There was nothing to fear from any enemy. Nothing at all. 'Well, I can't argue, but I won't wait for then. Soon Jael Furyck will come. I have seen her ships being readied. You could turn back and defeat her first, though it would be a far greater victory if you'd already conquered the Vilanders. There would be many more warriors at your disposal then.'

It was a hard choice, and Gudrum frowned intensely as he thought it over. 'Tell me what you see of Jael Furyck. She's a dreamer, last I heard.' He laughed then, still surprised by that. 'A warrior dreamer.'

'She's not the only one,' Gysa murmured, thinking of Alys. 'Though potentially, she's the most dangerous.'

'So Jael knows what's coming? Knows I'm here, waiting? Does she see through our little game?'

'I don't imagine so. Harran is bound to me now, oblivious to anything but my words, my voice. And that scroll was covered in symbols, unseen by the naked eye. The words written on it would have rung with the echoes of truth. There would've been no doubt in Jael Furyck's mind when she read them. And besides, it's no secret her dreams left her after the Vale. Rumours of that have been whispered for some time.' Gysa saw the concern furrowing Gudrum's brow, and leaning towards him, she lowered her voice. 'You needn't worry about her. The queen will come because she's a warrior first, born and bred to fight. She won't run from you, I assure you. But, in the meantime, you must decide. Who shall be first? For if you are to secure Alekka's throne, you cannot let either Reinar Vilander or Jael Furyck live.'

Gudrum was unable to decide, but then he laughed, thinking how fortunate he was that Raf had left him and Gysa had found him.

It didn't matter which enemy he chose.

With the dreamer by his side, he would defeat both with ease.

***

Puddle lived.

Barely.

It wasn't the first time she'd carried a limp and wet Puddle in her arms, Alys thought, remembering trying to revive the puppy out at sea. But this time, he seemed so much weaker. Almost lifeless.

Jonas had plied him with a little water, and now he laid his cloak on the ground and taking the limp puppy from his granddaughter, he wrapped him in thick woollen layers until only that black nose was once again poking out.

Lotta and Magnus looked happy and scared and worried most of all as Jonas lifted the bundle, holding it close to his chest, hoping to shield Puddle from the worst of the rain, while they hurried back through the forest, heading for the fort.

***

Jael had enjoyed a reprieve from her dreams for three years, but now, as her husband prepared to depart for Alekka, she felt the absence of them acutely. She was used to leading, to making the decisions, and though she trusted Eadmund, she felt unsettled as she stood on the black stone beach, watching as, one by one, Oss' extensive fleet was sailed into the harbour. Before The Freeze, they'd taken the ships around to Tatti's Bay, locking them in secure sheds to protect them from winter's worst. And now, with the sea melting, they were once again returning to the harbour. Though not for long.

Jael watched her sandy-haired husband thumping around on *Sea Bear*, which she was kindly letting him take to Alekka. *Sea Bear* was her favourite of the fleet, and they'd survived much together, so Jael thought it made sense for at least one of them to go with Eadmund.

Oss' master shipbuilder, Beorn, stood next to her. 'Strange you're not coming,' he decided gruffly, eyes on the ships. 'Though likely Eadmund will give us an easier time.'

Jael's eyes skipped from Eadmund to Thorgils, who was laughing with his uncle, Bram. If Bram's wild hair hadn't turned as white as snow, she was sure they would have looked like twins. As it was, they were still giants. Still big and broad and booming. 'I'm sure he will. Though best you keep an eye out, make sure he's fully informed. He won't see everything.'

'Not if you stay here, he won't.'

Jael turned, suppressing a sigh. 'I'm happy with my decision, Beorn. Just keep an eye on Eadmund. On the sea. On any problems. I'm relying on you.' And not wanting to get drawn into yet another debate about why she wasn't coming, Jael headed across the stones to where Thorgils' wife, Isaura, was trying to corral their children, who were mostly getting in the way of the men lugging sea chests down the muddy slope to the beach.

'Selene!' Isaura called, blonde hair sweeping around a fretful face. 'Come here! Move, girls! Bo Skalleson!'

Jael laughed. 'You need a shepherd's crook!'

Isaura turned around with a smile, tucking her hair behind her ears. Her six-month-old daughter was strapped to her back, and she was already pregnant again. It would be her sixth child, and she felt ready to fall over, unsure how she was going to manage another.

'Careful,' Jael warned as Isaura's only son started chasing the dogs around her in circles. 'Mads! Do you want to knock your mother over? She might be carrying a brother in there, you know.'

That had Mads looking up with interest, for he'd grown bored with his sisters, none of whom wanted to play with him anymore. Mads wanted a brother more than anything, and turning away, he led Ido and Vella down to the foreshore, charging through the water.

'Thank you, Jael,' Isaura sighed wearily. 'I do wonder what I'm doing having another. Though the gods have a plan, I suppose. And mine is to have the biggest brood on Oss!'

Jael smiled at her. 'I have some seeds you can take after this one arrives, if you like? They stop you falling pregnant.' She hadn't revealed that to anyone before.

Isaura looked surprised. She was a shy woman, and it had taken some time to become friends with Jael, though even now, she felt slightly nervous around her. 'Don't you want more children?'

Jael quickly shook her head. 'No.' She shook it again for good measure. 'Not a chance. Eadmund's lucky he's got two. I've done my part. I'll leave you to have all the babies now.' And reaching out, she grabbed hold of Isaura, sensing that she was about to lose her balance.

Isaura glanced up at her. 'Thought you weren't a dreamer anymore?'

'I don't need to be a dreamer to know that a pregnant woman on slippery stones isn't a good idea. Come on, I'll walk you up the hill.'

Isaura was grateful, not noticing the puzzled look on Jael's face as she led her away.

***

Stina and Solveigh hurried to the sodden figures who had flung open the door and rushed into the cottage, seeking the warmth of the fire. Then, seeing Jonas unwrapping his woollen bundle, both women threw their hands over their mouths in shock. And then relief.

Stina took over, instructing Solveigh to look after a complaining Agnes, Alys to gather up the furs to make Puddle a bed by the fire, Jonas to head outside for more firewood, and the children to generally move out of the way.

'Sausages,' Lotta mumbled. 'If he smelled a sausage, it might wake him up.'

Alys agreed, reaching into her purse, though Jonas beat her to it, handing two bits of silver to the children, who disappeared back into the rain.

'What happened?' Stina asked, shaking her head as she lay the limp puppy on the bundle of warm furs. Puddle barely stirred as she slipped Jonas' cloak out from underneath him, handing it to Alys, who hung it over a stool to dry.

'A boy,' Jonas told her. 'Someone paid a boy to stuff him in a sack and throw him into the quarry. Lucky for Puddle, he wasn't very thorough. He didn't notice the sack had landed on a ledge. I guess he just scampered back to the fort for his coins.'

'What?' Stina looked horrified. 'Someone wanted to hurt Puddle?'

'Perhaps the sausage seller?' Jonas joked, though looking at the lifeless puppy, he wasn't smiling for long.

'Perhaps it wasn't Puddle they wanted to hurt?' Alys whispered, and with a shiver, she turned to stare at the door, now rattling in the wind.

CHAPTER TWENTY ONE

There'd been no sign of Gudrum for either Eddeth or Raf during the day, which wasn't surprising. Sometimes, they saw visions while the sun was out, but most useful information was uncovered during the night. Eddeth grinned, happy in the darkness, not interested in sitting around drinking with the likes of Ollo and Ilene. She'd avoided them entirely since Ollo's outburst, and she hurried Raf past them, towards where Ludo and Helgi had brought an enormous fire to life.

'You still awake, Eddeth?' Ludo grinned, looming like a death collector over the flames.

'Well, that stew's sitting in my belly like a lump of amber, so I imagine I'll be up for some time yet. Think I may have to take over cooking duties tomorrow. Someone's got a rather heavy hand.' She lowered her voice, peering around. 'Tough as boots that meat was.'

Ludo agreed, still picking it out of his teeth. He had no intention of going to bed either. Not while there was ale to drink and company to be had.

Eddeth sat down next to him. 'What are you going to do about Stina then?' she blurted out. 'Poor woman will lose her mind if you don't do something soon.'

Ludo didn't know where to look, but he certainly didn't look at Eddeth.

Berger burst out laughing, and beside him, Helgi appeared confused. 'Alys' friend,' his cousin explained. 'The one with the long face. Brown hair. Always looks miserable.'

'What?' Ludo hit Berger. 'What?'

Berger laughed some more. 'Come on, Eddeth's right. Poor Stina. After what she went through with Torvig? She's not getting any younger, you know. Better get on with things before there's no chance.'

'No chance of what?' Ludo wanted to know.

'Children. I expect you'll want some of those when you're married.'

Ludo's face burned with embarrassment. 'Talk about yourself. Leave me alone,' he mumbled, receiving a raised eyebrow from Berger, who poked Helgi.

Helgi didn't say anything, not fond of playing games when it came to love. If it was love? The way Ludo was acting, perhaps it was, though he didn't know any of them well enough to truly understand what was going on.

Leaning back with a loud yawn, Eddeth eyed the tapestry of stars twinkling above her head. 'What do you think Sigurd's doing?' she wondered, not noticing the foul look Raf shot her way. 'Watching us? Perhaps trying to find you?' She grinned, turning her head, finally seeing Raf's unimpressed face. And realising she was making one mistake after another, Eddeth decided that sleep was probably the wisest choice after all. 'I hope Alys is looking after Agnes,' she muttered, scrambling to her feet, suddenly worried about her goat. 'And Rigfuss. He had a sore paw, he did. I should have mentioned that!'

'The woman's mind's a nest of fleas,' Berger decided as Eddeth scuttled away from the fire.

Ludo glared at him, still simmering over his comments about Stina. 'Well, I'd wager that woman's done more to help us than you. Dreamers are different. Their minds are their weapons. They have to store so much knowledge in there, not to mention all the dreams that come.' His eyes rested on Raf, who quickly dropped hers to her lap where her fingers were busy picking her nails, thick with dirt.

Berger ignored a simmering Ludo, instead opening up his

pouch, where he pulled out a fine sliver of well-worked bone, handing it to Raf. 'Easier if you use this.'

She looked at the little tool in confusion, hesitant to take it.

'There's never been a more well-groomed man than my cousin,' Helgi smiled. 'He doesn't usually share his precious tools, though, so I'd take it quick. Those nails will be clean in half the time.'

Helgi's smile reached his hazel eyes, which were kind, Raf saw, not calculating like his cousin's. And nodding, she took the bone tool with a shy bob of her head. 'Thank you.' She looked past Helgi to where Eddeth had slipped inside their tent, tempted to join her, though it was still early, and she felt wide awake. She heard the laughter of men huddled around fires, some enjoying the company of the servant girls. She saw that horrible Ilene smirking at Ollo. Reinar was off with his father. Vik was nowhere to be seen.

And as Ludo, Berger, and Helgi talked about horses and weapons and nothing she was interested in, she lifted her head to the stars, thinking of Sigurd, wondering if she'd ever see him again.

***

Sigurd stood before Hyvari, holding a hand in her rushing water. He wanted to feel real cold. Here, in Gallabrok, he felt nothing but comfort. Mostly, he didn't notice, but sometimes, the desire to feel something less than perfect was overwhelming. He wanted to feel human again, to be part of a world where much was unknown, where discomfort was a way of life.

'You look as though you want to run away,' Valera smiled as she approached, dressed in a plain black cloak.

Sigurd jumped in surprise. 'I...' He turned to his sister, seeing both warmth and sympathy in her eyes. She was so different from Thenor. His father's face was a mask, revealing little. He was friendly at times, authoritative and stern at others, but mostly, Sigurd had the sense that he would never truly know him. Valera was more open, more inviting, and he felt relaxed in her presence. 'I hate feeling blind,' he admitted. 'It's hard not knowing what's happening. *If* something's happening. I don't understand why I can't...' He stopped, remembering everything Thenor had said about why he couldn't get involved. It wasn't that he didn't understand. It was that he didn't want it to be that way.

He didn't want to be a god.

'I am sorry for you, Sigurd,' Valera said gently. 'You have been cut off from all you know, and that can't be easy.'

'No,' Sigurd agreed, 'it's not. I understand why I can't interfere, though it's not that. It's that I can't see at all unless Thenor's here. Unless he brings Hyvari to life, I'm blind.'

'There are other ways to see,' Valera smiled. 'Hyvari is Father's, but there are other ways. Every god is born with the ability to see beyond what lies before our eyes. It is merely about finding your own way.'

Sigurd was shocked. 'You mean I could see by myself?'

'Not here,' Valera whispered. 'Not in Hyvari, for she is Thenor's alone. But yes, if you find something, somewhere that feels right, you could. Water opens a window, and when we become at one with it, it enables us to reach beyond, to see as far as we desire. I could... show you,' she offered, half fearing that her father would be cross with her. But one look at Sigurd told Valera that he would never flourish in Gallabrok if he felt suffocated. He would never let go of his old life then. 'I am just going on a little journey, but when I return, I will show you how to open a window.'

***

Alys heard the wind squealing through gaps around the windows, whistling under the door. It stopped her falling asleep. Worry for

Puddle did too. She didn't understand why she hadn't seen the danger the puppy was in or why she hadn't been able to find him. And why hadn't Ragnahild come to her? Surely she could have raised the alarm?

Finally fed up with being the only one still awake, Alys got out of bed and padded to the fire, wanting to check on Puddle. And seeing that the fire was mostly embers, she added another log, kneeling down beside Puddle's bed of fur, stroking his head, now fluffy once more. He snuffled but remained where he was, curled in a ball.

'Stupid little thing!' came a familiar growl, and Alys looked up to see Ragnahild peering at her from the other side of the fire.

'Are you alright?'

'Me? Pfft! That puppy! Never has there been a greedier creature. Or a dumber one! Following after that boy as though he had good intentions? I don't know what he was thinking!' She dropped down onto a stool with a frustrated groan.

Alys hurried to sit beside her. 'But couldn't you stop him?'

Now Ragnahild became still. 'No, not at all. I was powerless. Utterly powerless.'

'But why? How?'

'That I don't know, but there's no time for it, Alys. Not now! You need to bundle up that puppy, pack your bags and prepare to leave!'

'What?' Alys glanced around, though no one had stirred. 'Leave for where?'

Ragnahild was immediately off the stool, stomping around the fire. 'What is happening, I don't know. I truly don't, Alys. Some things are amiss, others are afoot, most remain a mystery, but Alari is certainly up to something. Her new pet, Gysa, is a weapon she is wielding to propel Gudrum to victory.' She took a deep breath. 'And Reinar will die without you. I have seen that very clearly, so you must go, Alys. You must go in the morning!'

***

The following day dawned on Oss with real hints of spring in the air. Rather than the usual palette of greys, the sky had a slight tinge of blue and even some pink. Though the wind was still fierce, and Jael had both hands on her flapping hood as she stood on the beach, saying goodbye to her husband. 'Don't die,' she said with a kiss.

Eadmund laughed, pulling her closer, seeing fear in her eyes. 'You don't think I can do this without you?'

'Likely not,' she said, trying not to smile as their children clung to Eadmund's legs, begging to be picked up. 'You need to be careful.'

Eadmund felt happy to have Jael in his arms, though he felt a twinge of unease about her words. 'I won't die,' he promised, leaning in until their noses touched. She stood entirely still before him, which was most unlike his wife, and frowning, he stepped back. 'You haven't seen something, have you? Something in your dreams?'

Jael shook her head as the children held their arms aloft, jumping up and down with impatience now.

Eadmund bent down, scooping up one in each arm. 'You be good for the queen,' he grumbled sternly. 'No nonsense. No stealing food and blaming the dogs. No playing tricks on Biddy.' He saw Biddy swaying in the distance, not knowing what to do with herself as Ido and Vella chased off every bird attempting to land on the stones.

'We'll be good, Papa,' Sigmund promised, tears glistening in his eyes. 'But don't die.'

Eadmund kissed his red cheek, trying not to smile. 'Why would I do that? No chance.'

Bo burst into tears, clinging to her father's neck. 'Miss you, Papa.'

He squeezed her back, feeling how tiny she was, seeing how much she looked like Jael. Eventually, he placed each child back on the stones. 'I'll miss you, too, but think how excited we'll be to see each other again? And I'll bring you something back from Alekka. What would you like? The head of a rebel lord? On a spear?'

Jael shook her head, certain that both children would be waking up crying from nightmares. 'Hmmm, that's helpful.'

Eadmund grinned, snatching her hand, motioning Biddy over. 'Good luck without me, Biddy.'

She looked teary-eyed, handkerchief in hand. 'Oh, no luck needed here. It's you who needs all the luck without Jael.'

Jael laughed loudly, seeing the surprise on Eadmund's face. Eadmund, who realised that Biddy was entirely serious.

Thorgils was bellowing in the distance, and Beorn was on *Sea Bear*, shouting at the crews. They'd pushed the ships into the water, calling out their last farewells to those waiting on the beach.

Biddy grabbed the two children's hands as Eadmund waved to them before turning away, walking Jael down to the foreshore.

'Be careful,' she warned, seriously now. 'Your father may have made an alliance with Ake Bluefinn, but that was years ago, so do your own thinking. You don't know what you'll be walking into over there.' She felt strange. Her people were leaving, her friends were leaving, Eadmund was leaving. Part of her wanted to go, though she was doing her very best to ignore that part. She glanced over her shoulder, seeing the children with Biddy. They would be well cared for if anything were to happen to her or Eadmund, she knew. Biddy would go back to Andala, where Sigmund and Bo would find a loving home with her family.

It wasn't that.

It wasn't the children, and Jael knew it better than anyone.

But she couldn't go. She couldn't.

Kissing Eadmund, she held him close. 'I'm sorry,' she breathed in his ear. 'For being strange.'

He laughed softly, kissing her cold lips. 'You've always been strange, though I like you that way.'

She didn't speak, still clinging on.

'The wind!' Beorn was barking from *Sea Bear*. 'We'll lose the wind!'

Jael smiled, kissing Eadmund one last time. 'You'd better go then.'

He nodded, staring into those beautiful green eyes. 'I better had. But don't worry, I'll see you soon.'

***

After Ragnahild's disturbing appearance, Alys hadn't slept. The spirit dreamer's words had echoed back to her in the darkness, keeping her wide awake and fearful. She felt sick with worry for Reinar and then confused, sifting through her options, trying to decide what to do.

Her first thought was to contact Eddeth. Remembering the pouch Eddeth had left with hair from both her and Raf inside, Alys searched for it, though it was nowhere to be found.

Which made no sense.

She had secured it in the saddlebag she kept under her bed. Everything else was in there, she could see, but no pouch.

Unable to sleep after that and more on edge than ever, Alys tipped out the contents of the saddlebag and started packing.

By dawn, she was fully dressed, slipping out of the cottage to find Jonas, and a few hours later, she was standing in the square with Stina, Solveigh, and the children, waiting for the horses.

Stina had rushed around packing and organising food as soon as Alys had said they were leaving. She stood beside her now, peering at the cottage, wondering if she'd thought of everything. 'Are you sure we should be taking Puddle? He's so unwell.'

Alys looked up at the first drops of rain. She glanced around, feeling the need to find Lief and explain why she was going. And Agnette. She wanted to talk to Agnette too. 'He is, but it's better if he's away from the fort and whoever's trying to hurt him. And besides, we need Ragnahild with us. She insisted upon it. Winter will be here, which means Salma will look after things. We just... we have to go, Stina.' Then dropping her bag to the ground, she swallowed. 'Can you watch the children? I need to go to the hall.'

Stina nodded, eyes on the children who were arguing over who would carry Puddle on the journey, but arriving with a stable hand, four horses and two ponies, Jonas snapped at them both. 'Well, it's not going to be much fun if you carry on like that! And as for Puddle, your mother and I'll take turns with him. Stina too. He's small, but the weight of him will be too much for you two to bear for long. So enough about that, and come over here and help me pack these saddlebags.'

Alys tapped his arm. 'I just have to speak to Lief, then we need to go.' Jonas nodded, and turning away, Alys hurried through the square, her mind once again returning to Reinar and whether she would reach him in time.

***

After a mostly sleepless night and an early start, Reinar felt irritable, yawning as he drew Riga's reins into his lap. Snow swept around him, the wind blustering his hood against his frozen cheeks, making it even harder to see as they rode down a steepening path. This was the most dangerous part of their journey, for the horses had to be sure of their footing, especially those pulling the sleighs. No one could afford them to lose control, so Reinar had sent twelve men to manage each sleigh while he led a slow pace from the front, wanting to keep everything steady.

'What's wrong with you?' Berger grinned beside him, his auburn beard white with snow. He was oddly cheerful, despite a late night and an early departure. 'Missing Alys?'

Reinar's head snapped around, blue eyes full of fire. 'You want me to tip you over the cliff?'

Berger laughed. 'You wouldn't do that, Reinar Vilander. You need me. And so does Solveigh. You wouldn't do that to her either.'

Reinar wasn't so sure. 'You think you're what's best for Solveigh?'

'I do. She deserves to be protected and cherished. I'll keep her safe.'

'From Tarl Brava? He won't leave her alone for much longer, I'd say. Now the sea's flowing, I expect we'll hear from him soon. He'll want his child.'

Berger licked frozen lips, brushing the snow from his beard. He'd thought about that, too, slightly less enamoured with The Thaw than everyone else. 'I think he'll have other things to do,' he decided. 'He won't head south without a plan. And he'll need time to find one. More men and ships too. I've got time.'

'To do what?'

'Build my reputation, grow my fortune. Make you a king.'

Reinar frowned. 'What does it matter to you?'

'You as the King of Alekka suits me better than any other. Me as one of the top advisors to the king? A prominent lord? That's where I belong.'

'Is that so?'

Berger nodded. 'And if you're the king, you'll have to fight Tarl Brava one day, and I'll be right by your side.'

Reinar laughed as Bjarni rode up to join them.

'Stellan says to slow down!' he grumbled, shuddering with cold. 'We're moving too quickly.'

Realising that he had sped up, Reinar tugged Riga back, slowing him down. 'Everything alright back there?'

'Mmmm, spose. Eddeth's still mounted, which is something. Vik's riding beside her, trying to keep her focused.'

Berger laughed. 'Poor Vik. Not sure he was expecting to become Eddeth's minder.'

Reinar grinned, imagining Vik's face, and then Berger was yelping, hands working the reins with speed as his horse skidded on a patch of ice. 'Focus now, Berger Eivin. Wouldn't want to lose one of my top advisors, would I?'

A few rows back, Vik's frown finally eased. 'That's better,' he sighed, feeling everything slowing down again. He rode on one side of Eddeth, Ludo on the other, both men fearing that Eddeth would get into trouble on such a deadly descent. It was better if she was watched, and not just by Raf, who rode behind her with Helgi and Ollo.

'I don't think you need to worry,' Eddeth insisted, though she was enjoying Vik's company. 'I didn't see us dying on this mountain!'

'No? Where did you see us dying then?' Ollo wondered.

Eddeth didn't answer, not having forgiven him for his rudeness. And sensing that, Ollo muttered something under his breath, which Raf heard perfectly clearly, and she glared at him.

'If you want to fix things with Eddeth, being angrier and meaner isn't the way,' she hissed. 'She's right to warn you about Ilene. We're dreamers. You should try and listen.'

But Ollo didn't want to. He'd set his sights on Ilene Gislar, and nothing anyone said was going to change his mind.

He'd kissed her once.

A drunken kiss and a quick fumble, which had almost led to something more in a dark alley, though it hadn't, and he was left with a burning desire to impress the woman he so desperately wanted to be his. 'Listen to what? Advice from you two? About love? Ha!'

Raf went quiet again, which suited Ollo.

Helgi was tired of the arguing and sniping. He wanted to talk about battle. And edging his horse away from Raf, he stopped alongside Vik. 'Why did you choose Salagat?' he wondered. 'It's years since I was there, though I don't remember it fondly. An abandoned village, a boggy field, and a hill. That's about it.'

Vik looked pleased to be talking about something other than dreams and Ollo. Though just as he was forming his response, he heard a strange noise.

So did the horses.

Helgi's eyes snapped right, finding only sheer cliffs smothered in snow.

Vik's head turned left, though that way led to a sharp drop down into a thick maze of white-tipped fir trees.

'What was that?' Eddeth wondered loudly. 'Sounds like... crying?'

Vik's head didn't stop moving, his ears straining to hear anything.

'Sounds like screaming,' Helgi offered.

'Must be a forest cat,' Stellan decided, and now his eyes climbed the cliff, not wanting an angry cat jumping down on them. His horse threw up its head, long mane flashing. Vik's and Helgi's horses were just as unhappy, shifting around beneath them.

Though not as upset as Rofni and Wilf, who made moves to escape. But Vik was quick to grab Wilf's bridle, holding him tightly as Eddeth slipped in the saddle. Raf cried out as Rofni barged into Ollo's horse, though Ollo was on hand to get him under control.

'We keep going!' Stellan demanded, sensing everyone panicking before him, fearing those panicking behind him. 'Hold your nerve and keep going!'

The strange noises sounded again, high-pitched and urgent.

Threatening too.

'Hold on!' Reinar bellowed from the front. 'Keep your reins tight!' Riga wanted to bolt, and he was working hard to keep him calm. Beside him, Berger looked worried as his own horse whinnied nervously.

As did Bjarni. 'What is it?'

'Cats,' Reinar insisted, though after their last forest experience, he felt on edge, fearing that wasn't true. 'Just cats.'

CHAPTER TWENTY TWO

Alys saw the basket of kittens sitting in front of the enormous hearth as she waited for Lief, though it was Agnette who found her first, having been visiting Falla and the baby.

'Are you alright?' she asked, hurrying forward. 'Did you see something?'

Alys quickly shook her head. 'No, well yes, but not about Bjarni. It's just that I... I need to go after them, Agnette. I had a dream. I need to leave.'

Agnette was stunned, gripping Alys' hands. 'But something must be seriously wrong if you're leaving?'

Alys knew she wouldn't be getting her hands back without an explanation, so lowering her voice, she whispered in Agnette's ear, telling her about Puddle and Ragnahild and her fears for Reinar. When she'd finished, Agnette released her hands with a low sound.

'And the children?'

'I'll be taking them. Stina and Jonas too.'

'But the fort?'

'I want you to look after Solveigh. In fact, could you move into the cottage? Keep a close eye on her and the cats? After what happened to Puddle, they need to be watched carefully, and it's a lot to ask of Solveigh.'

'Of course, of course I will.' And filled with purpose and trembling with fear, Agnette took Alys in her arms. 'You must look after yourself, Alys. It's all well and good worrying about everyone else, but please, keep yourself safe first.'

Alys nodded, and once again lowering her voice, she left Agnette with a warning. 'Be wary of Elin. Watch her closely.' She blinked, not wanting to say anything further, and pulling herself out of Agnette's arms, she turned to see Lief Gundersen heading her way.

***

Gysa brimmed with confidence, bolstered by how much faith Alari had put in her. She rode entirely alone in the covered sleigh now, having rid herself of her nattering servants. More than anything, she needed to think. There was no point in being powerful if you made decisions like a fool; if you didn't plan and ponder and search for trouble. For there was always trouble lurking where you least expected it.

She'd been taught at an early age that dreamers didn't see all things. A dreamer received only those messages that served a purpose. It was not a dreamer's duty to prevent every tragedy or to help someone achieve their greatest desires.

A dreamer, she'd been warned, was never to place their finger on the scale.

Though after her family was murdered and she was raped, then burned alive, Gysa had abandoned all thoughts of behaving as a dreamer should. Instead, she intended to focus on her own needs, on searching for every clue pertaining to her future happiness. Having been brought back to life, she was more determined than ever to place not just a finger but her entire hand on the scale.

The bones scattered over the floor of the sleigh had her concerned. She wanted to advise Gudrum, to show him the paths to victory. Yet one of those paths was now blocked, thanks to Jael Furyck choosing to remain on Oss. It was a surprise, and not one Gysa had anticipated, for Gudrum needed to defeat both the Queen of Oss and the former Lord of Ottby to secure the throne.

But now?

Lurching forward as the sleigh hit a rock, the bones swept away from her. Gysa snarled in fury, but in the next moment, it was as though dark clouds had shifted, revealing the most glorious sunrise.

And she smiled.

***

'Enjoying the day?' Fyn wondered with a grin as he rode back from training with Jael. They headed to his old cottage most mornings, looking to escape the attention that training in the Pit would garner. Jael had taught Fyn everything he knew about weapons. She had trained him to be a skilled warrior, and because of that, he was loyal to her above all others. He owed her his life, so he tried not to let his disappointment show at being forced to stay behind while everyone else sailed to Alekka.

The weather had quickly reverted to its usual bleakness, and Jael laughed. 'Enjoying? No. Enduring? Always.'

'It's quiet, though,' Fyn decided, looking down at the harbour as they rode up the hill to the fort.

Jael agreed, already dreading the return to the clamour and noise of the square, everyone eyeing her with unspoken questions, wondering whether to approach their notoriously sharp-tongued queen with some nagging problem. She shook her head, feeling Tig struggling up the hill. The snow was melting, and it had been a fast ride, both Jael and Fyn hoping the cold air would blow out the cobwebs. Though colder than ever and with aching ears, Jael was certain her mind was still thick with them.

She tried to distract herself. 'What will you do about Fria?'

Fyn blushed a deep pink, his embarrassment quickly colouring the tips of his frozen ears. 'What?'

'You only waste time by being shy,' Jael said, slowing Tig down, sitting back in the saddle. 'And there's no time to waste while you live, so say what you feel. Don't hold back. Don't waste a moment.'

Fyn turned to her with raised eyebrows.

'What? I'm not talking about me. I'm married. I've got children. No need to worry about me.'

Fyn smiled. 'Though you don't say what you feel, do you, Jael? Not all of it.'

Jael felt annoyed he knew that about her. 'I'm just trying to help you find a woman. Find her and keep her.'

'Why?'

'Because you're twenty-three,' Jael went on. 'Yet you're still too shy to talk to a girl. In the past year alone, Lilla Solberg married that idiot, Orm, and Siggy married Abel. Both girls you liked. And they both liked you.'

'They did?'

'Yes! Even Thorgils could see that. He was trying to help you, remember?'

'I thought he was just stirring up trouble, embarrassing me,' Fyn said.

'He wanted to help, I promise. I tried to tell you, Eadmund, too, though you didn't want to listen because listening would mean having to do something about it.'

Fyn frowned, focusing on his horse and the steepening climb. 'Fria's different,' he decided. 'She doesn't like me at all. Surely you can see that?'

Fria Sanvik was new to Oss. Her family had arrived from Bara before The Freeze, and Fyn had quickly become enamoured with the comely girl. Jael thought she was dull and preening, but Fyn was entranced. Entranced but, as usual, silent and shy. He watched Fria from afar and mostly mumbled, staring at his boots whenever she was around. Jael was beginning to worry that he'd be alone for the rest of his life if she didn't give him a sharp shove in Fria's direction.

'She likes you,' she promised. 'Who wouldn't like you?'

Fyn blushed further. 'Well...'

'We've all this time without the army. Just a garrison of old men left behind. None of them are competition for Fria's affections. It's the perfect time to do something.'

'*Do* something?'

Jael laughed. 'Come on, let's get inside. I want a fire!' And thinking about the hot pool outside the hall, she imagined sinking into it with a nice cup of ale. Her mind quickly left Fyn and his problems behind, drifting to Eadmund, wishing she knew where he was and what he was doing.

Hoping he was alright.

***

The island of Bara was tiny, and Thorgils hoped they wouldn't have to wait there for long. Gulvi Lundberg, Lord of Bara, had the worst ale. 'Like piss,' he grumbled, almost tipping the contents of his cup onto the floor.

'Shut up,' Eadmund hissed, certain Gulvi would hear.

'And not even nice piss,' Thorgils went on.

They were joined by Beorn, who looked as pleased to be on Bara as Thorgils. 'You've had nice piss?'

Eadmund glowered at the pair of them as Gulvi approached with his wife. 'We're grateful for the ale,' he said, enjoying the warmth of the fire.

Gulvi nodded, though he looked embarrassed. 'Tastes a bit like piss, I'm afraid. Though it's the best I can do, my lord. It's been a long winter.'

Thorgils snorted loudly, enjoying the look on Eadmund's face.

Gulvi appeared awkward, as did his wife, who was a young woman, shy in the presence of the king and his men. She had recently given birth, not expecting to be inundated with warriors and ships at such short notice.

'Lucky for you, we've brought good Oss ale with us,' Thorgils grinned. 'I'll organise a few barrels to be brought up.'

'Will you now?' Eadmund wondered, eyeing his best friend.

'Certainly! I imagine you'll have a lot to discuss. It's the least I can do for my king.' And slapping Eadmund on the back, Thorgils headed to *Sea Bear*, knowing exactly where the barrels of ale were stored.

Eadmund stared after him as the hall doors opened, seeing the ships dug into Bara's stone beach, feeling the absence of his wife.

Ake's man, Harran, approached with some of his crew. 'My lords,' he said, bobbing his head. And turning his attention to Eadmund, he spoke in hushed tones. 'How many more of your men can we expect? And how quickly?'

Harran was an impatient man, always looking to catch Eadmund's eye, to have a quiet word, to urge him on. There was a palpable tension in the man, though Eadmund didn't blame him. Harran feared for his king and his people. He had every right to want to hurry them along. 'Two more lords, so perhaps another day? Lucky we did bring our own ale.' He grinned at Beorn and Bram, catching a glimpse of Harran's fretful face. 'Don't worry, they'll be eager to get here. We've had little to do these past few years. Everyone will be itching to stretch out their sword arms again.' Eadmund didn't feel as confident as he sounded. He didn't know Alekka, so he already felt at a disadvantage.

Still, Ake Bluefinn would be there and having met the famous king, Eadmund was confident he would make them feel at home.

***

After reaching the end of the treacherous descent down Mount Norvist, Reinar had been looking forward to an end to the mournful cat-like noises, though they'd only intensified. Now they were deep in forest again, heads swivelling, bodies twisting in saddles, eyes darting through the trees, fearing an attack.

Reinar became so on edge that he sent Bjarni back for Eddeth and Raf, though when the dreamers arrived on whinnying, wild-eyed horses they had no ideas between them.

'What are we going to do?' Eddeth bleated. 'Those cats are following us!'

Raf knew forest creatures better than any of them, and even she felt a dark foreboding that trouble was coming for them.

'You're supposed to tell *me*, Eddeth,' Reinar complained. 'That's why you're here!'

Eddeth shrugged. 'I can tell you my dreams, but what's out there?' She shivered. 'It doesn't sound magical. Not something I can help you with.'

Reinar peered at Raf, who appeared to be holding her breath. 'What do you think? You're from The Murk. I don't recognise that cry at all. It sounds like a forest cat sometimes, other times... I don't know.'

'It's not cats.'

Bjarni blinked, immediately looking around. 'No? Sounds like cats to me.'

Eddeth felt just as confused. 'What is it then?' She thought of her own cat, hoping Alys had remembered to check on him. Rigfuss was old and slow now, less able to catch his own food, especially with a sore paw, and she started fretting, forgetting about their conversation until another long cry rang out, sounding closer now.

Reinar tightened his hold on Riga's reins, the back of his neck tingling. 'All we can do is keep alert. The scouts will come back soon, but you need to try and see something,' he urged, turning to eye both dreamers. 'We need some warning.'

Eddeth blinked, wanting to stop and take a moment to order her thoughts.

'We'll stop at the river and decide what to do,' Reinar said. 'The horses can't focus, and I don't think we can either. But we need to. We need an answer.'

Raf nodded alongside Eddeth, though she was distracted, realising how strange it was that neither she nor Eddeth could sense what was out there, following them.

***

Despite their best intentions, it had taken some time to leave Slussfall, and Alys was feeling on edge as the afternoon lengthened, fearing they hadn't made much progress. 'How far ahead of us are they?' she asked, Ragnahild's words echoing around her in the dark forest.

Jonas turned to his fretting granddaughter with a smile. 'They can't move as freely as we can or as quickly.' He glanced over his shoulder at his great-grandchildren. Despite constant pleas for food, the children had generally kept their complaints to a minimum, and they'd been able to move with speed throughout the day. Though Jonas could see that the ponies didn't have much more in them. Stina rode behind the children, Puddle strapped to her chest like a baby. He'd mostly kept his complaints to a minimum too. 'I'd say we'll catch them within two or three days if we use our time wisely. The quicker we find a campsite and get to sleeping, the earlier we'll be back on the road again. Food shouldn't be a problem, thanks to Stina. As long as the children don't get their hands on it!' Despite the weather, which had been mostly damp, and the cold, which had clung to them, Jonas was in a good mood, enjoying spending so much time alone with his family. He felt excited, too, looking forward to catching up with Vik and Stellan.

Alys could tell, feeling some relief that her grandfather had been freed from the fort and more relief that he was riding beside her.

'You're worried,' he decided, scanning the trees for a path, somewhere that would lead to a clearing. 'What did Ragnahild actually say?'

'She fears for Reinar,' Alys said, and seeing that Jonas'

attention was wholly focused on her, she lowered her voice. 'Raf had a dream before they left. Gudrum was victorious, and Reinar was dead.' She swallowed, fixing her eyes back on the road, feeling tears coming.

Jonas quickly replaced his wide-eyed shock with a look of calm thoughtfulness. 'It sounds worrying, of course, but if Ragnahild is sending you after him, she must see some hope. Some chance of turning things around.' Ragnahild had been Eida's grandmother, a prickly old woman with a big heart. Eida had adored her, and Ragnahild had tried to help her, Jonas knew, warning her about what Mirella would become. He blinked himself away from that dark place, not wanting to become distracted by the past.

It was Reinar they needed to focus on now.

Reinar, and Gudrum's plans for him.

***

Gudrum joined Gysa in her covered sleigh, enjoying the privacy of the walls and the shelter of the roof. The wind had terrorised him all morning, and his ears were throbbing as he slid in beside her, kissing her slowly. Leaning back, he stretched out his legs, smiling. 'So much for spring. We may as well be in the depths of winter again!'

Gysa agreed, leaning against him, entwining her hand with his, though she didn't care either way. It wasn't what she wanted to talk about. 'There is a problem,' she said sweetly. 'Nothing to worry about, just a little... wrinkle in our plans.'

'Wrinkle?' Gudrum jerked forward with a frown, turning to her.

'Your friend, Jael Furyck... she... isn't coming.'

'What?' Gudrum's frown deepened, and now he released Gysa's hand. 'Not coming? I'd say that's more than a wrinkle!' he snapped. 'Not coming?' He was furious. 'Why not?'

Gysa shrugged. 'Oss' fort is warded against me. A clever dreamer has been working hard there. But I saw her on the beach, waving goodbye to her husband while she remained behind.'

Gudrum was flabbergasted, having known Jael since she was a girl. No one had been hungrier for a fight than her. Except him. 'I don't understand. Did your plan fail? Does she know the truth?'

Gysa wasn't sure. 'The fleet sailed. They left Oss.'

'Heading for where?'

But Gysa only snorted. 'For the sea!' she laughed. 'I don't know. When I have more information, I will share it.'

Gudrum grabbed the back of her neck, pulling her towards him until his lips were touching hers. 'Do you think this is a game for me? Just a little game?' he growled. 'But Jael Furyck is everything, as you yourself said, *Gysa*. You may be a powerful dreamer, but I am the king of this entire land. Displease me? Fail to serve me?' He shrugged, shoving her backwards. 'There are other dreamers.'

Gysa was furious, humiliated, her neck throbbing. She reached for it, shocked to think that only moments earlier, Gudrum had been kissing her with warmth in his voice and softness in his lips. This man was different in every way. She remained holding her neck, trembling with fear, which quickly turned to rage. 'There are most certainly other dreamers, though you will struggle to find anyone with my skills,' she snapped, every part of her on fire now. 'Alari gifted me sight greater than any dreamer in Alekka. With unrivalled power amongst those who follow her and –'

Gudrum cut her off with a bitter laugh, his eyes narrowed and full of threat. 'And? How does that help me? For now I have what? Her pointless husband? When I wanted *her*!' He stared at Gysa for a moment, who held his gaze, and then the tension left his face entirely, and his smile came back, broader than ever. 'Her husband,' he breathed, dropping his shoulders as everything became much more interesting. 'Jael Furyck's husband.'

***

By evening, no one was happy.

Everyone was unsettled, shooting nervous glances at the dreamers, wanting to know what was happening and what the strange noises were. Eddeth and Raf hurried into their tent, hoping to find the answers. A brazier burned, encircled by tree stumps, and Eddeth wobbled on one, picking her wart, trying to pull ideas out of the darkness.

Raf was just as lost, though one thing kept bothering her. 'If we can't see what's out there, that should tell us what it is. Not the noises,' she decided. 'But that we can't see anything.'

They heard the noises again, howls now, coming from every direction.

'Oh, but how will we sleep?' Eddeth cried in despair, ready to pull out her hair. Then she wheeled around to Raf. 'What was that? The thing you said? Something! It was something!'

'That we're locked out?'

'Oh, we are. Yes, we are!'

Raf turned to her, lifting her slumped shoulders. 'Which means it's not forest creatures. It's a dreamer.'

'Or a goddess,' Eddeth fretted. 'Could be a goddess.'

'I think it's Gysa,' Raf whispered, glancing over her shoulder at the flapping tent opening. 'Trying to help Gudrum. She'd want to frighten us, to slow us down.'

Eddeth sneezed, thoughts bursting in her mind like bright flashes of sunlight. 'Oh yes, she will! She's the king's dreamer. She won't want to lose her place by his side. The most powerful man in Alekka? Oh no, she'll do anything to cling to that, won't she? Which means she'll have to be working away at his enemy.'

Raf agreed, suddenly hungry. She could hear Eddeth's stomach rumbling; she could smell the rich tang of roasting meat in the air. 'But if we don't know what it is, what can we do?'

Eddeth shrugged, and though she, too, felt hungry, the answer was obvious. 'We must try and dream!'

CHAPTER TWENTY THREE

Gysa remained in her own tent that night, mostly in a daze.

Her servants had fussed around their mistress for a time, though she hadn't welcomed their interest in her, and eventually, they'd retreated to a corner, where they sat, whispering quietly to each other.

'My lady?' the youngest servant murmured, approaching the dreamer, who'd sat silently before the brazier for some time now. 'Shall we bring you some food? Or wine?' She had asked before, being sharply rebuffed, but time had passed since then, and so she dared to ask again.

Gysa swung around as though surprised to discover that she wasn't alone. 'Of course!' And then she was up, leaving the chair behind, stalking the furs and pelts spread over snow and grass. Hers was a luxurious tent with an inviting bed, though it was not Gudrum's bed, and that unsettled her. That he had turned on her so suddenly? So quickly?

So violently?

At first, she'd felt angry and vengeful, but now she just felt hurt.

Gudrum ducked his head, sweeping into the tent with a wink at the youngest servant, who reminded him of Raf, though this girl was a lot cleaner, and smiling. 'You're staying in here?' he growled, though there was humour in his eyes, Gysa saw as she turned around. 'Hiding?'

'I am not hiding, no. A dreamer must be alone to think. No visions will come if I am constantly engaged in chit chat.'

Gudrum laughed, hearing the coldness in her voice, seeing her stiffness. 'Chit chat? Is that what we do when we're alone?' He came towards her now, grasping her hand. 'Surely you're old enough not to act like a child, Dreamer? Sulking after being told off? Like a little girl?' He stepped closer, lifting her hand to his lips, kissing it softly, then leaning forward, he trailed his lips across her cheek, watching her eyes. 'What I want most of all is Jael Furyck's head. You were right about that. I had thought that meeting was years off. I knew I'd take revenge on the bitch one day, but when you showed me what was possible?' He shook his head. 'So after what you saw, I thought my chance had gone. Though it's better than I'd ever hoped for. It's perfect!' He kissed Gysa's lips now, seeing the surprise in her eyes before closing his own.

Gysa didn't kiss him back, standing before him like a statue. 'I'm no dog to be kicked when you're cross,' she said darkly, stepping away. 'I'm not that girl, Raf, either. If you want me by your side, you will show me respect. I demand it.'

Gudrum lifted an eyebrow, conscious of the three servants watching them. 'Demand it? Of a king?'

'A king of my making,' she reminded him. 'A king who will need me if he wishes to keep hold of his throne, if he seeks to defeat every one of his enemies. Your little ruse with the Islanders will falter without me.'

Gudrum knew that to be true, and though he felt a surge of anger at the presumption of the woman, he was also excited by her strength. She didn't cower in the face of his anger. She was everything he'd been looking for, every bit of fire and fury that he needed. 'Agreed,' he breathed, stepping towards her, hands open in supplication, a smile creeping across his face. 'I agree entirely.'

***

They had brought along a tent, which Jonas had managed to erect with help from Magnus. Alys and Lotta had gathered wood and set a fire inside a little circle of stones while Stina prepared a cold meal. She had thought it made sense to eat quickly rather than taking the time to prepare a stew or broth, though after such a cold, wet day on the road, she regretted not having attempted to make something hot.

Alys didn't care about food. She was exhausted, having barely slept the night before, sore and stiff from the long ride, too, and she crawled under her furs early, eager to close her eyes. She heard the children arguing over who would sleep with Puddle. In the end, Magnus kindly agreed that Lotta could, though Stina wanted to ensure that Lotta wasn't going to suffocate the puppy with too many furs.

'You'll keep that saddlebag between you and Puddle, won't you, Lotta?' she asked, though Lotta was fussing over the puppy and didn't turn around. 'I don't want you rolling onto him. He's weak. He probably wouldn't make enough noise to wake us up.' Stina yawned, doubting anything would wake her up. 'Lotta?'

'I will,' Lotta insisted, tucking Puddle in beside her. 'I will.'

They were the last words Alys heard. The next thing she knew, there was no tent, no children, no Puddle. She stood at the top of a flight of stairs, peering down into the darkness.

Alys hadn't liked the dark as a child, imagining that as she got older, her fears would lessen. And though she had her own children now, she still felt a tremor of terror when she blew out her lamp every night, listening to the odd creaks and groans of the cottage. The snuffles and snores, the wail of the wind, the rain on the roof were familiar sounds now, but the darkness?

Alys felt a desperate fear of it.

She heard voices, though that didn't encourage her to walk down those stairs. Something frightening waited down there, she was certain, so Alys turned away, only to be faced with the exact same flight of stairs again.

Everywhere she turned, only stairs.

Eventually, heart thumping, she started down them, every

footstep reluctant, every breath a smoky snake, soon trailing behind her. The voices had been muffled, unfamiliar, though as she approached, she recognised them both: her grandmother, Eida, and Mirella, her mother.

Now she stopped, fearing what was coming. Turning back, she looked for those stairs again, heart racing.

But they were gone.

'You are making a mistake, Mother,' Mirella hissed. 'Thinking you can stop any of this? But even the gods support Jorek. His grip on the throne is secure, his sons are by his side, his lords are loyal. I have seen it. He will hold onto the throne. Surely you've seen the same?'

Eida was incredulous. 'You support a family like that?'

'Your precious Thenor supports them!' Mirella snarled.

Alys stepped into the room, shocked to see how young Mirella looked; her hair a lighter blonde, tied back from a furious face.

'How would you know?' Eida taunted. 'You can't presume to know Thenor's mind!'

Mirella closed her mouth, turning away from her mother towards the great stone hearth, where she watched the flames for a moment before spinning back. 'I will not allow your interference,' she warned, her voice laced with threat now. 'My husband –'

'Your husband is an evil man, like his evil father, and you would support them both? I don't need to be a dreamer to see what he does to you, Mirella. It is all over your face!'

Mirella's face was quickly scowling as she reached a hand to her cheek, still lightly bruised. She had thought she'd covered it up, though her mother's eyes were as sharp as always. 'What Jesper does –'

'You can come back here,' Eida insisted, wanting to touch her daughter, hoping to see some small hint of the girl she'd once been. 'With us. We will protect you, Mirella. Keep you safe from all of them.'

Mirella's eyes almost softened, as though she believed it was possible, though they just as quickly hardened further. 'Jesper loves me, as I love him. I want nothing from you, Mother. You tried to force me into being someone I never was. You picked away at me, trying to turn me into the daughter you wanted. You couldn't let me be me!'

'Yet you chose me to raise your own daughter,' Eida reminded her. 'Why is that, Mirella? Because you feared what Jesper would do to her? What Jorek would do when he discovered his son had fathered a girl?'

Mirella hesitated, but not for long. 'It was a mistake. We weren't married, but now that's all changed. I want Alys to come with me. She's not a baby. They will not hurt her.'

Alys gasped.

Eida nearly fell forward, her legs trembling. 'What?'

'She's my daughter, mine to care for. You have raised her well, I'm sure, but she was never destined to be with you forever, Mother. I just needed time –'

'No.' Eida glanced over her shoulder at the stairs. When she'd seen that Mirella would come, she had sent Alys to hide under her bed, making her promise to stay out of sight. To keep quiet as a mouse and not to come out, no matter what she heard. No matter what happened.

Alys remembered hiding under that bed in the dark, fearing it would collapse on top of her.

'You can't keep me from my own daughter!' Mirella growled. 'Why would you? You're not a cruel woman. You're not. You wouldn't keep a mother from her only child!'

Eida straightened her shoulders, pushing her boots against the floorboards. 'I will do everything in my power to keep Alys away from you, Mirella. When you gave her to me, you were lost. Lost, but there was still enough of you in there to know the right thing to do. Now, though...' Eida shook her head, strands of golden hair escaping a loose bun. 'Now you aren't there at all. My daughter is gone. You are Alari's, you are The Following's, you are not my Mirella!' Tears ran down her cheeks, fear throbbing in her chest.

Mirella eyed the stairs herself, seeing a glimpse of the girl hiding beneath the bed. 'She is mine.'

'She was never yours! And if you have any heart left, you will not take her to that family. They will destroy her. *You* will destroy her! She is...' Eida's tears flowed with greater force now. 'She is mine. Mine and Jonas' to care for. And we have. And we will. You cannot have her!'

'Get out of my way,' Mirella warned. 'Do not try to stop me.'

Alys panicked, fears rising. The angry voices swam around her until she couldn't move, imprisoning her, forcing her to watch. She couldn't even close her eyes against what she knew was coming.

She remembered hearing this. She didn't want to see it.

Eida was trying to block the stairs, Mirella trying to get past her.

They tussled.

It wasn't magic, Alys realised, watching in horror. Since she'd discovered the truth about her past, she had always assumed it had been magic.

Mirella was wild with anger before her, seeking some form of control in a life very much out of control. 'You will not stop me!' she screamed, pushing her mother out of the way. And turning to the stairs, she heard an odd noise, a heavy thud, a cry almost impossible to discern. She spun back with horror in her eyes, seeing her collapsed mother, eyes open, head bleeding on the stone hearth.

Tears streamed down Alys' cheeks as she watched.

Mirella ran to Eida, dropping to her side, lifting her head, cradling it in her lap. 'No!' she sobbed. 'You can't die! No! Mother! No, please! *Mother*!'

Alys wanted to turn away. The pain was new and fresh, grief tearing her apart. She saw the woman who had loved her and the woman who had abandoned her.

She felt Mirella's pain as she wept over her dead mother.

'Why?' Mirella cried, rocking back and forth, the blood leaking from Eida's head soaking her dress, flooding the floorboards.

Alys finally managed to close her eyes, and when she opened them, she was standing by her bed, listening to the whimpering girl beneath it, and then footsteps, coming up the stairs. She froze, expecting to see Mirella, but instead, she saw Thenor.

'Come, Alys,' he said, reaching out a hand. 'There is much we have to discuss.'

***

After what felt like hours, Reinar gave up on sleeping, and throwing on his fur cloak, he headed to the nearest fire, where his father sat, prodding the flames with a long, charred stick. 'Didn't know you were on watch. No need to be. We've got enough men with us. I'm sure you could get a full night's sleep.'

Stellan grinned. 'Ha! Not sure when I last had one of those. Not even when I was stuck in that stupor. My legs twitch, my mind jumps, memories lurching out of the darkness. Better to have something to do, and there's no wall for me to walk anymore, so I thought I may as well come out here and keep an ear out.'

'For those noises, you mean?'

Stellan nodded. 'I kept thinking something would pounce on us today. They seemed to be getting closer for a while, whatever they were. It's unsettling not to feel the ground beneath my feet. Nothing makes sense to me since Hector came to Ottby, since Ake died. I don't recognise this Alekka.'

Reinar took a seat on the log opposite his father. 'No, and Slussfall isn't home. I don't want to run back there if it all goes wrong. I want to go to Ottby.'

Stellan sighed sadly, missing the old fort as much as his son. 'Though home for you will hopefully soon be Stornas. It's what Ake wanted for you. What I want too. Leave Ottby to me. It's too small for a man like you.'

Reinar remained unconvinced. 'I don't feel worthy of commanding a pebble, let alone a kingdom,' he admitted, eyes searching the flames. His father despised weakness, Reinar knew, so he'd been reluctant to admit it, though he'd felt it for some time. He had grown up seeing Ake Bluefinn as a hero, akin to a god, and now to try and fill his place? To sit on his throne and wear his crown?

Reinar wasn't sure he'd ever feel worthy.

Stellan smiled at his son. 'Ake felt the same. I felt the same, too, just taking on Ottby. I didn't want the responsibility. I didn't think I'd stick at it, though I never told Ake that. He'd wanted to reward me, make me a lord, give me a great prize.' Stellan laughed, though it hurt his heart to think of his friend. 'He knew I didn't want it, but he also knew I'd be good at it, that I'd grow into it, and that it would grow on me. And it did. Took some time, mind, but eventually, Ottby became a part of me. Now it's the only place I want to be. Out on that wall, protecting my people.'

Reinar yawned. 'It's where you belong. I never felt right taking your place.'

'No, and you wouldn't because there's a different future waiting for you in Stornas. We both know that now. It won't be easy, but I'll be there every step of the way. Though it's you who has to defeat Gudrum. Only then can you proclaim yourself the true king.'

Reinar nodded. 'If Gudrum comes, and so far, there's no indication of what his plans are. And after his games in Orvala, I don't feel confident.'

Stellan looked around, hoping to see some sign of where a barrel of ale might be lurking. Or a handy servant. Though he saw only tents, heard only Vik's snores in the distance. Or perhaps that was Eddeth, he thought with a chuckle. He turned back. 'Gudrum will come. I'm no dreamer, but I feel it in my bones. It's what any lord would do, any man who calls himself king. You can't leave a rival out there. Any rival or enemy has to die. Gudrum won't make Ake's mistake.' It was hard to say but true, for Stellan knew that if he were here, Ake would have admitted it himself.

'I will kill Gudrum,' Reinar promised, though he saw Raf's vision in his mind, fearing that somewhere the Goddesses of Fate were laughing at him.

***

Gysa had been making plans for days, thinking of ways to disrupt the Vilanders. Though after how Gudrum had treated her, she doubted the wisdom of helping him at all. He was callous and cruel, ambitious and single-minded.

Though what was the alternative?

Alari had demanded that she help him. And after the generous gifts the goddess had bestowed upon her, there was little Gysa could do but continue. Though she did it with a twisted mouth and angry eyes.

She would help Gudrum Killi because it helped her.

She would help him by hurting his enemies.

***

Thenor took Alys into a forest. It was dark enough that she could barely see him. She felt afraid, not understanding what was happening.

'You have seen that Mirella had a heart once,' Thenor said, offering her a seat on a mossy boulder. 'She didn't mean to kill your grandmother. Eida had feared she might, but Mirella hadn't come to kill her. She had simply come for you. I often think of that moment, wondering what might have happened if Mirella hadn't made that choice. That reckless, violent choice.'

'What do you mean?'

'Perhaps, eventually, she would have returned to Eida and Jonas. To you.'

'But she was –'

'Mirella was still in there then. You saw that. She was a frightened woman trying to keep her husband happy. He hurt her and blamed her for not helping him and his father. She was bruised and scared, trying to offer him something, trying to find ways to get him to show her more warmth and caring.'

Alys blinked, unable to see Mirella that way.

'There were no children.'

She sat up straight.

'Mirella wouldn't risk it. She knew how to keep herself free of children. She didn't want to bring another Vettel into the world.'

'How do you know all of this? Why?'

'I watched the Vettels closely over the years, though I delayed my final judgement on their reign far longer than I should have. I had thought your mother would bring a change, especially once Jorek was overthrown by Ake, though Jesper crushed her, and Eida's death took what was left of her heart. After that, she hardened into the creature you met in Orvala. She has walked so far into the darkness now that there appears no way back.'

'But why didn't she take me with her? That day?'

'I suspect she saw the sense in what Eida had said, the truth in her words. The Vettels would have destroyed you and, yes, perhaps even killed you, for they had no desire for daughters. Instead, Mirella left you with a neighbour. Do you remember? She told you to go inside, though she didn't go with you.'

Alys didn't remember that. She was still too shocked to think much at all. 'But why are you showing me this now? I... don't understand.'

'She gave you something that day,' Thenor said. 'Do you still have it? A brooch. A silver crane eating a fish.'

Alys was stunned, not realising the brooch had come from Mirella. 'I... yes. I thought it was Eida's.'

Thenor looked pleased. 'No, it was Mirella's. When she left you outside the neighbour's house, she pressed it into your hand. I don't know why, but it's a way to her, and right now, Alys, we need a way to Mirella most urgently.' Thenor took a deep breath, taking her hand. 'There are many enemies, I know. I sense your desire to dream of Reinar and ways to help him, but whatever you may think of what will come to pass now, there is no greater threat to Alekka than Mirella Vettel.'

***

Gudrum lay in bed alone, thinking of dreamers. He thought of stiff and prim Mirella, wild and prickly Raf, and beautiful Gysa, with fire in her eyes and a body so soft and curvaceous that he felt breathless around her.

She had barely spoken to him all evening, returning to her own tent rather than lingering in his. It amused him to think that she could be so easily offended, and feeling a twinge of regret that his behaviour had caused him to be lying in bed alone, he sighed. Though getting distracted by women was never a good idea, he knew, once again revisiting his mistakes in Orvala.

Mirella had tricked him, and Raf had betrayed him, and Gysa...

Gudrum closed his eyes, thinking of her full lips, wondering what his newest dreamer would do for him.

Or, he frowned, wide awake now... to him?

***

Vik checked the horses.

It was hours before dawn, though he'd been woken by another of those strange cries, his weary mind trying to discern what it was and where it was coming from.

Ollo joined him, stretching his arms above his head. 'How's anyone supposed to sleep with that din?'

Vik imagined few were. It was the sort of sound that churned your guts. As though demons from the depths of Vasa's Cave were sweeping through the forest, warning of torture and death to come. It was one way to mess with their minds, he supposed. One way to keep them from sleeping, from being alert and ready for the battle ahead.

He turned to Ollo, squinting, and then he was running past him, looking for where he'd last seen Stellan talking to Reinar. Before he could reach them, though, someone screamed. And turning to glance over his shoulder, he saw Ollo down on his haunches, gripping his leg. Vik ran faster now, calling out, trying not to trip over barely revealed obstacles, though the dark camp was littered with unexpected traps, and soon he was down on his knees, biting his lip. 'Reinar! Stellan!' Back on his feet quickly, one sword drawn, Vik spun around as Berger rushed past him with Helgi, heading for Ollo.

'We're under attack!' Ollo panted, wanting to get the damn arrow out of his leg. Though looking down, he saw it was no arrow at all, just a small dart.

Berger pulled him to his feet. 'Leave it! We've got to get moving!'

Ollo agreed, and drawing his sword, he gritted his teeth, turning after them.

CHAPTER TWENTY FOUR

Raf shook Eddeth, who was muttering to herself between loud snores. She'd slept in her clothes and was fully dressed, trembling with both cold and fear as she stood over Eddeth's bed.

Eddeth didn't wake, so bending down, Raf shook her again, wondering if she should slap her face or yell in her ear. And then Eddeth sat bolt upright, smashing her head into Raf's, sending the little dreamer flying onto her arse.

'Ow!' Eddeth groaned, lifting both hands to her head, now ringing like a bell. 'Ow!'

Bright shards of light flashed before Raf's eyes, and she blinked as she pulled herself up on Eddeth's bed. 'We're under... attack!' she cried.

'What? Attack?' Eddeth almost fell out of bed, groaning at the stiffness of her hips after so much riding. Her legs were aching, too, and moaning and yelping, she found her way to her cloak and staff, tugging on her boots.

They could hear screams of surprise and confusion in the distance.

That howling cry again too.

Eddeth picked up her staff, feeling a sense of certainty in the darkness. 'That dreamer's got a hand in this, wouldn't you say? We can't see at all! Not with our minds or our eyes!'

'But we need to! We need to do something!' Raf felt afraid, turning as the tent started blowing around them, hearing those screams coming closer.

And then Raf was screaming as an axe-wielding creature rushed inside, lunging for her.

***

Reinar ran through the camp, trying to decide what was happening. They were under attack but was it Gudrum? The Ennorians? Those guarding the perimeter hadn't raised a warning, the dreamers hadn't either, leaving Reinar to wonder if magic was at work. He'd retrieved his shield and was now brandishing *Corpse Splitter* as he ran into the night. 'Shield walls!' he shouted, though hearing Eddeth's panicked screeching in the distance, he quickly realised that their enemy was already inside the camp.

And then it was his father crying out beside him as a small black-eyed creature flew out of a tent, springing up at Stellan like a cat. Clinging on with long fingernails as sharp as claws, it aimed its pointed teeth at Stellan's neck.

'No!' Reinar bellowed, raising his sword.

But Helgi Eivin beat him to it, flicking two small knives through the air, taking the creature in the neck. With a high-pitched squeal, it dropped onto its back, immediately flipping over, and now on all fours, it ran at Helgi with surprising speed until, drawing his sword, he lopped off its head.

'They're fjaladen!' Reinar roared, certain in his assumptions now. 'Cut off their heads!'

Stellan shook his own head beside him, forcing away the pain. 'No shield walls! We need to get after them!'

Reinar agreed. 'Kill them!' he ordered. 'More fires! We need to see!' There was no time to even look at the moon, but Reinar sensed it was lost behind clouds now, obscuring their vision further.

Ludo came running up to him, bleeding from the neck. 'I'll get the dreamers!'

'They'll need a fire! Help them, Ludo!' Reinar called, heart thumping as he ran after his father, calling his sleeping men from their tents.

***

Despite the viciousness of the fang-toothed fjaladen, Eddeth felt hesitant to hurt it, for the snarling little creature was the size of a child. She held her staff in two hands, trying to keep it at bay. But Raf had heard Reinar's screamed orders, and though she only had her eating knife to hand, she was working hard to kill it.

The fjaladen cried plaintively as Raf stabbed it in the back. Its eyes were big and black, moist with liquid as it stared up at Eddeth in misery. Eddeth drew one hand away from her staff, reaching it to the creature, who immediately dropped down onto all fours and sprang up at Eddeth, taking her hand in its mouth. She shrieked, dropping her staff, swinging both her and the creature around in a frantic circle, the fjaladen's fangs digging into her hand. Dropping low, Raf scooped up the staff, cracking it across the back of the creature's head. It didn't react, so she hit it again and again until eventually, the fjaladen dropped Eddeth's hand and spun for Raf. Though Ludo burst into the tent, sword out, and swinging at the howling creature, he sent its head flying into the tent wall.

Eddeth staggered, slightly dazed, her trembling hand dripping blood. She stared up at Ludo, who was already heading out of the tent.

'You need to come to the fire. We need to see. *You* need to see!' Ludo called, disappearing outside.

But ignoring him, a bleeding Eddeth bent over, and taking her staff back from Raf, she gently prodded the headless fjaladen. 'Poor little thing.'

'No time for that!' Raf growled, grabbing her arm. 'Come on!'

***

Stellan spun away from Vik, taking a creature in the neck, though he soon felt little hands around his own neck, claws piercing flesh, and he threw himself forward, trying to loosen its hold. The creature clung on, its claws digging in deeper, and now Stellan screamed until his ears rang with the sound of his own pain.

Vik couldn't reach him. He had both swords out, whipping them around at a cluster of pouncing, biting fjaladen. He was surrounded, seeing no way through, but Bjarni was there, quickly sheathing his sword. And with two hands, he grabbed Stellan's attacker by the hair, tugging until its claws released. It flew through the air like a sack, tumbling with a screaming crash of flames and sparks into the nearest fire. Trapped there, flames licking its body, the fjaladen burned alive.

'Fire arrows!' Stellan called, spinning around to Bjarni, who didn't hesitate, charging off towards their supply sleighs.

Reinar was felled by two creatures, one who'd jumped onto his back, while another pulled at his legs until he was face down in the slush. Rolling with speed, Reinar headbutted the black-eyed fjaladen, now trying to chew off his ear. And as it released its hold on him, squealing and slightly dazed, he sat up, spearing the one crawling up his legs with his sword. They were deadly creatures but thankfully light, and Reinar was up on his feet quickly, the impaled fjaladen dangling from his blade. He drove it down into the earth, and pulling out his sword, he chopped off its head.

Ludo ran past him with a handful of archers, who formed around the camp's largest fire. It bloomed in a circle of rocks in the centre of the tents, the perfect place to gather everyone together. And now, as those archers took up their positions, Bjarni came running back carrying an armload of fire arrows. Dropping them to the ground, he started handing them out, and before long, the archers were setting the fjaladen alight.

***

Her reluctance to help Gudrum had made Gysa hesitant, but the thrill of the fjaladen spell had her body tingling as she sought to do real damage to Reinar Vilander's army.

She'd sent her servants from the tent, wanting no word of what she was doing relayed to Gudrum or his ever-present shadow, Edrik. Her help, Alari had warned, would need to be discreet, for she could see what Gudrum was truly about. She hadn't been wrong, Gysa realised with a snort, and then her focus sharpened.

She had stoked the brazier, watching dark orange and red flames rising out of its iron cage. And smiling now, Gysa lifted her hand up high, clasping a bone. She held it there as she chanted, the symbols etched along the bone's edge glowing white. She felt the heat of the flames on her arm as they twisted higher, almost touching the bone. And then, opening her fingers, Gysa let it fall into the fire, sparks flying, the high pitched howl of an animal rising into the air.

***

Eddeth and Raf headed towards the central fire, slipping between the archers, relieved to have some protection and light as they got to work.

Eddeth hung over the fire, struggling to breathe. Visions came to her like great drops of rain, a deluge of images that had her unable to move forward. Her hand throbbed, blood dripping onto the flames, though there was no time to see to it. She had to do something to stop the attack.

Raf couldn't see anything herself, blinded by panic and noise. The archers were spearing the attacking fjaladen with their fire arrows, sending them wailing and flaming around the camp. And quickly seeing the threat those arrows posed, some of the creatures started attacking the archers. Crawling along the ground, they sought to escape the burning arrows, blowing darts at the archers' legs. Others jumped onto boulders, flinging rocks with great force, aiming for heads.

'They.... h-h-have....' Eddeth stammered, and then she was down, falling onto her knees, struck in the head by a rock.

Raf spun around, unable to see through the wall of archers, though some were now screaming, falling away. '*Eddeth*!' Dropping to the ground, Raf touched her shoulder. 'Are you alright?'

'Aim for their heads!' Ludo bellowed. And then he was crying out, too, struck in the neck, almost losing his footing.

'Eddeth?' Raf moved around to face the dreamer, gripping her hands, trying to get her back on her feet. 'We have to do something!'

The pain in her head had caused even more confusion for Eddeth. Ominous noises swelled around her until she felt as though hands were squeezing all the air from her lungs. She kneeled in cold snow, trying to think, and then she did see a pair of hands around Raf's neck; dirty little hands, squeezing hard, claws glinting in a rare burst of moonlight. 'No!' she yelled as Raf was pulled away from her, dragged through the circle of archers, kicking and screaming, scraping along the ground.

***

After returning from her journey, Valera had taken Sigurd deep into Gallabrok's extensive forests, showing him to a tiny grove wrapped around a pool of water. It bubbled soothingly, fed by a natural spring running down from the mountains. She had spent some time with him, showing him how the pool could reveal what was happening in the realm of the humans. She had brought that water to life herself, in the same way Thenor could turn Hyvari into a window. And Sigurd had seen Slussfall and then Stornas. He'd even seen Ottby. Valera hadn't shown him his brother or his father, though, which unsettled him. So when she'd sat back, encouraging him to try on his own, Sigurd had fixed his mind on Reinar, wanting to see where he was. Though the water wouldn't yield to his demands. And eventually, he'd convinced Valera to show him herself.

What he saw had him in a panic.

'Send me there!' he demanded, eyes on the fjaladen attack. 'You can do it!' He wore his cloak, *Fire Song* tucked beneath it, nestled in her scabbard.

'Thenor wouldn't allow it,' Valera insisted. 'Eddeth and Raf will help your brother.' She ran her hands over the matching silver bracelets clasped around her wrists. 'I...' And now Valera closed her eyes, knowing her father would likely be less angry at a little interference on her part. 'I can guide them. Just... give me a moment.'

Sigurd watched impatiently as Valera opened her eyes, and with the sweep of a hand, she closed the trees around the grove, moving them closer and closer together until they were locked within a dark circle.

***

Vik fought back to back with Ollo, who was struggling to put down a dark-haired fjaladen with a hideous gash through its mouth. The creature held a long chain attached to its ankle, and swinging, it hit Ollo repeatedly.

Vik was fighting off two hissing fjaladen. They fought with claws, slashing viciously, ducking every blow he tried to land. He attacked with both swords, aiming for their heads, though they moved with speed, slipping under his blades, launching themselves at him.

'Aarrghh!' Ollo howled, the chain slapping his knees. 'You little witch!' And dropping his sword, he grabbed the chain in both hands, yanking the creature forward. It started crying, a wail so piercing and loud that Ollo almost let go of the chain. He wanted to put his hands over his ears, to make the noise stop, though he knew it wouldn't stop until he killed it.

'Ollo!' Vik shouted, and glancing over his shoulder, he saw that Ollo had the screeching fjaladen's chain, though no sword. He wheeled away from his attackers, who clung to him like leeches. 'Duck!' And swinging backhanded, Vik took off the crying fjaladen's head. He was immediately hit in the back of his own head, falling onto his knees, just keeping hold of his swords.

Ollo quickly retrieved his dropped sword, ears still echoing with that howl, taking one creature in the neck. Chopping once wasn't enough to sever its head, though, so he drew back his sword again, and with a yell, he sent it flying into the night.

The remaining fjaladen looked at Ollo, then Vik, both men panting and bloody-faced before it. And leaping up, using its claws to climb, it sunk its fangs into Vik's neck.

***

Eddeth bounded after Raf, head down, drawing little notice from the attacking creatures. Over the cacophony of terror, she heard a breathy voice in her ears, though she couldn't make out who it was. Raf was screaming before her, and then Berger and Helgi were there, Berger swinging at Raf's abductor, Helgi pulling the little dreamer to safety.

Back on her feet, a dishevelled Raf immediately looked to Eddeth. 'We have to get back to the fire!' And seeing that Eddeth had turned her head away, she raised her voice. 'Eddeth?'

Berger looked cross. 'Eddeth! Do not make me throw you over my shoulder!'

Eddeth ignored him, closing her eyes, trying to hear that voice.

'*Eddeth*!' Raf pleaded.

But Eddeth held up a hand, and Berger's attention was immediately diverted to Helgi, who'd been knocked over by a chain-swinging fjaladen.

'Raf!' he cried, turning away. 'Watch Eddeth!'

Raf didn't even nod, too terrified to move as swarms of black-eyed creatures swept through the camp, at first like shadows, calling their mournful song, and then running and snarling, searching for prey. She saw filthy faces, broken chains around ankles and wrists, hair matted, hanging over big eyes, and those gleaming claw-like fingernails most of all.

Berger was quickly surrounded as he pulled Helgi back to his feet, sword wobbling in his hand as a creature jumped onto his back, biting his shoulder. He felt a dart pierce his skin, and clamping his hand around his neck, he yanked it out. His legs buckled, and with his next breath, he fell onto his knees, toppling face first into the snow.

Helgi wheeled around, grabbing a spitting fjaladen. With a growl, he wrung its neck, throwing it away, and rushing to Berger's side, he tried to see what had happened to his cousin.

Reinar ran towards them, quickly staggering to a stop. He saw Eddeth with her eyes closed beside a screaming Raf. Helgi was yelling over a collapsed Berger, who showed no sign of moving.

Stellan joined him with Ollo and Vik.

'What the...' Ollo's mouth fell open. 'Who's that?'

Reinar lifted his eyes to see a taller fjaladen in the distance, holding its arms out from either side of a gaunt frame. Unlike the rest, its head was shaved. It wore no weapons, carried no rocks or darts, though it didn't need to, for it was flanked by six white forest cats. They growled menacingly, heads bowed, teeth bared.

'Their leader,' Raf said. 'I can hear him calling to them.' She turned around, seeing the smaller fjaladen lifting their dirty faces. And soon they were creeping forward, eyes fixed on their leader. She saw Eddeth, lips moving as she turned around, staff in hand.

'I can stop them!' Eddeth promised with a croak as Valera's

voice faded. 'I can!'

'Surround the dreamers!' Reinar ordered. 'Shield wall!' He quickly moved out in front, his father on his right, Vik on his left. Helgi dragged his unconscious cousin into the circle as more shield-bearing warriors joined it, leaving him at Raf's feet.

'What do we do?' Raf wanted to know, urgent puffs of cold breath wrapping white clouds around them both. 'Eddeth?'

But Eddeth spun away, for she could hear the cats coming.

***

'Can Eddeth do it?' Sigurd wanted to know, gripping Valera's arm, the rush of leaves becoming a crackling hum around them. 'She's... Eddeth.'

'And a skilled dreamer, who only needs to believe in herself a little more,' Valera said calmly. 'But hush now. I must guide her.' And though her eyes were closed, she felt Sigurd almost jumping with impatience as he peered into the pool of water beside her, watching Reinar and his men trying to fend off the fjaladen and their giant cats.

***

Gysa's delight filled her like a goblet of good wine. She felt a deep warmth radiating from her chest, down her arms, pulsing in her fingers as she watched the flames. Fear and panic were a tonic for her fractured mood. The palpable terror of Gudrum's enemies as they tried to escape certain death had lifted her spirits. She smiled, knowing that every enemy she defeated was one less to stand in Gudrum's way. And though she wasn't quite ready to forgive her king yet, she knew that helping him was the only way forward.

The only path she wished to take.

***

'They were abandoned by families who didn't want them, who couldn't feed them, who left them out, left them to die,' Eddeth explained as she quickly carved three symbols onto the mostly bare end of her staff. 'And when they were dead, Vasa claimed them. She keeps them in the forest. They are hers. Ow!' Knocked into by Vik, as he fought off one of the growling cats, she fell against Raf, who steadied her. 'Hold onto me now. I must finish!'

'Hurry, Eddeth!' Stellan urged, taken on the arm by a snarling cat. 'Aarrghh!' The cat's long fangs pierced his leather arm guard, driving into his skin. Reinar was there, though, smashing his shield boss at the cat's face, following it up with a jab of his blade. The cat, impaled and disoriented, loosened its hold on Stellan, who stumbled away, shaking his left arm, bringing up his sword before the next cat could get anywhere near him.

Eddeth flung up her head, poking her staff through the huddle of men. 'Let me out!' she blustered, elbows working to clear a path.

Raf was close behind her, Berger's knife gripped firmly in her right hand. She glanced down at Berger, who still hadn't moved, though there was no time to help him now. She slipped through the circle after Eddeth, breath trapped in her throat, body quaking in fear.

Eddeth ran her fingers over the knobbly end of the staff, bringing the protective symbols to life, and banging the staff onto the ground, she hurried to draw a small circle around her and Raf. 'We're safe in here!' she called to Reinar, catching a glimpse of Ollo's bulging eyes as he was knocked onto his stomach by a jumping cat.

Reinar wished the rest of them were. Vik went down, teeth

clamped around his ankle. Helgi was trying to protect Berger. Stellan had two cats on him. Ollo had scrambled back onto his knees, fighting off the cat, though a fjaladen blew a dart at him, immediately knocking him unconscious.

The noise swirled like water, and Eddeth tricked herself into believing that she was standing on a beach, listening to the rhythmic flow of waves. They rippled in warm sunlight, surging towards her. She could feel the sand, wet and grainy, between her toes, the sunbeams on her face.

The noise was water, peaceful, soothing water.

And she was safe.

Now she brought her staff into the air, aiming it at the fjaladen leader, for it commanded all the creatures and every one of those wild forest cats. 'You will return home now,' Eddeth breathed, as though he stood immediately before her, instead of far in the distance, aggravating the chaos from a boulder. 'Home, where you are safe. Back to your caves, where food and light await you. Home. It is time for you to go home.' She repeated the last word again and again. It was, at first, a suggestion, her tone light and warm, and then an order, firm and direct, like a stern mother telling off a child.

Eddeth started chanting the words Valera had whispered in her ear, knowing that she had to keep steady. She couldn't fall now.

Steady, toes in sand. Steady.

Water, rushing back and forth. Soothing, calm water.

Eddeth banged the staff onto the ground, one, two, three times, then pointed it at the fjaladen leader, seeing those newly carved symbols, now glowing blue like Valera's walls.

This was Valera's magic, Eddeth knew, and her confidence rose as she saw that blue light burst from her staff, shooting into the darkness. It hit the fjaladen leader in the chest, exploding in a sudden flash so intense in its brightness that Eddeth had to shield her eyes. She held her ground, though, feeling Raf behind her, pressing a hand to her back, keeping her in place.

And then the light was gone, and Eddeth lost her balance, tumbling forward, the darkness around her complete, the camp falling silent.

Everything stopped for a moment, and Eddeth lifted her head, glancing around, amazed to see that all the creatures were gone.

***

Sigurd held his breath.

Eventually, Valera opened her eyes, sweeping a hand over the pool. Its water stilled again, the moonlight casting an icy sheen over its surface.

'Eddeth,' Sigurd said at last. 'Did that?'

Valera smiled, though she felt uneasy, fearing what Thenor would say upon his return. 'Yes. It has always been within her, but fear can be like a mountain some are too afraid to climb. Though Eddeth is growing stronger. She sent those creatures away. They are gone now.'

Sigurd's relief quickly gave way to worry. 'But now Reinar has to fight Gudrum with fewer men. Injured men too.'

Valera nodded gravely. 'Though there has never been an easy path for the one who wishes to be king.'

Sigurd's laugh was bitter. 'Seems to me Gudrum strolled up to Stornas and helped himself to the throne, thanks to a vengeful dreamer and a bit of luck. He wears that crown as though he's worthy, but he's not even Alekkan, not Ake's heir, nothing more than a lucky prick. And you think his path was difficult?' Though Sigurd wasn't mad at Valera. He was mad at Thenor and the gods who removed themselves from everything that mattered to Alekka's future.

They picked and chose how and when to involve themselves.

That magical line moved at Thenor's command.

He sighed. 'What will they try next? Vasa? Alari? Gudrum's dreamer?'

Valera felt concerned, though she didn't want to worry Sigurd further. 'I expect Gudrum will want a real victory, not some contrived dreamer spell. He will fight Reinar himself. I'm certain of it.'

Sigurd hoped so.

He wanted to watch his brother kill that grinning shit.

CHAPTER TWENTY FIVE

Reinar retched into snow-covered leaves. He was doubled over in the trees, needing a moment to catch his breath. A lack of sleep and the shock of the attack had him feeling rattled. He'd been struck by one of the darts, too, and his stomach still twisted in painful knots.

Bjarni came back from the latrines, tying up his belt. 'You alright?' he asked, patting Reinar on the back, listening to him retch some more.

'Fine,' Reinar sighed eventually, straightening up with a wipe of his blonde beard. 'Better than some,' he added, seeing the worry in Bjarni's eyes. 'I should have known. We don't tend to have much luck in forests these days.'

Bjarni dropped down onto a log, wanting to catch his own breath. He shook his head. 'Those creatures were no bigger than children.'

'But they weren't,' Reinar said, joining him. 'Keep hold of that, Bjarni. We weren't killing children.'

Bjarni nodded. 'Mmmm, and thanks to Eddeth, they didn't kill us.'

'Have you seen Berger?'

'Back there, shitting himself silly. Whatever was in those darts was potent. Ollo's with him. Doubt we'll see them for some time.'

Reinar grinned, though his eyes remained blank. He felt fear, knowing he had fewer men than before, worried that his dreamers weren't as powerful as the one they were facing. Though remembering how Eddeth had saved them from even worse carnage, his smile grew, sparking a hint of hope in his eyes. 'We'd better get moving then, have something to eat.'

Bjarni looked at him in horror. 'Eat?' He blew out a long breath, though his mind immediately turned to thoughts of breakfast, wondering if there was any bacon.

***

Alys woke up late, surprised that everyone was already packing to leave. She emerged from the tent with squinting eyes, feeling as though her head was stuffed with straw.

'She lives!' Jonas called from where he was preparing the horses. 'Thought you might be trapped in a dream. Stina said we may just have to throw you over your horse and get going!'

Alys peered at him, wrapped in her bed fur, eyes on the children, who briefly looked her way before turning their attention back to Puddle. The puppy was on his feet, drinking from a trencher of water, and the children were discussing what they might give him to eat.

Stina rushed towards her with a bowl of porridge. 'It's cold, I'm afraid, but you'll need something in your belly for the ride.' The fire was still burning, so she set the bowl down on a log before it, hurrying into the tent. 'We have to get moving!'

Alys nodded, though she stayed where she was.

Stina poked her head outside. 'Did you see anything in your dreams?' She'd had a worrying dream about Ludo and had slept fitfully after that.

Alys blinked, remembering exactly what she'd seen in her dreams. She dropped her head, fiddling with her purse. 'Nothing, no.' Though she'd sounded so unconvincing that she looked up. 'I had other dreams last night. About my grandmother,' she explained quietly, not wanting Jonas to hear. 'It was nothing about the army, I promise.'

'Oh.' And with disappointment in her eyes and a forced smile on her face, Stina ducked back into the tent.

Alys left her to see Puddle, who trotted towards her with a wiggling body and a wagging tail. 'Hello, there,' she smiled, bending down, preparing to be licked, though the puppy sat down and then lay down altogether. Trying not to feel worried, Alys turned to her daughter. 'Lotta, do you still have that brooch I gave you?'

'The snake one?'

Alys stared at her daughter, whose mouth was full of porridge. 'Snake? No, it was a crane.'

Lotta shook her head with great certainty. 'It's a snake,' she insisted. And handing the empty trencher to her mother, Lotta opened her purse and stuck a sticky hand inside, ferreting around for some time, eventually pulling out a tarnished silver brooch. 'See!'

Alys took the brooch, clearly seeing the crane, but for the first time since she'd given it to Lotta, she saw that there was indeed a snake. It curled around the crane's body, trapping it, crushing it.

Alys wrapped cold fingers around the brooch, smiling at her daughter, who quickly turned back to Puddle. 'I'll keep it now.'

***

There were many injured to attend to, so there was no point rushing through breakfast, though few had much of an appetite. Especially not Berger and Ollo, who sat by the fire opposite the dreamers, wiping their beards, occasionally spitting.

'I can still hear those chains,' Helgi said, carrying a jug of ale and a stack of cups towards them. 'Scraping along the ground.' He shuddered.

'Who knew children could be so terrifying?' Ollo snorted. He couldn't feel his leg where the poisoned dart had struck him. It was entirely numb, though every other part of him throbbed. He'd been knocked down, scratched by the forest cats, slapped with chains, had rocks launched at every part of him. He felt ready for his pyre. Though, he realised, as the pile of bodies grew behind him, he was one of the lucky ones. He glanced at a sneezing Eddeth Nagel, who had the most annoying way of saving his life.

He wasn't sure why he kept forgetting that.

Sniffing, he looked around, wondering where Ilene was.

'They weren't children,' Eddeth reminded him, digging out another spoonful of porridge. She was starving, already onto her second bowl. 'When they died, they became something else, something evil, thanks to Vasa. She has many creatures, none of them pleasant.'

'But why did they attack us? Did Vasa send them?' Ollo wondered, taking a cup of ale from Helgi.

'No idea!' Eddeth grinned, relief thumping like a drum inside her body. Relief that she hadn't made a mess of everything. She lifted her head, then quickly lowered it, realising that she hadn't seen what was coming. Both her and Raf were here to prevent disaster, to help Reinar and his men overcome Gudrum. And eyes drifting to the mounds of bodies, and ears open to the cries of pain, she sighed, feeling as helpless as ever. 'But whoever sent them was trying to frighten us. Frighten us and then kill us!' She stood with a weary groan. 'I must get back to the injured. Raf, you stay and finish your ale.' She spun around with another sneeze before bounding away, staff in hand.

'She's a useful woman,' Helgi noted, watching Eddeth go. 'Worth standing near if something like that happens again.'

Berger nodded, only half awake. Eddeth had given both him and Ollo something for the poison, but it felt as though it was still flowing through his veins. He felt confused, his limbs resting heavily upon the log. He thought about heading into the forest again but feared he didn't have the energy.

'Eddeth said you need to drink water,' Raf muttered. 'To rid yourself of the poison. To piss it away.'

Ollo laughed. 'Well, water, ale, it's all the same.' And ignoring Raf's frown of disapproval, he poured the contents of the cup into his mouth.

Reinar joined them, looking impatient. 'We've got to get going before the sun reaches its peak. Help me get the injured into the sleighs.' It had been a difficult decision – whether to bring sleighs or wagons – for though the first hints of spring had been in the air when they'd departed Slussfall, Reinar knew it would likely be a month before the snow was fully gone. And even then, it could often return. Now, though, when he looked at the ground, more earth than snow, he knew the poor horses were going to have a hard journey. The morning was cold but not icy, and no snow had fallen overnight. 'We need to leave!' he called, eyes on the dead, knowing he had to see to them quickly. 'Wherever Gudrum's lurking, if he's got his dreamer by his side, he's already celebrating his first victory. We can't afford to let him have any more!'

***

Gudrum Killi ate a breakfast fit for a king, though he was thoughtful, remembering Hector, whose charred bones he'd left back in Stornas, stuffed in a box.

It could all end so quickly.

That was the lesson he would take from that surprising turn of events.

It could all end in the blink of an eye.

'I was surprised you didn't return to my tent last night,' he said between mouthfuls of smoked pork and onions. He was taking his time, savouring each bite, resisting the urge to get his men moving again. They had marched in the dark, led to a sheltered clearing by Edrik, whose extensive knowledge of Alekka was proving useful.

Gysa glowed before him. The sun was out, and though the light streaking through clumps of clouds was weak, she shone in it like a radiant goddess. All thoughts of his displeasure at her were gone, and Gudrum stared, transfixed.

'I had work to do,' was all she would say. 'You and your men might sharpen your weapons and train, but dreamers must prepare too. There is always something to do. I cannot simply entertain you every night, my king. Surely that is what the servants are for?' She offered a small smile now, carving off a generous wedge of cheese. It was pungent and ripe, and she added it to the flatbread she had cut in half and filled with hard-boiled eggs.

'Though I have no servant to compare to you,' Gudrum grinned, knowing that to be true. 'No reason to settle for second best, either. Do your work during the day. At night, please your king.' His eyes were full of mischief, for he felt confident sitting in his chair, at his table, in his tent, with his dreamer. Servants bustled in and out, following his sharp-tongued steward's orders. He saw his armour laid out on the bed beside a fresh tunic and trousers. His boots sat together on the floor of furs, polished until their dark leather gleamed.

Gudrum had nothing to do but eat and admire the serene loveliness of the simmering woman sitting opposite him.

Gysa finally put down her flatbread, offering him her full attention. It was impossible to forget how he'd behaved, though she had to. She did. It was her job to protect him for Alari, and though she felt more inclined to throw something at him, it wouldn't serve her to cause problems now. 'Well, I wouldn't dare disobey a king,' Gysa purred, forcing a smile as Gudrum reached out a hand to stroke hers.

'And what did you do last night? Something to amuse yourself?'

Now Gysa's smile was genuine, for though that Eddeth woman had put a stop to her fun, she'd managed to turn Reinar Vilander's camp upside down. 'Yes,' she breathed happily. 'I did.'

***

It was nearly midday before Reinar got his men back on the road, and despite the size of the army, there was little noise. Even the horses were oddly quiet. Most were on edge, watching the trees, ears open, eyes alert. Stellan knew he needed to stay ahead of whatever trouble awaited them next, though he rode on one side of Reinar, often feeling his eyes closing. Then Eddeth would sneeze behind him, and he would blink, reminding himself that danger didn't only lurk in the dark.

'We should talk about what will come next,' Reinar decided, happy to have experienced men like his father and Vik flanking him. 'We can't worry about goddesses and dreamers, for that will only distract us from Gudrum and whatever he's planning.' Magic was disruptive, destructive, and there were more powerful dreamers than Raf and Eddeth in the wind now. He couldn't expect his dreamers to see everything coming their way. They would work to stop whatever tried to stop them as best they could, but it was what they could do to stop their real enemy that Reinar wanted to focus on.

Riga snorted, black mane flashing, once again irritated by the plodding pace. He liked to be given his head, set free to run fast, though here, walking through the forest, there was nothing to do but keep a steady pace for those following behind. He flicked his head once more, inviting a pat from Reinar, who turned to his sighing father.

'Well, we're at more of a disadvantage than ever. Not just less men but injured men, and, worst of all, frightened men.' He inclined his head towards his son. 'It's hard to command frightened men. They're likely to turn and run if given a chance. Or simply freeze and be no use at all.'

Reinar didn't react.

So Vik spoke. 'There's no denying that's true. It's hard to be brave in the face of what you can't explain. Fjaladen? Enchanted cats? Dark magic?' Vik felt unsettled himself, head snapping around at every sound, wanting to ascertain if it was nature or something more sinister. Sunlight leaked through endlessly grey clouds, though it wasn't warm, and they shivered as they rode, the wind a constant reminder of the lingering winter.

Stellan turned in the saddle, smiling at Raf, who rode between Ludo and Bjarni. 'Well, there's none braver than those dreamers. We're lucky to have them with us. Both of them,' he said loudly, turning back around.

Raf heard him, and feeling herself flushing in surprise, she didn't know where to look, though Rofni was quickly demanding her attention, attempting to nip Ludo's horse.

'I think he's half-blind, that one,' Ludo decided, edging his horse away.

'Or hungry,' Bjarni put in, regretting that he hadn't eaten his fill of breakfast.

Raf didn't speak. She was happier on her feet, and it took some time to refocus Rofni back on the path.

'I thought we'd see Sigurd last night,' Bjarni mused, watching the dreamer. She hunched beneath her hood, inviting no conversation, revealing nothing about herself at all. 'When those cats came charging for us, I imagined Sigurd and his flaming sword fighting them off.' He frowned, remembering the last sighting he'd had of Sigurd. 'Though perhaps he's still a prisoner?'

Ludo looked worried. 'I wish we knew, but maybe it's a bad sign? He would have come if he'd been free. He would've tried to help us.'

Raf had nothing to say to reassure either man.

Alari had finally taken Sigurd Vilander, and Raf feared there was no way back for him now.

***

After he'd walked Valera back to Thenor's hall, Sigurd had returned to the quiet grove, remaining there for some time. It was a wonderfully private place – already his favourite in all of Gallabrok. The trees wrapped around the pool of water like walls, hiding him away. He'd thought about going to see Tulia, to talk over what had happened with the fjaladen, though he knew she didn't want to see him. That felt odd. He was stuck in Gallabrok until Alari was caught or killed, and now he'd alienated the one person whose company he enjoyed the most in the entire prison.

Sigurd knew that Thenor wouldn't have wanted Valera to help save Reinar. He wouldn't have wanted him to be in the grove, trying to spy on his brother. The gods, Thenor had warned him, were the caretakers of Alekka. Eutresia had made the mistake of favouring kings above all others, and Thenor was determined not to let that happen again. Though Sigurd felt the opposite, wanting to do everything he could to see that the right king was placed on Alekka's throne.

Bending forward, he saw his reflection in the still water. It surprised him, and his bearded mouth dropped open, his blue eyes full of confusion. He almost didn't recognise himself. He looked older. Wary. His frown was deeper. His hair was now shaved at the sides, braided over the top. He cocked his head to one side, not convinced that it suited him. Tulia hadn't said, which, he realised with a wry smile, should have been a clue.

Dipping his fingers into the water, he swished it around, not wanting to see himself anymore. He wanted to know what was happening, for if he could find a way to see like Thenor, he knew he could help his brother.

Rocking back on his heels, he took a deep breath, letting every thought drift out of his mind. It needed to be empty and open, free of constraint. He had to become at one with the water, to let his thoughts flow as though they were clouds. There could be nothing in his way, nothing stopping the rhythm of his breathing, the rhythm of time, of life...

But as Sigurd opened his eyes, exhaling slowly, he stared down into the pool, seeing his miserable face once more.

***

When they stopped for a break, Jonas sought to have a word with Alys. 'You look pale today,' he said. She had barely spoken since they'd left their camp behind, answering his questions with a few mumbles but nothing more. 'Is something wrong?'

Alys shook away his concern, smiling broadly. 'No. Likely just a lack of sleep.' And shivering, she ducked her head, walking into the trees.

They'd stopped so everyone could stretch their legs and relieve themselves, including Puddle, who appeared to be enjoying the escape from his swaddle. He padded across the snow towards Magnus, who held a flatbread in his hand, trying to tempt the puppy to run around.

Alys left them all behind, needing a moment to think without the constant chatter. Her dream had peeled away another layer of her past, and she felt further displaced. It made her feelings for Mirella more conflicted than ever and inconvenient, too, as she needed to be dreaming of how to help Reinar. Reinar, who Ragnahild had warned, just as Raf had warned, was in grave danger.

She almost screamed, slamming both hands over her mouth as Thenor slipped out from behind a tree.

'You remembered your dream?' he asked quickly, glancing around. 'It's why I came.'

'But Alari? Mirella?' Alys panicked, glancing around herself.

'They may see me here, though they won't know what we're discussing. Not unless we tell them, Alys. I merely came to enquire about your dream and whether the results of my request were... fruitful?' He peered into her eyes, seeing a flash of recognition.

'They were. Very.'

'Good. I wanted to say goodbye for now. I will find you again in your dreams. Be ready for me, Alys, for soon we will have much work to do.'

He was gone before Alys could open her mouth, hoping he'd been talking about the brooch.

Wondering what he expected her to do.

***

They were aiming for Salagat, an abandoned village nestled at the foot of the Silver Mountains. It was a particularly lush area of central Alekka, with plentiful forests, rivers, and streams to supply their weary army and horses, and Gord's Field, perfect for battle.

If they could get there first.

Eddeth was back on Wilf, once again full of noise as they pushed their way up the column to reach Reinar.

He was pleased to see her, though the worry in her eyes concerned him. 'What did you see?'

'Trouble!' she announced, surprising no one.

Ollo rolled his eyes, certain he couldn't endure any more trouble. 'What's happened now?'

'The ship you sent? To Oss?' Eddeth was quickly breathless. 'Never made it!'

'What?' Reinar spun around so quickly that he nearly toppled out of the saddle. 'What happened?'

'A terrible storm! Shipwrecked, it was! Nothing left but broken strakes and bodies drifting to the bottom of Hartu's sea!' Eddeth shivered, remembering that feeling. When *Dagger* had sunk, death had felt closer than at any moment in her life. The cold had been impossible to fight against. She had almost given up, lost in the hypnotising chill.

Reinar tapped her arm. 'Eddeth?'

'Oh! Yes!' She gathered her drifting thoughts together again, well aware that everyone was waiting on her. 'The sea wrecked the ship. The message didn't get through. The Islanders don't know that we need their help. We're all alone! We'll be all alone!'

'Eddeth!' Stellan hissed. 'Not so loud!' Though he was being equally loud and taking a breath, he tried to calm his own rising tension. 'After last night, we need to give our men a moment. Keep this to ourselves a while longer.'

Ollo was leaning forward, wanting to hear everything, though, and when Berger and Ilene rode up to join him, he quickly filled them in on what was happening.

Ilene looked furious, then worried. 'What are we going to do now? Go back?'

Ollo shrugged.

'We can't go back,' Berger scoffed. 'A king can't go backwards.'

'Reinar's not the king yet,' Ollo hissed. 'Likely won't be now.'

Ludo rode ahead of them with Raf, and hearing Ollo's not-so-subtle whispering, he spun around. 'Shut up. You won't make anything better with that sort of talk, Ollo Narp. Reinar forgave you. He brought you in, gave you another chance, so show him some respect. And Ake. He chose Reinar. Our job is to help him get to Stornas, not to chip away at any confidence he might have left. At any hope he's clinging to. How would you feel if you were him?' And sensing his temper exploding, Ludo clenched his jaw, turning around to Reinar.

Who was staring directly at him. 'You alright, Ludo?'

Ludo nodded, attempting to get comfortable in the saddle, aware that Rofni was once again trying to nibble his horse's ear.

Reinar forced himself to smile through the horror of Eddeth's news and Ollo's muttering, though his confidence was quickly sinking, and turning back to the path, he felt his destiny ebbing away.

PART THREE

The One True King

CHAPTER TWENTY SIX

Gudrum could afford to take his time. He was the king. He had an army no one in Alekka possessed. No lord, no pretender to the throne commanded even half the men he did.

So he could afford to take his time.

And enjoy himself along the way.

The small fort had put up some resistance at first. Gudrum had sent Edrik on ahead to enquire about food and weapons, but the flags flying from the ramparts declared that the Lord of Skolman hadn't thought through the ramifications of proclaiming his loyalty to Reinar Vilander. So, no longer interested in ale and arrows, Gudrum decided to make him pay.

Gysa looked on disapprovingly as Gudrum and the Lords of Ennor and Borken, along with the ever-loyal Tudashi under their new king, besieged the wooden palisade, surrounding it with archers, quickly taking down every man in sight. Then, wanting to further demonstrate his superior strength, Gudrum used fire arrows to burn Skolman's thatched cottages, hoping to terrorise those inside.

'I only wanted a side of pork!' he laughed from his horse. 'A round of cheese and some ale!' Screams grew, panic consuming Skolman. He turned to Edrik, whose pale eyes shone in the glow of the flames dancing from the roofs of thatched cottages, brightening the grey spring morning. 'Smell that?'

Edrik looked confused. 'My lord?'

'Surrender,' Gudrum grinned. 'Another of Reinar's allies is now mine. Any men Reinar Vilander may have sought to claim himself, any weapons, all mine. Mine!' His confidence had soared as he'd made his way north, knowing that soon the only lord left standing would be the former Lord of Ottby. And wouldn't he get such a fright to see the size of the mountain he had to climb?

For it was growing more formidable by the day.

Gysa tapped his arm, hoping to claim his attention. 'I've had a vision,' she said, jaw clenched, unimpressed with the pointless diversion. Gudrum had more men than he needed – this was just indulgent arrogance. 'I have seen where Reinar Vilander is waiting for you.'

***

Jael woke with a sick feeling in the pit of her stomach. She heard the wind and felt her frozen toes, aware that her mouth was dry and her head hurt.

She felt terrible.

And she hadn't had a dream.

Opening her eyes, she saw Vella peering at her, and then, reaching out a furry paw, the little dog patted her on the head.

Jael closed her eyes, hearing the children complaining outside the door and Biddy's loud ssshing.

It was how most mornings went.

Something was wrong, though, or was she just fretting because she wasn't beside Eadmund, telling him what to do? Since Eirik's death, they'd ruled together, arguing about who had the right of things, though mostly Eadmund tended to agree with her.

And now? Without her?

He was perfectly capable, Jael told herself. He was a smart leader, a skilled warrior, a sharp tactician. He had finally turned into the man his father had longed for.

Jael smiled sadly, wishing Eirik were here to see it.

And not only Eirik...

'Bo!' she called. 'Sigmund!'

The door flew open, two little Skallesons running to the bed, pulling themselves up on the furs, scrambling towards Ido and Vella, whose tails snapped back and forth, happy to see them.

'Mama!' Bo called, wriggling towards her mother, kissing her head. 'Cake for breakfast?'

'Cake?' Jael looked up, seeing a stern-faced Biddy rolling her eyes in the doorway. 'Why not!'

***

They'd arrived at the ruins of Salagat as night was falling, pleased that Gudrum's army wasn't waiting for them, though slightly concerned that he may have decided to bypass them altogether and head directly to Slussfall. Though the morning brought word from the dreamers, confirmed by newly returned scouts, that Gudrum was close. Although according to the scouts, the proclaimed King of Alekka appeared in no hurry, leaving a trail of destruction in his wake, casting aside his enemies, tearing apart villages, installing his own loyal men. Reinar wasn't surprised, knowing that with Gudrum ranging below him, the Ennorians and Borkens with their strongholds in the East, and Tarl Brava in the North, he was quickly running out of Alekkan land to call his own.

'This battle will decide everything,' he said, admiring the view of Gord's Field from the hill that bordered it. 'It will decide who sits on the throne.'

'Perhaps,' Eddeth mused, struggling with her footing on the slippery hill. She followed Reinar's gaze, confident they were staring at the field Raf had seen in her dream. And though her fear blazed at the thought of it, Eddeth didn't want Reinar to sense her concern. 'I remember how many times Ake confronted Jorek Vettel.

It was always touted to be the final encounter. A battle for the ages! But it took Ake ten years to finish off the stubborn old buggar! So don't pin every hope on this battle. If you can wound Gudrum and damage his reputation, perhaps that will be enough for now?' She was reaching, not really knowing about battles and lords, though she wanted to reassure Reinar that this wasn't necessarily the end if it all went wrong. 'As long as you live. That's all that matters now.'

Reinar shook his head. 'Do you know what it feels like? To think my men are expendable? Just arms and legs fighting for me? Their lives worth nothing more than a shield or an axe? How many bodies am I going to leave down there, just so I can succeed?'

'Well,' Eddeth sighed, wishing there was somewhere to sit. It was raining again, and she tucked her hood around her face, trying to keep it out of her eyes. Looking over her shoulder, she saw the dark wall of mountains capped with snow. 'Land's bought with blood. That's the cost. You want the land, you pay in blood. It's been that way since the beginning of time. Even Thenor would tell you that, I'm sure. Whoever started it had the wrong thinking, but since then, it's been the only way. And how do you stop and talk it out with a man like Gudrum? How do you defeat him without men?'

Reinar peered at her. 'With magic?'

Eddeth didn't reply, staring into his eyes until he looked away. 'Magic has its uses, but you need to be a king who uses it for good. A king whose dreamers aren't witches with dark intentions. Power corrupts, and nothing's more powerful than magic.'

Reinar nodded. 'I know, Eddeth. I know.'

'I've been searching, oh yes, and Raf too. Looking for ways to help. Gudrum's confident. I've seen that smile, and it's good news for you, for an overconfident man will make mistakes. Though his army's growing, too, which is the bad news.'

'Keep looking,' Reinar urged, the rest of his thoughts remaining unsaid.

But Eddeth heard them loud and clear. She peered down at the mucky field below. It sloped, at first, then levelled off, soggy and boggy, leading to a thin snake of a stream, and beyond it, a wall of forest, dark and foreboding. 'Vik's been doing a lot of thinking,' she promised. 'He's got ideas!' She didn't know what they were, but she felt confident that Vik would know the right things to do. Stellan would too. Still, it was the tense man beside her who had to make all the decisions.

The man who would be king.

***

Gudrum returned to his horse, the taste of blood bitter in his mouth. He grabbed the waterskin from his steward with a frown, feeling in the mood for wine. Then remembering how fond Hector had been of wine and looking at Gysa, who had poisoned Hector's wine, he tipped the skin up, dribbling water into his mouth. Spitting, and wiping his beard, he eyed the dreamer. 'Should I simply walk into Reinar Vilander's trap? He'll have thought it through, knowing the terrain will give him some advantage, so should I accommodate him? Give him what he most desires?' Patting his horse with a bloody hand, he turned away, leaving his steward to refill the waterskin and Gysa to lift her cloak out of the muck and follow after him.

'You have more than twice the number of men Reinar Vilander has, so how much of an advantage can he gain? Truly?'

It was a fair point, Gudrum thought, kicking a whining dog out of the way. The limping creature whined some more, and eventually, after a few steps, it fell to the ground. Gudrum didn't break his stride, irritated that Gysa kept following him, remembering a time when he'd had a dreamer who wanted to be left alone. 'What?' he snapped, needing to be with his men. And realising that he couldn't accomplish that with Gysa tagging along, he wheeled around with a growl. 'What do you want from me?'

Gysa stopped as though struck, surprised by Gudrum's vicious snarl. They had once again been spending every night together. He'd kept her close, soft and gentle at times, demanding and urgent at others, but never angry. That Gudrum seemed to vanish with every dawn, revealing a raging warrior far less enamoured with her company. 'I... I am trying to help you, to advise you. You wish to defeat your enemy, and I –'

He grabbed her arm. 'Exactly! You have that right. I do. I do wish to defeat him. I *will* defeat him. I've led armies, Gysa. I've killed men and taken forts, achieved fame and riches. I have come from nothing to be crowned a king! *Me*! A dreamer didn't do that for me! *I* did!' He ignored all memories of Raf, not prepared to acknowledge how much she'd helped him or that Gysa had helpfully killed Hector. 'I made all the decisions, I took all the action. *Me*!' Seeing the hurt and surprise in the dreamer's eyes, he lowered his voice. 'I'm not a puppet like Hector was. I won't be. I want you with me, but you will not lead me. You will not whisper words in my ear, commanding me from a distance. No! I have my own ideas, my own insights. And most of all, I have experience! Tell me everything you see, and then I'll decide what to do, just like Raf did.'

Gysa started, not wanting to be compared to that forest dweller. '*Raf*?'

The jealousy in Gysa's eyes pleased Gudrum, quelling his anger, and he smiled, taking her hand. 'I have to go. Edrik's likely pocketing everything for himself!' He laughed, though Gysa's expression was unwavering. 'I could've gone after Raf if I'd wanted to. I could have taken her back, but she was a lying little bitch. She betrayed me. She was a stupid girl who fell in love with my enemy,' Gudrum growled, suddenly wanting reassurance of Gysa's loyalty. He pulled her close, knowing he was splattered in blood and gore, pleased to see that she didn't flinch. 'And you are nothing like that pointless girl, are you, my sweet Gysa?'

Gysa didn't speak, listening to his thoughts rather than his words, knowing how much more work lay ahead of her. It didn't matter what Gudrum said or thought he wanted, for if he was going to secure his place on Alekka's throne, he was going to need her help.

***

Jael had happily left her dreams in the past, though in truth, she'd never welcomed them in the first place. She had always been proud to be called Furia's Daughter, for Furia was the Brekkan Goddess of War. She'd never wanted to be a dreamer like her grandmother; it didn't suit her at all. But, she realised, brushing Tig, whose muzzle was buried in a pail of oats, having dreams had been a way to see what was happening. Now she had no idea if her husband was alive. No hint or clue. Not even a feeling.

'Are you sure?' Biddy wondered beside her. She'd put both children down for a nap and headed to the stables to bring Jael the last piece of honey cake. 'Sure you can't see anything? Not even if you tried?'

Jael laughed, moving around Tig's black rump. 'You don't think I've tried? It's been three years, Biddy. You don't think I've tried to bring back my dreams?'

'I most certainly don't!' Biddy snorted, taking a seat on an old stool, still holding the plate of cake. She broke off a corner, nibbling and frowning. 'You were different when you came back from the Vale. I don't think you wanted them back. Not after what happened.'

Jael kept brushing.

'But now you need to see, don't you? You need to know what's happening.'

'Though what good would it do? I'm here, not there.' Jael had been around Tig twice, and he gleamed like polished ebony, so there was no point hiding in the stables any longer. She left the brush on the shelf and headed out of the stall, eyeing Biddy sternly. 'Where are the children?'

'Sound asleep, or roaming the fort like wild animals. I'm never entirely sure with those two. Maybe we need a lock on their door?'

Jael grinned, taking the plate. Then looking down at Biddy, she pushed it back to her. 'You have it.'

Biddy stood with a crooked grin, feeling as creaky as the old stool. 'Why? Did you read my mind? Maybe it's a sign? Your dreams might be coming back!'

Jael laughed. 'No, you just had that look in your eye. You take the cake. I'll go and find Fyn, see if he's had a word with Fria yet. That should keep me busy till supper.'

'You know he won't have,' Biddy said, stumped by the puzzle of Fyn Gallas herself. Nothing she or Jael did brought him out of himself when it came to women. He was too shy to even open his mouth most of the time. Unlike Jael, she thought with a chuckle, who'd never had a problem on that front.

'What?'

'Oh, nothing,' Biddy mumbled, biting into the cake. 'It's good, you know. Shame you didn't try it.'

But Jael had no appetite for cake. She'd struggled to find her appetite since Eadmund had left Oss, for despite her lack of dreams, she was growing ever certain that something was terribly wrong.

***

Ludo stopped beside Raf, who sat on a log in the drizzle, sharpening her knives. She'd collected another knife after the fjaladen attack and now had two. She had never been confident with weapons before but was afraid enough of what was coming to want all the protection she could get. Helgi had been showing her how to better focus her aim, and they'd made targets on trees, practising throughout the morning. He liked to talk and was more inclined to share his time and his thoughts than his cousin. She saw him in the distance, watched by Ilene, and rolling her eyes, Raf turned back to Ludo. 'What do you want?'

Ludo almost spat out his mouthful of ale. 'What? I didn't even speak.'

Raf shook her head. 'Sorry. I... thought you asked me something.'

Ludo laughed. 'Not out loud, I didn't, but I suppose I was wondering about Sigurd. About whether you've seen him? Or Alari?'

Raf dropped her head, focusing on the small whetstone Helgi had given her, running it carefully down the blade. She saw the sharp edge gleaming in a sunshower, and heartened by that, she kept going, wishing Ludo would go away.

'Perhaps you don't want to say? I just... worry. Sigurd's like family to me. My own didn't want me. They sent me to live with the Vilanders when I was ten. Reinar was older, busy with his friends, but Sigurd took care of me. He always took care of me.'

Raf looked up, seeing the sadness in Ludo's eyes. 'I'm sorry, but I can't help you. Sigurd is a god. No dreamer can find gods. They find you.'

Ludo mulled that over as the fire sizzled before them, fighting the rain. 'And Alari? Does she find you, Raf?' Ludo had heard the rumours. They weren't even really rumours, he thought.

Raf didn't say, though she hunched over further. 'Alari took Sigurd. That's what Reinar saw. She came and took him away, and that's all I know. She wanted me to help her when I was with Gudrum. She promised she wouldn't kill Sigurd if I helped her.' She looked up, afraid of what Ludo would say.

But he simply nodded. 'So you tried to?'

'I did. I sent Gudrum to Stornas instead of Ottby. I thought it would help Hector like she wanted, but mostly I... hoped it would save Sigurd.'

Ludo thought that through. 'Likely it did. If Gudrum had arrived at Ottby before us, who knows what might have happened.'

Raf sighed. 'There's nothing I can do for Sigurd. Alari, she... threatens me.' Raf didn't know why she was saying things to Ludo Moller that she hadn't even told Eddeth, but there was something about his eyes. About his pain. It was a shared grief she knew he understood.

'To betray us?'

Raf shrugged. 'Alari doesn't want Reinar to succeed.'

'And will you help her?'

Raf didn't answer for some time. She stopped her sharpening, though her eyes remained fixed on the blade. 'I won't betray you,' she whispered.

Ludo watched her for a moment before standing, fearing she didn't mean it. 'Good,' he replied anyway. 'Sigurd will find a way back. He will. And he'll want you to be here, too, Raf. Remember that. No matter what you think or see, we were with Sigurd when he was missing you. They were real, those feelings. Whatever you might think, Sigurd cares for you.'

Raf's eyes remained fixed on her blade, leaving Ludo to turn away, the hollow feeling in the pit of his stomach growing bigger by the moment.

***

Thenor's absence from Gallabrok and his call to gather every loyal god and goddess into the fortress had meant that Sigurd was suddenly surrounded by unfamiliar faces. Valera had organised a feast, wanting to introduce him to everyone, though Sigurd felt so overwhelmed by the sheer number of ethereal beings that his head was spinning. Tulia had been there, for a time, though she'd barely looked his way. He didn't blame her, but he did miss her company.

In the end, he slunk away to a corner, where he hoped no one would notice him.

Ulfinnur approached with two goblets and a bright smile. 'You look ready to disappear. I don't blame you, though. All these gods? It's like being in a room full of children. They all hate each other. Most of them do, at least.'

'Do they?' Sigurd was surprised, not having picked that up at all. The hall was lit by soft candlelight, the melodic plucking from lyres and harps accompanying the murmuring voices of those gathered in groups around the fire or sitting at tables. Sigurd saw no tension and heard no raised voices in the genial atmosphere.

Ulfinnur laughed. 'You need to work on your senses, my friend. I can hear everything they're not saying.' He handed Sigurd one of the goblets, tapping his head. 'I wish I could turn it off sometimes. Not everyone cares to protect their thoughts. Perhaps they don't know how?'

'And could Alari read yours?'

Ulfinnur threw back his mead, drinking deeply. 'She tried to, of course, as I imagine she tried to read yours, though Valera is more skilled than Alari ever realised. She couldn't get in.'

Sigurd knew how he was feeling. He still woke from nightmares where Alari loomed over him, her single blue eye like a beam of light in the darkness, flicking that menacing knife. 'Do you think Thenor has gone to find her?'

Ulfinnur looked surprised. 'I thought you'd know that. I imagined he would have told you.'

Sigurd shook his head as Valera approached with Tikas, who looked in his element. His head twisted this way and that, ears open, searching for gossip, busily storing each tidbit away. The loss of his eye was still a shock, though he didn't shy away from it, wearing a white silk eyepatch, which drew attention to his youthful face. 'No, but I'm glad he didn't. The less information I have up here,' Sigurd decided, tapping his head, 'the better.'

Valera eyed Sigurd with a frown. Her discomfort at helping Eddeth had made her wary of approaching him again. He was so like Thenor that she found it hard to say no. His thoughts were guarded, but his emotions were intense, and she could feel every one of them. The loss of his family pained him greatly. He missed them all. He wanted to be there with Raf, with Reinar, with his father and friends. She dropped her eyes to her goblet, not speaking as Ulfinnur drew Tikas away.

'You're unhappy with me,' Sigurd decided when they were alone. 'For making you help me.'

Valera looked up, smiling. 'Well, there's your first mistake, Sigurd, for you cannot make a goddess do anything she doesn't wish to do. We are immovable, I promise.'

He grinned. 'Though I asked too much.'

'No, though I cannot help you again. I won't. It must be as Thenor wills it. I cannot go against him. His knowledge is so much greater than my own. He has the weight of two worlds on his shoulders, responsible for balancing everything. I am no Alari or Eskvir. I will not go against him.'

'I never wanted to cause problems for you or to disobey Thenor. It's just....' Sigurd glanced around the hall, seeing dead warriors mingling with gods. It often struck him how ridiculous it all seemed, how far away from Ottby. 'This is all you've ever known, who you've always been. But me...' He shrugged, not wanting the mead. It was potent, and without Thenor at Gallabrok, he felt the need to command his senses. 'I was something else once, someone else, and I miss it. I miss being me. I knew I was different growing up, but I didn't care. I just wanted to belong. And to belong, I had to help my family. And now I can't. I may be Thenor's son, but I was raised by the Vilanders, and in my heart, I'll always be one of them. Thenor is asking me to abandon them, and I don't know how to do that.' He saw Hyvari over Valera's shoulder, and his tension increased. 'I can't see what's happening, but I'm sure it's nothing good. Reinar's going up against Gudrum, who has twice as many men. He needs me. I want to be there.' Sigurd noticed more than one unfamiliar face looking his way, and he dropped his head, sighing.

Valera could feel her resolve unravelling like a ball of yarn. 'You must keep trying then,' she murmured. 'I can't help you, Sigurd, but you can. You were born a god, and everything you need is there, inside you. If you truly want to help your brother, *you* must find a way.' She placed a hand on his shoulder, squeezing it gently. 'You spent your life wondering who you were and what you were capable of. And now it is time to find out.'

CHAPTER TWENTY SEVEN

Reinar hadn't stopped all day, trekking from one side of Gord's Field to the other – up the hill, across the stream, into the surrounding woodland. He wanted to understand every part of the terrain; to imagine it both dry and wet or covered in snow; to see where the wind was weakest and strongest; to determine what trouble the archers would have with the sun if it continued to shine, or their strings if they were deluged with rain or blanketed in snow. He needed to think about whether to use horses or where to keep them safe. The list of questions grew longer as he walked, finding more problems, deciding on some solutions, but generally never feeling comfortable at all.

Stellan managed to catch him as the sun reached its peak. He'd taken off his cloak, enjoying the spring day, though the melting snow had made a real bog of the field, and he almost wished the sun would go away and bring back some clouds. 'You're hard to find!' he called with a grin. 'Not even Bjarni knew where you were!'

Reinar wasn't smiling. 'Bjarni can't walk fast enough. I left him down with Ollo and Vik, talking to the archers.'

Despite his smile, Stellan was on edge. He feared for his son, who had to stand at the head of them all, and though the thought of it terrified him, he wanted Reinar to know that he wasn't alone. 'I'd rather be you than Gudrum,' he said, falling in to walk beside him. 'You've got good advisors around you. Experienced men. Funny thing is, Hector was the most experienced man Gudrum could have leaned on. He could've told him all about the problems he'd face here.'

'He probably would have told him not to come. We're here first. Hector would've known what that meant. We can take our pick of where to place our men.'

Stellan nodded. 'Though Gudrum will have a new Lord of Ennor. No doubt another Bearsu. And there's that deaf old troll from Borken if he's still alive. They know this place better than most. If Gudrum's smart, he'll listen to them.'

Reinar wondered if he would, guessing he would likely listen to his dreamer most of all.

'You can only work with what's before you,' Stellan reminded him, listening to voices raised in anger behind them. And glancing over his shoulder, he saw Beggi and Torfinn breaking up a scuffle. 'Don't waste a moment wishing for things you don't have. If we wake up in a storm, keep going. If we're attacked by dark spirits in the night, kill them, and keep going.'

'So you're saying I should keep going?'

Stellan grinned broadly, pleased to see that his son wasn't merely sinking into a pit of fear and worry. 'I think we're up against it. Can't deny that. But think of the throne and Stornas and how much it mattered to Ake that he left it in good hands. Not corrupt, greedy, evil hands. Gudrum and his dreamer and his men.... what intentions do they have for Alekka? Likely they've plenty for themselves, but Alekka?' Stellan shook his head, his mood as changeable as the spring sky, which had once again darkened overhead. 'I'd wager Gudrum wants gold and power like most greedy lords do, but I doubt he'll want a headache. Remember that above all things. Who wants the prize the most will claim the victory, for a determined man can achieve many things with a strong mind.'

***

Rain streamed down on Gudrum's men as the afternoon lengthened, though turning around, he saw that many were still marching with purpose and vigour, seeing the Silver Mountains reaching above the tree canopy in the distance. After a number of crushing victories on the journey, they were in fine spirits. Optimism flowed, conversations were loud, smiles brimming with confidence. There was talk of a victory so resounding that it would be the greatest ever sung about. So, despite wet boots and aching backs, despite the weight of armour and weapons, they marched at pace, eager to get to Salagat.

Gudrum rode at their head, flanked by Edrik, and Bor Bearsu. He'd quickly realised that Bor was much better company than the spitting Lord of Borken, who was well past his best and reeked of piss, or the new King of Tudash, who Gudrum couldn't understand at all.

'They'll have taken the hill, my lord,' Bor said gravely, though they were still some way from their destination. 'Reinar Vilander will want to make you climb.'

Gudrum turned his way, still fascinated by the man's nose, which had been broken so many times that it angled in more than one direction. Mostly it was flattened against his ruddy face, notable for the misshapen nose and a pair of black eyes which peered at Gudrum from beneath a thick forest of brows. He was serious, always intense, and very direct.

'You don't think we can climb in a little rain?' Gudrum laughed, feeling as optimistic as his men. Numbers gave him confidence, and he had so many men riding and marching behind him that he knew no one in Alekka was capable of challenging him now. Jael Furyck was a problem he was eager to turn to, but first, he had to defeat his one remaining rival for the throne. And not just defeat him, Gudrum knew. He had to pummel Reinar and his men into the earth until they were nothing but blood and bone. There would be no mercy shown. Not by him. This battle would be a sacrifice to Alari and Vasa and all those gods who supported him. A great sacrificial offering, guaranteeing his luck for years to come.

Bor didn't smile. 'You are confident, my lord,' he stated,

saying nothing further, though his gloved hands tightened around the reins, jaw clenching.

Gudrum saw a great hole in the road ahead. After all the snow and now rain, their path had been dotted with such holes, though none of this size. He nudged his horse towards Bor, moving around it. 'I have reason to be, so I'll use that to spur our men on. A cautious man can be defeated by fear, even when there's no reason to feel fear at all. No, I see what is behind me as well as what lies before me. I see it all so clearly.' He looked up, eyes on the mountain range in the distance. 'Whether we're traipsing across bogs or running up a hill, with me at the helm, we're guaranteed a famous victory. I need not think further than that. To do so would only aid our enemy. Mind games are games I have no intention of playing. I will enter this fight strong and leave it the true King of Alekka.'

It was hard not to be impressed by that, Bor decided, though he still felt tremors of worry that the cocky king hadn't foreseen all the troubles that lay ahead. Though there was time, he knew. Once they made camp, there would be plenty of time for him to point each one of them out.

Gudrum laughed some more, seeing the Lord of Ennor's perturbed face, not stopping as the sky opened above them, sending forth a violent deluge of rain.

***

'I want to kill them all! Every last one of the foul wretches!' Alari raged, head flung back, throwing a curse at the ceiling. Lumps of rock crumbled in the distance, showering over Vasa's table.

Alari wasn't alone in her anger.

Vasa was mourning the death of her beloved wolf, Ulura, still in shock that her most loyal companion was actually gone. No magic Alari tried had worked, and nothing Vasa could do would bring the wolf back. She was dead. Killed by Thenor. Her body still lay where it had fallen, abandoned on Alari's island. 'We will, Sister, we will,' Vasa growled. 'With Gysa's help, Gudrum will defeat Reinar Vilander, and with a loyal king on the throne, Alekka will be ours.'

They stood in Vasa's cave, listening to the ravens flapping and fighting over scraps. Angry ravens, dripping ceilings, and the ever-present howl of the wind. It was a grating, noisy, oppressive irritation, though after Thenor and Sigurd and their helpers had tainted her island, Alari had left with no intention of returning. The tower could fall into the sea for all she cared, though the smell of her sister's cave was repulsive, the constant noise of her ravens maddening. 'It will,' she agreed, picking an apple out of a basket. 'Though we can never discount Tarl Brava. Gudrum's greatest mistake may end up coming back to haunt him.'

'Perhaps, though by then, Gudrum will be a king of many, more powerful than a mere lord. Gysa did you a favour there, Sister. Hector Berras wouldn't have fared well against Tarl Brava, no matter how many men stood behind him.'

Alari wouldn't admit it, though she was tempted to agree. She had never considered Gudrum as a contender for the throne, for he wasn't even Alekkan. Though he had proven himself stronger than every Alekkan-born contender, so she couldn't discount him any longer. He was fuelled by hunger and desire, by brute strength and cunning. He had everything within him to crush the Vilanders. She grinned, biting into the apple. 'Our Father has no idea what he's up against.'

Alari's confidence finally managed to lift Vasa's dour mood. 'And nor does Reinar Vilander. With Gysa by Gudrum's side, he stands no chance at all.'

***

The sick feeling in Alys' stomach had intensified as they approached the Silver Mountains. She had hoped to catch the army before it reached Salagat, and though she'd seen the odd glimpse of Reinar in her dreams, she wouldn't feel any relief until she saw him in person. Puddle's kidnapping and the missing pouch had kept her on edge, wondering what it could all mean. Though Alys knew she had to keep her mind on Reinar above all things. Ragnahild had warned as much.

She was here to save him.

Jonas rode beside her. Stina was further back with the children, a wriggling Puddle strapped to her chest.

Alys' eyes were peeled open as they rounded the corner, weary horses blowing as they fought against the rain. 'See up there! The Silver Mountains!'

Magnus' eyes brightened considerably, though he was less enamoured with the mountains and more eager to see Vik and Ludo and some of the older boys who had left with the army. 'We're here? Really? Do you think we're too late?' As the journey had worn on, he'd become fearful that they'd miss the battle altogether.

So had Alys. 'We are. Here.' She turned back to Jonas, mostly holding her breath.

'Looks safe,' he decided, ears open, eyes scanning the path ahead, where the trees finally ended, and a stretch of open meadow, sprinkled in snow, waited. 'Best I go ahead, though. Unless you can see something? I don't want to expose the children to any danger.' He smelled smoke, perhaps even meat cooking, when he inhaled sharply. He heard the faint hum of people in the distance, but this far out, it was impossible to know who it was. He couldn't even see a banner, though he knew they'd be there.

'I can't see anything,' Alys said, and swallowing, she turned back to the children again. 'We'll wait here. Jonas will go ahead!' Magnus opened his mouth, though having read his thoughts, his mother lifted an eyebrow in his direction, pleased to see him tug Daisy's reins, pulling her to a stop.

***

Vik stopped to stretch out his back. Sleeping on the ground was becoming less desirable as time marched on, and he thought of his cottage at the lake for the first time in days. It wasn't much, he knew, though it had suited him. There'd been plenty of room for Jonas to share, and they'd managed things between them well. He'd enjoyed the company, and now when he thought of the lake, he looked forward to building more cottages. Alys and the children would come with Stina, maybe Solveigh. Hopefully, Estrella and the girls too.

Someone shouted his name, and turning around, he saw Ollo tottering towards him with an armload of stakes, calling out for help. Guessing he'd only tried to carry that much to show off to Ilene, Vik was tempted to let him topple over, needing something to laugh about. Though the hours of moaning that followed wouldn't be worth it.

'You took your time!' Ollo panted when Vik had helped him drop the stakes to the ground. 'I nearly didn't make it.' His boots sunk into the mud. 'What are we doing here?' he sighed, eyes sweeping the bank of the hill, which rolled into the boggy field. 'It's the wrong season to be fighting. May as well prepare for mud wrestling.'

'Well, it'd be more fun to watch!' Vik laughed, and hearing his name called again, he spun around in surprise. 'Jonas?'

Ollo swung around with him, one of his boots remaining behind. Grumbling, he wobbled with his arms out, balancing himself as he retrieved it. Though by then, Jonas was off his horse, embracing Vik in a bear hug.

'Miss me?' Jonas grinned.

Vik was stunned. 'You left Alys and the children?'

'No, they came with me. Stina too. Thought I'd ride on ahead first, though, check you're not Gudrum.'

Vik and Ollo glanced at each other, then back to Jonas.

'You brought the children here?' Ollo didn't know what to

make of that.

Jonas' joy at seeing his old friends was short-lived. 'Alys had to come. She said it was important she was here, and you know Alys. After all that's happened, she's not leaving her children behind. Especially after what happened to Puddle.'

'Puddle?'

But then Reinar was approaching with an arm in the air, a look of confusion on his face. 'Jonas! Has something happened? What are you doing here?' He couldn't help but look behind Jonas, surprised that he'd left his granddaughter behind.

'Nothing's happened, no. Alys just.... she wanted to come.' Jonas smiled broadly, hiding his own worries. The field was a bog, the hill a slide. And thanks to the long winter and the size of the enemy they were facing, they were going to have a hard time of things.

'Alys?' Reinar grabbed Jonas' arm, looking around again. 'Where is she?'

***

Feeling the need to take charge of her supper, Eddeth had dragged Raf on a foraging mission, disappearing into the area of woodland linking Salagat and Gord's Field, where they collected a basket of mushrooms and nuts, some wild leeks and garlic too.

Raf had barely spoken a word, which was nothing new, and as they made their way back to camp, Eddeth sensed something was wrong. 'Are you nervous? About what will come?' she asked gently, nudging the girl as they walked.

Raf supposed she was, but that wasn't why she was quiet. 'I feel Gudrum,' she admitted. 'As though he's standing on that field over Reinar. Over Reinar's body.'

Eddeth gulped, nose twitching. 'You still see that?'

Raf nodded. 'It's all I do see. I don't know why I'm the only one to see it. Why I *keep* seeing it.'

'Well, because you're a dreamer, that's why! Dreams give us an opportunity to change course, don't they? We're lucky in that way, seeing what's coming.'

'I'd rather see how to stop it. If Gudrum's victorious here, it will mean the end of everything. He won't be kind.' Raf felt real fear then, imagining what Gudrum and Gysa might do to her and Eddeth. 'You should ride away. If it starts going wrong, if Gudrum kills Reinar, you should go back to Slussfall.'

'What? Not without you!' Eddeth insisted, slipping her arm through Raf's. 'Oh no, I won't. If it all goes wrong, we'll leave together.'

Raf stopped, wanting Eddeth to hear her. 'No, we won't. You'll go on your own. I won't be coming.'

'But why?'

'Gudrum wants me. He won't care about you. If I stay, he won't care about you at all. You'll be able to get to Slussfall and help Alys save everyone.' She blinked at the red-nosed dreamer before her. 'Agnes and Rigfuss and the horses too. You'll need to get back to Slussfall and help.'

Eddeth couldn't deny that it was a sensible approach, though the thought of leaving Raf behind unsettled her. 'Listen to me now,' she said in a low voice, rumbling with a confidence she didn't feel. 'We're here to help Reinar and save a kingdom. *Our* kingdom. It doesn't belong to Gudrum, who stole it from Hector, who stole it from Ake, the rightful king! We can't run or ride away! And I won't leave you. Alys will have help, and I know Stina and Solveigh will care for our animals.' She blinked, suddenly seeing the most curious sight. And dropping her basket, she squeezed Raf's hand, hurrying her away.

***

The sight of a sodden Alys brightened Reinar's day in a way he hadn't imagined possible. His tension eased, his serious face breaking into a beaming smile. All thoughts of Gudrum and his impending demise left him as he stared at her.

Catching his eye, she became flustered, and after holding his gaze for a moment, she turned back to help Stina with the children and Puddle.

Puddle?

Reinar frowned, coming forward as Stina released the unwrapped puppy onto the ground.

Puddle didn't move, legs trembling. He looked ready to fall over.

And then he sat down with what appeared to be a sigh.

'What happened?' Ludo wanted to know, immediately bending down, hand out. 'Something's wrong.'

'A long story,' Stina said as more people gathered around them. 'He's been unwell. Getting better, though.' She smiled as Lotta scooped up the puppy. 'Best you keep a close eye on him, Lotta. We'll set up our tent, and he can have some water. Something to eat too.'

Lotta nodded, already looking around for somewhere they could put their tent, though the campsite was mostly full of both tents, trees, and a handful of crumbled old cottages. It wouldn't be easy to find a good spot.

Bjarni arrived with Berger and Stellan and then Helgi, all of them looking from Jonas to Alys, wanting to know what had happened in Slussfall.

'You left Solveigh?' Berger was shocked, unsettled too. 'Both of you?' He turned back to Stina.

'She'll be fine,' Alys promised. 'Agnette's moved into the cottage. She'll take care of Solveigh.'

That had Berger feeling slightly less troubled. 'But why? Why are you here?'

Alys watched as every pair of eyes turned her way. She tried not to look at Reinar, though she could feel him watching her intensely. 'I had a vision. A dream. It didn't reveal much except a...

message. That I was needed here.'

Stellan scratched his chin, aware of how desperately Alys was trying not to look at Reinar. In fact, neither Jonas nor Stina were looking at Reinar either, and it had his senses on high alert. 'Let's get you a tent!' he announced loudly, wanting a moment alone with Jonas. 'Come!'

'I've brought my own,' Jonas told him. 'The women and children can have it. Somewhere to put it would be good, though.' And with one look back at Alys, he followed Stellan, inhaling the welcome tang of ale in the air, his eyes busy, taking in every aspect of the sprawling camp.

'My dreamer!' came a bellowing cry as Eddeth bustled past him, almost pulling Raf off her feet. 'You're here!' She staggered to a stop, breath smoke sweeping around a mottled face, teeth showing. And then she was frowning. 'But whatever has happened, Alys? Why are you here?'

CHAPTER TWENTY EIGHT

Gysa had remained ensconced in her sleigh all day, and though her anger at Gudrum lingered, eventually, she started to miss him.

He joined her as the army made what she hoped would be its final stop at yet another village. There was no fort here, no palisades to get in the way, so Gudrum simply sent his men forward to take ale, weapons, and men. Food too. He didn't join them, curious as to why his dreamer hadn't emerged during the day. 'You're still mad?'

She smiled at him, trying not to look mad, and seeing his smile, she almost stopped feeling it entirely. 'You are stubborn,' she began.

Now Gudrum's smile grew, and leaning forward, his lips lingered on hers, not quite kissing her, just waiting, watching her eyes. 'I am,' he breathed, and now one hand crept up her back, resting on the nape of her neck, holding it there. 'Stubborn and determined to get what I want.'

She eyed him with a hint of mischief. 'Alone.'

'I'm here, aren't I? Do I look like I want to be alone?'

'Don't you have to go and see to your men?'

Gudrum's other hand had been resting on her knee, and now it worked quickly, bunching up her cloak and dress and shift until her legs were exposed in the cold sleigh.

'That's why I have Edrik and all those ambitious lords out there. Let them do some work for a change. We're nearly at the mountains, and once we arrive, I'll have to lead. Until then, I think I need a little time to myself, a little... relaxation.' He kissed Gysa, feeling her weaken beneath his hands, every hint of anger now replaced with urgent desire.

***

Jael kissed her protesting children, who Biddy was trying to shepherd into bed. 'But if you don't go to sleep, how will you have the energy to get up and run around tomorrow?' she tried, though neither child was listening, protesting some more. Eventually, both women started growling, and the children were forced to admit defeat, led to their beds by an exhausted Biddy.

'And I thought you and Aleksander were a handful!' she laughed, turning after the children.

Jael stood in the hall, watching the green curtain. The hall was emptying behind her as the servants cleared up, though Jael didn't hear any of it. She was back in Andala with Aleksander and Biddy. With her brother, her mother.

Her father.

Ranuf Furyck had meant everything to her. His loss had left a hole in her heart that would never be filled. He had taught her, pushed her, scolded her, and loved her in that stern, gruff way of his.

She missed him every day of her life.

But turning back to the table for her cup of ale, it was Aleksander's face she saw as he ran to her on that field of bloody snow.

***

Feeling greatly relieved to have arrived before Gudrum, Alys sat around the fire that night enjoying the conversation, happy to see Reinar's familiar silhouette in the distance. He hadn't stopped all afternoon, not having spoken more than a few words to her in passing, and even now, as everyone flocked to the campfires, he seemed reluctant to come near her.

She was occupied, though, with Lotta nattering in one ear and Helgi in the other. Stina sat opposite her, talking to Bjarni and Ludo; Jonas and Vik near them. She heard someone singing nearby, laughter and hooting behind her.

It felt almost festive.

'What did you see to make you come?' Helgi wanted to know. 'Something bad?' He'd seen her watching Reinar since she'd arrived. 'Something about our future king?' His gaze swung away from the fire towards where Reinar and Stellan were talking outside a tent.

Alys smiled. 'I mostly see bad things.'

'But to come all the way here?' Helgi's voice was low now, his breath warm on her face as he leaned towards her. 'It must be very bad.'

Alys squirmed, seeing how persistent he was becoming. She turned to him, hoping to end his hunt for information. 'It's nothing about you. I haven't seen anything about you.' And then she did: flashes of blood and bared teeth, howling noises and a hairy chest.

'Now you have,' he whispered, touching her arm. 'Haven't you?'

Alys never knew how to act around Helgi. He was a man on the edge of his emotions at all times. It was hard to rouse some people. They spoke and moved as though half asleep. Others hid behind walls of pain, their feelings and words barely connected. But Helgi Eivin's heart had a direct path to his mouth, and everything he felt tumbled out before he'd given much thought to what he wanted to say.

There was some clarity in that, Alys realised. His honesty was affronting but also refreshing.

'I saw you fighting,' she said simply. 'Nothing more.'

And he believed her.

Lotta had turned away, stroking the puppy, who appeared asleep, and Helgi edged even closer. 'I don't know if I want to die,' he admitted. 'After what happened in Napper, I immediately decided I did. I headed for Berger when I heard what was happening. To die fighting? Before the gods?' He snorted. 'Better than taking my own life, I thought. Now though?' He peered at the beautiful dreamer. 'I wonder what else the gods might have planned for me.'

Alys blinked, and Helgi laughed, and then she smiled. 'I'm not sure I've ever met anyone as... interesting as you.'

'You're saying I'm more interesting than Eddeth?' Helgi shook his head. 'I doubt it's possible to be more interesting than Eddeth.'

Reinar's attention snapped away from his father towards the sound of Alys' laughter. He stared, surprised by how close Helgi was sitting to her. Even more surprised by how much Alys appeared to be enjoying his company.

And after everything they'd said in Eddeth's cottage?

Eventually, Berger tapped his arm. 'You want to go over there? Punch my cousin in the mouth? He's got a big one, I know, but I wouldn't recommend it.'

Reinar turned to him with a scowl, but Berger held up a hand. 'Alys deserves to be happy. You can't keep her in a cage so you can look at her, but no one else can touch her.'

Reinar glared at him, though his rush of anger was quickly dampened by the sympathy in Berger's eyes. It was so surprising that he stepped away, catching his breath. 'You know nothing about Alys and me.'

'Course I don't, but I've got eyes, Reinar. We've all got eyes.'

Reinar turned back to see that Alys was leaving the fire with Lotta and Puddle, and without a word, he headed off after them.

***

Sigurd returned to the grove, wanting to be alone, though he wondered if he was ever truly alone, surrounded by gods and goddesses who could see and hear everything he did. He bent to the pool, dipping a finger into the still water, desperate to reveal an image or some clue as to what was happening. The water was cold, and he saw nothing more than ripples as he stirred it around. Eventually, he yanked off his cloak and sat down. He knew he stood no chance of seeing anything while he held himself back, slightly removed, only half-believing the truth about who he was. He'd half-believed everything his entire life, doubting most things, suspicious of everything. Even now, here, at Gallabrok, he still didn't completely believe he was Thenor's son. He couldn't bring himself to commit to anything with his whole body and soul. And if he couldn't do that, how could he make magic?

'You must let go.'

Sigurd twisted around, though no one was there, and he quickly realised that the woman's gentle voice was inside his head.

'You have been afraid of the truth since you were a child, Sigurd. You feared the truth was something to be ashamed of, but the truth of who you are is wonderful, something to be proud of. But now, to truly become yourself, you must let go of that old fear. It won't serve you now.'

'Who are you?' Sigurd demanded with a frown. He kept turning, looking around the grove, but no one answered him.

No one was there.

Though the woman's words lingered as he fixed his attention back on the water.

***

It was raining and almost dark when Gudrum dismounted, leaving his horse with his steward, walking through the forest with Bor Bearsu, Edrik, and a handful of his men. The Tudashi king had become a reluctant ally, it appeared, for he'd refused Gudrum's offer to accompany him, preferring to remain behind in their camp, wanting to ensure that his men would be sleeping and eating well that night. But brushing the irritation away, Gudrum walked with energy, for though he was weary and wet from his journey, his body was tingling in anticipation for the coming battle.

'As I predicted, my lord,' Bor smiled, lifting one side of his crooked mouth as they stopped, peering through the trees. 'They have taken the hill. The more amenable side of the field too. They'll be in the woods, I imagine, and beyond, enjoying what Salagat still has to offer.' He pointed to the stand of trees to the west of Gord's Field, where they both saw tiny figures moving around.

Gudrum licked his lips. They were some distance from the enemy, though he felt the urge to grab his horse and spur him across the field to where Reinar Vilander and his army were likely making their plans, sitting around fires, drinking and eating.

He could end it all so quickly.

Kill the man who would be king, capture his people, conquer Alekka and turn back to face the Islanders...

He laughed, the visions receding, smiling at Bor, whose frown had only deepened. 'No doubt their dreamers will alert them to our presence. That will give them a few nightmares!'

Bor didn't smile. 'And you intend to do what, my lord?'

'Retire to my tent, change my clothes, drink some ale. I hope to see my dreamer and hear her thoughts, perhaps enjoy a meal. And then, I shall invite my warlords in for a little chat, and we will make our plans. But for now, Bor, I'm too wet and cold to think!' He winked at Edrik and turned back into the trees. 'Stop worrying!' he called over his shoulder. 'Soon we'll give the gods a battle worthy of their attention!'

Bor Bearsu watched Gudrum go, hearing his laughter, unable to relax his frown.

***

After shepherding Lotta and Puddle into the tent, a distracted Alys left them with Stina and went in search of Magnus. It wasn't late, but she hadn't seen him since supper.

Instead, she found Reinar standing beneath a tree, watching her.

She approached him with a smile, feeling oddly hesitant after their conversation in Eddeth's cottage. 'Have you seen Magnus?'

Reinar nodded. 'Earlier, yes. He was with some of the older boys. Gulli Forvast's sons.'

That saw the end of Alys' smile. Those boys were big and rough, far too old for Magnus. She didn't like them at all.

'He'll be fine,' Reinar promised. 'Gulli will have a close eye on them. Magnus won't be sneaking off anywhere.'

Alys hoped not, knowing how eager her son was to become a warrior.

And at eleven?

Though remembering that he'd helped her kill that man in Orvala and watched as she took off his father's head, she supposed she wasn't surprised.

'Gudrum is close,' Alys said. 'We all feel it. Like a storm on the horizon, waiting to strike.'

'We're prepared,' Reinar assured her, the memories of their goodbye in Slussfall flooding his mind. 'Though now you're here, perhaps you can organise Eddeth and Raf? Eddeth keeps a lot to herself, as does Raf. It's been hard to get any sort of plan out of them. I still don't know how they intend to help or what they can do.'

'I can try, though I imagine we won't know what to do until it happens.' She saw flashes of the field: Reinar's body, Gudrum's victorious face. 'But you'll have three dreamers now,' she went on, strengthening her voice, hoping to inspire confidence. 'Three pairs of eyes. We'll all be watching you.'

He frowned. 'Not just me. I hope not.' Glancing over his shoulder, he saw no one watching them, and touching Alys' arm, he walked her around the back of her tent, walking further until they were well out of earshot. There was little to hear but the trickle of the stream and the rustle of creatures ferreting about in the underbrush, checking whether it was safe to come out. 'I meant what I said, back in Slussfall, in the cottage.' Now Reinar stepped forward until his face was shadowing hers. 'It's not fair on Elin to keep living a lie. I can't keep pretending I don't feel these things for you. She's not a fool, and she doesn't deserve a husband who treats her like one. And you, you deserve more than feeling as though you have to hide away, afraid to show your face.'

Alys squirmed, feelings of guilt rearing their head again. 'But she's your wife, Reinar, and once you're in Stornas, you will... you will...' She saw flashes of Elin Vilander vomiting in the garden, talking to Agnette, rubbing her rounded belly. And horrified, she stumbled backwards.

'What? What did you see?'

Alys' mouth was open, though no words came out. She stared at Reinar, wide-eyed, debating what to do.

And then she dropped her head.

Reinar blinked in confusion. 'Is it Helgi?'

Alys looked up. 'What?'

'He seems fond of you. He's always where you are.' Jealousy was in Reinar's voice, his jaw clenching. Never before had he experienced jealousy. Elin had always been his. He'd never felt the pangs of anger that flared whenever Helgi Eivin looked at Alys.

Alys shook her head. 'No, it's nothing to do with Helgi. It's... your wife.' She kept shaking her head, certain it wasn't her place to tell Reinar about the baby, fearing that he shouldn't have it on his mind before such a crucial battle. 'You're married, and it matters. Your oath to her matters. It shouldn't be something you can just change your mind about.' She was stumbling over her words, trying to edge away, feeling strange all over. 'You owe Elin. We... it will be different when we're not in Slussfall. You'll be able to move on, to forget everything. We both will.' Alys' eyes blurred with tears, her heart pounding. 'This... it's not what we should be talking about, Reinar. There's too much to do and I... need to find Magnus.'

Reinar backed away, feeling an odd distance between them

now, as though Alys had put up a wall.

'I need to find Magnus,' she repeated. Reinar looked hurt, and she never wanted to hurt him, though she turned away from him, knowing what Ragnahild had warned and Raf had seen.

What she had seen herself.

Elin was carrying Reinar's child, but it was Alys who had to save his life.

Reinar was too stunned to move. He had woken every day since he'd first laid eyes on Alys, thinking about her. At first, when he'd taken her from Ullaberg, when they were making their way back to Ottby, he'd told himself that he was interested in how she could help him as a dreamer. Though it quickly became so much more. And even when Elin returned, he still woke every morning with that face in his mind.

Alys' face.

He didn't understand what had happened between Slussfall and here. Or what Alys had truly seen. He stood frozen there for some time, the conversation echoing around his confused mind, mingling with the one in Eddeth's cottage. He remembered kissing Alys, telling her he loved her. And now he saw her almost running from him, desperate to get away.

It didn't make sense.

Eventually, the sounds of the camp brought him back to life, and resettling his cloak, he realised how cold he'd become, deciding to head to the nearest fire in search of ale.

***

It was all about timing, Alari knew.

Her fiery rage had dampened, though it would never stop burning until her father and those he supported were dead. She stirred the embers of her brazier with a poker, watching first one army and then the next. She knew how easy it would be to interfere, to insert herself into the tedious affairs of the humans.

She wanted a say.

She very much wanted a say in who would rule Alekka.

But to empower a dreamer like Gysa and then do all the work herself?

It was all about timing, Alari knew, dropping her shoulders.

And sitting back, she closed her eye, smiling.

***

Returning to the tent with a reluctant Magnus, Alys left Stina with the children, all three of them yawning, Puddle flopped over Lotta's arm. She would spend the night with Raf and Eddeth, for there were plans to make and dreams to be had. Jonas had gone to stay with Vik and Ollo, so Stina would hopefully enjoy a night uninterrupted by snores and nightmares.

Alys wrapped her cloak tightly around her chest as she walked, feeling the rain intensifying again. Ludo caught her, and turning to look up at him, she smiled.

'You're not staying with Stina?'

'No, I need to be with Eddeth and Raf now. Stina will look after the children. They know what to do if something happens.'

'I'll keep an eye on them too,' Ludo promised.

Alys placed a hand on his arm. She had spent so long thinking of her own aching heart, though she wasn't the only one struggling. And feeling bad for not having tried to help Stina before, she felt the need to do so now. 'You should say something to Stina.'

Ludo blinked, hearing thunder rumbling nearby. He curled over slightly, shoulders lifting. 'Say something?'

'Perhaps I'm wrong, but I think you like each other. Maybe more? It feels that way to everyone watching, at least. It's not my place, but Stina... she likes you.'

Ludo looked shocked. 'She does?'

'You're surprised?'

'Well, I thought she'd rather be with someone older. Like Vik.'

'Vik?' Alys laughed, shaking her head. 'No, Stina likes you.'

Ludo didn't appear convinced.

'I promise she does.'

'But what happened in Ottby? We captured you, locked Stina in a barn and Torvig...' The thought of what had happened to Stina under his watchful eye often kept Ludo awake at night. 'I should have protected her.'

'I'm a dreamer, and even I didn't see it, so you can't blame yourself. And Stina doesn't blame you, I promise. She just wants to know how you feel.'

'Alys! Over here! We're over here!' came Eddeth's squawking voice.

Alys turned away, holding up a hand. 'You don't have to do anything, Ludo, but if you do, you'll make Stina very happy.' And with that, she was hurrying towards Eddeth's familiar silhouette, wanting to put all thoughts of love and romance far behind her.

***

Jael fell asleep with her children, who had both escaped their own beds not long after she'd fallen into hers. They were missing Eadmund, and she was missing Eadmund, and the dogs were missing Eadmund. And having eaten an enormous supper after a long day of training with Fyn, Jael was too exhausted to move. So Sigmund lay on one arm, Bo on the other. Vella was curled up by her feet, guarding the door, and Ido was having a dream on Eadmund's pillow, which he'd spent at least an hour licking.

Jael couldn't move. And though her arms were numb and she preferred to sleep on her side, she found her eyes closing, unable to stop herself falling asleep.

CHAPTER TWENTY NINE

After his conversation with Alys, Reinar took to his bed. There was a raucous, almost joyous mood in the camp. He felt neither and didn't want to linger by the fires, ruining everyone's good time. The ale was flowing, the hunters having returned that afternoon with stag and elk. That had kept the servants busy, and now those gathered around flaming fire pits and crackling braziers had greasy fingers and beards, but more importantly, full bellies, as they sat back listening to stories about heroes of old, wondering if one day such songs would be sung about them.

Reinar lay in his cot bed, arms rigid by his sides, trying to take his mind off his conversation with Alys by entertaining thoughts of anything and everything but her. It was a chilly night, though he felt almost warm beneath a generous stack of furs. His steward had been issued strict orders by his mother to keep him warm, so Reinar wasn't cold, but he felt frozen by fear.

A king was just a man, a queen just a woman.

They were no different in how they felt and what they thought.

Their responsibilities were vastly greater, though their hearts and minds?

They were exactly the same as anyone else's.

Reinar was afraid that he'd fail to defeat Gudrum. In fact, he feared he most certainly wouldn't be able to overcome Gudrum's distinct advantages and that he was making a mistake to even try. To risk the lives of his men because he thought he should be king?

Because Ake had willed it? Because Ragnahild had seen it?

There were always bad kings. Between the mostly good ones, there was always a rotten apple or two. A mad king, a cowardly king, a corrupt, greedy king, a cruel, malicious king. Reinar wondered which one Gudrum would be if he conquered all of Alekka, realising that as much as he wanted to pack up his army and head back to Slussfall, he couldn't.

He had to try.

For Ake and Thenor, he had to try. For those Alekkans who had lost their homes and loved ones and feared for their futures, he had to try.

He saw himself dead on the field, his mind wandering to how it would go, to the way his life would end. He knew he should embrace it – the idea of a warrior's death, the honour of his sacrifice before the gods – but lying there all alone, he thought instead of pain, fear, and sadness. He wished he'd said more to Elin when he'd left. His obsession with Alys had corrupted his feelings for his wife, and now he didn't see her as the same woman anymore. Perhaps she wasn't, though that was likely his fault too. He wished he'd taken the time to talk more to Agnette, to hold her baby, or to listen to his mother's words of advice.

He was afraid of dying.

Seeing Alys' face, Reinar closed his eyes, seeking his brother instead.

'Sigurd,' he whispered, hearing joyous whooping noises in the distance. 'I need you. Wherever you are, I need your help. Never thought I'd say that,' he grinned suddenly. 'But, Brother, I do. I really do.'

***

The boy held an arm around the dog's throat.

The dog whimpered.

The boy squeezed tighter.

'No!' Jael shouted. 'Let her go!' She ran forward, but now it was Biddy, and the arm was wrapped around her throat.

The man held her tightly, threatening her with a knife.

'No! Stop!' And lunging, Jael fell through the darkness, tumbling, hands flailing, and then she was lying on her back, staring at the stars.

'I'm going to kill him,' the voice beside her growled.

'No, she was my dog,' Jael said through tears. 'I'll do it. Ronal killed her, and now I'll kill him.' She felt a hand on her arm, and turning, she looked into Aleksander's dark eyes.

'But your father...'

The voice crashed over her like thunder.

'What were you thinking, Jael? You killed Ronal Killi over a dog? A *dog*?'

It was her father's voice, scathing in anger.

Jael shook her head, and Biddy was there again, whimpering before her, that knife now scraping her throat.

'I'm going to gut you, you smug bitch. Gut you and bleed you so you can feel yourself die.'

Jael blinked, and she was on the field of snow and mud and bodies, and a man was running towards her, arm out.

And it was Aleksander.

She had loved him and lost him and turned away from him entirely, and now he was before her again, and she didn't know what to do.

Reaching her, he pulled her into his arms, holding her tightly. 'Don't go this time. Stay with me, Jael. Please. You must hear me!'

She didn't squirm. She didn't move at all.

'Stop running away. Stop, please.'

'I...' She started crying on his shoulder. 'I....' The tears kept coming. She couldn't make them stop.

'You're the strongest person I know, Jael Furyck. You did your best at the Vale. You always do your best, so don't run anymore. Not from what you did or didn't do. Not from who you were or are. Be here now. You have to be.'

Jael pulled back, staring at Aleksander, holding a hand to his face. She'd spent most of her life staring at that face. 'I miss you.'

He smiled. 'I know, but you have work to do.'

'Work? What do you mean?'

'Jael, it's Gudrum. He's back.'

***

Stellan thought about Sigurd as he tried to get comfortable, hoping his son was safe. It was a fleeting thought, for there was nothing he could do to help him. Not here. Not now. He had to fix his mind on what the morning would bring, and to do that effectively, he was going to need some sleep.

Ollo and Jonas were already snoring, but Vik didn't appear ready to join them. He'd found a jug of ale and made himself comfortable in front of the brazier he was now adding more logs to. Eventually, Stellan decided to join him, unable to find anywhere comfortable to lie. He'd happily given up his tent to the Lord of Fasta, who had arrived that afternoon with two hundred men, and after their long journey, he wanted the lord to have some comfort and privacy. The lord had brought his wife along, and they both seemed to appreciate Stellan's gesture.

Vik smiled at Stellan as he pulled up a stool. 'Sleeping on the ground's losing its appeal.'

Stellan chuckled. 'You're not wrong.' He reached for the cup of ale Vik had poured him. 'So that's all that's keeping you awake then? Or is it those two wild beasts back there?' He flicked a hand at the snoring duo in the corner.

'It's almost like I can't hear it now,' Vik admitted. 'Though it's neither, really. I've been going into battle for more years than I can remember, but this is the first time where it feels as though something's on the line.'

Stellan frowned at him, too tired to sense his meaning.

'Estrella,' Vik sighed. 'She needs me.' He shook his head, seeing glimpses of Estrella's flaming eyes. 'Well, likely she doesn't need me, but after losing Ake, I don't want her to lose me too. Not with a baby coming and the two girls to worry about.'

Stellan knew better than most how much Vik had always loved Estrella. And love like that was powerful enough to last a lifetime, he imagined, never having experienced it himself.

'I've never really fought that way before... caring if I die. Now though...'

'But you have to fight the same way,' Stellan insisted. 'If you let fear in, you become less effective. There was always a chance you'd die, it's always been there, but you shut it out. Now you can't afford to let it in. You can't, Vik. None of us can. Not if we want to win.'

Vik nodded, sipping his ale.

'Jonas has to shut out Alys and the children, though I imagine it's all he can think about. Reinar has to shut out his people and his fears of what will happen to us if he falls.'

'And you?'

Stellan blinked, eyes on the flames, seething with intensity now. 'I have to shut out my son. To be able to fight alongside Reinar, I have to shut him out entirely. Yet I'm his father, and he's my boy, and every instinct tells me to protect him, to save him. Though I can't.'

'And Sigurd?'

'I can't think about him at all,' Stellan said softly. 'We can only focus on what lies before us now. And soon that will be Gudrum.'

***

Jael shook Biddy's arm until she shrieked, sitting up in a panic.

'What? Jael! What are you doing?' Biddy panted, grey curls bouncing around a crumpled face. She was immediately shivering, the cold night air raising the hairs on her arms; the sight of Jael looming over her too. 'Whatever has happened?'

'It's Gudrum. He's...' Jael wanted to scream or fly. She had to be in Alekka now. *Now*! 'He's the King of Alekka. Ake's dead. Gudrum tricked us!'

Biddy's face wrinkled in confusion. 'Gudrum? Gudrum Killi? A king?'

Jael nodded. 'I have to leave. I have to go after Eadmund.'

Biddy remained confused. 'What? *Now*?' She looked around, blinking in the darkness.

Jael grabbed her arms, trying to focus her. 'Eadmund's heading for Gudrum. Gudrum, who tried to take something from me before. Gudrum, who wants revenge more than anything. And what do you imagine he's going to do to my husband?'

Biddy blinked at her in horror. 'You have to leave! But will you be in time? Jael?' She pushed Jael out of the way, wriggling to the edge of the bed.

'I don't know,' Jael said, standing up. 'I've woken Fyn. He's organising a crew. We'll leave at first light. I'm sending you to Andala. You and the children and the dogs. I don't know what else Gudrum's planning, but I can't leave you here to find out.'

Biddy was thoroughly flummoxed but wide awake now. 'Don't you worry about the children, just get going. Do what you can. It's all you can do, Jael. What you can.'

Jael strode to the door, fur cloak pinned to her right shoulder. She lifted the hood over her dark braids, shaking her head. 'No, this time, I need to do more. This time, I have to end Gudrum Killi.'

***

As dawn was breaking, a wide-awake Gysa joined Gudrum in his tent.

'Why so nervous?' he wondered with a laugh, noting the tension in her eyes, seeing her inability to stand still. 'Haven't you seen what's waiting for us? It's like Oss trying to defeat all of Brekka! I remember Eirik Skalleson thinking he could touch us, but he was a little fly, and we were a mighty horse. He was nothing more than an annoyance. Easy to swat away.'

Gysa tried to smile. 'I don't like war. It's ugly.'

'It's pure joy,' Gudrum countered. 'Bloody, horrible joy!' He pulled her close, wanting to feel her lips, her arms, every warm and soft part of her. After days of being drowned in rain, shivering with cold, he desired some comfort.

She came to him willingly, feeling oddly panicked. 'I fear what your arrogance will do.'

He swung back as though struck. '*Arrogance*?'

Gysa saw her misstep and quickly sought to begin again. 'Arrogance is no insult,' she insisted with a full, beaming smile. 'For a king must swagger. He must inspire confidence by projecting his own. No, you mistake my meaning.'

Gudrum lifted an eyebrow, inviting her to go on.

'Confidence is necessary, but believing you are invincible? Acting like it? That could harm you. Your enemy could use it against you.'

Now Gudrum laughed until his eyes watered. 'Have you seen this face? This body? All that's been done to me? All those famous warriors who've tried to kill me?' He held his belly, the laughter hurting now. 'I'm stitched together like a cloak! But stitched together, I am. Full of life and power and strength, and luck most of all. Don't you see, Gysa? I *am* invincible!' It wasn't true, and Gudrum knew it, but he wanted her to believe it because she was looking at him as though he was an old man, soiling his drawers.

'Of course I see it, I do,' Gysa smiled patiently, taking his hand, saying the opposite of what she was thinking. For it wasn't what she thought that mattered now, she realised. It was what Gudrum believed. And that belief would carry him to victory. 'I lost everything. All that I loved died before my eyes. I don't want that to happen again. When I see the future, it is...' She didn't go on, feeling foolish.

But Gudrum was intrigued. He had quickly become attached

to the dreamer, and it pleased him to know that she felt the same, that her fears for him were personal. He kissed her. 'I'll go and meet Reinar. We'll discuss things. And when I feel so inclined, I'll finish him, and then there'll only be one enemy to face. And that one I look forward to most of all.'

***

Having left Fyn organising a crew for one of the two remaining ships beached in Oss' harbour, Jael woke Thorgils' wife, Isaura, who immediately knew something was wrong. And after explaining her dream, Jael had hurried her back to the hall. With Biddy's help, they organised a fire and herbs from the kitchen garden, which had thankfully shown signs of life over the past few days.

'But it's been years,' Biddy muttered anxiously. 'Years since you did a dreamwalk. How can you even remember what to do?'

Jael couldn't, though she didn't plan to tell either woman that. 'I remembered the herbs. So did you. The words will come. The main thing is my connection to Eadmund. And I have this,' she said, holding out one of his tunics. It smelled like her husband, and Jael started blinking as fear rose its head once more. 'You keep feeding the fire. I'll close my eyes and try to slip away. Isaura will drum.'

They were in Biddy's chamber, sitting on the floor opposite the fire pit, candles and lamps flaming on tables around them. Though only enough to see. Jael wanted it to be dark. It had been over three years since she'd attempted a dreamwalk, and she vibrated with the worry that she wouldn't know how to fall into a trance.

'Close your eyes,' Biddy hissed impatiently, dropping a handful of mugwort into the flames. They spat and crackled, sparks flying. She took a deep breath, reaching for more herbs, watching as Jael closed her eyes.

***

'Oh, that Hykka hates us!' Eddeth exclaimed, wet hair clinging to a fretful face as dawn broke over the Silver Mountains. 'Doesn't he? I may as well take off my boots and walk around in bare feet.' She slipped off a boot and poured out a trickle of muddy water. 'What do I need these for?' she grumbled, brandishing it at Jonas.

Jonas and Ollo had come looking for Reinar, but mostly they wanted to know if the dreamers had seen anything, especially about the atrocious weather.

'And will it continue? The rain?' Ollo asked. 'Surely it doesn't help either side?'

'Well, we all need rain,' Eddeth said pragmatically, thinking things through. 'So perhaps Hykka doesn't have us in mind at all? Though it's rather inconvenient to be drowning us now!' She turned to Raf, reaching out a hand to steady herself on the little dreamer's shoulder while she shoved her wet boot back on her muddy foot. 'What I wouldn't give for some sun! Perhaps yesterday was it? Spring's done and dusted, and now it's just rain and misery till next winter?'

'Eddeth,' Jonas smiled, seeking to calm her down. She was a bundle of nerves, nattering away endlessly. 'You dreamers need to think about what to do with yourselves. Perhaps you can head back to camp with the servants? That's where Stina and the children will be.'

Raf looked at Eddeth, who straightened up.

'Oh no, that would never do! What use can we be tucked away with the servants? No, we need to be with you.'

'What?' both Ollo and Raf exclaimed at the same time.

'You can't be with us, woman,' Ollo laughed. 'You and your stick in a shield wall?'

'Not *next* to you,' Eddeth snorted. 'I didn't say that, did I, Ollo Narp?' She glowered at him for a moment, eyes jumping with tiredness. 'No indeed, that's not how it will go at all. But we dreamers need to be close enough to help if needs be. To get a message through quickly. You don't want me trying to roll down that hill, do you?'

Jonas grinned at the thought of it. 'Perhaps placing you on a hill isn't a good idea,' he agreed.

'Then where?' Raf wanted to know, not keen to be in the middle of a battle. 'We can't get too close.'

'No, you can't. We'll need you,' Ollo decided. 'What?' he grumbled, seeing three surprised faces. 'We know Gudrum's got a dreamer. I doubt he left her behind, did he? Why would he? So we need our own dreamers keeping her busy.'

That was true, though the thought of facing Gysa didn't fill Raf with any confidence. She felt relieved that Alys had arrived, bringing the puppy, though worried, too, fearing that she was only here because everything was about to go horribly wrong.

'We'll make a circle!' Eddeth decided. 'A circle in the mud! It will keep us safe and lock that Gysa woman out.' She spun around, pointing to the wooded area to the west of the field, nestled at the base of the hill. 'There! We'll be safe over there!'

No one looked sure about that.

'We will. I promise we will!' Eddeth insisted, turning away to sneeze. And when she turned back around, her mouth dropped open. 'He's coming soon. Gudrum! I sense him. And that dreamer too. We'd better get to work! No time for that!' She tore the ale cup out of Ollo's hand, throwing it to the ground in a fluster. 'Move, move! We have to move!'

***

Fyn was waiting outside the hall when Jael emerged into the half-light. A fine day was dawning, though the wind was blustery, which was nothing new on Oss. 'What happened?' he asked as Jael stalked past him, heading for the gates. 'Jael? The dreamwalk?'

'I couldn't get through to Eadmund. There was no way through.' At first, Jael had feared that she'd done something wrong, but eventually, she'd realised that a wall was blocking her. And nothing she did could move it. Whatever games Gudrum was playing, he had dreamer help. And not feeling much like a dreamer anymore, Jael didn't know what to do about that.

'Are we leaving?'

She nodded. 'I just need to go over things with Halli first. He'll have even less men to keep Oss safe now, and with me sending Biddy and the children to Andala, he'll have no ships for awhile.' She'd said goodbye to a tearful Biddy, urging her not to wake the sleeping children until she'd gone. She had kissed them both goodbye, and the dogs, knowing it would be harder to leave if they were all awake, clinging to her.

And her clinging to them.

'Should we take horses?'

Jael had initially felt hesitant about that. Though, in the end, she knew they had to move quickly, and there was no guarantee how long it would take to find horses once they landed. 'I've sent Askel to bring them down. Leada and Vili too.'

'Tig won't be happy.'

Jael knew that to be true, though she didn't smile.

'Was it a dream then? How you knew about this Gudrum?'

Jael glanced over her shoulder at the great hall commanding the square – hers and Eadmund's hall – and she nodded. 'More of a nightmare, really. Gudrum is...' She dropped her head. 'A mistake I have to correct. If there's time.'

Fyn followed after her, cloak flapping around his legs, feeling a flutter of excitement. Fear too. He thought of Eadmund and Thorgils and Bram, wondering what trouble they were all in.

CHAPTER THIRTY

Alys had spoken to Stina, going over what she needed to do if anything went wrong. She didn't know if Gudrum and Reinar would choose to fight quickly or whether they would take more time to prepare, but she had a feeling that it wouldn't be long now.

Crouching down, she tapped Lotta's nose. 'I'll be back later.'

Lotta frowned. 'Later when?'

'Later when I'm done,' Alys promised with a smile. 'And you'll be here with Puddle and Stina and a nice hot fire, please. Some stew and ale too.'

'And pancakes,' Lotta huffed, hating to be left behind. 'Stina said we're going to make apple pancakes.'

Magnus was pleased about that, but turning to his mother, he threw his arms around her neck with fear in his eyes. 'You need to come back.'

'I do,' Alys agreed, squeezing him tightly. 'And I will. No matter what happens, nothing will keep me away from you.'

'And me?' came Lotta's tearful voice as she wrapped her arms around her mother's back.

'You too. Of course, you too.' Alys released one arm from Magnus, bringing Lotta in close. 'Stay with Stina, don't leave the camp, and whatever you do, don't let Puddle out of your sight.'

They heard a nervous cough, and looking up, Alys saw Ludo looming above them all.

'Stina's gone to talk to the servants,' Lotta said immediately, pulling herself out of her mother's arms. 'I can walk you there.' And not waiting for Ludo to speak, she took his hand and tugged him away.

Alys smiled as she stood, though Magnus remained frowning. 'Your sister –'

'Never listens to me! Never ever.'

'I was going to say that she's a dreamer, so you should listen to her.' Which, she could see, wasn't what he wanted to hear. 'If she sees something, you'll need to tell Stina, and if not Stina, then find a servant, someone who can get a message through to us.' And then, reading his thoughts, Alys placed her hands on his shoulders, staring into his eyes. 'But not you. Not you at all.'

Magnus finally smiled, burying himself in his mother's arms again.

'Go and get your sister, Magnus. Ludo and Stina need to talk, and I...' She kissed his head. 'I'll see you soon.'

***

It had quickly been relayed to Reinar that his enemy had arrived, though they didn't appear in any hurry to attack him.

Scouts had been tracking Gudrum for days, returning in waves with the news of his progress, so it wasn't a surprise that he was finally here. In fact, Reinar decided, eager to begin, it was a relief to know that Gudrum had chosen to come to Salagat and face him rather than slipping around him to try and capture Slussfall.

Mercifully, the rain had stopped, though they were all still squelching through mud and snow, knowing that what lay ahead was going to be miserable, ugly, and very, very wet.

'Gudrum seems like an impatient man,' Bjarni decided. 'Doubt he'll sit around for long, enjoying the view.'

Reinar laughed as his father, Vik, Ollo, Berger and Helgi joined them. 'You never know. He's had a long journey, and he's not a young man. Likely he could do with a sit-down and some hot milk.'

Stellan didn't think that sounded like a bad idea himself. 'Well, once he's finished that, I expect he'll make a show of listening to whoever's got his ear. If they've any sense, they'll be advising him against trying the hill. Against crossing the stream too. Though if the Goddess of Luck's with us, he won't listen. His giant ego will have him charging towards us.'

'Well, his giant something,' Berger grinned, lifting an eyebrow at Raf, who'd just arrived with Eddeth and Alys.

'I saw the woman! The dreamer!' Eddeth announced breathlessly. 'Oh yes, she's plotting something. Something dark!'

Everyone turned to Eddeth, who bubbled like a cauldron, though Reinar's eyes were on Alys, who turned to him with worry in hers.

'We have to go. The dreamers! We can't be here one moment longer!' Eddeth insisted loudly. 'We'll take that one-armed servant with us. What's his name? Dalmar? Dalman? Darin? He can run back and forth if we need messages sent. And he's useful with his left arm, isn't he? I'm sure he could swing an axe if he had to.'

Reinar shook his head, grabbing Eddeth's elbow as she made to leave. 'You'll need more protection than that, Eddeth. More help too. Bjarni, find at least eight men. They can guard their... circle?'

'Yes, our circle! It will be mightier than any shield wall!' Eddeth blustered, then shrieking, she spun around so quickly that she knocked into Ollo, who almost lost his footing in the mud.

'What are you doing, woman?' he growled.

'Arrows!' Eddeth shouted, heading for the hill. 'Run!'

No one ran with her.

They stood in the shadow of the hill, eyeing the dark forest opposite the stream, where they knew Gudrum and his men were camped. Their own archers had been practising since they'd arrived, knowing that, here, at the far end of Gord's Field, with no enemy archers even in sight, they were well out of range.

Raf glanced at the huddle of bleary-eyed, yawning men, then at a panicking Eddeth, and chose to hurry after the dreamer.

Alys watched them go, seeing Jonas coming towards her with an easy smile.

The arrows whipped into the air like a great flock of birds, just a hint of a whistle in the distance. No man held a shield as they stood their ground.

'*Move*!' Eddeth screeched, turning back around, boots stuck, going in opposite directions, and unable to move, she lost her balance, tumbling headfirst into the mud.

The arrows struck far below where they stood, near a group of men hammering the last stakes into the ground on their side of the stream. Though they'd heard the noise in time and had run out of range.

Reinar turned to see Raf trying to drag a muddy Eddeth back to her feet.

'Told you,' Eddeth grumbled, spitting out a mouthful of mud. And batting Raf away, she stomped towards the stand of trees, one eye on where those arrows had come from.

Reinar watched her go, and shaking his head, he turned to leave, catching Alys' eye. He held it for a moment, still confused, not understanding what he'd done wrong or what had changed between them. But ducking his head, he turned away, knowing that he couldn't think about Alys or Elin or Sigurd or anyone but Gudrum now.

Gudrum, who would come for him soon.

***

Ludo knew he didn't have time for distractions, but the approaching battle had filled him with an overwhelming sense of urgency.

And a small measure of courage.

Lotta had left him outside the servants' tent, though she lingered near a tree in the distance with her brother, watching. He turned around, seeing her frowning, urging him on with both hands. Magnus stood beside her, looking just as impatient. And turning back around, Ludo closed his eyes, taking a deep breath, hand on the tent flap.

Stina walked out, banging into him. 'Oh!' She almost fell backwards, but Ludo grabbed her with both hands, steadying her, and then, as she looked up in surprise, he bent down and kissed her.

The loud whoops from Lotta and Magnus didn't stop the kiss as Ludo gently clung to Stina, and she almost fell against him in both surprise and joy.

Eventually, he released her, stepping back, suddenly shy again. 'I wanted to... say goodbye.'

Stina stared up at him, too breathless to speak. She felt as though she could float. As though her limbs were made of clouds and she could simply float into the sky. She couldn't even blink. 'So did I,' she finally admitted. 'Though I don't think I would've been that brave.' She didn't take her eyes off him, and eventually, she saw his return to her.

'You didn't mind? After Torvig, I –'

Stina grabbed his hand. 'Torvig's dead.' And pushing up on her tiptoes, she kissed him again.

***

Alys shook her head, trying not to become distracted by thoughts of Reinar or her mother. She had slipped her hand into her purse, and feeling the brooch, she saw immediate flashes of Mirella.

It was unsettling and not what she needed to be thinking about now.

Helgi tapped her on the shoulder, and she jumped, crying out.

He blinked at her in surprise as she turned around to him. 'Sorry, I...'

Alys was embarrassed. 'I'm not very good with surprises,'

she admitted. 'I wish I didn't have to scream, though.' She felt her cheeks heating, sensing many pairs of eyes on her. And then Helgi's.

'You look upset,' he decided. 'Worried.' He felt a familiar thrumming in his body but no fear as he stood before her, ready for whatever Gudrum was planning. He felt cradled in the hands of the gods, confident that Thenor himself would determine his fate.

'And you're not?' Alys glanced over her shoulder at the circle where Eddeth was making a fire, arguing with the warriors who'd surrounded them on Reinar's orders, wanting them to move further away.

Helgi looked up at the sky, seeing hints of snow. And looking back down at Alys, he stepped closer. 'The gods are with us,' he promised softly. 'You said it yourself that Thenor supports Reinar. And Thenor's an army in his own right.'

Alys didn't want to dent Helgi's confidence, though she wanted to see more concern in his eyes. More hesitancy. So, grabbing his arm, she pushed up onto her toes until her lips almost touched his ear. 'You should be careful,' she warned. 'What we have seen, the dreamers... we aren't confident.' Stepping back, she kept her eyes on Helgi, who, she was pleased to see, finally looked a little disturbed.

'We've things to do!' Reinar bellowed as he approached. 'No time for chatting! No time for drinking or eating! We've things to do!' He stopped before Helgi, eyes flaring. 'Berger and Ollo need your help. We have to finish staking the base of the hill.' And resisting the urge to pick Helgi up and throw him far away from Alys, he inhaled a deep breath and turned to the dreamer.

Eddeth shouted Alys' name.

And then a horse.

It was hard to tell who was riding it, but with one lingering look at Alys, Reinar started for Riga, certain that it was Gudrum.

The rider was joined by four men, who rode just behind him, one carrying Gudrum's yellow banner. Reinar quickly chose Stellan, Vik, Bjarni and Berger to come with him. He would've picked Ludo, though he couldn't see him, and Berger quickly put himself forward, which wasn't a surprise.

'You look well!' Gudrum boomed as he reined in his horse some way from the stream. 'I am surprised. Tail between your legs? Running up North like a smacked child? You look much better than I'd imagined when I dreamed of this moment!'

Stellan kept his mouth closed, his expression neutral, though he quickly took the measure of the new King of Alekka – so very different from the last one. It was impossible not to stare at the horror of that mauled face . Impossible to ignore a twinge of fear that this man was going to be a real problem.

'You're dreaming of me?' Reinar grinned. 'I guess you're lonely now Raf's with us!'

That wiped the smile off Gudrum's face, and he jerked forward so abruptly that his horse stumbled, forcing Gudrum to rein him in. 'Raf?' He was quickly smiling again, though his eyes had hardened. 'She was a warm body in The Murk, but little else. You're welcome to her! I've replaced her with a real woman. A skilled, powerful, capable woman. Raf would've been out of place if she'd remained with me. Though I imagine your brother's pleased.'

Reinar wanted to focus Gudrum's attention on what lay before them. 'You've come to surrender?' he asked with a straight face.

'To you?' Gudrum's eyes gleamed. 'Why? Do you have another army hiding up that hill? Or perhaps you've dug up the dead? You're certainly going to need all the help you can get! Though not many want to fight for a doomed man. A man with no luck. An unlucky man, spurned by the gods!'

'Well, that depends on who you're talking to,' Reinar said, taking the bait, sensing his father glowering beside him. 'Though the gods aren't here, and you still have a chance to surrender before my men humiliate yours. Before I tear your head from your shoulders and shove it up your arse!'

'Well, that was parley!' Gudrum announced loudly, looking from broken-nosed Bor to handsome, pouting Edrik. 'Now let's do battle!' He swung his horse around, heading back to the forest. 'I look forward to your plans, Reinar!' he called over his shoulder. 'To all your surprises. If you've got any!'

Stellan looked after him for some time before turning to Reinar. 'Looks like he was spat out a giant's mouth.'

'Or shat out its arse!' Berger laughed.

Bjarni frowned. 'He's still standing, though. That's got to tell you something.'

'Only that he's not faced my son in battle,' Stellan decided.

Reinar glanced his way. 'Well...'

'Sea fighting's not real fighting,' Stellan snorted. 'Who can achieve anything on a rocking ship? No, this will be a proper fight. We'll get you to Gudrum. Get you there, and protect you while you defeat him. That's the plan. Drive that bastard into the dirt. Leave what's left of him for the crows.'

'Bor Bearsu looks up for a fight,' Vik put in. 'He's a leader. Less of a prick than Svein was.'

'Just means we'll have work to do,' Stellan insisted, not wanting anyone to wander down a rabbit hole of doubt. 'But we always knew that.'

Berger looked up for the fight, busy tidying his beard, but Bjarni felt ready for a quick dash to the latrines. 'Will he come now?'

'No idea.' Reinar was quick to turn Riga around, wanting to be ready either way. 'Let's get back, ensure all our defenses are in place. Berger, go find Ludo. It's time to get your men, gather them together, take up your positions.' Berger nodded, and spurring his horse across the field, he aimed him at Helgi.

Reinar turned to Bjarni. 'You ready?'

Bjarni inhaled quickly, spluttering out a cough. He couldn't speak, though he managed to nod. His need for the latrines was suddenly so demanding that he wheeled his horse away from Reinar without another word.

Reinar was inclined to follow him, though he couldn't disappear now. Turning to his father, Vik, and Jonas, he saw their grey hair and weathered faces, feeling like a boy before them, knowing all three men had done this before. They had battled a powerful army, outnumbered, fearful of defeat, afraid of letting their men down. Yet they had succeeded. They had lived.

They were legends.

Jonas smiled, feeling the familiar tremors of fear and excitement mingling in his limbs. 'Gudrum's not long for this world. He might think himself lucky, but I doubt Thenor has much patience for a usurper like him. And a Brekkan one at that. No, Gudrum's end is near. That cockiness?' He shook his head. 'Men like that are only trying to hide the truth. And the truth is that he was never born to be a lord, let alone a king.'

His voice was deep and authoritative, and Reinar wanted to believe him.

He saw Vik nodding.

'He might listen to his advisors,' Vik added. 'But just as likely, he'll ignore everything they're saying, trying to defeat us without thinking too hard at all. Men leading large armies often become lazy. It's the thinkers who stand the better chance. And lucky for you, you're surrounded by them.'

'I'm glad of it.'

Jonas and Vik took one final look at their future king and each other before heading away in opposite directions, leaving Stellan standing before his son.

'To be a real king, a man must ascend to a higher level of being.'

Reinar blinked. That sounded like something Thenor would say.

'It's what Ake once told me. You have to leave yourself behind and become something else entirely. A leader. A champion. A king. The one everyone looks to for guidance and inspiration. You have to shut yourself away now, Reinar, and lead us. Forget everything you've heard. All the whispers and the gossip and the dreams.' Stellan stepped closer now, gripping the back of his son's neck. 'And looking at your face, I imagine there've been some dreams. But ignore them now. Your destiny is out there.' Standing back, he motioned to the boggy field before them. 'Whatever has gone before, whatever has been seen doesn't matter. You can make your destiny today, Reinar. Ake is with you, I am with you. This is *your* day.' Stellan feared he would cry, which wasn't what he wanted to give his son. Reinar needed to feel nothing but strength, determination, and desire.

Reinar kept nodding.

'I saw Gudrum's eyes. He's afraid of you. He's come here because he's afraid of you,' Stellan went on. 'He wants to put you down because he fears what you'll become. So we'll make that work in our favour.' Bringing his son into his arms, Stellan held him tightly. 'There's no place I'd rather be. No place at all.' And letting Reinar go, he smiled. 'You've nothing to prove, just a lot of work to do out there!' And turning away, he didn't look back, leaving Reinar alone.

But not for long.

Soon his warriors were charging towards him, questions in their eyes, hands in the air, and Reinar was lost in the noise and hum of activity, trying to push his fears and worries about Gudrum away.

***

Eddeth and Raf remained in the muddy circle while Alys came and went, bringing firewood, a bucket of water, a jug of ale, cups and food. She couldn't stay still, her eyes constantly returning to the field, trying to find Reinar, regretting what a mess she'd made of their goodbye.

Raf squatted beside a fidgeting Eddeth, who was struggling with their fire. Her hood flapped against the back of her head, black hair sweeping across her face in the stiffening breeze. 'There's too much wind,' Raf muttered, thinking of the archers. Thinking about their fire too.

Eddeth looked up, mouth hanging open. 'Wind?' She hurried to her feet with a click of her hips and a loud sneeze. 'Wind!' And taking Raf's hand, she closed her eyes. 'The wind has a voice,' she bubbled, thoughts racing. 'And it's our job to hear it! Close your eyes now, and feel the wind, feel where it's coming from. Listen to the noises it makes, in your ears, in the trees. Let it enter your mind! Once we know the type of wind it is, we can try to wrangle it.'

Raf frowned, not understanding, though feeling the pressure of Eddeth's cold hand squeezing hers, she closed her eyes, taking a few shallow breaths. It was impossible to relax, though. She could feel Gudrum nearby; Gysa too. She guessed that Alari was watching, perhaps Vasa, and it distracted her, for they would never let Reinar be king. They would never let him defeat Gudrum, for he was now Alari's, just as Gysa was now Alari's.

'Oh, that's an angry wind! A dark, evil, angry wind!' Eddeth declared, eyes springing open. She didn't wait for Raf to agree, searching through one of her saddlebags. 'What did you hear?' she asked, looking up with a squint. 'Anything?'

Raf shrugged. 'Feels like a storm, though.'

Eddeth dropped her eyes to the rope she'd pulled from her bag. 'I have to bind it!'

Raf looked down at her in confusion. 'The wind? You can bind the wind?'

'I can try!' Eddeth grinned, knowing she had many things to think about and do, but Raf was right, that wind was a terror. And with half as many men as Gudrum, Reinar was going to be heavily reliant on his archers.

The wind needed to be with them.

So Eddeth had to try and command it.

CHAPTER THIRTY ONE

Bjarni returned to Reinar after his third visit to the latrines, and though he was jiggling on the spot, he didn't think he needed to head off again.

'Are you sure?' Reinar wanted to know. 'We've a lot to do, Bjarni.'

Bjarni knew that to be true. 'I can't think Gudrum will want to charge over here until he's gathered himself together. He won't just jump on a horse and pick up a spear.'

Reinar almost wished he would. If he killed Gudrum quickly, it would save a lot of lives. 'Either way, we're the ones who need to be ready. I don't give a shit what Gudrum's up to. We have to focus on our own plans now.' He started walking, pleased when Bjarni followed him. The mud was heavy going as they made their way past servants, whose heads remained down, trying not to fall over as they carried quivers of arrows to the archers and cauldrons of water to the fires. The morning was cold, but cloaks had mostly been abandoned now, everyone heated by panic and urgency.

Reinar and Bjarni wore mail shirts that hung to the tops of their thighs, cinched with full belts, knives and swords sharpened and waiting. Leather arm guards protected their wrists. Thick shoulder pads were secured across their upper torsos, covered by shields, which sat on their backs. They carried helmets in their left hands, leaving their right hands free for pointing and waving, which both men were doing plenty of.

'Kall!' Reinar called, turning to see his steward slipping and sliding behind him. 'Get this path cleared. I don't want anyone walking through here now. Keep to the sides. This is a bog!' He looked up, conscious of the menacing wind, fearing for his archers. But he quickly realised that though he needed to be aware of what was coming and what he could control, the wind wasn't one of them. 'Let's get to our position,' he said, taking a deep breath. 'I see nothing more to do now.'

And glancing around, Bjarni agreed.

'We'll get everyone ready, and then... I need to go and talk to our men.'

***

Ollo fussed around Ilene in a way that had her wanting to slap him. Since Berger had tossed her aside for the pregnant woman and Sigurd had disappeared, Ollo had become her constant companion, though Ilene was acutely aware that he wanted much more. She wasn't sure what she thought about that. He certainly wasn't handsome or young or as tall as the Eivin cousins, though he was a skilled warrior, brave in the face of fear. She'd seen that.

But did she really want to commit to one man? And an old one at that?

She wasn't sure it would matter soon, knowing the mountain of trouble they were facing.

'Why don't you wear a helmet?' Ollo snapped, tension mounting. Ilene strutted around as though she was off for a stroll. It was getting on his nerves.

'Don't want one. I can't hear what's going on with that metal over my ears.'

'That can be a good thing,' Ollo insisted. 'Blocks out some of the noise. A battle like this? It'll be hard to think soon, and you'll need to keep thinking.'

'But I want to hear everything,' Ilene said, the first hint of nerves showing now. 'I need to have some warning.'

'Agreed, but there's no guarantee you will, even without a helmet. Better to have one protecting you. You can suffer a blow to the back or the arm or the leg, but the head?' Ollo shook his own head, deciding not to take no for an answer. 'There'll be a spare helmet somewhere. Those men who died in the fjaladen attack won't be needing them, will they?'

Arguing and protesting came naturally to Ilene, and she opened her mouth to do just that, but seeing the concern in Ollo's eyes – Ollo, who had survived many battles – she nodded. 'Alright, but we have to hurry. Won't be long now.'

'Go to the stewards' tent. That's where everything will be. I'll meet you there.' And gripping his aching belly, Ollo hurried to the latrines.

***

Helgi stripped off his cloak and tunic, wrapping them up, leaving them near the row of braziers where the archers were discussing tactics.

Berger laughed at him. 'Looks like snow to me!'

Helgi snorted. 'What? You think I'm going to risk my luck by changing the way I fight? Today?' Though he had to admit it was freezing. His chest hairs tingled, his nipples ached, goosebumps rising over exposed flesh. But picking up his shield, he swung it over his back with a confident smile. 'No, Cousin, this is all I know. I won't walk away from it now.' He tied his swordbelt around his waist, settling his shoulders.

'You've a few new markings,' Berger noted, eyes on Helgi's arms, where swirling blue symbols rose up past his elbows like flames. 'Was that Vasir?'

Helgi nodded. 'The last ones he ever made.'

'Why? What happened?'

'Fight with his brother. The jealous prick cut out his eyes.'

Berger shook his head. 'Napper was always a shitheap. Glad we're out of it.' He saw a flash of unhappiness in Helgi's eyes; some regret too. 'We are out of it, aren't we?'

Helgi nodded, catching a glimpse of Alys. In the deepening gloom, her golden hair kept flashing like a beacon. 'Yes, we're out of Napper,' he assured his cousin. 'But let's hope today that Napper isn't out of us!'

And now they were both laughing, and Helgi was shivering, wanting to find a jug of ale before things kicked off.

***

Eddeth had swallowed a packet of flying powder by mistake. Thinking it was one of her mixes for settling her stomach, she'd tipped it into a cup of hot water, and now she was all over the place. Or nowhere at all. She couldn't decide. Finding it impossible to aim her mind in the direction she wanted it to go, she'd sent Raf out of the circle so she could fully concentrate on her spell to bind the wind. And not wanting to distract her, Raf walked into the woods, where she met Ludo coming towards her.

'Do you need something?' he asked, checking the circle, still counting eight guards. He wondered if it would be enough? Perhaps Gudrum would want his dreamer back? Or maybe he'd seek to get rid of her entirely?

Raf shook her head. 'Eddeth needs to be alone.' Her cloak lifted around her, and she snatched at it with fumbling fingers, trying to get it under control. 'She's trying to command the wind.'

Ludo looked surprised. 'Can she do that?'

Raf shrugged. 'I...' She glanced over her shoulder. 'I....'

Ludo sensed there was something on Raf's mind. She was usually reluctant to speak, but she certainly appeared to be trying to. He pressed a hand on her arm. 'You can tell me. Anything. I'll help if I can.'

Raf swallowed. 'I had a dream about Reinar before we left Slussfall. He doesn't want anyone to know, but I... he was dead. On a field. It looked like this field. It... was this field.'

Ludo's mouth gaped open. The wind howled through the trees. Raf's cloak snapped angrily before him.

'He was dead, and Gudrum sat on the throne. That's what I saw.'

'And Reinar knows?'

Raf nodded, and looking up, she saw tiny snowflakes floating through the air. Or perhaps it was ash from Eddeth's fire? Blinking, she focused her attention back on Ludo. 'It was just a dream.'

'But you're a dreamer. Your dreams aren't just dreams,' Ludo insisted.

'Sometimes they are.'

Taking a deep breath, Ludo saw Eddeth open her eyes, arms extended to the sky, holding a knotted rope in one hand.

'We'll try to help him,' Raf promised, 'but I... don't know if we can.'

Ludo was so stunned that he didn't know what to do.

'You should go, back to your men,' Raf said, pushing him towards the trees. 'Alys has been organising our supplies, but if we need anything else, the guards will help.'

Ludo started nodding, unable to stop. 'Do you see Sigurd coming?' he asked before turning away. 'Can he help Reinar?'

Raf blinked in surprise, then shook her head. 'I'm sorry. I can't see anything about Sigurd at all.'

***

Sigurd had joined Tulia for a training match, though his mind was elsewhere, and she finally held up a hand, coming towards him.

'Why are we doing this?' she sighed. 'You're not even here!'

He blinked at her in surprise. 'What? What are you talking about?

'I'm talking about you,' she hissed. 'What's wrong? I could have dropped you to the ground five times by now. And if my sword had an edge, you'd be dead, or whatever happens to a god.' She sniffed loudly, turning away. Thenor's chosen warriors were treated well by their benefactor, and there was always a table brimming with jugs of ale and wine to be found, food, too, though Tulia was rarely hungry.

Sigurd dropped his shoulders, letting the wooden tip of his sword touch the gravel. 'Something's wrong. I feel it, but I can't see it.' He followed Tulia, one eye on the warriors in the ring. 'Without Thenor, I can't see what's happening.'

'Why not?' she countered, spinning around. 'You're a god. A god must be able to see.'

'I'm trying, believe me.'

'Well, something's in the way then.' Tulia poured ale into two cups, handing one to Sigurd, whose frown deepened. He was her best friend, and when she'd realised that, it had become easier to stop being mad at him for breaking her heart. In truth, she'd always known that his feelings had never matched hers, and it was impossible to blame Sigurd for that. She took a long drink, moving away from the table, heading for the shade of a tree. 'But even if you saw what was wrong, what could you do? You're as much of a prisoner here as I am, aren't you? If Alari's hunting you and Thenor wants you to stay here, what can you do?'

'Something,' Sigurd insisted quietly.

'Can I help?'

'After what I did?'

'What did you really do,' she asked sadly, 'but follow your heart? And now you need to follow it again. You may be a god, but you'll never be happy while you're a prisoner. I know that all too well. I miss the freedom of being alive, of being a human. Stuck here like this?' Tulia shook her head. 'I'd rather be ash.'

Sigurd was shocked to hear it, though he didn't blame her.

Tulia Saari was like a wild horse, and being fenced in had never suited her.

'Do what you can to be yourself, for if you lose that, what do you have left? You can't be Thenor's servant. If he wants you to be a leader, Sigurd, you must be yourself.'

***

Gysa liked what she saw.

When she'd first met Gudrum, he'd been a bedraggled wreck of a man, rough and coarse. But now, in armour that shone, wearing new boots and trousers which fit him snugly, mostly clean and free of holes, he looked like a king. She smiled. 'You are ready, I see.' Holding a hand to his face, she ran her fingers over the thick rivers of scars. 'I feel Reinar Vilander's nerves. His heart pounds like a boy going into his first battle.'

Gudrum liked the sound of that. 'There's something to be said for being a creaking old warhorse,' he laughed. 'Though I had no problem beating him in the past.' He didn't dwell on the inconvenient fact that Raf had saved his life twice, which may have had something to do with it. 'And I'll take that luck into this battle too. Luck and the upper hand. I have everything he wants, and I'll remind him of that before I kill him. And then –'

Gysa held a finger to his lips. 'You mustn't get ahead of yourself,' she warned. 'Eadmund Skalleson is coming, I've seen that, but you mustn't think of him today. You need all your attention on this battle. Not the next.'

Gudrum hated being told what to do, though as his irritation receded, he saw the sense in her words, and he nodded.

His tent felt ready to blow away.

'The wind will make it fun,' he grinned, holding Gysa close. 'Fun for my men, at least. And what will you be doing while I'm ending Reinar Vilander's claim to my throne?'

Gysa remained silent while he kissed her, feeling oddly anxious. She was a dreamer with vision far greater than most, so she didn't understand her tremors of fear. She'd been feeling them for days, and looking into Gudrum's eyes, she tried to find an explanation, though nothing revealed itself. 'I will be floating like a cloud, hovering above you, going wherever I'm needed.'

Gudrum frowned, not liking the sound of that. 'You will remain in my tent, safe and out of the way. This is a battle of warriors. It's nothing to do with dreamers and nothing to do with magic.'

'Though Reinar Vilander now has three dreamers with him. They are looking to cause you trouble. I can't simply stay in this tent and warm my hands over the fire. I must do something to help if they act. I must!'

Gudrum wasn't used to being cared for, and though the dreamer's need to protect him grated, he found himself softening. 'Why?' he wanted to know, searching her eyes. 'Why do you worry about me?'

'I...' Gysa dropped her head. 'I... care.'

Lifting her chin with his finger, Gudrum smiled. 'I'm not sure I believe that,' he decided. 'Still, it's a nice feeling to have a powerful woman desiring my return to her bed.'

Gysa frowned, shaking his finger away. 'I do care,' she insisted. 'You will be a great king, and I want to be beside you. I care that you return, not to my bed, but to your throne. I want that for both of us.'

He saw her more clearly now, and his smile grew. 'An honest woman indeed, though you needn't worry. With the size of my army, we'll be able to take off the Vilanders' heads and march onto Slussfall before the day is done.' He slipped his arms around her waist, pulling her close, inhaling the intoxicating spiced oil she'd dabbed around her neck.

Gysa looked over his shoulder, feeling the pulsing strength in his arms.

Seeing how wrong he was.

***

Reinar's breath swept around him in white circles as he strode back and forth before the long shield wall his men had formed some fifty paces back from the stream. His army hadn't stopped working since they'd arrived at Gord's Field, though with a dreamer by Gudrum's side, he wondered what the point of all their preparations had been? It would be almost impossible to use the element of surprise.

His father would stay with him. Bjarni too. Berger would take his men to the western flank. Ollo would take the east. Jonas and Vik had led their men to the hill, where they'd command one side each.

Reinar shook his head, becoming distracted by doubts. He wanted to boost his men's confidence, to open their minds to the possibility that miracles could happen, that a man like Gudrum could be defeated. For what Gudrum had already done to Alekka during his short time in power was enough to destroy thousands of lives forever.

'We have three powerful dreamers! We have archers and catapults and spears! We have shields and swords and axes! And we have you!' Reinar bellowed, voice straining as he trekked through the mud, the icy wind numbing his face. He tasted snow in the air, and looking up, he saw grey clouds seething, becoming almost walls around them. 'The men of Ottby and Slussfall! Of Tromsund and Fasta and Goslund! The women too!' he shouted, seeing a smattering of shieldmaidens amongst the men. 'Gudrum has hired hands! Hector's men! Those he's threatened and bribed! And who are they fighting for but a greedy, self-serving mercenary? A man who wants to take and take until there's nothing more for Alekka to give! We stop him here, and this land belongs to us again! We stop him here, and I'll go on to Stornas and rule as the king Ake trusted me to be! As the king who'll put our kingdom back together again!'

Reinar watched as Stellan nodded his approval before turning to the drummers. The drummers had shields on their backs, swords in their scabbards, but first, they would thump out a beat to stir the blood. For war was glory, and war was destruction, and war was pain, but at its heart war was a battle for survival - nature in its most brutal form - and Reinar knew that only the strongest and smartest would survive today.

Bjarni came forward. 'Horses,' he said, pointing back to the treeline.

It felt like Orvala, Reinar thought, hearing those thumping drums and the pounding warning of horses approaching.

'First mistake,' Bjarni decided. 'Bringing horses into this soup?' He shook his head. 'What's he thinking doing that?'

Reinar rubbed his eyes, trying to clear his blurred vision. He saw Gudrum and his men quickly dismounting, leaving their horses to stewards and servants or sending them back to camp with a slap. The air felt heavy, a misty gloom descending upon the field. It wasn't snowing heavily yet, but the sky was darkening just when he needed to see clearly. Shoving his helmet onto his head, Reinar folded in the cheek pieces, and nodding at his father, he pulled Bjarni close. 'If anything happens...'

'What?' Bjarni sunk into the mud beside him, almost losing his balance.

'Look after Elin.' It wasn't what Reinar had been planning to say, but Alys had Jonas and Stina, Vik, too, whereas Elin had isolated herself, becoming increasingly alone, in no small part thanks to him. 'You'll need to help her.'

'Reinar,' Bjarni started.

'That's all,' Reinar said sharply, and though he spoke of Elin, it was Alys' face he saw. 'Care for my wife if I don't make it back.' And taking a deep breath, Reinar turned to where he could see Gudrum's men emerging from the forest in a massive line of shields and spears and banners, surging towards them.

***

Hearing the drums, Eddeth grabbed Raf, pulling her back into the circle, one eye on the guards, who kept glancing over their shoulders at them. 'You keep your eyes out there!' Eddeth snapped, pointing them back to the trees. 'We'll manage what's happening in here!' She crept towards the centre of the circle where their fire had finally burst into life. 'Eh? What about that then?' Eddeth grinned suddenly, flashing a crooked smile. 'I told you I could bind the wind!'

Raf wasn't convinced she had, though the wind had noticeably dropped. 'But what about the snow?' she wondered. 'What are we going to do about that?'

Eddeth didn't know, though the snow was barely a few flakes for now and her fire was blazing. 'You need to slip into Gudrum's head!' she decided, dragging Raf down to her knees, positioning her on one side of the fire while she moved to the other. 'Alys and I will keep our minds on Reinar now, but you must find a way into Gudrum's.'

Raf nodded, though she feared there was no way through. Gysa had been weaving spells around Gudrum since Hector had died, but following Eddeth's lead, Raf inhaled slowly, closing her eyes, hoping they could trust the guards protecting the circle.

Alys watched them from where she was saying goodbye to her grandfather. She had many feelings, most of them unsettling, and she clung to him as he kissed her cheek.

'You worry about Reinar,' Jonas told her. 'Vik will have my back. He always does.'

Alys knew they'd been distant for all those years because she'd made such a terrible decision, running away with Arnon as she had. She regretted how much time had been lost. Now she took Jonas' hand, not wanting to lose any more. 'I'll do what I can to keep you safe too,' she promised, tears in her eyes.

Jonas laughed. 'What? You're saying an old man like me has no business here? No business thinking he can stop an arse like Gudrum?'

Alys smiled. 'You're not that old, and Reinar's going to need all the help he can get.' She felt real fear then, seeing the snow sprinkling over Jonas, settling on his mail shirt. 'I won't be far,' she promised, inclining her head to the circle where Eddeth was shouting at the guards, hands flailing around. 'I'd better go and see what that's about.'

'Don't worry,' Jonas winked. 'We'll all be together soon. All of us. Safe.' He turned to go, holding her gaze for a moment.

Leaving Alys shivering all over.

***

Gysa sat alone in her tent, perched on a stool, eyes on the flames whipping around the brazier. They were angry and impatient – she could see that. She could hear it too. It was odd to be hiding away when Alari had made her the most powerful dreamer in Alekka – the woman she had chosen to protect her king.

And she would, Gysa knew.

Gudrum might think he could win the battle on his own, but he couldn't.

He wouldn't.

She wasn't going anywhere.

CHAPTER THIRTY TWO

The stream was in the way.

Gudrum laughed, knowing what Gysa had seen of Reinar's plans. Though had he really needed a dreamer to uncover the predictable traps his enemy had hidden beyond that stream?

He lifted his eyes to Reinar Vilander, who waited on the field in the middle of a long shield wall, hoping to lure his enemy into the range of his archers.

Instead, Gudrum swung up an arm, lowering it after a breath, and his own archers were the ones firing into the murky sky. The clouds were closing in on them like grey waves, promising heavy snow soon. He felt impatience, wanting to jump the stream and charge for that shield wall, shattering it until it broke. Instead, he whistled loudly, sending half his men east with Edrik, the rest west with the Lord of Borken, while he took his own men directly across the field.

It didn't phase Reinar, who knew that for every obstacle they'd put in Gudrum's path, he'd prepared backup options. He threw up his shield as the first wave of arrows struck, quickly followed by the second and then a third. He was certain Gudrum had enough archers to keep up the fast rhythm for some time, though no lord or king had an unending supply of arrows, so Reinar was happy to hold his ground, letting his shield do all the work. He heard Bjarni grunt beside him, foot sinking into the mud as he angled his shield higher.

'Snow's coming,' Stellan said on his other side. And hiding behind his shield, he calmly lifted the horn he'd slung around his neck to his lips, waiting for Reinar's signal. He thought he would struggle to be commanded by his son, doubting his ability to hold his tongue, but he knew they had a small chance of success, which diminished further if their communication wasn't clear.

It needed to be Reinar's voice and Reinar's timing now.

'Blow the horn,' Reinar ordered, eyes up as another wave of arrows darkened the sky.

And Stellan did, blowing loudly before he was forced to drop beneath his shield once more.

Vik heard the horn from where he stood on the eastern side of the hill, his attention immediately snapping to Jonas, standing far opposite him. They could both see that, as expected, Gudrum had separated his forces, for a man with an army that impressive and an ego that large wouldn't have just the one plan. He would have men coming at them from every angle, so it was up to all of them to spot attacks before they happened. He glanced back at the men waiting expectantly behind the fortifications they'd erected on the hill. They were out of range for now, and though Vik felt a bubbling need to get into the action, he let his boots sink further into the mud, nodding at Jonas. Jonas nodded back, and Vik took a deep breath, seeing snow, watching Berger and Ollo, stationed down on the field, flanking Reinar and Stellan, hoping that Ollo Narp wouldn't let them down.

Ollo saw Gudrum's flanks moving, and although he felt the sudden need to vomit, he turned around and winked at Ilene, who was fiddling with her new helmet behind him. 'I look forward to our great feast in Stornas!' he called. 'As guests of the new king!'

Ilene ignored him, fearing her helmet was too big and would drop over her eyes; that she wouldn't be able to pull her boots out of the mud. It sucked at them already, and she worried that she'd quickly end up fighting bootless. Though there was nothing to do about it now. There was nowhere to go but forward.

Ollo saw the banners of what looked like Borken, and the plumed helmet of the old man leading his men around at pace, hoping to outflank them. 'Let's move!' he roared, sword in the air. And nerves settling, his focus sharpened. 'Edge forward!'

With a quick look over her shoulder at the grey, nervous faces behind her, Ilene turned back around, following him.

Helgi loped alongside Berger as he marched his men towards the other half of Gudrum's forces. 'And where else is he coming from?' he wondered with narrowed eyes, body thrumming. 'Or perhaps he's holding the rest in reserve?'

Conscious of the need to have his ears open to everything that was happening, Berger ignored him, head swivelling, trying not to become irritated by the thick mud or the swirling snow. Helgi hadn't stopped talking, which was odd, he thought, his cousin being the last man Berger would have expected to get nervous before a battle.

'He'll have more men in reserve somewhere,' Helgi muttered, not letting that point go. He wore no helmet, his bushy hair ruffled by a now-moderate breeze, dappled with snow. Gripping his shield in one hand and axe in the other, he looked frozen solid, though his eyes were busy, watering in the cold.

'Ssshhh,' Berger hissed at him, trying to think. 'Keep marching and close your trap, Helgi. Your yapping's not going to help any of us now. Not with Gudrum coming. Eyes up! Mouth shut!'

Helgi nodded, then started moving backwards. 'I'll take the rear,' he decided suddenly. 'I'll be more useful back there!'

Berger turned in surprise, though there was little time for arguing. His cousin was quickly lost to him, and the taunting shouts of Gudrum's men drew his attention back to his enemy, now moving forward at pace.

***

'Men are coming!' Eddeth shouted at the top of her lungs, startling Raf, whose eyes burst open. She was quickly scrambling to her feet, away from the fire.

Alys spun around, squinting through the snow, wiping it from her eyes. She saw that Gudrum's men were moving around the flanks, that Gudrum himself was heading towards Reinar, and her heart thumped, arms trembling.

'We're far away here,' one of the guards promised calmly, eyes on the field in the distance. Two men waited expectantly near the woods, hoping to be given messages to pass along to those in the camp or to the leaders of the army, knowing that any insight the dreamers could offer would give them a better chance of living through the battle.

'No! No! Not the field! Up the *hill*!' Eddeth called, peering up at the towering man. He was taller than Ludo, as young as Aldo, and she felt a twinge of grief for the dead boy, who would've been standing guard with those men, wanting to keep her safe. 'You go and tell Vik! He's up there, he is! Go and tell him they're going to come in behind him! On the other side of the hill! Gudrum has more men coming from the north!'

Alys turned around, searching the hill for Jonas, fighting the urge to run and warn him herself. Though realising that she couldn't leave the circle, she closed her eyes, hoping to get through to him.

The guard nodded, beckoning one of the waiting messengers, and relaying Eddeth's warning, he sent him on his way. Turning back around, he urged his men to stay alert.

Raf seized Eddeth's arm, fearing she was about to leave the circle. They'd made it with every powerful symbol they knew, hoping to lock Gysa out. Though they feared there was nothing they could do to stop Alari.

Eyes open now, Alys spun back to Raf. She saw nothing but the snow and mud and that which lay before her. 'Have you seen anything, Raf? Any sign of Gysa?'

Raf shrugged. 'No, just Gudrum. He's coming for Reinar.'

Eddeth snorted. 'Well, I can see that with my own eyes! You need to see what isn't before us. You need to see inside Gudrum's mind. *Please*, Raf! We have to protect Reinar. You know what you saw! We have to do everything we can to stop it from happening!' Her attention darted to the field, seeing Reinar's long shield wall moving slowly backwards as Gudrum edged closer.

Raf nodded, looking from Eddeth to Alys, and seeing the fear in their eyes, she closed her own.

***

Gudrum's archers were in command, and Reinar let their assault go unanswered, wanting their confidence to bloom. Confidence, if unchecked by a disciplined leader, led to cockiness, quickly followed by poor decision making. So Reinar was happy to be on the receiving end of the arrow storm. Let Gudrum think he was being timid and hesitant. Let him think his dreamer had uncovered all their plans. Gudrum was the man who had taken Orvala in a bold move, only to lose it in the blink of an eye.

He was a man prone to making mistakes.

He wasn't the only one, Reinar knew, but still, he would let Gudrum make a few more.

He kept edging back across the muddy field, head moving left and right, eyes on his men, wanting to keep his shield wall intact.

***

Gudrum watched Reinar with a grin before turning to the Lord of Kurso, who was bright-eyed and red-nosed beside him. 'Hard to keep that up,' he laughed. 'Walking backwards? What say we make them run?' And now he lifted his sword in the air. '*Charge*!' he cried, scything his blade through thickening snowflakes, aiming it at the retreating Lord of...? Gudrum didn't know anymore.

It didn't matter.
Soon he'd be dead.

***

Ollo was struggling to stay upright. He'd attempted to keep his shield wall intact, but the mud had moved like a stream beneath his men, and now it was hand to hand combat, swords and axes flying forward in an angry song as they sought to keep Gudrum's men from running through them. Ollo heard Ilene screaming, headbutted to the ground, but unable to move, pinned in on every side, he couldn't reach her.

Mercifully, the arrows had stopped. Now that Gudrum's men were engaging their flanks, his archers had fixed their sights further afield, trying to pick off the men creeping backwards with Reinar.

Those men kept their shields close, defending themselves as they drew Gudrum and his army further across the field. And then, finally reaching the end of his game, Reinar spun around. 'Shield walls!' he roared, turning his head to carry his voice, as half of Ollo's and half of Berger's men turned back suddenly, shields locking into place like a wave of wood and iron. Then, just as quickly, Stellan was blowing his horn three times, inviting their archers to have a turn.

Gudrum was now surrounded on three sides, fenced in by shield walls, cut off from Edrik and the Lord of Borken, though he didn't appear fazed as his own men rushed their shields together, quickly forming three rows across the field, mirroring Reinar's walls. 'So you've decided to fight!' Gudrum laughed. 'If you think that's what's going to happen? A fight?'

The flaming arrows struck behind Gudrum's rear ranks in an almost perfect line, nearly every arrow hitting its mark: pitch-soaked bundles of herbs, wrapped in cloth, dug into a narrow trough. Smoke rose from the field in suffocating clouds, Gudrum's men immediately lost in it.

And then, so was Gudrum.

'Fuck!' he coughed, eyes stinging. He had no idea what was burning, but breathing immediately became a challenge. He couldn't see either, furious that in everything Gysa had uncovered about Reinar Vilander's plans, she hadn't seen this. 'Edrik!' he roared, hoping to carry his voice, though he was soon coughing some more. 'Edrik, come through! Break their walls! Move... forward!' But quickly disoriented in the smoke, Gudrum could no longer see where forward was.

The rising smoke put a smile on Berger Eivin's bloody face. His shield wall had been broken quickly, his men unable to hold their footing in the mud, forced back by a much larger foe. He'd seen no sign of Helgi. He was struggling to command his men whilst locked in a battle with a stocky lump of a warrior, who twirled two axes in the air with an arrogance that had Berger wild with rage. He slipped out of the arc of one of those swinging axes, smoke drifting across the field, the noise of battle swimming around him now. Blood streamed from his left arm, where the axe had nicked him, down to his fingers, threatening his grip on his shield. His right arm moved with speed, though, working to defend himself. But seeing that his opponent was struggling, the now-grinning axeman started hammering on Berger's shield, shattering the boards.

Hearing a shout behind him, Berger ducked as Helgi flew through the air, growling like a bear, teeth bared, axe in two hands as he took off the man's head with a vicious blow. Falling to the ground, he was quickly up on his feet, flinging his axe around in a killing frenzy, clearing space. And lifted by that, Berger threw away his broken shield, spinning around, taking one of Gudrum's men in the nose.

***

Vik received Eddeth's urgent message, immediately running to Jonas, where, after a quick discussion, they changed their formations. Jonas ordered his men to spread out, mirroring what Reinar was doing on the field, while Vik turned away, leading his men up it with as much speed as he could muster. But as he neared the peak, he saw that the climbing Tudashi were already running towards him, howling with joy. 'Break!' he called, backing down the hill. 'Harald! Go right! Dalren, left! Join with Jonas!' The hill was less muddy than the stomped-over field, so they could move with speed. And they did, going sideways like crabs, until they'd opened a great mouth for the screaming Tudashi to run into, banners flying.

Vik turned his men around to face them, shield up, Jonas quickly bringing his men in from the flanks. They couldn't let the Tudashi come down the hill and crush Reinar from behind.

'Hold them here!' Vik shouted at his men, pushing his sword through the gap in the shields. 'We hold them here!'

***

The smoke had given Reinar a chance to retreat back to the hill, which he very much wanted to do. Eager to lead Gudrum away from the more accommodating field, he sought to tempt him towards the hill, where Vik and the archers were waiting.

And if he could just get Gudrum within range...

Though peering over his shoulder through the smoke, eyes lifted to the hill, Reinar was horrified to see a battle already taking place. No one there appeared to be focused on the field. He saw blue cloaks and banners, spiked helmets.

And his heart sank.

Quickly turning back to the smoky wall masking Gudrum's men, he knew he had no choice now but to go on the attack. 'Push forward!' he cried, smoke burning his eyes, drying his throat.

'Pin them here! *Push!*' Through the twirling snowflakes and the suffocating clouds of smoke, Reinar saw a glimpse of Bjarni's blinking eyes. He held his friend's gaze for a moment, then, with a nod, he ran forward.

***

Alys didn't know where to look.

She couldn't see Reinar on the field because she couldn't even see the field, but he was in the smoke somewhere, as was Gudrum. She could almost feel Reinar's heart pounding, hearing the sound of his ragged breath in her ears.

And then her grandfather's face.

Despite knowing how capable Jonas was and fearing how much danger Reinar was in, she found her attention lingering on the hill, trying to see what was wrong.

Something, Alys could feel.

Something was terribly wrong.

CHAPTER THIRTY THREE

Gysa hung over the brazier, tension in her body, nibbling her lips.

It was going wrong for Gudrum, and she feared that his hubris would only cause things to unravel further. Her attention shifted to the dreamers, and though she could see them, hard at work, she couldn't reach inside that circle. They were free to work their magic. Free to do what they could to hurt Gudrum and help Reinar.

Unless they were forced to leave it...

***

The battle was blood and gore and noise and terror, and Eddeth had to work hard to shut it all out of her already muddled mind. The flying powder was still affecting her, and sometimes she wasn't even sure where she was. She'd laid traps all over the field, doing her best to mask her intentions from Gysa, though she felt certain that the powerful dreamer would be one step ahead of her nonetheless.

Raf sat on the opposite side of the fire, taking charge of topping it up with wood, hoping to keep it shielded from the snow. She closed her eyes occasionally, trying to see something useful about Gudrum. Sometimes, she saw glimpses of Ludo or Reinar. Other times, Ollo and Ilene. She saw their eyes and heard the frantic rhythm of their thumping hearts. Some were lost in a battle trance, like Helgi Eivin, who was possessed by the spirit of the bear. She'd seen men like that in The Murk. He was almost foaming at the mouth, dripping blood as he slashed and kicked, throwing himself through the air with little care for his life.

Then she saw Gudrum.

He peered at her through a mask of bloody mud, the whites of his eyes as bright as snow. He was furious, teeth gnashing, his scars pronounced and angry, and yet she remembered how he had found her and saved her. She remembered all those nights in his tent, feeling his arms around her. She tried to remind herself of who he really was and how he'd really treated her, but nothing bad came to mind.

Wrenching open her eyes, wanting an escape from it all, Raf blinked at Eddeth, who was rocking back and forth on her knees beside her. She turned to look at the guards, who were muttering to each other, hands gripping swords and spears, eyes sweeping the smoky field. Alys stood on the edge of the circle, her head in constant motion, watching the hill and then the field. Raf swallowed. 'They're coming closer.'

Dropping her head forward, Eddeth sneezed. 'What? Who?' Her eyes were quickly open, and swaying from side to side, trying to see between the guards, she saw hints that the battle on the field was edging towards their circle. 'Nothing to fear,' she promised, nerves fluttering. 'They can't touch us. We're safe in here!'

Raf turned away, trying to see what was happening herself, but she was small, and the bulky guards mostly blocked her view.

'What about Gysa?' Eddeth wanted to know. 'I can't see her. Can you?' Raf didn't answer, and Eddeth frowned. 'Raf?'

Raf turned back with blurry eyes. Her head pounded. She felt odd, fighting the urge to run just as much as she was fighting the urge to sleep. 'I... I can't.'

Eddeth hurried to her feet, and striding towards Raf, she grabbed her arm. 'We're only here because we can help, so we need to *help*! They need us!' She felt Vik's panic rising, certain that if a calm man like Vik Lofgren was experiencing panic, something was going badly wrong. And turning her attention to the hill now, she saw the fear on Alys' face. 'I have to help Alys. That's where we'll focus now. If those men come down the hill, they'll pen Reinar in!' She blinked, seeing more than one of the dark-haired dreamer. 'We need you, Raf. You have to try and find something to help!'

Raf stared up at her, seeing Gudrum's face once more, but she nodded, wanting to be alone. And when Eddeth had bounded away to join Alys, Raf turned her attention to the field. 'Move,' she grumbled at the guards. 'I need you to move!'

***

Unable to sleep, Sigurd had gone for a walk in the forest, ending up kneeling before the pool of water in the grove. But once again, it had revealed nothing. His foreboding feelings had intensified, though, and he'd made his way back inside the hall, seeking some wine to calm himself down. Though as soon as he'd fixed his eyes on Hyvari, he'd forgotten about wine altogether. Instead, he stood before the giant stone bowl, watching the flowing water rushing into it, wishing Thenor was standing beside him, revealing what was happening with his brother.

'It's something,' he whispered, holding out a hand, feeling the cold water numbing his fingers. The hall was silent, not even a creak or a hint of the wind. It was as though he was entirely alone in the world. He stood perfectly still, his heartbeat slowing, his eyes blinking at half speed and then closing altogether.

His brother's face immediately entered his mind.

'Forget Gerda,' Reinar said with that familiar frown. He was a boy, Sigurd could see. His hair was long and braided; they had both worn it that way once. 'She doesn't know what she's talking about. You *are* one of us, Sigurd. You'll always be a Vilander.' He tousled Sigurd's hair, grinning broadly. 'If you're ever in trouble, just think of me, and I'll be there. That's what brothers do. They look after each other. Don't forget now, Sigurd. No matter how old we get, no matter where we go, you'll always be my brother.'

Sigurd felt tears coming, and opening his eyes, he held both hands in the water now, seeing Reinar's bloody face.

***

Reinar could hear Gudrum, but he couldn't see him. The smoke had mostly cleared now, though he saw no sign of the king as the shield walls, under pressure from warriors who couldn't move with speed in the mud, collapsed. And as much as he wanted to get to Gudrum, there wasn't a moment to think. Reinar was struggling to stand, crushed between his enemies. He had to escape the melee to find out what was happening. He needed to get higher, wanting to see. 'Move!' he screamed, butting helmets with one man, spinning tightly to take another in the leg with his knife. He tore flesh, watching the man fall away. And finally able to free his shield arm, he banged the rounded boss into an elbow, breaking it, knocking another of Gudrum's men away, slashing his throat.

He heard horns blaring through the snow, now falling in thicker clumps. It was hot, though, or he was, feeling the weight of his mail and his mud-heavy boots as he tried to pull away from another man, whose sword arm wasn't long enough to reach him. Then Bjarni was there, piercing the man's throat, and Reinar was free to move. 'I have to see what's happening!' he croaked. '*Duck*!' And the sword aiming for Bjarni's head flew over it. 'You take charge!'

Bjarni didn't have time to even nod, his attention quickly on the bellowing voice of Gudrum Killi, who was calling Reinar's name.

Gudrum felt as though he was sinking into the mud and gore, certain that soon it would be up to his knees, though he was still smiling. He knew how many men were waiting in reserve, but he was sure that this was all Reinar Vilander had, so he was happy to let the fool tire out his men, killing and injuring as many as possible. It wouldn't take long before he would fence him in, crush his dreams, and then end him entirely. He took a man in the cheek, the man's screams quickly cut off as the Lord of Kurso hacked at his neck. Gudrum winked his thanks, and lifting his own head, he was pleased to see the battle on the hill exploding as the blue tide of Tudashi washed over Reinar's men, seeking to take the rear of the field. Looking west, he saw the Lord of Borken's forces engaged in a furious struggle for the left flank, and to the west, he saw another evenly matched battle.

It was hard to tell who held the upper hand, which surprised Gudrum, knowing how greatly outnumbered his enemy was. And then he saw Reinar Vilander pushing away from him, heading for the hill.

It would make sense to stay and lead his men, Gudrum knew, hearing Hector's mumbling voice in his ears, advising a cautious, steady approach. But Gudrum shook all thoughts of Hector away, turning until he found a familiar face. 'Edrik!' he shouted, sword in the air. 'Hold here! You have command!' And with that, he was away, slashing and snarling towards Reinar Vilander.

***

Alys and Eddeth had turned away from the field, becoming increasingly concerned that something odd was happening on the hill. The Tudashi appeared to be concentrating their efforts on the western side, where Jonas commanded.

Though it quickly became apparent that it was much more than that.

'They're all aiming for Jonas!' Eddeth shouted, reading Alys' mind.

A panicking Alys stepped out of the circle, though Eddeth's hand was immediately on her arm, pulling her back.

'No! We can help him from here! Where we're safe,' Eddeth insisted, tugging Alys further back inside the circle. 'Do you think all those warriors picked Jonas out of everyone? That it's a coincidence?' Eddeth felt dark magic in the air, and she drew Alys away from the circle's edge, finding a patch of snowy earth, where she dropped to her knees, thoughts swirling around her in a most revealing way.

Alys didn't sit with her, wanting to keep her eyes on the hill, but Eddeth grabbed a handful of her cloak, yanking her down.

'Hold my hand,' she grinned. 'I've got that flying powder in me, I have, so let's fly!'

***

Gysa watched, amused, for though Alys and Eddeth weren't leaving their circle behind, they no longer had their eyes on Reinar Vilander...

***

Thenor's waterfall revealed everything happening on Gord's Field, and Sigurd stumbled in surprise, hearing a gasp from behind as Valera entered the hall.

'How did you...?' she wondered, coming forward. She hadn't been able to sleep herself, having walked the gardens for much of the night, wondering where her father was, fearing for his safety. And then she'd felt the pull of her brother and had immediately returned to the hall, where she now feared for them both.

Sigurd shrugged. 'No idea.' But his attention was quickly back on Hyvari's perfectly clear water, which showed him what he'd been suspecting for some time: Reinar was in trouble. He saw the battle – Stellan, Vik, Jonas, Ollo and Berger. He saw his friends, his family, and looking down over the field, the hill, and the woods, Sigurd could see how truly outnumbered they were. 'I have to help them,' he decided at once. 'I have to go!'

Valera realised that perhaps her sense of dread and doom had been about this all along. Her fear that, eventually, she would have to contend with Sigurd's desire to leave. 'But you cannot enter a battle amongst the humans. You cannot interfere. None of us can.'

'Do you want Gudrum to win?' Sigurd was wild, and though he knew it wasn't Valera's fault, he needed her help. 'Fine, don't do anything, but please, take me. Just take me there. Let *me* help!' Thenor had shown him many things, but knowing how impulsive his son was and how desperate he was to get back to his family, he had never taught him how to move between the realms.

Valera shook her head. 'I cannot, Sigurd. You must remain here. Thenor would say the same. He would. You know he would.'

Sigurd pounded his fists against his thighs, eyes fixed on the battle, seeing Gudrum charging after Reinar. And closing his eyes, Sigurd tried to reach his brother himself.

***

Jonas didn't understand what was happening. He couldn't move. It was as though he was slathered in honey and the Tudashi were hungry bears. They all seemed to be aiming solely for him. He wondered if he was imagining things, becoming paranoid, lost in the churn of noise and terror. But everywhere he turned, he was met by the swinging blade of another howling Tudashi.

He felt an unfamiliar stirring of panic, hearing Eida's voice in his ears. 'Vik!' he shouted, though he was quickly knocked to the ground, trampled by boots, hit with shields, and then an axe, swinging for his head.

***

The herbs smoking in their fire had kept Alys and Eddeth in a near trance-like state for much of the morning, so it had taken little time to fully immerse themselves.

Alys could hear the drumming of her heart, and then her grandfather's as he fought to avoid the swarming Tudashi. She heard Vik's urgent voice in the distance, though she knew he couldn't get through to help. Those men were bound to Gysa; Alys felt it strongly. She saw their glazed eyes fixed on Jonas. It was as though they saw or felt nothing but the need to kill him.

She knew they had to act quickly, so slipping into the darkness of her mind, she focused on finding Eddeth, surprised to see her sitting on a log, patting a purring Rigfuss, who lay curled up on her lap.

'Eddeth!' Alys shrieked, rushing forward. 'What are you doing? We have to help Jonas!'

Eddeth blinked up at her in confusion, and then Rigfuss was gone, and they were standing in a snow-dappled field, ringed by warriors, all of them shouting and bellowing. She picked her wart, thoroughly disoriented, as though she was being pulled in two.

Alys stood before her yelling, but those warriors?

What did they want?

Despite her own panic, Alys was clear-eyed and pulling her knife from her belt, she dropped to the ground, drawing symbols. 'Ragnahild showed me this,' she said, immediately thinking of Reinar and her need to get back to him.

But first, she had to save Jonas.

Eddeth was nodding behind her, eyes on those bellowing warriors, not listening at all. Not to Alys, at least. She heard panicked voices, familiar ones, and her attention was quickly torn away.

'Eddeth?' Alys looked around as she bent to the symbols she'd drawn, but Eddeth had gone. And having no time to wonder what that meant, she sliced her knife across her palm, dipping a finger into the beading blood.

***

Vik heard Jonas' screams of agony, lost in a huddle of blue-cloaked Tudashi, and though he had the entire hill to worry about, at that moment, he only cared about saving his friend. '*Jonas*!' he roared, two swords flying, working hard to get through. 'Help me!' he called to his nearest men. 'Help me!'

Jonas was heartened to hear Vik, though he feared his friend would be too late. Lying on the ground, fighting for his life, he saw Eida's face. He saw Ake. It felt like an ending. Blades had torn through his trousers, slashing skin, no matter how many times he'd rolled away. He pushed himself up onto his knees, panting, elbows working to make room. He couldn't bring up his arm to use his sword, but he still held his shield, so using that to protect his left side, he pulled out his long knife and started stabbing.

***

'They're coming through the trees!' Eddeth shrieked, snapping out of the trance, spinning away from Alys, who was kneeling by the fire, eyes closed. She could still hear those noises in her head, as though a hundred horses were running through a forest, though it wasn't horses, she knew. She immediately attracted the attention of the nearest guard, pointing him towards the woods. 'Men are coming through there! I hear them! Hundreds of them!'

'Stay in the circle,' the guard ordered as Eddeth hovered behind him, standing too close. 'Get back!' And sword and shield at the ready, he turned to his men. 'We hold them here. Engage, but do not leave your post!'

Raf remained oblivious, lost in a trance, kneeling before the flames. She heard voices echoing around her, though they sounded like rushing water, pushing her deeper into the trance. She had tried to find Gudrum, but instead, she'd found Gysa. The dreamer held a sword, and Raf frowned, not recognising it. It shone like new, two sharp edges gleaming with threat. Raf saw the way Gysa was mesmerised by it, drawing it back and forth through the flames twisting in an iron brazier. Symbols sparked, showering the air with bright orange and red light. Gysa was chanting something Raf couldn't understand. She moved further into the tent, trying to see the symbols.

Eventually, Gysa drew the sword out of the brazier, holding it up, eyes fixed on the three symbols glowing near the blade's tip.

They were familiar, Raf thought, certain she'd seen them before.

She crept closer, fearing that at any moment, the dreamer would sense her presence.

Behind her, the tent flap opened, and a young man stepped nervously inside. 'My lady?' he mumbled. 'The king is ready to leave.'

Gysa smiled, eyes on the sword, its symbols extinguished, invisible now. She turned it, aiming the hilt at the man, who looked relieved to have it back. 'Ensure you place this directly into the king's scabbard,' she purred, dark eyes frozen with menace. 'Do not let it touch another soul.'

'I... I won't, my lady,' the man stammered, stepping back until he reached the tent flap, and spinning around, he disappeared.

As Gysa turned around to the brazier, Raf closed her eyes, seeking to leave, and then a hand on her arm had them springing open, and she was staring at Gysa's angry face.

The dreamer snarled, squeezing her arm until it burned. 'You dare come here, spying on me? Searching my memories?'

Raf felt real fear, then she remembered Mirella's red book, and all that she'd learned in her dreams, all that Eddeth had taught her as well. 'You're no goddess!' she spat, yanking her arm away. 'You're no better than me!'

'Are you sure about that, Raf?' Gysa purred, and sweeping her hands around, she sent Raf flying through the air.

Raf's head thumped on the ground, and she shook it as she rose to her feet, not seeing Gysa now.

Then the dreamer was laughing behind her. 'But I am better than you in every way. I know it, Alari knows it, and Gudrum knows it too.' She pulled Raf's hair, dragging her backwards until Raf's eyes were watering.

Raf closed them. 'It's just a dream,' she panted. 'Just a dream, and I'm not your prisoner!' The flames spat and crackled, Gysa hissing in her ear, but Raf shut it all out, forcing her mind back to Eddeth and Alys and their circle near the woods.

And Gudrum's sword.

***

Jonas bellowed loud enough for the gods to hear as he swung around with his shield, making room, hoping to give Vik enough time to reach him. Hoping to save himself.

And then Alys' voice roared in his ears. '*Get down*!'

Not arguing, Jonas dropped where he stood. Shield over his head, crouching now, he heard what sounded like an explosion. The noise immediately blocked his ears, as though his head had been stuffed with pillows. Everything became distant, oddly slow and blurred, and then Vik was there, hand on his arm.

'Up!' he urged, pulling a dazed and bleeding Jonas to his feet. 'Up!' He'd sheathed both swords, leaving his men watching his back as he helped Jonas get himself together. 'You're alright,' he smiled, patting him on the back, and seeing that Jonas could stand and that his wounds didn't appear debilitating, he turned away, running through the scorched circle burned into the hill.

Jonas stared after him for a moment, blinking and swaying. Then his eyes drifted to the circle himself, realising that he stood in it alone. Outside it lay the bodies of nearly thirty Tudashi, who had moments earlier been attacking him. Not one of them was moving. And seeing their open eyes and frozen bodies, he doubted they ever would.

CHAPTER THIRTY FOUR

Reinar found his father.

'We're holding them on both flanks! The hill's a problem, though!' Stellan panted.

Reinar spun around. 'Head up there and help them! Where's Ludo?' He saw the sea of men twisting and screaming before him but no sign of Ludo, who was supposed to be coming through the woods, bringing their reserves into the fight. 'He would've heard the horn.'

Stellan agreed, shield up as Gudrum's archers snapped another flock of arrows into the air. 'Something's wrong then.' He felt the worry he saw in his son's eyes. 'Nothing to do but dig in. I'll help Jonas and Vik with the Tudashi. You need to bring Berger and Ollo back to your side. Pull back to the base of the hill. We'll reengage there.' Then realising he wasn't the man Ake had chosen to be king, he stopped. 'If you agree?'

Reinar did. 'Go! I'll pull everyone back!' He glanced towards the woods where he knew the dreamers had made their circle, certain he could see trouble flowing their way.

***

The Tudashi surged down the increasingly muddy hill, pushing towards the field, trying to break their line. Vik saw a few of his men tumbling past, knocked off balance, and unable to regain it, they rolled like boulders. Snow drifted across the hill, and he shivered, one eye on a limping Jonas, half lost in the dance of death. Vik felt it coming towards him at times, seeking him out like one of Vasa's death collectors. And then he would turn and twist out of its path, leaving it to claim another soul.

Those death collectors were busy, Vik could see.

He kept blowing his horn in two short bursts, wondering why there was no sign of Ludo and Torfinn with their reinforcements. Then he saw Stellan, hearing him bellowing urgently for his men to take to the hill.

That hadn't been their plan, though fighting uphill was what they knew best of all, and Vik dug in hard, balance steady. He swept his shining blades around, carving through the snow. 'Stellan's coming!' he barked at Jonas, who had his back to the field, trying not to tumble down towards it. Though it was a losing battle, Vik saw, as his old friend slid further down the hill until they were fighting side by side.

'You think we're ever going to find some good weather?' Jonas grinned, happy to still have a chance to fight. His bleeding nose had turned his moustache red, matching his blood-soaked tunic and trousers. Though the demanding threat of the Tudashi kept most of his pain at bay. He swung his sword with both hands, taking a flying Tudashi in the chest, stopping him mid-flight.

Vik heard a familiar shriek, and ducking a spinning knife, he turned to see men emerging from the woods near the dreamers' circle. Squinting, he spotted Ennorian banners. 'Fuck!' he yelled, inclining his head for Jonas to see the trouble.

'Go!' Jonas urged. 'Save the dreamers!' Then thinking of dreamers, he swung around, fearing for Alys.

***

'Reinar Vilander!' Gudrum shouted, moving like a wolf, eyes fixed on his prey. 'Have I got you on the run?' He smashed an elbow into the face of one man, jamming his sword into the throat of another. Drawing it out, he was immediately showered in blood. 'But what did you expect, thinking you could come for my crown?' Gudrum felt unstoppable. He saw the Ennorians swarming through the woods, the Tudashi wreaking havoc on the hill, certain that the scales were heavily weighted in his favour now. Confidence shot through him like sunbeams, heating him up from inside. He felt like one of those ancient kings. Immortal. Though he was determined to remain focused, not wanting his victory snatched away as Hector's had been.

Whatever happened, he would never let someone take the pleasure of killing Reinar Vilander away from him.

***

Reinar felt torn.

He needed to command his army, to make decisions and lead, though he'd plenty of capable leaders to step up in his place. He heard Bjarni yelling from the front ranks, lost in the smoke. He saw glimpses of Berger and Ollo. He knew his father had joined Jonas and Vik on the hill. He thought of the disastrous sea battle, which had cost Bolli's life. And now he had so many more lives to protect. Screams reverberated around him, cries of terror and pain and panic all seeking to distract him. He couldn't save everyone, but if he didn't stop Gudrum this time, Alekka stood no chance.

So, steadying himself, Reinar turned away from his men, lifting his shield to his shoulder, squeezing his frozen fingers around *Corpse Splitter's* hilt.

Waiting for Gudrum.

***

Fearing they would be overrun, circle or not, Eddeth turned her attention away from the woods and the men guarding them, wanting to wake Raf out of her trance. The little dreamer had been sitting with her eyes closed for some time, and Eddeth needed her back on her feet, ready to leave at a moment's notice. She dropped her staff and rushed to Raf's side, grabbing her arm, giving her a shake, though she couldn't wake her. No matter how loudly she yelled, Raf remained frozen, eyes closed, head tucked down to her chest. So, leaving Raf in her trance, hoping she was doing something useful, Eddeth worked to help those men trying to guard the circle. Whatever happened, she had to keep it intact.

Alys was busy. Raf was busy.

They couldn't be overrun now.

Then suddenly remembering the knotted rope, she fell back to her knees, digging around in the snowy mud. Eventually, finding the rope, Eddeth started fumbling with the first knot, chanting softly. She felt tears of terror pricking her eyes, but blinking them away, she undid the knot, holding the rope in the air, swinging it around in a circle, watching as the wind picked up.

***

Ludo had been leading a group of Reinar's reserves through the woods, weaving through the trees with as much stealth as warriors dressed for battle possessed. He'd used hand signals, coordinating their slow march towards Gord's Field. The plan was for them to emerge through the trees near the base of the hill, reinforcing Reinar's men. Torfinn was leading another group of men around the hill from the east. Together, they would work to bolster their much smaller army's rear flanks.

Though Ludo hadn't counted on coming across the Ennorians.

And now he was surrounded by them, fighting on every side, trying to hold them back, quickly realising that it wasn't Reinar's forces running out of the woods to support their leader.

It was Gudrum's.

***

The men coming through the woods was a problem Reinar had no choice but to let go of, for now Gudrum was before him, and those around them were making space as they could, sensing that both men wanted to fight one on one.

Gudrum was full of cocky noise, which Reinar tried to ignore. Neither man had a serious wound, though they were both drenched in mud and blood, struggling to stand, to move, to see clearly.

The wind howled in the distance, a threatening noise, snow blustering around them. It wasn't ideal, though Reinar knew he'd succeeded in worse conditions. He kept those thoughts at the forefront of his mind, swinging back to avoid Gudrum's first strike, his long blade gleaming like new through layers of gore.

'You will die here!' Gudrum taunted, confidence making him bold. He almost skipped forward, teeth clenched, two hands cradling his golden hilt. It was a sword for a king, and he'd never felt more like one as he launched it at Reinar's head.

Reinar swayed out of reach, slipping in the mud, but quickly righting himself, he jabbed at Gudrum's thigh. Gudrum wanted a performance, but Reinar just needed to put him down, and a man couldn't stand if his legs wouldn't hold him up. He heard the Ennorians behind him, the wind becoming more intense, the shouts from the hill and Bjarni's horn.

But he shut it all out, knowing that he just needed to put Gudrum down.

***

Alys was back on her feet, confident that she'd seen off Gysa's attack on her grandfather, hoping he knew to retreat back into the circle if Gudrum's dreamer tried anything again. Now her attention moved away from the hill to Raf, who appeared to still be in a trance, and then to Eddeth, who was on her knees, fiddling with a rope. She heard the scuffle of warriors, the clashing of blades, suddenly realising that they were surrounded by Gudrum's men. 'Eddeth!' she shouted as one of their guards went down, an arrow through his throat.

'Not now, not now!' Eddeth barked, trying to focus. Her gentle breeze had quickly progressed into a strong gale, and now she moved to undo the third knot, hoping to unleash a furious storm. Up on her feet, she swung the rope around in bigger and bigger circles, conjuring up a whirlwind.

The Ennorians threatening the dreamers' guards were immediately knocked off their feet, and trying to pull themselves up on each other, they were quickly falling again. The force of the wind swirling around the circle was nothing they could withstand, and soon they were blown away. Eddeth, Raf, and Alys remained untroubled inside the circle, though Eddeth belatedly realised, and with some regret, that they'd lost the guards who'd been watching over them.

The wind had knocked them away too.

Alys spun around in surprise, mouth gaping open. She saw Reinar's men fighting the wind, bodies bent almost at right angles, hands and weapons pointing forward, trying to gain some ground, though many were soon defeated by the force of that wind, tumbling and rolling away.

Eddeth shrugged at her. 'We're safe for now!' she promised loudly, though she could barely make herself heard. 'Now we can try and help Reinar!'

Alys saw a shouting Ludo emerge from the woods, and turning around, she heard Vik bellowing just as loudly. Between both men, the Ennorian forces were coalescing. Alys saw glimpses of how many were surging through the woods. 'Vik!' she shouted. 'Hurry!' They had to hold this flank, to keep those Ennorians back. If it broke, Reinar's army on the field would be swallowed whole.

***

Reinar turned Gudrum around, and with both boots trapped in the mud, he couldn't twist back with any speed. So moving quickly, Reinar cut Gudrum's thigh, slicing through his trousers, knocking him off balance.

But not for long.

Gudrum had been fighting for more years than Reinar had been alive. His body was his greatest weapon, his most reliable ally. Held together by scar tissue, it had never let him down. 'Ha!' Gudrum was as bullish as ever. 'You think I've never been cut before, Reinar Vilander?' He laughed some more, skipping forward, his blade just missing Reinar's thigh.

Reinar tried to move quickly, though the mud had hold of his boots, and he pulled out his right leg, leaving the boot behind.

Gudrum kept smiling, though he was struggling just as much in the muck, not helped by his bleeding legs. 'We can always wrestle!'

'Or you can just go back to Brekka!' Reinar panted, trying to get into Gudrum's head. The man was too confident, too certain of his victory, so Reinar sought to flood him with doubts. 'Go back to your own people! No one wants you here! Or perhaps the truth is, no one wants you anywhere!'

Gudrum hated being reminded of Brekka and everything he'd left behind, and enraged now, he caught Reinar's mail with the tip of his blade.

***

Raf screamed, rocking forward until her hands nearly touched the flames of the struggling fire. She'd finally escaped Gysa's hold on her, but turning around, she saw the chaos consuming the circle. It felt as though they were trapped in a storm, the howling wind so loud that she barely heard another noise.

Men swarmed around the circle, banners flapping above screaming, bloodied faces. Raf stood, trying to see Reinar or Gudrum, or Ludo, who was supposed to be here, she thought. Though quickly realising there was no time for any of it, she left the circle, forcing herself through the whirlwind, away from a gaping Eddeth.

Alys spun around, sensing Raf leave, and now she felt it herself.

Reinar.

***

Gysa was alert, leaning over the brazier with sharp eyes, having lost hold of that brat Raf in her dream. She dipped her hands into the flames, stirring them higher, needing to see what was happening with Gudrum.

***

'Reinar!' Raf shouted, almost catching a swinging axe in the face. She was small, though it was still hard to move through the warriors, who were tussling and punching, slipping and falling in the mud. She ducked and stumbled past them, over them, the dead and injured lying in her way making it impossible to move with any speed. 'Reinar!' she tried again, immediately knocked off her feet, and thumping down on her arse, she bit her tongue.

Pulling herself up quickly, Raf turned sideways, slipping between armoured bodies, trying to avoid slashing weapons. '*Reinar*!' she screamed. 'Reinar, stop!'

***

Reinar swung high, slicing his blade across Gudrum's nose and cheek. He saw blood spurting through the snow, listening to Gudrum's roar of agony as he staggered backwards.

'*Fuck*!' Gudrum was angry now, blinking rapidly, forcing the pain away. Though the burn? That burn brought tears to his eyes.

The space around the two men grew wider as more realised who was fighting. Some stopped their own battles to protect that patch of churned over mud. Others took a brief moment to watch, sensing that Reinar Vilander had the upper hand.

Reinar thought he did too.

Gudrum was struggling to stand, and now, with flashes of white light bursting before his eyes, he was struggling to see. He limped before Reinar, mud hampering his movements, and, just like Reinar, he'd lost a boot.

Reinar pushed forward, taking full advantage now, swinging his blade at Gudrum's neck. Gudrum parried, face aching, bleeding legs trembling, though his balance remained as solid as ever. Confidence had a way of steadying a man. He was a king, he was strong, and he took the blow like a wall of stone.

Though Reinar quickly followed with another and another, pummelling Gudrum in fast strokes until he was tumbling backwards, Gysa's urgent voice loud in his ears.

***

'Raf!' Sigurd looked into Hyvari in horror, seeing that familiar little figure pushing through the warriors surrounding his brother. She was moving closer, lethal blades sweeping around her, threatening her life. 'What is she doing?' he cried, turning to Valera, who appeared to be holding her breath. 'I *have* to go! Please, you must help me!' Gripping her arm, he stared into her eyes, thinking of all he had learned and all he had lost.

And then he was gone.

***

Reinar lunged forward to finish Gudrum, who was struggling to get up now. But hearing him coming, Gudrum kicked out with his bootless leg, trying to trip him.

Hearing someone calling his name, a distracted Reinar nearly fell.

It wasn't Alys. The voice wasn't in his head but nearby.

It confused him momentarily, then he realised that it must be Raf.

'The... sword!' Raf shouted, running out of breath as she tried to get closer, though the warriors surrounding Reinar and Gudrum rose like a shield wall before her. She used her elbows, trying to force her way through. 'Move!' she shrieked. 'Fucking *move*!'

Gudrum scrambled up onto his knees, distracted by both that familiar voice and then Gysa's.

Reinar saw Gudrum's neck and swung for it, but Gudrum dropped back to the ground, reaching out, aiming his sword at Reinar's ankle.

He only needed a touch, Gysa assured him.

Just a touch.

'Reinar! His sword! It's –' Raf finally made it through the wall of warriors. '*Cursed*!'

Reinar saw Gudrum's sword coming for him. He tried to pull his leg away, though the mud had hold of his boot, and he screamed as the tip of the blade touched his leg. Light exploded before him, so bright and intense that he no longer heard or saw anything as he fell, *Corpse Splitter* dropping from his hand.

Gudrum was on his feet, dragging his bleeding legs out of the mud, moving in to claim his prey.

'No!' Raf lunged in front of him, arms extended, trying to shield Reinar. 'You can't kill him! I won't let you!'

Gudrum snarled at her. 'Get out of my way, you disloyal bitch! You'd try and help *him*? Save *him*? After what I did for you?' And seeing that Reinar wasn't even moving now, Gudrum aimed his sword at Raf instead.

CHAPTER THIRTY FIVE

Alys forced her way out of the circle after Raf, leaving Eddeth behind.

Jonas and Stellan were gaining the upper hand on the hill, though Vik and Ludo were being overrun by the Ennorians, who continued to surge through the woods. Some rushed to help the Tudashi, but most were heading for the field, though Alys couldn't stop to help any of them. Raf's voice was screaming in her ears, warning that Reinar was in danger. And though Alys couldn't see it herself, she could feel it. But no one would let her through.

She couldn't get through!

So, dragging her sword from its scabbard, she started clearing a path.

***

Berger's men were being pushed back towards the hill, forced into a retreat, though glancing over his shoulder, he saw Ennorian banners behind him now. Gudrum's reinforcements were coming from everywhere, it seemed, as men on horseback rode out of the forest, charging across the field, aiming for the stream. 'Where's Reinar?' Berger panted, spitting out a tooth. He looked up at the hill, seeing the familiar figures of Stellan and Jonas fighting the Tudashi.

Helgi didn't know, wiping snow from his eyes as he tried to catch his breath. 'Something's happening over there!' he called, inclining his head towards rows of men seemingly at a standstill. 'Maybe that's him?'

'Ollo!' Berger yelled, surprised to see him so far west. 'What's happening!'

'Retreat!' Ollo was screaming, eyes bulging, swinging his head from side to side. 'Ennorians are coming through the woods! More surging on the eastern flank. The Tudashi too!' He ducked as a wave of arrows whistled overhead. 'There's... no hope!' Then straightening up as the arrows landed far behind him, his eyes shifted to the line of stationery men too. 'What's that?'

Berger shrugged. 'We need to form again at the base of the hill. Join together, get another wall going!'

And realising that it was impossible to retreat on his own without looking like a cowardly fool, Ollo nodded. Though Helgi shook his head, fearing what other surprises Gudrum had in store. 'We should head for the flanks. If the hill falls, we'll be overrun. Leave the archers where they are, get around the flanks and start moving up the hill!'

Berger agreed, but hearing a woman's voice screaming Reinar's name, he turned towards that row of men and ran.

***

'I saved you!' Raf cried as Gudrum circled her, sword out. She saw that Reinar was unconscious, knowing he'd been cursed, fearing he was dying. She didn't want that blade touching her, but she wouldn't let Gudrum kill Reinar. She couldn't.

'Saved me?' Gudrum laughed. 'Once! But now you seem set on saving him. Get out of the way, Raf, or I'll kill you! You'll not stop me taking his head! I *will* have his head!' he roared, barging forward.

Raf kept her arms moving, trying to hold him back. She'd heard about Alys' wall in Tromsund, and remembering Valera's, she tried to make something happen herself, sensing that Alys was on her way.

And if she could just distract Gudrum...

***

Alys faced an uphill battle to get to Reinar, and realising that her sword wasn't doing anything more than attracting angry warriors to turn her way, she sheathed it, throwing back her hood, curling cold hands into trembling fists.

Ragnahild came to her then, bellowing like a horn in her ears. 'Use your magic, Alys! Hurry! Gudrum will finish Reinar! You must hurry!'

That was all Alys needed to hear. And lifting those curled fists into the air, chanting until the words hummed in her chest and surged through her arms, she launched a great ball of light at the men before her. Some fell away, screaming. Others stumbled out of her path as Alys kept her arms extended, running forward now.

***

'You never cared for me!' Raf raged, tears stinging her eyes. 'You never helped me. You *used* me! Took what you wanted from me! You would've killed me if I wasn't a dreamer!' Gudrum made to get past her, but Raf spread her arms wider. 'Back!' she sobbed. 'Get back!'

Gudrum laughed, his anger boiling now, furious that Raf had turned against him. There was no doubt anymore, no question at all. He was enraged, and, drawing a knife from his belt, he flung it at her throat.

Raf felt a pain, a sharp prick in her neck, then her heart started throbbing, beating so loudly she feared it would burst.

She fell, seeing the snow twirling, hearing a loud hum in the distance.

The pain coming like a wave now.

And then nothing but darkness, swallowing her whole.

Sigurd was roaring as he landed near his brother, touching the ground with the tip of *Fire Song*, his balance solid. He looked down, first seeing Reinar and then Raf.

Then, lifting his head, he saw Gudrum.

Gudrum blinked, stumbling back in surprise.

He wasn't the only one.

Valera was quickly by Sigurd's side, taking in the situation. 'You mustn't interfere,' she warned, though her lips didn't move, not wanting Gudrum to hear. Sigurd didn't respond. 'Promise me,' she urged. 'I will take Raf. I can save her.' And seeing the hint of a nod now, Valera turned away, scooping Raf's body into her arms, quickly disappearing.

Leaving Sigurd with Reinar and Gudrum.

'Get back,' Sigurd warned darkly, brandishing *Fire Song*, whose blade glowed like molten iron.

'Oh,' Gudrum laughed. 'I forgot you're a god now. That's what they say! A god with a fire sword! Is that what you are, Sigurd? The new God of Fire?' His swagger masked his fear of what Sigurd could actually do, having heard the stories about Tromsund from Bor Bearsu. Though he couldn't back down now.

Sigurd sheathed his sword, shaking his head.

Fire Song was a powerful, magical weapon, though he'd quickly discovered that she wasn't as powerful as him. 'One day soon I'll be the God of War, and we might meet again, Gudrum. If you live that long. So go before I kill you. Leave here and take your men before I burn you all.' Sigurd's threat was delivered quietly, as though he stood alone before Gudrum; quietly but full of the threat he could feel coursing through his body. He saw Bjarni, and then Berger and Ollo. 'Berger, get Reinar out of here. Get him to safety,' he ordered, eyes fixed on Gudrum, arms vibrating by his sides. 'Bjarni, you're with me.'

Alys pushed through the warriors, eyes on a fallen Reinar. She bit back her tears, her regrets, and her fears most of all. And as Berger rushed forward with Helgi and Ollo, Alys joined them, her eyes quickly finding a small hole in Reinar's trousers, just above his boot. She saw no other wound. He barely looked injured, though his eyes were closed, his face oddly pale.

'A curse,' Ragnahild breathed in her ears, defeat in her voice. 'Reinar has been cursed.'

Alys looked up at Bjarni, who motioned for Berger to take Reinar's feet. And helped by Ollo and Helgi, who each took one side of Reinar's shoulders, they hoisted him into the air. Alys moved ahead of them, unsheathing her sword, carving a path for the men to follow.

The noise of the wind died down, the hum of battle lessening now, though the cries of the wounded became louder and more urgent.

'Go,' Sigurd warned Gudrum again, his blue eyes intensifying in the gloom. 'Leave here.'

Gudrum was incredulous, holding his ground. He had defeated his enemy. His army was on course for a resounding victory. And now he was supposed to turn away without any spoils? Because a man masquerading as a god told him to? He laughed, simmering with anger.

'I won't kill you if you retreat,' Sigurd promised, struggling to mean it. 'I'll let my brother do that when he's back on his feet. So leave this field, Gudrum Killi! Leave and return to your camp!' Sigurd finally raised his voice as he lowered his right hand, wrapping it around *Fire Song's* hilt. Heat surged through the sword, up his right arm, down to his left hand, and lifting both arms, he shot a stream of fire past Gudrum, watching as Gudrum's men scattered, screams of terror shattering the silence. Lifting his arms higher now, Sigurd sent those flames showering over the field like burning rain. 'Bjarni, get everyone behind me! You need to retreat!'

Chaos swirled, the waves of fire scorching the field and any who stood in its path. Those who had heard about Tromsund started running.

Though Gudrum remained standing before Sigurd, reluctant to move. Face dripping blood, snow dusting his beard, he scowled, daring Sigurd to steal away the victory he'd earned. Curling his lip in defiance, he lifted his sword, daring him to take it all.

So Sigurd did.

Inhaling deeply, Sigurd brought his hands back to his chest, holding them there for a moment before pushing them down to the mud. And lifting them up, he turned his palms to the leaden sky, drawing fire up from the earth itself, from one side of the field to the other. Only fire. Fire as far as anyone could see.

Thenor had taught him how to command fire with his hands.

It was useful when wanting a meal in a forest or seeking some warmth.

Or needing to terrify your enemy.

The wall of fire grew until sweat poured down Gudrum's forehead, running into his wounds. He screwed up his face in fury and in pain, and reluctantly dragging himself around, he bellowed at his men. 'Retreat!' he called, hesitantly, at first. And then, feeling the heat of those flames intensifying and seeing the determined look in Sigurd Vilander's glowing blue eyes, Gudrum dragged his legs out of the mud. '*Retreat*!'

Sigurd watched him go, bringing the two sides of his fire walls together, uniting them. And now, he pushed the great wall forward, like lava rolling down a hill, hot and charred and hungry, wanting to ensure that Gudrum and his men would leave the field of battle entirely. He felt the pull of wanting to be with Reinar; the need to get back to Gallabrok to find out if Raf was alive; the fear that he was going against Thenor; the certainty that Alari would come again.

He looked over his shoulder, seeing Bjarni herding his men away.

'We've got Reinar! We've got him!' Bjarni promised.

Sigurd nodded, wanting to go with him, but remaining where he was, he lifted the wall of fire even higher, sending flames up to the clouds, melting the falling snow. And though he felt the heat of the fire himself, he shivered, fearing for his brother. 'You must save him,' he breathed, seeing Alys' face. 'You must save him, Alys.' And eventually, knowing that he'd done all he could, he dropped his arms, leaving the fire wall in place, following Valera back to Gallabrok.

***

No one could explain what was happening. It was pure chaos.

Once Gudrum had ordered the retreat, the horns had started, the Tudashi quickly abandoning the hill, scattering as though they'd never been there. Stellan took charge, hearing that Reinar had fallen in battle to Gudrum. And though waves of grief and fears for his son nearly paralysed him, having to focus on getting everyone to safety helped steady his mind. 'Back to camp!' he bellowed, attempting to make himself heard over the noise. He turned, looking for reliable warriors, wanting to pass the message along.

Jonas joined him. 'Vik's taken Eddeth to Reinar. They'll go back to camp.'

Stellan barely nodded, arms waving, moving everyone towards the woods. 'Help the wounded!' he urged, seeing Ludo and Ollo. 'Get everyone up on their feet! Back to camp! Retreat! Let's move!'

They'd been given a chance by Sigurd, and both Stellan and Jonas knew that they couldn't afford to waste it.

***

Gysa was furious as she watched the great wall of fire in the distance, wondering where Alari was. She had tried breaking it herself, to no avail. That was god-magic, and not even a dreamer as powerful as she now was could extinguish it.

Gudrum had been forced to turn back, to walk away from victory. He would be furious. *She* was furious, not understanding why Thenor would allow his son to interfere so recklessly.

And then Gudrum's first warriors came trudging back into the camp. They passed her by with barely a glance, caked in mud, limping and bleeding, smoke-dry throats in need of ale. Weapons hung from aching arms, shoulders drooping as they filtered past her like broken men.

Gudrum followed, slightly stunned, mostly confused.

Seeing Gysa, he grabbed her by the elbow, pushing her towards her tent, his anger suddenly as bright as Sigurd Vilander's eyes.

'What was that?' he snarled, throwing her inside, unable to stop coughing.

Gysa didn't understand.

'The sword... *my* sword! What did you do to it? I told you not to do anything! Not to help me!'

Gysa inhaled sharply. 'He would have killed you. I feared it would come to that. In my dreams... I... wasn't as confident as you.'

'So you put a spell on my sword?' Gudrum sneered. 'Bringing a god into my fight? Ruining everything! And Raf?' He'd killed Raf. It didn't seem real. He'd flung that knife at her throat as though she was some faceless enemy. But she hadn't been. She'd been his. For years, she'd been his. '*You* did this! We were one blow away from victory!'

Gysa was incredulous. 'You were one blow away from death! Reinar was about to end your life, to take your head to Stornas, to hang it from the gates! I saw it all. I saved *you*! Now you live to fight another day. Reinar Vilander won't. That curse will kill him if it hasn't already!' Gudrum had her arms, and she squirmed in his grasp until he let go of her entirely, pacing the tent like an angry bull.

He didn't know what to think. 'Sigurd Vilander's a fucking god!'

'Which you already knew. And yet he held himself back. He could have ended you, but he didn't. He came to protect his brother, not to kill you.'

'But he could have,' Gudrum realised, still heated by those flames, still seeing the menacing glow of Sigurd's eyes.

'Any god could. They don't, for the most part. Thenor doesn't allow it. Though perhaps for his son, he has other ideas?' Gysa didn't think that was true, though she wanted Gudrum to feel truly threatened, for only then would he realise the size of the mountain he sought to climb.

Despite having half as many men, those who fought beneath Reinar Vilander's banner were backed by Thenor himself.

Gudrum licked his lips, suddenly aware of the burning agony of his face, the weak trembling of his slashed legs. He saw Gysa staring at his nose. 'You will fix me. Heal me. Stitch me! I need to...'

'You need to stop,' Gysa said calmly, sensing his anger cooling ever so slightly. She took a step towards him, hand out. 'Stop now. We have time to gather everyone together. Time to wait.'

'For what?' Gudrum wanted to know, his thoughts fractured, unable to get Raf's face out of his mind.

'For reinforcements.'

PART FOUR

New Friends, Old Scores

CHAPTER THIRTY SIX

In the aftermath of the Battle of Gord's Field, Stellan had led the army back to their camp at Salagat, quickly tripling the men guarding its perimeter. They needed to hold here, to tend to their wounded, to try and save Reinar's life. They couldn't afford to be pushed back now, forced to turn and run, leaving Gudrum free to advance towards Slussfall.

Stellan's mind was awash with more worries than what Gudrum would do, though. He was watching Eddeth, who hovered over Reinar's bed, belching and sneezing and making all sorts of strange snorting sounds.

His son hadn't woken since he'd been carried from the field.

He was breathing but unconscious and, according to Alys, very much cursed. It made sense to Eddeth, who had quickly decided that Raf must have seen the danger that blade had posed. The little dreamer had risked her own life to warn Reinar and then gotten herself killed trying to protect him.

Thinking of Raf, Eddeth sniffed loudly, overcome with emotion. Neither she nor Alys had slept much in the last two days, and it showed as Alys came back into the tent with a steaming cauldron, her face as crumpled as her cloak.

Stellan looked around, his nose wrinkling at the smell. 'What's that?'

Alys wasn't sure. 'Something to try and wake him up.'

'And you think it could work against a curse?'

Eddeth was quickly in front of Alys, shooing Stellan out of the tent, wanting to get on with things. They didn't need to be answering questions and Stellan needed to be taking charge of the camp, and finding ways to keep them safe from Gudrum. 'We can try, we can try!' she barked. 'Yes, yes, but it won't help us to have you as an audience. Off you go now!' And giving Stellan a final shove, she nudged him towards the tent flap.

Stellan knew Eddeth was right, and though he wanted to stay until his son opened his eyes, he needed the dreamers to get to work. 'Send word if anything changes,' he murmured, disappearing outside.

Alys watched him go, holding back tears, struggling to keep control of her mind, which wandered with tiredness and fear. They had taken turns caring for Reinar, though there'd been no change in his condition. He was mostly cold to the touch, perfectly still, and breathing. That was something, she supposed, sighing wearily.

Eddeth took the cauldron from Alys, sloshing hot water over her trousers. 'Remember when we had to help Hakon Vettel?' she chuckled. 'Stuck in a tent, fearing he'd find out the truth about you?'

'And you did help him,' Alys reminded her.

Eddeth lifted the cauldron onto the table, where she'd lined up her bottles of herbs. 'With a few maggots! Though I doubt we'll find some magical curse-breaking maggots around here.' Her smile was gone as she pulled the cork from the first bottle, inhaling the acrid scent of sea holly. All her herbs were dried, many folded into little linen packets. She'd spent hours in Slussfall's forest with Raf and sometimes Alys, searching for fresh herbs, and when she'd stumbled across them, she'd dried them, storing them away, not knowing when spring would arrive to bring new hope. Now it had, though she had no time for foraging, not wanting to be away from Reinar's bedside for even a moment.

'We need to think, Eddeth,' Alys said quietly. 'About more than Reinar. Gudrum will come again, won't he? We have to be able to warn Stellan about what's coming next.'

Eddeth knew that to be true. 'I...' She glanced around the tent.

'Can you do it? I have to find a way through this curse. I can't ask Raf what she saw.' And tears in her eyes, she blinked up at Alys. 'I need to help Reinar.'

Alys nodded, though she was desperately worried about Reinar too. 'Don't worry, I'll search for Gudrum and Gysa. I'll try and find a way to see what they're planning.' She thought of Raf, too, wondering what had happened to the little dreamer.

***

Valera wouldn't let Sigurd see Raf.

She had acted on impulse bringing Raf's body back to Gallabrok, quickly realising that she'd only made everything worse. Though she'd desperately wanted to save the dreamer. As the Goddess of Dreamers now, Valera needed one as talented as Raf – a dreamer who had sacrificed her life to save a future king. So, holding her hands to Raf's torn throat, she had brought her back to life, leaving her to recover in the privacy of a comfortable chamber while she thought on what to do.

'Where's Thenor?' Sigurd wanted to know, seeing Valera emerge from Raf's chamber. He felt annoyed, desperate to get inside, though Valera seemed just as determined to keep him out as ever. She led him away from the door, leaving two of her father's men to guard it.

'I have no idea. He does not wish to be found. Whatever he is doing, he doesn't want anyone following him. It will be something to do with Alari or Eskvir, I'm certain.'

Sigurd hoped their father was safe, knowing how eager Alari was to play her games. Ultimately though, she wanted to kill him. And knowing Thenor genuinely feared that his time was nearing an end, Sigurd felt concerned, though his mind quickly returned to Raf. 'What will you do about Raf? Send her back?'

'I must. She does not belong here.'

'Yet you've kept her here,' Sigurd frowned. 'Why?'

'I...' Valera pulled Sigurd close, seeking to keep their conversation private, for despite Gallabrok's intricate security, Valera never underestimated Tikas' talent for uncovering gossip. And no gossip was more sought after than Gallabrok gossip. 'I want to help her, to guide her. She will go back into a war, and Reinar will need her. Gysa is powerful, and if Gudrum sets her free, she will be dangerous. Unstoppable. Eddeth and Alys are going to need all the help they can get.'

***

Gysa wasn't gifted with healing magic. It wasn't something Alari valued. Her dreamers knew the dark arts: curses and spells to hurt and maim. Their magic was weaponised. But to heal? Alari had little use for such things, so Gudrum had been forced to rely upon his healer to tend to his wounds. The woman was perfectly capable, and he'd been stitched up in no time, slathered in honey and all manner of sweet-smelling balms. The healer had suggested he cover his face with a bandage, though Gudrum had balked at that, wanting to look like a man who'd waged a war, only denied his victory by a vengeful god. Not like an invalid ready for his pyre.

Gysa sat opposite him with an irritated look, Edrik slumped on her left, noisily crunching some pork crackling. She had sat patiently through his meeting with the disgruntled warlords, who had spent two days licking their wounds and pointing fingers as they'd counted their losses. And after piling up the bodies of the dead, stripped of anything of value, and lighting the pyres, they had come up with suggestions for how to move forward. Gudrum had listened, or attempted to, though he'd felt hemmed in, reminded of watching a squirming Hector enduring Svein Bearsu's neverending tirades. Eventually, sending the lords away,

Gudrum had sought to order his thoughts, inviting Edrik's and Gysa's advice.

'You should choose your own path. You don't need to listen to any of those lords,' Gysa insisted as Edrik raised an eyebrow in surprise. She turned slowly to the man, her lips pressed together. 'You don't agree? But Gudrum is the king. His way is the only way.'

Edrik was more pragmatic, having spent nearly twenty years learning and listening at the elbows of lords and now a king. There was diplomacy, and there was battle, and if a king wanted to succeed, he needed to be adept at both. 'If you dismiss their ideas, they'll talk amongst themselves. Maybe they'll band together and decide that a Brekkan shouldn't be the King of Alekka after all... my lord.'

Gudrum glowered at him, leaning forward until his elbows were resting on his knees. His back ached, but then his thighs stung where they'd been stitched, and irritated on all counts, he sat up straight. 'What have you heard?'

Edrik was pleased to have claimed his king's attention, enjoying the dreamer's irritation as she fidgeted beside him. 'There is unhappiness, my lord, mutterings of displeasure. But with no victory, that's to be expected. Your Southern allies remain loyal, but they're not as powerful or influential as those in the North. The Lords of Ennor, Kurso, and Borken are neighbours, and close ones at that. Their families are connected through many marriages. They know each other better than they know you.'

Gudrum nodded, seeing how quickly things could unravel. 'Well, perhaps my new allies will help?' he grinned, moving his attention to Gysa.

'The Islanders? But why would they fight for you, my lord?' Edrik wondered, then seeing the way Gudrum had turned to smile at the dreamer, he nodded. 'Oh, I see.'

***

'What we need is that Gysa here, before us!' Eddeth announced, throwing back her head, eyes on the shadowy light dancing across the tent roof, realising the day had run away with them. 'We need to know what she did! How can we undo a puzzle we can't even see?'

Alys jumped in fright, having thought Eddeth asleep in front of the brazier.

They'd remained in Reinar's tent as a storm lashed the camp and day turned to night. Alys thought fleetingly of the children, though Stina had assured her that between Ludo, Jonas, and Puddle, they were well occupied. 'What did you see?' she wondered, leaving Reinar behind to join Eddeth by the fire. And picking up a handful of branches, she added them to the dying flames.

'I saw everything that happened, all over again. As though I was standing right there, watching Gudrum stab Reinar with his sword.' Eddeth stood with a groan. 'Horrible, it was! Though I found no answers for how to reverse the curse. Nothing useful at all.'

'You've stopped curses before,' Alys said, thinking of the trees in Ottby.

'I have,' Eddeth agreed. 'More than one since we met. Oh yes, but the world's a much darker place these days, Alys. Brimming with evil! I don't remember it being that way before, do you?' Though not waiting for an answer, Eddeth rushed to Reinar's bed, feeling all of a fluster. And resting a calloused hand on his forehead, she ploughed on, turning to peer over her shoulder. 'I think Alari's unbalancing things, working with that sister of hers. The creatures coming out of the darkness? The rise of cruel men again?' Eddeth's eyes bulged. 'It's always been there, I know, lurking in the shadows, though I had hoped not to live through a truly dark time.'

'Dark time?'

'Oh yes, for there can be no light without darkness. And I thought we'd escaped the Darkness a few years back, but here it is in Alekka, rearing its evil head again. Its evil, evil head. And what can we do about it, Alys? You and me?'

'We have to help Reinar,' Alys insisted. 'We can't let Gudrum and Gysa remain in power.' She stood then, joining Eddeth by the bed, wrapping her fingers around Reinar's wrist. She wanted to see something, to glimpse a clue, anything they could do to help him. It was so frustrating to watch him deteriorate. Though feeling nothing but the unnatural coldness of his skin, Alys released her fingers, trailing them down his leg, all the way to just above his ankle, where Gudrum's sword had pierced his skin near the bone. 'It feels hot,' she murmured, touching that small hole.

Eddeth nodded. 'And not just his ankle. He's on fire up here. The rest of him's like ice, but his head and feet are flaming.' Bending over, she whispered the words of a healing chant in Reinar's ear. Symbol sticks were buried beneath his neck and under his wrists and ankles, and every few hours, she would try to ignite their healing powers, hoping to spark a change.

Alys placed both hands on Reinar's wound now. It wasn't festering. And apart from the odd little mark, there was no obvious sign that he'd been injured. He didn't flinch when she touched him, though she knew her hands were cold. And closing her eyes, Alys let Eddeth's voice drift away as she searched the silent darkness for answers.

She immediately saw a blue eye glowing before her. Just an eye.

And then a voice.

'He doesn't *want* your help?' Alari laughed. 'But what does that matter? Most lords and kings don't know what is best for them. Most men don't either! But you must help him, Gysa, for you've already killed one of my kings, and I won't let you lose another!'

'But how? Gudrum will see everything I do.'

'If that's true, I have wasted my time on you entirely! Do you really imagine that to be the case? Ha! But some of the most powerful work a dreamer does is invisible to the eye. It is always better to make our magic in the shadows, and there is nothing more suited to the darkness than a curse.'

Alys blinked open her eyes, staring at Eddeth.

'What? You saw something?' Eddeth breathed, creeping around the bed towards her, placing a hand on Alys' arm.

'I...' Alys nodded. 'The curse. It isn't Gysa's. It belongs to Alari.'

Eddeth blinked with real fear then. 'Alari? Oh dear, but what are we going to do now?'

***

Stellan didn't know what to do.

Nor did Jonas and Vik. They were in an untenable situation. They didn't have enough men to hold back Gudrum's army, yet to retreat over the mountains, back to Slussfall? It wouldn't only take time but serious effort, and after the battle there were many injuries and many more dead.

Bjarni was chewing a sliver of salt fish before him, tired eyes darting about. 'If we go back to Slussfall, we'll have the walls to protect us, a chance for reinforcements. We can send another message to the Islanders.'

Stellan frowned. 'You think so? That our ship sinking was just a coincidence? And if we lock ourselves into Slussfall again with no help coming?' He sighed. 'Besides, I don't want to carry Reinar back to Slussfall. I'm not sure he'd survive the journey.' Stellan cleared his throat, any emotions he felt remaining firmly hidden behind an iron-strong door. 'Reinar's destined to be the king. We can't forget that. So while he's recovering, we must ensure that we make the best decisions possible on his behalf, to prepare ourselves for his return. After what he's been through, he'll want to kill Gudrum even more. If he wakes up to find he's back in Slussfall, I doubt he'll thank us.' There was little confidence in his voice, and Stellan realised that he was mostly trying to convince himself that Reinar was going to be alright.

Only Ollo spoke what they were all thinking. 'But if he doesn't? If he dies?'

Stellan wanted to slap him, but he couldn't deny it was a question that needed asking. 'If he dies, I'll lead us. Perhaps I'm wrong, but I believe it's what Ake would have wanted. Reinar too.'

Jonas nodded. 'Without a doubt, Stellan. It would have been you.'

Vik and Bjarni agreed.

Ollo was happy to still be standing with those deciding what to do, not dying in a tent or a corpse on a field, picked at by crows. He'd come close to losing his head on more than one occasion, lucky to have escaped the battlefield with nothing more than a sprained ankle.

'So we stay here,' Stellan announced with a heavy sigh. Though quickly hearing the defeat in his voice, he lifted his chin and thought of Ake, who had faced his death like a true king, with courage and dignity. And now Stellan had to follow in his footsteps, putting Alekka first. Always Alekka first. 'We'll hold our position here and try to reach the Islanders again. Bjarni, find messengers. Get three. Organise horses while I write out notes. We'll send them to Goslund, to Erpstad, to Trova. They'll each need to find a ship. One will be sure to arrive. And if not, we'll turn to our dreamers, to Thenor, to whoever we need to. Whatever we have to do, we'll do it. We will not gift Gudrum the prize of that throne!'

***

Gudrum would never trust a dreamer again.

First, Raf had betrayed him, then Gysa had disobeyed him. He remembered Mirella, too, who had wound him in magical knots, ultimately humiliating him, helping Tarl Brava return to reclaim Orvala.

There were so many games and too many manipulative dreamers playing them.

He walked through the dark camp with Gysa, feeling the chill of the night air creeping under his cloak. Then, seeing the familiar silhouette of Bor Bearsu coming towards him, he abruptly changed direction, slipping between two rows of tents, wanting to remain alone with his dreamer. 'I have no need for your help,' he began as Gysa hurried to catch him, lifting her cloak and dress out of the mud.

She looked surprised, having expected him to say the opposite.

Turning around, he eyed her sharply before continuing. 'Though I will allow it *if*, as before, you see trouble coming my way. I will allow your interference, but understand that my victory over whatever is left of Reinar Vilander's army will belong solely to me. I don't want any songs sung about magical beasts and mythical dreamers. Or you. Whatever you choose to do, be discreet.'

'You needn't worry,' Gysa promised, suppressing a smile. 'I am used to working in the shadows.'

***

Raf wanted to see Sigurd, though Valera wouldn't let her.

She'd been confined to a chamber, which, though luxurious in both size and adornments, made her feel like a pig in a pen. 'Is Sigurd here?' she wondered, eyeing the door. 'Or perhaps he doesn't want to see me?'

'Sigurd belongs here,' Valera smiled, though her voice was firm. 'And he will stay here, but you will soon leave. Seeing Sigurd wouldn't help you now.'

Raf didn't agree.

Valera sat on the bed beside her, patting her leg. She had gifted Raf a new dress. It was dark blue, made from finely spun wool, embroidered with silver coils at the nape and sleeves. It set off her dark hair and blue eyes, though Raf was yet to feel comfortable wearing it.

She didn't feel like this person. She didn't belong here.

'I will help you before I send you back,' Valera said softly, almost conspiratorially. 'Alari is guiding Gysa, gifting her advanced powers, showing her many things. Goddess things. So while you are here, I will teach you ways to counter whatever magic Gysa employs against you.'

'What about Reinar? Is he alive?'

Valera nodded. 'For now. Alys and Eddeth are trying to save him, though they are not confident.'

'But can't you save him? Like you saved me?' Raf glanced at the door again, feeling Valera's hand pressing down on her leg.

'I cannot. Gysa's curse comes from Alari. I saw the same symbols you did, though I have no way to undo the curse. Not yet. I will try to find an answer, though, for Alekka needs Reinar Vilander.' Once again, Valera imagined her father glowering at her, and with a tense smile, she stood. 'I will have food and ale sent. Though perhaps you would prefer wine?'

'No,' Raf said quickly, wriggling in the uncomfortable dress.

'It suits you,' Valera smiled as she walked to the door. And stopping, she turned back. 'You are not who you think you are, Raf. You are so much more. Though realising that will only come from within and with time. You saved Reinar's life. If Gudrum had cut him again, or deeper, he would have died on that field as you saw in your dream. Because of you, the curse barely touched him, though it is powerful enough that it may claim him in the end.' Valera felt a great sense of uncertainty. It was as though they had entered a new world. And with Thenor's son having a human family, she knew it was going to be impossible to hold that magical line for much longer.

CHAPTER THIRTY SEVEN

They made land in the middle of a hailstorm.

Thorgils peered at Eadmund through dripping tendrils of red hair. 'Wish we still had those little houses Jael built. Remember those?' The hail was as big as pebbles, and he ducked back under his hood as *Sea Bear* surged towards the beach. 'Not the most auspicious start to this little venture of ours!'

Eadmund smiled, wet through and shivering, though he felt much the same. 'Reminds me of Oss, so I'd say the opposite's true. It's just like being at home!'

Beorn was barking at his rowers as white-capped waves rolled them towards the shore. 'Keep her steady now. Steady! What? Are your ears full of hailstones? I said *steady*!'

Twenty-eight ships were looking to find their way to the wide-mouthed beach through streaming rain and pounding hail, and no one wanted to be last, for rows of cottages lined the beach, and the promise of shelter and ale was a prize everyone wanted to be first to claim.

'Well, here's hoping that Harran knows where his lord is,' Thorgils grumped. 'I don't fancy trekking up and down this miserable place looking for the king.'

Eadmund laughed. 'Glad I brought you along. You really know how to lift our spirits, don't you?'

Thorgils sighed, shoulders dropping. 'I'm just hungry. I can't remember when I last had a meal that filled me! Isaura knows how to take care of me. There's always food in our house. Always something to eat.' He couldn't stand still, fidgeting with his cloak pins.

Bram rolled his eyes. 'Your poor wife. When she's not popping out babies, she's as skinny as a broom. Now we know why! I bet she's sitting at the table, enjoying a full meal for a change. Ha! Here's hoping our hosts are prepared for your giant appetite.'

Eadmund felt slightly awkward about seeing Ake again after what had happened when they'd last met on Oss.

Knowing what had happened to Orla Berras.

He wondered if that was why Hector had turned against his king? He felt the unfamiliar sensation of nerves fluttering in his chest. After returning from the Vale, there'd been little need to leave Oss, and apart from the odd visit to the islands or to Osterland to see friends and family, they hadn't. Eadmund and Jael had hibernated away, strengthening their defenses, building their family, and recovering from what had been an arduous first year of marriage.

This was the first time they'd been apart since then, Eadmund realised, missing that scowling face.

'And what do you think Jael's doing?' Thorgils asked as the hail finally eased, the beach coming at them quickly. He grabbed the nearest rope, preparing for impact. 'Likely she won't even know you've gone!'

Eadmund laughed, imagining that was true.

'She'll be enjoying the peace and quiet, not having you two lumps moping about the place, that's for sure,' Bram decided. 'So we'd better go and show her what's she missing. Can't go back with some pitiful tale about getting defeated, humiliating ourselves, kicked out of Alekka for being no use at all.'

Eadmund lurched forward, clinging to a rope. 'True. We need to do something of note.'

'Of note?' Thorgils scoffed. 'What? You think this is going to be some piddling arm wrestle? No, from what Harran said, this is all out war. And Jael's missing out on that?' He shook his wet hair, flinging great drops of water at his uncle. 'Makes no sense to me.

Hopefully, our queen can sort out her thinking before we get back. She needs to!' And impatient to get onto the beach, Thorgils made his way down the deck.

Eadmund stared after him, receiving a slap on the back from Bram.

'Ignore the big oaf. Jael knows what she's doing. We can handle this and get back before she starts missing you.'

Eadmund smiled, nodding as he followed after Bram.

Hoping he was right.

***

Eddeth had spent the night sitting by Reinar's bed. He appeared to be getting weaker, and they didn't want to leave him alone. When Alys had come to relieve her, she'd stumbled out of the tent, needing sleep, almost hoping no dreams would disturb her. Though it was only an hour later that she was bounding through the camp like a hare, searching for Stellan Vilander.

After a few wrong turns and a quick trip to the latrines, she found him talking to Berger, Ilene, and Ollo. 'I... I saw...!'

Stellan grabbed her arm, heart thumping. 'Is it Reinar?' He led Eddeth to a tree stump, where he forced her to sit down, wanting her to catch her breath, hoping it would help her reveal what she'd seen in a way that made sense.

'Gudrum!'

'Gudrum!' Ollo was quickly glancing around. 'Here? Is he coming here? *Now*?'

'Calm down,' Berger grinned. 'We'd have had some warning if he was. Don't you think? We've scouts out there. We've set signal fires too.'

Stellan nodded. 'What about Gudrum, Eddeth?'

'The Islanders,' Eddeth panted. 'They've come to help him!'

'*What*?' Stellan was horrified, his horror immediately reflected on the faces of the three warriors before him. 'They're in Alekka?'

Eddeth nodded, gathering steam again, and standing, she stared up at Stellan. 'I... saw them. They brought their ships. I saw them! They talked about the king. About coming to help the king, but, but...' There was more, but her excitement had tied her tongue, and it took some time to untangle it. 'They think the king is still Ake!'

'Why?' Berger wanted to know. 'How?'

Eddeth didn't know, the memories of her dream already becoming a little hazy. 'They talked about coming to help the king! About helping Ake!' she repeated. 'There was a man!'

'What man?' Ilene wondered with a sigh, fed up with Eddeth's meandering explanations.

'A man was with them, talking about Ake. About how he would... lead them to him!'

Stellan scratched his cheek, which he had a habit of doing when he was worried. 'They think Ake's the king? And this man? He did too?'

'No! Yes! No!' Eddeth couldn't decide, beginning to feel muddled. 'The man! I saw his eyes. Dazed, they were. Dark and dazed. There was something wrong with him!'

Stellan thought he might have an understanding of what was happening. 'The Islanders were Ake's allies. There's no reason for them to help Gudrum unless they don't know who Gudrum is. Unless they don't know whose side he's on.'

That rendered them all silent.

'We have to tell them,' Berger decided. 'Send men to find them, to warn them. Maybe they've changed sides? We need to know.'

Stellan agreed. 'We do. And maybe if we can get through to them, tell them the truth, they'll switch back to us.' He peered at Eddeth, hoping for more, though she only looked confused and eventually shrugged.

Ollo was almost on his way. 'I'll find some men. Scouts will go.'

Stellan nodded. 'But where are they, Eddeth? Do you know?'

Eddeth's mouth opened, though no answers came out. She

turned, looking at the three men, pointedly ignoring Ilene. 'I... couldn't say,' she eventually admitted. 'I couldn't! They landed their ships, but I don't know where. A beach. Just a beach!'

Stellan patted her shoulder. 'You've done well, Eddeth. Now make Reinar as comfortable as you can. If the Islanders have truly decided to take Gudrum's side, we'll need to move quickly, so please, do what you can to help him.' Everything was falling apart, and Stellan was struggling to hold onto even one thread now. 'There's an answer in this somewhere,' he muttered, turning away. 'Somehow. We just have to find it.'

***

Magnus and Lotta brought Puddle to visit their mother, who had barely emerged from Reinar's tent since he'd been carried into it.

Puddle and a bowl of porridge.

Though the smell almost had Alys gagging. 'You can have it, Magnus,' she said, wrinkling her nose.

Magnus frowned at her. 'Stina said you'd say that, and I'm supposed to stay until you've eaten it.' He felt annoyed about that, for his friends had talked about going fishing, and he didn't want to miss out.

Reading his thoughts, Alys smiled. 'I promise I'll eat it. You can tell Stina I had some.' And reaching for the spoon, she shovelled some porridge into her mouth. 'There!' she announced, trying to gulp down the unappetising lump. 'Now you can leave.'

Magnus looked ready to bolt, but his sister shook her head. 'That's not enough, Mama. You need to eat more.' Dropping Puddle to the ground, Lotta dug her hands into her tiny waist, cocking her head to one side.

Alys stared at her eight-year-old daughter. 'Or maybe I'll just tell Stina how you tip her stews back into the cauldron when she's not looking?'

Lotta looked horrified, immediately straightening up, scowling at her laughing brother. 'Well, we can go then,' she decided. 'But you can have Puddle. He'll keep you company, and maybe Ragnahild will come?'

Alys hoped she would. 'What will you do then, Lotta? Magnus will be off fishing, so maybe you can find Stina?'

Magnus was eyeing the tent flap as Lotta shook her head. 'Stina just wants to kiss Ludo.'

'What?' That was news to Alys. 'What?' She looked from Lotta to Magnus, who nodded, rolling his eyes.

'They can't stop,' Magnus muttered. 'Kissing.'

Alys shook her head. 'How did I miss that?'

'Because you've been in here for so *long*, Mama!' Lotta sighed, shoulders dropping. 'I want you to come to our tent tonight and sleep with me.'

'I will,' Alys promised, then looking over her shoulder at a silent and still Reinar, she wasn't sure that was true. Turning back to her daughter, she shrugged. 'At least I'll try to.'

Lotta wrapped her arms around her mother's waist, squeezing. 'You'll find an answer. You'll save Reinar. I know it. It's why we came. You're meant to save him!'

Alys swallowed, knowing that Reinar lay in that bed solely because she hadn't saved him.

The children swept out of the tent, ignored by Puddle, who was on his belly, crawling beneath Reinar's bed, looking for something to eat. Alys turned to the bed herself, eyes resting on Reinar's chest, relieved to see it still moving, before drifting up to his face, which remained so still and pale.

She placed a hand on his forehead, trying to bring images to her mind, looking for some way to help him. But all she saw was the hurt in his eyes as they stood beneath the tree that night. She'd seen that his wife was carrying his child, but Reinar had never known that. She should have said. She shouldn't have let him think he'd done something wrong or that she didn't...

'You came into my life for a reason,' she whispered, lowering her face to his, remembering their kiss in Eddeth's cottage. He'd said he loved her, and though she felt the same, she hadn't said it back. Yet time never stood still, and moments passed as quickly as sand falling through fingers. Moments that often never came again. 'You captured me, I know, but what you really did, Reinar, was set me free. All those years of being Arnon's prisoner, trying to escape, and you took me away from it all. You changed my life, and now...' She sniffed back tears. 'Now I'll save yours.' With one look at Puddle, who was staring up at her, she bent forward and kissed him. 'I will save yours.'

***

'What news?' Gudrum called with a forced smile as his dreamer approached. His face and legs were mostly numb. The healer had been rubbing butter, honey, and various balms on his burns and wounds, and though they'd stung initially, they had taken away the pain. He almost felt like himself again. 'My lords grow impatient for news. As do I! Three nights and no useful dreams? I may have to find myself another dreamer.' He winked at Gysa, knowing that she'd seen many things, though nothing he wanted to reveal to his allies, who perched on chairs beside him.

They were eating on their laps, enjoying the sunshine and the ale, which Gudrum's steward was hurrying to keep the three men's cups filled with, though there was tension in the air. Tension and the first hints of disease taking hold. It had snowed, at first, then rained for days, and now rot was setting in. Gudrum could smell it. He needed to make a decision about what to do quickly.

He hoped Gysa could help him.

'The Islanders have arrived in Alekka, my lord!' she called. 'They are here, marching to you!'

Gudrum lifted his cup to the Lords of Borken and Kurso and the sullen King of Tudash, who mostly refused to look his way. 'As I was saying, why make a move now when we could add another thousand men to our numbers? The loss of those we left on that field hasn't helped. Better to head for Slussfall with fresh arms and legs. We'll send the Islanders up to the first rank!'

Bor Bearsu frowned, ignoring the dreamer, who shook her head as Edrik offered her some ale. 'The Islanders are expecting to find Ake Bluefinn waiting for them. And what are you going to do about that, my lord? How will you convince them to fight for you instead?'

Gudrum turned to Gysa. 'There are ways. None you need concern yourself with, my lord, for my dreamer and I have that well in hand. The important thing is that they are coming. They are coming to me.'

***

Valera had prepared Raf as best she could. The girl was healed and strong again, with no sign that she'd ever been killed by Gudrum's knife. She had new clothes, greater knowledge, and a real sense of purpose.

But there was one thing missing, and being the Goddess of Love, Valera found it impossible to ignore. 'Come with me, Raf, and I will take you to the hall.'

Raf scrambled off the bed, surprised by the invitation. She knew Valera would send her back to Alys and Eddeth, but she hadn't expected to be allowed out before then.

'Though what you see and hear is nothing you will reveal, understood?'

Raf nodded eagerly, and following Valera out of the chamber, she was immediately awestruck, tilting back her head to take in the enormously high ceilings, and dropping it, she saw the warm glow of hundreds of tiny lamps flickering in the walls. She heard the sound of running water, and confused by that, she was frowning as she entered the great hall.

It wasn't as she'd imagined. It was warm and bright and decorated with beautiful ornaments and tapestries. She had thought it would be a cold place, commanded by a serious god, though she wondered if perhaps Valera had had a hand in things?

Turning back to her, Valera winked. 'Perhaps. Now I will leave you here, and you may eat and drink and...' She stopped, looking around. 'I will return shortly and take you back home.'

Raf looked confused. 'I don't have a home.'

'I thought you did? With Eddeth and Alys and the children and the animals. I thought you did, Raf?'

Raf blinked, remembering that stinking little cottage and the bleating little goat. She remembered lying opposite Eddeth, whispering in the night, waking up to find her breakfast on the table beside a hot cup of tea. There'd been a tea for every ailment, for every mood, for every part of the day.

Raf smiled.

Eddeth had darned her socks and repaired holes in her dress. She had slipped her arm through hers as they'd strolled the market, looking for anything that might take their fancy. She had walked her into the forest, teaching her about trees and plants and creatures. And though Raf had been raised in a forest, she hadn't known most of what Eddeth had shared.

She shrugged as Valera turned away. 'Perhaps.'

And then Sigurd was there, and all thoughts of Eddeth vanished from Raf's mind. Her lips parted, her breath caught in her throat. She almost coughed in surprise, seeing how different he looked. How handsome.

'I never thought she'd let you out,' Sigurd grinned, walking towards that familiar figure, taking in everything, from the top of her shining black hair, tamed for the first time, to the polished boots, free of mud. 'You look clean.'

Raf squirmed. 'I...'

'It suits you.'

Raf wrinkled her freckled nose, embarrassed in the silly dress.

Sigurd stepped closer with a smile. 'The dress is nice.'

'Your hair is different,' Raf blurted out, wanting to stop him talking about her.

Sigurd reached up, touching the newly shaven sides of his head. 'Does it make me look like a god?' he joked.

Raf wasn't sure. 'You... saved me.' She blinked up at him, knowing that Valera had only rescued her because of Sigurd. 'You saved my life.'

'And you saved Reinar's,' Sigurd said, taking her hand, staring deep into those eyes, now moist with tears. 'For a long time, no one knew what to make of you, not even me. But you showed me the truth in that moment. I watched you risk your life for Reinar, and I'll never forget it, Raf.'

Raf's tears spilled down her cheeks, feeling the comforting warmth of Sigurd's hand holding hers. 'I...' And then she was in his arms, and they were strong and gentle, and she buried herself into his chest, feeling the relief of being held by him; the sweet, unexplainable joy of it. 'I have to go,' she mumbled into his tunic, not wanting to trick herself into believing that this was anything more than one moment. He smelled of pine and mead, and she inhaled deeply, wanting to carry that scent back with her.

'You do, but not yet. I need to hold you some more.' Sigurd lowered his head until his chin touched Raf's hair. 'You smell nicer than I remember.'

She smiled, not replying.

'I'm glad you finally gave up on Gudrum.'

Raf pushed herself out of Sigurd's embrace, turning her face up to his. 'He turned out to be exactly who I knew he was,' she admitted with some regret. 'I just... hoped he'd be different. I thought I owed him my loyalty. But, in the end, I saw that I'd helped him more than he'd ever helped me.'

'And he did kill you.'

Raf smiled. 'There was that, yes.' Now she pushed herself up onto her toes, kissing him. 'How long do we have?'

'Not that long,' Sigurd laughed between kisses. 'Valera will come to take you back soon.'

'Will I ever see you again?'

Sigurd stepped back. 'I don't know,' he admitted, heart

throbbing, body filled with need. 'Alari remains a threat. I'm supposed to stay here until she's dead.'

'But you can't kill Alari. She sees everything. She knows everything. Her magic is greater than anyone's!'

'Don't worry, we know more than she realises. We aren't giving up. Thenor...' But realising that he couldn't talk to Raf about Thenor's plans, Sigurd abruptly changed the subject. 'You're leaving,' he said with sadness now. 'I won't speak to you again.'

'Forever?'

Sigurd shook his head. 'Not forever, Raf. I couldn't live with that. I couldn't.'

'Then you'll come and find me again? One day?'

'Do you want me to?' He was a god who felt like a boy. A strong, tall man feeling as small as a faerie before an ogre. Though Raf was no ogre, he thought, stroking her sweet face.

She nodded. 'I'll wait for you, Sigurd.'

He kissed her. 'Then I'll come for you. I'll find a way we can be together. There'll be a way. If a god can't make things right, then who can?' He wiped away the tears rolling down her cheek. 'There'll be a way, Raf. There will.'

She wasn't sure she believed him, though she wanted to.

'You have to help Reinar,' Sigurd added. 'He needs to live.'

'I'll try. I'll try everything I can.'

'Don't forget Gudrum killed you.'

Raf laughed. 'I won't. Don't worry, I'll never forget that.' And now, more tears came as Valera approached again. 'I'll never forget... you.'

'You won't need to,' Sigurd whispered, bending to her ear. 'I'll see you again soon, I promise.' He kissed her ear, her cheeks, her nose, her lips. And bringing her into his arms one more time, he lifted her off the ground, squeezing her tightly, wanting to remember this brief, fleeting moment forever.

'It is time,' Valera said solemnly, hands clasped in front of her cloak. 'We must go, Raf.'

Raf nodded, untangling herself from Sigurd's arms, barely able to tear her eyes away from him. 'Stay safe,' she pleaded, 'from

Alari. She wants to hurt you, Sigurd. She wants to hurt you all.' And before she could say another word or Sigurd could offer a reply, she was gone, and Sigurd was left standing alone, staring at the waterfall.

CHAPTER THIRTY EIGHT

Eddeth made the familiar trek back to Reinar's tent to find an exhausted Alys sound asleep on the floor. And realising that she might be having a dream, Eddeth decided to let her sleep a little longer. She crept back outside, knocking into Helgi, who was carrying a bucket of water, which he promptly tipped all over her.

'Oh, it's c-c-cold!' Eddeth exclaimed loudly, staggering backwards, her wet cloak immediately clinging to her in the stiff breeze.

'Sorry! I think I was mostly walking with my eyes closed,' Helgi admitted, having been thinking about Alys as he passed the tent.

'Likely you were,' Eddeth grumbled, eyes on the tent herself, hoping all her noise hadn't woken Alys, for she'd appeared to be having a good dream.

***

'You are a Follower,' Alari breathed, her blue eye sparkling with interest as she studied the young woman, turning her, scanning every part of her lithe body. 'And that makes you perfect for what I have in mind.'

Mirella didn't understand. 'I left The Following,' she admitted. 'I left them. At least I... wanted to come home. To be with my parents. To be home.'

Alari slipped an arm around the girl's back. 'But home needn't be that small little hole in Torborg. No! After your adventures in Osterland? With the knowledge you gained there? The great minds who taught you? The gifted, gifted dreamers? No, Mirella, sweet girl, you can never go back there.'

Mirella felt torn. She was seventeen. The years away from her parents had been hard on her, and though she'd enjoyed her time in Tuura's temple, she felt as though she was meant for something more. Though she also wanted to be part of a family again.

'And you will be,' Alari purred. 'Your own! I have found the perfect husband for you. The man you are destined to be with. I have seen your future, and it is the most majestic sight! You will help your husband, and I will help you. I will teach you all I know, and you will help me save Alekka.'

Alys sat up, gripping her throat, the menacing glow of Alari's eye like a beam of light in the dark tent. She blinked, glancing around, seeing that the fire had burned to ash and embers, and shivering, she sat up, immediately worried about Reinar. Scrambling to her feet, she placed a hand on his chest, checking to ensure it was still moving. And finally confident that he was breathing, she stepped away, sitting on a stool.

Her dream rushed back to her in urgent waves.

Mirella had been Alari's apprentice.

As a girl, Alari had taken her under her wing, introducing her to Jesper Vettel.

Alys pulled the brooch from her purse, staring at what now looked like a snake killing a crane. She had treasured that brooch as a child, but now it made her afraid.

Alari had taught Mirella everything...

Was that true? And if it was, could her mother help her find a way to save Reinar? Alys didn't know, but one look at Reinar told her that she was quickly running out of time.

***

A dripping Eddeth had rebuffed any help from Helgi, who eventually left her behind and continued his journey to Stellan's tent. Reinforcements had arrived overnight, and there was a sense of optimism that hadn't been present the day before, though it was only a hundred-odd men. They weren't even back at the beginning, for surely they'd lost more than that in the Battle of Gord's Field.

'What do you think?' Vik was saying to Ollo as Helgi entered with a nod to the men gathered around Stellan's table. 'That we can sneak up on Gudrum's camp? With that woman watching?' He glowered at Ollo, who had grown impatient with the whole mess, just wanting to take some action.

He wasn't alone.

'What about Eddeth?' Ollo asked. 'She said she could hide us when we were in Stornas, so maybe she can keep us hidden from the dreamer?'

'And you want to risk that?' Jonas asked, feeling surprised. 'You?'

'Well, I wasn't suggesting I go,' Ollo stammered. 'What? I'm a leader here. I can't go!'

'A leader?' Stellan wondered wryly. 'First I've heard of it.' And enjoying Ollo's spluttering noise, he remained silent for a while, eventually holding up a hand. 'You are, of course, and a leader will be needed to take those men to Gudrum's camp. It's risky, but if we could cause some damage, maybe set a few fires, we could start to unsettle him, push Gudrum to rethink his plans.'

Berger looked unconvinced. 'A few fires? What good will that do?'

'Well, a big fire then... we could cause some real damage. But we'd only have the one chance,' Stellan decided.

Vik agreed. 'They'd double their defenses, and the dreamer would be on watch after that. But one run at them might upend their cart a bit. I'm happy to go along if Ollo needs some hand-holding?'

Ollo looked suitably insulted, thumbs tucked into his belt, belly protruding. 'Hand-holding? Well, if you're keen to get out of here, I'm happy for the company, but you can hold your own hand.'

Vik laughed, though Stellan had already turned his attention back to the map. 'It doesn't make sense to try anything if Eddeth can't hide you, though,' he warned. 'So go and find out what's possible, Ollo, Vik.' He glanced at Berger and the newly arrived Helgi. 'Any other volunteers?'

Both men shook their heads, and Stellan nodded, agreeing with that.

They had to do something while they waited to hear about Reinar and the Islanders, though it wouldn't be without risk. He couldn't afford to lose useful men like Berger and his cousin.

'I'll let you know what Eddeth thinks,' Vik said, tugging Ollo's sleeve. 'Come on, can't change your mind now.'

'What? I'm not doing any such thing,' Ollo blustered, following Vik out of the tent, suddenly consumed by the need for ale.

***

After their journey across the wild Akuliina Sea, Thorgils was happy to be on a horse, though he wasn't enamoured with being so wet. It hadn't stopped raining since they'd landed in Alekka, at a shitheap Harran had called Ullaberg. The small fishing village had offered little in the way of food and ale, and desiring to keep moving, Harran had insisted on keeping a fast pace.

It had hailed and rained, then rained some more, and after nearly two days, Thorgils had finally had enough. He rode next to Eadmund, who was plying the king's man for information. Thorgils had started listening, bored with the landscape, which didn't excite. It was like Brekka, he thought – all rolling hills and flat fields. They were skirting a range of mountains to the north, heading through the slush and slop towards where the new king was camped.

The news of Ake's death had been relayed to them by Harran, who'd been informed by the Ullaberg villagers of the sudden change in things.

After hearing that, Bram had felt the need to pull Eadmund aside. 'What do we know of this new king? Gudrum? How can we trust him?'

'He's fighting Ake's enemies,' Eadmund insisted.

'But our alliance was with Ake,' Thorgils put in. 'Not whoever this king is.'

'What? You want to take our ships and go home?' Eadmund hissed, glancing back at Harran, who was watching them closely. 'We came to hold up our end of the alliance. If we were in trouble and called on the Alekkans we'd want them to do the same. We can't just change our minds because Ake's dead. They still need our help.' He felt slightly concerned himself, but a change in leadership didn't necessarily imply a change in approach. Still, he saw the concern in Bram's experienced eyes.

'And who's this Gudrum?' Beorn muttered, joining them. 'What do we know about him?'

Eadmund shrugged. 'We ask as we go and decide when we get there. If we don't like the man, we can leave.'

'But how many days is that going to take?' Thorgils grumbled. 'Too many, I'd say! Too many to have to go back on ourselves. All the way back to that shitty beach?'

'Best you shut up then so we can get going,' Eadmund snapped, striding away from his moaning friend.

'This isn't going to end well!' Thorgils decided loudly, aiming his mouth Eadmund's way. 'Mark my words. Jael will be ruing the day she let you off the leash!' Which only incensed Eadmund further, he could see, and smiling now, Thorgils nudged Bram and trotted after him.

***

It had rained all day, and finally tired of shivering and dripping, Eddeth headed back to her tent to change her wet clothes, disappointed to discover that she'd nothing dry to change into. So she'd set a fire, and when it was blazing, she'd made herself comfortable on a stool before it, wrapped in both hers and Alys' bed furs, quickly falling asleep, chin on her chest, head lolling.

There had been so many sleepless nights, so many nights searching for dreams rather than seeking rest, and Eddeth hadn't realised how bone-weary she actually was. The fire was comforting and warm, the furs enclosing her like a baby bear in its mother's embrace.

She screamed as the hand touched her shoulder, lashing out in surprise, both arms flailing, furs falling into the brazier, though the flames had long since died.

'Eddeth! Stop! It's me!' Raf pleaded. 'I'm back!'

'*Back*?' Eddeth stared at her, mouth wrenched open, eyes full of sleep and confusion, and then surprise. 'I thought you were dead! Dead and gone with that Valera! And now you're back? Just like that?' She looked doubtful, narrowing her eyes. 'Or perhaps it's just a trick? An Alari sort of trick?' Glancing around, she found her staff and scooping it into her hands, she aimed it at Raf's belly. 'I see no scar! No sign you were ever hurt!'

'Valera saved me. She healed me.'

'Where?'

'In Thenor's hall. Gallabrok. I saw Sigurd.'

Now Eddeth was too curious to feel suspicious. 'You did?'

Raf nodded.

'But why are you back? How did you get here?'

'Valera brought me. I... wasn't allowed to stay. She showed me some things, ways to help us, to stop Gysa. Though I don't know how we can stop Alari.'

Eddeth threw her staff onto the bed, pulling Raf into her arms. 'Oh, I'm so glad to see you again!' she declared, bursting into tears.

'I thought I'd lost you too!'

Raf was surprised, though not unhappy to have been missed. 'Gysa cursed Reinar. I saw the symbols she put on Gudrum's sword. She wanted to help Gudrum. I don't think he knew.'

'You *saw* the symbols?' Eddeth could barely contain her delight. And grabbing Raf's hand, she dragged her out of the tent, shouting at the top of her lungs. 'Vellum! I need vellum! And some ink! Bring me some ink right away!'

***

Gudrum ate supper with Gysa, just the two of them in his tent. His desire for her company as a woman had remained constant, no matter the problems he'd had with her as a dreamer. At times, it felt as though they were wrestling for control of the situation, perhaps even for the throne itself, though Gudrum was slowly coming to realise that Gysa truly wanted to help him succeed, for helping him would, in turn, help her. Still, after what had happened with Raf, he remained cautious.

'Raf has returned,' Gysa said, reading his thoughts, a hint of displeasure in her eyes.

Gudrum spat out a chunk of pork, hitting Gysa in the throat. And seeing her throat, he remembered stabbing Raf in hers. '*What*?'

'Alive and well, returned to the Vilanders' camp.' Gysa watched Gudrum's eyes with interest, feeling the heat of jealousy rising up her neck. 'By Valera, I assume, for the goddess obviously saved her life. Returned her back, as good as new.'

'You saw that?'

Gysa nodded, cutting her pork with a trembling hand.

'Why? Why save a pointless thing like that? Some raggedy child I found in The Murk? What point is there to her?'

'I would think the answer is obvious. She is a dreamer, and dreamers are valuable, not pointless. It's a wonder you haven't realised that by now,' Gysa snapped.

Gudrum didn't argue, too stunned to offer any further reply. 'What about Reinar Vilander? The curse? Can Raf save him?'

Gysa snorted. 'Why would she be able to save him? The magic of those symbols belongs to Alari. Only Alari knows how to break that curse, and I assure you, she won't.' She picked up a silver goblet, gulping down her wine. 'Do not let the girl become another distraction.' She saw Gudrum's eyes sharpen, though she carried on. 'There can be no distractions now. What you intend to do requires a clear purpose, a singular vision. I will do everything within my power to help you, but it won't matter if you lose your focus.'

Gudrum rolled his tongue around his mouth, not enjoying being dictated to by a dreamer. But realising that he faced mounting problems on many fronts, he knew he needed her help. She had pacified the Lords of Borken, Kurso, and Ennor, who had become restless, discussing options amongst themselves. She had wound a spell around Harran, who was leading the clueless Islanders to him.

And, of course, she had cursed Reinar Vilander, who would surely soon die, if he wasn't already dead.

Though there was one problem she was yet to help him with, Gudrum realised. 'And Jael Furyck?' he murmured, leaning across the table to stroke Gysa's hand. 'How can you help me there?'

***

Tig hated sailing, so Jael stood by him for much of their journey across the Akuliina Sea. Fyn's horse, Yara, was an agreeable chestnut mare, so docile that she slept for much of the time, ignoring her irritable travelling companion. Leada was Eadmund's mare, used to Tig's moodiness, and Vili was Thorgils' stallion, who unsurprisingly spent most of his time nudging her for food.

Jael held a hand to Tig's smooth, cold cheek. 'Another adventure for us,' she breathed as he tossed his head, feeling unsure about that. 'What do you think? Can we find Eadmund in time?' She wished she could find Eadmund in her dreams. She'd tried to propel herself towards him, but despite her best efforts since they'd left Oss, she'd found no way through.

The idea that a dreamer was waiting for her in Alekka made her feel oddly nervous. She had no great skill as a dreamer, or, at least, no skill she'd worked to master the way she had as a warrior.

And how was she going to counter that?

Fyn touched Jael's arm, offering her a cup of ale. The salty air had dried her throat, but the rocking ship had kept her desire for any form of liquid at bay, so she took it with a tight smile.

Fyn sighed, bored with the journey now, impatient to be in Alekka. 'And what will we do when we get there?'

'Ask around,' Jael said. 'Hard to miss an army of strangers traipsing through your midst. We'll find them quickly enough.'

'And then?'

Jael sipped her ale, which was so cold that she shuddered. 'And then I kill the King of Alekka.'

***

The excitement of Raf's return wasn't enough to prevent Eddeth from quickly falling asleep again. So leaving her snoring softly by the brazier in Reinar's tent, Alys drew Raf away to the table where Eddeth had collected all her potions, salves, and herbs. Raf had drawn the symbols she remembered seeing on Gudrum's sword, and they studied them, searching through Eddeth's book, which had once been Salma's. Eddeth hadn't let it out of her sight since Alys had given it to her, so it made sense to call it hers from now on. There was nothing similar to what Raf had seen, though. No clue as to how to break the curse.

'Couldn't we carve the symbols onto Reinar?' Raf suggested. 'Would that help?'

Alys didn't think so. 'Likely Alari's magic will be more complicated than that.'

Raf agreed. 'If only we had her book.' She smiled as she said it, then seeing Alys freeze before her, she blinked. 'What is it?'

'Alari taught Mirella everything she knew. Or, at least, she promised to. Perhaps she did? I... I need to try and find Mirella.'

Now it was Raf's turn to freeze. 'No,' she whispered, 'you don't. I can.'

Alys didn't understand.

'Mirella showed me her book. A red book filled with symbols and magic and chants. She was trying to trick me. She thought I couldn't read it, and I couldn't when I was in her chamber in Orvala. But when I was in Stornas, I had dreams of that book. Mirella wasn't there, but I could open it on my own and turn the pages. I could read the spells. I knew what the symbols were for. There was no Mirella, but I could read it.'

Alys glanced at Eddeth, who was starting to lean towards the brazier, though the fire was mostly out. She grabbed Raf's arm. 'You need to go back into the dream of that book and see if you can find the symbols. If the curse is in there, it might show us how to break it.'

Raf nodded, feeling nervous, though seeing how pale Reinar looked, she knew there was no time to waste.

Alys smiled at her, hoping to instill her with some confidence. 'Eddeth and I will be there, beside you. It will help, I'm sure. I'll just go and see the children and get more firewood. We're going to need it.' She could see Raf looked relieved that she was leaving, though she understood the need to be alone.

Heading out of the tent, Alys immediately bumped into Stellan, who was shocked to hear her news.

'Raf?' Stellan's tiredness made him confused. He rubbed both hands over his beard, frowning deeply. 'Is alive?'

Alys nodded. 'And she might be able to find an answer, a way to help Reinar.' She suddenly became conscious of standing in the main thoroughfare, warriors and servants milling about in the dark. She heard a few songs being sung, but generally a quiet, sombre feel was in the air. 'We need more guards on Reinar's tent. No one can come in.' She thought of Gysa, too, hoping the dreamer wasn't watching.

Stellan nodded, and as Alys turned away, he touched her arm. 'Will it work? Alys, I...' Stellan had held his emotions at bay for days, but his fears for his son were becoming impossible to ignore. He could hear the desperation in his own voice now. 'Will it work?'

'I don't know, but we won't stop trying. We'll break this curse. We'll find an answer. I promise.'

CHAPTER THIRTY NINE

When Alys returned with an armload of firewood, they woke a snoring Eddeth, who was too sleep-addled to understand what Alys and Raf were talking about. She was still shocked to see Raf back in the tent with them, amazed that it hadn't simply been a dream.

She was glad it hadn't been a dream.

'But this red book? You're sure it's real, not just an illusion? Some game Mirella was playing? She's a clever dreamer, isn't she?' Eddeth peered at Alys, who nodded. 'What if it's just a trick?'

'It's not,' Raf insisted. 'I used one of its spells when I was in Stornas with Gudrum. It worked.'

Eddeth rubbed grainy eyes, remaining unconvinced. Though knowing they had to try everything to save Reinar, she pushed her doubts to one side, determined to do whatever she could to help.

As night settled in, the camp became quieter outside, and Alys let the hum of the two women drift away behind her as she sat by Reinar's bed, holding his hand. She closed her eyes, trying to see anything useful, wondering if she could find a way into his dreams.

Wondering if he was having any dreams.

Candles glowed softly above her head, swinging from the rafters in shallow bowls, though Reinar's skin remained blue-tinged, almost translucent. Lifting a hand to his forehead, Alys could feel how hot it still was. 'Don't worry,' she whispered, 'Raf's here now. She's come back to save you, and she'll find a way. She saw Sigurd. He's alive. He came to help you. Both him and Valera. And soon you'll be back on your feet, and you'll go and finish Gudrum.' She wiped away a tear, not wanting to lose control, though sometimes it was impossible. Her fears rose like waves, and there were moments she felt she might drown in them.

'Alys?' Raf called from where she sat in front of the brazier Eddeth was adding a few herbs to. 'Will you come?'

Alys nodded, and with one last look at Reinar, she turned away, thinking of her mother, hoping Raf could find her way back to Mirella's red book.

***

It was dark when they arrived at the camp and hard to see, though the man who greeted them looked like he'd dragged himself out of the Otherworld, Thorgils thought, raising an eyebrow at Eadmund, who was busy tidying himself up after their soggy ride. Thorgils and Bram flanked their king, backs aching, hoping the formalities would be over quickly, for both men wanted to head off in the direction of whatever that meaty smell was.

Thorgils' stomach growled noisily, long past satisfied with a few flatbreads and slivers of salt fish. Eadmund glared at him, though Thorgils did his best to look innocent, staring around and then down at his boots.

'My lord king, my lords,' a younger, smaller man said.

He had the look of a simpering ferret, Eadmund thought, reminded of Osbert Furyck.

Remembering what had happened to Osbert Furyck.

'My name is Edrik. Please allow me to introduce you to the new King of Alekka.'

Gudrum stepped forward, working hard to contain himself. Here was Jael's husband and, according to Gysa, one of her closest friends too. He looked up, eyeing the big red-headed man, who peered down at him with confusion in his eyes.

'My lord,' Eadmund said, working hard to avoid staring at the prominent wound that had almost sliced the king's face in two. 'I was sorry to hear about Ake. That was a shock. We hadn't heard anything about it.'

'No,' Gudrum said gravely as Edrik ushered them towards a table and chairs set up outside his tent, surrounded by glowing braziers. 'What with The Freeze lasting for so long. The king had tried to seek help for some time, though, in the end, it was too late. He was dead not long after the messenger left for Oss.'

Eadmund frowned, hearing Bram muttering something on his left. 'And he chose you as his heir? I... haven't heard of you. Haven't met you before.'

Gudrum had been expecting that, and his answer came without hesitation. 'My king had no son. His own had recently died. And with Hector Berras threatening to unleash havoc, he chose who he believed stood the greatest chance of bringing his people together. And that was me.' He smiled through the lie, his scars stretching further across his face, which ached.

'And you are from where, my lord?' Bram wondered.

Gudrum's look of surprise as he turned to the old warrior had Eadmund intervening. 'Bram lived in Alekka for many years.'

Gudrum's grin froze on his face. 'Is that so?' He saw Edrik almost stumbling out of the corner of his eye, and not wanting to draw attention to any unease, he quickly resumed his easy manner. 'Where was that then?'

'Moll,' Bram said, eyes narrowed, determined to get his answer. 'And you are from, my lord?'

'I came down from The Murk, made my way to Stornas. It was only when Hector Berras abandoned his king that I was able to stake my claim. To take a more prominent role.'

Gudrum turned away from Bram's searching eyes, motioning with his hand for Eadmund to walk beside him, and quickening his pace, he let Bram, Thorgils, and Beorn fall behind.

Eadmund saw the spread and comfort waiting for him,

knowing that Thorgils would be impatient to get to a chair and pick up a goblet. Though he felt hesitant. 'My men have had a long few days, my lord. I appreciate your hospitality, and believe me, it is not unwelcome, though it's my men I must see to first. I need to find them shelter, food, ale. They need fires and somewhere to dry off. If we're to be of any use to you, they must be seen to.'

Gudrum stopped in his tracks, a hint of irritation in his eyes, though his smile remained firmly in place. 'Of course. Edrik, find Paki. He's my steward,' he explained. 'A man who'll know where to put everyone. And when you're happy, I look forward to your return.'

Eadmund nodded slowly, feeling uncertain about everything. 'And Hector Berras?' he asked. 'Where is he?'

'Nearby,' Gudrum said. 'Camped at the foot of the Silver Mountains. We battled his men at Gord's Field some days ago, suffering great losses. Your timing is impeccable, my lord, for now that you're here, we can try another assault. Your men will boost our ranks considerably.'

Eadmund saw a man hurrying towards them with a deep frown.

'Ahhh, and here's Paki now,' Gudrum announced. 'I will wait here for you, my lord. Though don't worry, there'll be plenty of food and wine left for you and your men.'

Eadmund nodded, seeing Thorgils' relieved face. And grabbing his friend's arm, he led him away, keeping pace with the scurrying steward.

'Sure he's not a dragur?' Thorgils whispered hoarsely. 'With that face? Sure he's even alive?'

Bram whacked him. 'You really want to make an enemy of a king?'

'Well, you didn't look so fond of him yourself, asking all those questions,' Thorgils grumbled.

'We need to know what we've gotten ourselves into, wouldn't you say? No point holding a bag over our heads,' Bram snapped. 'Jael wouldn't be pleased to find out we'd made a mess of things without her.'

Eadmund smiled, thinking of his wife, wondering what she would have made of the new King of Alekka.

***

As soon as Raf entered the trance, she found a corridor. It was Tarl Brava's hall in Orvala. She remembered these walls, made of thick logs. Torches flamed, lighting her way, and she started walking, hoping to find Mirella's chamber. Though every wall revealed nothing but long, rounded logs.

There was no door to find at all.

She felt panic then, fearing she was losing control of the trance. Her mind wandered back to the tent, hearing Eddeth murmuring beside her, tapping the drum.

She saw Reinar lying in bed, recognising the dark wound on his leg.

And then she saw Gysa standing over him, stroking his hair.

Looking up, Gudrum's dreamer smiled. 'Did you imagine you could outthink me? That I would *let* you?' Gysa strode around the bed now as Raf tried to blink her away, wanting to get back to Orvala's hall. To the corridor and the book. She needed to find Mirella's book!

But stepping forward, Gysa laid a hand on her arm. 'I hear everything, I see all, and I'm not about to let you go digging for clues, girl. To save Reinar Vilander? You may have turned your back on Gudrum, but I never will. I'm doing everything I can to protect him, and soon he'll be victorious, and I will find a way to kill you!'

Gysa lunged at her, hands around her throat, and Raf saw her burned face. Her skin was melted and scarred, her mouth half gone, as was one eye. But the other eye was staring at her as though it would consume her alive.

Raf screamed, arms flailing, trying to escape.

And then Alys was there, and she had hold of Raf, pulling her close. 'Ssshhh,' she soothed. 'It's alright. You're back here with us. It's alright, Raf. Ssshhh now.'

Raf tried to push her away, but Alys' voice calmed her, bringing her back into the tent. Then Eddeth was there, too, one arm around her back.

And she was safe.

***

There was no word from the scouts they'd sent to try and reach the Islanders, and the mood in the camp was as dark as the stormy morning sky rumbling above their heads.

Stellan knew a choice had to be made. Ollo and Vik had been preparing to make a run at Gudrum's camp, hoping to cause some trouble, but the latest report from the dreamers had stopped them in their tracks. If Gudrum's dreamer was listening to everything they were planning, whether to help Reinar or attack Gudrum, they would only be putting their men at risk. And those men who'd been looking forward to escaping the confines of the camp and taking a bite out of their enemy were not pleased. Especially Ollo Narp, who, after his initial reservations, had been hoping to do something to lure Ilene's attention away from Helgi Eivin. Having seen him fight, bared chested and wild as a bear, she'd become transfixed. It had left Ollo in a complete tangle, irritated that Stellan was being so cautious, depriving him of the opportunity to impress her.

'What good would it do for us to lose more men?' Stellan snapped at him, tired and long past needing something to eat. He'd had no appetite for days. He felt weak, his trousers hanging off him, but every morning he rolled out of bed, thinking only of whether Reinar had opened his eyes.

With Raf's return, his hopes had lifted, but now?

'If we go back to Slussfall,' Bjarni began.

'What?' Ollo was as tired as the rest of them but far hungrier. 'After coming all this way? After risking everything?'

Stellan sighed heavily, hands on the map table, almost holding up his body. He heard the servants preparing breakfast, though his appetite didn't stir. Still, he wouldn't be able to swing a sword if he didn't eat soon.

'We can't go back, Stellan. There's no one else to call on. This is our last stand,' Vik insisted. 'Here.'

And Jonas nodded.

Berger looked caught somewhere in between, eyeing his cousin. Who spoke.

'Seems to me, if you don't mind the interruption, that you could do with a different kind of conversation.'

Everyone turned, staring at a blinking Helgi. 'Until we know the dreamers can hide us, we're just whispering in Gudrum's ear. His dreamer will tell him everything we're saying in here, won't she?'

Jonas was quickly on his way. 'I'll find Alys and see what they can do.'

Stellan didn't want him to. He wanted the dreamers to focus on helping Reinar, though likely there was little they could do now. He thought of Gerda and of Sigurd, wondering if his youngest son was watching.

Wondering if he could do something to help?

***

'What can we do?' Sigurd demanded, turning from Valera to Tikas to Ulfinnur. Gallabrok was still heaving with gods and goddesses, all awaiting Thenor's return. And apart from his continued absence, the main topic of conversation was the imminent death of Reinar Vilander.

Which had Sigurd in a frantic state.

Valera sighed. 'I showed Raf ways to fight against Gysa, but I cannot break that curse. It is Alari's magic. She taught it to Gysa, and that woman is doing everything she can to prevent the discovery of any answers.'

'You could kill her,' Sigurd suggested. 'Gysa.'

'Which wouldn't save Reinar,' Tikas reminded him, feeling caught in the middle. He felt Sigurd's pain and shared Valera's concern, but without Thenor advising them, they were at a loss to know what to do.

'I saved Reinar to give the dreamers a chance to heal him. And you saved Raf,' Sigurd said, frowning at Valera. 'Did it mean nothing? It must have meant something!'

'But what do you expect us to do?' Ulfinnur asked, trying to bridge the divide. 'It is not our place to intervene, Sigurd. Enough has already been changed.' He eyed Valera, who looked overwrought. 'If Gudrum succeeds, then he is meant to rule Alekka.'

'But isn't the king chosen by the gods?' Sigurd snapped. 'That's what I grew up believing. That the gods have the final say in who becomes the king. So why let it be Gudrum? It doesn't have to be!'

'The problem comes in choosing a king who was defeated,' Tikas said carefully. 'And Reinar was beaten by Gudrum, so to lift him up as the king now? Thenor supported the Vettels because they achieved great success. They vanquished enemy after enemy. They strengthened Alekka, made it a formidable kingdom. He stood by them until Ake was victorious. And no one worked harder for his victory than Ake Bluefinn. He was a true king. The finest in memory.' Tikas fiddled with his eyepatch, seeing how incensed Sigurd was becoming. 'Your brother was defeated, Sigurd, and I'm afraid there is nothing the gods can or should do about that.' Having made his point, he abruptly turned away, not wanting to become further embroiled in the heated debate.

Ulfinnur followed him, knowing that, ultimately, this came down to Sigurd and Valera.

Who smiled at her tall, stern brother. 'Reinar *is* fighting. He still lives because he is strong enough to withstand the worst of the curse. It should have killed him outright. And Eddeth, Raf, and Alys are trying everything they can. We have to trust that one of them will find an answer.'

'Trust?'

'It's what Thenor would say. I believe that with my whole being. We must trust that the Goddesses of Fate have a plan.'

Sigurd felt powerless, though ultimately, he knew it was still his choice to remain in Gallabrok. He could go, be with Reinar, but something was holding him back. And eventually, Sigurd realised that it was his brother.

Deep in his heart he knew that this was Reinar's fight.

***

'Symbols are powerful!' Eddeth cried.

Jonas blinked at her in surprise. 'Yes, I agree.' He had joined the dreamers in Reinar's tent, where they sat around the brazier, fractious and fretful, heads in their hands, rubbing their eyes, trying to find solutions.

'So why can't they stop this woman?' Eddeth grumbled. 'Why can Gysa see past them all? Everything my grandmother showed me? None of it's worked! There's no way past her wall, yet no way to shield us from her view.'

Jonas picked a log out of the woodpile, adding it to the brazier. 'It's cold in here,' he said, eyeing his granddaughter, who looked to be eating as little as Stellan, her soft face appearing oddly gaunt. 'You need to stay warm. It won't help you think if you're cold.'

No one appeared to care.

'We've done so much thinking, yet we're still wandering aimlessly in a forest!' Eddeth huffed. 'I...' She picked her wart. 'I'm at a loss. I truly am.'

'Don't let Reinar hear you say that,' Jonas frowned. 'He's relying on you.' Which made all three women look even worse.

And realising that he wasn't helping, Jonas stood. 'What we need is a way to hide from Gudrum's dreamer. Perhaps turn your attention away from Reinar for a while and look for an answer to that. His dreamer will be sitting there, listening to every word.'

'But not for long!' Eddeth warned, jumping off her stool to check on Reinar. 'She'll be busy helping Gudrum plan his next attack now that those Islanders have arrived!'

Jonas stared at her. 'What?'

Alys and Raf stared at her, too, and eventually, Eddeth turned around with a puzzled look on her face. 'What is it? What's happened?'

'You never said the Islanders are with Gudrum. *Now*?' Jonas was incredulous.

'Didn't I? Oh, I'm sure I did. I'm sure!' Eddeth insisted, sneezing loudly. 'Oh well, yes. They are!'

Jonas glanced at Alys. 'You need to think about leaving.'

'What?'

'Take the horses, head back to Slussfall. You have to get the children to safety.'

Alys shook her head. 'And do what? I'm not leaving you. I'm not leaving Reinar.' Her voice trailed away, and she fought the urge to turn around and look at him. 'No. We can't give up yet. We can defeat Gudrum.'

'With what army? With what weapons? With what magic?'

Raf looked down at her hands, feeling oddly responsible. Valera had helped her and given her another chance at life, and yet she still couldn't save Reinar.

'I have to go,' Alys announced suddenly, grabbing her cloak. 'I can't sit in here anymore, sinking in defeat! I, I need to get some air!' She pulled her cloak tightly around her shoulders, and with one final look at a lifeless Reinar, she swept out of the tent.

CHAPTER FORTY

Eadmund quickly decided that he didn't like Gudrum.

The new King of Alekka never stopped smiling. To all appearances, he was an affable, generous host who treated him and his men with respect, going out of his way to ensure that they were well-fed, as dry and warm as possible, with more ale than they could wish for. Eadmund guessed that Gudrum was taking from his own army's stores to feed them. He smelled sickness in the air, and that bothered him, though the king made it clear that he was trying to improve conditions.

He told them that they needed to attack Hector's men, to break through their line and push further north. There were more settlements on the other side of the mountains. And those settlements would have food, ale, and weapons. They just had to make a move, and now that Eadmund was here, Gudrum was confident they could.

Eadmund, though, wanted some time. 'I need more of an understanding of your plans,' he began calmly, seeing the blustering Lord of Borken frowning opposite him. 'And what you intend to do about Hector Berras.'

The Lord of Ennor joined the Lord of Borken in his frowning.

Gudrum picked up a leg of pork, wielding it at Eadmund. 'Well, that's a good question, my lord. Hector? I'll kill him. As I'm sure you'd agree, you can't leave an enemy behind. I'd never be able to look over my shoulder. I'd have to keep calling you back!'

He turned as Gysa entered the tent, dressed in a dark red cloak, the fur trim brushing her face as she dropped her hood. 'Ahhh, my dreamer. I wondered when you'd come to reveal some news!'

Eadmund looked further surprised. 'I thought Ake's dreamer was an old woman?' He felt Bram's tension on his left, and though Thorgils was gnawing his own leg of pork, he sensed some unease about him too.

'She was, my lord,' Gysa said, lowering her eyes, dark eyelashes fluttering demurely. 'But sadly, she was killed.'

Gudrum didn't blink, though he dropped the pork chop and picked up his goblet of wine. 'Drink up, please. Drink! I think you'll find this wine better than any you've tried before. I'll be more than happy to reward you with a few barrels to take back to Oss.'

Eadmund stiffened, eyes narrowing on the grinning king, who sat across the table wearing his garish crown. 'Hopefully, you'll have more in mind than that, my lord.' He sipped the velvety liquid, happy to take some back to Oss, but there had to be more to this alliance than a few barrels of wine.

'Of course!' Gudrum laughed, watching him closely. 'Now do drink up, and I'll be happy to tell you all about my plans.'

***

Alys walked into the trees. She didn't intend to go far, though she felt a burning need to be alone. She felt exhausted from a profound lack of sleep. Her footing was uncertain, her eyes were grainy, her body heavy, but she needed to see with clarity, and to do that, she had to be entirely alone.

She walked until the camp noise was little more than a whisper, and choosing a clear spot, Alys sat down, pressing her back against a lichen-covered trunk. She slipped her hands under her cloak, breath smoke streaming from her mouth, and pulling her hood over her hair, she slunk back beneath it. Letting it drop over her face, she closed her eyes, looking for all the world like a dreamer trying to find a dream.

And she was.

Sliding her right hand into her purse, keeping it concealed beneath her cloak, Alys gripped hold of her mother's brooch.

***

Upon hearing Eddeth's great revelation that hadn't appeared like a revelation to Eddeth, Jonas had hurried her to Stellan, who quickly gathered everyone into the map tent.

A panicking Ollo was immediately huffing and puffing. 'And how many men have they got? The Skallesons? Why are we taking one more breath in here? We should be packing!'

Everyone turned to him in surprise.

'We should!' Ollo insisted. 'If we get to Slussfall, we live to fight another day. What? You want Jael Furyck coming after you?'

Stellan was tempted to agree. No longer the hot-headed risk-taker he'd once been, he now tended to err on the side of caution. He looked to Vik, who'd turned his attention to the map.

'The Islanders will replenish Gudrum's army, for sure,' Vik began. 'They'll bring fresh arms and legs, maybe new ideas, but we still hold the high ground. We've still got everything Salagat has to offer.'

'You're not saying we stay and fight?' Ollo snorted. '*What?*'

'Are you getting so old that you've forgotten how many times we fought outnumbered beside Ake?' Jonas growled, moving forward to join Vik. 'I remember you complaining just as loudly then! But despite all your noise, we went into most battles undermanned. We didn't run away because it felt too hard. We fought with everything we had. Fought and won!'

Berger glanced at Bjarni, who looked hesitant, and at Ludo, who appeared caught. 'Jonas is right. What use are we to Alekka if we go home when it gets hard? Why would any Alekkan want us leading them into the future?'

Vik nodded. 'And you think this is as hard as it gets? Now? What if Tarl Brava's on his way? And you want to give up now?'

That had Berger back on his heels, thinking of Solveigh.

'But why would the Islanders fight for Gudrum?' Bjarni wanted to know. 'Makes no sense to me.'

'Or me,' Ludo agreed. 'Do you think the dreamer has a hand in it?' he asked, turning to Eddeth.

'Oh, I think that woman has a hand in everything! I wouldn't be surprised. No, I wouldn't!'

'Then stop her, Eddeth. Find a way to kill her,' Ludo implored, feeling much more like fighting since he'd heard Sigurd was alive.

Eddeth blinked. She'd never killed anyone in her life, but if Gysa wasn't stopped, she would help Gudrum destroy Alekka, and everyone in the tent would be dead. 'I will,' she croaked, throat tight with nerves. 'I... will try.'

***

'Be prepared to kill,' said the voice.

Alys turned around to Alari, though the goddess wasn't talking to her. She was walking towards a table where Mirella sat. A younger-looking Mirella, Alys thought, stepping closer. There was nothing to see but the table and her mother and the goddess. But then, leaning forward, she saw that Mirella had a quill and a pot of ink.

And a book.

Mirella looked surprised. 'Kill who?'

'Every enemy you face. And mine. You must protect the Vettels, for many wish to hurt them, including your own mother.'

Mirella looked nervous. 'She isn't a powerful dreamer. She doesn't know real magic.'

Alari burst out laughing. 'You know that's not true, so why lie, Mirella? Eida is the granddaughter of Ragnahild One Eye. You know exactly how powerful your mother is!' She took a deep breath, not wanting to become distracted. 'Now, did you draw those three symbols?' She came towards the table to see.

Mirella nodded, showing her. 'Yes.'

'You did well,' Alari purred. 'First, you will make symbols in ink, then with knives, hands, and finally, with your mind. That is when you will be at your most powerful, Mirella. When your magic is created in your mind.'

'And how do we break the curse?' Mirella wondered, quill poised over the vellum.

'Break it?' Alari was confused. 'For what purpose?'

Mirella looked just as confused. 'To... save the person?'

'But why would we want to do that?'

Alys felt herself riding a wave, looking on silently, hoping for answers that, almost offered, quickly slipped out of reach. She saw the symbols Mirella had drawn, and they were the ones Raf had seen on Gudrum's sword.

But how to break the curse? To reverse it?

'Why should I help you, Alys?'

Alys stumbled, mouth gaping open as she swung around to her mother.

'Do you think you can enter my memories and help yourself to anything you want?' Mirella asked coldly. 'Did you really believe Ragnahild knows more than me? That she knows how to keep me out?'

Alys felt afraid. The young Mirella still sat at the table, Alari frozen before her, but it was an older Mirella who commanded her attention now – the one she remembered from Orvala. 'I want to save Reinar.'

'So he can be the king?' Mirella sneered, shaking her head. 'Reinar Vilander was never fated to be the king, but Tarl Brava is. Whatever Ragnahild told you, the truth is that Tarl will unite Alekka. He is the one who will rule.'

Alys felt chilled to the core, barely able to speak. 'But Alari and

Gudrum? And Gysa?'

'Are problems to be solved, I admit. Though as enemies, what can we do about that, you and I?'

'Help me,' Alys pleaded, seeing signs of hope in her mother's eyes. 'Help me defeat Gysa and Alari.'

Mirella looked tempted. 'And then what?'

Alys wanted a mother who loved her, who looked at her with warmth and affection. But she had this woman, who had been broken by life. Or perhaps she'd always been this way? Alys didn't know.

Though Mirella was the mother she had, and she needed her help.

'I could work with Alari to defeat you, or you could work with her to defeat me. But I'm certain that above all things, you want to stop that goddess, so let us work together,' she suggested.

Mirella turned to see the girl she had once been and the goddess who had taken her to Jesper. Alari had shielded the truth about who the Vettels really were. She had led her into a cave of bears, and Mirella had never been safe again. She looked back at her daughter. 'We don't have to be enemies, Alys. I don't wish you to become me. I wouldn't wish that on anyone. I just don't want you getting in my way.'

'Show me how to break the curse then, please. If you bring Reinar back, we have a chance to rid Alekka of Gudrum.'

Mirella knew what Tarl would think about that, though it was a distraction neither of them needed. 'This is the choice you wish to make?'

'Yes. Help me save Reinar.'

Mirella stared into those familiar-looking eyes, tempted to hold out a hand, though both arms remained stiffly by her sides. 'You are a talented dreamer, Alys, but still too timid. You have killed, though you have no appetite for it, and that will be your undoing in the end.'

Alys stared at her imploringly until Mirella curled a finger in her direction.

'Come then, and let us... negotiate.'

***

As the day wore on, Gudrum's plans became clearer, and Eadmund found himself becoming more convinced by the new King of Alekka. He left Gudrum's tent with a yawning Thorgils and a frowning Bram.

'He grows on you,' Eadmund decided with a grin. 'Seems like a man who wasn't looking to be king, but thrown into the role, he's doing his best with what he has.'

Thorgils agreed. 'That dreamer's a nice woman. And the wine? We have to take some of that back to Isaura and Jael.'

They walked down the main thoroughfare, which, turned over by thousands of boots, had become a mucky slop, though neither appeared to notice.

Bram stared at the two men in confusion. 'What are you talking about? You really believe that? I doubt Jael would if she were here.'

Eadmund stopped, grabbing Bram's fur-covered arm. 'You don't think Gudrum's plan was sound?'

'You don't like that nice Gysa?' Thorgils added. 'What's gotten into you? Ohhh, and the pork. Did you try the pork? How are they cooking that?'

'The tents are spacious,' Beorn added, still thinking about the wine.

'Are you alright?' Bram snapped, feeling concerned by all three men. 'What are you yapping about? Wine and tents and pretty dreamers?' He pulled them to one side as a boy hurried past, pushing a handcart full of wood. 'I don't know how you can trust that Gudrum so easily.'

'He's our ally,' Eadmund insisted, irritated by Bram's sour mood. 'What's wrong with you? You've been like this since we left Oss. Something's eating you. It's not Gudrum, that's for sure.'

Thorgils nudged him. 'It's Ayla. Got to be Ayla.'

Bram spun away. 'You're not thinking!' he barked, tapping his head. 'Jael would slap you all! You need to start thinking!'

Thorgils and Eadmund turned to each other in confusion, both men then turning to Beorn, who shrugged.

'Wine?' Thorgils suggested. 'We should find that steward. See about getting some wine sent to our tent.'

'Good idea!' Beorn grinned, patting him on the back.

And all three men headed off, leaving a gobsmacked Bram staring after them.

***

The buffeting wind had made their journey to Alekka fast, though incredibly rough.

Jael walked all four horses towards Fyn, certain she wouldn't feel like food for some time, and watching Fyn, bent over, spitting on the sand, she was sure he'd agree.

The afternoon was darkening rapidly, but she could clearly see the great line of familiar-looking ships dug into the sand. She'd seen glimpses of this beach on her journey, complete with a dripping Thorgils and a smiling Eadmund.

It was impossible to remain focused when she saw her husband's face, so instead, Jael sought to keep her mind fixed on Gudrum. She hoped to find a guide in the village to lead them to Eadmund. They needed to get riding immediately, making some progress before they stopped for the night. She would need sleep and some dreams, for once their ship returned to Oss, they would be two against an army of what she could only guess would be thousands.

Gudrum Killi?

Shaking her head, Jael saw how quickly a single mistake, seemingly small and insignificant, could turn into an unmitigated disaster.

And if she didn't defeat him now?

'We need a guide,' she said, handing Yara's and Vili's reins to a still-spitting-Fyn. 'I'm sure someone will be happy to help us out for a pouch of silver. Ernst and the crew can camp on the beach. They'll leave at first light.'

Fyn blew out a long breath as he started walking, clicking his tongue for the horses to follow. 'You don't think we should keep them with us?'

Jael shook her head. 'Oss can't be without a full garrison. We don't know what Gudrum's plans are. And not just Gudrum. Anyone harbouring ambitions would be pleased to hear Oss has been left in the hands of twenty-odd men, and mostly useless ones at that. I won't risk it.'

Fyn nodded. 'Though how will we defeat an army, Jael? Just the two of us?'

She smiled at him. 'We're not here to defeat an army. We're here to kill one man.'

***

'Jael Furyck,' Gudrum breathed, kissing Gysa's exposed neck. It wasn't as elegant as Mirella's or Solveigh's, though it belonged to a far more reliable woman. 'Is coming? You're sure? Certain? She's coming here? To me?'

Gysa kept nodding, revelling in his delight. He'd almost skipped around the tent like an excited boy when she'd revealed the news.

'And what else?' Gudrum wanted to know. 'What else do you see? Is Reinar dead? What of Sigurd? What of their army? Will they run back to Slussfall now?'

Gysa held up a hand, laughing. 'I only have one pair of eyes! I only see what you need to know.'

'Well,' Gudrum said, stepping away from her, returning to his map. 'I need to know all of that. How else can I choose what to do?'

Gysa smiled. 'Jael Furyck is coming here. Your greatest enemies will be in one place, and soon you will defeat them both.'

'Not with magic,' Gudrum warned, turning to hold a finger to her lips. 'Understood? You will not interfere when it comes to Jael Furyck. She is mine. Only mine.'

Gysa nodded, knowing how much it meant to him. Still, she was rigid beneath his finger, her jaw clenched. 'I understand.'

Gudrum laughed. 'I may not be a dreamer, but I don't believe that!' He lifted her chin, staring into her eyes. 'The balance of power must never be in your favour, Gysa, for I am the king. I want you with me, beside me, but you will follow me. Not the other way around.'

Gysa nodded, though there was tension in her eyes. A rebuke, whether delivered with a snarl or a smile, was still a rebuke, and she felt anger stirring like hot coals in a brazier. Though at the same time, she knew that a king was necessary, for she had no desire to rule a kingdom. 'Of course,' she sighed, eventually. 'I agree.'

***

Alys headed back into the camp, vibrating with nervous energy.

What Mirella had shown her...

She wondered if it was real? If it was truly possible?

Or just another game?

But knowing that Gysa was likely watching, she couldn't reveal anything yet.

Lifting back the tent flap, she saw Raf sleeping with her head on Reinar's bed. A servant was knitting on a stool by the brazier. There was no sign of Reinar's steward.

She hurried to Reinar, lightly pressing a hand on his chest, relieved that it was still moving.

'What?' Raf woke with a start. 'Oh... I....'

'Go back to your tent, Raf. I'll stay with Reinar now,' Alys smiled. 'It's my turn.' Her attention shifted to the servant. 'You go, too, Svea. You both need a proper rest.'

The servant looked hesitant, though Alys fixed her mind on her so strongly that within a heartbeat, she had put down her knitting, bundled up her cloak and hurried out of the tent.

Raf watched her go, surprised, feeling as though she was walking up a mountain. Every part of her felt too heavy to move. 'Are you sure?' she yawned.

'Yes, yes, I've had a nap. I'm refreshed. You need to be strong enough for tonight, though. We must try something tonight.'

Raf blinked. 'Oh, alright.' And then she was following after Svea with another long yawn. 'Eddeth will be here soon.'

Alys nodded patiently, waiting for her to leave, and when the flap fell closed, she turned back to Reinar with a frown, knowing she wouldn't have much time.

If Gysa was watching, she wouldn't have much time at all.

'I'll rub one of Eddeth's magical balms on you,' she said loudly. 'Your body is wasting away. I need to wake it up a little. But first, I'll take off these furs. It might get cold, though perhaps that will help wake you up?' It was all a performance, though Alys was no performer. She worried that her voice sounded different, her movements unnatural, but she kept going, not wanting Gysa to suspect a thing.

***

After their talk, Gudrum had left the tent to train with his men. He didn't want them sitting around eating and drinking all day. He wanted them fired up with purpose, anticipating and preparing for what was coming, setting a good example for the Islanders. So Gysa took the opportunity to study the flames. She waved a hand, wanting to bring those images to life that were of greatest importance, eager to find answers to all of Gudrum's questions.

She immediately saw Reinar Vilander. Dying, pathetic Reinar Vilander.

Gysa didn't hate him the way she'd hated Hector. In fact, she didn't care about him at all. But he stood in the way, so she needed him gone.

It was taking some time, though, and she was becoming impatient. He was a skeleton, a ghost, but still hanging on. Frowning, she leaned closer to the flames, wondering what Alys was doing.

***

'First, you will make symbols in ink, then with knives, hands, and finally, with your mind. That is when you will be at your most powerful, Mirella. When your magic is created in your mind.'

Alys rolled those words around her own mind, trying to fill herself with confidence as she rubbed Reinar's chest and then his arms. His body was wasting away, and the tears that fell from her eyes dropped onto pale skin, barely covering bone. She shook her head, wanting to remain focused, not on mourning Reinar but on saving him.

Pulling down his tunic and rolling down his sleeves, Alys covered his torso with furs, focusing now on his legs. He wore thick woollen socks, and she gently pulled those off, tucking them into a ball. And then she gave her attention to his trousers, rolling them up until they sat just above his knees. It was upsetting to see him this way. A prisoner. A patient.

Near death.

She felt that most strongly of all as she started rubbing Eddeth's salve over his legs. The scent was soothing and intense, and Alys' tension calmed as she massaged Reinar's legs, trying to remain focused.

***

Gysa watched, quickly growing bored as Alys wept over her lost love. It was as though she was saying goodbye. Gysa didn't feel sorry for her, though. She felt no empathy at all. Her own loved ones had been torn from her on a bloody, horrific night. She had never seen them again. They were lost to her forever; there'd been no goodbyes for her.

And finding herself becoming angry with the pathetic woman and the irritating Reinar Vilander, who refused to die, Gysa flapped a hand at the flames, looking for something more interesting.

***

Alys reached Reinar's ankles, seeing the mark where Gudrum's swordtip had pierced his flesh. She rubbed around it, massaging both ankles, then back up his legs to his knees and down again. And then she closed her eyes, focusing on the wounded leg and that dark mark, remembering Mirella's words. She saw the symbol in her mind. It was just the one. After much debate, a young Mirella had drawn a way to break the curse out of Alari. Mirella had smiled telling Alys that, pleased to know that beating Gysa would mean defeating Alari.

Alys hadn't cared what Mirella's motivation was. She just needed to save Reinar.

'And you will,' her mother had assured her. 'I saw what you did in Tromsund, Alys. Your mind is already powerful, so just focus it on what you want most of all. Knowing how you feel about Reinar Vilander, it shouldn't be hard. Focus, and hold him in your mind as you draw the symbol.'

So Alys did.

She saw Reinar sitting on the throne in Stornas, a crown on his head. She saw his father and mother standing behind him, smiles of both pride and relief on their faces. She saw how strong he looked, how different.

And she held onto that image as Mirella's symbol sparked to life.

CHAPTER FORTY ONE

The debate had raged for hours, and eventually, everyone had convinced themselves that staying and fighting was the only choice they had. It was the choice Ake would have made. That Reinar would have made too.

Even Ollo had finally agreed, knowing that no matter what he might say, he was never going to turn tail and run away.

They would stay and fight Gudrum.

'Eddeth, you must find a way through to the Islanders yourself,' Stellan urged as they walked to Reinar's tent. 'They can't be fighting with Gudrum because they want to. They can't know who he truly is.'

Eddeth had rolled up her still-damp trousers to avoid the mud, though they'd fallen down as she walked, and now she was fussing over them, trying to roll them back up, nearly falling over and certainly not listening.

'Are you listening?' Stellan grumbled.

'I...' Eddeth straightened up, seeing Alys running out of Reinar's tent, blonde hair streaming in the wind.

Stellan froze, fear rippling through his body.

But Eddeth saw joy in those eyes. Joy and shock and tears, too, as she bounded away from Stellan towards Alys. 'He's saved!' she cried, jumping on the spot, her trousers unravelling all the way into the mud now. 'He's saved!'

Alys nodded, unable to stop crying. 'He is. I think he is!'

Pushing her to one side, Eddeth rushed into the tent, leaving Alys to go to Stellan.

'Are you sure?' Stellan asked, not believing it to be true. He felt his heart pounding as he took her hands, tears in his own eyes. 'You broke the curse? You?'

'I had some help, but yes, Reinar's awake.' She smiled then, relief flooding her body. 'Reinar's awake!'

***

Sigurd drank with Tulia that night, unable to stop smiling. 'No one knows how Alys did it. Not even Valera. Perhaps not even Alys? But if anyone was going to save Reinar, it was always going to be her.'

Tulia knew that to be true. 'It was a luckier day than Reinar ever realised when he decided to kidnap that woman.'

Sigurd frowned, still feeling bad about that. Though many good things had come from it, he realised, thinking of Stina and Ludo and Alys' dead husband.

'But if he's still weak, what will they do now?' Tulia mused.

Sigurd didn't know, though, as usual, he was left fighting the urge to leave and join his father, his friends, and his brother. 'I want to know everything. Everything they're planning, everything they're thinking. Gudrum, too,' he admitted. 'Though maybe it's better if I stop looking?'

'I promise you it is,' Tulia said wryly. 'It's better not to know.'

He nudged her, enjoying her company. She almost looked relaxed. Or perhaps that was the mead?

'Why are we here?' Tulia asked after a long silence.

Sigurd glanced at her. 'What? In the hall?' They were alone in the hall – the last two. Everyone else had left hours ago while they remained, happy in the silence.

'No, in Gallabrok. The warriors. Why are we here?'

Sigurd shrugged. 'To fight with Thenor?'

'Against who? And when? There's been no war in centuries. That's what the others say, those who've been here the longest. It's just training, drinking, eating, day after day, year after year. Some don't mind it, though I want to kill them all and run away.'

Sigurd laughed. 'Sounds like you.'

'I thought Amir would be here,' Tulia admitted sadly. 'I had hoped for a... friend.'

'Well, that tells you something about yourself, surely?' Sigurd said. 'Amir was a good warrior, but not a great one like his sister. Thenor told me himself that he only chooses the finest warriors. And he picked you.'

'But not Ake Bluefinn? That makes no sense. Where is he?'

That was a question Sigurd had no answer for but something he'd wondered himself. Many times. 'No idea, though hopefully at rest. He deserves to be for what he did for Alekka.'

Tulia nodded, finishing her ale. 'I've had enough of today.' She stood, staring down at him, knowing he wouldn't be coming with her. Not anymore. He'd told her about Raf's visit, struggling to stop smiling, his feelings now perfectly clear. It hurt, though it almost felt better not to keep wondering. 'Not everything works out,' she murmured. 'Not everyone gets what they want, but I'm glad your brother is going to be alright, Sigurd.' And with a sad glance around the hall, she headed for the side door leading to the gardens.

Sigurd watched her go, feeling sad himself, wishing he could be there, celebrating Reinar's return.

***

Reinar didn't know how he felt.

The steady stream of visitors exhausted him quickly, though, and Stellan was forced to order the guards watching his tent to keep everyone out. Though he remained, still in shock that his son's eyes were finally open. 'You look terrible,' he grinned. 'Though having had a curse on me, I know how it feels.'

Reinar blinked slowly at his father with heavy eyelids. 'I... need to... know everything.'

Stellan patted his hand. His son still looked gaunt, his cheekbones shockingly pronounced, though colour had come back into his face, he was pleased to see. 'Seems to me you need to rest most of all.'

'But I...' Reinar tried to raise his head. 'The curse?'

'Alys lifted it,' Stellan said, beaming with joy about that.

Reinar closed his eyes, slumping back onto the pillow. 'Alys.' He saw her face and smiled. 'How?'

'No one knows. She's not saying. Perhaps she can't? All that matters, though, is that she did.'

'Sigurd?' Reinar wanted to move, though he could barely lift his arms.

'He saved you too. Raf stopped Gudrum and then Sigurd... he was fire itself.'

Reinar's eyes flickered.

'He pushed Gudrum's men back with walls of flames, forced them into a retreat so we could get you to safety. So we could retreat ourselves.'

'And now?'

'Now we're preparing for another round. Another battle.'

Reinar sighed. 'I can't... I need to...'

Leaning forward, Stellan placed a hand on his son's forehead, moving it down over his eyes. 'I could put you to sleep when you were a wee boy, just by running my hands over your face. Do you remember?'

Reinar did, and he didn't reply as his father swept his hand over his face in gentle, repetitive motions until everything slipped away.

***

The news was good but not perfect, for Stellan had sent word that though Reinar was awake, he hadn't magically returned to his old self. He remained an invalid, so they were going to have to fight their next battle without him.

'But he's back,' Bjarni breathed. 'He's back!'

Helgi rubbed his nose, mind whirring as he sat around the fire with Berger, Bjarni, and Ludo. 'Which doesn't help us against the Islanders. And what will we do about them?'

Bjarni shrugged. 'We can't send more messengers. They wouldn't get through.'

Berger agreed. 'More magic then?'

Ludo laughed. 'We may as well go back to Slussfall, let Eddeth, Raf, and Alys fight for us.'

Berger laughed, too, though thinking about Solveigh, he was quickly frowning. 'We can't let Gudrum past. Can't let him get a sniff of Slussfall.'

'He's got an ego,' Ludo said. 'He wants to defeat Reinar. And now Reinar's back, he'll be motivated to strike again.'

'Especially now he's got help,' Helgi added. 'A lot of help.'

'We should be on guard,' Bjarni decided, standing up with a wobble. He'd felt in a celebratory mood when he'd sat down and was suddenly aware that he'd drunk more ale than usual. It felt good, though, not to be fearful for a moment. Or, at least, as fearful as he knew he should be. Whatever waited in the darkness was terrifying, threatening their very existence. This could easily be one of his last nights. He'd enjoyed sharing it with friends, sitting around a hot fire, drinking cold ale. And now he wanted to crawl into bed, hide beneath his fur and dream of his wife and daughter.

Berger was nodding. 'When Gudrum finds out Reinar's curse is broken, I doubt he'll hold back for long.'

It wasn't the thought to end on, but as the fire died down and the voices in the distance became quieter, and eventually silent altogether, the four men made their way to their tents, fearing what the night would bring.

***

Gysa was furious that she hadn't paid more attention to Alys, for what that irritating woman had done was a mystery. Whatever it was, it had broken her perfect curse. The curse of a goddess. Alari's curse.

And now she had to tell Gudrum.

She waited until they were in bed, and Gudrum's trousers were on the floor, and he was kissing her with urgency, propped up on an elbow, one hand roaming her body.

'The curse has been broken,' she said simply. 'Reinar Vilander will live.'

Gudrum froze, lips touching hers, eyes widening with fury. '*What*? How?'

Gysa shrugged. 'They have three dreamers. One of them found a way through. They pulled an answer out of somewhere.'

'You don't *know*?' Gudrum rolled away from her now, lying back on the pillow, staring at the billowing tent moving like dark clouds above them. 'Why don't you know?'

'He has not recovered,' Gysa hurried to add, not answering his question. 'He's as weak as a dead man, as frail as a grandmother. He's not coming back in a hurry. You have nothing to fear from him.'

Gudrum wasn't so sure. He rolled back towards Gysa, all desire gone, his mind buzzing. 'But his dreamers? If they can outthink even Alari, what does that mean for us?'

Gysa turned towards him, stroking his scarred cheek. 'It means that, eventually, solutions will be found. The knowledge Alari has, or I have, is not sacred. As dreamers, we create magic all the time. Symbols are our tools. We weave them as the Goddesses of Fate weave the threads of destiny, so a clever dreamer will often stumble upon a solution. There's nothing surprising there. And, as I said, Reinar is weak, an invalid. He may die anyway.'

Gudrum frowned at her, and with a grunt, he rolled away, reaching for his trousers. Quickly jiggling them on, he pulled on his boots, secured his swordbelt and strode out of the tent.

***

After Stellan had left Reinar's tent, Alys returned. Someone needed to keep a close eye on him. The curse may have been broken, though it would take some time for him to recover, so he needed to be watched closely in case Gysa or Alari tried something else.

Alys felt overwhelmed with tiredness, but she was so stunned by what had happened that sleep wouldn't come. Instead, she sat by Reinar's bed, watching him sleep.

'You,' he whispered.

She blinked, wondering if he was dreaming.

'I can smell you... Alys.'

He didn't open his eyes, and Alys took his hand, feeling warmth there for the first time in days. 'That doesn't sound good,' she grinned.

'Honey. You smell like... honey.' Reinar opened his eyes, turning to blink at her, though the tent was so dark that he saw little but her face, glowing warmly before him.

And those eyes.

He smiled. 'You saved me.'

'Then we're even,' she decided. 'You saved me too.'

Reinar tried to laugh, though he didn't have the energy for it. He closed his eyes again. 'What... now?'

'Eddeth's got two broths boiling away outside, servants watching over them all night. Full of bones and herbs and who knows what. She's going to help you get stronger.'

'Hmmm, but Gudrum?'

Alys felt fear then. 'He will come soon, but don't worry, your father will lead us.'

'Not you,' Reinar said. 'Stay safe.'

'When Gudrum comes, we'll have to try and stop his dreamer. Once she discovers I broke her curse, Gysa will try something new.'

Reinar moved his hand until it touched Alys' again, wanting to feel her. 'Thank you,' he whispered as the darkness came for him again.

Alys sat there for some time, a whirlwind of emotions keeping her wide awake. She couldn't imagine sleeping, and finally, turning towards the fire, she thought that there were more important things to do than sit and stare at Reinar Vilander.

Gudrum would come, and Gysa would come too.

She had to be ready.

***

Eadmund had been in the middle of a very pleasant dream when he was shaken awake by Bram.

Bram had been woken by a nightmare, and fearing it was no nightmare at all, he'd rolled out of bed, padding over to his king. 'We need to talk.'

Eadmund mumbled, tongue stuck to the roof of his mouth. He rubbed his eyes, flinging an arm out as he rolled over. 'What?'

Thorgils snored loudly opposite him, mouth wide open, one leg hanging out of bed. Beorn was even noisier, tucked into a cot bed near Eadmund's feet. The noise was horrific.

'Not surprised you can't sleep,' Eadmund grinned, though his head ached, and he remembered the wine.

'It's not Thorgils keeping me awake,' Bram whispered. 'Things aren't right here. I lived in Alekka for years. I know it well. I know the men and the politics. I know the lords. Nothing Gudrum said makes any sense. And did you see the way those other lords looked?

Like they were biting their tongues, afraid to speak. Something's off.'

Eadmund blinked at him. 'I thought the same, at first, but it was just a surprise, that's all. Gudrum's the king now, and we're here to help the king. What are you saying? That you want to sneak out in the night?' Eadmund lifted his eyes to the tent flap, hearing voices outside. 'That you want to run away?'

Bram nodded. 'Yes. Something's wrong.' And he tapped his chest. 'I know it, in here. You need to trust me, Eadmund.'

Eadmund didn't move. He didn't speak.

'What would Jael do?'

'Jael?'

'She wouldn't trust anyone she didn't know. Wouldn't believe everything they told her. You need to think this through. I'm not saying we run out in the night, but we have to make sure we're doing the right thing here.' Bram wasn't sure why he felt so unsettled, but something about Gudrum had his senses on high alert. The new king didn't appear overly familiar with Alekka. He didn't speak like an Alekkan. Bram doubted he was from The Murk at all.

Eadmund was struggling to keep his eyes open, but Bram's concerns weren't something he could ignore. 'I'll talk to Gudrum in the morning,' he promised. 'I will. See if you can get some sleep, though, Bram. Nothing we can do about things now.'

Bram watched as Eadmund's eyes closed, and within moments, he was snoring just as loudly as Thorgils and Beorn.

***

Neither Raf nor Eddeth could sleep. They spoke about Reinar and about Alys, who had saved Reinar. Eddeth wouldn't let that go, desperate to know how she'd done it. Alys had sworn it would remain a secret, which had her even more determined to find out.

One day.

For now, they had to focus on stopping Gysa.

'Ludo said I should kill her,' Eddeth whispered.

Raf didn't even blink. 'It's not in you, Eddeth. It's not who you are.'

Eddeth remembered fighting off that murderous couple up North. She remembered how hard she'd fought to save those she cared about, and if that had meant killing, she was certain she could have done it.

Couldn't she?

'*I* need to do it,' Raf insisted. 'Let me do it. Valera showed me things. I could try.'

Eddeth wasn't so sure. 'You just died!'

'But now I know more than before,' Raf whispered. 'So much more.'

They could only assume that Gysa was watching and listening, though surely the dreamer needed sleep as much as everyone else? Still, it kept both women guarded and cautious. Even Eddeth, which surprised Raf, given the time they'd had recently, and the exhaustion of caring for Reinar. And nothing loosened Eddeth's tongue as much as tiredness.

'Gysa won't hesitate to kill,' Raf warned. 'And nor will I.'

'And Alys?' Eddeth wondered.

'She won't be pleased with Alys breaking the curse,' Raf smiled, happy to think of Gysa being so miserable. 'Nor will Gudrum. I doubt we'll have long to wait now. We should sleep.'

Eddeth agreed, and they lay perfectly still, eyes wide open, neither saying a word. The wind snapped the tent, an owl hooting in the distance, someone crying out in pain.

Eventually, Eddeth rolled over. 'Or we could plan? Come up with more ways to stop that Gysa?'

Raf rolled towards her, smiling. 'Yes, we could.'

***

The second time Eadmund Skalleson was woken that night, he was in a far less agreeable mood, but seeing that it was Gudrum's man, Edrik, he got out of bed quickly. And after dressing, he left the tent with a yawning, stumbling Thorgils and a quiet Bram and Beorn behind him.

'Is something wrong?' Eadmund wanted to know as he entered Gudrum's tent, seeing the warlords gathered around the king, all dressed for battle, the fragrant scent of wine in the air.

'We will attack Hector Berras' camp tonight,' Gudrum said gruffly, stalking back and forth behind his table. 'Before further allies reach him. He has requested help, and my dreamer sees danger ahead if we don't act now.'

Eadmund could sense Bram glowering behind him, and reminded of their conversation, he stepped forward. 'I'm still struggling to understand the motivation,' he admitted, causing Thorgils to raise his eyebrows so high that they touched his curly hair.

Gudrum looked both furious and surprised. Whatever spells Gysa had woven around their allies were obviously not as strong as they'd believed. 'I thought we had... cleared up any confusion?'

Eadmund shook his head, not taking the wine offered to him by Gudrum's steward. 'You were very forthcoming,' he began, 'though we haven't brought a dreamer with us. In fact, on Oss, I don't even have one.'

'But I thought your wife was a dreamer?' Gudrum said lightly. 'We all heard about the Vale of the Gods and what you achieved there. Quite a feat that was. It certainly made your wife famous outside of Brekka.'

Eadmund saw a glint of something in Gudrum's eyes, which made him even more inclined to trust Bram's instincts. 'My wife isn't here, and her dreams are not your concern... my lord.'

'Though if she were still having them, I wouldn't have been able to lure you here.'

Bram froze.

Eadmund blinked. 'Lure? I don't understand.'

Gudrum's smile stretched his scars across his cheeks like

ribbons. 'No, you don't. You see, thanks to my dreamer, and let me tell you how useful it is to have a dreamer!' He came forward until he was breathing in Eadmund's face, his men closing in. 'Thanks to my dreamer's unrivalled skill, she has bound your entire army to me, so I don't need you to command your men anymore. Now, they'll simply follow their new king!'

Memories of the past returned, rushing over him like a wave, and Eadmund was immediately back in the Vale.

On the wrong side of things again.

Thorgils spun around, eyes snapping to the axes and swords wielded by emotionless men. He turned back to Eadmund with tense shoulders. 'Feels familiar.'

Eadmund was no dreamer, though he felt certain they wouldn't be alive much longer. He thought of his wife and children, and then his wife again, who would be furious to hear that he'd led everyone into a trap.

'I intend to kill your wife.'

Eadmund blinked some more.

'And it will be so much more rewarding to kill you when I have her here. So, for now, Eadmund, you and your friends are my prisoners. I know Jael cares for each of you, so you'll remain here, and I will take your men. They'll go into the front ranks, every last one of them. They can take the arrows while their king sits in here enjoying wine and cake. Paki!' he called. 'Do bring my guests some cake!' And leaning forward to peer into Eadmund's stunned eyes, Gudrum lowered his voice. 'Your bitch wife took someone from me, someone I cared about more than any other, and now, finally, it's time to make her pay.'

PART FIVE

Vengeance

CHAPTER FORTY TWO

Puddle barked.

At first, it sounded as though he was having a dream, for it was his softer, clucking bark, but then he jumped onto Stina's bed, paws on her chest, barking loudly in her face.

Neither child enjoyed being woken, and it generally took a long time to drag them out of their slumberous states, but the sound of Puddle's urgent barking in the dark tent had Lotta and Magnus out of bed in a flash. They ran to Stina, who pushed Puddle onto the floor and sat up blinking. 'What's happening? Puddle, ssshhh!' she grumbled, trying to hear.

'I'll go and see,' Magnus offered.

Now Stina was wide awake. 'No, you won't! Pass me my cloak, and I'll go. You'll stay here with Puddle.'

But it was too late for that as a still-barking Puddle wriggled on his belly, quickly escaping the tent.

'No!' Lotta cried after him, and throwing Stina's cloak at her, she raced for her own.

***

Raf hurried to warn Alys while Eddeth ran into the centre of the camp. 'They're coming!' she bellowed into the silence, still half in her dream and wobbly with it. 'Gudrum's coming!' She heard barking and soon saw Puddle racing towards Reinar's tent. There was relief in that, Eddeth thought, still constantly second-guessing her dreams.

Ilene had been walking back from the latrines, and she stumbled to a stop, looking first at the puppy and then back at a panting Eddeth. 'What? Gudrum?' Spinning around, she saw no one. She heard nothing but the hoot of an owl. 'Are you sure?' she snapped, convinced that Eddeth was likely sleepwalking.

Eddeth was acutely aware of what Ilene thought of her abilities, so ignoring her, she rushed away, calling into the night. 'Gudrum's coming! You must wake up! Gudrum's coming!'

Ilene drew her sword, moving quickly now, hurrying back to her tent.

Just in case.

***

Alys lifted her head off Reinar's bed as Raf burst in, almost tripping over Puddle, who rushed up to Alys, pawing her leg. She didn't need to hear Raf's words to know that something was happening.

Reinar woke up quickly, unable to even move. 'What?' he croaked, his throat like sand.

'Gudrum's coming,' Raf said breathlessly. 'We have to go!'

Alys glanced at Reinar. 'I have to stay.'

'No,' he told her. 'Go, Alys... go. Help... Stellan.'

She nodded with some reluctance, and grabbing her black cloak, she drew it around her shoulders, taking one final look at him before following Raf and a barking Puddle outside.

'Don't let anyone in,' she warned the men guarding the tent. 'I'll send help. You'll need more help.' Looking up, she saw fire streaming across the dark sky. Though blinking, it was quickly gone, leaving her to wonder if it had truly been there at all.

***

The news of Reinar Vilander's resurrection had incensed Gudrum so much that nothing else entered his head but the desire to end his rival's claim to the throne. He would not wait, would not delay. With the arrival of the Islanders, now bound to serve him, thanks to Gysa, there was no reason to wait another moment.

So he hadn't.

He'd roused his warlords, who had quickly woken their men, and preparing for battle with urgency and some excitement after days of sitting in boredom, they had marched away from their camp, heading across the field, aiming for the Vilanders.

Stealth and silence were necessary, so weapons were secured and horses left behind. They had moved with speed, despite the mud, wanting to reach their enemy before dawn came to announce their presence. And now they stood, waiting in the woods, the nearly thousand-strong spellbound Islanders forming the first shield walls on the north, east, and western flanks. They would attack on three fronts at once, aiming to quickly crush Reinar's men.

Rage had propelled Gudrum forward. Rage and frustration and the desire to take matters into his own hands; not waiting, not playing games, not dreaming or scheming. He wanted an end to this pointless folly.

It no longer interested him at all.

Gripping his sword with a sweaty hand, he surged through the trees, shield on his back, left hand pushing away branches, searching for unseen obstacles. Edrik was right behind him, and knowing he had another pair of eyes in the darkness gave him confidence.

He heard a few shouts now, listening closely, trying to ascertain if Reinar's camp had had some warning, or perhaps it was merely a few drunks searching for their beds? He couldn't tell, and moving forward, eyes sweeping the silhouettes of trees coming at him like ramparts, his mind started wandering.

He imagined a weakened Reinar, still bedbound, unable to move.

He would finish the foolish boy himself. A weak, foolish boy.

He thought of Jael and Eadmund, and Ranuf Furyck, who had taught him that you always pushed the hardest when your enemy was at its weakest.

Ranuf had ruled Andala with an iron fist, victorious in every battle.

There had been none like him, though his ambitious daughter had always sought her father's throne...

Focus, Gudrum reminded himself, snarling now. In the dark, it was easy to become immersed in your own thoughts, though he was quickly yanked out of his as a bright light burst above his head. 'Fire arrows!' he screamed, turning back to Edrik, who had swung his shield off his back, aiming it skyward.

Gudrum drew his own shield from his back, looking forward to taking Stellan and Reinar Vilander to join the rest of his prisoners. Though perhaps he wouldn't bother?

Better to just take their heads.

***

'We've no chance!' Eddeth panicked when Alys and Raf joined her beneath one of the great oak trees marking the entrance to the camp.

A few men glanced her way as they ran to their positions.

'What? Why?' Alys wanted to know, though she quickly saw glimpses of the army coming through the woods herself. Gudrum's surprise attack wasn't necessarily a surprise, yet most of their warriors had been asleep. It was hard to respond to such urgent danger in the dark. And despite the great fire burning in the centre of the camp and braziers lining the paths, they were mostly cloaked in darkness.

Stellan and Bjarni ran past them, followed by Jonas and Vik.

'Alys!' Jonas skidded to a stop, turning back for her. 'Ludo's with Stina and the children!' He took her hand. 'He's got men with him. You need to join them!' Though he already guessed what she'd say about that.

Alys shook her head. 'Nowhere's safe,' she warned, pushing him away with a worried look. 'I'll do what I can. Be careful!'

Eddeth grabbed hold of her panic and then Alys' hood, pulling both her and Raf close. 'Alys, we need your sword. We can try to stop Gudrum, but you have to keep us safe. Oh yes, that Gysa will be watching! And how will we work while she's got her hands in the flames?'

Alys looked surprised and slightly confused. 'My sword?'

Eddeth nodded. 'Raf and I have a plan! A way to keep us safe! Something we've been working on, but you... you need to watch over us. Protect us in case Gudrum's men come. Oh yes, he's got those Islanders now! They're his, and what can we do if they break through?'

Alys patted Eddeth's arm, trying to calm her down, sensing Raf shuddering before her. And unsheathing her sword, she stepped back. 'Alright, but let's hurry. We can't let Gudrum and Gysa get the upper hand.'

***

Berger and Helgi stood on the eastern edge of the still-growing shield wall protecting the main entrance to the camp. Helgi was fighting the pulsing need to unleash his bear spirit, though he knew how vital it was to keep the shield wall intact. Berger was beside him, shouting orders in a steady stream of noise. They had shieldmen and those wielding axes and swords, but what they needed now were men with spears.

And archers, Bjarni decided, standing behind them, relieved to see a few bows in flashes of moonlight. 'Archers!' he screamed. 'Form up behind! Fire at will!'

It was chaos, which was surprising given how many times they'd practiced responding to a night attack. Though it was quickly apparent that the darkness was an enemy in its own right, and there weren't enough braziers in all of Alekka to reveal every danger coming for them now. It sounded as though they were surrounded, the noise loud enough to drown out every other thought.

The man beside Bjarni went down screaming, an arrow driven into his face. Bjarni shuddered. 'Stay down!' he called as the wounded man tried to get back to his feet, in shock and panicking. 'Help will come. Stay down!' Turning, he saw the three dreamers out of the corner of his eye, standing beneath one of the oaks, surprised they were so exposed. 'It's not safe!' he shouted at them, though his words were quickly drowned out by another roar from the enemy, busy thumping shields and chests, aiming to unsettle them.

Hearing the sudden wails of panic and pain, Eddeth became distracted, wanting to help, but Raf grabbed her arm, holding her close. 'We can't help one man. We have to help all of them,' she insisted, pushing her towards the oak tree's twin on the other side of the main thoroughfare. 'Alys will go with you. I'll stay here.'

Though Alys didn't like the sound of Raf being alone. 'Torfinn!' she called, seeing a familiar silhouette nearby. 'Can you help Raf?'

Raf usually found it impossible to ask for or accept help, though realising there was no time for feelings of any kind, she touched Torfinn's arm. 'We're going to help. You need to watch my back.' She turned away from a nodding Torfinn, drawing her knife from her belt.

Alys took a deep breath before turning after Eddeth, hoping the two dreamers knew what they were doing.

***

Jael rolled onto her aching back, having forgotten how uncomfortable it was to sleep on the ground and the muddy, slushy, snowy ground at that. Her guide, Milla, had led them off the main road, into the trees, which sheltered them from the worst of the wind.

Jael felt grateful to have found the girl - a skinny seventeen-year-old with bright eyes and a toothy smile. She was an expert horsewoman and hunter, eager to share her knowledge of the land and of the dramatic events surrounding Ake Bluefinn's recent demise. Jael had mentioned Salagat, certain that Eadmund had been heading there, and Milla had happily told her all about the abandoned village, separated by woodland from a famous field where armies had often spilled blood.

She knew it well.

It was going to be silver well spent, Jael realised with some relief, and opening her eyes, she saw bright lights in the sky. Not stars but flames. Tiny balls of fire sweeping through the darkness.

She heard Tig whinnying in the distance, the rush of water rippling in the stream they'd camped beside. And at that moment, Jael knew she existed in two places at once.

Not speaking, not moving, she let her thoughts lead her, suddenly aware of how slow her breathing had become, how light her body felt. The discomfort of lying on the ground disappeared as she became as light as air.

It was cold, which wasn't a surprise, Jael thought wryly.

She could never escape the cold, not even in her dreams.

Was it a dream?

She saw a tent emerging through a wall of trees, heavily guarded, banners staked into the ground around it. The banners snapped, blowing angrily in the wind, but Jael was sure she saw two crossed axes. She thought of the amulet she wore around her neck. Those were Furia's axes.

Blinking, she was immediately inside the tent, where she saw more guards.

And prisoners.

She counted four, heart sinking, suddenly back in her childhood home of Andala.

Jael's dog, Asta, had been her best friend.

Gudrum's son, Ronal, had been her greatest enemy.

And finally fed up with being defeated by Jael in the training ring, embarrassed in front of his father and his friends, Ronal had killed Asta. He had taken her dog and slit her throat while his friends held Jael's arms, making her watch.

So Jael had killed him.

Jael and Asta had slept together every night, gone everywhere together since she was a little girl, and Asta was a puppy. They'd been inseparable. And Ronal Killi had always been more adept with his twisted little mind than he ever was with a sword.

He knew how to hurt her...

Jael shivered, standing amongst the trees now, seeing familiar faces wielding the bows launching fire arrows into the sky. Her men. Hers and Eadmund's. She let herself sink further into the vision, entranced by its clarity, desperate not to lose it before she found what she was searching for.

The voice was familiar, a rasping growl.

Years after Ronal's death, Gudrum had tried to kill her, and she had tried to finish him.

They had both failed.

And now?

Jael's fears multiplied as she walked deeper into the chaotic darkness, following the sound of that voice until she saw him.

Gudrum Killi.

***

Reinar tried to move. He heard arrows whistling in the distance, fearing that Gudrum was getting closer. He didn't even know where they were. His last memory was of fighting on Gord's Field. Now he was an invalid, half-alive, stuck in a bed, unable to move.

One of his guards hurried inside with two trembling servants. 'They will dress you, my lord. In case we have to move you.'

Reinar hated the sound of that, but he nodded, lifting his eyes to the tent roof, seeing bursts of light through the fabric. 'Shields,' he said as the servants took up positions on either side of him. 'Get... more men. Be... ready with... shields.'

Following the gaze of his lord, the man bobbed his head, disappearing outside, coming back with two shield-bearing men, all three of them gathering around Reinar's bed, ready to protect the lord and his servants.

***

Magic became potent when more than one dreamer joined a spell, Valera had taught Raf, explaining why her blue walls had been so strong when they'd united in Orvala. Raf had become embarrassed knowing that she'd been the weak link in those walls – the one to let Alari escape. Though Valera had smiled kindly, not mentioning a word about it.

Now, Raf hurried to put all memories of mistakes behind her, quickly carving symbols into the oak's generous trunk.

Torfinn remained with her, wanting to ask questions about what she was doing but just as quickly aware that more danger lurked in the sky. Gudrum's archers had the range, and they were shooting waves of fire arrows into their camp. A few tents had already caught fire. A few men, too, by the sound of things. He heard blades clanging on iron bosses, axes striking shields. The sounds surrounded him, and he kept moving, seeking warning of a breach in their defenses. Both Reinar and then Stellan had prepared them to defend an attack on all four fronts, day or night. He just hoped they had enough men to withstand whatever Gudrum and his allies were throwing their way.

'Ssshhh,' Raf grumbled, turning around. 'Your thoughts are too loud. I need to find Eddeth!' Turning back to the two symbols she'd drawn, she placed a shaking hand on each, and with a deep breath, she closed her eyes, searching for Eddeth in the darkness.

***

Eddeth had initially been confident about the symbols Raf had shown her. They had been two of the many taught to her by Valera, and they'd discussed how they would use them to protect the camp from an attack. Eddeth had drawn them repeatedly, tucking the scrap of vellum into her purse, looking at it often.

Until she'd lost it.

And now she was struggling to remember one of the symbols entirely. Happy enough with the first symbol, she had started on the second, eventually stopping, doubting it was the symbol at all.

Alys turned back to her. 'What's wrong?'

'I...' Someone screamed in agony, more fire arrows lighting up the camp, and Eddeth shook all over, teeth chattering. 'I... m-m-might have forgotten one of them.'

'A symbol?' Alys could barely see what Eddeth had marked on the tree. 'Eddeth, I... you have to focus. Close your eyes and shut out the noise. Trust in what you see, in what you remember. You have to hurry!'

Eddeth nodded, sensing that to be true. And quickly closing her eyes, she pressed her hands against the hastily carved symbols, trying to determine whether they were correct, and then she saw Raf's symbols in the darkness. They were a perfect match, glowing orange, warm like fire.

And smiling with some relief now, Eddeth brought her own symbols to life.

Alys sighed, filled with a sense of relief herself, though only momentarily, for spinning around, she saw men running into the camp, wielding axes. They weren't Reinar's men, Alys was certain, watching as they charged past, roaring a war cry. So, firming up her grip on her sword, she stepped closer to Eddeth, away from the revealing beams of moonlight.

Though suddenly, there was nothing but light as the dreamers' symbols exploded in waves of colour. Eddeth didn't turn around, focusing on controlling the symbols, but Alys did, realising that some of those men were now coming her way.

CHAPTER FORTY THREE

Armed with his trusty sword and set free to cause chaos, Gudrum was enjoying himself. He stood ankle-deep in frosty mud, shield at his chest, stabbing through gaps in the shield wall with his long knife, making his opponent work hard to stay alive. In this perfect moment, he wasn't a king or a lord, he was a warrior, the taste of blood in his mouth, the sound of his enemy's terror in his ears.

Death was all around him, but he'd never felt more alive.

***

Gysa watched.

Reinar's dreamers were hard at work, though Gudrum had his eyes on what lay before him, oblivious to the danger on the horizon. She bit her fingernails, pacing her tent, returning every few steps to the brazier where the flames revealed precisely how things would go.

Gudrum had made it perfectly clear that when it came to battle, he wanted no interference. No help from her at all.

And if he didn't want her help?

Gysa sighed, shoulders tense.

If Gudrum didn't want her help, what could she possibly do?

***

Raf felt the power of the symbols moving through her. They rippled like water, and her body felt as though it was moving with them. She pushed down with her feet, fearing she would float away. Though it wasn't her body that was moving, she eventually realised.

It was her mind.

They were mind symbols, and Valera had warned that while the symbols worked to trick the mind of her enemy, she had to keep total control of her own.

She couldn't afford to get lost now.

***

Stellan commanded their western shield wall, though he feared it would soon break. He heard Ollo snarling and spitting beside him. 'You need to get out of the wall, Ollo! Get down the line! Secure our right flank. It's turning. I feel it!'

Ollo could, too, and he called to Ilene on his right. 'Close up! I'm going!'

'What? Where?' Ilene didn't understand, but as Ollo slipped away, she hurried to link her shield with Stellan's, immediately losing her momentum, pushed back through the mud.

Stellan held his ground in the centre of that wall, screaming men all around him, wide awake now. The weight pushing against his shield was immense. He wondered how Ilene could stay upright. She was surely only half his weight. His thighs were burning as he worked to stay on his feet. 'Hold!' he roared to his men, wanting to give them some encouragement. 'We hold here! Let them try and come in! We'll take their heads!' Though his own head was quickly spinning, sensing movement behind him. He saw tents on fire, men running into the camp, and not his own. Their weapons were raised, and they were cutting people down. 'Ilene!' he barked, turning back, shoulder braced against his shield. 'Get into the camp! Find Bjarni, Berger, anyone! They need to break away, form again inside the camp! I can't... leave!' The more shield walls they held, the more men they kept out. 'Go!' he shouted as Ilene pulled back. 'Hurry!'

***

The axeman swung for Alys' head. Alys ducked, then using her feet, she skipped forward, holding her father's sword in both hands as she brought it down in a chopping motion, taking off the man's foot. He looked up at her in horror, almost too afraid to move, not wanting the truth of what she'd done revealed. Alys tried not to feel sorry for him as he started hopping, howling in agony, which distracted her from the next man, who aimed at her belly.

She swayed back, then dropping low, she hacked at his leg with a grunt. Stumbling into a hole, she lost her balance, tangled in her cloak, but the now-injured man was slow to turn. So, rolling up onto her knees, Alys took him in the groin with a vicious blow that stopped him entirely. He puffed out his cheeks, eyes bulging, dropping back onto his arse.

Turning quickly, Alys saw the footless man swinging his blade. He was still hopping, realising that he needed to protect himself, but his balance was unsteady, and there was little power in his strike.

Alys parried it, scrambling to her feet, and before the footless man could swing again, she swept her blade low, into his neck.

He screamed and fell, and then silence.

And not wanting to think about any of it, a panting Alys turned around, sword dripping, wondering who else would emerge from the shadows.

***

Jonas was out of breath, fighting in their eastern shield wall. His attention swung between what lay before him and what he'd left behind. He hoped Alys was safe, his mind wandering to the children, and then a knife slid between the shields, taking him in the leg, just above his boot.

'Jonas!' Vik was there quickly, leaning over to budge his friend upright.

Jonas growled angrily in response, annoyed that he'd lost focus. He needed a strong mind. To defeat an enemy cloaked in darkness, he had to keep his mind clear of every other distraction, no matter how important.

The screaming before him became deafening. No longer threatening and taunting, filled with rage and urgency, it was simply loud and frantic.

Vik didn't understand what was happening, but Jonas lifted his eyes a little higher, aware that he could see more. Dawn was hours away, but the light in the sky wasn't just a shower of fire arrows now. It was a surreal orange glow. 'Dreamers,' he breathed. 'The dreamers are helping.'

***

The power of the spell was such that Eddeth feared she would fall down or lose her grip on the symbols entirely, though Raf's voice was comforting and supportive in her ears.

'Listen,' Raf breathed, full of awe. 'Listen, Eddeth, it's working.

Keep going.'

So Eddeth stopped panicking, opening her ears to what she could hear in the distance. The balance was shifting. The voices of those defending the camp were ascending, and now it was Gudrum's forces bellowing in confusion and panic.

And terror.

***

Gudrum suppressed a scream, though he felt real fear coursing through his body. His head moved, snapping left and right, looking over his shoulder, then back at the moving shield wall before him. His men were panicking, retreating, and taking their shields with them.

He didn't understand what was happening, though he feared the danger of hesitating for too long.

The earth was coming apart around him. The sky was on fire above him.

His mind raced, keeping pace with his galloping heart, struggling to piece everything together.

A volcanic eruption is what he pulled out of the darkness, like the one that had destroyed Osterhaaven all those centuries before. His ancestors had escaped that melting, burning mess, leaving for the land they would steal from the Tuurans, eventually naming it Osterland.

'Volcano!' he screamed, eyes on the fiery sky. 'Run! We... have to run! Retreat! Move back to camp! *Retreat*!' Though as he turned to run, shield arm dropping, Gudrum felt a stabbing pain in his side. He thought about lunging back, trying to hurt whoever had wounded him, but instead, as the ground started shaking beneath his feet, he turned and ran, urging his men to follow him. 'Hurry!' he yelled until his throat burned. '*Run*!'

***

Gysa could have stopped it.

Watching closely as the two dreamers played their little trick, she knew she could have stopped it all.

Though as Gudrum and his allies turned tail and ran, she sat perfectly still before the brazier, hands folded in her lap.

***

Berger didn't understand why their enemy had scattered. 'Hold!' he barked as his men became restless, wanting to go after them, threatening their shield wall. 'Hold till we know what's happening!'

'They're seeing things,' Helgi decided beside him. 'Look!' And he pointed at the orange light in the sky. 'Something's happening.'

Berger felt as though his arm could fall off, thrilled that something was happening.

To the enemy.

He watched as Gudrum's men vanished into the darkness, hearing Stellan barking at them, urging them to hold. He didn't want anyone running after them.

They had to protect the camp.

Helgi's weary face broke into a smile. 'It's the dreamers. They're using magic.'

Berger was happy to watch, pleased that it wasn't being done to them, though in the back of his mind, he knew that Gudrum's dreamer was the most powerful one of all.

***

Alys sensed Eddeth vibrating behind her, worried that soon she would collapse.

Every man that had thought about threatening them, every enemy that had infiltrated the camp, had suddenly turned and run away, some even leaving their weapons behind. Though Alys tightened her grip on her sword, keeping watch, just in case. She was certain the magic Eddeth and Raf were weaving was working. They just had to keep it up until every last one of Gudrum's men had gone.

***

Gudrum pushed two men out of the way, knocking them over. And not caring to help them up, he ran on, stumbling over roots, falling into holes. The flames in the sky felt hot enough to melt his skin. The ground undulated around him, trying to knock him over as he fought to move forward, banged into by those men he was trying to outrun. He bled from the wound in his side, though he didn't feel anything but terror.

The volcano would kill them all.

He felt it, as his men felt it, and they ran through the dark forest, tangled in bracken, banging into trees. They twisted ankles, losing boots. It didn't matter. It didn't stop them.

They had to escape before it was too late.

***

Eventually, Stellan dropped his shield.

Their enemy had gone.

Gudrum's men, running and howling in terror, had disappeared into the night. Above them, the sky had a warm orange tinge to it, but apart from that, it was pure darkness.

And soon there was nothing and no one to see but each other.

He turned around as Ollo came back to them.

'They've all gone,' Ollo said, shaking his head. 'Why?'

'Is it a trick?' Ilene wondered.

'I think it is,' Stellan decided, shoulders dropping in relief. 'But not one of theirs.'

***

Eadmund, Bram, and Beorn sat around the brazier, chained together, all three men too troubled to fall back to sleep. Thorgils sat with them, though his head had dropped onto his chest so many times now that he'd finally given in to his tiredness, snoring noisily on Eadmund's left.

'Gudrum said Jael's coming,' Bram murmured, trying to shut out the pain in his wrists, his ankles, his back. 'So did she receive a messenger? Or are her dreams back?'

Eadmund hoped for the latter. 'I don't want her walking into his trap. If she's seen what he's doing...'

'Well, if she's seen what he's doing,' Beorn said, barely moving his lips, trying to be discreet. A guard had popped his head inside the tent, and having checked that the prisoners' restraints were secure, he'd brought a stool inside, deciding to keep a close eye on them. 'If she's seen something, she's coming. You know Jael.'

Eadmund did, and it worried him.

'He's got a grudge against her, that's for sure,' Bram whispered, trying to wriggle free of his restraints. He'd been pulling against them for hours now, the only result of all his hard work being bruised wrists. 'To go to all this trouble?'

Eadmund didn't want to think about Gudrum's plans for Jael. 'But what can she do? Walk in here with what? At most, she can bring two shiploads of help. Two shiploads and Fyn. Though I doubt she'd do that. She wouldn't want to leave Oss exposed.' He felt sick, so tired that he couldn't think straight, but he could feel, and what he felt was pure terror for his wife, and their men, who were under the spell of Gudrum's dreamer.

'You have to try and reach her,' Bram said, seeing Eadmund's eyes closing. They were all uncomfortable, legs numb, wrists and ankles bound in iron fetters that pinched their skin, but as much as it was painful, it was also exhausting. He found his own eyes threatening to close.

'Me? I'm no dreamer.'

'No, but you're her husband, so if you try and focus on Jael, she might see you. She might see what's happened before it's too late.'

Eadmund nodded, thinking it sounded like the best idea.

Well, it was the only idea, he realised.

They were trapped, imprisoned.

And if he couldn't find a way through to her, Jael was about to join them.

***

By the time Gudrum and his men made it back to their camp, the spell had lifted, and they didn't understand what had happened or how they'd ended up back where they'd begun, turned around by the enemy they'd been so confident of defeating.

They had run and stumbled away from the Vilanders' camp and were now scratched and bleeding and limping. Their clothes were torn, many had dropped their weapons.

Others hadn't returned at all.

They milled around their king, who looked as confused as the rest of his men. The Tudashi gathered around their own king while the Ennorians turned to Bor Bearsu, who strode towards Gudrum.

And shaking his head, Bor peered at him. 'What happened? I don't understand what that was.'

'You were attacked by dreamers,' came a calm voice as Gysa stepped through the mud, looking elegantly serene in the cold light of dawn. 'They played with your minds, made you see things that weren't there. It was a very skillful trick indeed.'

No lord liked to be told that he'd been made a fool of, no king either, so Gysa had tempered her scorn, eyes sweeping the dazed men, eventually resting on Gudrum, who didn't seem fully there. No one did. The servants and stewards were rushing back and forth, bringing trays of wine and ale. There were towels and bowls of water for the lords. Plates of cheese and cold meats too.

Though no one looked their way. No one attempted to take off their helmets or their armour. They simply stared at the dreamer as though she wasn't there.

***

Even Ollo was pleased with the dreamers.

They gathered outside Stellan's tent, where an exhausted Raf and Eddeth had been led to a log near a fire, offered ale, which neither woman took.

They were still trembling, still half lost in the trance.

'What will they do now?' Bjarni wondered, taking a long drink of ale himself. 'When they realise it was just a trick?'

'I don't imagine they'll come again quickly,' Stellan decided, looking at Jonas and Vik.

Vik nodded. Jonas was busy having his leg tended to by Alys. The children were hovering behind her, ignored by Stina, who was trying to find Ludo.

'Depends on how long it takes them to get a grip of themselves again,' Vik sighed, taking a seat beside Eddeth. Dawn was struggling to break through the darkness, and he suddenly felt weary, as though his body was trying to drag him back to bed. 'We should remain alert either way.'

'He won't be happy,' Ollo chuckled. 'Gudrum? Ha! He won't be happy at all.'

And though everyone agreed, no one else smiled.

***

Gudrum wasn't smiling as he pushed Gysa inside his tent, turning her to him with an angry snarl. 'What was that then? Your little *performance*?' He felt unsteady on his feet. His ears still rang with the screams of his men, the clang of blades and shields clashing in his mind. He felt displaced and fearful, and his anger ignited. 'Tell me!' he hissed. 'Tell me all about your games, dreamer!'

Gysa blinked slowly, not daunted by his flying spittle. 'The games were not mine, I assure you.' She didn't back down in the face of his fury, for despite his anger, she felt his fear, sensing how much he needed her now. 'You may wish to fight with iron-forged weapons, but they have three dreamers, so why wouldn't they use them? Gifted creatures like that? But they are the greatest weapons of all, for they can control minds!'

Gudrum could feel that, though he still found it impossible to believe that what had happened hadn't happened at all. That the ground hadn't been shuddering, that the sky hadn't been raining fire, the forest running with hot lava. His frown intensified, his head thumping. 'All of it?' He dropped Gysa's arm, turning to the brazier. 'All of it was just an illusion?'

Gysa quickly concealed a smile, pleased that Reinar Vilander's dreamers had helped her out so much, for she needed Gudrum to submit to her, not keep her at a distance, unable to truly help him. 'No, just an army of frightened men running through a forest, fearing for their lives.'

Gudrum shook, realising how cold he was. It was as though

his body could suddenly feel again. He held his hands over the brazier, entranced by its flames. 'So you think I'll let you have a say? Is that it, Gysa?' He swung around, eyes narrowed to slits. 'You think they did you a big favour? That I'll let you fight beside me now?'

Gysa hoped the surprise didn't show in her eyes; surprise that he could read her so easily. 'You have never been up against just an army of warriors. Three dreamers are worth thousands of men. They can upend your plans whenever they choose to. If they were skilled enough, they could take your life.'

Gudrum stepped towards her. 'And you are offering to do what?'

Gysa took his filthy hands, staring into his eyes.

And smiled.

CHAPTER FORTY FOUR

Eadmund hadn't slept since Gudrum's men left their camp.

Gudrum's men and his men.

And now they were back, but something was wrong. Something was off.

'Dreamers,' Bram murmured beside him. They'd both had their ears open, trying to listen to what was happening. There were no guards in their tent now. They'd been removed, stationed outside, and the four men had been left alone to sleep. Though only Thorgils and Beorn were managing it. Eadmund and Bram had remained wide awake.

'Dreamers?'

'They're talking about the earth moving. About fiery skies and flaming ash,' Bram said.

'Sounds like a volcano.'

'It does, but I barely smell smoke, and the only thing moving the earth is Thorgils' farts. Got to be dreamers up to no good.'

'Or up to some good since we're on their side,' Eadmund decided. 'Or would be if we weren't stuck in here.' He pulled against the fetters again, wishing his hand was slimmer or that he had fewer bones. And sighing loudly, he relaxed his body, knowing that no amount of squeezing would make any difference.

'If they've got dreamers with them, they must see the mess we're in. Perhaps they'll help?'

Eadmund wasn't so sure. 'We can't let Jael walk into this trap.

I can't, Bram.'

'Trust your wife,' was all Bram would say. 'It's important, Eadmund. We can't do anything except be ready for when Jael comes. Trust your wife knows what's happening, that she knows what to do. You know Jael. She's always got a plan.'

***

They woke as dawn was breaking, gulping down handfuls of tart raspberries and the last of the soft cheese they're brought from Oss. It wasn't much, but neither Jael nor Fyn had any appetite. Their cheerful guide, Milla, had offered to catch some fish, but they just wanted to get on the road. So, leaving Jael and Fyn to talk, Milla headed for the horses, who were nuzzling through the snow, searching for shoots of grass.

'What will we do when we get there?' Fyn wanted to know, eyes sweeping the trees. 'To their camp?'

Jael shrugged. 'No idea. Rescue everyone?' She smiled. 'Rescue everyone, kill Gudrum, go home.'

Fyn laughed. 'Sounds easy. I imagine Warunda would sing another song about you then.'

'Ha! About us,' Jael decided. 'You're going to be there too.' She felt nauseous, her confidence shaky in the early morning light. The wind was wild, promising a stormy day. She still felt at sea, quickly regretting having eaten anything at all. Though mostly it was worry, she knew.

Worry that they wouldn't arrive in time.

'Take this,' she said, handing Fyn a smooth river stone painted with a symbol. 'Keep it for a while. I want my friend to see I'm coming. Say nothing, though. Not about our plans. Not until I have it back.'

***

Reinar sipped from the spoon Eddeth held to his lips. It wobbled in her distracted hand, and he peered up at his dreamer, wondering what was wrong. Though with broth dribbling into his mouth, he couldn't speak.

'Are you alright, Eddeth?' Ludo asked instead.

Eddeth turned to him in surprise, spilling broth down Reinar's chin. 'Sorry,' she mumbled, turning back to wipe his beard with a filthy hand. She moved her hand down over his tunic, wiping some more, unaware that both beard and tunic were now smeared in the broth.

Reinar spluttered, unable to decide if he wanted to sneeze, vomit, or cough.

'Help me prop him up,' Eddeth said, dropping the spoon back into the bowl, freeing two hands to help her patient, who grunted as Eddeth's coarse nails dug into his armpit, pulling him forward. 'Sorry,' Eddeth grinned as she let go of Reinar, turning to the pillows behind him. And lifting them up, she batted and shook each one, resettling them to make a tower of feathers and linen, which Ludo then lay Reinar back against. 'There! Much better!'

Ludo, who had never received an answer to his question, asked it again. 'But what about you, Eddeth? Are *you* alright?'

Eddeth sighed dramatically, plopping down onto a stool as Reinar closed his eyes. 'Alright? No, I'm not. I fear we opened the mouth of the beast last night, and now who knows what will come our way? For all that we did to help, Gudrum's dreamer isn't going to be happy. And what will that mean for us?' She looked up at Ludo with bulging eyes. 'What will she do now?'

'But there's three of you, only one of her.'

'Mmmm, but that's like saying there's three humans against one goddess, for I fear the woman's powerful enough to be one.'

Reinar opened his eyes. 'But what can you do?' He spoke with ease for the first time since he'd woken, wondering if Eddeth's broth had actually helped.

'We've drawn symbols everywhere. All that we know,' Eddeth muttered, fearing they wouldn't be enough. 'Symbols to keep the woman out.' She saw concern in Reinar's eyes, hearing Ludo's loud and doubting thoughts. 'And they will!' she insisted, standing with a sneeze. 'Oh yes, that Gysa woman doesn't know what trouble awaits her if she tries to tangle with us!' And knowing that bravado would get her nowhere, Eddeth left Ludo with Reinar, deciding to call a meeting of the dreamers.

Urgently.

***

Gysa had left a furious and still-dazed Gudrum to deal with his equally dazed and furious warlords while she took to her bed. The weak dawn light wasn't enough to disturb her, and her tent remained mostly dark. The howl of a building storm blocked out the noise of the camp, and the heady fragrance of the herbs she'd added to the brazier helped her slip into a dream.

She hoped to find Reinar Vilander's three meddlesome dreamers.

And though she did find a dreamer, it wasn't one she'd been looking for.

***

Alys left the children in Jonas' care, heading after Eddeth and Raf. Stina was busy tending to the wounded, and Jonas wasn't up for much with a bandage wrapped around his leg and a weariness in his battered body that only a good night's sleep would cure. That and a proper bed, he thought with a crooked grin as he eyed the two children.

'I want to go with them,' Lotta complained, trying to pull her hand out of her great-grandfather's.

'Not going to happen,' Jonas said sharply. 'No, it's not. You may be a dreamer, Lotta, but this is dangerous. This is war.'

Magnus walked on Jonas' other side, wanting to leave as much as his sister, though he knew his great-grandfather planned to keep them close. He remained where he was, not needing his hand held.

'But I can still help!' Lotta insisted. 'I see things too.'

Jonas looked down at her. 'Then I'm sorry for you, Lotta, because that can't be very nice for a little girl. You should be dreaming about...' He didn't know. It had been too long since Alys was a wide-eyed girl now. And longer still for Mirella.

'Sausages?' Magnus suggested wistfully.

Jonas laughed as Ollo approached with Berger and Helgi.

'Time for a meeting with Stellan,' Ollo said, scowling at the children. 'You can't bring them.'

Magnus looked insulted on his and Lotta's behalf.

Though Jonas agreed. 'I need you to watch your sister, Magnus. Likely she'll try to run off.' He eyed Lotta sternly before turning to her brother. 'Or you will.'

Magnus shook his head. 'No, we won't. I'll keep Lotta safe.'

Lotta quickly looked annoyed by the thought of it, slipping her hand out of Jonas' to cross her arms and pout. She felt lonely. Stina was always busy with the wounded or with Ludo, her mother was always with Reinar Vilander, and Magnus was bossy and annoying.

'Good,' Jonas said. 'We'll be in that tent over there.' He pointed to the largest tent in the camp, its walls rolled up, revealing a table with many men standing around it, pointing and waving their arms. 'So don't go far. I'll pop my head out to check you're still here.'

Magnus sighed, though Jonas' voice was hammer-like, so he had no choice but to nod. 'We won't go anywhere,' he promised. Though looking at his sister, who appeared to have other ideas, he frowned.

***

Gudrum discovered that Reinar's dreamers had caused more problems than he'd first realised, something which had been angrily brought to his attention by the crotchety Lord of Borken, who'd arrived with Bor Bearsu to inform him that a number of their men were still missing.

'And where are they?' Gudrum wanted to know, arms in the air.

'Lost?' Edrik offered beside him.

The two lords and their king looked furious.

'Whatever those witches did it was powerful magic!' the Lord of Borken bellowed. 'I'm surprised any found their way back here. I didn't think I would. Didn't know where I was at all!'

Bor Bearsu agreed. 'Your dreamer needs to get to work, my lord. Why have the woman if she can't help us? How are we expected to fight against dreamers?'

That surprised Gudrum, who hadn't imagined that anyone would desire Gysa's help. Though he was quick to pivot. 'She is hard at work already, my lords.' He smiled broadly, ripping hot, moist flesh off the bones of a freshly-caught trout. 'Though while she dreams, we must find those missing men. Whatever happens with the dreamers, we must be prepared to fight.' He looked up as Gysa pulled back the tent flap.

'My lord,' she said, then looking around, she bobbed her head. 'My lords.'

'You have seen something?' Bor wondered quickly, not about to be sent from the tent without knowing what was happening.

Gysa was hesitant to speak, though Gudrum motioned for her to go on. 'I have, my lord, yes. I have seen Jael Furyck. She has landed in Alekka. She is coming here, for you.'

***

After her meeting with Alys and Raf, Eddeth returned to Reinar's tent, shocked to discover that he'd decided he was well enough to get out of bed. Though not according to Eddeth, who pushed him back down with both hands. 'You're like a sapling, you are. One stiff breeze, and you'll topple over!'

Reinar snorted. 'You think I should lie in bed some more? And what good will that do?' He was quickly out of breath, though, slumped over, fighting a determined Eddeth, who felt strong enough to knock him down.

'Well, I think it would give you enough energy to breathe, for one,' she chortled. 'And I don't imagine you want to go out there and faint in front of everyone. Gudrum's dreamer will be quick to tell him about that!'

That had Reinar frowning. 'But I need to kill him, Eddeth. End this. Just... kill him.'

'Oh, but a man like that won't be easily killed,' Eddeth said, joining him on the bed, patting his knee. 'And not by you.' Reinar jerked his head in her direction. 'Not like this, at least. What? You think you could lift a sword for more than one blow?' Now she sneezed, wiping her nose on her sleeve. 'Don't worry, Stellan has everything under control out there. He's prepared.'

'For what?'

That had Eddeth blinking. 'The next attack?'

Reinar frowned. 'I need to get up, Eddeth. I may not be ready to face Gudrum, but I'm still our leader. I can still lead.'

Eddeth supposed that was true. 'Well, you sit there then, and I'll bring everyone to you!' She jumped up, eyeing Svea, busy darning socks by the fire. 'You watch the lord,' she grinned at the servant. 'I'll round up his men!'

***

Taking a break from caring for the injured, Stina and Ludo had rescued a bored Magnus and Lotta, all four of them carrying buckets to the stream. It was usually a pleasant walk, though the wind was fierce, and Stina stopped to drop her bucket. Tucking her hair down her dress and unpinning her cloak, she secured it more tightly across her chest.

Ludo picked up her bucket, and they carried on, listening to Puddle barking at a pair of ducks swimming down the stream. Stina kept her eye on the puppy, though he didn't appear keen to jump in after them.

'He seems better,' Ludo smiled. 'He was so quiet when you arrived.'

Stina nodded. 'You should have seen him when they brought him back from the quarry. I feared he wouldn't make it.' She saw that Lotta had abandoned her bucket and was now chasing Puddle, who had taken off after a rabbit. And with one look back at Stina, arm in the air, Magnus disappeared after them.

'I'm glad you came,' Ludo said, turning to her. And now he dropped the buckets to the ground, taking her hands. 'I should have said something before I left Slussfall. I wanted to go back, to make sure you knew how I felt in case something happened to me.' He shook his head, becoming shy. 'Sometimes, I think too much. I think my way out of saying what I feel.'

Stina stared into his gentle brown eyes, utterly transfixed. It was as though no other person existed in the world, though she suddenly heard Lotta cry out in the distance.

So did Ludo, but he kissed Stina before bringing her into his arms. 'When we get back to Stornas or Slussfall or wherever we end up next, we need to talk, make some plans. I don't want to waste another moment.'

Magnus came running up to them. 'Lotta's fallen over! She says she's broken her ankle, though I can't see anything's wrong. She's always making things up. I doubt she's hurt at all!' Though he looked over his shoulder with concern in his eyes and then back up at Stina, wanting her to hurry.

She nodded at him. 'We'll come, don't worry.' Though she didn't move with any urgency, knowing Lotta's cries well enough to guess that Magnus was right. He ran away from her, back to his sister, leaving them behind. 'Plans would be good,' she murmured, thinking about children. 'Very good indeed.'

***

When they were all gathered in Reinar's tent, Stellan spoke at length about what lay before them, the state of the camp, their missing scouts, the Islanders joining with Gudrum. He laid it all before Reinar, who sat up in bed, Eddeth hovering at his elbow, blinking at them all.

'We need a plan,' Reinar decided, eyeing Ollo, who wriggled as though he had a flea in his trousers. 'What? What aren't you saying?'

Stellan turned to Ollo himself, lifting a weary eyebrow.

'How do we even speak of plans? Gudrum's dreamer will find a way to hear us, no matter what you might say,' Ollo said, holding up a hand as Eddeth started spluttering. 'We may have turned them back with some magic, but it won't be long till they come at us with magic of their own. We can't hold them out forever. We can't stay here!'

Reinar knew that to be true.

'And we can't attack them,' Berger added, with some regret. 'Not with the Islanders beside Gudrum.' He shook his head, unable to see any plan that helped them to victory. His thoughts kept turning to Solveigh, fearing that she would soon be in danger in Slussfall. 'Perhaps it's best if we head north? Go back to Slussfall? With the sea flowing again, we could find some ships, send the women and children away? Get more help?'

Reinar didn't dismiss his fears; he shared them.

He looked back at Eddeth, who had gone completely still. 'Is there anything you can do to get through to the Islanders? To their king and queen? I imagine they're both there? They say Jael

Furyck's a dreamer. Can you get through to her?'

Eddeth's mouth dropped open at the thought of it. 'Well, I...' It was nothing she'd discussed with Alys and Raf, though it was certainly worth considering. 'We can try, though she may have a different way of doing things. I...' Eddeth wasn't sure why she had suddenly become nervous, but the thought of trying to reach a famous queen like Jael Furyck?

She was shivering all over.

'You need to try, Eddeth,' Vik said, watching her picking her wart, avoiding their eyes. 'We need a path out of here. We need help now.'

***

Milla Ulfsson loved to talk. She'd quickly brushed aside Fyn's shyness, smiling and chatting on regardless of whether he answered her. Jael was amused to see it. The girls on Oss were more reticent, waiting for Fyn to talk to them, which he rarely did. But Milla ploughed into every conversation with the enthusiasm of a child. And soon Fyn was answering her in complete sentences, his shoulders dropping away from his ears, occasionally lifting his eyes to meet hers.

Fyn was telling Milla about the Slave Islands as they set a fire, neither looking her way, so Jael headed to the horses, where she held a small sack of grain out to each one in turn. Vili tried to have more than one helping. Tig was hungry, though he appeared more tired than anything. The other two politely waited their turn.

Jael's mind wandered to Eadmund, knowing how close he was now.

How close she was to him.

She could almost smell his smoky beard, almost feel his finger smoothing the scar beneath her eye before he kissed her.

Though what was she actually going to do when she reached

Gudrum's camp?

Closing her eyes, she sighed, trying to relieve some tension. She immediately saw her grandmother's sweet face, remembering sitting in her cottage on the little stool by the fire. Edela would've had some advice for her, she was sure, trying to hear what that might be. Though it was only her face she saw, only the crackling fire she heard.

But those familiar twinkling eyes said everything.

So, turning away from the horses, Jael eyed her bedroll, knowing it was time to go searching for a dream.

***

Eddeth, Alys, and Raf sat around the brazier, all three of them yawning. The disturbed nights had taken a toll, and it was proving impossible to come up with any useful ideas.

'I don't see how we can find Jael Furyck,' Alys decided. 'We don't know her. We have no connection to her at all. Nothing of hers to use. No reason for her to let us in.'

Raf agreed. 'Though we should still try. All of us should. I don't know anything about her, do you?'

Alys nodded. 'She was the daughter of a famous Brekkan king. When he died, everyone thought she would take the throne, but her uncle stole it instead. At least that's what Jonas told me. She was sent to marry Eadmund Skalleson. His father was the King of the Slave Islands. Oss is their home.'

'She's a warrior,' Eddeth put in. 'And a dreamer. A powerful woman indeed!'

'But if that's the case, how did Gysa trick her?' Raf wanted to know. 'Because if she's fighting for Gudrum, she must be under some sort of spell. Mustn't she?'

Alys and Eddeth shrugged.

The camp was quietening down, and Alys wanted to go

and say goodnight to the children. She had promised Lotta that she'd stay with her tonight, though she was equally conscious of needing to focus on her dreams, and a tent with Puddle and Lotta in it inevitably made it impossible to focus. 'I won't be long,' she promised, standing with another yawn. 'I'll just see the children and be right back.'

Raf nodded, and Eddeth turned to her bed with a look somewhere between desire and trepidation. 'Don't be long,' she warned. 'We need to get to dreaming, and I think the only hope of finding Jael Furyck is if we're here, all three of us together.'

Alys stared at her, hoping she was right.

***

Stellan took leave of his son with a pat on the shoulder. 'Get some rest,' he urged. 'You never know what tricks Gudrum might try to play tonight.'

The thought of another attack from Gudrum filled Reinar with dread, for though he'd gotten up and moved around the tent that afternoon, there was little he could offer in the way of defense. Not even of himself.

'I'll ensure those men outside know to keep their eyes open,' Stellan reassured him, seeing the tension in Reinar's face. His son was usually impatient, much like he was, Stellan thought with a smile, though being mostly an invalid, it was sure to be driving him mad.

'Good.'

Stellan cocked his head to one side. 'We'll get out of this mess. There'll be a way. And I say that with the confidence of a man who's been in many messes in his life. And yet here I am, still standing!'

Reinar smiled. 'It's hard not to feel helpless stuck in here.' He heard the wind howling outside, seeing the tent walls moving like waves. 'What can I do?'

'You can think. And thinking's the hardest thing of all. Making decisions, looking for paths to victory. You don't need arms and legs for that!' And turning to the tent flap, Stellan took a deep breath, wanting to instill his son with confidence. He looked back over his shoulder with a smile. 'We only have now and what comes next, so forget Gord's Field, forget Ottby. Close your eyes now and find us a path out of here.'

Reinar watched him go, Stellan's words lingering long after his footsteps had faded away. He stared at the flames dancing in the brazier, entirely wide awake, doubting any sleep would come.

***

Alys returned to the tent to find Eddeth and Raf sound asleep. Eddeth was muttering loudly to herself, as though having a conversation. Raf was perfectly silent and still. And sighing, Alys sat down on her bedroll, running cold hands through the fur.

It was hard not to give in to fear. It took constant effort to fight back against frightening thoughts, which became more pronounced when night took hold. She heard her mother's threatening voice, saw Gudrum's grinning smile, and Gysa's burned face. She knew they were outnumbered, that Reinar was weakened by his injuries, that Alari was watching them all.

'Though you are not alone, Alys,' said a voice.

Alys turned around, seeing no one. It wasn't Ragnahild, who had a grumbling, gravelly sort of voice. This voice was gentle and familiar.

'Grandmother?' she asked into the silence, though no one answered, and eventually, Alys lay down on her fur, pulling another over her black cloak, closing her eyes.

CHAPTER FORTY FIVE

Jael watched Gudrum's camp, looking for opportunities, though it was dark in her dream, making it hard to see. She saw glimpses of Islanders, seeing the glazed eyes that were so familiar – the look of bound men. And moving further into the camp now, she searched for a plan.

The woman coming towards her was a surprise.

A dreamer, Jael recognised immediately. Strands of dark hair hung around a ghoulish face, as though she'd been thrown into a fire and dragged back out again. Jael shuddered, moving aside as the dreamer strode by. She heard the woman muttering, perhaps chanting, and turning, she followed her to where a man stood, stroking his beard.

'Gudrum wants to see you,' he said with a hint of a sneer.

He didn't like the dreamer, Jael could tell, and she watched as the woman swept into the tent, leaving the man behind. He turned with a scowl, almost bumping into an old man, who looked much like one of the Island lords she was so used to dealing with.

'And what will they do now?' he grumbled at the younger man. 'Spells? Is that what this mighty army will be reduced to? Following a dreamer?'

'I doubt that, my lord. Gysa has the Islanders bound to her, for they would surely not fight for our king otherwise. Though he won't want her to do more. He wishes to win this battle with his sword, as I know you do.'

'Of course!' the old man blustered. 'But when? It's all well and good holding all these meetings, but if nothing gets resolved? If we never get anywhere?' And realising that he'd get nowhere talking to Gudrum's minion, the Lord of Borken stormed away.

'Excuse me?'

Jael watched the younger man, once again tugging his beard. He rocked on one foot, then the other, deciding what to do. His eyes moved to the tent the dreamer had disappeared inside, then dropped down to his boots, and eventually, he headed off after the old lord.

'Excuse me?' came the voice again, followed by a loud sneeze.

And eventually, realising that the person might be talking to her, Jael spun around to a strange-looking woman. She frowned, peering closely at the wild-haired creature, who stooped slightly, jiggling on the spot. 'Hello?'

'You can *see* me!' Eddeth cried, hands up to the moon. 'Oh, oh!' And overcome with delight, she forgot to introduce herself. She forgot to confirm who she was talking to, though every sense in her body said that this was the woman she'd gone searching for in her dreams. She couldn't see the colour of her eyes, though she knew they were famously green, and seeing a hint of a scar under the woman's right eye, she clapped her hands together in victory.

'I can see you, yes,' Jael said carefully. 'And you can see me.'

'Yes, yes, it's wonderful, isn't it? I've not been a dreamer very long, you know. Well,' Eddeth considered, picking her wart. 'I suppose I've been a dreamer my entire life, but realising it? No, that didn't happen until recently, when Valera herself came to me. Just one night, into my dreams. Oh, I've never been more surprised in my life! Surprised and then relieved, for it couldn't have come at a better time. No, it couldn't. I saved Alys, I did!' Eddeth shook her head. 'Well, I think Reinar saved Alys in the end. But I helped him get there. Yes, indeed!'

Jael's mouth had fallen open and stayed there as she tried to keep up, though she saw no way into the one-sided conversation.

'I came to find you!' Eddeth finally announced, barely able to draw breath. Reaching out, she placed a hand on Jael's arm. 'Your help. We need your help!'

It wasn't what Jael had been hoping to hear at the end of the rambling speech. 'I need help myself, I'm afraid. My husband's a prisoner in this camp, and my men are bound to Gudrum's dreamer. I doubt there's anything I can do to help you.'

Realising how rude she'd been, Eddeth bobbed her head. 'I... my lady, I, do forgive me. I'm Eddeth. Eddeth Nagel. I'm the king's dreamer! Well, the man who will soon be the king. Reinar Vilander! I'm with him. Not far from here, oh no, we're not. Camped in Salagat, over the field and through the woods. Just by the mountains, we are!'

'Reinar Vilander?'

Eddeth nodded with great vigour. 'Ake Bluefinn chose him as his heir when he knew death was coming for him. He did, yes! Hector Berras killed Ake, then Gudrum, oh that horrible Gudrum, killed Hector!' She frowned then, feeling slightly embarrassed. 'Alekka's not usually like this, I promise.' Though thinking of the terrible Vettels and the many awful kings before them, she went silent, picking her wart.

Jael thought quickly. 'Eddeth? Your men are camped nearby? How many?'

Eddeth opened her mouth, eyes bulging as she tried to pull a number out of her memory. 'Not enough,' she decided eventually. 'Perhaps half Gudrum's number? And that was before your Islanders were tricked into helping him! Oh no, Reinar doesn't have enough men at all. They're deciding what to do, fearing they need to retreat back to Slussfall. Unless we can get help.'

'Well, if we can break the binding spell, my Islanders will fight for this Reinar. Things will even up quickly then. And once I kill Gudrum, I doubt his men will have much fight left in them.'

Eddeth's eyes bulged some more. '*You* want to kill Gudrum?'

'I'm *going* to kill Gudrum, but I need you to break the binding spell. Can you do that?'

Eddeth stared at her for some time.

Eventually, Jael stepped forward, shaking her arm. 'Are you still here?'

Eddeth jerked out of her daze. 'Yes, yes! Though Gysa, Gudrum's dreamer... she was gifted powers by Alari herself!'

Jael shrugged, not understanding.

'The Goddess of Dreamers, the Goddess of Magic. The most powerful goddess of all!'

'Though a binding spell can always be broken if you kill the dreamer who cast it.'

'I...'

'Kill the dreamer and free my men, Eddeth, then your lord will have his victory. I'll enter Gudrum's camp as dusk is falling, and you will kill the dreamer then. That's the plan.'

'The plan?'

'Yes, my plan.' And thinking quickly, Jael pulled a stone from her pouch and pushed it into Eddeth's hand. 'You must remember this symbol. It's the only way to shut out powerful dreamers. A Tuuran way, but hopefully, it will work here. Draw it on every stone you can find, give it to everyone before you tell them of my plan. It won't work if that dreamer finds out. Understood?'

Eddeth nodded vigorously, and then she was staring at an old man, who waddled towards her, swigging from a jug. She spun around, peering into the darkness, wondering what had happened. 'My lady? Are you still here?'

***

Reinar woke in a sweat, and sitting up, still half in his dream, he touched Alys' hand.

She smiled at him, gently coaxing him back down to the pillows. 'I think you were having a nightmare.'

Reinar blinked. His ears were buzzing, the noise of the camp filtering through to him. 'It's morning?'

Alys nodded, pointing to Lotta, who held a trencher of hotcakes in her hands. 'We brought you breakfast.'

Lotta smiled at Reinar. 'You need some strength to get out of bed. That's what Mama always says to me. I don't mind hotcakes, but I hate fish. Whenever we have fish for breakfast, I don't want to get out of bed at all.'

Reinar felt disoriented. His nightmare had been horrific. He'd been on his knees in Ottby's hall, his dead son in his arms. He'd heard that old dreamer cackling in his ears, Elin lying dead before him on the floor. Blood everywhere.

He blinked at a rosy-cheeked Lotta, trying to smile.

'Perhaps we'll leave them by the bed, and you can eat later?' Alys suggested.

Reinar quickly shook his head. 'I want to get up. Today's the day to decide what to do.' And realising that his nightmares hadn't led him to any decisions about that, he frowned. 'Did you have any useful dreams, Lotta? Anything to help me choose which path to take?'

Lotta shook her head. 'I dreamed of a lake, and it was cold, and Puddle was swimming it in. There were fish in the lake, and Vik caught one for supper.' She shuddered.

Reinar laughed, turning his attention to Alys. She looked tired, he thought, though he didn't imagine he looked any better. 'How about you?'

'Not me, I'm afraid, but I left Raf and Eddeth sleeping when I went to see the children. Perhaps they found something?'

***

Eddeth woke with the energy of a puppy. Her first thought was to race out of bed, cold be damned, running through the camp to find Stellan. They would go to Reinar's tent, and she would –

She clamped her lips together, eyes darting around her own tent.

Always the last to wake, Raf lifted an arm in the air and then another, stretching her arms and legs until her toes poked out from the fur. She quickly pulled her legs into her waist, folding herself up like a baby. Then, sensing someone watching her, she opened an eye, staring at an oddly still Eddeth. 'What's wrong?'

Eddeth shook her head, lips remaining clamped together.

'Eddeth?' Now Raf sat up, pulling the fur around her shoulders, breath smoke streaming from chattering teeth. 'Did you have a dream?'

Eddeth didn't even nod.

They sat like that for some time until, eventually, having some inkling of what was going on, Raf reached for her boots. 'Pick up your staff, Eddeth. We need to go and see Reinar.'

Eddeth's eyes bulged, but without a word, she slipped on her boots, picked up her staff and followed Raf out of the tent.

***

Jael was so pleased with Milla's help that she planned to give her twice the amount of silver she'd initially offered. She was a poor girl, she realised, seeing her raggedy cloak, remembering the ramshackle village she'd come from. Her boots appeared to have been stitched together more times than was sustainable, her tunic was too small for her. Her cloak didn't even graze the top of her boots.

She was helpful and considerate, full of wisdom and not afraid of hard work.

And Fyn seemed to like her.

Jael would have smiled if she didn't feel so tense.

'I don't want to put you in any danger, Milla,' she said as Fyn kicked dirt over their fire. 'You should return home when we get close to Salagat. Once we see where we need to be, we won't need you.' And drawing the two pouches of silver from beneath her cloak, she handed them to the girl.

But Milla shook her head, pushing them back to Jael. 'You'll need help when you get there, my lady,' she decided, glancing at Fyn. 'What about the horses? You don't want them disappearing, do you? Or making noise, drawing someone's attention?'

That was true, Jael thought, having felt concerned about merely tying them to a tree, knowing how difficult and determined Tig could be. Still, she inhaled sharply, not wanting to put her at risk.

Milla, though, could almost read the queen's mind. 'I don't want to go back to Ullaberg. Ever. It's...'

Jael saw glimpses of Milla's life in the village, seeing a pock-faced man shouting at her, twisting her arm. And now, looking at the scrawny girl, she saw defiance in her eyes.

'My father wants me to bring him the silver, but I don't want to go back at all.' She glanced at Fyn again as he stepped towards them.

'Jael's right,' Fyn warned. 'We'll be walking into danger.' He saw the spark in Milla's bright hazel eyes, undaunted by anything he said. She reminded him of Jael in that way, and he turned towards his queen with a shrug.

Jael made her decision quickly. 'You'll keep the horses quiet then, but that's all. You'll stay with them and wait for Fyn. Understood?' Milla nodded, looking at Fyn once more. 'And whatever you do,' Jael warned. 'Don't lose your symbol stones.'

***

After an entirely silent journey through the camp, where Eddeth had ignored Stina's greeting and Vik's raised arm, they arrived at Reinar's tent.

Ushering Raf ahead of her and pleased to see both Stellan and Alys, Eddeth jumped into action. Unsheathing her knife, she dropped to the ground, and pushing away the pelts covering the grass, she started drawing the symbol Jael Furyck had shown her.

It still didn't seem real. Jael Furyck?

Realising that she was becoming distracted, Eddeth bent back to her work, occasionally turning around to lift a finger to her lips, warning no one to speak.

And when she'd completed an entire circle of the symbol, she popped her head outside, ordering the men guarding the tent not to let a soul inside. 'Now!' she puffed, turning back around and scurrying to Reinar's bed. 'Now I can finally speak!' Though it was all too exciting, too unexpectedly, overwhelmingly exciting, and it took some time for everyone to understand what Eddeth was trying to say.

'Jael Furyck wants us to kill Gysa?' Alys repeated. 'But if we could do that, we wouldn't be sitting here at Gudrum's mercy.' She hadn't meant to speak so bluntly, and looking around, she saw everyone watching her.

Though it was true and Raf nodded. 'But how, Eddeth?'

'You, Alys. You've killed a dreamer! That Mother Arnesson. Valera showed you! We must be able to do it again. I remember how it went, I... think?' She frowned now, retreating somewhat.

Reinar sat up, feeling energised. He saw hope in Eddeth's dream, though his father, he could see, looked more hesitant. 'If you can kill the dreamer, we'll have the Islanders with us. It would be an even fight.'

'Not if Jael Furyck can kill Gudrum,' Eddeth crowed. 'If she can kill Gudrum, you'll have the upper hand!'

Stellan blew out a long breath. 'It's a lot to take in, Eddeth. A lot of hope and a lot of dreaming.'

'Though it's nothing we haven't done before,' Reinar told his father. 'And listening to dreamers makes sense. They open doors for us to walk through. Besides, what's the alternative? That we stay here in Salagat? But soon disease will find us, or Gudrum will. Men will peel away, wanting to return home. Eventually, we'll be forced back to Slussfall, if we live that long. No, Eddeth's right. This is what we need to try. This path. The dreamer's path.'

Stellan's shoulders felt ready to break in two as he stared at his son before turning to the three dreamers, one of whom was hopping up and down like an excited child.

And he nodded.

***

Gudrum's lords were becoming impatient, though he kept them compliant with promises of more gold, knowing that, eventually, someone would find the Vettel hoard in Ottby. And well aware of how impressive it was rumoured to be, the Lords of Ennor and Borken bit their tongues and focused on keeping their own men happy.

The Tudashi king had been far less tolerant, deciding that he'd had enough of Gudrum entirely, so it wasn't the greatest surprise to wake that morning and find that he'd left, taking his eight hundred men with him.

Having received the news from a tense-looking Edrik, Gudrum spun around to Gysa. 'You didn't see this coming?'

She was irritable, longing for the comforts of Stornas' castle, tired of lords and kings who acted like toddlers. 'Surely I don't need to dream about what is before your own eyes? I'm trying to get through to Reinar Vilander's dreamers. Can't your men see what is happening in their own camp?'

Gudrum placed his goblet on the table, mouth opening in surprise.

And realising that her temper had gotten the better of her, Gysa smiled sweetly. 'The Tudashi were useful, of course, but you have the Islanders.'

'*You* have the Islanders!' Gudrum snapped. 'They fight for me because of you.'

'True.' And that made Gysa happy, for despite what Gudrum might say, she knew he was as resistant to her help as ever. Yet to defeat both his enemies, he was going to need her more than he realised.

'And all this time that you've taken, searching for answers? What have you found?' Gudrum was just as desperate for a proper bed. One that didn't move beneath him like a pile of sticks. He longed for walls that kept out the wind and a hearth that blazed with hot flames.

'I have some ideas for those dreamers,' Gysa promised, revealing nothing. 'Though, of course, I shall wait until you are ready.'

'Yes, you will, for my plans are *our* plans, so you will hold yourself in reserve until I give you the signal.'

Gysa bit her tongue, seeing Edrik smirking by the tent flap. Her relationship with Gudrum had become a daily battle, and she was growing tired of his games. The leash he kept promising to release still chafed in a most irritating way. 'Your prisoners,' she breathed, leaving her goblet behind to join Gudrum by the brazier. 'You will keep them alive? As what? Bait?'

'Of course they're bait,' Gudrum grinned. 'Bait that has lured that bitch away from her warm little fort, all the way to this heap of slop. What? You think she'll come to rescue a few corpses? Risk her life for that?'

Gysa didn't care about Jael Furyck, though it was all Gudrum thought about now, all he talked about. The battle with the Vilanders was no longer at the forefront of his mind. Every waking breath was focused on how he would kill Jael Furyck.

Gysa herself saw little of the woman, apart from those eyes.

Green and sharp and full of fire.

***

Milla slipped back, leaving Jael and Fyn to talk as they rode closer to Gudrum's camp. They had entered a dark forest, which brought back both good and bad memories, and Jael tried to distract herself by going over her plan with Fyn once more.

He seemed nervous as he rode beside her, and she didn't blame him.

'It will be dangerous,' she said, eyeing him closely.

'I know.'

'So you'll have to use everything I've ever taught you. As soon as you find Eadmund, give him all the symbol stones. That will shield them from the dreamer immediately, or, at least, I hope it will. We can't be sure the symbol will work on Gudrum's dreamer, but we have to try. I'll give you mine when we get there.'

Fyn nodded, glancing back at Milla. The girl was eager for adventure, he could see, but having had a taste of it himself, he knew how terrifying it could be.

Especially if it went wrong.

They rode in silence for some time, and though Jael couldn't read his thoughts, she could imagine what Fyn was thinking. He had confidence in her but little in himself, which was understandable. It had been years since they'd done anything more than chase each other around a training ring. 'You'll be fine,' she promised, hoping her sword was sharp enough.

The sword with no name.

It had never killed, never drawn blood, and despite years of practice, it still felt oddly unfamiliar in her hand.

'And you?' Fyn wondered, gulping down some bile. 'How will you be fine? What you're suggesting doing?' Shaking his head, he tried to focus on the road, though it didn't hold his attention for long and frowning, he turned back to her. 'I don't understand what you think you can do? Alone?'

Jael shrugged. 'You have to trust me, Fyn. You used to.' Jael hadn't told him everything about her dream, and she wouldn't, for if the symbol stones didn't work on Gudrum's dreamer, the woman would hear everything they were saying.

'I do trust you,' Fyn insisted. 'I do, Jael. I just... what do I do if you're killed? What do we do?' he asked, inclining his head back to Milla.

'A good question!' Jael grinned. 'Run for your lives, I'd suggest. Find a ship, get to Andala as fast as you can.'

'Andala?'

Jael nodded, serious now. 'That's what you'll promise me, Fyn. If it all goes wrong, I need you to go to Andala. I can't guarantee Oss will stay safe. Without a dreamer, without a king, a queen, and a fleet? But Andala's a fortress, with neighbours ready to come to her aid. You'll be safe there with my family. You both will.'

Fyn inhaled sharply, listening to the rhythmic hooves of five horses thundering down the road, though none of them sounded as loud as his thumping heart.

CHAPTER FORTY SIX

The dreamers spent the morning inside the circle in Reinar's tent. He was up, moving around, trying to get used to walking with the crutch Vik had made him. He felt so oddly weak, and becoming irritated by that, he didn't stop moving. Eventually, though, Eddeth forced him back onto the bed, trying to ply him with a warm chicken broth. She'd been boiling bones and herbs for days, and now those healing liquids were ready to get to work.

Reinar took the broth without argument, wanting to do whatever he could to regain his strength. And leaving her compliant patient on the bed, Eddeth returned to her stool between Raf and Alys, where they were drawing symbols onto the great stack of stones the children had collected.

Throughout the morning, they'd brought various people into the tent, giving them a symbol stone before revealing Eddeth's dream and their own plans. But they needed to make more, so many more. And while they sat before the brazier with inky fingers, it left them plenty of time to talk about how to kill Gysa.

'We've got till dusk,' Raf reminded them. 'We have to kill her at dusk.' She felt panicked then, fearing that Gysa would see through the symbol, that she would find a way to hurt them instead. She lowered her voice. 'If you think we can?'

Alys was the only one of the three to have killed a dreamer, and though she shared the same fears as Raf, she nodded with some confidence. 'We can. I can. I've done it before, and we remembered the symbols, didn't we, Eddeth?'

'We did! We can't cause a fuss, though. Not before dusk. If we do, we might unbalance things altogether. That's what I think. Dusk is when everything happens. We just need to be ready in time.' And seeing Lotta and Magnus arrive with more buckets of stones, Eddeth's shoulders dropped, realising how much more work lay ahead of them. Then her attention was on Stellan, who arrived with Berger, Helgi, Ollo, Jonas and Vik, everyone squeezing into the circle.

'Any news?' Vik wondered, looking from Reinar to Eddeth.

'According to Alys, the Tudashi are heading for home,' Reinar said through sips of broth. He put the cup on his bedside table and reached for his crutch, pushing himself up until he almost matched his father's height.

'That's good news.' Though Stellan didn't raise much of a smile. He was tense, still worried about relying on Eddeth's dream. At times, it seemed so implausible that he found his mind wandering down dark paths leading to ambushes and certain death. Though seeing that Reinar was firmly back in command, he stopped himself from voicing his fears.

And watching Stellan clamping his lips together, Reinar began. 'The Tudashi's departure helps us, but we still have to break the spell on the Islanders. We can't have them lining up against us.'

'How do you know the Tudashi aren't coming to surround us? Attack us?' Ollo suggested, wobbling on a stool, gnawing a piece of salt fish. 'Maybe it's a ruse?'

It was hard to know for sure, but Alys had the distinct impression that the Tudashi king had been angry as he left. He'd muttered to his men, grumbling and growling. They weren't being quiet. They hadn't looked to be doing anything other than departing. 'I can't say, but I think it's not.'

'Though we can't be certain,' Reinar decided, hoping Ollo was wrong. 'It's easy enough to play games.'

Everyone was nodding, including Eddeth. 'Tudashi or not, we have Jael Furyck on our side!' she exclaimed, feeling happy about that. And then, realising how loud she'd become, she bent over, focusing on her stone.

'But how can she help us?' Ollo sighed. 'One woman?'

'Well, she's not just one woman,' Helgi put in, having heard as much about the famous Brekkan warrior as everyone else. 'Is she?' He smiled at Alys.

And seeing Alys smiling back, Reinar had to work to keep his focus. 'We have to prepare to attack them at dusk. That's the plan.'

Ollo straightened up. 'What? Based on what? A dream? Eddeth's dream?' And now he peered at Eddeth with incredulity in his eyes.

She didn't look his way, too busy drawing symbols to care what he was huffing and puffing about now.

Jonas stepped in. 'But what else do we have at this point, Ollo? We can't sit here for much longer. We have to make a move either way. We have to go home or get going, and I'd rather get going.'

Berger nodded, pleased to have someone voice his own desperate need to do something. 'Attacking them makes sense.'

'Attacking them makes no sense,' Ollo argued, looking to Vik.

Vik scratched his nose, frowning. 'If the Tudashi have left and Jael Furyck's got a plan, then now's the time to move. If our dreamers kill his dreamer, Gudrum will be distracted. He'll be slow to react without her insight.'

'He'll still have the Islanders,' Stellan warned. 'There's no guarantee they'll change sides.'

'But they're Jael Furyck's men,' Jonas added. 'And she's come to get them back. No, Reinar's right. We've waited too long. We must act. Today.'

***

Thorgils feared he would lose his mind. Truly lose it.

He'd been stuck in the tent for days. He couldn't remember how many now. Sometimes, he thought three, other times, he wondered if it was four. Though perhaps it was only two? His ankles and wrists were ringed in sores from the iron fetters rubbing against his skin, and those sores were bloody and filled with pus now. He felt oddly hot, sometimes cold, and mostly ready to scream.

Bram nudged his quiet nephew. 'You alright? What's happened to all that complaining then?'

Eadmund grinned, though it took some effort. He was in agony, no longer able to get comfortable. Every position he tried made his bones and joints burn. He saw the same pinched agony on Thorgils' face, though he tried to prod his friend back to life. 'I wouldn't mention it, Bram. He'll only start moaning again.'

'Why are we still here?' Beorn croaked. 'Do you really think they're waiting on Jael?'

'I bet Jael went to Andala and got the Brekkan fleet,' Bram said, closing his eyes. 'She might be sailing here to save us.'

Now Eadmund laughed. 'She'll be a while then, so we may as well get comfortable.' His aching shoulders slumped, and he longed to rest his head against a wall or his back against a chair. His chair, in his hall, with his wife beside him, his children chasing the dogs under the tables, Biddy chasing them all. 'Best thing we can do is stay quiet and calm, conserve our energy. Something will happen soon, and likely we're going to need it.'

Thorgils closed his eyes, working hard to ignore his discomfort. In the darkness, he saw a familiar pair of eyes, praying that Furia would send her angry daughter to rescue them all.

***

While the army prepared to depart with Stellan, Eddeth worked hard to remember everything she'd done to help Alys kill Mother Arnesson. Though it felt like years since Ottby and years more since that memorable dark night. She kept dipping a finger into the pungent mixture before her, dabbing it on her lips, quickly screwing up her nose. 'It's not right, it's not,' she fretted to Raf, who sat beside her, afraid to say anything.

They both had a symbol stone secured in their pouches, though Raf didn't feel confident it would keep Gysa out. The sun was setting, the air cooling, and she began twitching, wondering where Alys was.

Eddeth stood, tipping the potion onto the ground. 'I'm starting again!' she declared, and with the bowl tucked under one arm, she stomped through the camp, heading for her tent.

Ludo approached Raf with questions in his eyes, but she could only shrug, not wanting to reveal out loud what Eddeth was doing. 'Are you going with them?' she asked instead, seeing the men forming into columns, hearing Stellan's booming voice rising above the general noise.

Ludo shook his head. 'I offered to watch the camp.'

He looked almost bashful then, and Raf smiled. 'Stina will be pleased about that.'

Ludo looked up, grinning. 'Well, only if I do a good job of it. Though we've no idea what Gudrum's dreamer might throw our way, or even Gudrum himself.' He felt concerned, fearing that Stellan wasn't leaving enough men to protect the camp, though he couldn't ask for more, for they needed every sword, every arrow and axe to try and defeat Gudrum.

'Everything,' Raf warned quietly. 'If she feels threatened, if she thinks Gudrum's in danger, Gysa will attack.' And turning away from Ludo, her eyes drifted to the fire, its burning flames fighting the wind.

***

Magnus said goodbye to Jonas with fear in his eyes. His great-grandfather was bruised and bandaged, and he feared that this battle would be too much for him.

Jonas ignored the concern he could see in the boy's eyes. 'Got your knife?' he asked quietly, so that Alys and Stina didn't hear.

Magnus nodded, patting his cloak, where he could feel it secured against his leg.

Jonas winked at him, pleased to hear it. 'I got you another,' he added. 'Another knife.' And now he pulled the wrapped knife from his cloak, where he'd been keeping it safe, tucked into his own swordbelt. 'You can wrap this around your waist. Shouldn't be too big. One on each side, I'd say.'

Magnus' eyes shone.

'What's that?' Lotta wanted to know, but Magnus hid the knife beneath his cloak before she could find out. She stared at him with big, worried eyes as the armoured men marched past, following those on horseback.

'Nothing for you to worry about,' Jonas told her. 'You've got work to do helping Stina and staying out of the way.'

Lotta wrinkled her nose. 'That doesn't sound like work. Anyone could do that!'

Jonas laughed, his attention shifting to Alys, who was giving Stina some last-minute instructions. The atmosphere was tense, for no one knew what they'd be marching into or what would come for those in the camp while they were gone.

'If things go wrong, you need to leave,' Alys told Stina. Turning around, she gripped Lotta's hand, pulling her closer. 'As soon as it turns in any way that's dangerous, I'll let you know, Lotta. And you'll tell Stina.'

Magnus looked cross. 'But why?'

'Because your mother wants you to be safe,' Jonas said. 'That's what mothers do. They send their babies to safety when they're threatened.'

Now Lotta looked cross too. 'But we're not babies!'

Alys smiled. 'You're not, but Jonas is right. I want to keep you with me always, but sometimes the danger becomes too great. If that happens, you'll need to ride away from here and find your way back to Slussfall. I believe you can. We've been up and down those mountains a few times now. You'll find the way.'

Magnus nodded, feeling a sense of responsibility as the eldest.

'Will you come with us, Mama?' Lotta asked.

Alys glanced at her grandfather, who, she could see, needed to leave. She saw Raf by the oak tree, fussing around the fire. 'I'll be over there with Eddeth and Raf, doing what I can to help. I need to protect all of us, and Reinar.' Reinar wouldn't be able to join the fight. He could stand now and walk with a crutch, but even he could see that there was nothing he could offer in the battle to come.

It was better that Stellan fought without him.

'Will Gysa come?' Lotta frowned. 'For you?'

'I don't know, but keep your mind open, Lotta. Help if you can, but more than anything, I need you to be my daughter. My eight-year-old daughter, who will listen to Stina above all things.'

'And if anything happens to Stina, you'll need to listen to me,' Magnus added sternly.

Lotta looked at him as though he was speaking Tudashi.

'He's right, I'm afraid,' Stina said. 'But Magnus, you can't ignore what your sister says because she's younger than you. She sees a lot, so you must listen too.'

Alys regretted bringing them along, though she was relieved that Stina was there. 'Go and find Puddle now. We need to keep him safe. I'll have a word with Jonas and Stina, then I have to go.'

Lotta kissed her mother, throwing her arms around her neck. Magnus knew this wasn't goodbye yet, so he just smiled before running off to find Puddle. And finally, with a reluctant sigh, Lotta turned after him.

Alys watched them go. 'I shouldn't have brought them.'

Stina shook her head. 'I'm glad we're not stuck in Slussfall. How horrible would that be?'

Jonas laughed, taking his granddaughter in his arms. 'Go and be a dreamer, sweet Alys. Stay safe, and I'll be back for you soon.' He kissed the top of her head, feeling a shudder of fear ripple through his body, though when he stepped back to look at her, his eyes were twinkling, his smile bright.

Alys grinned at him. 'I...' She shook her head suddenly, feeling odd, as though someone had placed a hand on her shoulder. And shivering, she turned around.

Stina peered at her. 'What's wrong? Alys?'

'Nothing,' Alys said, shaking her head, though she felt certain it was finally time to begin.

***

Gudrum strode back to his tent after a long tour of the camp. Mostly, he'd been pleased with what he'd seen. The Tudashi may have gone, but the Northern lords seemed happy that their share of any booty had risen considerably. Still, a fracturing army wasn't something to celebrate, and Gudrum scratched his beard as he walked, forcing a smile.

Edrik kept pace beside him. 'Word of the Tudashi's departure will unsettle many, my lord. Eventually, we'll have to show ourselves. Why else wait here? You have to defeat the Vilanders if you hope to secure the throne, and there's no time like the present.'

Gudrum's head snapped around, his lips curling venomously, but he managed to stop himself spitting out furious insults, knowing that Edrik was one of the only people trying to help him and not themselves. Though, he realised, staring closely at the man, everyone was ultimately trying to help themselves. 'We will move soon, of course! We'll crush and defeat them. They know that. We all know that!' Now Gudrum was smiling, striding through the mucky centre of the camp, hearing the odd shout and groan. He saw men training, others throwing axes at targets they'd carved into trees. Many sat around fires, sharpening already sharpened blades, trying to pass the time. 'It's only a matter of when.'

'Exactly, my lord,' Edrik murmured. 'I had thought the dreamer would be more helpful.' It was a risk to speak against her, he knew, for Gysa was both terrifying and powerful, though he'd become concerned by her growing influence over his king.

The Gudrum Edrik had known for three years had never been dictated to by a dreamer. Raf had helped him, shining a torch on both problems and possibilities, but she'd never gotten in the way. She'd never imposed her will upon her lord.

But Gysa?

Though Gudrum didn't break his stride. 'Gysa is the reason I'm here.' That was hard to admit, but something that was becoming increasingly obvious as the days wore on. 'She saved my life on that field. She killed Hector. We're here now because she had the vision to see what was possible and the desire to help me achieve it.' He was surprised by his need to defend a woman who'd frustrated him more than any other; who he appeared locked in an endless battle of wills with. Though just thinking of her had his mind wandering, and soon his smile was back. 'You stay here, Edrik. I'll go and speak with our dreamer. See what she has to say about things.'

The sudden hush behind him had Gudrum doing the opposite, and instead of heading off to find Gysa, he found himself standing perfectly still, watching the woman walking towards him, arms held out on either side of her, palms turned skyward.

Everything stilled, the camp falling silent now, and Gudrum felt as though he was back in Andala, bereft, consumed by anger and grief. He pushed his boots into the earth, feeling the weight of his sword on his right hip.

Though all his attention was on her.

Jael Furyck.

***

Having heard about the predicament the queen's husband was in, Milla had ridden to the nearest village with a few silver coins, returning with some useful tools, which Fyn had wrapped in cloth and now carried in the saddlebag, concealed beneath his cloak.

He'd taken enough symbol stones to give to each man, keeping two for himself, just in case.

He gagged, walking past the camp latrines, trying to look as though he was supposed to be there, just another of Gudrum's men. And then, suddenly, he wondered what would happen if an Islander spotted him? They hadn't thought about that. And deciding it was better not to find out, he pulled up his hood, dropping his head as he moved forward. It was growing dark, the sinking sun now swallowed by thick clouds, and Fyn felt some relief about that. He tried to get his bearings without revealing too much of his face. Jael had drawn a map of the camp in the dirt, marking which tent she believed Eadmund, Thorgils, Bram and Beorn to be in, and now he just had to find it.

***

Gudrum had warned Gysa that this wasn't her fight, so whatever she saw or heard, he hoped her attention remained on Reinar Vilander's dreamers, not on this.

This moment was all his. At last, Jael Furyck was his.

He walked forward, holding his breath until Jael stopped some distance from him. A great muddy puddle blocked their path, a bird swimming around in it, wings flapping, ducking its head into the water, oblivious to the tension in the air.

'Not quite how I imagined things going!' Gudrum laughed, his eyes fixed on the tall woman before him, dressed for battle. Her dark hair was long, braided at the sides, just as he remembered it. He saw the tiny scar beneath her eye, the scowl on her face. It was as though no time had passed since they'd last met in Andala.

'Nor I,' Jael agreed, lowering her arms until they rested by her sides. 'Though the Goddesses of Fate were always going to draw us together again, weren't they?'

Gudrum agreed. 'But I doubt you were expecting to face a

king!'

Jael laughed. 'Is that what you call yourself? From what I've heard, you're just a usurper, squatting on a throne that doesn't belong to you. The rightful king's over there, waiting to finish you off!' She saw familiar faces – Islanders – though she didn't let it distract her. There was no obvious reaction to her sudden appearance from any of them. They looked on blankly.

It was a terrifyingly familiar feeling.

Gudrum had been enjoying the attention of a wrapt audience, though he hadn't been counting on the big-mouthed Brekkan bitch to turn on him so quickly. 'Ha! Says the Queen of the Slave Islands! What a sad and pathetic fall for Ranuf Furyck's famous daughter! Imagine what he'd say if he were here now?' Anger sharpened his words, though Jael looked calm and still before him.

'I imagine he'd say the same as me! That he should have killed you before he ever inflicted you upon Alekka. That he regretted ever having a piece of shit like you by his side!' Jael's expression remained neutral, her voice steady, though inside, she was vibrating, remembering Ronal Killi and what he'd done to her dog. Though there were other memories too. Gudrum's son had caught her in the forest once. He'd thrown her to the ground, fumbling with her clothes, and if Aleksander hadn't arrived...

'I'll always be with you.'

She heard Aleksander's voice as though he was standing by her side.

Smiling, she watched as Gudrum lost his temper, stomping through the puddle, scattering the bird away. And sneering now, he slapped her face.

'So no more talking?' Jael asked, blinking through the pain.

'You, *bitch*, are going to know what it feels like,' he hissed, leaning forward. 'What it feels like to lose those you love. I'm going to make you burn with pain, squeeze your heart until it breaks.' And stepping back, Gudrum motioned for his men to seize her. 'Take her sword. Hold her there!' And when his men had stripped Jael's sword and knives from her belt, Gudrum pushed her down to the ground, onto her knees. 'So arrogant! How are you Furycks so fucking arrogant? To come here alone?' He narrowed his eyes, looking around, doubting that was true, though there was no sign of anyone else. 'Alone? Ha! Arrogant and foolish. What did you imagine? That we would talk, and I would simply set your husband free?'

'Why not?' Jael asked, face burning. She blinked through watering eyes, arms twisted behind her back. 'I'm a queen, a powerful, useful queen. You might have bound my men to fight for you, but then what? You kill me, a Furyck, and what do you imagine will happen next? My family will come for you. My allies too. And I have many now. All of Osterland supports me. All of it. Every kingdom in that land is loyal to me. Every king is my ally. And finding out that you killed me?' Jael shook her head. 'Why make such a deadly mistake so early in your reign? I came because I truly believed you weren't stupid, Gudrum Killi. You might want to avenge your son, though it won't bring him back. It won't make you feel anything but empty.'

Gudrum had much to say, though he saw that, despite being on her knees, Jael Furyck appeared to have enthralled the entire camp. He, too, remained silent, hanging on every word.

'You have my husband, my friends, my men. Let them go, let me go, and we can talk. Perhaps I can help you?'

Now Gudrum laughed. 'You nearly had me for a moment, but that? Ha! That's a step too far, Slave Queen. You want to *help* me?'

Jael just needed to keep Gudrum busy. She saw a woman approaching - the dreamer, she knew - though Jael had warded her thoughts. The journey from Oss had given her plenty of time to remember what she'd been taught about dreaming.

Gudrum saw Gysa, too, and scowling, he willed her away, hoping she'd remember his order not to interfere.

She would certainly regret it if she tried.

'Why *wouldn't* I help you?' Jael snorted, hoping to reclaim Gudrum's attention. 'What happened was years ago.' She tried not to look revolted by his face or curious about which scars she'd given him, though it was impossible to ignore his appearance, which was more gruesome than ever. 'How does it serve either of us now? We both rule kingdoms. We both need to keep them secure.'

Gudrum laughed, clapping his hands, turning around to see his men looking his way. He saw the Lords of Kurso and Ennor, and Edrik too. 'You are quite the performer, Jael! A warrior I knew, a dreamer I'd heard, but a performer? That is new and so impressive!' He turned, motioning to Edrik, who came forward quickly, and now his smile was gone. 'Bring the prisoners. Bring them here now!'

CHAPTER FORTY SEVEN

Fyn panicked.

Three men were having a conversation outside the tent.

Having finally gotten his bearings, he was confident that this was the tent holding Eadmund and his friends. He'd casually wandered around its perimeter, seeing a handful of heavily armed guards positioned outside the tent flap. And walking around the back of the tent, he let the shadows lengthen, preparing to slip under the tent wall.

And now these men?

Not wanting to draw attention to himself, he kept walking, occasionally looking over his shoulder, hoping they'd leave.

He didn't fear fighting them – he'd certainly have a go – but he feared the noise they'd make, the alarm they would raise as he tried to kill them.

Jael needed him to be a ghost – in and out of the camp as though he'd never been there. And looking up suddenly from where he stood beneath the awning of an unoccupied tent, Fyn saw two of the men raise their hands and leave.

He started walking, keeping to the shadows, hood down.

The last man remained behind, a cup in one hand, a jug in the other.

Fyn turned, hearing a rumble of noise as more people started moving away from the tents, heading for the centre of the camp. He felt sick, imagining that Jael was now there, hoping she hadn't been hurt by Gudrum.

Throwing back his hood, he straightened up, and helping himself to an empty cup sitting on a table, he strode towards the lone man still swaying by the tent wall. 'What's going on?' Fyn called, raising his cup, inclining his head to the left. 'Where's everyone going?'

The man turned towards him with confusion in his eyes.

It was dark, and Fyn couldn't see them clearly, though by the smell, he imagined they were bloodshot. 'Here, let me help you,' he offered. And stepping forward, he drove his knife into the man's belly.

The shocked man grunted, unsure what had happened, but Fyn laughed. 'You need to sit down, friend!' he called loudly, dropping his cup, and with the knife still in the man's belly, he eased him down to the ground. 'There, you sit there, and I'll be right back.' And now he leaned over the man as he started to stir, pulling away from him, and drawing out the knife, Fyn lifted it higher and stabbed him in the heart.

The man jerked, his body in spasm, and then it stilled, though Fyn remained with him a while longer, wanting to ensure he was dead.

***

Reinar dropped down onto the tree stump outside his tent, trying to catch his breath. After saying goodbye to his father and friends, he'd hobbled around the camp with his crutch, wanting to show everyone that he was still there, still in command. Though he imagined he looked ready to fall over.

Alys was hurrying down the main thoroughfare towards the oak tree where Eddeth was hopping about when she saw him. 'Has something happened? Reinar?' She headed towards him, seeing how pale his face was as he lifted it to her.

Reinar waved away the two guards who remained on call

outside his tent, encouraging Alys to sit beside him.

She looked hesitant, her eyes lifting back to the oak again.

'Please.'

Sighing, Alys sat down, fearing what he was going to say. Or ask.

'Have you seen anything?' Reinar wondered, turning to her. He wanted to take her hand, to hold it while he stared into her eyes, but she kept both hands tucked near her legs as though she was reading his thoughts.

Perhaps she was?

'Jael Furyck's there, with Gudrum.'

Reinar's eyes widened. 'You saw her?'

Alys nodded. 'I have to go and start the spell.'

'Of course, I just...' And now Reinar reached for her. 'In Eddeth's cottage, I thought...'

Alys didn't give him her hand, but she did give him her full attention now. 'In Eddeth's cottage, everything was different,' she agreed. 'But in the camp, when we spoke, it all changed.'

Reinar knew that to be true. 'But why?' He was almost whispering, afraid of her answer.

'I had a vision when we talked. Elin is... carrying your child.' Tears flooded her eyes, the great well of hopelessness rising up to claim her again. Her lips wobbled, but she held her chin in the air, staring into his eyes.

His shocked blue eyes.

'You saw that?'

Alys nodded.

It was like being punched in the stomach, Reinar thought, seeing a fist coming for him again and again, knocking all the air out of his body. He felt breathless. 'A child?' Reinar dropped his eyes to his hand, still extended, and he drew it back onto his lap. 'I see.'

'The Goddesses of Fate have spoken,' Alys said, standing now as Eddeth started bellowing her name. 'And who are we to argue?' She turned then, leaving him on that tree stump, staring after her with an open mouth.

***

After an unexpectedly long wait, a tense-looking Edrik returned to inform Gudrum, very quietly, that the prisoners had escaped.

There was no sign of them.

And not wanting anyone to hear or for Jael to discover this unfortunate turn of events, Gudrum turned to Gysa with venom in his eyes. 'Take our guest to my tent!' he roared, spinning back around. 'And she and I will continue our parley in private!' Stalking towards Gysa, he smiled at her, leading her away from the centre of the camp and the hundreds of pairs of curious eyes and ears. 'You couldn't see that they'd escaped?' he hissed, grabbing her arm when they were out of sight. 'What are you even doing? I gave you permission to see for me, to be my eyes, to help guide me, and you couldn't see *that*?' He was furious, caught between the need to have the camp searched and the embarrassment of losing his prisoners. 'Edrik!' he bellowed, and when he was by his side, Gudrum bent to his ear. 'Search the camp and find them. They can't have gotten far.' He eyed Gysa, who looked on in confusion, and when Edrik was gone, she stepped forward.

'I saw nothing about the men escaping. I don't even see them now.' That surprised her, unsettling her too. Her focus had been on the Vilanders' camp for days, preparing everything she needed to defeat those pointless dreamers when the time came. Gudrum had warned her off even thinking about Jael Furyck and his prisoners, so she hadn't given them another thought. Yet surely she should have been alerted to their escape? Or, if not her, someone else?

Gudrum's thoughts became disorderly, fuelled by rage, and realising the trouble that would soon create, he sought to gain control. 'Get to your tent. Look for them in your flames. Send word to Edrik if you see anything. I'll deal with Jael Furyck myself before she, too, escapes!'

***

None of the men moved with any speed, though Fyn felt only urgency to reach Milla and the horses. He hadn't stopped worrying about the girl since they'd said goodbye, concerned that he'd left her exposed with five horses to care for and nothing more than a knife to protect herself with.

Despite his fears for Milla, Fyn's attention was mostly on his king, who appeared ready to head back to Gudrum's camp, though he wouldn't be able to do much with bound wrists. Using Milla's tools, Fyn had removed the fetters from everyone's ankles, wanting to get them moving with speed, but after days bent over and bound, exhausted and starving, they were a wobbly, slow bunch.

'You can't go back,' Bram panted, echoing Fyn's unspoken thoughts. He was already out of breath, though they'd only just made it into the trees, and there was still some way to go to the horses.

Jael had told Fyn that as soon as he'd rescued everyone, they were to ride towards the field, where they would hopefully encounter the Vilanders' army, but Fyn quickly realised that he was going to have problems getting Eadmund there.

Eadmund heard horses snorting in the distance and then a soft whistle. Fyn whistled back, but Eadmund turned away, not liking Jael's plan.

'We have to go,' Fyn tried, one hand on his king's back.

'You think I'm going to leave Jael there?' Eadmund turned to growl at him. 'Leave her with Gudrum? Fuck!' He looked down at his bound wrists. 'Take these off, Fyn. I'm your king, so take them off!' He turned back, peering through the trees, heart thudding, hearing his wife's voice in his ears for the first time. There was only one word. 'Go!' But still, he hesitated. 'I can't leave her there.'

'Jael has a plan,' Fyn insisted.

Thorgils snorted. 'Haven't heard that in a while.' He glanced at Eadmund, feeling much the same as his best friend, but he knew

Jael. 'Eadmund, if she's got a plan you have to trust her.'

Eadmund did trust his wife. He did. Though his legs wouldn't move.

He still saw the camp through the trees.

'We have to get going!' Bram growled, cutting through all the noise in Eadmund's head. 'Come on! Once we get to the horses, get these fetters off, we'll be able to ride back with an army behind us. You'll do no good going back there on your own. Think, man!'

And finally feeling Eadmund's body relax, Fyn dragged his reluctant king away.

***

The three dreamers sat around the fire, attempting to reenact the spell Alys had used to kill Mother Arnesson, though in the back of everyone's minds was the fear that Gysa was a far more powerful dreamer.

There was no sign that Valera would come.

Raf was sure she wouldn't, though Eddeth remained hopeful.

They'd decided that since Alys had been the one to kill the old dreamer in Ottby, it made sense for her to cast the spell. Alys agreed, though she still felt nervous as she swallowed Eddeth's magical flying powder. In all the time they'd known each other, Alys had never discovered what it was actually for, but as soon as she'd gulped it down, her senses started to sharpen and then unwind altogether.

She stood, leaving Raf and Eddeth chanting over the fire, making her way to the oak tree, knife in hand. Questions jumped out of the darkness, seeking to distract her. Her heartbeat became loud, almost painful in her chest. She heard her mother's taunting laughter, Alari's, too, though that was nothing new. And shutting them both out, she took a long, slow breath and started carving symbols into the tree.

***

Burning with rage, Gudrum flew into his tent, eyes on the three guards watching his prisoner. 'Out! Get out!'

The men didn't hesitate, slipping past their king with eyes lowered, arms by their sides. It was dark now, the wind whipping the flames in the braziers, making a howling noise outside. But Gudrum could clearly see the kneeling woman, bound and helpless before him.

Helpless? He narrowed his eyes.

Was Jael Furyck ever truly helpless?

Drawing his knife, he bent down, checking that her ankles were bound, her wrists secured.

'So this was your plan?' he sneered, bringing his blade to her throat.

Jael could smell him.

She heard raised voices, hoping Fyn had managed to get everyone to the horses. She felt her heart racing, working hard to keep hold of every thread. For there were many, and every one needed to be handled with great care.

Inhaling deeply, Jael worked to show no sign of discomfort, though nearly bent backwards on the floor, with Gudrum's mauled face almost touching hers, she felt plenty. 'My plan? My plan was to save my husband, to get my men to safety. It didn't have to be like this. We could have put the past behind us.' She didn't smile, didn't blink. There was no expression in her eyes at all.

Her father watched over her. Ranuf.

He'd been a man with a temper as explosive as hers, despairing that she'd never be able to control herself.

Control. It was all about control now, she heard him say.

'You? Jael Furyck? So willing to forgive? Ha! But you couldn't forgive my boy? Couldn't forgive him?'

Jael saw Ronal's face, his hideous smile as he tore his knife across her dog's throat. She closed her eyes. 'I was a child. I made a child's mistake.' She kept listening, only half her attention on

Gudrum's knife. 'It didn't bring back my dog, didn't erase my pain. It was a... mistake.' She swallowed through the lie, all her attention on that knife now as Gudrum pressed the blade to her neck, drawing blood.

'Do you fear dying?'

She tried to smile, though now he was pushing her head back until she thought her spine would snap. 'Dying? Killed by you? No, I don't fear that at all.'

Standing up, oblivious to the noise outside the tent, Gudrum ran his eyes over Jael's body, seeing her dirty tunic, muddy trousers, legs locked tightly together, ankles secured by iron fetters.

And glancing around, he found a ring of keys on the table. Working quickly, he released Jael's legs. And knowing that was likely to cause problems, he quickly squeezed one hand around her throat, unbuttoning his trousers with the other.

Jael wriggled, feelings of panic threatening to distract her. But quickly forcing herself away from the past, she became acutely aware of the feel of Gudrum's body, his hand, his breath. 'You've got problems out there,' she croaked as Gudrum fumbled with his trousers. 'Can't you... hear it?' She was struggling to breathe as he squeezed the air from her throat, though she needed to distract him. Quickly. Panic came again like shivers of lightning, the fear of no air overriding every other need. She tried to swallow again and again, unable to breathe now, things starting to go black. 'Listen!' she rasped. '*Listen*!'

Though Gudrum heard nothing except his angry, throbbing need to take everything this woman had and destroy her.

***

Upon returning to her tent, Gysa became even more flustered. It was as though a great darkness had descended on the camp, and she couldn't find a torch. She added small branches to the brazier, and grabbing an iron poker, she prodded and stirred it until embers sparked, and the flames flowed freely, able to breathe.

Though they revealed nothing.

Her body started vibrating, and she swung around, eyes on the tent flap, thinking of Gudrum. He was taking care of Jael Furyck, she knew, but what about his other enemy? The one with the army and the three meddlesome dreamers?

Clasping her hands together, Gysa imagined Alari watching her, and she smiled serenely, reminding herself that a blind dreamer could still act.

She was powerful.

She had lifted Hector Berras up until he achieved his greatest desires and then brought him crashing down, exacting her revenge so expertly, so perfectly.

So cruelly.

Gudrum had risen to the throne because she'd willed it. Because she had desired a strong leader to rule the kingdom; a powerful warrior who would attend to all those matters which didn't interest her; a man who would serve Alari's interests as well as her own.

She had seen what would come, the path to victory revealed by beams of light so bright and certain. It had all come together seamlessly, so she would not let the sudden loss of her sight upend her plans.

She blinked at the flames, still hoping to see something revealed, though they merely burned before her. So, turning around, heart racing, she lifted a handful of bones from a small silver bowl.

***

Eadmund felt relief to be on Tig, though the horse appeared just as unhappy about riding away from the camp and Jael as he did.

Fyn had joined Milla on her horse, giving Yara to Bram. Beorn took Leada, Thorgils was on Vili, and with their arms free, they rode with real pace across the boggy field.

Though not for long.

Eadmund yanked the reins, forcing a whinnying Tig to stop. He glanced at Fyn. 'What do we know about them?' he asked, eyes on the army marching towards them, led by rows of men on horses. 'This is who Jael told you about? The Vilanders?'

Fyn nodded. 'They're Gudrum's enemy. Their lord's the one Ake chose as his heir. We have to wait for their dreamers to kill the woman who's bound our men. And once our Islanders are free, we'll join forces.'

'That's good enough for me,' Thorgils decided, lifting an impatient eyebrow at Eadmund. 'Come on, the quicker we meet up with them, the quicker we get back to rescue your stubborn wife.'

Eadmund felt more hesitant, already having made a mess of things once, but seeing Fyn's nodding head, he nodded his own. 'Let's go!' And he spurred Tig forward, hoping Jael had found a way to distract Gudrum.

***

Jael moved like a rocking horse, not about to let Gudrum rape her. Though he appeared determined to do just that, seething with anger, pulling her hair, tearing her trousers. She wriggled, trying to roll away from him. He punched her in the face, drawing blood, and now her head was ringing, her right eye shutting. Coughing and gagging, she heard screams, fearing they were in her own head.

Gudrum breathed in her ear, finally getting his hands on her. 'I'm going to make you bleed.'

Swinging her head forward, Jael broke his nose.

'*Fuck*!'

Head thumping, barely able to see, she rolled up onto her knees as Gudrum dropped back, grunting in pain. And finding her balance, she released her right leg, swinging it at his head.

Slightly dazed, squinting in the dark tent, Gudrum didn't move in time. Jael's ankle hit his cheekbone, and the knife she always wore tucked down her boot broke it. She thought quickly, seeing no victory yet, for no one was more likely to escape death than Gudrum Killi. She had to give him more than a few scars this time.

This time, she needed to take his head.

Screaming in pain, Gudrum lunged for her with both hands, but now Jael had wriggled up onto her feet, hands still bound behind her back. Face aching, she almost smiled, remembering that she'd only just walked Fyn through this very scenario.

'You bitch!' Gudrum snarled, eyes watering, though they were clear enough to see that smile. He unsheathed his sword, but Jael flung up her leg, kicking his wrist, knocking it away. And now she stood, panting before him, hoping he'd draw his knife.

***

Stellan held his position as the horses charged towards him.

He sat atop his grey stallion, flanked by Jonas and Vik, all three men pushing back tense shoulders, turning their heads.

'You think it's them?' Ollo called from behind.

Stellan didn't answer. The men riding towards them carried no banners, though if it was Gudrum's men, they wouldn't stand much of a chance. Stellan could count five horses. Five horses and five men. He squinted, seeing a woman now.

It was definitely them. So, arm in the air, he moved his army forward.

***

Alys held her bloodied hands to the symbols, confident she'd drawn them correctly, certain she had the chant right. She had gone over it many times during the day, having brought the vision of that night in Ottby's square into her mind.

But now?

Eddeth sensed a problem, and cocking her head to one side, she peered up at the tree. 'What's happening?'

Alys didn't know, but the symbols weren't glowing. Swallowing, she turned around. 'It's not working.'

Eddeth was on her feet in the blink of an eye, cloak swirling around her, Raf quickly by her side. 'Why? Why not? Those are the symbols, I'm sure of it!'

So was Alys.

'She's too powerful,' Raf whispered. 'Maybe she's stopping us?'

'Or maybe the symbols only worked on that old bat?' Eddeth cried in despair, and arms in the air, she called out. 'Valera! Valera! Hello? Valera!'

Raf grabbed her. 'Eddeth, she won't come. I promise you, she won't. After everything that happened on the field, she swore as much. She can't. Thenor won't allow it.'

'Well, I...' Eddeth sneezed, and looking up at Alys, she tried to think.

But Alys almost knocked her flying as she suddenly ran away from the tree, eyes on Reinar's tent. 'Do something!' she called over her shoulder. 'Find a way to fix the spell!'

Eddeth frowned after her, wondering what was happening, but Raf quickly claimed her attention.

'Eddeth, there's no time. If we don't kill Gysa now, the army won't stand a chance! Gudrum will kill them all!'

***

Gudrum drew his knife, but before he'd even steadied his hand, Jael ran at him, head down, hitting him hard in the stomach. He was wearing a mail shirt, and it felt like hitting a wall, but as Gudrum fell backwards, winded, Jael landing on his chest, the knife slipped from his grasp. Jael rolled away from him with speed, onto her back, pawing at the furs covering the grass, until, at last, she cut herself on the blade. Moving quickly, she wrapped her fingers around the haft, wriggling and grunting back to her feet. 'Listen!' she panted, not wanting to give Gudrum time to think. 'You're under attack! *Listen*!'

Gudrum ignored her, and staggering back to his feet, he dropped his eyes, looking for his knife or his sword.

Jael stepped back, almost knocking into the brazier. Its flames were warm but fickle, blowing about in the wind. She kept moving until she was behind it, Gudrum's knife clamped between two sweaty hands, trying to think, though her head felt as though it was filled with socks. Thick, woolly socks.

She could only see out of one eye.

And what she saw was a dark silhouette approaching.

'I'm going to slice you up,' Gudrum promised, scooping up his sword. It hurt to talk, he couldn't breathe through his broken nose, and remembering how many times Jael Furyck had cut his face, he roared at her. 'You think I care about what's happening out there?'

Though he did, and he sensed that he had to hurry.

***

Raf and Eddeth were trying to fix the spell.

They had taken themselves into a trance, holding hands by

the fire, searching for answers in the darkness of their minds. The spell had worked on one dreamer, so why not this one? What was wrong with it?

Alys hoped they could find an answer, but she couldn't find it for them. Something was out there, surrounding the camp. She couldn't hear it or see it, but she felt it. In the growing darkness, her body was tingling, her senses heightened. She stalked the camp, needing to be everyone's eyes and ears. She had to protect Reinar, mostly helpless, hobbling around; the servants and women who had come along.

Her children and Stina.

Ludo saw her. 'What's wrong?'

'Something's coming,' Alys warned him. 'Alert your men. Get word to your men.'

'What is it?'

Alys didn't know. 'Just be ready. Is someone guarding the children?'

Ludo nodded, though Alys didn't look comforted. 'I'll check on them myself,' he promised, running away from her.

Her sword hung by her side, banging against her leg, and every moving shadow made Alys twitch, fighting the urge to unsheath it. Magic was her real weapon, Ragnahild had insisted, though she feared it wasn't as reliable as a blade. Ultimately, though, she still didn't feel confident with either.

It had been months since Arnon's death, months without him yelling at her, saying that she was nothing. Nothing.

Just nothing.

Yet she still heard his mocking voice. The voice that had rung in her ears for nearly eleven years.

She still believed him.

Shivering suddenly, she spun around, hearing branches snapping on her right. Images exploded in her mind: Ragnahild's face, Eddeth sneezing, Mirella's symbol.

Gysa chanting.

And then she heard a blood-curdling growl.

CHAPTER FORTY EIGHT

After listening to Eadmund Skalleson's hasty outline of Gudrum's camp, Stellan divided his men into four groups under Bjarni, Vik, Berger and Ollo, ordering them to flank the perimeter, holding their positions until he gave the signal. And that signal would come as soon as they were certain the Islanders had been freed from the dreamer's binding spell.

But seeing that the King of Oss wasn't going to be swayed from trying to immediately rescue his wife, Stellan offered a hundred of his own men, and together they spurred their horses directly into Gudrum's camp. Jonas joined them, squinting in the darkness, shield banging on his back, keen not to get in any trouble while the bulk of their army remained out of reach.

Eadmund led the way on Tig, trying to see anything familiar, though he'd spent most of his time in the camp imprisoned within a tent.

And in the dark?

He swung his head from side to side, holding the reins close as Tig fought to go faster. Spurred on by the noise, Jael's horse wanted to get involved, and Eadmund had to pull him back as he reared up, avoiding the blades of two familiar faces. 'Arl! Ervor!' Eadmund called, though neither man responded, both of them trying to slash Tig with their axes.

Eadmund turned him away, not wanting to engage. He spun around to Thorgils. 'They're still under the spell! We can't hurt them! Find Jael!' He turned back to Stellan Vilander. 'Do not engage my men!'

Stellan could barely see, let alone know how to differentiate between the Islanders and Gudrum's men, though he nodded. 'Find your wife! My dreamers are working to free your men!' He swallowed, hoping that was true, certain they should've been able to achieve it by now.

Eadmund turned away, fighting with Tig, who seemed to have a clear idea of where he wanted to go. And finally given his head, Jael's horse immediately aimed for one tent in particular.

***

Gudrum lashed out with his sword, and with long arms and a longer blade, he nearly reached her, but Jael had the use of her legs, and she moved away from him with speed. He was blocking the tent flap, his hulking body filling the space before her, though she had no thought of running and none of escaping. She saw flashes of Tig, certain she could hear him, wanting to know that Eadmund was riding him away to get help.

She hoped he was.

Blinking, head thumping, she sharpened her focus as Gudrum lunged forward again, and this time, she stepped back, seeking balance. With her hands locked into the heavy fetters, it was challenging, but finally, feeling a sense of stability, she kicked the brazier, sending flames and ash showering over Gudrum. Screaming with rage, he flapped at his cloak, which quickly caught fire. He tore at it then, trying to pull it off, though it was secured well with heavy brooches. And then Jael was there, snapping her leg at him. He swung his sword, one sleeve on fire now, missing, and they both lost their balance, tumbling to the flaming ground.

Jael moved quickly, conscious of the fire, sensing that her own cloak was alight. She swept her bound arms around, smashing her elbow into Gudrum's broken cheek. And not giving him a chance to recover, she swung at him again, feeling the crack of her elbow on his broken nose. Gudrum grunted in fury, grappling for her arms, trying to grab hold of something. The pain of the flames melting his skin and his mashed face made it hard to breathe, though nothing was as demanding as his need to kill Jael Furyck. She was wriggling away from him now, and he finally seized a handful of her hair, yanking her backwards onto his lap.

'Your fucking son killed my dog!' she roared. 'You tried to take my horse! To kill my friend! To kill my husband and me!' And stabbing down with Gudrum's knife, still secured in her hands, Jael drove it deep into his thigh, dragging it down in a tearing motion. Rocking and wriggling, she was back on her feet, stumbling, almost falling back onto him, knowing she had to hurry. Her cloak was burning, but she had no hands free to whip it off.

Gudrum was shouting, trying to stand, but Jael turned and kicked him where he sat. Over and over again, she kicked him in the head, in the face, in the throat, until he was barely moving at all. 'I will kill you!' she croaked. '*You* will bleed!'

The sides of the tent went up in a whoosh of orange flames, sparks flying, the smoke rising in a wave that had her choking, and quickly dropping to the ground, Jael rolled, trying to put out her cloak. The tent was a flaming wreckage, barely holding its shape. Gudrum was crying out as the flames consumed his flesh. 'You could die like this,' Jael panted, rising onto her knees beside him, still clutching the knife. 'But why give the pleasure of your death to the fire? No! You've done this because of me, because I let you go. And now?'

'Fuck you!' Gudrum snarled. 'Fuck –'

Jael spun, dropping back down to him, and lifting the knife, she stabbed it into his chest, taking away his breath, the pain so intense that he forgot about the fire, though everything suddenly bloomed brightly before him.

And then a face as Jael turned to look at him.

A green-eyed, snarling face.

He saw that small scar glowing beneath her eye, and he

thought of his son.

And then nothing.

Jael watched Gudrum's eyes bulge and then freeze, she smelled his bowels giving way. And then her own eyes bulged as her husband came rushing into the flaming tent.

'*Jael*!' Eadmund took in the scene, eyes immediately fixed on his mess of a wife, who appeared to be on fire. Grabbing her arm, he pulled her to her feet as the tent poles crashed to the ground, flames shooting into the night in a great column of light.

Jael stumbled beside him, coughing and panting, then finally, pulling against him. 'No! Wait! I need the key!'

***

Alys had seen many terrifying things since leaving Ullaberg, though the creatures surging out of the trees almost paralysed her. They ran like men, though they looked like wolves. Their arms were long and hairy, hands clawed, poised to strike.

Skeplukka. Wolf men.

'Reinar!' she shouted, hoping Ludo had made it to Stina and the children in time. 'Stay where you are!' She saw Reinar standing outside his tent, fumbling with his crutch, trying to secure it under his left arm so he could free his sword. But two skeplukka leaped over his tent, landing just before him. The bigger one turned, and with an open mouth, fangs gleaming, it tore out the throat of one of Reinar's guards. The other grabbed the second guard in both hands, snapping him in two.

Alys ran faster as both creatures now turned to Reinar. She heard nothing but her heartbeat, felt nothing but the soft fabric of her hood fluttering against her face, and seeing a symbol glowing before her, as big as a cloud, she quickly drew it with her mind.

Letting Reinar go, she fixed her eyes on the terrifying skeplukka, and, hands pushing away from her body, she sent a great wall of light through the air. It sparkled like ice, white and cold, deadly to the touch. Both creatures were knocked flying, and once down, shimmering white now, they didn't move.

Still running, Alys reached Reinar, quickly steadying him. 'You need to stay with me!'

He was breathless, lips parted, wishing he could offer more help.

'We need to save Raf and Eddeth!' Alys cried, and turning them both around, she could see the dreamers still sitting before the fire with their eyes closed, oblivious to the danger. 'We have to help them, then I need to get the children!'

Reinar nodded, trying to move with speed, though he could only hobble along beside her. 'Eddeth! Wake up!'

Eddeth's eyes popped open in confusion, surprised to hear Reinar screaming her name. She looked back at Raf, who was still lost in the trance. But quickly hearing odd growling noises and seeing the hideous monsters prowling the camp, Eddeth dug her staff into the frozen earth, pulling herself up to her feet. Thinking quickly, she ran one hand up and down the staff, and when her symbols were glowing, she got to work. 'Come here!' she cried to a slow-moving Reinar and Alys. 'Into the circle! I'll keep us safe!'

Raf heard nothing but a gentle hum in the distance, for in the darkness of her mind, she had found Gysa. The angry dreamer stood over a brazier, holding a bowl in one hand, a small hazel switch in the other. Occasionally, she would dip the switch into the bowl, stirring it around before splashing some dark liquid onto the flames. They sizzled, twisting and rising, almost white with fury.

Gysa didn't look up, her attention remaining fixed on those flames.

She was chanting, Raf heard, and realising that she hadn't expected to get this close, she started backing away, not wanting to be caught again.

But then Gysa was behind her.

'A powerful dreamer can have many cauldrons on the boil,' came the purring voice. 'Do not think I am only here before you, Raf. You want me? Is that why you came? Thinking you could do what? Spy on me? *Hurt* me?' She laughed, though she felt only tension and an urgency to return to her work. 'But by coming here, you only hurt yourself. Yourself and your dreamer friends.' Gysa laughed, squeezing Raf's arm. 'Don't you know what is happening in your camp?'

But thanks to Valera, Raf wasn't the same dreamer who'd been trapped before, and she spun around in a tight circle so that her body was right before Gysa's. And reaching out a hand, she slapped Gysa's forehead, holding her hand there until, waking up her senses, the snarling dreamer flung it away.

Then Raf was gone, and Gysa was left blinking in confusion.

She lifted a hand to her forehead, though she felt nothing but smooth skin.

And shaking her head, she heard panic in the distance.

She saw a glimpse of Gudrum, dead, his tent consumed by flames. The shock was so great that she couldn't move, couldn't think. She stared at the flames for some time, unaware of anything but the great loss of hope, the earth shifting beneath her feet, sweeping away all her dreams.

But this was her second chance, and she wouldn't lose it.

She couldn't.

So, throwing her cloak around her shoulders, Gysa ran out of the tent, into the night.

***

An unbound Jael threw herself onto Tig, who immediately rose up on his hind legs. She clung to the reins with her left hand, tightening her sword grip with her right.

Eadmund ran ahead of her.

'Islanders!' Jael bellowed. She saw Thorgils and Bram, though no one else she recognised. Then Fyn was beside her on Milla's horse.

'They're trying to kill us!' he called. 'Our men! And the Vilanders are trying to kill them!'

'Shit! They haven't killed the dreamer!' Jael roared, spurring Tig on. 'Get in between them. Protect our men! I'll kill her myself!'

***

Edrik found a dazed Gysa standing outside the burning wreckage of Gudrum's tent. 'You must do something!' he urged, and getting no response, he shook her by the shoulders. 'Gysa!'

Gysa barely heard him. The reverberations of Gudrum's death kept coming back to her, making it impossible to focus. The skeplukka would decimate Reinar Vilander's camp, though without Gudrum, who would lead?

'Gysa!' Edrik shook her again. 'You must help us now! We can get out of here if you stop –' A riderless horse knocked him down, trampling his body into the muck, bones snapping, head crushed, just missing Gysa, who ran out of its path, slipping between the tents.

***

Raf jerked out of her trance to see Eddeth jumping around their circle, staff swinging, trying to protect a wobbling Reinar. And eyes snapping to the snarling, man-sized monsters terrorising the camp, Raf was immediately on her feet, screaming. 'Her hair! Her hair! I have Gysa's hair!'

Reinar was busy shouting orders, pointing Eddeth this way and that. Alys was beside him, trying to make magic with her hands, though Eddeth kept getting in the way.

No one turned around.

'*Eddeth*!'

'Move, you beast! Reinar, *duck*!'

And realising there was no time for talking, Raf burrowed beneath her cloak, searching for her purse. It was full and messy, everything stuck beneath the big symbol stone. She threw that onto the ground and then everything else.

'Stay behind me!' Eddeth bellowed, staff working hard, sparks flying, trying to move Reinar out of the way. '*Behind* me!'

And finally finding the lock of Gysa's hair, now just a few dark strands, Raf bent down, looking for the bowl of potion.

Alys turned around, seeing what she was doing, realising that she had to leave and find Stina and the children before those creatures found them. 'Eddeth! You must look after Raf! She's working on the potion!' She blinked at Reinar, fearing there was little he could do to protect himself. 'And Reinar!' she cried, drawing her sword as she started running. She saw more skeplukka leaping through the air, pouncing on their prey. She tried to shut out the noises, though the agonising howls of broken, bleeding, dying men had her fearing the worst.

Ludo had wanted Stina and the children where he could see them, so when the attack had begun, he'd called them out of the tent, pushing them into the centre of the circle he'd made with four other men. Three of those men were now dead, Lotta was screaming behind him, and Magnus had unsheathed both knives, moving around his sister and a shaking Stina, trying to keep them safe.

Alys saw them, taking everything in as she ran, arm in the air. 'I'm coming!' she screamed until her voice broke. 'Hold on! *I'm coming*!'

'Mama!' Lotta sobbed. 'Hurry!'

And then she heard Puddle barking as he ran out of their circle towards her mother.

***

The night was illuminated by the glow of the spreading fire, fanned by a gusting wind. Horses whinnied in protest, feeling the heat of those threatening flames, skittering and skidding across the muddy surface, now littered with bodies.

Some riders fell, their horses charging away, lost to them.

But not Tig, who liked a battle as much as Jael.

The Lord of Ennor had gathered his men beneath his banner, calling more to join him. Stellan could see that as he spurred his stallion towards the dark-haired woman on the black horse. And when a tent went up in flames behind her, he saw the mess of her face, inhaling her singed hair and cloak. 'My lady? I'm Stellan Vilander. I command these men.'

'Gudrum's dead!' Jael called, barely looking his way as she turned in the saddle, trying to sense where that dreamer had gone. 'Get the word out! Gudrum's dead! Take your men –' Inhaling a smoky breath, she yelped, fearing she'd broken a rib or two, and starting to cough, she was sure of it. 'Take your men to the perimeters! Keep them back while I save mine!' Eadmund was out there with Fyn, Thorgils, Bram and Beorn, trying to gather their bound men together. 'Do not get in my way!' And narrowing her one open eye on the man, Jael swung Tig around, disappearing into the blazing night.

Jonas rode up to Stellan, who appeared momentarily stunned, though he saw the sense in the queen's orders. 'Get our men back. All of them! To the flanks! We stand down till the Islanders are freed from that dreamer's spell! If we're to claim victory, we'll need them, so let's not kill them!'

***

Alys ran towards her sobbing daughter, eyes on the creatures. She heard Puddle barking, and then Ragnahild was before her.

'Take my hand!' Ragnahild urged, reaching out to her. 'I will help you!'

Alys pulled up, knowing that Ragnahild was only a spirit, but that spirit suddenly grabbed her hand with strength and power.

'Close your eyes and find that symbol again. To kill them all, we need to draw it over the entire camp. See the moon, Alys, and draw Omani's powerful light to you. I'm here, with you. We'll do it together.'

'Alys! Help us!' Stina pleaded.

Only Lotta could see Ragnahild. She knew what her mother was doing. 'We have to hold on!' she cried to Stina. 'Mama's helping!'

Magnus lunged in front of her as Ludo's last man was knocked over, torn apart and thrown away like a carcass. '*No*!' Magnus felt frightened, body shuddering as a yellow-eyed skeplukka loomed over him, fangs dripping blood. And then it lashed out with an arm, aiming to bat the boy away.

But Ludo threw himself between them, sword flashing in the moonlight, twisting his blade as he fell, dragging it across the skeplukka's hairy belly.

He didn't see the creature's friend coming from his left.

'Ludo!' Stina screamed as Lotta buried her head against her stomach. '*No*!'

And as Ludo fell to the ground, both creatures jumped on top of him.

Stina couldn't do anything, Alys had her eyes closed, Lotta was clinging to her. And Magnus?

Magnus started stabbing.

Ragnahild's voice was calm, despite the terror swirling around them. 'Draw the symbol over the entire camp,' she kept repeating slowly. 'Wider now, much wider. Bring that light over the trees, Alys, there you go. Wider still!'

Alys heard her crying daughter, she felt Ludo slipping away, and gritting her teeth, infused with the power Ragnahild was sharing, Alys drew that symbol into a bigger and bigger shape until soon it covered almost every part of the camp.

***

Gysa was breathless as she hurried past flaming tents, wondering where Alari was, fearing that she would come.

Though, admittedly, she needed her help.

Her skeplukka were under attack in the Vilanders' camp. Gudrum was dead, Edrik, too, and more besides, though she saw Bor Bearsu rising up out of the chaotic mess of noise and flame. And they still had the Islanders, bound to her, forced to fight for Stornas.

Thoughts of Stornas fuelled Gysa's tense body as she ran to the nearest brazier, dipping her hands into the flames. And lifting her burning arms to the moon and the clouds sweeping across its pale face, she started chanting. Bringing her right arm down, she swung it east and then her left, throwing it to the west. She buried her arms into the seething flames again, touching embers, and this time she threw the flames north and south until the entire camp was fenced in by a ring of fire.

***

Ollo's horse reared up at the sight of those flames, and he had to work quickly to stay in the saddle.

Vik was beside him, eyes glowing in the fire. 'We can't get through!'

'Whose magic is this?' Ollo growled, patting his panicking horse, turning to the men lined up behind him, arms ready with bows and swords, with axes and spears. 'Whose?'

'I imagine it's Gysa's.' Vik saw Stellan riding towards them. 'What can we do?'

Stellan's throat was full of smoke, and he coughed out his reply. 'Jael Furyck's in there! Gudrum's dead! I'm guessing she killed him by the look of her. We have to wait now! Wait until the Islanders are free! There's no choice. There's no way through!'

Vik turned back to Ollo, who looked ready to burst, but with a wall of flames blocking their way, what could they do?

***

The Islanders were fighting their own king and queen.

Eadmund couldn't see how to stop the two men he considered friends without hurting them. He was on the ground now, sword flying, parrying each strike.

'Eadmund!' Thorgils bellowed, riding past on Vili, forcing the two men to scatter. 'Keep out of reach!' He pointed to where Fyn and Bram were riding away from running Islanders, skirting the flaming tents and the hollering warriors, hoping something would change soon.

Fearing it wouldn't, Jael aimed for the dreamer.

Gysa saw the queen coming on her big black horse, and dropping her hands back into the flames, she shot some Jael's way. Though being a dreamer and having seen what the witch had done earlier, Jael had already nudged Tig out of her path, and now she dismounted, slapping him away. 'Find Eadmund!' she called. Then turning around, 'Eadmund! Take Tig!' And drawing her sword, she ran at the woman, who drew her hands back to her chest, twisting and turning them, readying another strike.

Jael's body throbbed with memories. None of them good.

She felt oddly hesitant, then remembering Aleksander's words, she charged, sword swinging, knowing that the blade without a name was protected with symbols.

The dreamer wouldn't break it, she told herself.

She wouldn't.

Jael edged closer, anticipating every strike. 'You think you can defeat a dreamer?' she taunted, hoping to distract the woman, sweeping her sword back and forth across her body.

Though Gysa was no Gudrum and her mind remained alert to the danger before her, the danger in the Vilanders' camp, and the danger in her own.

Jael kept going, knowing that she might be able to play the game of catching magic on her blade, but what was she going to do when she reached the dreamer?

Dropping to the ground, Gysa pushed her hands through the mud, chanting, her fingers alive with energy, pushing and pushing until the earth was rolling towards Jael Furyck.

And not having sensed that coming, Jael was quickly knocked off her feet as the ground rippled beneath her like a storm-wracked sea. She tried getting up but couldn't keep her balance, seeing those around her falling, horses stumbling, tossing thick manes as they fell onto their sides.

Jael wriggled onto her knees, bringing her sword into two hands, slashing quickly, still keeping the dreamer's magic at bay. She heard a familiar sound in the distance, and up on her feet now, she saw Eadmund approaching on Tig, sword out. 'You!' she screamed, seeking to command the dreamer's attention. 'Bitch!' she roared until Gysa's head snapped back to her.

Eadmund brandished his sword, aiming for her back, but Gysa immediately swung around, shooting both hands at him.

'*No!*' Jael bellowed, and fearing what was coming, she threw herself forward, over the brazier, sword reaching ahead of her, blade tip glinting as she drove it into the dreamer's back.

Gysa grunted, falling onto her face just before Tig, who reared above her, hooves pawing the air.

And then she was rolling, up on her feet, arms extended, facing down two enemies now, and not about to hesitate.

***

Having mixed Gysa's hair into the potion, Raf turned back to the oak tree, but one of the skeplukka broke through the circle, slipping past Eddeth, knocking her down, potion spilling everywhere. Raf crawled away from it as Eddeth howled in anger, and Reinar flung a knife at the creature's head.

Feeling around on the ground, Raf dipped her fingers into the remnants of the liquid, and up on her feet again, she ran to the tree, tracing the symbols Alys had carved into the bark.

They were Valera's symbols, and though the goddess wasn't with them, Raf could almost hear her soothing voice in her ears. She steadied both her finger and her mind, letting the words of the chant come to her, seeing the symbols begin to glow.

'Raf!' Eddeth screeched as Reinar was knocked into her, both of them falling over. '*Hurry*!'

Raf closed her eyes, shutting out Eddeth's screams, Reinar's grunts of pain, and Gysa's taunting voice. She took herself back to Gallabrok and Sigurd's arms and then Valera's face, her words so gentle and yet so deadly.

Eyes springing open, Raf started chanting. Over and over she repeated those three simple words, holding her hands to the tree as Eddeth howled, bitten by a skeplukka, and Reinar roared, on his knees, hacking at its throat.

As the clouds swept away from the moon.

And the night sky exploded in bright white light.

***

The dreamer was dead, though not killed by her sword, Jael could see, eyeing the symbol glowing on the woman's head.

Eadmund stood beside her, one hand on Tig's bridle.

Turning to him, Jael saw relief in his eyes. And feeling it herself, she kissed him, face aching, the waves of panic receding now. 'Get the men together. It's time to change sides!' Reaching for Tig's bridle, she grabbed a handful of reins, throwing herself into the saddle, arm trembling, smoke trapped in her throat, knowing the job wasn't done.

CHAPTER FORTY NINE

'You are teaching dreamers to kill,' Thenor noted, his voice icy with disapproval. 'I wasn't aware that was something the Goddess of Dreamers did. Not my goddess, at least.'

Valera had opened her chamber door expecting to see Ulfinnur, surprised instead to see her father. She pulled the door open wide, ushering him inside, though Thenor was stiff and thin-lipped, not appearing pleased to see her at all.

'Things have changed in the brief time I was away, if that is the case.' And turning, he glowered at his daughter. 'Do you think we should engage in war with the humans now? Fight battles beside them? *For* them?'

Valera was, at first, embarrassed and hesitant but then quickly defensive. 'I think your magical line moves as you will it, Father. You have not always kept behind it.'

'Eutresia –'

'Not Eutresia,' Valera interrupted, holding her ground, though Thenor appeared to have grown in size before her, his thick eyebrows jutting out over disapproving blue eyes. 'You help when you feel the need to, you know you do. Alekka is ours to watch over, to guide and guard. We cannot simply throw up our hands or tie them behind our backs. You remember what Daala herself did, only recently, and what you did, helping Alys and Reinar in Orvala. We must defeat those gods and goddesses lining up against us, I know, but what about the humans they weaponise?

We cannot simply turn our heads. Evil has no place in Alekka. Not the poisonous evil fuelled by Alari and her allies. I had no choice.'

'You *had* a choice!' Thenor boomed. 'To follow *my* rules! My rules, which keep us safe! Which keep the humans safe!'

Valera was too incensed to back down. 'But haven't you seen, Father? They are not safe! Not anymore! Alari has caused more trouble in Alekka than any of us could have imagined, even one year ago. She must be stopped! *We* must stop her! In both our realm and theirs! The war is here, now, and we mustn't shy away from it. Not for a magical line. Not for archaic rules!'

Surprised by Valera's outburst, Thenor fell into silence, his daughter's words echoing around him like a whirl of ravens. He stepped back, trying to think. First, Sigurd demanding he help the humans, and now, Valera?

He was facing disrespect, disruption, and disorder.

And by his own family? In his own hall?

Yet order was his to command. *His*, as the Father of the Gods.

It was he alone who could control the chaos.

Sweeping his cloak around, he headed for the door, seeing no reason to talk further, not until they both had hold of their tempers. 'You will think carefully about your next step, Daughter,' he said sharply. 'And when you have done so, I will be waiting to discuss this further. You helped kill a human tonight. A dreamer, maybe, an evil witch, for certain, but a human nonetheless. And you will have to answer for that, Valera. You will have to answer to me.'

Valera watched him go, the heavy wooden door closing with a bang.

She stood staring at it for some time before looking away, wondering what she had done.

***

Ragnahild had gone, the skeplukka lay dead around the tent, and

Ludo wasn't moving, his armour torn off him, his body awash with blood. Stina was screaming over him, Lotta by her side. Magnus stood nearby, too shocked to move.

'We...' Alys was out of breath. The effort of drawing the symbol had her wobbling on her feet, and though the horrors before her were demanding, her mind immediately went to Reinar. 'I'll find Eddeth,' she said, limbs trembling as she turned away. 'Lotta, get into the tent, find cloth, a tunic or dress. Anything. Tear it into strips. Magnus, get water. I... I'll be back soon.' And hearing the distant sound of Ludo's failing heart, she started running.

***

Gysa's walls of flames were gone as though they'd never been there, and free to move forward, Stellan led his men into Gudrum's camp, having no idea what he'd be facing. Or who.

He was quickly greeted by more flames and smoke, waves of it surging towards him in the darkness. But riding through it, he saw the now familiar figure of Eadmund Skalleson and his red-haired friend, relieved to hear that the Islanders were free.

Allies at last.

Eadmund had quickly corralled his men, leaving Jael to cause chaos, which, despite the mess of her face and her broken ribs, she seemed quite keen to do.

'We need to crush them!' Stellan warned. 'They're rallying under the Ennorians, and they won't give up easily.' He turned to Vik, who immediately pulled away, aiming his horse at Jonas and Ollo.

Eadmund's men were behind him now, slightly confused but well aware of which side they were on, and he pointed them forward. 'Come on!' he urged. 'We need to head in the right direction now that we're on the right side!'

***

Thenor strode into the hall, vibrating with anger, and finding an ashen-faced Sigurd staring into Hyvari, watching what was happening with his family, his rage burned. Sweeping a hand over the waterfall, he removed every image, every hint of water, and then he spun to face his son. 'You have been busy while I've been gone. So very busy!'

And though surprised by the sudden return of his father, Sigurd was just as wild with anger. 'What choice did you leave me? You didn't show me how to see! You didn't show me how to leave. You don't even want me to!'

'It is not safe! Alari –'

But Sigurd didn't want to hear about Alari. 'What use am I to Alekka if I hide here, where everything's so comfortable? Where I'm warm and safe and well-fed, while everyone I love is risking their lives!' He thought of Ludo, wanting to see more, to know if he was going to be alright.

He hadn't looked alright.

'We have a place,' Thenor tried again. 'A very important place. Parents cannot suddenly act like their children, and we cannot suddenly behave like humans. There is an order to things. My order! Why can't you see?' His cheeks flamed, his beard trembling. He wanted to grab Sigurd and make him understand that his way was the only way. The only way Alekka could survive.

Sigurd turned away, knowing he could leave.

He'd done it before.

Looking over his shoulder, he glowered at Thenor. 'I used to lie awake dreaming as a boy and even as a man, wondering who my real father was. Especially on those nights I was mad at Stellan for something. I used to imagine my real father was better than any man alive. Someone I could grow up to be like, someone I could be proud of.' He shook his head, feeling disgusted. 'You rage about order and control, yet you hide away from your daughters and your brother, who all want to kill you! That's not control, that's cowardice!' And not wanting to waste another moment trying to convince an old god that there was a better way, he turned his head and almost ran out of the hall, wanting to find Tulia.

***

Reaching the oak tree, Alys saw Raf and Eddeth trying to hoist Reinar onto his feet. He was weak, covered in blood, unable to stand on his own. His crutch lay in pieces, but quickly looking around, she found a spear, offering it to him.

'Did you do that, Alys?' Eddeth asked, shaking so much that even her eyebrows were trembling. 'That light? The creatures? They're all dead!'

Alys nodded. 'With some help.' It was dark again now, and though she couldn't see the injured, she could hear them screaming for help. 'I need you, Eddeth. It's... Ludo.' She saw Reinar stiffen as he took the spear, leaning his weight on it. 'He's hurt.'

Eddeth blinked, seeing glimpses of that herself, and then she was bounding away, heading for Stina's tent.

'Go with her, please, Raf,' Alys urged. 'I'll bring Reinar.'

'How bad is he?' Reinar wanted to know, watching Raf run after Eddeth.

Blood streamed from his shoulder, down his chest, and Alys thought she could see bone. Though quickly looking away, she encouraged Reinar to lean on her. 'I can't tell, though he's luckier than some. There are... body parts everywhere.'

'But it's over?' Reinar asked. 'It's truly over?'

***

It was a rout.

With the Islanders organised behind their king and queen, Stellan's men had the reinforcements they needed to quickly overcome the ambitious Lord of Ennor, who proved to be no Gudrum in the end. He wasn't even as capable as Hector Berras, Stellan could see, as more and more men threw themselves at his feet, bloody hands in the air, begging for mercy.

Which he gave every one of them, for these were Reinar's people now, and they needed to know that his son would be merciful.

Merciful, though not stupid, he thought, watching a panting Ollo come to a stop beside him.

'Smoke's bad,' Ollo rasped through a coughing fit.

Stellan nodded, seeing the Queen of Oss coming his way.

'You've got problems back at your camp,' Jael said shortly, wiping her nose and wincing. 'There was an attack. Some sort of creature.'

Stellan froze, his fears for Reinar rising.

'Though not your son,' Jael assured him, feeling certain about that. 'He's the king now.' And glaring at the man coughing beside Stellan Vilander, she handed over her waterskin. 'Take this,' she offered and not waiting for a spluttering Ollo to reply, she disappeared into the flaming night, looking for her husband.

'She killed Gudrum,' Berger said, joining them, taking the waterskin from Ollo, swigging from it to clear his own throat. 'Killed him with her hands bound behind her back, from what I heard.'

'What?' Ollo looked surprised, then immediately doubtful.

'Someone saw her coming out of his tent, hands bound in fetters. And Gudrum wasn't following her.'

Stellan raised an eyebrow. 'They're an ally worth keeping, that's for sure.' He saw the King and Queen of Oss embracing in the distance, and staring for a moment, he thought of his miserable wife, feeling no desire to go home to her; no desire to pull her into his arms in that moment when you realised you'd escaped death and lived to fight again. When Stellan thought of that feeling, it was foreign, as though he'd never experienced it before. And shaking his head, he realised that the man who'd harped on about having a heart of stone had obviously got what he asked for.

He slapped a still coughing Ollo on the back. 'Let's get going. The sooner we round up our prisoners and see to the wounded, the sooner we get back to camp and find out what mess Gudrum's dreamer made of it.'

***

It took every bit of willpower Sigurd had not to leave Gallabrok.

'But why can't you?' Tulia wondered beside him. They sat on Sigurd's bed, fearing for Ludo, talking about what to do. 'Why can't you go and see Ludo?' Tulia had her hand on Sigurd's leg, trying to calm him down, which was the opposite of how things usually went, she thought wryly.

Sigurd jumped up, pacing the spacious chamber. He kicked out at a stool placed before the fire. The stool of a god, the chamber of a god. And spinning around, he threw his arms in the air. 'This? I didn't want this! I didn't ask for this!'

'But Thenor –' Tulia stood, going to him.

'Is a god! He's always been a god! It's all he knows, all he wants, but me? I had a life! *Have* a life. It's mine! I don't need this!' Sigurd spun around to Tulia, grabbing her hands. 'Thenor hasn't even told me who my mother is. After all this time, I don't even know if she's alive!' He was vibrating, unable to stand still, and dropping Tulia's hands, he strode to the hearth. 'I'm not going to stay.' Though as he said it, he felt the fear of what that would mean to both Thenor and the Vilanders. 'I'm not going to stay,' he whispered, head dropping now. 'I don't want to hide away anymore.'

***

Stellan had sent Bjarni back to check on their camp, though when he returned, it was with the shocking news of what had happened.

Stellan had struggled to speak after that, fearing for Ludo, who no one was confident would live. He fought back tears, flooded with memories as he stood in the centre of Gudrum's ruined camp, ordering his men about. Without Reinar, he had to, he told himself, though eventually, Vik found him.

'You go back. Everyone will need you, Stellan. Reinar and Ludo certainly will.' He thought of Stina, feeling his own wave of sadness. And swallowing, he patted Stellan on the back. 'I'll sort everything out here.'

Stellan didn't argue, trudging towards his horse, his body aching, heart heavy.

Vik turned back to the mess as snow started falling, thinking of his cottage by the lake and Estrella. He would ask her to come and live there, he decided. They hadn't discussed it except in passing, though he very much wanted to care for her and her children. To get them away from all of this. To escape all the fear and death and misery.

And loss.

Turning away, he saw the Islanders piling the bodies of their dead, their king and queen standing over them, almost leaning against each other in exhaustion.

'Mistakes can be costly,' Eadmund sighed, seeing the frozen faces of more than one friend amongst the bodies. 'Magic can be deadly.'

Jael nodded, feeling the weight of her own failure to see the truth in time. It could have been worse, she knew. She wouldn't even be standing beside her husband if she'd been too late or if she hadn't come at all, but still, it was no real consolation. She'd thrown away the lives of her men once again.

'Because you are a queen.' She heard her father's voice, gruff as always, though perhaps with a hint of pride. 'We never throw lives away, Jael, but sacrifices for the greater good will always be needed. No leader can hide from it. Not from the death they must preside over. Not from being a queen or a warrior.'

Jael slipped her hand into Eadmund's, her voice just a whisper. 'It's my fault. All of it. Gudrum being here, you being here. All my fault. My dreams... I pushed them away. After the Vale, I didn't want to be a dreamer anymore.' She smiled then. 'Though I never wanted to be a dreamer.'

Eadmund turned to her, gently touching her swollen eye. 'You can't keep running from who you are.'

Jael mumbled something he couldn't understand.

Eventually, she looked up and repeated it. 'Or from you.'

He looked sad. 'I'm not who you want. Not really. I'm not who you want to be with.'

Tears pricked her eyes, and for a moment, Jael imagined Aleksander standing by a tent, staring at her. She shivered, then blinked him away. 'What? You think I'd have gone through all this to rescue someone I didn't want?' She pushed herself towards her husband, arms protecting her broken ribs.

Eadmund laughed, kissing her for some time, until she had to take a pained breath. 'I'm glad you did come, if only to save me from Thorgils' moaning. He never shut up the entire time. I almost hoped Gudrum would kill him first. At least it would've given me a moment's peace.'

Jael shook her head, shoulders dropping, relieved that it was over. 'Gudrum Killi. What a cunt.'

***

Raf blamed herself for not remembering Gysa's hair earlier. If she had, many would still be alive.

Eddeth comforted her, which felt better than giving in to her fears for Ludo. She'd done what she could, cleaning and stitching every wound, though they were extensive and grievous, like nothing she'd seen before. She feared he was slipping away. Tears leaked into the deep creases around her weary eyes, and she sniffed, squeezing Raf's hand. 'We did what we could with what we had, with what we knew. That's all we can hold onto now. The rest, I'm afraid, is in the hands of the gods.' She hoped Sigurd would have some say in things, for surely he wouldn't let anything happen to his best friend?

Alys entered the tent with a loud sigh. 'Stellan's back. He's with Ludo.'

'Where's Stina?' Eddeth asked. 'Poor woman. Poor, poor woman.'

'With the children. They're trying to cheer her up, though...' Alys felt tears coming. 'Though they're upset themselves. And Reinar's no better.'

Eddeth nodded. 'We'll all find a reason to blame ourselves, won't we? Something we did or didn't do. I know how that was with Aldo. I...' And now she dissolved in a flood of tears, and it was Raf's turn to comfort her.

Alys wiped her eyes. 'We need to organise the camp. Everyone's in a daze, but the injured need our help. People need to eat and get warm. It's snowing too.'

Eddeth wiped her nose, and creaking to her feet, she pulled Raf after her. 'Of course, of course. We can't sit around here feeling sorry for ourselves.' Though her tears kept flowing, and her nose kept running. 'I wish we could've saved more. Done more.'

Alys felt oddly fearful. 'Next time,' she said, strengthening her voice. 'We'll do better next time. We'll do more.' She saw Mirella's face, and her mother was smiling. 'So much more.'

Raf nodded, boots pressed firmly into the earth. 'We will. There's a lot we can learn to get stronger, more ways to help Reinar.' She thought of Sigurd, wondering why he hadn't come, imagining how he was feeling, trapped in Gallabrok, wishing he could help.

Eddeth made to sneeze as a snow-speckled Lotta popped her head into the tent. 'Ludo's awake! Stina said to come!'

And with a quick look back at an open-mouthed Eddeth, Alys rushed outside.

***

'Knew you wouldn't be able to keep away,' Thorgils smirked as he rode beside Jael towards the Vilanders' camp. They'd left Beorn and Bram in charge of their men and Milla helping the injured while they made a necessary visit to their ally, the new King of Alekka.

Jael snorted. 'It's true. I missed your big mouth. Oss was just too quiet without you.'

Thorgils peered at his queen, wondering if that was a compliment. 'He made a mess of your face, that Gudrum. Typical Brekkan shit.'

Jael laughed, then gasped in agony. 'You're blaming Brekka for Gudrum? I don't think so. He was always an arsehole. Doesn't matter where he came from.'

'Spose so,' Thorgils grudgingly agreed, wishing Fyn and Eadmund would ride faster. 'Got anything to eat?'

Jael turned to him with a frown. 'What am I? Your mother? No, and if I did, I wouldn't share it with you.' She fixed her eyes on her husband's back, trying not to smile, hoping just as much as Thorgils that they'd reach the camp quickly.

She was starving.

***

Stina knew she should be helping the rest of the wounded, but she needed more time with Ludo, not wanting to leave his side until she felt some certainty that he would live.

He tried to reassure her, though he couldn't speak and mostly kept his eyes closed, murmuring and groaning as she held his hand.

Lotta sat beside her, placing both hands on Ludo's leg.

Eventually, surprised by her continued silence and stillness, Stina turned to the little girl. 'What do you see, Lotta?'

Lotta stared at her with tired eyes. 'I see a cottage, lots of cottages. And you're there with baskets of berries.' Now she closed her eyes, wanting to go back into her vision. 'Puddle and Winter are there. Ilyia and Maia too.' She opened one eye, peering at Stina, not sure how she felt about that, but seeing Stina's fretful face, she closed her eye again.

'And Ludo?' Stina whispered, seeing that Ludo had fallen asleep.

Lotta searched through all the people. She saw Jonas and her mother. Magnus was with Vik and Estrella, carrying fish out of the smokehouse. There were tables arrayed with cups and jugs and delicious-looking food, and the sun was shining. She saw it glittering off the enormous lake where she knew she would go swimming. She kept turning, and then she saw a tall, thin man hunched over at one of the tables, motioning for her to come closer.

It was Ludo.

And opening her eyes now, Lotta looked up at Stina with a beaming smile.

CHAPTER FIFTY

Deep into the night, the fires bloomed brightly. The snow had finally stopped, leaving a thick white blanket over the ground. The air was chilled, though the wind had died down, and those fires blazed intensely.

Ollo sat next to Berger and Ilene, starting his fourth cup of ale, though he felt just as cold and empty as when he'd sat down. Ilene ignored him, peering around, no doubt searching for Helgi. Having heard he was a man with land as well as battle prowess, she hadn't stopped looking Helgi Eivin's way.

And Eddeth's words came back to Ollo like a nagging cough.

Though he would never admit that the dreamer had been right. Shaking his head, he knew he'd never admit that.

Berger looked up as Vik and Jonas joined them, carrying two more jugs of ale. 'Just in time!' he boomed, holding out an empty cup. 'Nothing's touched the sides so far!'

Vik smiled. 'Often feels like that after a battle.' He filled Berger's cup and then Ollo's and Ilene's before sitting down.

'The last battle for a while,' Ilene decided with a groan. 'Now that Reinar's the king.'

Vik laughed. 'You think so?' He glanced at Berger. 'You don't think Tarl Brava's going to stay up in Orvala, do you? That he won't come looking for Solveigh and his child?'

Berger squirmed. 'Well, he can come to Stornas, see how easy it is to get in there. We'll work on those walls as soon as we arrive.

I'll help Reinar. He won't get in.'

Jonas frowned, thinking of Mirella, who, while she lived, remained a threat. 'You'll need to keep your dreamers busy too. It won't only be Tarl Brava coming your way.'

'What will you do?' Ollo wanted to know. 'Go back to the lake?'

Both Jonas and Vik nodded.

'There'll be more than enough help for Reinar in Stornas,' Jonas decided. 'And my family deserves a break from all the chaos. Those children do, that's for sure. I'm going to build them a house.'

'I'm sure Elin will be happy to hear it,' Ilene laughed.

No one laughed with her.

Berger saw Helgi and Alys walking together past a fire. Turning his head a little more, he saw Reinar sitting beside Jael Furyck, watching them. 'I know someone else who'll be happy to hear it,' he said, inclining his head to Helgi, pleased to wipe the smile off Ilene's face.

Helgi was trying to cheer up Alys but failing miserably. 'If you saw everything that was coming you'd be a goddess,' he grinned, nudging her arm.

She turned to him with a frown. 'But what's coming next...'

Now Helgi was frowning. 'Next? But we killed Gudrum and his dreamer. They're dead, the Ennorians have surrendered, Reinar's the king, Alekka's free.'

Alys shook her head. 'I've just... it's been a long few days. I'm not making much sense.' She didn't want to let her fears take away from their victory. Reinar was the king, and that was something to celebrate. They'd faced an enemy twice their number, and despite devastating losses, won.

It was something to smile about.

Though Alys couldn't.

Nor could Reinar, who felt awkward sitting beside Jael Furyck, knowing she'd done what he couldn't.

He felt less than he should have.

Not a real king; one who'd earned his throne.

And reading his very loud thoughts, Jael sighed. 'Gudrum

was only ever my problem to deal with,' she admitted, turning to Reinar. 'He escaped Brekka because of me, came to Alekka because of me.' She shook her head, feeling awkward herself. 'I failed to kill him when I should have. It was all on me.'

She stared at Reinar with one big green eye, and Reinar felt oddly shy, knowing her reputation. 'Did you really kill him with your hands bound behind your back? In fetters? That's what I heard.'

Jael lifted her head, meeting Fyn's eyes. He sat across the fire, mediating between Thorgils and Eadmund, who were involved in another argument. Rolling his eyes at her, Fyn smiled. 'It's worth practising,' Jael decided, drawing her attention back to Reinar. 'Though it was harder than I'd imagined.' Now she laughed, holding her ribs. 'And a lot more painful.' Keeping her smile fixed on her face, Jael tried to shut away the memory of Gudrum's hands ripping open her tunic, his breath in her ear, his tongue in her mouth... 'He's dead.' She blinked, feeling the relief of it. 'And you're Oss' newest ally, Reinar Vilander.' Lifting her cup, she knocked it into his. 'I didn't know Ake Bluefinn, but I heard he was a good king. A famous warrior. A hard man to follow.'

Reinar nodded, holding her one-eyed gaze. 'The best.'

'Then take my advice and forget him. You'll never be him, never replace him, never measure up to any standards he might have set. From experience, I know that you just have to follow your own path, be your own king. It's the only way to move forward. The only way to sleep at night.'

Reinar listened attentively, those words settling over him like a mantle. 'Sleep would be good.'

Jael heartily agreed, looking up as Eadmund joined them. 'But first, more ale.'

***

Thenor drank alone in his hall.

He'd returned after a revealing journey, yet it appeared no one had missed him. Or, at least, his children hadn't. That much was obvious. Valera had remained in her chamber, Sigurd in his, yet he urgently needed to talk to them both. What he'd discovered in his travels to the Northern Reach was of great importance, a threat so grave that there was little time to waste on squabbles and hurt feelings.

But how to get Valera and Sigurd back on side?

Thenor stood, pushing away his plate, having had little appetite, and taking his goblet, he carried it to the fire. Hyvari's rushing water reminded him of Sigurd and his desperate need to leave to be with the Vilanders. To be with his friends.

To be human.

Thenor rubbed his beard, feeling old and troubled. And then, he remembered his mother, Daala. It had been centuries since he'd sought her out, but what was coming was a problem greater than any he'd faced since tearing Alekka in two.

Looking up, he blinked, seeing Ulfinnur waving at him as he headed out of the hall, no doubt on his way to see Valera.

And just thinking of his stubborn daughter had Thenor scowling again.

***

Tulia had left, giving Sigurd a chance to think. And now he knew he had no choice but to leave Gallabrok. He wouldn't disappear, though. He owed Thenor more than that. Despite his anger at his father, he wouldn't slip away without a word. But he couldn't stay. He couldn't give him what he wanted. Valera was Thenor's daughter, a clear and calm leader. She would be his heir. She had to be. He would be no use, for he wanted to be human, to be *with* the humans.

It would never work.

Tulia would return soon, and he would say goodbye to her. And then Thenor and Valera and...

Sigurd pushed back his shoulders, trying to ignore the image of Thenor's disappointed face. He saw it strongly as he unsheathed *Fire Song*, laying her on the bed: his father, holding out a hand, calling to him.

But turning away, he shut it out.

***

Valera stood, her body heavy with regret, knowing that Thenor deserved an apology. She'd had time to think, now realising that he was right. She had let her desire to help override every other consideration. It wasn't Sigurd's fault, but the more time she'd spent with him, the more she had begun to feel his pain. She'd begun to want what he did – to have a greater say in Alekka's future.

She had lost control.

Thenor was right. The gods were the gods, the humans the humans. They could not fall into Eutresia's trap. Eutresia had become mired in her desire to please the humans, to show them her fealty, her beneficence. Everything that came after could be traced back to that single error in judgement, that great loss of control.

Valera smoothed down her dress, running a hand over her hair, and feeling both foolish and embarrassed, and desperate to make everything right, most of all, she headed to the door.

Hearing a knock.

Imagining it was Thenor, she called out. 'Come in!'

Ulfinnur pushed open the door with a smile, though seeing her disappointment, he frowned. 'You were expecting someone else?'

Valera nodded. 'My father. I... need to make it right.'

'I thought as much, though you seem to be in a better place

now. Perhaps?' He came forward, taking her hands, and lifting them to his mouth, he kissed them. 'He looked so sad out there. So lonely.'

Valera felt worse than ever. 'It's my fault. He expected more from me, and I let him down.' Pulling her hands away, she smiled at Ulfinnur, narrowing her eyes. 'Wait here for me. I promise I won't be long. I just need to talk to Thenor. I won't be long.'

Ulfinnur let her go, following her to the door. 'Wait!' he called. 'Valera, there's something I...'

She turned around to him as he stepped forward, driving the knife into her heart, watching those pretty lavender eyes widen in horror and surprise.

Mostly horror, he saw as her body staggered, trembling before him.

He held onto that knife, feeling her panic, her pain, sensing how desperately she wanted to speak. And now he pulled the blade out of her, stepping back, seeing the shock in her eyes intensify.

Though as much as she tried, she couldn't speak.

She swayed for a moment before collapsing to the floor.

'Your father,' he hissed, bending down to her ear, wanting her to hear one last thing as her body jerked its final movements. 'Will die.' And straightening up, knife sheathed, Ulfinnur left the chamber.

Heading for the hall.

***

Reinar found Alys.

Despite knowing Elin was pregnant and the rearrangement of his thoughts and plans, which had quickly followed that news, his jealousy kept flaring every time he saw her with Helgi. Though he was surprised to discover that he didn't hate Helgi Eivin. He'd wanted to, but it had proven impossible. Helgi was smart and useful, a skilled warrior and a kind man. 'Jonas said you won't be coming to Stornas.'

They stood by an ash tree, hidden from the moon, just the two of them. Reinar wobbled before her on unsteady ground, irritated by his weakness and his reliance on the crutch, which dug into his armpit, making him want to scream.

Alys didn't notice. She felt dizzy from too many cups of ale and so exhausted that she could barely see. 'No, when Ludo's well enough to travel, we'll be going straight to Burholm. We'll be living there.'

'Eddeth will miss you.'

Alys smiled. 'I'll miss her.' And thinking about it more deeply, Alys realised how much she really would miss Eddeth, her mad horses, her irritable cat and human-like goat. 'But we'll visit.' Though she didn't know if she meant it.

Reinar dropped his head, fighting the urge to say what was in his heart. 'Ludo will need you all.'

'He will. And once he's on his feet, there'll be plenty to keep him busy. We'll take good care of him, I promise.'

Reinar nodded, not doubting it for a moment. 'I wanted to thank you, Alys. After what I did, taking you from your home. You didn't owe me your help or loyalty or... but you saved my life. If you hadn't come after me, if you hadn't broken the curse...'

Alys had shed enough tears for one day, though in the darkness, she felt more coming, knowing that this was finally goodbye. 'You were born to be the king, Reinar, and now you are. It doesn't matter how you got here or who did what to help you. What matters is what you do now and what sort of king you choose to be.'

He took her hand. 'I –'

But Alys pulled it back. 'When I ran away with Arnon, I lost myself. I forgot who I was. I became someone else, someone I didn't recognise. Someone I ended up hating.' Tears rolled down her cheeks. 'You're married, Reinar, and now your wife will give you a child. You were never mine, and I was never yours.' She stepped back. 'I'm tired of being less than I should be, someone I'm not proud of. I can't keep playing this game. I have to be better than this.' She stepped back again, hating herself because Reinar was in pain, and so was she.

But he was married. Reinar was married.

And not to her.

'I can't be this person anymore. I won't. I...' Turning away, Alys still saw his face, hearing the thumping pain of her heart, trying to tell herself that she was doing the right thing.

Reinar watched her go.

He stood there for some time until, eventually, there was only darkness, and ducking his head, he dug his crutch into the snow and turned away.

***

Thenor turned to Ulfinnur with a smile. 'Come to cheer me up, old friend? Come, come and share a cup of ale with me.' Thenor had had many now, which was unusual. The ale was potent, almost as strong as the mead, and he felt a lightness not usually present in his ancient body. He would talk to Valera and Sigurd in the morning. They would find a way to exist where all three of them could be happy. He was certain they could. If only they would listen more.

Though once he told them what he'd found up North...

Turning to the table, he poured ale into an empty goblet, holding it out to Ulfinnur, who shook his head.

'I'm on my way to bed,' the God of Winter smiled. 'Perhaps tomorrow?'

Thenor was surprised, then stepping closer, he frowned. 'Something's wrong? You seem upset.'

Ulfinnur shook his head. 'Wrong? No, just that daughter of yours. Her heart is broken.'

Thenor sighed. 'Well, that would be my fault entirely.' He sipped the ale himself. 'Though I can make it right now.' And turning away, he patted Ulfinnur on the shoulder. 'Thank you for pointing me in the right direction. Better not to put off till tomorrow what you can make better today.'

The knife struck him in the back, and as he spun around in shock, horror in his eyes, Ulfinnur stabbed him in the chest too.

'No!' Sigurd yelled, running into the hall, Tulia by his side.

Ulfinnur let go of Thenor, turning to face Sigurd.

'Run.'

Sigurd heard his father's faint voice in his ears.

'Leave this place.'

Thenor couldn't hold himself up, knowing the knife that had struck him was magical. He hadn't seen it coming. He'd had no warning at all. He collapsed to the flagstones, falling onto his side, the stone cold beneath his ear. He felt that most of all, confused as to why he was so powerless. He couldn't leave his body. He couldn't rise to defend his son.

His son.

'Go North... Sigurd... the...Reach.'

Sigurd's hand hovered near where *Fire Song* should have been, surprised by the sudden emergence of Alari and Vasa, who arrived at the hall in a rush of feathers and cloaks.

'Oh! A family reunion!' Alari declared, her eye snapping to Thenor's dying body, watching as Sigurd pulled a woman close, one arm around her waist. 'What? Did you really think I would just let Ulfinnur go? Or you? No, Brother, I needed Thenor to come for him, to bring him back here. For whatever Ulfinnur was is gone, but that shell is all mine. As you will soon be. If only Valera or our father had been so useful.'

'Valera?' Sigurd heard the echo of his father's faint voice in his ears. 'You hurt Valera?'

'Not hurt, no. That would be too kind. No, the bitch is dead. Dead!' Gudrum's defeat and Gysa's demise had barely broken Alari's stride, though it had prompted her to act. Now she bent to her father, breathing in his ear. 'Do you feel it, Father? That helplessness? That sudden fear of the unknown? You have no power, no vision, no abilities at all. You are almost human!' And now she laughed, looking up at Sigurd. 'Just like your pathetic son and saviour here.'

Thenor closed his eyes, wanting Sigurd to see everything. Alari was right, he had nothing left that made him a god but his thoughts, and with his last breaths, knowing that Valera had gone, that Ulfinnur was no more, that Alari was here...

He had to show Sigurd everything.

Though the darkness came quickly, and he soon felt himself being propelled towards a familiar voice.

A dark, venomous voice.

His father's, he realised, body failing him, hope gone.

'No!' Sigurd shouted, horror in his eyes. He squeezed Tulia's hand, pulling her close.

And then they were gone.

***

Their injured were secured in Gudrum's sleighs and wagons, hitched onto horses. Thorgils was fussing over how much more food he could fit into his saddlebag, which embarrassed both his king and queen, who pretended they didn't see him as they said their farewells to the Vilanders.

Tig butted Jael in the back, and Fyn erupted into a coughing fit, and eventually, Eadmund decided that they needed to get on their horses and leave, for it was going to be a long ride back to the coast. Though thankfully, they had Milla to show them the way.

'It's a pity you can't come to Stornas,' Stellan smiled. 'You'd be welcome, I'm sure.' He looked at a sombre Reinar, who nodded beside him.

'Perhaps another time,' Eadmund said, glancing at Jael, who'd woken early from a dream, tight-lipped and worried, wanting to leave in a hurry. He couldn't get out of her what was wrong, but it was obviously something.

'Thank you,' Reinar said, raising a hand, his eyes on the

bruised and battered Queen of Oss. 'We won't forget.'

Jael nodded, slightly distracted. 'We really must go.' And turning to Eadmund, she sucked in a cold breath. 'We need to get to Andala.'

Reinar stepped away, dragging his crutch out of the snow, eyes on the woman who had finally killed Gudrum and, by doing so, gifted him Alekka's throne. He thought of the walled city of Stornas, knowing he would be going there without Sigurd, without Ludo, and without his father, who had made plans to return to Ottby.

Stellan nudged him. 'I think we should get moving ourselves. What do you say? Time for a new adventure, my king?' He shivered, seeing a glimpse of Ake's face, though he tried to smile. 'Time to get you to your new home?'

'Come with me,' Reinar urged. 'To Stornas. I'll need you. I want you there with me.'

Stellan was ready to argue, to insist that Reinar didn't need him at all, but he saw the desperation in his son's eyes, and he found himself nodding. 'Stornas? Well, a change would be good, I suppose. Your mother would certainly like it. And I'm sure you could find someone useful to take charge of Ottby. At least for a while.'

Reinar's eyes drifted from his father to Bjarni and then to Berger. 'I'm sure I could.'

The Islanders left Gudrum's camp in a slow waddle, mud and snow and manure flicked up by plodding horses, grim-faced warriors weighed down by the odd memories of what they were leaving behind.

Turning around, Jael raised a hand, catching Eadmund's eye.

'Andala?' he asked. 'What's wrong there?'

Jael wouldn't say, though he thought he saw the glitter of tears in her eyes.

***

Eddeth sniffed through the packing of Wilf's saddlebags. She sneezed, too, feeling odd not to see Ludo hovering around her, wanting to know if she needed anything. Raf was quiet beside her, preparing Rofni, though Eddeth could tell that she was upset about saying goodbye to Alys and the children.

But she wasn't, Eddeth insisted as the tears kept flowing.

No, she wasn't.

Then Lotta's arms were around her waist, and Magnus was hugging her, and Alys was there, with Stina beside her, and Eddeth was a blubbering mess. She saw Vik coming and tried to compose herself. 'Oh, this spring air!' she sniffed loudly, lips quivering. 'Can't stop sneezing! Must be the grass. Oh yes, I always have a problem with grass in spring! Just as well we're leaving. I hope they don't have any in Stornas!' Eddeth had chosen to go with Reinar, leaving Raf to go back to Slussfall with Bjarni to sort everything out.

Vik stopped before the spluttering, sneezing, crying dreamer and pulled her into his arms, holding her tightly. Eddeth was so surprised that she became completely still. 'I will miss you, Eddeth Nagel. You are so much more than I ever expected. A complete wonder and surprise. I'm very glad I met you that day in the forest.'

He released Eddeth with a kiss on the cheek. 'You'll come and visit us, I hope? Bring us news of Stornas?' Eddeth's face flushed a deep pink as she stood before him, mouth open, unable to think of anything to say. Eventually, she nodded, and Vik laughed. 'Good, now let me help you up onto that horse.'

Alys raised a hand to Eddeth, holding it there as she wrapped her other arm around Stina. 'I'll see you soon, Eddeth. In my dreams.' And blinking, Alys didn't know what that meant, though Eddeth appeared oblivious to everything but the feel of Vik Lofgren's rock-like arms as he boosted her into Wilf's saddle.

'Yes, yes,' she muttered to anyone and no one at all. 'I'll see you soon.'

Lotta and Magnus turned away, Magnus quickly finding his pony, and Lotta hurrying to her mother's side, slipping a hand into hers. 'It's goodbye,' she said quietly, 'but not for long.' And looking up at her mother, she felt a tremor of fear.

Alys' eyes had wandered away from Eddeth and Vik to where Stellan and Bjarni were helping Reinar onto his horse. Reinar wasn't making it easy on them, fighting to manage on his own, and turning irritably in the saddle, his eyes met hers. Alys stared at him, trembling beneath his gaze before turning away, leading Lotta back to Ludo's tent. 'Yes,' she agreed, fears rising, mingling with grief and exhaustion; sadness too. 'Not for long.'

THE END

EPILOGUE

Mirella held her hands on either side of Tarl Brava's head, watching as he closed his eyes.

'Will it hurt?' he asked, opening one eye to peer at her.

She laughed. 'Of course it won't hurt. Do you want to be a king or not?' They stood beside the small pool of water Mirella had carved out of the ice. Their breath flowed in thick clouds, nearly masking the dark water. 'You wanted to see, so I'm going to show you.'

They'd been trekking through the Northern Reach for months. Months of ice and frostbite and cold so intense that Orvala appeared tropical in comparison.

A clearly still hesitant Tarl closed his eye again.

Mirella smiled before him, feeling elated. All their searching, their deprivation and struggle had finally led them here.

To a lake.

A frozen, hidden, majestic lake, as big as anything she'd seen in her life. She closed her own eyes, feeling the magic embracing her, holding and singing to her like a melody. A dark, mysterious melody that only she could hear. Drawing symbols with her mind, she felt her shoulders loosen, her breath coming in lengthened, rhythmic waves, until finally, she felt a warm glow. And opening her eyes, she tapped Tarl's arm. 'There. Look.'

Leaning over the water, Tarl blinked, surprised to see the great beam of light revealing what lay beneath the surface.

'Do you see it?' Mirella breathed, unable to stop smiling.

Tarl wasn't sure what he saw.

He cocked his head to one side, seeing a shape come into sharper relief as the sand settled and the water became clearer.

'That is the Sun Torc,' Mirella said, turning him to her. 'It's everything. The key to healing The Rift, the key to the throne, the key to Alekka!'

Tarl's smile grew, watching the happiness in his dreamer's eyes. 'And my wife and child?'

'Oh yes, it's the key to claiming them too.' She squeezed his hand, hurrying to her feet. 'Come now, we must find Ulrick. It is time to begin!'

WHAT TO READ NEXT

If this was your first time meeting Jael Furyck, read *The Furyck Saga* and see how she ended up in that famous battle at the Vale of the Gods.

To find out what happened the last time Jael and Gudrum met, read *Kings of Fate, The Furyck Saga*'s Prequel Novella.

ABOUT A.E. RAYNE

Some things about me, the author:

I live in Auckland, New Zealand, with my husband, three kids and three dogs. When I'm not writing, you can find me editing, designing my book covers, and trying to fit in some sleep (though mostly I'm dreaming of what's coming next!).

I have a deep love of history and all things Viking. Growing up with a Swedish grandmother, her heritage had a great influence on me, so my fantasy tales lean heavily on Viking lore and culture. And also winter. I love the cold!

I like to immerse myself in my stories, experiencing everything through my characters. I don't write with a plan; I take cues from my characters, and follow where they naturally decide to go. I like different points of view because I see the story visually, with many dimensions, like a tv show or a movie. My job is to stand at the loom and weave the many coloured threads together into an exciting story.

I promise you characters that will quickly feel like friends, and villains that will make you wild, with plots that twist and turn to leave you wondering what's coming around the corner. And, like me, hopefully, you'll always end up a little surprised by how I weave everything together in the end!

To find out more about A.E. Rayne and her writing
visit her website: www.aerayne.com

Printed in Great Britain
by Amazon